I0736646

DARKEST SIN

SIN DEMONS COLLECTION

PART 2

MILA YOUNG

HARPER A. BROOKS

Darkest Sin, Part 2 © Copyright 2022 Mila Young & Harper A. Brooks

Cover Design by **Joy Book Design**

Visit our books at
www.milayoungbooks.com
https://harperabrooks.com

All rights reserved under the International and Pan-American Copyright Conventions. No part of this book may be reproduced or transmitted in any form or by any means, electronic or mechanical, including photocopying, recording, or by any information storage and retrieval system, without permission in writing from the publisher/author.

This is a work of fiction. Names, places, characters and incidents are either the product of the author's imagination or are used fictitiously, and any resemblance to any actual persons, living or dead, organizations, events or locales is entirely coincidental.

Warning: the unauthorized reproduction or distribution of this copyrighted work is illegal. Criminal copyright infringement, including infringement without monetary gain, is investigated by the FBI and is punishable by up to 5 years in prison and a fine of $250,000.

CONTENTS

TO HELL AND BACK

Chapter 1	3
Chapter 2	11
Chapter 3	19
Chapter 4	32
Chapter 5	39
Chapter 6	48
Chapter 7	58
Chapter 8	70
Chapter 9	84
Chapter 10	97
Chapter 11	107
Chapter 12	121
Chapter 13	130
Chapter 14	138
Chapter 15	145
Chapter 16	156
Chapter 17	163
Chapter 18	170
Chapter 19	175
Chapter 20	188
Chapter 21	196
Chapter 22	207

WHEN HELL FREEZES OVER

Chapter 1	221
Chapter 2	226
Chapter 3	232
Chapter 4	243
Chapter 5	252
Chapter 6	261
Chapter 7	269
Chapter 8	279
Chapter 9	289

Chapter 10   297
Chapter 11   305
Chapter 12   314
Chapter 13   322
Chapter 14   331
Chapter 15   341
Chapter 16   349
Chapter 17   360
Chapter 18   372
Chapter 19   381
Chapter 20   390
Chapter 21   403
Chapter 22   416
Chapter 23   425
Chapter 24   438

HELL ON EARTH

Chapter 1   451
Chapter 2   456
Chapter 3   468
Chapter 4   477
Chapter 5   487
Chapter 6   499
Chapter 7   509
Chapter 8   524
Chapter 9   539
Chapter 10   549
Chapter 11   560
Chapter 12   572
Chapter 13   589
Chapter 14   597
Chapter 15   609
Chapter 16   615
Chapter 17   625
Chapter 18   635
Chapter 19   645
Chapter 20   653
Chapter 21   662
Chapter 22   671
Chapter 23   684
Epilogue   697

HELL OF A GOOD TIME
BONUS SCENE

Hell of a Good Time	709
Snowball's Chance in Hell	717
Hell or Highwater	719
Sin Demons Series	721
About Mila Young	723
About Harper A. Brooks	725

DARKEST SIN

Falling in love can be Hell...
As the danger increases around me, Sayah's
darkness grows inside me.
Scariest of all... I'm starting to like it.
My sin demons will risk it all to save me from
eternal damnation. But my biggest enemy
may not be Lucifer.
It may be the monster that lurks inside me.
And when we meet the devil at the gates of
Hell, will I be strong enough to make the
ultimate sacrifice to save us all? Or will I lose
everyone I love to the fire?

TO HELL AND BACK

SIN DEMONS

They were trying to get back to Hell... But Hell showed up at our door.
None of us expected a visit from the devil himself, but after Lucifer comes a-knocking, we know things are about to heat up fast. According to the demons, the only way to protect me is to bind us all together. Forever. Something I'm not sure I'm even willing to do. But with Greed's ring still on my finger and Lucifer's sights set on making me his next play thing, what other choice do I have? When I'm dragged to Hell against my will, I'm determined to find a way topside again. But the darkness within me is enjoying this deadly vacation a little too much, and my powers only seem to grow the longer I stay.
My demons will risk it all to save me from eternal damnation. But after going to Hell and back, will *I* still be the same in the end?

ONE

"We are each our own devil, and we make this world our hell."
— *Oscar Wilde*

"Lucifer!" The name rolls off my tongue and past my lips unintentionally, but to be standing in front of him leaves me utterly terrified. My mind is spinning. I can't believe he's sharing the same breathing space as me. The Prince of Darkness, Beelzebub, Father of Lies, or simply Satan... My mouth falls open in shock.

"Oh, she has a voice," he says, amused, and here I am struggling to calm my racing heart. Let alone respond.

He studies me, while my skin crawls under his gaze. Even in his black suit and red shirt, looking more like a businessman than the devil in charge of Hell, I can see similarities between him and Cain. Both impeccably dressed. Lucifer is older, though his mustache and beard don't conceal his handsome face. An air of regalness clings to him, a confidence that I've seen so much in Cain, too, but while Cain is poised and strikingly calm in most situations, behind Lucifer's eyes I can see the insanity lurking there, so close to the surface. This man is unhinged.

Cain, Elias, and Dorian remain close by, while Maverick stands near his father. My anger still tumbles inside me after learning his true intentions with me. And that Joseline foolishly made a deal with him. I want to shake some sense into her. Maybe give her one hard smack upside the head, but is that going to change anything? No. It'd make me feel better though.

But really, is what I did any different? I trusted Maverick and let him trick me by putting this ring on me. I thought he was an angel when he's Cain's brother, for hell's sake.

Looking back, it's so obvious now I want to punch myself too. I allowed myself to fall because I'd been desperate to find a solution to Sayah. My fear overcame my common sense, and he knew that and used it against me.

Stupid.

Stupid.

Stupid.

"What are you doing here?" Cain breaks the heavy, oppressive silence, his voice dark and brimming with fury.

When Lucifer sweeps his gaze from me and over to his son, I stand cautiously.

Why is Lucifer even here? Why had Maverick worked so hard to get the ring on me and get Joseline under his thumb? I can't see the connections yet.

"Is it wrong of me to pay my son a visit? It's been so long." Lucifer's lips pull into a wicked grin, revealing the tips of his canine teeth have been sharpened. The lines at the corners of his eyes deepen, and it's clear with the way he stares at Cain, how much he's enjoying himself. How this is exactly what the devil wanted—to scare us with his presence.

His gaze roams the room, his nostrils flaring. "What a... *quaint* little place you have here," he says as he steps further inside. "So unlike you."

Cain squares his shoulders, his voice like venom. "Everything you do comes with purpose, Father. So, why are you here?"

Dorian and Elias are stiff, ready to jump into action in a split second if Cain calls to them.

"I am so much more than I allow you to see, I am everywhere, and I have been hearing rumors about you," Lucifer says, his jaw clenching. He takes a step toward me, and Elias is suddenly in front of me. A massive demon shield.

I try to breathe but fail miserably. Joseline hasn't moved, but tears run down her cheeks. I'm pissed at her for what she did, but the terror on her face makes guilt spin within me, too. I hate seeing her this way, as angry as I am with her. Despite everything, I still care.

"The moment you threw us out of Hell is when we severed ties. You are nothing to me," Cain growls.

To hear the way Cain talks to his father, with hatred and agony in his voice, undoes me. The bits of information the demons have told me about his past doesn't even compare to the tension between Father and son. Let's not forget that Maverick is Cain's brother and did absolutely nothing when he was tossed out of their home.

I'm burning up with anger for Cain, for Dorian and Elias, for Joseline, for me being used.

"You have been busy on Earth," Lucifer begins, speaking so casually that he reminds me of a serial killer who is waiting for the right moment to make his move and jab his blade into his victim's heart. He completely ignores Cain's earlier comment and keeps talking. "Secrets have a way of betraying you." His attention turns in my direction momentarily, leaving me covered in goosebumps, then back to Cain.

"You got something to say, then do so and get out," Dorian states, his words fueled by fury. My light-hearted and carefree Dorian... It's strange seeing him like this. And scary. "We had a movie night planned and your presence is killing the whole fun vibe."

Lucifer seems caught off by that, but it only takes seconds for him to shake off any sense of distraction, and that perfect mask of illusion slips back over his face.

"Insolent, impertinent, and disgraceful. These are who you associate with, and you wonder why you lost your chance at my throne."

I note Maverick's nose wrinkling with disgust at hearing his father's words. Is that why he betrayed Cain? At his own chance to eventually inherit the title of the King of Hell? Except, can Lucifer even die?

"What the fuck do you want?" Cain snaps, and even I flinch at his fury.

"There has been talk that you have intentions of returning

home uninvited." The devil breaks into loud laughter that booms off the walls.

Maverick watches his father and brother, not saying a word, and I can't for the life of me work out what he's thinking. His expression has fallen blank.

"It's hilarious to think you can return," Lucifer muses, still laughing, making him sound more like a lunatic when no one else makes a sound.

I nibble on my lower lip. He's completely bonkers.

Elias growls under his breath and jolts forward with tremendous rage and speed, but he doesn't even get close. Suddenly, he's flying across the room in the opposite direction and slams into the wall with a thunderous bang. He slumps to the ground, groaning.

Dorian snaps forward too, his sharp nails sweeping out so fast, I barely have time to breathe. But just as quick, he joins Elias, thrown against the wall like they are nothing.

Lucifer didn't even lift a finger. Didn't even blink. Only his eyes follow the demons. He's too powerful. How are any of us meant to stand against Lucifer himself?

Those short thoughts are all I have time for before he turns on me.

I recoil, my stomach knotting up, and a scream involuntarily rises to the back of my throat.

Cain lunges at his father, but Lucifer's hand moves with unimaginable speed and grabs him by the throat, lifting him off his feet. Cain's dark eyes widen, his fingers clawing at his father's iron grip.

"Son, you will learn the hard way. This I can promise you." He tosses him aside like he's nothing and stands a breaths distance from me, moving so fast I missed him coming at me completely.

He grabs my chin, sharp fingernails digging into my cheek. "These demons may be the darkness in your light, but when your time comes, I will swallow you whole."

Then, in the blink of an eye, he pops out of existence, no longer standing before me.

I gasp and stumble backward until my back hits a chair, and I seize it to stop myself from falling over. My breaths come too fast, fear slicing right through my chest. That's when I notice Maverick is also gone.

Joseline is on her knees, crying into her hands, while my three demons are getting to their feet. They each have fire in their eyes.

I don't know exactly what to expect—them to lash out, erupt into a fit of curses and flames—but they don't do any of that. They're stiffly silent, in shock.

A shiver slides down my spine.

Lucifer, himself, was in our home.

CAIN

I MAY HAVE my father's blood in my veins, but I am nothing like the bastard. I will return to Hell and finish what I started. Eradicate the filthy from power and show my brothers that I am the one they will bow to. I will get revenge on them for standing against me. Especially my weaselly brother, Maverick. The spineless prick. It's been clear for centuries that Father is no longer fit to rule over the underworld, and it appears the war I've sought has finally made an appearance, even if it comes sooner than I expected.

My pulse hammers after seeing my father after all this time. I loathe him as much as I did when I left home. My hands curl into fists. The smell of the crackling fireplace reminds me of home, of the constant stench of burning darkness. Of the innocent deaths he caused.

It doesn't matter that I'm on Earth. His presence has leached into me, poisoning me, and he's all I can think about again.

And that's exactly what he wanted.

I lift my chin and glance over to Aria, who is back kneeling next to her crying friend, and a different emotion wraps around my heart. Pain... It yanks at me to know I've put her directly in my father's sights. I tried so hard to keep it from Aria, but she was in danger the moment we brought her here. It was selfish of me to want to keep her, thinking I could somehow protect her from my father's wrath.

All I want is to adore her, save her, care for her, and I may have brought Hell down on her instead.

Fuck!

I cross the room and crouch beside Aria, placing my hand on

her lower back. Her soft, dark eyes flare with panic. My heart thunders louder, banging in my chest to see her scared.

"You are safe here," I tell her, although I'm not so sure if it's the truth.

"For how long?" Her hand trembles as she tries to wrench Maverick's ring off her finger. She groans, her whole body quivering in her attempt.

"Aria, it's not going to come off without Maverick removing it," I say.

She looks at me, exasperated, tears pooling at the corners of her eyes. "I ruined everything."

"Demons are tricksters," Elias answers to try and calm her. "There is no greater thief than a demon."

"That doesn't make me feel any better."

Joseline presses her shoulder up close to Aria, whispering, "If we're going for the most dumbass award, I'm pretty sure I take the cake." Her attempt at a grin comes out lopsided and awkward.

But my thoughts drift to my father and how close he came to Aria. If anything happens to her, I'll never forgive myself. Just the idea of him hurting her, torturing her, for the sake of controlling me, has me shaking all over. I wouldn't put it past him at all. The thought alone drives me to the point of insanity.

Dorian and Elias step into my view, distracting me from my darkening thoughts. Both stand tall and broad like sentinels. Rage radiates from them in waves, and I don't blame them. Elias's upper lip curls, his chest heaving madly for breath, while shadows gather under Dorian's eyes like he's about to burst. I am under no illusion that if we had a way back into Hell, they'd already be on Father's heels for revenge.

I stand and clear my throat. "Elias, escort Aria's friend to a spare room. She's to be watched at all times," I command. He nods.

Aria's on her feet, bringing her friend with her off the floor by an arm. "Joseline can stay in my room," she insists, her eyes imploring I give her this.

Except this girl with mousey blonde hair reeks of magic, and the deal she made with Maverick makes her a ticking time bomb.

Aria's glistening gaze melts me, but on this point, I will not bend. "That is not a wise idea," I explain, then turn to Elias with a knowing expression.

He nods. "I got this," he says, and he understands the danger Joseline poses to Aria, to all of us, which is why we keep her with us for now.

As Elias approaches Aria, she offers me a wry glare. "Joseline's scared."

"And she's compromised," I reply. "We don't know yet if Maverick controls her, if he uses her as eyes and ears."

Joseline's head tilts upward, her eyes red from crying meeting mine. There's trepidation in her gaze. Good, she should be scared, because if it wasn't for Aria, I'd have the witch locked up in the basement. She has no idea what danger she's brought to our door, or that she teeters on the edge of death by making a deal with a demon.

"Go." I wave for Elias to take them, and he does.

Now alone, Dorian paces in front of the fireplace in the parlor, and I join him by the hearth.

"Your father's been watching us." The corners of his mouth tighten, his expression taut, and he breathes rapidly. His demon side is creeping to the surface, his hair lightening and his nails long. He runs them over the bricks, making an ear-grating sound. "I'm itching to rip Lucifer and Maverick apart with my bare hands."

I stare at the deep scratches in the stone. It's not the first time the place was damaged. It's just usually Elias causing the mess.

The last time I'd seen Dorian this angry was when we were first kicked out of Hell, when he felt so lost in the world. He'd almost lost part of himself to rage at one point and compensated by fucking every supernatural and human he lured to his side. Sex consumed him then. It was the only way he could cope.

"Lucifer does nothing without reason," I answer. That's how the devil works. I've seen him in action through the years, the games he plays, the strings he holds over everyone. Anyone steps out of line, and he sends his hellhounds after them to rip them to shreds. Elias was one of the best, so I have no doubt there is a special torture waiting for him for abandoning the Infernal Legions of Hell if my father gets his way.

"He wants us dead," Dorian answers, his voice bitter and dark. "That's his reasoning. He's a fucking lunatic."

I shake my head, knowing the devil too well for it to be that simple. "If that was all, he would have done it by now. I suspect it involves Aria."

Silence chokes the air in the parlor, and I look up at Dorian. He and Elias are the demons I call brothers, over my own flesh and blood. And with Lucifer's appearance, this is not the time for secrets. I have to tell him about the vision I had while I was under the necromancer's power. The one with Aria and Hell.

"There's something you should know," I admit.

Dorian stares at me with trepidation in his eyes. "I'm not going to like this, am I?"

"You better take a seat," I answer. "Elias will join us shortly."

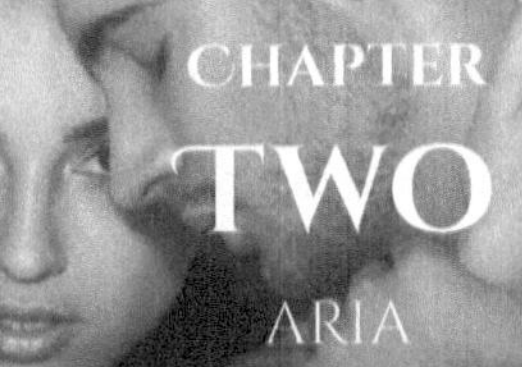

Elias, Joseline, and I walk up the many steps to the top floor. Instead of continuing down the hall to my bedroom, Elias stops at the first one on the right. He throws open the door and steps aside for us to step through.

Like mine, the room has a large bed, clean linens, sparse furniture, and an attached bathroom. Everything is neat and orderly, kept expecting a guest any day. I turn back to Elias.

"Are you sure she can't just stay with me?" I ask him. "We've been roommates before."

Staring down at me, he frowns. "Like Cain said, it's not a good idea right now."

"Can she at least have a room closer to me then?"

But he's already shaking his head. "We don't know the extent of Maverick's contract with her. He may have her under his influence in some way."

Annoyance prickles up my neck. Can't he see that she's scared for her life? Not to mention that he's talking about her like she's not standing right there. "Joseline would never hurt me."

"You don't know that." His gaze slides her way. "Anymore."

Wow.

Okay, I know Elias isn't good with social cues, but that was cold-blooded.

"Aria..." Joseline whispers softly beside me, and lightly touches my arm. "Maybe he's right."

Confused, I blink at her. "What do you mean?"

"This is my fault. I'm the stupid one for trusting Maverick and signing my soul away for money and power. I should've never agreed to it in the first place," she says.

"I trusted him enough to let him put this ring on my finger, so I'm just as stupid," I reply. The truth of Maverick's betrayal stings still, but not as much as my own self-loathing for falling for his tricks in the first place. "He played us both."

"Maverick has always been a slimeball with the uncanny ability to manipulate a person's emotions, an ability he uses every chance he can get. It makes it easier to persuade others to do his bidding," Elias explains.

"Emotion manipulation? You mean like Dorian?" I ask.

"Dorian can only heighten sexual desires. Maverick can take your fears and make them the only things you see until you go insane or pitch yourself off a bridge. He can bring you comfort and lull you into a false sense of security. Or heighten your rage until you strangle someone with your bare hands..." He glances at Joseline again, obviously implying that this is a fear he has with her. She swallows roughly. "And there's no way to fight it. He can make you lose yourself completely with just a single touch."

A touch. No wonder Cain had warned me not to let Maverick touch me.

Now that I think about it, I did feel strange whenever his hands were on me. Like when we were flying or when he'd first tried to "help" me with Sayah. It was like he was amplifying my happiness in one situation and drowning me in fear in the other. Really, he'd been influencing me from the beginning.

The asshole.

"I still think Joseline should be closer to me. If Maverick is that dangerous, as you say, she'll need protection."

Elias opens his mouth to argue, but Joseline is the one to respond first. "Aria, it's really okay. I'll be right here. I don't want to cause more trouble than I already have."

"Listen to the witch," Elias quips, and I throw him a glare, still not happy about the idea. Not backing down, he pulls his shoulders back. "Until we figure out what we're doing next, we need to be prepared for the worst." Then he turns to Joseline. "In the meantime, I'll have some food sent up for you."

Just then, the bald-headed guard who I'd seen many times in front of my bedroom door and in Purgatory reaches the top of the stairs. Throwing a nod to Elias, he takes his place against the wall.

Really? A guard? I understand they're worried about Maverick using her in some way, but is this necessary?

It feels more like the demons are keeping her prisoner until they figure out what to do with her, and that thought alone shakes me to the core. I mean, what if they decide we'd be safer with her dead?

I do everything I can to shove that terrible thought from my head. It's not like I'd let them do such a thing anyway. Even if Joseline and I hadn't left off on the best of terms before this, she was still my friend. The closest one I had. My foster sister.

"If you need anything, Byron will be here to help you," Elias says. His gaze lingers on me for a few seconds more, sending me a silent warning, before he heads down the steps and out of sight.

The moment he's gone, I look at the guard I just learned was named Byron and push Joseline further inside the room. He doesn't say anything, even when I close the door behind us, but once we're alone, Joseline becomes scared once again.

"Aria, if the demons don't want you around me..." she begins.

"Oh, fuck that," I say. "They don't own me." I pause, realizing the irony behind that statement. "Well, I guess technically they do, but they *own* me, own me. Does that make sense?"

Her brows pinch in a 'no.'

"I can still do what I want, and if that means catching up with an old friend or getting into some deep shit with another demon unknowingly, that's up to me."

"Well, let's hope those two things don't coincide with each other anymore," she replies with a short laugh, but the humor drains away immediately, and she moves to the bed to lean against it.

Crossing her arms over her chest, her gaze drops to the floor and she rubs her lips together, something she usually does to prevent herself from crying.

"Hey," I say as I move closer to her. "Don't take what Elias says to heart. He has as many social skills as a wet paper bag. He doesn't understand—"

"He's right, though." Her voice hitches from the restrained emotions. "I led Maverick and Lucifer straight to you. And why? Because I was jealous. I wanted some of this for myself. What kind of friend am I?"

When the tears come, she presses her palms to her eyes and her entire body trembles. "I should've told you the truth from the beginning. I shouldn't have been so selfish. I should've never said all those terrible things to you at my apartment."

Watching her this torn up makes my chest ache. She's beating herself up over this more than I am. I don't care anymore about the things she'd said. That's all water under the bridge.

There's only one thing I'm concerned about now, and that's how we're all going to get out of Lucifer's sights alive.

Not sure how else to comfort her, I rub a hand up and down her back. "You're safe now," I tell her, because that's what matters. "I doubt Maverick will have the balls to show up here again after that little stunt. You just need to lay low for a bit until we can sort this all out."

She smiles up at me, her eyes glistening with tears. "I really am sorry. For everything. For calling you a whore."

I shrug a shoulder. "Eh, maybe I am." With everything else going on with me, that's honestly the least worrisome thing I could be.

To my surprise and relief, Joseline laughs. "You've definitely changed since you've been here."

"Huh? What do you mean?"

"Not in a bad way," she assures me, wiping her wet cheeks. "More confident. More center-stage and less in the background."

I guess that's a good thing, right?

"Look, you're even wearing more color, too," she says, and points to my dark burgundy top. I had paired it with my typical dark jeans, so not completely out of my element but it is something different. "When I saw you in heels before, I thought you'd been possessed or something."

That makes me snort. "That was part of my work uniform. Still can't walk in the damn things, though."

There's a low whining sound and scratching at the door. Joseline freezes, still a bit jumpy after our ordeal in the foyer. I, however, know exactly who it is who's come to visit.

Quickly, I move across the room and open the door. Cassiel shoves his way inside, all overgrown gray fluff, and pushes his head against my legs. He's so big now, he almost sends me toppling over.

Joseline squeals with fright and scrambles onto the bed. "What in the world is that thing?" she cries out.

"Calm down. This is Cassiel. He's a lynx." More interested in the ear scratches I'm giving him, Cassiel doesn't even look Joseline's way. When I stop, his tongue licks my palm, asking for more. I chuckle. "He won't hurt you. He's just a kitten."

"That's the biggest baby lynx kitten I've ever seen. Didn't even think grown lynxes get that big."

That's true. Cassiel had grown significantly in the last few days, with the help of a warlock's magic potion and a necromancer's enchanted grave dirt. He is almost as tall as me while on all fours.

"He eats his Wheaties," I say, taking his massive head in my hands and rubbing our noses together.

"You aren't afraid he'll eat you?" she asks.

"Me? No. But he is pretty protective of me though. I wouldn't put it past him to make a meal of someone else if they tried anything funny."

"If the demons don't get to them first," Joseline says, and carefully gets off the bed, eyeing Cassiel.

"True."

Her gaze roams around the room again, eventually settling out the arch window where more snow has begun to fall. "Do you like it here? With the demons?"

Her question throws me off guard. Maybe it's because I've only just decided to stay, at least for a bit longer. The goal had always been to help the demons track down the rest of the relics, gain my freedom from the contract, and then move on with my life. But now, I'm not so sure. Thinking about leaving Cain, Dorian, and Elias causes my lungs to squeeze and makes breathing more difficult. When the time comes, I'm not even sure what I'm going to do.

But to Joseline's question, do I like it here with the demons now?

Do I like being manhandled and threatened by the King of Hell? No.

Do I like almost dying like every other day? Absolutely not.

Do I enjoy living in constant fear of losing someone I care about? That's a hard no, too.

But, do I like living here? I'd have to say yes.

I know, it sounds bizarre, but it's true.

Since I'm not even sure how to explain myself, I simply nod my answer to Joseline. "It's a far cry from a ritzy apartment on the upper eastside though," I say.

She huffs. "Yeah, but I'd take a shithole like Murray's over it any day."

A smile tugs at my lips at the memories that stir at the mention of our old foster father. It feels like years since we were living under his leaky roof, both stuffed in a single bedroom, going to bed hungry every night. But there were good times, too. Like staying up super late while Murray was out gambling our money away and watching horror movies on a grainy, box tv. Or making each other Christmas gifts, which usually involved us trying to top each other for the "Most Awful Gift Award."

Out of all my foster families, Joseline was the only other person I'd connected with. Growing up in the system had been rough for both of us—we'd seen our fair share of fucked-up stuff—but we made the best of it. Together.

Joseline must be thinking the same thing because she says, "Could you imagine if we actually did move in together after your birthday? Like we'd planned?"

Cassiel pads across the room and curls up in a ball in the center of the rug. Within seconds, he's snoring. *Sweet life.*

"Sleeping in sleeping bags and eating ramen for the rest of our lives as we scrape to get by?" I laugh.

"But we'd be roughing it together," she says. "It sounded like living and luxury whenever we'd talked about it."

She's right. We knew we'd struggle to stay afloat after moving out but, somehow, it seemed like a dream come true.

How much things have changed since then.

"Maybe we can still do that. You know, after things calm down." The words leave my mouth without thought.

Joseline's head snaps my way, a grimace on her face. "How though? Both our souls are contracted..."

"First, we're going to find a way to get you out of yours."

"Is that even possible?"

I nod. "Cain once told me that a soul contract can be broken by the responsible demon's death."

She deadpans me. "You really think your three demons are going to be okay killing one of their own? Or Cain killing his own brother?"

"Did you see what happened downstairs? Not exactly *The Brady Bunch* going on there."

Joseline's pinched brows tell me she still isn't buying it.

I touch Maverick's ring on my finger and fury flares again at the fact that I'd let him dupe me. I've never wanted to strangle someone with my bare hands so much in my life. "And if they don't, then I will," I say, through clenched teeth.

"And what about you? How will you get out of yours?"

"Cain and I made a deal. Sorta. An adjustment," I reply.

Her head tilts. "Oh?"

"If I help them find these magical objects that they're looking for, then they'll release me."

"Huh... That's odd." She quickly realizes what she's said may be offensive and scrambles with the rest. "I mean, just because you're an ordinary. It makes me wonder why they want your help. No offense."

I'd been living secret-free with the demons, I'd almost forgotten no one else knew about Sayah or my inner dark-magic detector. Joseline still thinks I'm plainer than sin.

As much as I want to tell her, it's safer if I don't. Especially with her now involved with Maverick and Lucifer.

"No offense taken," I assure her. "And who knows why. But it's a deal I was willing to take."

"I don't blame you. You have a way out."

There's a subtle knock at the door. Cassiel's head pops up and he sniffs the air.

"Come in," I call, and a second later, in strolls Sadie with a cart full of food. Steak, roasted potatoes, steamed vegetables, grilled chicken, rice, and three different kinds of cakes. Joseline's eyes light up at the sight of the feast before her, and I chuckle, remembering the first time I'd been faced with a meal here. It was enough food to feed a small army—certainly more than a starving foster kid had ever eaten in one sitting.

"Thanks, Sadie," I say to the maid. She waves and walks out just as Cassiel stretches and makes his way over to see what goodies he can beg for.

"This is all supposed to be for me?" she gasps in disbelief. "I can't eat all this."

Smiling, I snatch one of the rolls and take a bite. As expected, it's warm and buttery and absolutely delicious. After all of the crap that's happened between the two of us, I'm beyond thrilled to have my friend here with me again, catching up and joking like our lives weren't super f-ed up at the moment. It feels normal. Refreshing, even.

"No worries," I say, and take another bite. "I'm here to help."

Cassiel creeps closer to the cart, his tail swiping the air and his tongue darting out of his mouth as he eyes the array of foods in front of him. Joseline jumps at his closeness, and I laugh.

"And I'm sure Cassiel would just love to take some of it off your hands, too."

On cue, he uses his nose to nudge a plate of gravy off the tray. Glass breaks, the gravy splattering all over the floor, but Cassiel laps it up happily, making pleased purring noises as he does. Joseline and I burst into a fit of laughter.

"Are you going to spill already, or is this a guessing game?" I ask Cain sarcastically, needing to know what could possibly be worse than Lucifer making a surprise visit.

Cain sits perched on the edge of the couch, legs parted and hands rested on his thighs. When he gets like this, so lost in his thoughts, he's a hard one to talk to. But his stiff and silent demeanor makes me anxious.

"I had a dream about Aria," he tells us.

Dorian bursts out laughing. Slaps his knee and all. "Wait, you're joking, right? Here I thought this was going to be all doom and gloom, but instead you're telling us you had a fucking wet dream?"

Of course his mind goes straight to sex.

I resist the urge to roll my eyes.

Cain's gaze narrows on him. He's suddenly on his feet and moving in front of the fireplace. Body rigid, he turns and stares at us.

Dorian plops down in his spot on the couch, while I stand behind him. I don't understand what's so worrisome about a dream, but if Cain's concerned, there's reason to take this seriously. Not much can disturb a prince of Hell.

"Okay, so what happened in your dream?" I ask, hating the waiting.

"It started with me and Aria in a binding ritual, about to be bound together for eternity."

"So it *was* a sex dream," Dorian says. "I knew it."

Cain gives an exasperated sigh. "It may have started that way, but we were quickly thrown into my father's grand room in Hell, full of people. You two were there, along with all my brothers. Everyone was witnessing my union with Aria. Doesn't bother me. At least, not until she's sitting in Lucifer's throne, eyes black and demonic, with his crown on her head. As if she's the new ruler of all the underworld."

My heart climbs into my throat. Aria—our Aria—the Queen of Hell?

"What does it mean?" I ask.

"Nothing," Dorian says with a dismissive wave of his hand. "It's just a dream."

"I'm not so sure," Cain replies.

"I have dreams I'm being railed from behind by a person in a bunny costume. But I don't see the fucking Easter bunny here anywhere. Do you?"

I side-eye him. "I hope you're joking."

"I wish I was," he says. "It's why I don't eat chocolate before bed anymore."

But from the hard look on Cain's face, this was more than just an ordinary dream. "What do you think about it, Cain? It's clearly gotten to you."

"I can't stop thinking about it," he confesses. "It felt like something else to me. Not just a dream, but a glimpse into the future."

"You mean a premonition?" Dorian asks.

Cain doesn't move for a long moment as he considers his words. Then, his head dips in a nod. "I believe so, yes."

I blink, stunned. "You think Aria—"

"I don't know for sure, but it is curious," he replies. "My concern is that it's linked to my father. I saw the way he studied her. It's as if she'd always been in his vision. It's been a plague on my thoughts, and then paired with my dream, I'm certain his visit was for one purpose. To assess her."

I clench my jaw. "He's seeing her as a threat now?"

"It's near impossible to ever know what that madman is thinking." Dorian's legs bounce, suddenly antsy.

Cain nods. "Lucifer likes to play with his food, so I would not be surprised if this is part of his way to torture us. But at the same time, the dream suggests he may know something we don't. I fear he'll try to control her. Use her. Why else get Maverick involved?"

Feeling too stiff all over, I crack my neck and roll my shoulders. My hellhound is aching for a fight, to rip and tear someone apart. Preferably Lucifer or Maverick. "We can spend weeks speculating what he wants from her, but there's only one immediate solution. Make it impossible for that fucker to get his hands on her."

"Agreed." Dorian's head jolts up.

"There's only one way for that to happen, as you all know," Cain mutters. "Is that something we're prepared to do?"

"She's going to be pissed," Dorian states the obvious.

"We won't hide it from her. She needs to know," I insist.

Dorian pushes himself from the couch and heads for the door. "I'm going to collect her now so we can talk to her." He's gone before Cain or I have a chance to say otherwise. But it's better this way.

I sift my attention to Cain. "Something needs to be done about Joseline. We don't know how deep your brother's claws are in her or what influence he has, what information he's attempting to uncover. In truth, I don't feel comfortable having her here."

Cain meets my gaze, and for a split second, I swear I see fear cross his face. It terrifies him, the thought of losing Aria. I'd heard it in his voice when he spoke of his father and his dream, and I don't blame him. Since moving in with us, she's crawled under my skin and gotten into my veins. Everything I smell and touch and think about reminds me of her. She's affected all three of us alike.

"I'll find a way," he says.

Footfalls scraping the wooden floorboards have me turning to the parlor entrance. Aria walks inside, dressed in black skinny jeans and a tight burgundy shirt. I can't ignore how perfectly the fabric hugs her breasts, my gaze following every curve that has my fingers twitching with a desire to take her for myself.

Fuck, she's breathtaking, and a growl rises through me, my hellhound responding to her presence, wanting her pressed up against me.

She catches me staring, and I reward her with a wink. Her lips look fuller today, they are redder too, as are her eyes. I picture her in my arms, the tender, small thing who doesn't deserve to be in the middle of so much chaos.

Shoving past Dorian in the doorway is Cassiel, seeming to not realize he's now four times his normal size.

My lip curls upward at his presence. Damn furball, but Aria adores him, so for her, I make an effort to tolerate him.

Aria's mouth purses as she pauses several steps into the room. "You wanted to talk to me about Lucifer?" There's a quiver in the tone of her voice, and she rakes her fingers through dark, tousled hair that falls past her shoulders.

"Come, take a seat," Cain implores.

She moves across the room quickly and flops down into the corner of the sofa before grabbing a small cushion and hugging it to her chest. Cassiel leaps up next to her, making himself cozy but taking up the rest of the room on the cushions.

"Did something else happen?" she asks. "You're all scaring me a bit right now."

Cain approaches her and crouches in front of her, taking her hand in his. The tenderness in his approach is the opposite of the demon who rarely showed empathy, but Aria means the world to him. Dorian and I have both noticed the change after his brush with death.

"We're concerned with how easily my father appeared. If he's managed to get out of Hell once, it's possible he could return again."

"What do you mean?"

"He's supposed to be trapped. Hell is meant to be his prison. Coming up to Earth is supposed to be nearly impossible for him, yet he was able to do it. Who knows if he'll be able to again," he explains. "But it proves he's stronger and more clever than we originally thought."

She places her hand over his, and a sting of jealousy plunges into me. I wish she was looking at me that way. With such longing. "You're worried about me." It's a statement. Not a question.

"Of course I am," he whispers. "We all are. But we will do whatever it takes to keep you safe. You must know that."

"That's what I'm afraid of..." She glances at me and Dorian before sighing. "I just don't understand. Why would Lucifer want me? Is it because of Sayah?"

"It could be, but we don't know for sure," Dorian adds. "He's paying you a bit too much attention for my liking."

"This is my fault, isn't it?" She pulls her hand away from Cain's and curls up on the couch. Cassiel snuggles up against her side and puts his massive head in her lap. The lynx really has become attached to her. "I let Maverick trick me, and now I've got fucking Satan stalking me. Not exactly what a girl wants to hear."

"Of course not," Cain insists.

There's no shame in admitting fear, none what-so-fucking-ever, and right now, my little rabbit is shaking like a leaf.

Dorian sits on the armrest beside her and wraps an arm around her shoulders, drawing her to him.

When Cain stands, his expression darkens, the muscles of his jaw clenching.

"There is a way to keep you protected," I say, to break the growing silence. She turns to me.

"What is it? I'll do anything."

Well, that's a good place to start. "A binding ritual. It will ensure Lucifer can't get his hands on you."

"Binding... ritual?" Unsure, Aria stares up at me, then looks around to Cain, Dorian, and back at me again. "But? There are always buts."

"But," Cain begins, "it can only be done on a full moon, which is a few days away."

Silence permeates the room, and a sense of tension thickens the air. Aria isn't a fool. She knows there's more to this, yet Cain has only drip-fed her information, to not scare her. But time isn't on our side. She needs to know the full impact of what we have to do.

When Cain doesn't continue, I clear my throat, drawing his attention. "Are we going through the details now?"

He pinches the bridge of his nose. He probably didn't want to tell her any more than what he had, but oh well. I understand wanting to protect her and not scare her, but she'd want to know. We can't deceive her with something like this. It's no simple task.

Am I scared we're even offering the ritual as a solution to this? Fuck yeah I am. It's the same thing I'd gone through with Serena, the woman I swore was my soulmate but ended up betraying me. Betraying all of us. The guilt of it still sits like a mountain on my shoulders. I had been the one to ask Cain and Dorian to help me with the ritual, and as my friends, my brothers, they agreed, even though they didn't believe Serena was loyal to me. I hadn't wanted to listen, but ultimately, they were right, and because of my foolishness, Lucifer knew of all our plans before we could even do them, which landed us here. Banished.

It took me too fucking long to get over Serena's betrayal. So, was I hesitating to go through this again and risk it all on a woman we met only months ago? Yes. But am I willing to do whatever it takes to protect Aria? Even if it kills me in the process?

Absolutely.

Without hesitation.

Maybe I haven't learned anything at all.

"What is it? Tell me what?" Aria persists, looking between the three of us. "I need to know what I'm in for." Her gaze lingers a little longer on Cain. "No secrets, remember?"

Dorian and I wait for Cain to explain, but he says nothing.

"Tell me what happens. Will it lock my soul with yours? Curse me into another dimension? And what about our new deal?" The last part was directed to Cain again. "You said if I helped you find your relics, you would release my soul. What happens to that?"

He glares at me, but I shrug it off. I don't care. He can be angry with me all he wants. Aria needs to decide this for herself. It's her soul on the line here.

"Give us time to work out the details," Dorian answers to break the rising tension.

I sigh loudly. You know, to really let my annoyance be known.

"Why are you being such a prick?" he barks at me.

"A prick? Me? Never."

"What's going on?" Aria asks.

"Listen," Cain says. "We think we have a way to keep you protected, but nothing with demon rituals and deals is straightforward. Like Dorian said, give us a day to sort out the best approach and then we'll lay out all the details for you. That way you can decide if this is something you want to do."

Aria untangles herself from Cassiel and pushes up to her feet. The way she looks at us with glistening eyes has my heart squeezing. Fuck, this isn't what I wish for her, and yet, to save her from Lucifer, we have no other options.

"I don't want to play games," she says. "After everything we've gone through together, I deserve the truth."

"And you will have it." Cain moves to stand before her, and he cups her face. "I would never allow anything to harm you. This is why I need to make sure there are no other options. The ritual is irreversible."

She blinks at him, and I expect her to ask him what it is again, but she doesn't. Resignation settles over her expression, and she pulls free from Cain.

"I'm going to my room."

She walks out, her hands deep in her pockets, and her shoulders curved forward.

The tapping of her feet against the floorboards outside the room fade with her distance, and I turn to Cain and Dorian.

"Fuck, why did we even bring her down here to talk about it if you were not going to actually *talk* about it? If you wanted to terrify her, you did an incredible job," I snap.

"I know I'm going to regret saying this, but maybe Elias is right here, Cain," Dorian replies. "I know you want to protect her, even emotionally, but she should know."

"You think I don't know that?" he bites back. The cords in his neck move with each word. "But my father is a terrifying son of a bitch, and she's in more danger now than ever before. If she knew what he was capable of, if she saw it..." He trails off, as if the thoughts are too much to bear. Then, after a long moment, he says, more certain, "We hold back until the very last minute. I want to explore a couple of other options I've heard about that might be helpful but won't bond her to us. Less... permanent."

"Would it be so bad if she was?" Dorian asks, straightening.

Cain hesitates, while my stomach lurches.

"You heard her mention the promise of her freedom again. How do you think she'll react when she discovers that'll be taken away?"

"Even if it means saving her life?" he asks. "What's her other option? We give her freedom only to have Lucifer swoop in and steal it from her? You will live with that regret on your mind for the rest of eternity."

"I want what's best for her. Even if she doesn't."

I could understand that, but still. "I say we lay everything out for her and let her decide. It's only fair."

"We need to tread carefully," Cain replies to Dorian. "We push her too far and she'll hate us forever."

"And if we don't push enough, we'll lose her forever," Dorian reminds him.

Shit. Is anyone listening to me?

A growl bursts out of me, snapping both their gazes my way. Finally.

"Why do we have to choose for her? Why can't we have her choose her own fate?" I blurt out before one of them can cut me off. "She should have a say."

They remain rigid for a few minutes, but finally Cain sighs, rubbing his temples.

"We will reconvene on this later," he says. "By then I hope to have confirmed if my backup plans have any merit. And if not, then we tell Aria everything." He doesn't ask for our agreement but marches out of the parlor. Headed to his office, no doubt. Shaking his head, Dorian leaves shortly after him.

Cassiel's soft snores fill the silence, and I curl my hands into fists until my knuckles turn white. I stare into the flames, hating that even outside of Hell, Lucifer poses such danger to us.

A flash of movement catches my attention from outside the parlor, and there's the faint creak of a floorboard.

Curious, I head out of the room, my mind consumed with finding that weasel Maverick spying on us. What I would give to finally get my chance to break his face.

Around the corner, I find Aria creeping away. She'd been eavesdropping. I should be angry, but instead I smile to myself. Of course she's spying on us. I shouldn't have expected anything less from her.

I march after her as she heads down the hall, and when she twists around at my thumping footfalls, her eyes widen at my approach.

"How much did you hear?" I ask.

"Enough." She stumbles around to look at me.

The air between us thins as she sweeps a tongue over her lips.

"You know we only want the best for you."

"But it's my decision at the end of the day, not any of yours."

Her response flies out fiercely. "You all treat me like I'm glass and about to break, but I'm a lot stronger than any of you realize."

She's so powerful yet so vulnerable, and all I want to do is hold her close to me, keep her so guarded that nothing can ever touch her. Staring into her eyes undoes me. When did I fall this hard for her?

If I really thought about it, I could answer that question with half a dozen scenarios, but where the truth lies is much simpler than that. Her very presence calls to me. My inner hellhound responds to her in ways I cannot describe. It didn't even respond like this to Serena. So what I'm feeling with Aria is new and fucking terrifying. But I'll never back away from her. I can't.

"I promise you, no matter what happens, I will keep you protected," I say.

Her chin quivers, and that's not the response I expect. Instantly, my chest clenches with guilt.

Fuck! I should've never said anything.

I drag her into my arms, and she buries herself against my chest, crying softly. I hold onto her, and my insides shatter. She talked about her not being glass, and right now I feel like I'm the fucking brittle one who is splintering as I listen to her cries.

Swallowing, I wrap my arms around her tiny waist and lift her up against me, to bring her as close to me as possible.

"My little rabbit, you're breaking me. Don't cry."

She holds onto me desperately, her touch trembling, I guide her legs around my hips, then I embrace her so we are as close as humanly possible.

"I'm sorry." I never thought I'd say those words in my lifetime, but she deserves them, and so much more. "I fucking hate that you are in this situation. If I could stop it all, I would have done it already."

She quiets down and pulls back to look at me. I reach up with one hand, while holding her with the other, and wipe the tears tracking down her cheeks. "I know you're scared, but we will find a solution, just as we did when we saved Cain."

She half-shrugs and nods, then turns her head to look back down the corridor where the light from the windows light up the entryway and parlor. "Elias, I'm still pissed off at the three of you but... I can't take anymore chaos after everything." The way she tilts her head to the side, her gaze falling to my mouth, I can't ignore the temptation she's offering me. The unspoken message of what she wants me to do.

I lack willpower when it comes to resisting Aria. Having her wrapped around me drives my impulse. When she leans in and takes a kiss, I stop fighting what I should do and follow on with what I damn well want to do.

Quickly, I walk her up against the wall and return the passion three-fold, desperation to claim her consuming me.

My gut tightens while my cock hardens, thickening in my pants. My little rabbit rubs her groin against me, igniting fire between us. My breathing grows ragged, captured in a whirlwind of emotions.

I pin one hand against the wall over her head as she clings onto me, and with the other, I grip her chin and force her to look at me as I break our kiss. "You are the most exquisite thing, and I cannot possibly say no to you. My hunger for you is insatiable."

"Then fuck me and stop talking," she says, her hand gliding to the back of my head where she fists my hair and forces me back to her lips.

Hell, a moan bleeds out of my lungs at her aggression, at how wild it drives me.

With a growl, I kiss her hard, our mouths clashing, and I dip my hand between us, my fingers sliding in under the elastic of her pants and underwear. My touch reaches her drenched pussy, wetting my fingers, and she shudders in my arms.

Her breaths quiver out of her, and I can't think beyond the steam in my head.

I push into her, and she's gripping my shoulders, already rocking herself over me, her sweet little pussy sucking on my two fingers deep inside her.

Her eyes are fluttering backward as she arches against me. The harder I drive into her, the louder she groans, and I see the climax rising in her across her flushed cheeks. I sense it in her tightening body but it's too fast. She seeks release, but I'm going to make her remember us, to never forget what it's like being fucked by me.

I slide my fingers out, to her protest, and grip her waist as I lower her feet to the floor. I kneel in front of her and am already pulling her pants down her gorgeous legs, taking her thong too.

My attention locks on her glistening lips in front of me, her scent intoxicating and I lean in, taking a lungful, imprinting her scent on my soul. As she steps out of the clothes, I push my face to her delicious pussy and flick my tongue out across her moisture.

She moans, collapsing back against the wall.

Electricity roars through my body, and I push my hand up under her top, finding her stomach, reaching for her breast. I tug down the fabric of her bra, and find the softest orbs, filling my hand.

I press my tongue to her pussy, licking her in long strokes, while tugging and pulling on her hardened nipples.

Her moans fill my ears as I devour her, pushing and pushing her to the edge of an orgasm. With my other hand snaking around her hips, I grab her ass and draw her closer and she widens her stance for me. I push deeper, driving my tongue into her, loving how sweet she tastes, how her scent envelopes me and makes me feel like we're one. Like I could never forget how this goddess smells.

When her legs start trembling, I know she's close, and I pull back.

She collapses against the wall, breathing heavily. I eye the desire in her eyes, how her inner thighs glisten from her arousal.

"You have no idea what you do to me," I say, while I unbuckle my belt and drop my pants, then tug my T-shirt up and over my head.

I'm standing before her butt naked, and she's eyes me, licking her lips.

I groan in response to her hunger. "I'm going to fuck you," I breathe heavily, then I kiss her, our bodies merging, my cock nestled against her lower stomach. My balls ache with the need to release.

"Please, Elias. I can't wait much longer."

Hearing her begging for sex is my elixir, and I drag her back up into my arms, her sweet legs curled around my waist. We're tangled together, kissing, our bodies sliding against one another.

There's no ceremonial build up. Instead, what I feel for her is primal starvation, and I need to be inside her. I'm so fucking hard that I guide my cock to her entrance. She stiffens against me in anticipation.

"What are you waiting for?" she asks, and seems to be holding her breath, waiting for me to push in further.

I smile. I'm so in-fucking-love with the way she demands sex, her legs wide and me between them. My response comes in the form of me thrusting into her. There is nothing soft about the way I plunge into my little rabbit, in the way I force her open to accommodate my size.

Her cries echo around us, and I take her with a force that makes her moan louder. I bury myself in her to the hilt.

"Fuck, Elias," she almost purrs as her back arches, her fingers digging into my shoulders, holding on as I fuck her.

"Show me your tits," I demand, and she smiles, tugging up on her top, before pulling down on her bra. And those cherry red nipples dance beautifully each time I slap into her.

There's not a thing in the world that compares to sex with Aria. To how fast I'm falling apart and letting her take me over. I grip onto her hips and pound into her hard, my dick sliding in and out, the whole time I hold her stare.

I watch the euphoria wash over her face, stare at her parting lips with each cry, and everything about her swallows me whole.

She breathes erratically, matching my own, with every stroke, every thrust that has me slamming up against the innermost wall.

The hallway fills with the hungry sounds of sex, her moans, the slapping of me pounding into her tight pussy. I won't be surprised if the others come down and find us here, but I don't give a fuck. Aria is the type of girl I never imagined myself drawn to, yet she's everything I've ever wanted.

A spark of energy races up my arms in the same second my sweet Aria shudders and convulses with her orgasm claiming her. Her eyes clamp shut, and the concentration on her face is the most beautiful thing I've ever seen.

I barely hold on as her pussy squeezes around my cock. There's only so much a man can take, and I'm soon tumbling over the shuddering edge. I roar, my heart thundering. Sparks burst behind my eyelids. I release inside her, pumping every last drop as I groan.

Finally, as we're both locked in a lover's embrace, our brows press together, I stare at her and the satisfaction in her smile.

Hell, I'm proud of my handiwork. I bathe in the scent of our sex, in the afterglow of Aria's grin, in the sticky sweet fire between her legs.

She laughs and collapses against me. "That was everything I wanted."

Still throbbing inside her, I find my voice doesn't work. Instead, I wrap her in my arms and hold her against me, enjoying the ride down from the high of so much sexual hunger coursing between us. I'm going to have to eventually put her down, yet something inside me insists I hold onto her for as long as possible. That I don't let her out of my sight.

I hoist her up a bit more and walk with her down the hall, me still buried inside her.

"Where are we going?" she whispers, not lifting her head from the curve of my neck.

"To your room so I can wash you."

She hums. "I'd like that."

Here I thought I was bringing her relief, but in truth, it was just as much about finding peace in my mind as it was for her.

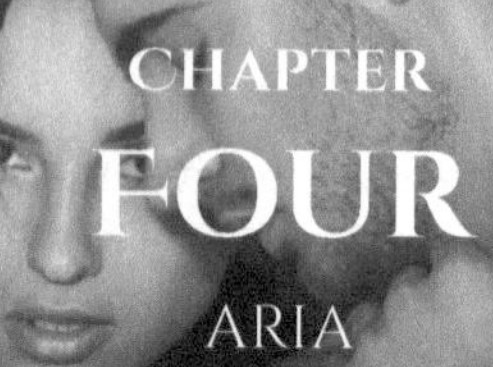

When I walk into Purgatory the next day, I head straight for the back room behind the bar to hang up my coat and grab my apron for my shift. When I step into the small space filled with my coworkers' lockers and a variety of extra bar supplies, a soft sniffling sound catches my ear. It's coming from the broom closet.

Carefully, I creep closer and see movement through the cracked door. Someone's inside and they're crying.

"Hello?" Slowly, I open the door and I'm shocked to see the thick, long blonde curls and shiny blue eyes of Charlotte sitting there on a turned over mop bucket, looking horrified that I'd found her hiding spot. Jumping to her feet, she hastily wipes at her wet cheeks, smearing makeup across her face.

"Oh! Aria!" She sniffs and blinks rapidly to combat the tears. "You're here early."

I have no idea what I've just walked into, but seeing her upset has my heart clenching with worry. "Cain had to come in, so I figured I'd just hitch a ride with him for my shift."

She pushes past me, head down, clearly trying to avoid the question hovering in the air all around us. With trembling hands, she snatches her apron from the hook and quickly ties it around her waist. That's when I see the deep purple smudge under her right eye. Not from running makeup, either. It's a bruise.

I grab her shoulder and force her to turn to face me. Her head snaps up, and I gasp. Her eye is puffy, purple, and irritated, something that could only happen if someone hit her.

Oh my god. Someone had punched her.

My stomach twists into a knot.

Wait. That purple I'd seen under her necklace the other night. She'd been trying to hide it from me, too.

Viktor... Could it be? Is he the one doing this to her?

Anger ignites inside me. The idea of anyone putting their hands on her like that enrages me beyond words. I can only stare at her, mouth agape, my heart pounding in my ears.

"It's nothing," she snaps, glancing away. "I just... I just..." Her voice hitches as more tears well up in her eyes, and immediately my fury is replaced with heavy sympathy and sorrow. I step closer and rub her back, hoping it'll give her some comfort.

I continue to stroke her back as she cries, my chest aching for her. I can't bring myself to ask her who did this to her or what happened. Not now. She's too distraught.

After a few minutes, I whisper gently, "You should just go home. I'll cover your tables tonight."

She shakes her head, blonde hair spilling over her shoulders. "I can't do that to you," she hiccups between sobs. "That's cruel."

"Hey, I'll be fine. It's only Tuesday. Can't get too crazy in here. And if it does, I'll drag Sting out from behind the counter. We'll make it work."

"But... but Cain..."

"I'll handle Cain," I reply. "You need to go home and relax. Take a hot bath. Then come kicking ass tomorrow." And I didn't just mean that figuratively. Tomorrow, I'll be drowning her in questions about this because if it is Viktor hurting her, you bet your sweet ass I'll be sharpening some stakes and knocking on the vamp's cave door.

Charlotte peeks up, considering it. The sounds of more voices drift from the bar just outside the back room, and fear passes over her face. She's afraid of more people seeing her like this, something I can understand. She doesn't want anyone else to know.

"Go ahead," I assure her. "Sneak out the back. I'll cover for you."

She hastily grabs her fur coat from the hook beside mine and shrugs it on. "Thanks, Aria. I owe you one."

I wave the comment away. "You've covered my ass more times than I can count. It's about time I return the favor."

She smiles at me, but it's one weighted heavily by sadness. "Thanks."

I move to the door that leads to the alley and the club's back parking lot. Opening it, the frigid winter air rushes inside. "How do you normally get home? Do you have a car?" I ask her.

"I take the bus, or a taxi sometimes. Or..."

Or Viktor, she's going to say. Well, that's not going to work now, is it? There's no way I'm letting her go home alone.

Bright lights illuminate the alley as a black limousine makes a U-turn in the parking lot. The driver has his window all the way down, and when I recognize Holmes behind the wheel, I praise my luck. He hasn't left yet after dropping me and Cain off.

"Holmes!" I shout, waving him down. He looks my way as I rush over to him. Without my coat, the chill slides over my skin, raising goosebumps, and I hug myself for warmth.

"Why, Miss Aria. Did you leave something in the back?" he asks.

I glance over my shoulder to see Charlotte making her way over to us. "No. But I do need a favor from you."

"Of course. What can I help you with?"

"This is my friend, Charlotte," I say, gesturing to her as she steps up beside me. "I need you to take her home *safely* for me."

He looks her over, his gaze lingering longer on her swollen eye, and as if understanding exactly what I mean, he nods stiffly. I'm sure with working for the demons for so long, this guy's seen his fair share of shit, so it's nice that I don't need to explain things further.

"Absolutely." He nods.

I walk over and open the back door for her to get in. She hesitates but eventually climbs inside.

As I hold the door open a moment longer, I say, "Call the club if you need anything, do you hear me? And I mean *anything*. I'll check on you later."

"Okay." The moment she closes the door, the limo starts to pull away.

"Take it easy but take no shit!" I yell as I watch it spin around the parking lot and toward the exit.

Hugging myself, I stand there in the dark until the car's lights disappear around the corner. I'm shaking all over, but whether it's from the cold or the mixture of anger and sorrow from my friend whirling inside me, I don't know. At least I know she'll be getting home safe with Holmes, so that's one less thing to worry about. But, as to what comes after, I have no idea. My only hope is that she hung up some crucifixes and didn't invite Viktor into her place.

I'll have to get her number from Antonio later and make sure to give her a call. To check up on her.

My mind is a jumbled mess, I spin around and march back inside. I find my order notepad and grab a few rolls of toilet paper to restock the bathrooms before heading out into the club. The moment I step onto the main floor, a deep male's voice comes from behind me.

"Should I ask?"

I don't need to turn around to know it's Cain. I'd know his smooth baritone anywhere. I also know that I shouldn't be surprised that he's been hovering around the entire time, watching and observing from the shadows as he normally does. Just how much he's seen is the question, though.

As I turn to face him, I know it's best if I tell him the truth, even if Charlotte wishes I wouldn't. If Viktor ever came here to cause a scene, Cain should know. He could protect her.

"I had Holmes drive Charlotte home," I begin, voice low. Since it's still early in the night, the place isn't too crowded yet, but I also don't want to take the chance of someone else overhearing. "She's... run into a bit of trouble."

His brows raise at that. "Trouble? What do you mean?"

"I think it's Viktor. He's hit her. Her eyes all bruised and swollen, and I found her crying in the broom closet, trying to hide. She was really shaken up by it."

Cain becomes as rigid as a statue, his face a mask. It reminds me of when Lucifer stepped through the door, like all his fury was sunken into himself and wound tight, ready to explode at any moment. A passerby may think he's just being indifferent, but I know him better than that. I can see the small twitch in his cheek where he's clenching his jaw. His pupils dilate in size as he fights for control of his demon. He's beyond furious.

"Viktor." It's only one word, but it comes out of him in a half-growl.

Afraid to poke the bear anymore, I nod.

"Are you certain?" he asks, entire body stiff.

"I can't see who else it could be. The other night, I'd seen bruises on her neck, too. Like he'd tried strangling her or something. And not in a kinky way," I say. "She hides it well, so who knows how long it's been going on."

He doesn't reply. Just stands there, cloaked in a foreboding silence.

After a long moment, I ask, "You're not mad at me for letting her go home, are you? I figured she needed the break."

"No. You did the right thing. But I don't like the idea of her being in her apartment alone."

"Me neither." Which is true.

He turns toward the closest bodyguard, one who's taken his post beside the bar, and gestures from him to come over. He does. Like most in his position, he's a massive man, more than six feet in height, and made of solid muscle, which he shows off through the sleeveless vest he wears. With shaggy hair and honey-colored eyes, I guess he's a shifter of some kind, which most of the guards in Purgatory seem to be, now that I think about it. Makes me wonder if Elias had his hand in picking the lot of them to protect the place. Wouldn't be surprised if he had.

"Quinn, I need you off the floor tonight," Cain tells him.

Understanding what that means, his eyes light with excitement. It makes me wonder what all these men the demons have on their payroll do when not tending to club matters.

Something tells me it involves more... illicit activities. Most likely things I'd rather not know about.

"House call?" he asks, voice gruff and scratchy.

"Not our usual, no," Cain replies. "I need you to check on one of the employees here. Charlotte."

"Char?" He blinks, confused. "Yeah, of course I can."

"Stay around and make sure she has no late-night visitors. Even Viktor."

Now he looks even more concerned. "Her master vampire boyfriend?"

"Will that be a problem?" he asks, jaw stiff. "You may ask Jared or Williams to join you if you're concerned."

He bristles at that. "Fuck that. Vamps are nothing. I'll handle it."

Clearly Cain poked his pride some with his comment because as far as I knew, vamps were high on the supernatural power hierarchy and were nothing to be scoffed at or taken lightly.

Cain's expression never changes. "Then go."

With that, Quinn is off and lumbering toward the door.

Alone again, Cain turns to me. "Don't worry, Aria. It'll be dealt with. You of all people know we protect our own."

By the time my head hits my pillow, I welcome sleep with open arms. And it overtakes me quickly, too. Much quicker than usual. Without Charlotte there to help me run the floor at Purgatory, I was sprinting around like a chicken with its head cut off, even for a "quieter" Tuesday night. I even had to drag Sting from behind the bar a few times just to help with the load.

I'll tell you one thing. It definitely made me realize just how much Charlotte does at the club and appreciate her more. I'll be voting for her as the next Employee of the Month for sure.

So, it comes to no surprise that once the club closed for the daily deep cleaning and I was brought back home, I didn't even have the energy to take off my clothes or shower before flopping face first into my bed and closing my eyes.

I'd worry about everything else once I woke up.

I sleep so deeply that my dreams are more like vivid flashes of memory. Of the encounter with Maverick, Lucifer, and Joseline in the foyer. Of the craziness with Charlotte at work. It's like I'm just reliving past events, seeing them again for a second time but not feeling the panic and stress I'd felt before.

Instead, I'm overcome with a soothing sense of calm. Peacefulness. Acceptance.

It only makes it easier for my exhaustion to drag me under.

For a long moment, I'm so lost in the feeling, that I almost miss the buzz of a person's voice at the very back of my mind, behind the replaying dreams. The only reason I don't miss it now is because it doesn't seem to match what I'm watching, yet still tingles with familiarity.

"I'm going to find out what you're hiding..."

Something featherlight and warm cascades over me, heating me from the inside out, and a single name springs to my mind.

Maverick.

My eyelids flutter open, and to my surprise, I see his face staring down at me. His silvery blond hair, sharp nose, and dark eyes hover over me, merely inches away.

I should be panicking. I should scream. The muscles in my throat clench as they try to work and make sounds, but the vibrating warmth spreads through me rapidly, forcing both my brain and my heart to remain blissfully calm. I'm still so drowsy, and my vision blurs as sleep presses down upon me again.

I know he's doing something to keep me weak—using his power to play on my relaxed state and overall tiredness. He must be.

"Goodnight, sweet Aria," he coos, as another wave of peacefulness washes over me. Like a sedative, it does its job and tugs me deeper into a sea of unconsciousness.

It's the strangest feeling. There's no fear, although there should be. But I can't fight what's happening, so I'm forced to only obey and sink down further, even though I know that's exactly what he wants.

"See you in Hell..."

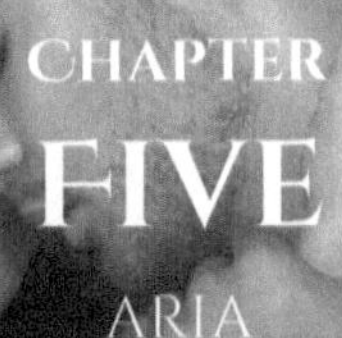

CHAPTER

FIVE

ARIA

When I open my eyes, the ceiling above me spins, and it takes me a moment to stop the world from tilting. With it come memories that leave me gasping for air.

Maverick had been in my room in the mansion, I know that now without a shadow of doubt, and as my mind catches up, I'm left teetering on his last words.

"See you in Hell."

That thought alone has me jerking upright and scrambling out of a huge, luxurious bed. The black silk beneath me has me sliding right off the mattress and landing on my knees onto the floor with a thump.

I'm sucking in desperate, shallow breaths, scanning the strange room. Dark stone walls draped in black curtains, and no windows in here that I can see. Iron chandeliers hang overhead, dripping with black crystals, and a mahogany wardrobe sits in the corner. A black unlit fireplace sits in the wall across from the bed, and above it is an oversized skull of a creature with curled horns. It's like nothing I've seen, and the more I stare at it, the more I'm convinced I am in Hell.

My heart bangs louder.

"You've got to be kidding me," I murmur under my breath, and cross the room to the door. It's black like everything else in this

39

place with ornate carvings in the wood. The iron handle is cold under my touch, and I press it down. To my surprise, it opens.

My stomach flutters with the possibility of sneaking out of... wherever I am.

Hell?

Shit, I hope not.

But where else would a psycho like Maverick bring me?

I feel so sick and scared that I might vomit.

But I've escaped difficult situations before, and this is no different. Just another challenge, I keep telling myself. Except, a horrible sensation rises through me that I'm fooling myself.

Slowly, I pull open the door, thankful the hinges don't squeak. Outside is a hallway, and I listen first for any sounds, any voices.

Dead silence.

I stick my head out carefully and peer down the hall, left and right. My eyes widen, and well, I'm confused. Both sides of the hallway stretch out for what looks like forever with no end in sight. Is this some twisted, terrifying house of horrors?

Even before I step out of the room, I hate this place. Hate it with a vengeance. Hate that I've ended up here.

Think, Aria. How the fuck do I get out? Thoughts sweep across my mind, ones where I could get Sayah to check out if the hallway goes anywhere. Except, that brings its own handful of problems, especially since Maverick's ring is keeping her caged somewhere inside me and I can't take it off.

We're also not exactly on the best of terms.

I chew on my lower lip, my heartbeat picking up its pace.

Alternatively, this could be all a dream—or a nightmare—and then I can sit in the room until I wake up. Except this doesn't feel like any dream I've ever had. This feels real, and I pinch myself hard on the forearm until I wince.

Okay, that hurt a lot. Definitely not asleep.

The building, the deranged hallway, and even me standing here, it all feels so fucking real that my head twirls.

I pace back and forth from the door to the bed, wondering what's with the black-on-black motif here. The longer I think about it, the more I'm convinced I'm in some kind of onyx prison.

If this is indeed Hell, how the fuck will I get out when Cain,

Elias, and Dorian have been trying for decades to get back in and failed? And that thought terrifies me because I am truly stuck.

It makes me clench my hands and anger flares within me that he tricked me. And I fell for it like an idiot. Like someone so desperate to find solace from Sayah, from everything I'd been going through since arriving at the mansion, that I truly believed he was an angel.

Talk about gullible.

He played on my desperation so he could get to his brother, Cain. I stiffen, loathing that I showed Maverick my vulnerable side, that I even let him almost kiss me. I want to scream with frustration at the whole stupid situation.

Movement from the corner of my eye grabs my attention, and I jerk my head up to a figure standing in the doorway. I flinch at first until my gaze settles on his face, and my chest squeezes with fear.

"What do you want?" I snap, my voice braver than I feel on the inside.

"Can I come in?" Maverick asks.

I huff an exaggerated breath. "Do what you want. Last time I looked, I was the one kidnapped and thrown into this macabre prison for the depressed."

He saunters inside, and the moment his foot hits the dark floorboards, the fireplace awakens, a blaze roaring and licking at the hearth. The whole room seems to come to life in his presence, from the skull hanging on the wall with golden eyes, to the chandelier flickering with flames. Even the black stone wall now seems to be patterned with fox-like silhouettes, who move only from my peripheral vision. That is unnerving. I preferred the room when it was just dull.

"The room isn't so depressing now," he says with a grin. Today he chooses to wear all black. Pressed pants, a matching button-up shirt open at the base of his throat, looking more like a lawyer than a sin demon. But I'm not exactly the expert on demonology, now I am? Unlike the last few times I'd seen him, there is no ethereal aura around him. Instead, he has darkness feathering around the edges. It's a complete contrast to his short, white hair, the front swept over his brow and that welcoming grin.

"Why the hell am I here?"

His deep mocha eyes study me, scanning me from head to toe,

and it's only then that I realize I'm still in my clothes from work. Short shorts and a white blouse that rides up high, exposing most of my belly. Great dungeon clothes. I might have laughed at myself, if I wasn't so unnerved.

"I put you in here because this is my room, where you'll be safe, Aria." His deep voice says my name smoothly, like it's passed his lips many times.

I blink at him, and his eyes twinkle from the fire. The corners of his mouth quirk upward. There is something almost stunning about the way he looks, the dark colors suit him so much more exquisitely than the white angelic appearance. I see that now. Every inch of his six-foot-two height screams predator, and yet I'm fascinated and can't look away.

"Is that meant to make you the good guy here?" I ask him with a huff.

He laughs at that. "Good guy? Oh, no. Never in my life have I been a *good* guy."

"Now, that I believe! You've already revealed yourself as a monster, and there's no stuffing that beast back into Pandora's box."

"You sure have a flair for the dramatic, don't you?" He crosses the room with long strides and sits on the bed, the bedsheet still on the floor from where I'd fallen out.

"Take a seat," he offers, gesturing for me to join him.

"I prefer to stand." I straighten my spine, unsure if I am pulling off the strong appearance with my cleavage on full display.

He draws a bent leg in front of him, and there's another glint in his eyes. Something he's hiding from me. Another part of him.

"You didn't answer my question," I say. "Why am I here?"

"It's complicated."

I laugh out loud, all for show. "Don't give me that shit. If there's something I've learned about demons, it's that they all have ulterior motives, always scheming something." I speak from a place of truth, one where my demons back in the mansion had their own agenda when I first arrived in their home. "You planned everything. Even dragging my friend, Joseline into it."

"Actually, that one just landed in my lap. Really, she did most of it herself by casting a spell with Clauneck, the demon who bestows wealth, and he is very well loved by Lucifer. So, you can imagine his surprise when Clauneck mentioned who Joseline was. Then, all I did was take over the contract. Easy."

I blink at him, unsure if I can believe him. "You lied to me about everything."

He is on his feet in an instant, sighing heavily, his head snapping up. "Aria, there are some big things coming and I couldn't have you in the cross-fire."

Fury burns me at the thought. "What are you going to do to Cain?"

"My brother can look after himself. It's Lucifer's intentions you need to fear, not mine."

I grind my teeth, eyeing the monster in front of me, the demon who pretends he is the innocent one, when that couldn't be farther from the truth. I suck in a shaky breath as he strolls over to me.

"Oh, Aria, if I didn't care for your wellbeing do you think you'd be here now? If I left it up to my father, you'd be in the darkest pit of Hell, sharing a cell with the deadliest beasts. I meant what I said about helping you with Sayah."

Sweat curls across my nape from the burning heat of the fireplace, from the trepidation of where this is leading.

He pauses inches from me, his chest quickening as if being this close affects him. But refusing to run, I stand my ground. Lifting my head to look into his deep brown eyes, I find the flicker of gold in his irises is more prominent than I remember. Being this close to him, the last time he came to my room returns to my thoughts, and suddenly the ring on my finger feels heavy and tight. I raise my hand and look down at the thick silver band embedded with a large emerald stone with thorny vines etched into the sides.

He places his hand on mine, and a charge of energy zips up my arm. I pull away, but his fingers curl around my wrist, holding me near. His grip is like iron when I wrench against him.

"I gave you my family ring to protect you from Sayah, as that's what you wanted."

"Then why can't I take it off? What else has it done to me?"

He stares down at my hand, the bridge of his nose bunching up. "My brothers and I were each given a ring from our father, and they carry their own magic. Mine has taken a special liking to you." His grin takes me by surprise at how beautifully menacing he appears, and that thought alone scares me. For all I know, this ring could be making me feel things for him I never would feel otherwise.

His thumb traces the back of my thumb, rousing feelings in me I don't understand and shouldn't be feeling. They don't belong between us.

"I give you my word that I will keep you safe from Father's wrath."

The earlier warmth morphs into a chill, covering me in goosebumps. "Then release me. Let me go."

He doesn't answer, and my chest tightens because the truth swirls behind his darkening eyes. He leans in closer to me, the warmth of his body embracing me. His whisper is barely a breath in my ear. "I had no choice once Lucifer found you, remember that."

His words leave me shaking. "I-I d-don't understand."

"You will soon." He pulls from me, his hand slipping from around my wrist, his warmth leaving me as well. As strange as it seems, I want it back, and clumsily fumble with the bottom of my shirt.

He makes his way toward the door. "There are fresh clothes for you in the wardrobe, and you can wash yourself in the bathroom. We aren't savages down here."

"I'd beg to differ," I throw back.

He ignores that comment. "I will return, and don't be foolish enough to think you can run. Or hide. Or stop Lucifer. It's better for you to just give into the darkness."

He walks out and shuts the door behind him, while I stumble on my feet, struggling to get air into my lungs.

Maverick is one thing, but Lucifer? He's a different beast entirely, one I fear beyond everything else.

And he has his sights pinned on me.

MAVERICK

I pause outside the room, her sweet scent filling my nostrils, the softness of her skin still lingering on my hands, and I half contemplate going back in and claiming what I want. But her venomous words don't leave me, the hatred in her eyes haunt me.

I shouldn't expect anything less, and it sure as fuck shouldn't bother me, but somehow, it cuts deep.

I've let her crawl under my skin.

Shit. I've made a colossal mistake. One that may end up costing me my life down the road.

My muscles tighten. She has no idea how much danger she's in, how much I am risking to protect her. And she'll never know. I'll carry that secret with me until the end of time if I have to. When my father pays anyone attention, it never ends well for them, and standing up to him almost always ends in bloodshed.

My interest in the girl was too rash on my part. I visited her initially with the intention to gain information on my brother, but there's something intoxicating about her presence I never anticipated. With each visit I paid her, it got harder and harder to keep her out of my thoughts. It was like she clung to my very soul, and I found myself conjuring up ways to keep her for myself.

Fuck Cain. He's already ruined so much since he betrayed Father, and now there's a deadly target on his chest. Lucifer never forgives. Why he banished him instead of killing him outright I'll never know. Maybe to prolong the torture. But one thing's for sure, no matter how much time passes, Lucifer will get his revenge.

I shut my eyes and draw in a ragged breath. This is becoming too complicated. With each inhale, I can still smell her honeyed scent, the fear of her perspiration, and beneath it all, a delicious darkness I crave.

Something in her veins is different, stronger, older than I've sensed before. Darkness stalks. The potential she carries is extraordinary, and I doubt even Lucifer realizes that yet.

I should leave her side, but instead I stand there, listening to my hammering heartbeat. Her eyes had watched me like she might strike, and a spike of excitement claws through me at the thought.

The only thing holding me back from staking my claim over Aria is my father. My brother and his men are simply competition, but an easier one to overcome. I never back down from a challenge. Right now, she may look at me like I'm the worst demon in the world, but Cain isn't innocent in the slightest, and if she knew the whole truth about him, she might not look at him so longingly.

She's fucking beautiful, high cheekbones, full lips, and a curved body that calls to me.

I growl under my breath, frustrated as hell, and I whip around to put more distance between my room and me. I swing toward the wall that splits open like rippling water instantly upon my approach. This is my palace, and everything in here responds to me. It's why I've made the place impenetrable to everyone else.

Stepping through the wall, I emerge outside in the oversized yard enclosed by a spiked metal wall. The sky bleeds reds and purples today, a promise of blood rain soon. Dried soil crunches under my boots, and I have a legion master to meet with, one who reports to me and has been keeping an eye on all my brothers. I may live in Hell, filled with the most deplorable demons, but the biggest danger comes from my family. And I like to keep track of who does what.

I march out toward the fiery gates that crackle and spit flames when from the corner of my eye, movement calls my attention.

I jerk my head to my right and catch the shadow of someone darting around my home.

Anger shoots through me.

There's no pause. I'm already sprinting in that direction, well aware that the soul-starved scavengers down here would have smelled Aria's presence. Her intact soul is like heroin to an addict. It's not like anyone can get into my palace, the fortified structure made of onyx, but that's not the point. Three oversized square towers are joined at the base by hallways that would make anyone lost if they somehow make their way inside. Plus, at the bottom of my home is where I keep all my wealth, I'm extra touchy about anyone breaking in.

I mean, I am the demon of Greed, after all. It's in my nature.

Now, some groveling fuckwit is about to find out what happens for crossing me.

I careen around the corner, speeding up on the demon before he even senses me approaching. Filthy vermin, the lowest ranked beasts who could only be compared to rats in the human world. Lanky things that walk on two legs, hunched over. Their skin is worn, like cracked leather, their heads round with two tiny eyes but a mouth that splits the length of their faces. If they stood straight, they'd tower over me, but the things have curved spines. They are nothing more than animalistic beasts constantly searching for food.

They plague Hell and somehow manage to survive the cullings. Along with getting into places they shouldn't. And by the rip across his back with black blood spilling down, he's risked crawling over my fence. Joke's on him, seeing that the enclosure is poisonous to the touch. Still, I can't let my catch get away, not when I'm fucking fuming that he thinks he can get anywhere near Aria.

I grab the blade from my belt and lunge at him just as he jerks around to see me coming.

His eyes widen, his fear causing his lipless mouth to drop open.

I smile, loving the way fear so easily paints his expression.

My skin always itches before a kill, in anticipation to finish off another fucker thrilling.

I crash into him with speed, both of us hitting the ground. My weight shoves him onto his stomach, his head cracking against the ground. He whines, already bucking to escape.

"You will pay for coming here to take what is mine." I tuck my hand around the front of his neck and swipe my blade across his throat, taking his existence with ease. For good measure, I stab him a dozen more times in the back, because these roaches are relentless bastards.

Fuck, it feels amazing.

Black blood splatters up my arms. I feel its warmth trickling down my cheeks.

When I stand up, I stare down at my handiwork and grin. I'm a fucking mess, but before I clean up, I need to put him on display out in front of my home to discourage any other vermin from thinking breaking in is an option.

I've missed the chase, the fight, the kill. Father's had us running around on menial tasks to ready everyone for his strike against Heaven, I'd almost forgotten how much I loved the adrenaline soaring through my veins. Plus, I need the practice.

And considering the chaos that will break out if Cain found a way back into Hell to claim Aria, well, I have to be ready for anything.

CHAPTER
SIX

CAIN

t's late. Or should I say, it's early.

As Dorian likes to say, it's the ass-crack of dawn, and my usual time of coming home from Purgatory. It's tradition that I stay later than everyone else and get whatever I need to do done, but after a full night of work and my body still not fully healed from my brush with death, I'm beyond exhausted as I step into the mansion just as the sun breaks over the horizon.

I know Aria went home before me and she's probably sleeping —as she should be—but she was so concerned about Charlotte that I debate waking her and telling her what Quinn reported to me before I left.

I suppose it *could* wait until she wakes for the day, but part of me craves her presence and that part always seems to win out, doesn't it?

Without my command, my feet begin to move me up the stairs to the third floor. Looks like they've made the choice for me, and I have no reason to object. After our run-in with the dragon, I've been so long without her, my need for her is greater than ever. Even after our time in the Red Room, I haven't had my fill.

As I head for her door, I notice one of the hallway windows is open. The bitter winter wind whips inside, tossing up the curtains and blowing snow across the rug and walls.

Strange. These windows are rarely opened, except during the

warmer months or when the servants do a deep cleaning of the house. And only one? That doesn't make sense.

I glance at Aria's door, left ajar, and a wave of fear ricochets through me. Something's amiss. I can feel it deep in my gut.

I charge, throwing her bedroom door open so forcefully it slams against the wall hard enough to rattle the walls. The resounding boom explodes through the house like a gunshot, and I immediately hear Elias's and Dorian's fast footsteps as they race up the stairs.

But my frantic heart won't slow because of what I'm staring at. An empty room. An empty bed.

Pacing across the room, I find the bathroom the same. No Aria.

Whirling around, I see Elias and Dorian standing outside the door, looking confused and a bit out of sorts. Must've woken them up or frightened them, but it's for good reason.

Dorian's eyes land on Aria's empty bed, and he pales. "Please tell me she's with one of you," he says, voice shaky with panic.

"I just got home," I reply, my throat tightening.

"She was supposed to be asleep," Elias says.

I gesture to the bed. I can't help the annoyance leaking into my tone. "Do you see her there sleeping?"

"She must be somewhere else in the mansion. Maybe the kitchen for a snack?"

Elias sniffs the air, following some smell we obviously can't sense, and heads to the open window in the hall. We follow him, and he crouches closer to the window's sill and inhales deeply. Then he leans out and searches the grounds below.

"Well?" Dorian presses against his uneasy silence. "This is not the time to be all broody and quiet."

Elias spins to us. "She's not in the mansion," he says quickly. "Not anymore."

"Fuck!" Dorian throws his hands up and begins to pace up and down the hall. "She's run off again, hasn't she?"

Ignoring him, Elias looks at me. "There's another scent with hers," he says, and his words make my blood run cold. Somehow I know the answer before he even needs to say it. Dread seeps into my bones. Even Dorian has stopped his erratic pacing.

We're all thinking about it. After our run-in in the foyer, it was only a matter of time...

Maverick.

He's come back to collect Aria. For Lucifer. I'm burning on the inside, fury spiking my pulse. Every muscle tenses with the need to destroy someone. They took my Aria.

"Fuck! Shit! Piss! Fuck!" Dorian spews every curse he can think of and runs his fingers through his hair. "What are we supposed to do now?"

Roaring, Elias crosses the hall in one long stride and throws his fist into the wall, popping a hole through the plaster. When he pulls back, his knuckles glisten with blood, but if there's pain, he doesn't show it on his face. There's only fury. "We should've done the ritual to keep her safe. Now she's fucked."

"*We're* fucked," I say, as I try to keep myself calm, but really, I'm just pissed at my brother's betrayal and how deeply he's sunken into his traitorous ways. I should've let Lucifer kill him that day instead of saving his pitiful excuse for a life. Pissed at my father for his role in this. As usual, he's the one pulling the strings. But most of all, I'm pissed at myself for not performing the ritual sooner. And for getting Aria involved in my family's mess.

This is my damn fault, and I'm fuming, hands curling into fists.

"What do we do?" Dorian's staring at me with a mix of desperation, fear, and determination in his eyes. Glancing at Elias, I find him waiting for my direction, too, his entire body vibrating with rage.

They're willing to do whatever it takes to get Aria back, and I'm right there with them. Problem is, there's no doubt in my mind Maverick took her to the one place we can't go. Hell. So that makes things a little more complicated.

But one thing's for certain. Once I get my hands on my baby brother, I'm going to rip him to shreds and watch the life drain from his eyes. It will be my absolute pleasure in finishing what my father had started in wanting to kill him, what I should've let happen.

"It's obvious, isn't it?" I say to my two *real* brothers. "We're going to Hell. Our trip has been fast-tracked."

"We've been searching for the relics for over a century. Without Aria's gift, how are we supposed to speed it up?" Elias grumbles.

We need to figure out something, because it's our only way back through Hell's gate.

"And what about Aria's soul?" Dorian interjects. "She's not like us. She'll be dead once she crosses through the veil to a nonliving plane. We might not even be able to bring her back."

Just the idea of Aria's soul being lost to us has acid churning in my gut. But, lucky for us, Maverick did one thing right. "The ring— Maverick's ring will protect her while she's in Hell. For how long, I can't say, but it must be why my brother put it on her in the first place. To keep her safe for the cross over."

"But why? That's what I don't understand. If Lucifer wants her, what does it matter if she's alive or if he just has her soul?" Dorian asks.

"It's clear he needs her alive for some reason." Elias rubs the blood off his bruised knuckles. "Do you think he knows what she is?"

"Maybe not entirely, but he's definitely curious. And that curiosity may be just what keeps her alive until we can take Lucifer down and drag her out." That's what I'm hoping for, anyway.

It looks like it's time to contact all our scouting teams and see if anyone has found clues to the missing relics. With the spine, we at least have four, and that means three more to go. We are going to really light a fire under our asses and be more proactive in the search. Aria's life—and possible afterlife—depends on it.

I push past Dorian and Elias and head down the stairs.

"Hey, where are you going?" Dorian calls out, following after me. Elias, too. "You can't just go all silent and storm off. We need to know what's going on. What can we do?"

"I'm going to my office to make calls to our search groups. See if any are close to finding another relic."

"Gathering all the pieces of the harp will take too long," Elias bites out, annoyed. "It's taken a hundred years to find what we have. We don't have that time—"

I spin mid-step and glare at him. "I know!" I snap, my voice deepening as my fury lashes out. "You think I don't fucking know that?"

Dorian hops two steps to get between us. "Okay, let's just take a breath here. We're all tense and on edge after what's happened.

We've been through a lot, and there's a shitload more to come. We need to keep our wits about us."

Drawing in a shaky breath, I try to push down my budding rage. I'm not really mad at Elias, of course, and Dorian's right. We have a lot of work ahead of us and not a lot of time. Better to look forward and focus on a solution now than tear at each other's throats. That's what my father would want, and I refuse to give him the satisfaction.

When I speak again, I keep my tone even. "If there was another way to get back to Hell, I would've found it by now. I've dedicated my entire time on Earth to finding a way back. I've read every book, studied every legend, and the harp is the *only* way we can return."

Elias huffs, still not satisfied with a non-immediate answer. "What if we summon another demon? Maybe one of your other brothers to help us. Nix might, if he's bored enough. Forget Raz. He wouldn't lift a finger unless he was guaranteed something in return. And Torryn—"

"What about Maverick?" Dorian interjects.

I'm not sure I've heard him right. "Maverick?"

He nods.

"The asswipe who just took Aria from us?" Elias clarifies.

He nods again. "He's the one with Aria. He's the one we need. I say we summon his ass back onto this plane and force him to bring her back."

"If I ever see that piece of shit again, I'll kill him," Elias growls.

I'm thinking the same thing.

"I'm right there with you, but we get him to bring us Aria first. Then we can have our fun with him."

"Problem is, we can't summon demons ourselves," I remind him. As Hell-creatures ourselves, we don't have the ability.

"We make someone else do it for us," Elias says. Clearly he's on board with this plan, too. More than the harp. "Bribe them. Threaten them. Whatever it takes."

Dorian taps the side of his jaw in thought. "What if we don't have to," he begins, an idea forming. "What if the best person for the job is here with us? Right now."

At first, I have no idea who he's talking about, but then it hits me. We'd recently gained a new guest. One who'd had her soul contracted to Maverick himself and is a perfect connection to the demon. "The witch."

Dorian touches his nose, telling me I got it. "Bingo. It'll be quicker than hunting down the last three relics and worth a try."

Elias doesn't reply. He's already leaping up the steps again three at a time to get back to the third floor where Aria's friend, Joseline, is staying. We hear Elias grumble at the guard, then open the door, and then a furious roar that sounds more animal than man.

Dorian and I run up to meet him. As we push our way into the bedroom, we see Elias leaning over the broken stained-glass window, the bedsheets stripped off the bed, tied into knots, and tossed out. Joseline is gone.

"Are you fucking kidding me? Again?" Dorian crosses the room and leans out the window to look down. "At least we know where Aria learned it. These foster care girls are resilient."

"It looks like the sheet didn't make it all the way down. She would've had to jump the rest of the way," Elias says. "I can bet money she's hurt. Broken ankle at least."

"That's going to slow her down." Dorian peeks up at him.

Seeming to be on the same wavelength, Elias starts to pull off his clothes and heads for the door.

Dorian hurries after him but pauses at the top of the steps to glance back at me. "You coming?"

Shaking my head, I wave for him to go on. "I'm still going to make those calls," I say. "Just in case."

"Good idea. I'll call you when we find her." He takes one more step but stops again and gives me a knowing, slightly sympathetic look. "Don't beat yourself up too much about this. Lucifer and Maverick's insanity isn't on you. We'll get her back."

"Oh, I know." I can feel my darkness swirling inside me as my power rises. "And I'll turn Hell inside out to do it."

ARIA

Quick footsteps echo outside the door, and I jump to my feet as they get closer. Knowing this is Maverick's room, in his house, I don't trust a speck of dirt here, just as much as I don't trust the man who owns it. Like Maverick, nothing here is what it seems.

An excited voice booms in the hall, one I don't recognize at all. "You didn't tell me you brought a *human* here, Brother! A living *human*!"

Brother? Fear spikes through my heart at knowing this stranger is talking about me, thrilled about my being here, and is related to Maverick. And therefore Cain. Another original sin demon? Has to be. And that means I'm about to be in even more trouble.

The bedroom door shoots open with such force, it slams against the stone wall and bounces back, only to be caught without struggle by a strikingly handsome man with long dark hair, almond-shaped eyes, and sharp, regal features. He steps inside, his eyes pinned on me with intrigue, and I find myself shrinking back further into the room. He's not just handsome, he's beautiful.

Soon, Maverick appears behind this beautiful stranger, looking annoyed at the intrusion, but he doesn't seem bothered in the least. His green eyes glow as they search me from head to toe, and I can't help but squirm under his stare.

"Oh, brother," this demon says, as if I'm a newly discovered treasure they've been longing to find. "You didn't say she was such a... scrumptious little thing, either. Mmmm."

I wrap my arms around myself, suddenly feeling more naked than ever before.

"Leave her alone, Nix. I told you not to come here," Maverick spits.

"But how could I resist?" the demon named Nix says. "A living human in Hell? It's only a matter of seconds before every infernal creature is knocking down your door."

If this Nix is really one of Maverick's and Cain's brothers, and a Sin, which of the seven can he be?

I look him over for any clues. Unlike the suits Cain normally wears, Nix wears skinny jeans and a deep V-neck T-shirt. Much more casual than the others. But that isn't what surprises me the most. There's a lingering hunger in his shockingly green eyes. Something I recognize from Cain's gaze when he's about to devour me. Sexually that is. But this demon carries that primal look with him at all times.

"How cute," Nix says unexpectedly. "She's trying to figure me out. Well, let me help you out a bit there, sweetheart. Don't need you to have an aneurysm. You've only just arrived." He clears his throat, ready to give me a more formal introduction. "I'm Nix. The third oldest brother, and the demon of Lust."

I almost choke on my own tongue. "Lust?"

"Is that so hard to believe?" He sputters a laugh. "Unlike my other siblings, I can drown you in pleasure. Show you things you never even knew existed and free you from all your inhibitions. And that's just in the first ten seconds!" He chuckles louder this time.

I, though, am not as impressed. "So you're like Dorian then."

His laughter stops abruptly, and instead, his lip curls up in a vicious snarl. "You insult me! An incubus demon? Ha! They can only touch the surface. I can reach into your very soul and pull out your deepest and darkest cravings."

"Nix," Maverick warns from behind him, but he only shushes him sharply.

"She doesn't believe me, Brother," he replies, disappointed. "I'm going to have to show her what I mean."

"Not in my house." Maverick's voice is a threatening rumble. "You will not."

Nix pouts and stands up straight, as if he'd been denied a chance to play with a shiny new toy. When he turns back to me, the skin across his face starts to ripple. It bubbles like his very muscles are boiling underneath. All the while, his eyes stay fixed on me and continue to glow with their own eerie light.

I hold my breath.

"Nix!" Maverick shouts, reaching for his arm to stop him, but he doesn't stop what he's doing. His flesh continues to move and change.

"Ah..." he muses as his face contorts. "I should've guessed."

My gaze flicks to Maverick for understanding. He's trying to wrench Nix away, but he's glued in place.

"This is almost too easy," he says. Then, his skin lightens, his hair shrinks back into his head, losing its lushness and length until it's cropped short on his head. His cheeks fill out to a strong jawline, his lips thicken, and his brows gain fullness. Last are his eyes, which switch from electric green to a shocking blue every time he blinks, and that's when I stare dumbstruck at the man before me.

No longer Nix, but Cain.

"C-Cain?" I stammer, unable to believe what is right before my eyes. No, it can't be. Not really. It's Nix in a Cain costume. A facade. The only thing that gives away his true identity are the clothes, which haven't changed from the jeans and tee, and the ring on his finger, which bears a brilliant red stone and engraved roses on the sides whose leaves create the rest of the band.

He holds his hands out, presenting himself again to me, only more proud of himself this time. "He is who your heart craves at this exact moment." He glances at Maverick, who has anger dancing behind his eyes. "Our oldest brother. Can you believe that? She's quite smitten with him."

Maverick clenches his jaw but says nothing.

"So you can turn into another demon at will?" I ask him. It's beyond strange to be facing Cain right now but knowing it's not really him. I saw the transformation myself, yet my heartbeat speeds up out of reflex, betraying me.

"Not just any demon, sweetheart. *Anyone.* Sky's the limit."

Wow. That's pretty cool and extremely horrifying at the same time.

He grins wide, and seeing such an expression on Cain is too odd for me. It's not him at all.

"Change back," Maverick growls under his breath.

"Ah, you're right, Brother," Nix begins. "Can't be walking around like this outside. Father would slaughter me on sight."

On cue, his skin begins to quiver and bubble, tanning in color, and his hair grows back to its waist-long length. His cheeks hollow, his jaw shrinking, and within seconds, he's the demon who'd burst into the room moments ago.

"That's a neat trick," I say, my voice heavy with sarcasm. "You're like a walking-talking multiple personality disorder."

He frowns. "Keep talking like that and you might just hurt my feelings."

"You poor thing."

Glaring, he tries to take a step toward me, but Maverick's hand is quick on his arm. "Leave, Nix. Now."

"She has a sharp tongue that needs to be wrangled," he replies. "She doesn't know who she's dealing with."

"Now," he says, firmer this time, and shoves him toward the door.

Nix isn't pleased, but he walks out without a fight. His eyes stay a bit longer on me, a warning lingering there. When they both disappear down the hall, the door shuts and locks behind them on its own, and a violent shiver shoots down my spine. Not only am I in this Hell funhouse, but now I have the other sin demons to worry about. Like Lust, a shapeshifting, cocky bastard who clearly thinks I should be amazed by his parlor tricks. And according to him, more Hell-dwelling creatures are sure to come a-knocking.

And they might not be as welcoming.

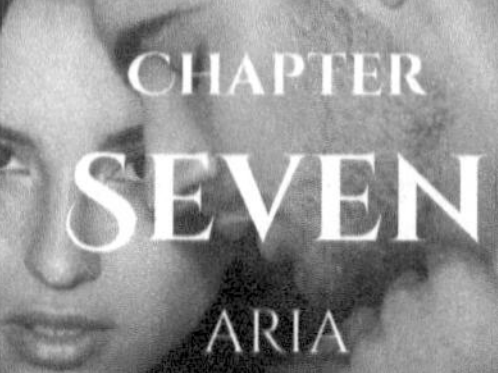

CHAPTER

SEVEN

ARIA

I miss Cassiel, as silly as that may sound at the moment. Especially trapped in Hell, surrounded by fire and brimstone, and who knows what else. But I've been left alone for what feels like hours now, and in that silence, I've been thinking a lot about the things I miss. Cassiel, for one. I could really use his over-sized, fluffy snuggles right now. Not to mention he'd probably tear Maverick's face off if he got too close, which is a comforting thought in itself.

Of course, there are the demons, too. What I wouldn't give to have them here with me. When Nix had turned into Cain, I almost lost it. Seeing him again, even if it wasn't really him, had my heart pounding. He, Dorian, and Elias must be losing their minds by now, after discovering I'm gone. Part of me hopes they were trying to find a way to get me out of here, but the other part hopes they stay away. After seeing Lucifer toss Elias and Dorian across the foyer without so much as lifting a finger, I didn't need them sacrificing themselves over me.

And, with Hell's harp and the other relics the only way to open the gate and get down here, I'm not sure how they'll be able to get to me. I may be dead before then.

I'll find a way out of this place myself. Somehow.

I glance down at the ring on my hand again. The emerald shimmers, mocking me, and I grip the thing for about the

58

hundredth time and try prying it off. As expected, it doesn't budge, and I curse.

"Fucking Maverick and his fucking ring!"

"That *ring* is what's keeping your soul intact right now."

My head jerks up to see him leaning against the doorway, arms crossed, looking amused by my struggling.

"What are you talking about?" I snap at him.

"Even if you could take it off, I wouldn't suggest it," he goes on, and pushes off the frame. "Living people can't cross into a nonliving plane without dying. My ring is allowing you to be here and keep your soul. Without it, your soul would be stripped from your body and trapped here."

Yikes.

I drop my hands. Guess the ring stays on, at least until I can find a way above ground again.

"So, you're protecting me?" I ask.

"Don't get yourself excited. It's only because my father wants it so. For now, anyway."

Well, that's reassuring.

"How does it feel being Lucifer's lap dog? Does he pay you in biscuits? Or does a good ol' ear scratch do it for you?"

His eyes narrow. "It'd be wise to keep your mouth shut while you're here, Aria."

I meet his glare head on and square my shoulders, despite the fear trickling through me. "I can't wait for Cain to tear you to shreds. I'm going to enjoy watching it."

In a blur of speed, he rushes at me and lashes out with an arm. I'm struck in the chest and thrown sideways. My head hits the black stones of the fireplace, pain ricocheting through my skull instantly. I crumple onto the floor, my vision darkening and my chest squeezes as I struggle to breathe. I groan, barely able to lift myself up on shaky arms as more agony rocks through my head and lungs.

Tears spring to my eyes. Feels like bruised ribs.

Touching the side of my head, my fingers come back shiny with blood.

Oh shit.

Maverick's polished shoes are in front of me, and I jerk onto my butt and find the wall to help me stand again. My head whirls again, and nausea rolls at the same time. A concussion, too? God, I hope not.

Trying to blink past the wooziness and stand steady, I look up at Maverick again. His silvery white wings are out, his skin deathly pale and almost translucent, and curved horns poking out of his white hair. He stands before me in his true demon form, and I don't know how I ever thought of him as an angel. There's nothing angelic about him.

His wings shoot out, caging me in on either side, and I press myself closer to the wall as he leans in. His hand reaches for the cut on my head, and with gentle fingers, he touches the blood there before bringing it between us so we both can see. He rubs his two fingers together, admiring my blood as if it's the most precious jewel.

"Let's get one thing straight right here, right now. I'm not like my pathetic brother. His time on Earth has made him soft. Unlike him, I won't hesitate to kill you."

"That-that makes two of us," I gasp past the pain.

He laughs, his shoulders bouncing. The sound only fuels my hatred.

Inside me, something dark and familiar stirs. A tickle of power awakening again.

Sayah.

I freeze. She's not nearly the strong presence she normally is, but I'm surprised to be feeling her at all, especially with Maverick's ring still on. Looks like Maverick's power over her is starting to wear off, or she's too strong for it.

Both are unsettling thoughts, but it is a bit of a relief to have her with me again, as unpredictable as she is. At least I'm not alone in Hell.

Peering down at me, Maverick's suspicious gaze roams over my face. Even though my heart is racing, I do my best to keep my emotions from my face. There's a good chance he doesn't know about Sayah's reemergence, and that means she may be a tool I can use for later. *IF* she cooperates.

Slowly, he eases away, his wings coming down from around me, and I suddenly don't feel like I'm suffocating anymore. I wish I knew what he or Lucifer wants with me. Surely it can't just be to hurt Cain. No, there has to be more to it. And since they both know about Sayah, I can't help but wonder if she's gained their interest as well. But is an unruly shadow spirit really worth all this? I can't see the appeal.

Maverick rolls his shoulders, reeling his demon back into place. He grits his teeth as if the action causes him a great deal of pain. Why suppress it at all? He's in Hell, not Earth.

"I'm not scared of you or your demon, just so we're clear," I say.

"Then you're a bigger fool than I originally thought."

Asshole.

No wonder Elias started punching him in the face the very second he walked through their door. I've never wanted to sock someone so much in my life.

"Why am I even here?" I bite out, my annoyance growing by the second.

"You'll have to ask Lucifer that himself," he replies.

"Okay then. Where is the bastard?"

A smirk quirks his lips, he moves over to the fireplace again and taps on the mantle twice. Icy blue flames erupt from the hearth, as tall as me, and I'm smacked in the face with intense heat. I step back.

"Just on the other side of this actually," Maverick says, enjoying my reaction. "He's been waiting for you."

All my fake bravado dies instantly, and fear fills me. I didn't expect to be meeting the King of Hell right now. At this exact moment.

"What's a matter, Aria? I thought you wanted to take your complaints up to the supervisor?" He laughs again, the blue light from the fire dancing across his handsome face.

I realize then that I hate his laughter. It grates on my eardrums. Inside me, even Sayah reacts, wiggling out from her dark corner a little more.

Maverick extends his arm toward the fire, gesturing for me to step through, testing my bravery. The pleased grin stays transfixed on his face the entire time. "After you."

I step closer to the fireplace. Although my insides are shaking, I don't want to give him the satisfaction of being right about me, and that part is winning over all out. Even my common sense, which is screaming, *"Don't walk into the fire, Aria. You're not like them. You'll burn to death."* Instead, I take a deep breath, lift my chin, and walk through the dancing flames.

Heat surrounds me, making me sweat, but nothing hurts. The fire doesn't actually touch me, just wraps around me, reaching for my skin but unable to make contact.

It reminds me of Harry Potter and how the characters would travel through fireplaces to other destinations, only a lot less cool and a whole lot more terrifying. Things definitely lose their charm when put in a Hellish setting.

When I come through the other side, I step down from another massive stone fireplace and into an equally colossal circular room draped in red and gold and constructed from polished black marble. Candles glow dimly from standing candelabras all around the place, and at the top of a dais, there's a gold throne behind an altar. At first glance, the entire set up reminds me of a church, with its domed ceiling and religious effigies and paintings on the walls, but when examined closer, I realize those aren't of saints or angels. They're of gruesome battle scenes with horned beasts, rivers of blood, and souls being tortured in unimaginable ways.

I force myself to look away, my eyes finding the man—no, the serpent—who runs the show down here. Lucifer himself is standing across the room in the same fancy getup I'd seen him in when he'd showed up at the house. His lips are twisted in a sly grin.

"Aria!" He welcomes me like an old friend, with open arms. "How nice of you to pop in for a little visit."

"It's not like I had much of a choice..." I say, eyeing him as he moves across the room. Maverick steps through the fireplace next, the blue flames extinguishing immediately. Without the fire, an icy chill settles over the room.

Lucifer's gaze swings to Maverick and then back to me. "I hope my son has been making sure you're comfortable here?"

What the fuck did he think? I'd gone on some lavish vacation or something? Because this was a pretty far cry from sipping fruity drinks in an oceanfront, five-star resort in Cancun, Mexico.

"You don't strike me as a quiet woman," he says, and looks me over from head to toe. "If you have something to say, just say it. This is a safe space." His smile widens.

He hasn't moved any closer to me, but a tingle of warning zips up my spine. His presence is large enough to fill the room, and I can't help but feel vulnerable before him. Like I've walked straight into a hungry predator's den and he's sizing me up for the eventual take down.

Even Maverick shifts closer to my side.

"Well?" Lucifer presses.

I try to rack my brain for all I had learned about Lucifer from the demons, especially Cain. It wasn't much, besides him being psycho, conniving, and evil as all hell. He'd created his seven sons to rule this underworld with him, ripping them each from a piece of his soul, but there was no familial love between them. No sibling bond between the brothers, either. And Cain, being Pride and the first made, was so scared to be like him, it ate at him, while Lucifer saw him as the biggest threat.

One thing I know for sure is that I'm not going to grovel before him or plead for my life. If he wanted me dead, he wouldn't have gone through this elaborate charade with Maverick posing as an angel, giving me his ring, and bringing me down here. He needs me for something. And I'm going to figure out what that is.

"Why am I here?" I repeat the question I'd originally posed to Maverick. "I don't want to be involved in your family drama."

He rubs his mustache and beard, dark eyes sparking with interest. "Oh? But you're living with my oldest son and his two buffoons, are you not? That automatically injects you into our little squabbles. Wouldn't you say so?"

"No, I was forced into it. My foster father traded my soul to free him from his contract." Just mentioning it again brings back bitter feelings of anger and loss from Murray. It may've been a while ago, but the wounds are still there, and they still sting.

"You don't say..." He begins to walk around the room. I want to move, too, keep the distance between us, but that would be revealing my fear and showing weakness. Two things I refuse to do, so I stay put.

He continues to stalk closer. "I might be able to help you with that, you know. Breaking the contract."

Cain had told me the only ways to free a soul from a demon contract was if the demon responsible changed the terms or if they were killed. And I am definitely not going to agree to him killing Cain, Dorian, and Elias to free myself. There's no way.

"No thanks. I already have it handled," I say. He's behind me and Maverick now, and I can sense Maverick tensing nearby, his muscles stiff like he's ready to strike his father if he gives him reason to.

Odd... And I thought these two were working together to cause havoc in my life, but if I didn't know any better, I'd say there's tension here, too.

Lucifer keeps strolling around the circular room, watching me and rubbing the dark hairs around his mouth and jaw. "Ah, then, if not you, then how about your little witch friend? Her soul worth anything to you?"

My heart plummets into the pits of my stomach and I choke out her name, "Joseline?"

He nods. "That's her. Yes. Joseline. She's gotten herself in quite a predicament, hasn't she? It's amazing what someone will do for a little bit of money." His eyes flick to Maverick, the sin of Greed. "Isn't that right, my son?"

Still, Maverick doesn't answer, and his silence through all this surprises me. I expected him to be licking Lucifer's boots or something. He was as stiff and quiet as a statue.

"Otherwise, when her debt is collected, she'll come down here, be flayed like a fish, her insides scooped out, and impaled on a hook for all to see. Forced to endure that pain for eternity, as were the terms she signed to."

Panic surges through me, and I leap forward. The images springing to my mind are nightmare inducing. "No!" There's no way Joseline knew any of that when she agreed to Maverick's deal. "You can't!"

"I'm sure Maverick would consider ripping up his ties to her, free her, if..."

"If what?"

Lucifer stops walking and climbs up the few steps of the dais to his throne. "*If* you join me."

"Join you?" What the fuck does that mean?

Again, he opens his arms wide. "You are special, Aria. Special and incredibly powerful. You're destined to do great things. Can't you feel it?"

The only thing I feel right now is confused and a bit sick to my stomach.

"I'm just an ordinary," I say, bringing back my old excuse. Even after all this time, it flows from my lips easily.

"No, my dear. You are *extraordinary.*" His voice bounces off the marble walls all around us. "The dark power inside you is an ancient one, unfamiliar to even me, and I've been here for all of time. It's just what I need to exact my revenge."

Ancient? He has to be lying. I'm only eighteen. But one thing is for sure, he wants to use me as a weapon. Or Sayah, I should say.

Maverick steps forward, his brow knitted. Is that worry I see on his face, or am I imagining it? "Father, you don't mean—"

"Quiet, boy!" Lucifer shouts, his eyes flashing black like Cain's. That alone has Maverick shrinking back again. When he turns back to me, his gaze is cool again, a smile plastered back on his thin lips in a show of fake sincerity. "My kingdom is vast, Aria, but it is under constant threat by the holy ones above. I've been waiting for my chance to strike, take back what's rightfully mine, and I think you can be what I need to make that happen. And when we've won, you can rule by my side, enjoy all the luxuries Hell has to offer."

"Like poor souls strung up on hooks?" I snap.

He's unfazed. "If that's what you prefer."

I don't reply. How could I? I shake my head to try and release the terrible images of my friend being tortured that way. I could save her by taking him up on his offer; I could set her soul free, but at what cost? Lucifer using me to raise some kind of demon army against Heaven?

This is absurd.

But another thought strikes me then. "What if I just kill Maverick?" I say. "That would break Joseline's contract, wouldn't it?" Then I wouldn't have to join anyone and their apocalyptic plans.

His laughter rolls over me, sending shivers across my skin. "You're right. It would." He grabs something off the altar and tosses it our way. It slides across the floor, bouncing off my feet and spinning to a stop. It's a dagger, deadly sharp and with a gold handle. I only stare at it.

"Go on," Lucifer encourages, the sick bastard. "Do it then."

He isn't serious... That's his son.

I twist to see Maverick scowling at me, a challenge in his gaze. "You can try," is all he says.

"Wait, you're right, Maverick. Let's help her out some, shall we?" He flicks his wrist and two massive men with bull-like legs, hooves, and wide torsos step out of the black marble pillars of the fireplace, as if they were created from the very material. They seize Maverick by the arms, trapping him. He wrenches and lashes out to try and free himself, but they don't budge.

"Father! What is this? Release me! Now!" He continues to fight against the creatures' holds, but nothing seems to be working.

Lucifer ignores him and continues to talk to only me. "There you go, Aria dear. I've even made it easy for you. Kill him. Save your friend."

The voice in my head screams, *He's insane! He'd have me kill his son? I'm not a murderer. I can't.* Yet, I'm bending down and picking up the dagger, examining the blade.

Inside me, Sayah rustles, liking the more poisonous thoughts leaking in. *He is right. Killing Maverick saves Joseline. And he tricked you! He brought you down here. He deserves it.*

My lingering anger tumbles forward, making the second voice louder. He'd turned his back on Cain, his own brother. He took me away from the demons, deceived me, took advantage of Joseline and took her soul. I can make it right.

"Come on, Aria," Lucifer says. "You know you want to."

Boy, do I want to.

Adrenaline shooting through my veins, I close the distance between me and Maverick, lean up onto my tiptoes, and press the blade against his throat. He snarls at me. Actually snarls. I lean into it, blood bubbling up from his skin, and coating the dagger.

My gaze rises from the knife to his lips and something inside me shifts. My heart pounds wildly in my chest. The need to crush my mouth against his collides with the need to slit his throat, just as powerful, and suddenly, I'm left struggling between them.

My body's reaction surprises and horrifies me at the same time. I shouldn't be turned on by the sight of his blood. Or by the idea of cutting him down where he stands, but I can't help staring at his mouth, wondering what he'd taste like, what his screams would taste like if I pressed the blade deeper. I can feel my pulse thumping between my legs just at the thought.

What is wrong with me?

But suddenly, Maverick's wings fly out from his back, tearing the two marble creatures off his arms and throwing them across opposite ends of the room. Now free, he seizes me by my throat, my air supply abruptly cut off. My knife doesn't waver, and we stand there, arms crossed, both inches away from a very quick death by the other person's hand.

Something sparks in his eyes, too, that same fiery hunger I saw before in his room, and I'm unsure if he wants to kill me or fuck me right here in the center of the room.

Scarier still—I'm not sure what I would do if it wound up being the latter.

A slow clap echoes all around us, and I remember we're not alone. As if snapped from a stupor, Maverick releases me and I drop the knife at the same time, sucking in air. He touches his throat and stares at his bloodied hand.

"That was quite a show," Lucifer begins with an impressed look at us both. "I quite enjoyed it."

"You're demented," I hiss at him. "Utterly insane."

"What did you expect, dear? Martha Stewart?" Throwing his head back, he laughs.

"You told her to kill me!" Maverick shouts at him, fury rumbling through his tone.

Lucifer's head snaps his way. "Oh, relax, boy. You can't die here, remember? Not while in Hell."

"I can with that blade," he bites back. "An angel blade!"

"Oh, that's right. Must've slipped my mind."

Maverick huffs, clearly not buying Lucifer's false innocence.

I peer down at the dagger on the floor. It's rather simple looking, with a slightly curved edge and engraved hilt. I can't really see what makes it special, but according to Maverick it can kill a demon. Even while under the protection of Hell. That would be a handy thing to have.

I reach down for it, but Maverick's hand snatches me by the shoulder and wrenches me away. "I wouldn't if I were you."

That strange tingle of energy begins again—the one that always comes whenever he touches me—but I'm not going to let him use his powers on me again.

Glaring at him, I shrug off his hold. "Don't touch me."

"She's a feisty one. I'll give her that," Lucifer chuckles.

I turn back to him. "My answer is no, by the way. No, I will not join your mission to take down Heaven, so you've wasted your time here."

"Let me apologize. I've misled you," he says, stepping down from the dais. His words may be sweet but his lips twitch like the facade might break at any moment as he strides across the room. He stops in front of me, head tilting, before seizing me by my jaw and squeezing tight. Pain shoots up through my temples. "I've made you think you've had a choice."

The strength of his hold increases, and I grasp his arm, crying out as my bones grind against each other. He's going to crush them with his bare hands. Sayah slides a little more out of her dark prison in my mind, shifting back and forth, wanting to help but not being able to yet. Maverick's ring must be holding some power over her still.

"Father, enough," Maverick barks, appearing at my side. "We have her here. She's not going anywhere. There's no need for this."

But he doesn't let up, and I claw at his arm with my nails raking across his skin, drawing blood as black as Cain's when he's changed into this demon. Lucifer doesn't even flinch.

"Father." He slaps a hand on Lucifer's upper arm, and for some reason, he releases me.

I rub my jaw to try and get some of the pain to ease. Between getting tossed around by Maverick earlier and now this, I have one hell of a migraine brewing.

His eyes dart to Maverick and a silent warning passes through his gaze, one I don't understand but Maverick seems to because he steps back.

Looking down at me again, the corner of Lucifer's mouth curls up. My stomach sinks. The demons hadn't exaggerated about him at all. He is one crazy, sociopathic bastard.

"I have a surprise for you, Aria," he sing-songs.

Oh no. I want nothing this man wants to give me. Not a damn thing.

His gaze never leaving mine, he holds up a finger and curls it, signaling for someone behind him to step forward. A man steps out of the shadows between two columns. His clothes are ripped and dirty, and he has mostly dark hair, except for the grays peppered throughout. He glances nervously at me with sunken eyes, and his mouth is thin and surrounded by a badly shaven five o'clock shadow.

Glancing between them, I can't seem to figure out what this is about. I have no idea who this man is; I've never seen him in my life.

"Ah, here he is!" Lucifer finally turns and waves for him to come over to us. Slowly, he does, limping as he walks. It's clear from his disheveled state that he's been in Hell for a bit, probably one of the many poor, tortured souls that reside here.

Grabbing the man by the shoulders, Lucifer shoves him the rest of the way and he stumbles right in front of me.

I search his face for something familiar, but find absolutely nothing. "I... I don't understand," I say to both demons. "I don't know who this is."

Lucifer grins and turns to the man again. "Why don't you tell the little lady your name."

The stranger raises his chin to meet my gaze. My chest clenches and I'm not sure why. Even Sayah sways back and forth, recognizing him before me. I still, for the life of me, can't find the connection.

"Tell her." Lucifer's voice booms, and he flinches.

His cracked lips part to speak. "Liam..." he wheezes, struggling to even form words. "Liam... Cross."

Cross? But that's my last name.

Who—

"That's right, Aria," Lucifer says, taking in my confused expression and grinning broadly. "It's your daddy-dearest."

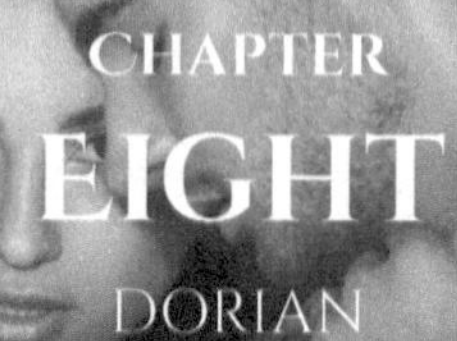

"She's gone." Elias scoffs. "The witch isn't in her apartment, and neither is her scent. So, wherever she went, it's not there. I even checked the old neighborhood she grew up in with Murray, but I didn't pick up her scent."

"Fucking great," I snarl. "Cain's got nothing on the relic front, and with Joseline gone, we're back at square one."

Cain sits silently at the desk in his office, while Elias stands in the doorway wearing just jeans, his hair wild like the wolf prowling behind his eyes. I press my back to the wall, irritation flaring over me that we'd ended up in a corner with no way out.

"So, what do we know so far?" I ask.

"That Maverick took her," Elias snarls, storming into the room, his chest heaving for each furious breath. "I'm going to murder him," he hisses through clenched teeth. "And we can't just waltz back into Hell. That's where we fucking are."

"We don't know what Maverick told Lucifer about her," Cain adds.

"Do you think it's about Sayah?" Elias asks, a question he'd raised several times earlier, and he's sounding like a broken record.

"Uh…" I hesitate, deciding I have to come clean. There's a lot riding on us knowing all the facts. Aria's life. Our future in Hell, and if there is one after Lucifer's appearance at our home.

"What is it then?" Cain asks.

"While in Scotland, Maverick paid me a visit." I pause as Cain stiffens and shifts to the edge of his seat, the questions on his face as plain as day. "He asked me if we were using Aria as a secret weapon."

Cain's on his feet in seconds, and he moves with lighting speed, the man moving in a blink and I don't respond in time. His hand clasps my throat and drives me hard into the wall.

Black lines wriggle under his skin, snaking across his face, and fury darkens his eyes completely. A reddish glow encases his other fist, hellfire.

"You've been keeping this from me?"

And I'd be lying if I say his aggression doesn't intimidate me slightly, but I hold my head up and look him in the eyes. Cain knows how to control his anger, but when he loses it, he's terrifying.

I swallow hard. "Fuck off, and I'll tell you."

"Speak," he growls in my face, his hand squeezing my throat, making it slightly harder to speak.

"Maverick told me, Lucifer knows about her power," I gasp out.

"What power?" he roars, his hand tightening, and I tense up, ready to shove my fists into his damn chest to dislodge him. He may be a sin demon, but I won't back down, and can give just as damn good.

"Don't think he can respond if you choke him to death," Elias pipes in, standing to my side, watching in utter amusement. "Want me to take over and maybe he'll talk quicker?"

Cain releases me with a growl, and I glare at Elias. "Get off me." I shove past both of them to catch my breath, filling my lungs, anger flaring over my chest.

I turn and face them. Two demons I'd lost my home with, experienced abandonment with, and found ourselves again. I remind myself they aren't the enemy but are just fucking pissed at Maverick and Lucifer.

"I asked him the same question about Aria's power, and the fucker vanished on me. So, Lucifer knows a lot more than it seems. As does Maverick."

"Or he's just lying to you. I mean he went to you out of us three, so he must think you're the gullible one."

My gaze narrows at Elias's direction, my anger fuming at his spiteful words. "You've always been a prick, never fit in back home, so don't spin me your jealousy bullshit."

Elias comes at me, a growl escaping his lips, but it's Cain who juts an arm out across his chest. "Not now. After we find Aria, go rip each other's heads off for all I care." His voice carries thorns, and his attention funnels in on me. "Now, tell me everything, and don't make me hurt you to drag out anything else you've kept from me."

Cain is a master at playing the calm guy, while the psychopath lying underneath is ten times more dangerous than Elias. Elias's emotions are always on his sleeve, so at least you'll know when he's about to kill you.

So, I reiterate every encounter with Maverick, every note, every visit, word for word. "He's visited me in the past, but mostly to dig up information which I gave him none, and he gave me zilch. I didn't think it was worth mentioning as it provided nothing but a nosy asshole who is clearly intimidated by his older brother."

"So, was he just talking about Sayah?" Elias asks.

"Don't have a clue," I say. "But if he's got his filthy hands on her now, he's going to find out."

"And knowing Lucifer, that will come in the form of anything to get what he wants."

A shiver races up my arms at the thought, as I'd seen Lucifer torture people for little things like walking in his path accidentally, and the bastard enjoyed himself. Not that I can complain as I had my fair share of hunting down rogue demons, but when I put that into the context with Aria, a chill sinks into my bones.

"Anything else?" Cain barks at me, and the distrust taints his words. I bristle at his tone, but my gut twists at the knowledge that I should have said something earlier. But shit's done and I don't live in the damn past when I can't change it.

"That's everything."

Cain pivots toward Elias. "What about you? Are you keeping secrets from me?"

Elias's shoulders rear back, disdain flashing over his expression. "Are you fucking kidding me? I'm insulted you'd even ask me that."

"Everyone outside our home is meant to be the enemy, but apparently snakes live inside these walls too, so yes, I'm asking."

Elias curls his upper lip in a silent growl, his gaze deepening at Cain. "I'm not a traitor."

Okay, that comment hit me hard. "Hell, Elias, take it down a notch."

Before he can respond with aggression, Cain's cell phone rings, and he grabs it from the table, staring at the caller ID and turns away from us.

"Speak," he answers.

He doesn't say a word but nods at first, and only a faint whisper comes from the phone from a male's voice.

"Are you sure? That doesn't sound right." Cain states.

Silence, and I glance over to Elias who's seething, his mood sour and when he looks at me, retribution crosses his face. Bring it on because after everything, I needed a good punching bag.

"Give me the location," Cain orders, then he hangs up as he stuffs the phone into his back pocket.

"What's going on?" Elias asks.

"One of my leads has picked up a strange energy source in Glenside."

I shrug. "So?"

"My team is searching for relics, and Zay said it was something they sensed. It might be nothing, but he wanted me to know. The guy is a fae with his strength drawing from elements, so he senses faint distortions in the air that radiate unusual energies."

"I doubt there's a relic in town, if that's what he's implying, or Aria would have sensed it by now," Elias says.

"That's my first thought too," Cain responds, moving to stand behind his desk and searching through the top drawer.

"And you're going to check it out regardless?" I ask.

He doesn't answer at first.

"Whatever it is, it's happening in our territory. We can't lose control of our hold on this city. Not to mention that if I stay here a second longer, I'll do something I'll regret, like slit your throat." The intensity behind Cain's glare tells me he meant every damn word.

"You two get back out there and find Joseline for fuck's sake," he orders.

"On it," Elias grunts under his breath and storms out of the room, his shoulder purposefully knocking against mine on his way out.

"Now, get out of my face, Dorian." Cain turns from me, and I storm out, fucking exhausted of talking to these emotional bastards.

Not like the information I had got us any closer to finding Aria, yet the guilt curling deep in my chest never subsided. Because tempers are already at their breaking point, and well, I had indeed fucked up.

CAIN

THE CAR HUMS as we sped through town, and I sit in the back listening to the radio Holmes had switched on. For a change, I welcome the distraction. Anything to get my mind off Aria, how we'd let Joseline out of sight, and then hearing Dorian's deceit topped things off. All this time, he's been keeping secrets. Maverick's visits and Lucifer's interest hadn't been as sudden as I originally thought. They'd been playing the game for a while, but through Dorian.

Here I assumed it had everything to do with me, but I'd been wrong. It's all about Aria. I shift uncomfortably, staring outside at the world as we blur past it. What pisses me off more is that I didn't spend more time working out what was different about Aria. She was with me this whole time and I'd been so caught up in everything else that I ignored the obvious. So much so that even Maverick and my father had seen her potential from Hell.

I clench my teeth, furious at myself more than anything else. I'd let her down, and that burns through me like acid.

An annoying, panicked voice on the radio bugs me, and I tune into what they're saying.

"Reports coming from the Glenside Chief of Police confirms twenty-two people died from an overdose this week alone from what authorities are calling Hush, a new drug on the streets. No further information has been released on this narcotic, or where it's come from. But from what eye-witness accounts have said, those who overdose experience extreme stimulation, loss of inhibitions, and a sense of euphoria that has them addicted from the first taste."

"Switch it off," I call out to Holmes, not interested in humans choosing to destroy their lives. I will do anything to retrieve Aria before it's too late, as I can't bear the idea of losing her.

Time goes by quickly, and soon we're rolling down a residential part of town, trees lining the sidewalks in front of Queen Anne townhouses, packed closely in next to each other, each a two-story home and in a different color.

I never understand why humans enjoy living so close to each other.

Holmes parks in an empty spot beneath a tree, shading us from the sunlight, and I peer outside to the house with number fifty-five stuck on the front door. The building is a pale sunset color with windows draped by dark curtains. The front lawn is overgrown, mail overspilling in the mailbox, the place appearing run down compared to the other homes nearby.

I push open the door while glancing over to Holmes in the driver's seat. "I won't be long."

My intention is to quickly see what's here, though in truth my initial instincts tell me it's a lost lead, and I'm wasting my time. But I won't live with this on my thoughts in case it's a clue— anything that might lead us to a relic.

Up on the front porch, I stare at the front door that has a strange marking painted on it in red of an upside triangle with a cross inside of it. Odd, but then again, the whole house looks like it's falling apart so no surprise the place is graffitied.

I knock on the door and wait.

No response, and I can only guess they're not home. It's in the middle of the day, so they could be at work. When another knock doesn't bring anyone to open the door, I try the handle. To my surprise, it creaks open.

Sunlight rushes inside from behind me, carving through the darkness, revealing a long, empty hallway and a set of wooden steps to the left. Like the outside, the place is worn, wallpaper peeling off the walls, one of the steps broken, and now I'm more convinced no one lives here. Well, except for squatters who've found a free home.

I step inside and peer into the first room to my right, dark with only slivers of light pouring in from the edges of the curtain. I move over and draw one open so I can better see more of the open room that leads into a filthy kitchen.

The furniture is torn and stained. I sniff the stuffy air that is tainted with a putrid stink and blood. The deeper I walk into the house, the heavier the metallic smell grows, and I can already taste it on the back of my tongue.

Curiosity rushes forward, shoving me to find out what's going on here, why the fae sensed unusual energy from this home.

I head down the long corridor, the first few doors I pass are locked, the last one slips open at my touch like the lock has long been broken.

A heavy smell of blood hits me first, so thick and ripe in the air, it suffocates me. I've seen my fair share of death and bloodshed, but to have it concentrated in a small room compounds it into a horrific stench.

My eyes scan the darkness as a faint trickle of light from behind me spills inside.

It's enough to show me the vampires.

Three of them suspended from the ceiling, upside down, their souls as dark as the pits they'd come from.

They dangle from beams that have been suspended across the ceiling, their clawed feet holding on like bats. With their arms wrapped around themselves, they hang there, looking like corpses, their faces deathly pale. In the corners of the room are slumped bodies, at least three of them, and by their ripped throats and putrid smells, they aren't newly created vamps, but food.

My stomach turns at the sight of the humans.

Viktor rules over the vamps in Glenside, and we'd agreed it was fucking illegal to kill humans from town to not raise suspicions. That was a big rule all the pack leaders in Glenside agreed to. He'd created special locations for his brood on the outskirts of the city, ensuring none of the blood-starved are near the humans. So, what the hell have I just found?

I retreat and shut the door, then slip back through the house, confirming more vamps and dead, while also using the moment to search for anything that might resemble a relic. I fall short on what I'd come here for. Instead, I'd found a nest of rogue vampires feasting on their neighborhood.

My heart squeezes at the deaths. I need Viktor to fix his fucking coven.

The thing about the undead is that they emit a vibe that hangs in the air like a bad smell. Put a clutch of them together and that energy intensifies, which tells me this might be what the fae had picked up on, not a relic.

With my pulse thundering that I've come to a dead end, I storm outside as a sense of hopelessness sinks through me. The notion of spending several more decades just trying to find the rest of the relics eats away at me. Even next week could be too late for Aria to be left in Hell, and fear climbs through me. Trepidation echoes with every thump of my heart.

I leap into the back of the Town Car. "Home."

Staring back at the house, I can't get the images of all those vamps and the dead out of my head. I check my phone for any messages from my team, but there's nothing.

I lift my gaze to Holmes in the driver's seat. "Let's take a detour by Viktor's estate."

He nods and I sit back, needing to make this visit quick, and I hope to hell Elias and Dorian have been more successful than me.

By the time we draw up to Viktor's estate and drive through the open gates of his mansion, something appears odd. There are no guards out front.

Holmes stops in front of the grand mansion, the marble columns in the front always made me feel like I'd stepped back in time. Vampires are terribly nostalgic about their past, and Viktor has Roman blood.

I'm out of the car and banging on the front door before I know it. A servant opens the door, staring at me, startled.

"I'm here to see your master," I instruct the young man who looks utterly terrified in my presence.

"Come in," a female's voice calls out from deeper in the house, and I lift my head to find Charlotte bouncing down the stairs in cut-off denim shorts and a loose-fitting blue tee with nothing underneath, based on the way her breasts jiggle. I've always thought she was a beautiful woman, but not exactly my style with her clinginess. When Viktor claimed her, it was like he brought out the happiness from the girl who'd grown up in a horribly abusive family. They've always been the perfect couple.

I'm a bit confused why she's here. Especially when Viktor is suspected to be the one leaving bruises on her body and making her cry. My next question is, why hadn't Quinn told me she'd left the apartment and come here? He'd be hearing it from me when I got out of here.

"Before you freak, Quinn's here," she explains. "I only came here to pick up some of my stuff, and he'd only let me go if he tagged along."

Good thing she'd said so because, in the mood I'm in, I was liable to tear him a new one.

The servant steps aside and I enter the enormous marble hallway that leads to an elaborate set of stairs that sweep to the right. The windows are all heavily tinted, blotting out most of the sunlight, while enormous chandeliers light up the place. Statues of women in flowing gowns flank the bottom of the steps. It matches the rest of the extravagant, Greek-inspired decor.

Charlotte throws herself into my arms, which I don't expect, and before I can say a word, she's got her face nestled against my neck, crying. Her whole body is trembling as she clings to me.

I grasp her by her waist and wait for her to settle down. When she does, she pulls back and wipes her face. "Oh, crap. I'm so sorry, Cain. But I've been so frazzled lately. I can't help it." Her eyes are red and puffy, and I doubt they are just from her crying session right now.

"Did Viktor hurt you? Where is he?" A darkness lines my voice.

Her chin trembles as she clasps her hands to her chest in a look of despair. "You don't know where he is either? That's why I thought you came over. That you had bad news or something about him."

I shake my head, and now my thoughts fill with what I'd witnessed at the vampire house. The humans, the blood... Could it be related to Viktor at all?

"When was the last time you saw him?" I ask, as Charlotte is tearing up again and shaking her head.

"Seven days ago. I'm used to him traveling and being out of town, but he always tells me where he goes. Except this time, I kissed him, went to work, and then haven't seen him again."

"Did he say anything unusual? Or has he spoken to you about a new vampire in town, or anything that might help?"

She blinks at me, while licking her lips nervously, and her hand moves to her neck, almost absentmindedly.

That's when I notice the dark bruise just below her ear, and another sticking out from beneath her top and over her collarbone.

"Who hurt you, Charlotte?" I reach over and pull her hand away so I can have a better look, and it hurts me to see the agony someone has caused her. I've known her long enough to care, as much as I don't like to admit such a thing, and no one touches those close to me.

She looks down, not meeting my gaze. "A couple of vampires."

"Which ones?" I ask louder this time, my chest tightening with the growing anger.

She tilts her head back and meets me with glassy eyes. "Two of the local ones under his command. Fucking assholes dared touch me when I asked them if they knew where Viktor was. They said if I asked about it again, they'd kill me."

"Are they new vampires under his command?"

She shook her head. "They'd been with him for years, but it seems like they've changed their allegiance." She cranes her neck to the side as proof. "This, paired with Viktor's disappearance... I'm worried something bigger is going on. If something's happened to Viktor..." Squeezing her eyes shut, she shakes her head, refusing to think about it.

I keep going over the vamp faces in the house, and not one looks familiar. I've spent enough time with Viktor and his followers to never forget a face. And those bastards are not from around here. So, does that mean they've infiltrated Viktor's brood and got rid of him? And are the rogue members of Viktor's coven who'd hurt Charlotte turning on him?

Something sinister is going on here, and I'm going to figure out what.

"Where do I find the two who attacked you?"

"They used to live on the grounds here, but I haven't seen them for a couple of days. It's like everyone is dropping off the face of the earth and forgot to tell me." She starts crying again and lowers her face into her hands.

My stomach hardens at her pain, at something big going down in the bloodsuckers' world, and it couldn't have come at the worst time.

There is only one solution... I'd take Dorian and Elias to pay the vamps in the house a visit, but really my priority is Aria. Not dealing with someone else's shit.

"Stay in the house, and keep Quinn close," I tell Charlotte, holding her by the arms and drawing her against me. "I'll look around and see what I can find out." I make sure to leave out the part about the other vampires to avoid terrifying her more than she already is. I have no doubt those fuckwits had a hand in Viktor's sudden disappearance. He's a friend of mine, but also a resilient vampire, so I am not ready just yet to count him as dead.

ARIA

Dad?

This man in front of me is supposed to be my dad?

I'm stunned beyond words. Beyond thought. All I can do is stare at the man before me and gape like a fish out of water.

Even he blinks rapidly, confusion flitting across his face. "Aria?" He glances at Lucifer as if he doesn't believe it, either. "My daughter, Aria?"

"It's a happy family reunion," Lucifer replies, grinning. "Little Aria is all grown up now."

When the man named Liam turns back to me, he's just as shocked as I am. He says nothing for a long moment, but then he licks his dry lips and says, "I haven't seen you since you were born."

"Since before you gave me up, you mean?" The vicious words snap from me like a whip, laced with bitterness and anger. I don't know why I even said it at all, really. This man could be anyone. This all could be a trick. I've never even seen a picture of my parents before, so I have no way of knowing this guy—this Liam Cross—is who he says he is.

He winces at the harshness in my tone. "I-I didn't know."

"What do you mean you didn't know?" My head pounds as I think back to the abandoned hospital and what Cain and I had found there—my name on a list for abandoned children. "You didn't want me. You left me at the hospital."

"I did none of those things. I died the day we brought you

home from the hospital. Only a few days after you were born," he explains.

I blink as his words sink in.

But if he'd died shortly after my birth, that meant...

"It was your mother, that heartless bitch," he snaps suddenly, hatred contorting his face. "I had a feeling she had a hand in my death, and now knowing she gave you up, too, I'm sure of it."

"She... killed you?" I asked.

"Isn't this exciting?" Lucifer cuts in and then looks to Maverick. "Every family has its dark secrets and problems."

Maverick huffs at that.

I'd honestly forgotten they were even there, listening in.

It seems Liam doesn't care either because he keeps talking, his words rushed in his anger. "Your mother was a piece of shit. Cheated on me multiple times. Loved to call the cops on me whenever she was pissed enough. Threw all my clothes in the garbage and lit them on fire..."

He's rambling, but I don't stop him. From everything he's describing, my mother seems like a real character, which could explain why she was able to toss me aside so easily. Her own daughter.

"I would've never given you up, Aria," he says. "She's fucked us both over. She's the one who should be here in Hell. Not us."

"Where is she?" I ask.

"I can answer that one," Lucifer adds. "She's not dead, yet. But she's been sent to a residential home for the mentally disturbed."

She's alive? My heart beats faster at finding this out. For so long, I made myself believe both my parents were dead as a way to deal.

"How do you even know that?"

He shrugs. "It's my job to know all souls damned to Hell. Once she dies, she's got a one-way ticket down here as well."

"But why?"

"Because, like Liam said, she killed him. Not directly, but that little detail doesn't matter when it comes to stuff like this."

I glanced at my father. "What does that mean? How did you die?"

"I don't know how exactly, but somehow, your mother was able to summon something. Something dark. And use it to kill me."

I didn't reply, too confused and shocked.

"I have no idea how she did it," he goes on. "She was human, like me."

I glance at Lucifer for confirmation, and he nods. "Definitely human."

"But she was able to use dark magic to summon some... shadow creature. It attacked me in the middle of the night. A black figure with a shifting shape... and glowing red eyes... And it dragged me into Hell. That's why I ended up here."

My blood runs cold at that. Shadow creature? Red eyes? Could he mean Sayah?

Lucifer is watching me intensely, dark eyes alight. He's waiting for me to make the connection myself. That the thing inside me could be the very reason my father is dead.

Sayah... Is it true?

She shrinks back, burying herself again in the unreachable places in my mind.

My heartbeat skips. I mean, I've seen what Sayah is capable of with my own eyes. She's been getting more powerful and less possible to control. Did I think she could kill someone? Absolutely. But is she the reason I was orphaned since birth?

There's a monster inside me.

"That creature is what lives inside you now, Aria," Lucifer says.

Oh. My. God.

"Do you know what she is?" I blurt out. "Or why she's inside me?"

"I don't know." He frowns, and I know he's telling me the truth. He's obviously not happy this is something unfamiliar to even him.

But if the actual King of Hell doesn't know what Sayah is, then how will I ever know?

"She's not a demon?" I ask. "Could this be possession or something?" I've considered that option before; it's the only kind of thing I can think of where a dark spirit takes up residence in a human.

Maverick steps forward. "Only some lower-level demons can possess humans, and it's never for a long amount of time. Soon the living body will start to break down, unable to house the concentrated darkness inside."

And Sayah's been with me since the beginning. Years.

"Wait… that *creature* lives inside… *you?* Now?" Liam gasps in terror.

"It's controlled," Maverick replies quickly, and glances down at the ring on my finger.

Oh shit. That's what he thinks. Now I'm not so sure it's a good thing I can feel Sayah again.

As my anxiety rises, so does my temperature. Heat prickles up my neck, and I want to throw up. Or faint. My vision grows fuzzy, and my knees wobble.

I'm going down.

"Shit! The creature's got its claws in her!" Liam says.

"She's overwhelmed." There's a presence close to me, pressing into my side, and I hear Maverick's voice buzzing near my ear. "That's enough for today. I'm taking her back."

My head swims and thumps at the same time, and I'm barely aware of anything but the pressure of Maverick's arms around me and the movement of the world around me as he picks me up and carries me toward the fireplace.

Exhaustion sweeping me up, my eyes drift close.

"Maverick." Lucifer's warning tickles at my consciousness.

"My ring can only do so much. She's not meant to be down here," he explains. "I'm taking her back."

There's a burst of light against my eyelids and a blast of heat as Maverick doesn't wait for Lucifer's response. Then, I'm lost to the darkness.

I wake to a room that's empty and surprisingly cold. A quick look around and I confirm I'm in Maverick's house again, laying in his bed, but alone.

How long have I been out?

I try to think back on the conversation leading to my fainting spell. Being in Lucifer's throne room with him, Maverick, and crazy enough, my father. I found out some things, like my mother was still alive, and my father had died before she'd dumped me at the hospital to be someone else's problem. She'd also found a way to summon a dark entity—Sayah, I am guessing—and sick it on him. Then, for some unknown reason, Sayah latched onto me and has been with me ever since.

What is Sayah exactly? I still have no idea. And apparently Lucifer doesn't even know, but that's not stopping him from wanting me to help him overtake Heaven. He thinks Sayah is the weapon he needs to do it.

But do I get a say in this? If I stay here, it's looking like a big, fat no. It's just another reason why I need to find a way out of here.

Climbing out of bed, a shiver races down my spine, then with it comes a strange sensation, one where I sense something rising through me, emerging.

Speak of the devil.

I watch as a black shadow slithers out of me and stretches

across the floorboards like a serpent. I stare at Sayah, then look down to Maverick's ring. Yep. The same damn thing's lost its oomph.

She slides across the walls, the ceiling, even inside the fireplace, despite it roaring with flames. With quick, jerky movements, she knocks over a bust of what looks like Medusa, and it shatters on the floor.

Shit. She's able to touch things here?

Better question is, why don't I feel that dragging, suffocating feeling I normally feel whenever she decides to go solid? Where's the orange glow that usually sparks through our connection?

Is it because... she belongs here?

Jerking away from the wall, she turns back to me and rears up, towering over me. Like she's no longer a shadow but a rogue entity.

Gasping, I back up until my back hits the wall. Trapped.

Two glowing red eyes blink into existence, and my throat tightens, remembering Liam's words. A shadowy figure with red eyes... That's what he saw before he died.

Is this it? Is she about to kill me, too?

She takes a more humanoid shape, mimicking my shadow, but with too long limbs and billowing hair. She doesn't move, though, just stands there, waiting.

"Sayah..." I say hesitantly.

Her chin dips in a shallow nod.

Okay, she's trying to communicate with me, like old times. That's a good sign, right?

Still too nervous to move away from the wall, my gaze flickers around the room. "As you can see, we're not in Kansas anymore."

Again, she nods once.

"I don't belong here," I tell her.

Another nod.

"Do you?"

This time, she doesn't move.

Okay then...

"Did you kill my dad?"

At first, nothing. But then her head drops in a yes.

My pulse speeds up. "But, why?"

In a flash, she throws herself toward the exit, flattening herself and shimming under the door, leaving behind just a thin black thread attached to me. I release a tense breath.

There were times when I'd often sit around with Sayah in the room with me, where I'd feel less lonely, where she filled the void... and now, I can't help but be scared. I hate that things have turned so sour between us, but to be fair, she's turned out to be terrifying.

She's a killer.

It seems like an eternity before Sayah finally returns. She zips back into the room and snaps back into me, curling herself back into that safe space in the back of my mind. She's decided she's done talking to me, apparently.

Fine. Whatever.

Feeling somewhat frustrated, I sigh and plop down onto my side in bed. I hate this hopelessness in my chest, not knowing what anyone has in store for me.

Most of all, I am starting to believe more and more that whatever Sayah is, she's way stronger than I'd ever imagined.

Coldness sweeps over my skin despite the blazing hearth, and I lay there, not feeling safe one bit.

MAVERICK

"Brother, how long do you plan on keeping the girl a prisoner in your house? I'd love to play with her," Nix almost purrs the words, which makes me furious. He's glancing over my shoulder and in the direction of my mansion. I'd been on my way to pick up a few things from the market for Aria, but I lost interest when Nix caught up with me in the local markets. A place where the chaotic demons aren't permitted, giving others living here a chance to buy some basic necessities. Not everyone in Hell is condemned... Some are here by retribution, by family requirements, by deals forcing them to carry out their duties. You'd be surprised how many humans end up here, trying to continue their existence all because of a little crossroads trade. I swear, those arrogant crossroad demons are some of the wealthiest for the simple reason that they bring in the most souls. The thing is, Father dearest pays demons per the soul they drag into Hell. It's a bitch fight too, a cut-throat industry down here, and as far as I'm concerned they can have it, and kill each other in the process.

When I glance over to Nix, he's still going on, his mouth never shutting, and his presence irritates me. "You're still talking?" I say, which only has him stiffening.

"You're a real bastard, you know that? You bring a new toy into Hell and suddenly you're the favorite. But then again, you've always been a greedy *sonofabitch*."

I laugh at him, mostly forced and to stop myself from driving my fist into his pretty face. Normally I don't let him get to me, but today I'm itching all over for a fight. "Father never takes favorites, and if he does, they are the ones to die first."

I push past him, finished with our conversation, and stride through the busy market. Black, charred buildings surround the courtyard from when a dragon had escaped the underground cells years ago. Let's just say he burned everything in sight. Father insisted on leaving the burned structures, as he liked to remind everyone that we were in Hell.

He hates these markets, but there are too many in here that don't belong deep in the pits, so it's a compromise he's learned to live with. I suspect he unleashed the dragon on these markets on purpose.

Six rows fill the courtyard, booths made of slabs of stone with a flat surface, since many here sell what they catch out in the wilderness, and this is where the butchering happens. One man in a torn cape is hacking away at something on his stand. He has an amethyst crystal as long and thick as my arm sticking out from the front of his chest. Clearly, it's what killed him and threw him down here. Now *he'd* be an interesting person to listen to over a few drinks.

Voices, singing, and even screams flood the air, and I find the sound rather calming.

Nix slips in beside me, striding along with me.

"No, you can't visit her again," I say.

"I wouldn't share her either, Brother."

"Why are you groveling?"

He doesn't respond at first, but saunters with me past a large cage with three horned pigs, snarling and fighting each other for escape. The soulless humans still like to feast on food, though it's not needed. Some habits are hard to break, I guess.

"There's something different about her, isn't there?" Nix finally breaks my concentration.

I cut him a sharp glare. "What are you talking about?" I had sensed something unusual about her from the first time we met, and while Father and I can't work out what it is that makes her different, it's clear we're not the only ones who've noticed.

"Come now, you don't think me a fool? I smelled the darkness on her the moment I entered the room. So, what is she? A recent fallen angel? Oh, we haven't had one of those in a long time. But seeing how much interest Father seems to have in her, could she be one of his own offspring?"

His words pause me for a moment, about the connection I feel for her, except if she had been Lucifer's, then we'd all sense it, as our blood unifies us. "Not possible. She's just a human with really bad luck," I answer. "Now get the fuck out of my face. I have places to be." Mostly, going back to my house. I turn down an alley for a short cut out of the center of the markets, when Nix's voice follows me.

"You know nothing in Hell remains innocent for long. So, how long do you really think she'll last, even with you hiding her? Our brothers are already whispering about her, and you know once Lorcan gets invested, he won't stop until he's got her."

Fury lashes me at the name. Lorcan. My brother, the demon of Envy, a dark bastard who'll destroy anyone and everything to get what he wants if he feels he's been left out.

I don't look back, just keep going, my heart thundering in my chest that Aria's time in Hell is short lived. I remind myself I shouldn't care, yet a chill races down my arms when I think of Lorcan laying a hand on her.

I emerge from the alley and head toward the gates into the community. A large angel skeleton is suspended from a pole near the entrance. One that Lucifer himself had dragged into Hell for crossing him. Now all that remains of her are bones, twisted wings, and torn fabric hanging off the frame.

When I look at it, all I can picture is Aria up there, and panic carves right through me, along with an urgency. I curve my shoulders forward, and a sharpness cuts across my shoulder blades as I call out my wings.

Skin splits, and I yank my shirt up and over my head. In seconds, silvery wings spread outward, casting a shadow over the land. Heads turn in my direction, but I don't give a shit.

My wings beat, wind picking up under them, and I'm lifting into the air, moving with speed. I need to get back to Aria.

The air burns across my face, a lot hotter than normal, which only means there's a swarm of new victims down below and the torturing is in full swing. Good. That means a distraction, as Father loves to watch.

When I reach my room, I step inside through the wall, only then remembering I ought to have knocked. Not that it matters when I find Aria curled up on my bed on the black fur blanket I'd left for her earlier.

Dark hair spills outward across the pillow, her hands curled in against her chest, her knees pulled up, and her pouty mouth is parted with her deep breaths.

I still don't know why my brother was the one bestowed to claim her soul. He is one lucky bastard, and I'd be lying if I said it doesn't burn me that I can't just easily keep her for myself.

I tried, obviously... case in point, why she's in here in my room. Father of course had a say in it, but it was my suggestion to keep her away from the scum out there. And I'm including my brothers in that generalization.

The thing is, I never expected to feel anything for her, so she was a nice surprise. But with knowing what is coming for her, I'm torn. Shredded to a thousand pieces.

I'm pacing before I know it. Leaving her here means she's at Father's mercy, but I maintain favor with him, to take his side and hopefully the throne down the track, this is the right thing for me to do. With Cain out of the picture, the opportunity lies wide open.

Well, that is, before this woman slinked into my life.

But to do the unthinkable comes with consequences. Father's wrath, and driving Aria right into the arms of the demon I tried to extract her from. Either way, I'm fucked really, and in truth, I've never been good at doing the right thing.

She hates me, and I ruined things by daring to lay a hand on her. The memory sticks to my insides like tar. When I watch her sleep, I see an angel amid the darkness, and she deserves better than that.

I pause by the bed, grinding my teeth. Time is limited for both of us, and what she brings out in me is unlike anything I've experienced. Anger, revenge, and hunger battle within me. But most of all, an addiction like never before swallows me when I think of her.

I'm beginning to understand why Cain is so protective of her, and thinking of him brings back memories I don't want to recall.

"You know what happens to anyone who steals from me?" my father yells, shoving his face into mine, the blade of his knife pressing into the soft flesh beneath my ribcage.

I suck in a breath, holding onto it from the excruciating pain as he breaks skin, and I hiss. It's not a matter of dying, as I can't with a normal knife, but that's not the point when it hurts like a fucking bitch. And when my father takes that as a challenge, there's a point where I wonder if he ever intends to stop or if I'll forever be in my own hellish nightmare.

"I-I j-just held them in a safe place. I w-wasn't stealing," I stutter between shaky breaths, the biting blade pushing into me ever so slowly by the psycho in front of me.

I grit my teeth, sweat dripping down the sides of my face. Anger rushes through me.

The empty room he uses for torture seems to close in around me, the walls made of flames, the flooring transparent, giving him a birds-eye view of the hideous creatures being whipped down below.

Heat pours over me while the crackle of flames surrounding us snap.

He grins, loving every moment of seeing me suffer.

His hand flinches, then he plunges the blade right under my ribs and into my heart. I shudder, groaning as I convulse. A devastating ache pulses across my chest, my heart constricting, and I can't breathe. Pleas drip from my lips, and I fucking loathe myself for showing Lucifer any kind of weakness. It's what he loves and has been waiting for.

He rips the knife back out as fast as he had jammed it into me, filling me with pain. I slump to my side in the chair he'd chained me to, shaking, blood gushing from the wound, down my leg and into the already darkening puddle.

I suck in ragged breaths, the pain so excruciating it blinds me as I shake uncontrollably. Already I start to feel the prick of my skin as it knits itself back together, as it has for the past dozen times he's already stabbed me. Fucking asshole.

He stretches his back, his bones cracking, then wipes the blood from his blade on my sleeve. "If you keep pushing me without an answer, I will bring out the angel blade. Won't that be fun."

I stare him dead straight in the eyes, and I stiffen, ignoring the shiver worming down my spine at his threat. Still, I won't give him the satisfaction of seeing my fear again. "They were four souls from your river of millions, new ones I intended to return. I saved them from escape."

His face contorts, and a harrowing expression grips him, replaced just as quick by an ugly hatred. I truly believe he loathes me enough to end my life over four damned souls I took after they lost their way. And I had every plan of returning the things after I had a bit of fun. After all, I found them, and without me, they'd be lost already. But my father notices even one of his precious souls taken from him. It's where he gains his strength from, we all know it, and that's why he'll kill anyone if they threaten that source of power.

"You think I'm a fool?" He tosses aside the blade, the metal clanging against the floor and vanishing into the flames. With the flick of his fingers, the blaze parts against a section of the wall that exposes a set of drawers, and from within he collects the angel blade. The corners of his thin lips quirk upward as he turns to me. "You leave me no option."

I clench my fists behind my back, fighting back the panic. He'll do it. He has six other sons, so I'm not a big loss to him. I've known this my whole life.

In that same moment, Cain emerges through the doorway that flickers with flames. He steps through them and brushes his perfectly pressed suit like it might get stained.

He's a replica of Father: tall, with a dangerous gaze, and both so prideful it makes me sick.

"This isn't necessary," Cain tells Lucifer with confidence, his chin high, his eyes intense, well aware that to confront Father on anything could lead to him ending up in my very predicament. So why would he take this risk?

Cain's gaze flicks over to me for a split second, no sympathy or emotion, yet he hasn't called for my execution either. So that's something.

"Don't get involved," Father growls.

"I wouldn't care if you make my brother suffer, but the truth is also something you stand for, it is not?"

Lucifer pauses, lifting his narrowing gaze at Cain. "I'm listening."

"I have it on good authority from the guards that the souls were indeed escapees and Maverick did you a favor by catching them."

The harsh light from the burning walls twists Father's features, clearly he's not a fan of Cain's reasoning, and would rather continue torturing me because that's what a bastard of a father he is.

His fingers curl tighter around the leather hilt that houses the angel blade, his knuckles turning white, and I can almost picture him jamming that thing into Cain for daring to stop him from having fun.

Cain, on the other hand, holds his composure like he's conducting a business transaction, something I've noticed he does often with our father. It works for him, and he's worked out how to ignore his emotions. While me, when I look at Lucifer's face, I want to rip his head off his shoulders. He doesn't get along with any of us, but we try to gain favor with him, as that makes our existence tolerable.

Lucifer's nostrils flare and he growls, the sound dark and angry. Shadows shift as he lifts the weapon in his hand, glaring at me, seemingly to decide between pleasure and doing the right thing.

The thing is, this is Lucifer and I expect nothing from him but destruction. The beast comes closer to me, my heart thundering, and I rear back in my chair.

He wipes a hand across his mouth with the hand gripping the blade, a gesture I am sure is nothing more than intimidation.

"Always remember this lesson, Son." His whisper is perfect and almost caring, and completely unexpected. Suddenly, the chains around my wrists drop, freeing me. And just like that, he turns and marches out of the room. "Cain, with me!" he commands, his voice filling the space. More shadows drift behind him and leave the room. The flames dwindle too, starting to dissolve to ash.

Cain looks at me, and my stomach clenches as I expect his payment for saving my ass. But it never comes, just a look of vulnerability, one that screams his understanding that we're just as much in Hell as all these souls, trapped and tortured slowly to madness by Lucifer.

Without a word, he marches out of the room as the last flames are snuffed.

In the darkness of the room, I stare at nothing, just trying to catch my breath and accept that, for some reason, Cain had saved my life tonight.

I pry open my eyes to the girl who's awakened a desire within me unlike anyone else, and has no doubt done the same with my brother. Cain saved me that day, and never once asked for anything in return, yet I took Aria from him. That sits especially heavy on my mind today.

A shadow falls over the bed she lies in and I lift my gaze to a dark figure standing across the bed from me. Watching me with bright red eyes, the rest of her features are almost imperceptible.

I let my gaze roam down her form, curious about this thing, tracing the silhouette of a female, all the way down to the thin, black thread that is linked to Aria's side.

Fear trickles through me at the sight of the creature. She's supposed to be locked away by my ring, but it seems even Hell's magic can't keep her bound for long. We may have severely underestimated her strength.

"Hello there," I say, looking back up.

She doesn't respond.

"I've wanted to meet you."

The edges of her form start feathering like she might disappear or change forms.

"You don't need to fear me, I won't hurt Aria. But I'm curious... Do you talk?" This poses an interesting opportunity to understand what Aria is living with, what she fears so much that she clung onto the idea that I was an angel back on Earth.

No response, which I take as no ability to speak. So, I reach across the bed for a connection. A small touch that will allow me to understand what I'm dealing with. But she's gone in a heartbeat, and when I look up, I find her plastered to the ceiling like a gaping black hole.

I lower my hand to the thread, my fingers going right through it, like she's nothing more than an actual shadow. No sensation floods me; my powers can't reach it, which leaves me more confused as to what Aria is. But while that fails, I draw in a deep breath, one that brings a flare of burned wood mingled with sulfur, and that smell is familiar. Whatever this thing attached to her is, it definitely originated in Hell, I am certain of this more than ever.

I lower my gaze to Aria's gorgeous face, and my chest clenches, heart racing at what she does to me. She makes me feel things I never should, makes me dream of her, when I doubt she holds the same emotions for me. She's a wicked little thing to make me fall for her. It's foolish of me to even contemplate needing someone like her. Yet my muscles tighten at the thought of never seeing her again.

I've always been broken, more psycho than normal, I admit, but with how easily I let myself soften around Aria, am I any better than Cain by giving myself to this little woman? Maybe it had been a mistake to convince Father we should bring her into Hell. I never should have gotten this close to her. Never should have let myself be captivated by her beauty, her courage, her fighting spirit. I see too much of myself in her, the darkness, the desperation to keep my head afloat, and the constant battle to never let anyone see that side of myself.

As if sensing my presence, she stirs and rolls onto her back, her eyes blinking to life. Stunning dark, brown eyes. In that instant, the shadow creature retracts, slipping back into her and disappearing.

She licks her dry lips as she pushes herself to sit up. "How long have you been watching me?"

"Does it matter?"

"What do you want, Maverick?" There's no hatred behind her voice this time, but she asks it more as a question of understanding. Something between us has changed, and when her gaze blazes in my direction with a strange look of both anguish and confusion, my body sags.

If only she knew my intention was never to bring her into such danger, that each time we spent together a new sensation rose through me, one of hope, of possibility, of happiness.

When I look back now at how everything brought us to this point, I hate myself that I dragged her into this predicament. Regret twists inside me and I deserve all the punishment coming my way.

But I know the longer I look at her, the more I go over everything in my mind, it becomes clear what I must do.

Of course, I shouldn't.

But I also can't sit around and do nothing either.

After all, regret is a bitch to live with for eternity.

"I never wanted you hurt," I say. "You weren't meant to be here, and I made a huge mistake in thinking it was the best decision for you."

She blinks up at me, rosy lips parting like she might ask a question, but the words never come.

"You are not safe here," I tell her, clawing guilt ripping at my insides that it has taken me this long to realize the truth.

"Was I ever?" She gives me a lopsided grin, and I take that as her attempt to not knock me down but make a joke. It's progress between us and I embrace it.

"No," I admit truthfully.

"Your father hates me. He would hate you even more for being nice to me. But you're scared he'll hurt me?"

"Yes. Everything I've done so far has been to survive. I lived with lies and distrust, accepting them as normality for so long, I forgot there was anything else. My father cares for nothing or no one but himself."

She watches me, not responding right away or moving away.

"Can I go home?" she finally asks.

I sit on the bed next to her. She doesn't pull away, and I take her hand in mine, the pull of the ring on her finger buzzing against my skin. It recognizes me.

I reach forward with my other hand and slide her hair behind an ear. She doesn't flinch away, but leans into my touch unexpectedly. "If that's what you want."

My fingers weave into her dark hair, curling around the thick luxurious mane around my hand at the back of her head. I meet her gaze, seeing the battle behind her eyes, the darkness, the desire, and she takes her lower lip between her teeth.

I'm still reeling from knowing what awaits her if she remains in Hell. That human saying comes to mind about adoring something so much you need to set it free. Not sure of the exact wording, but I feel that in my bones with Aria.

She tilts her head to the side, studying me.

"I might regret this," I explain.

"Me too, but I give you permission," she says breathlessly, which leaves me confused at first. That is, until she pushes herself closer to me.

Our lips graze, and with it comes a tremulous groan from deep within me, a long-awaited desire surging to the surface.

This time, I know I'm doing the right thing without a shadow of a doubt. I think back to our moment in the hot springs, when I'd almost kissed her then, and then when we were at each other's throats in Lucifer's throne room. That fire in her eyes as she held the angel blade to my neck. My cock hardens just at the memory of it.

Then with purpose, I kiss her back with a starved hunger.

My breath hitches from the way she pushes her body against mine, how her mouth parts, drawing me in to taste her.

From the beginning, I've wanted to hurt her, to make Cain suffer, to please Father and gain his approval. I'd been lost for so long... until now.

I take hold of the ring on her finger, and with a single thought call the energy to me. Then in an instant, I slide the thing off her hand and the world around us dissolves, leaving behind nothing but a worried knot in my stomach.

TEN

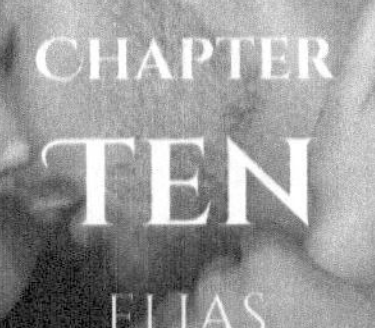

The three of us stand in front of a dilapidated looking townhome in serious need of a fresh coat of paint and a weedwhacker through the overgrown front yard. I could smell the stench of decay, blood, and putrefaction the moment we pulled up in the car. Multiple people were dead inside, and if Cain is right and this is a new vampire nest, I'm not surprised. Especially with the younger ones. They tend to be more sloppy and reckless with their kills.

It's why we had an agreement with Viktor's coven. If left unchecked, vamps would overtake a city in weeks. Like weeds. They could be an infestation and are extremely hard to get rid of.

From Cain's description, it seems something fishy is going on here. Viktor's clan has always been on the smaller side, and he's never had a problem with members going rogue before. But if he's missing—by his own doing or not—it could be why some decided to test their limits. Unless there was a mutiny situation and Viktor was taken out. Well... then we have a messier situation on our hands and some unruly vampires to dispatch.

First step is to go inside this house and teach these vamps a lesson. Then clean up the dead and all that—the less fun part.

But my attention is on the graffiti on the front door of a triangle with an upside-down cross inside it. "Never seen that before."

"It's just graffiti," Cain says and doesn't even hesitate but strides right through the front door. Glancing at me, Dorian grimaces, but we follow him inside.

The odor of death is so strong, my eyes water. And it's not hard to guess where it's coming from. Blood paints the walls and floors, like something out of a horror movie.

"It was a feeding frenzy," Dorian whispers, as Cain leads us down the hall. We peer into every room we pass but find no one. Well, no one living anyway. There are dead bodies everywhere, some even missing limbs or with their throats ripped out. Another sign of novice vamps, they're not as eloquent once the blood lust takes over. They'll do anything to satisfy that craving, which is also stronger the younger they are.

I remember Cain saying he'd seen vamps here asleep when he'd come last. So... where are they?

Cain must be thinking the same thing, because when he gets to the end of the long hall, he whips around, brows pinched in confusion.

"Maybe they left?" Dorian answers the unasked question we're all thinking.

"In the daylight?" I ask. "Wouldn't be the smartest idea."

"No, they have to be here. If there's a basement..." Cain brushes past us and heads for the foyer again. We hurry after him, and once we pass the staircase, there's a loud boom from the second floor. Our heads whip up to see three vamps perched on the landing's railing like some fucked-up humanoid birds.

To my surprise, I don't recognize any of them. We've been close to Viktor's coven for years. Any new vamp needs to be put in our database and recorded, but these three are completely unfamiliar.

Which means, these aren't from Viktor's coven.

Snarling, they leap for us with fangs bared. We split immediately. Switching into his demon faster than a blink, Dorian jumps on the wall and, using it to push off, hits one of the vamps mid-air. They land with a loud thud on the stairs and tumble the rest of the way down, punching and clawing at each other.

Cain doesn't bother changing forms. He simply grabs one vampire by the neck and slams him into the floorboards, splintering the wood. Blood explodes from his head, the skull smashed in.

As for me, my opponent—the only female in the group—hits the ground in front of me, crouches low, and rushes at me in a blur of speed. Vampires have always been speedy creatures, and can put up one hell of a fight, but those skills come with age and these babies are sloppy at best.

I track her movements easily. As she pounces for my neck, I seize her by the front of her shirt and hurl her across the room, using her own momentum plus my strength to really send her flying. She hits the front door with a terrible bone-crunching sound and collapses in a heap on the floor, her neck twisted at an odd angle.

Unfortunately, a broken neck won't be enough to kill her, but it's sure to paralyze her for a while. Not to mention, it'll hurt like a bitch when it heals.

When I turn around to assess the others, I find Dorian covered in blood with his vamp's throat ripped out, bled out. Cain has thrown his onto a bench near the entryway, his body slumped forward but making gurgling noises in his semi-conscious state. Like with mine, a smashed skull isn't enough to kill a vamp either, and it looks like Cain is banking on using this one to answer a few questions.

"Oops, I didn't know we were supposed to keep them alive," Dorian says, wiping the blood off his face with the back of his sleeve. He glances down at the bloody mess he made and shrugs. "My bad."

"We only need one," Cain says as he studies the one in front of him. His skull is melding together, the head reshaping as the inner wounds heal first. "And it looks like this one's going to be able to talk soon."

Dorian and I move closer. It doesn't take much longer for the vampire to lift his head and blink his eyes open. Seeing us, he flashes fangs and hisses.

"Oh, stop with that nonsense," Dorian snaps as his demon recedes. "Theatrics."

He tries to hop to his feet, but I slap a hand onto his shoulder and shove him back down. "Stay," I growl.

His confused gaze flicks to me and then to Dorian and Cain. "What are you?" he asks. Even his voice is boyish, and if I were to guess, I'd say he's no older than sixteen. A real baby baby vamp.

He's obviously never met with demons before, and he doesn't know how we were able to take him and his friends down.

"We rule this city," Cain says coolly. "Both Glenside and Storm, and what we want to know is who you are. And your master."

He huffs a laugh, and his lack of fear strikes a nerve with me. I curl my fingers more into his shoulder and grip harder. He gasps. "Hey!"

"I suggest you answer our questions, or there's a nice little pit in Hell with your name on it."

Hesitating, the vamp looks us all over again, more color draining from his face. "H-Hell?" he stammers. "You are the... demons?"

"Ah, so you have heard of us." Dorian smiles.

"Viktor warned us we'd be meeting you soon."

"Viktor?" Cain repeats, exchanging looks with us. We can see what he's thinking, Viktor's been making new vampires without us knowing? Not only does that break our agreement, it means war. "Is he your master?"

This time, the vampire bursts into near hysterics, laughing so hard he snorts. "That Dracula wanna be? Absolutely not."

Well, there goes that idea.

Cain's patience is wearing thin. He nods my way, giving me the okay to do what it takes to get him talking. Excited, I let the power of the shift push through me, but limit it to my arm still gripping his shoulder. My fingers elongate into claws, the nails pushing into his flesh and puncturing it. Blood darkens his shirt.

His laughter stops abruptly, and he tries to leap away, but I hold him firm.

"If not Viktor, then who made you?" Cain asks in a low rumble, capturing his attention again. "Who is your master?"

He peers up at him with mock interest. "You don't know?"

Little shit. He's really pushing the boundaries with us. Especially Cain. I can see his pupils enlarging, almost engulfing his eyes entirely.

With my temper rising, I jerk my claws, tearing at the skin and muscle in his shoulder and making him cry out. "I'd fucking talk if I were you. Unless you have no use for this arm anymore."

"Fuck you!" He spits in my face. The slimy loogie slides down my cheek, and my entire body boils with rage. My inner hellhound leaps forward.

With a roar, I embed my talons into his throat and wrench with my other hand with all my strength. Blood splatters everywhere as the vampire's head rips clear off his shoulders. It drops with a loud thud on the floor, rolling across the wood to Cain's feet.

Chest heaving and shoulders rigid, I look up at him and Dorian, the fury deflating out of me like a balloon. I let the headless body flop to the ground.

Dorian grins broadly. "I'm glad it wasn't just me this time."

Cain kicks the head to the side with a sigh. "It wasn't a loss. He wasn't much help anyway."

A low groan comes from across the room, capturing all our attention. The female vampire. She must be coming too.

"No biggie," Dorian says. "Two down, one to go."

It doesn't take too much convincing to get the girl vampire to sing. Especially after seeing her two friends ripped apart. The guy who mastered them is named Stephan. So, definitely not Viktor, like we originally thought. But that brings up another slew of problems. If Viktor didn't betray us, then that meant a new coven was trying to move into his territory. Meaning *our* territory, and obviously not playing by the rules.

We run this city. Hell, we run some of the areas around it, too, and our presence here on Earth is known throughout the supernatural community, so this vamp sure had some balls trying to overtake us.

It's a mistake he'll soon be regretting.

When we are done questioning the vampire girl, we let her go, hoping she'll send the message to her master that we have him in our sights. If he's smart, he'll get the fuck out of our town, but since he's been threatening Charlotte and making an army of young vamps, I doubt it's going to be that easy. This Stephan fellow is gearing up for a fight.

Then there's the fact that Viktor is missing. He could very well be dead, and if that's the case, well... things have just gotten a bit more complicated.

Tired and annoyed, we head home. The vamp problem is just one more thing we have to add to our to-do list, with getting Aria out of Hell as the top priority, of course. And with the witch, Joseline, missing, that only leaves the harp's relics as our way to her. But that takes time—time we certainly don't have.

We open the front door to the mansion and stride inside, only to be stopped short by the sight before us. Aria and Maverick, the two last people we expected to see, stand there at the bottom of the staircase, staring at each other, their faces close. Their heads whip our way the moment we enter, and Aria steps back instantly, causing Maverick's hands to slide off her arms.

She runs for us, collapsing in Cain's arms and holding him fiercely, like she's afraid of what might happen if she lets him go. Dorian comes around and strokes her hair, whispering something comforting to her in her ear, something I don't hear because my sights are set on Maverick, who's still standing in the middle of our foyer, watching her with longing in his eyes.

Fury surges through me again, wild and untamable, and I'm flying across the room before I can even register what I'm doing. I seize Maverick by the shirt front and wail my fist into his face so hard, he flies back onto the steps, smashing the back of his head and gripping desperately for the railing. The scent of blood hits my nose, and he tries to haul himself up to stand, but I leap on top of him and pin him down. I nail him again in his pretty-boy face, crunching his nose easily. More blood pours from his nostrils.

"Elias, no!" Aria's shouts behind me take me off guard. "Stop! Get off him, please!"

She doesn't want me to kill this asshole for stealing her away from us? I don't understand.

Maverick takes those two seconds that I'm distracted to throw his entire body into me and tackle me onto the floor. We roll together, fists flying, knees kicking. He ends up landing a good jab to my chin, but I manage to get my feet under him and use my legs to propel him off me and across the room. He slams into the entry table and knocks over a vase. The glass shatters everywhere.

"Wait!" Aria continues to yell. Cain holds her firm as she tries to get closer to him, but I'm on my feet in the next second.

"I know you like to play with your food, but kill him already,"

Dorian encourages me, despite Aria's protests. "The asshole doesn't deserve to live a second longer."

Maverick's head lifts, a new gash in his cheek spilling more blood. I'm ready to repeat what I did to the vampire kid and rip his head clean off his body. To hell with the consequences.

I trudge over to him, my beast shoving to the surface, wanting a part in his demise. A fierce growl tears from my throat, but before I can get too close, Maverick glances once more at Aria before blinking out of existence. The smell of sulfur lingers behind.

Throwing my head back, I roar, letting all my anger and frustration out at once. The pictures rattle on the walls, and my entire body shakes from the force of it.

Dorian runs over to the spot Maverick just was a second ago and kicks the broken pieces of wood and glass. "Fucking shit. He's always got to run away with his tail between his legs. What a worm."

I try to settle myself and calm the rabid animal inside me, but it's harder this time. Maverick was just here—in our house—and he got away *again.* It's like he's mocking us now. Being able to pop in and out whenever he feels like it, steal Aria, and do whatever he feels like. This is our home, our territory, and I'll be damned if I'm going to let him come here again and leave alive.

There's no fucking way.

Cain spins Aria and grabs her by the shoulders, looking her over. "Are you hurt? Did he touch you? His ring—did he take it off?" He snatches her left hand. Surprisingly enough, the ring is gone. His brows knit in confusion. "He... did."

Dorian turns. "Wait, what?" Walking over, he peers down at Aria's hand, too. "He took off the ring *and* brought you back? I don't understand."

"I-I don't either," Aria replies.

"There's something more to it," I snap. "There has to be."

"I agree. This is Maverick we're talking about here," Dorian says.

My fists clench at my sides. I'm itching to ram them into his face again. Over and over. I hate that he's able to stay one step ahead of us all this time. It's infuriating.

Dorian rubs his jaw in thought. "We need to figure out what

he's up to before he pops back here again and fucks us. What aren't we seeing?"

"I don't think he will," Aria says suddenly, making us all look at her. "At least, it didn't seem that way to me."

As usual, Cain's remarkably calm, despite everything that's happened. Maybe he's just relieved to have Aria back. But for me, that's not enough. I want blood. I want to make sure this can never happen again.

"Why do you think that?" he asks her, hovering close.

"I mean, he had no reason to bring me back here. Lucifer had plans for me. He wanted me to stay—"

"What?" Cain's pupils dilate at the mention of his father, enlarging until nothing is left of his irises but complete blackness. "Plans? What plans?"

"He wants to use me somehow—and Sayah, of course—to take over Heaven. He didn't explain the details, but I got the feeling he wants to weaponize me in some way," she explains.

"He's still on that pipe dream?" Dorian shakes his head.

I growl. "Of course he is. And he wants to use Aria to do it."

"Maverick... defended me, in a way. At least that's what it felt like," she goes on. "And then, without warning, he brought me back."

"You can't trust him to do something good and without self-motivation. That's the way he's always been," Dorian says.

"Lucifer won't give up that easily," Cain interjects. "His ability to leave Hell may be limited, but if he doesn't send my brother to retrieve Aria, he'll send others. We need to be prepared."

"We should've done the ritual," Dorian replies through clenched teeth. "The full moon's passed."

But this time, Cain nods, agreeing.

"Don't I get a say in this?" Aria asks, annoyance coating her tone. "It is my soul that we're talking about here."

I can't believe this is still an argument. Even after everything.

"That depends. Would you rather be dragged back to Hell again with us having possibly no way to get to you? Used as Lucifer's plaything?" Dorian says bluntly, his entire body rigid. It's not like him to be the intense one, but I guess after his fuck-up with Maverick, he's really feeling the guilt and danger now.

She swallows back her words.

"That's what I thought."

"Or we can go with the original plan and use the witch's connection to Maverick to summon him. Then get more concrete answers," I suggest.

"We still need to find her," Cain says.

Aria's eyes widen. "Joseline? Find her? Wait, where is she?"

"We don't know," I reply. "She's run off."

Dorian turns to her. "Unless you have any idea of where she might be hiding?"

She shakes her head. "If she's not at her apartment or work, then I really have no idea. The dark magic has changed her. I wouldn't even know where to start."

"That's what I was afraid of," Dorian grumbles.

"We have to find her," Aria says, looking between the three of us. "What if she's in trouble?"

"Then she shouldn't have run," I say blandly, which wins me a deadpan look from her.

"We'll find her," Cain adds in. His eyes return to their normal blue, and his shoulders sag. "But first, I want you to tell me everything that happened while you were in Hell. Especially with Lucifer. I need to know."

"Uh, okay."

He presses a hand to the small of her back and leads her toward the parlor. "We all have a lot to catch each other up on."

Dorian goes to follow but pauses when he sees I haven't moved. "You coming?" he asks, as Cain and Aria disappear into the front room.

My skin is itching, like a million ants are crawling underneath it, and I know that after our run-in with the vamps and now with Maverick, my hellhound needs to be released. It'll tear through me if I don't give it the freedom it craves.

I pull off my shirt over my head. "I need to run."

He glances at the door and then at me again. "Are you sure this is the best time?"

My jaw tightens. My muscles are already tightening and bulging just at the prospect of the change. "Yes."

He sighs heavily. "Very well. Don't disappear though. This isn't the time."

I want to bite back at him for the comment, but I know he's

right. It is my known pattern after all, and with Aria's life and ours still very much in danger, I can't lose myself to the beast again.

A quick run through the woods. Maybe a short hunt to get the need for blood out of my system, and then I'll be back.

I nod once in agreement and head for the door. The animal takes over before I even hit the gravel, and within seconds, I've changed and am running full speed on all fours toward the lake.

"Sayah killed your father?" Dorian's voice is low while his gaze is focused on me, like somehow he can see inside of me to where I harbor the monster.

I sit uncomfortably on the couch in the parlor while only two of the three guys remain close around me. Elias is nowhere in sight, but Dorian is perched on the armrest of the couch, one leg propped up on the cushioned seat. Cain is by the fireplace, still as a statue, yet there's fear, anger, and other emotions in his eyes.

I nod, brushing a few rogue strands of hair out of my face. I'm squirming in my seat, my insides still jumpy after everything that's happened. I've never been the person to drink tea, but I might need a cup. Or a Benadryl—something to calm these bouncing nerves.

"So not only did my mother summon Sayah to kill my father, but then she put her inside me before deciding I wasn't worth it and abandoned me at the hospital." The words pour out of me, and I still don't know how to feel about it all. It's been on my mind a lot lately.

Maybe I ought to be crying, to feel torn, but in truth I feel empty when it comes to my past. I've shed so many tears about them, so now that I know the truth, I don't know how to react. Maybe I've made myself numb, or maybe I'm still in shock, I don't know.

Before the guys respond, I give them a complete run down of the whole conversation with my father and Lucifer.

"Well then..." Dorian says, running a hand through his hair. "And I thought my parents were jacked up."

I huff out a breath. "It explains why I'm broken on the inside." I half laugh, which only comes out awkward.

Cain strolls over and takes a seat next to me, his arm around my back. "There is nothing broken about you, Aria. Not a single thing. We can't pick our parents, we can't pick our past, but we can become better from it, and that's just what you've done."

His words are sweet, but I don't know how true they are. I certainly don't feel like I'm better.

Elias strolls in then, his shirt off, his pants hanging off his hips, hair a mess. Blood is smeared across his mouth. He's been hunting outside.

Silently, he moves across the room to his usual spot by the bookshelf and crosses his arms.

Cain strokes my arm and I lean against him. "I always knew my parents had abandoned me for some reason, but it never occurred to me it might be because my mother was psycho and had cursed me."

Dorian is next to me suddenly, taking my hand in his. Elias kneels before my feet, his hands on my legs.

"You will always have us. And I'll gut Lucifer if it's the last thing I do," Elias tells me.

Having all three of them surrounding me, showing me the kind of affection I never expected, has my eyes pricking. It's so much all at once, but the emotions roaring through me are about how close I've become with these demons. Where I doubt I can be without them, and they seem to share the feeling.

"Everything is going to be okay," Cain tells me, his arm holding me tight. "And we can go find your mother if you'd like. See if what your father said is true."

Maybe it's the way they look at me, Cain's words, or the thought that my father might have lied to me, but my chest tightens. I'm trembling, and I bite down on my lip to stop myself from bawling. I squeeze my eyes shut, but tears leak out from the corners.

I can't stop them if I try, but I know why it's hit me so hard.

I've been holding on, being so strong for so long because I don't want to fall apart. Yet I've been seeing myself drifting deeper and deeper into trouble, my future so dark I can't stand it, and I keep telling myself I will catch myself. But maybe I've been a fool. Maybe this is too much for me to keep pretending all will be alright.

My heart thunders and a silence engulfs us.

I curl in against Cain, and he holds me as I cry, my chest feeling like it's torn open, unleashing everything I've kept inside me. The truth of my past is a blade, slicing me to hundreds of pieces. I don't try to stop myself this time because I need to face my fears.

Unsure how long I've been crying, we stay like that until I finally calm down. I pull back from Cain and wipe my tears. "I'm sorry. I didn't mean to lose control like that," I whisper.

"There's nothing to apologize for." Dorian reaches over and catches a tear as it rolls over my jawline.

"I'd be more concerned if you didn't feel anything after what you've been through," Elias adds.

"What if there is more wrong with me than just Sayah? What if my mother is really crazy, and what if—"

"No," Cain interrupts me. "Don't even entertain the thought. You're nothing like your mother. I've seen how much love you have for your friend, how you rescued Cassiel, how much you worry about us. That is who you are."

I blink at him, and we all sit there in silence, them watching me. And me... well, I feel loved. It's the only way to describe that sensation where there's no more awkwardness in my body, just a sense of contentment settles in my bones.

There's something unimaginably beautiful about having this kind of security.

I finally nod. "I know you're right. I guess I'm paranoid."

"We're here for you, no matter what," Dorian says.

"Anytime," Elias tacks on.

"You are all too good to me." I wipe at my eyes, and I offer them a soft smile, then recline against Cain once more, enjoying the time out.

Dorian and Elias exchange looks, silent words passing between them.

"What?" I ask them.

"Just that we have to check up on Charlotte and her vamp problem," Dorian says.

"How is she holding up?" I ask him.

"She's okay. Things with Viktor have gotten more complicated though."

"We don't want you to worry about that," Elias says quickly. "We have it under control."

Good. Because I don't know how much more I can handle right now. My shoulders slump. "As long as she's safe."

Elias nods. "She is. And besides, I think Cain wants to talk to you about something about the ritual, too. Alone."

Cain glares at him, but he shrugs it off.

When I look up at Cain, he sighs heavily. Defeated. "He's right. I do."

Dorian rises to his feet and blows me a kiss before he and Elias head out of the parlor.

Now alone, I shift a little farther from Cain but remain in his arms.

"I've missed you," he confesses, his voice a whisper soft. "I've been driving myself mad with you gone."

His words hold more weight because I knew that if it weren't for his brush with death, he would've never admitted such a thing.

"I've missed you, too. More than you know."

He sits up a bit straighter, his hands sliding away from me and onto his lap. "I hold a lot of guilt for everything that's happened to you. My brother... My father..."

"You shouldn't," I say to stop him. "I don't blame you for anything."

He glances away, conflict warring on his face. He holds so much responsibility on his shoulders, it breaks my heart.

"I've tried to protect you, Aria. From everything that can hurt you. Even the truth. And that's been another grave mistake I've made." He sucks in a deep breath. "You and Elias are right. You should know about the binding ritual because it will affect you and ultimately your soul. It needs to be your choice and your choice alone."

The ritual... The thing the demons are convinced will be the best thing to keep me out of Lucifer's clutches.

"Okay, I'm listening."

He waits a long moment as he struggles with how to begin. "The binding ritual is just what it sounds like. It'll bind you to the three of us for the rest of eternity. Like how humans like to pretend their traditional wedding ceremonies do, but this is in the literal sense. Our souls will mesh in a way, and that'll allow us to sense where you are at all times. We'll be able to tell when you're in danger, even if you're miles away."

"Will it... change me in any way? If our souls are meshing?" I ask. I already feel so out of touch with myself with Sayah. I definitely don't need more of that.

"Maybe meshing was the incorrect word," he replies. "More like intertwine. And no. You will just be able to sense us as we can sense you."

Scary. But could come in handy... But for eternity? Really? That's a long time. Am I willing to make that kind of commitment to these demons?

"Is there any way out of it down the road if I change my mind?"

"Unfortunately, no," he replies. "Elias is still linked to Serena because of it, and it tortures him every day. The only way to break it would be with their deaths."

His words sink into me, stirring jealously unlike I've ever felt before. Elias had performed the ritual with that bitch? The one who ripped his heart out? No wonder he's still traumatized by it. He thought she was his soulmate and she'd used him. With the jealousy comes another emotion too... one of surprise to hear that he had felt so deeply for someone else, that now I worry I can never compare. How can I be better than the first person he gave his heart to? Especially if he is still somehow connected with her. Does he still think of her and miss her? I don't know how to feel knowing he will always have this other woman linked to him.

"Dorian and I helped him with the ceremony, but didn't complete all the..." He pauses, looking for the right word. "*Requirements* needed for it to work on us in the same way."

What in the world does that mean?

I eye him suspiciously. "What requirements?"

Again, he pauses. "First, we needed a full moon to perform the ritual, but..."

"We missed it," I conclude, knowing I was in Hell when the moon was at its fullest.

He nods. "Waiting another month isn't really an option. Too much can happen in that time."

"So, what? That's it?"

"Not exactly. There is one more way, but it involves blood... And a lot of it."

My nose scrunches just at the thought. I'm not sure I like the sound of that. "Are we talking human sacrifices?"

"No. It'll be our blood."

Still gross. The fact that he can say it so calmly freaks me out a bit, but that's a demon for you.

"The blood will strengthen the bond between us. It makes the ritual more effective than if we used the full moon," he goes on. "And then the sex."

I choke. "The what now?"

"The sex," he repeats. "It's the requirement Dorian and I skipped with Serena, but Elias indulged in. The final step to seal the bond."

I blink. "I have to have sex... with all three of you?" My belly tightens just at the thought of all three demons having me at once. Talk about a girl's dream scenario come to life.

Wait. What was the downside to this again? I can't seem to remember anymore.

"Aria," Cain turns fully to me and stares into my eyes with concern. "This is no easy feat. This ritual involves some of the most ancient and darkest magic ever constructed. It's so powerful, it's rarely used, even by demons, but it's the best way for us to be able to keep you safe from Lucifer. Or any other threat to you for that matter."

He means Sayah. I can see her name hovering in his gaze. But eternity is a long time, and really, I just met these men a few months ago. Sure, we've been to Hell and back together, and that short time feels like ages, but am I willing to link myself to them permanently? Forever?

I'm not so sure.

Weddings come with divorces. The only way out of this is death.

And what does that mean for the freedom I was promised after helping the demons find the relics? Was that then null and void? Had to be, right?

"You said that if I helped you—"

"Find the relics, I'd set you free," Cain finishes for me. "Yes. I knew this question was coming."

"Well?"

"It would no longer apply technically, since our souls will be linked. However…" He trails off, his expression turning grave.

Dipping my head, I try to catch his eyes again. "However, what?"

"If you want it to be, I promise we will sever ties with you in all other ways. We may still be able to sense each other through the bond link, but we will never contact you or interfere with your life in any way again. I…" He clears his throat and corrects himself. "*We* will do everything possible to make sure you never see us again."

My chest burns at the thought. Have no contact with the demons? None whatsoever?

Yeah, my life may become less crazy and I wouldn't be staring death in the face every second of every day, but to have them erased from me? Completely? I don't know about that.

"I will hold up my end of our deal either way," he continues. "You just need to tell me what you want to do, and I'll make it so."

Problem is, I don't know what I want.

This is a massive decision.

"Can I have some time to think it over?" I ask in a whisper. "I know the clock is ticking, but this is… a lot."

He frowns but nods. "Of course."

He moves on the couch, and at first I think he's going to get up and leave me, but instead, he shifts closer and puts his arm around me once again. The gesture is a bit stiffer now, and I know he's still struggling with showing his emotions, so I meet him the rest of the way and lean my head against his shoulder.

"I wasn't lying with what I said before, Aria," he murmurs into my hair. "With you gone, I've thought of nothing else but seeing you again. I missed you more than humanly possible."

That draws a small laugh from me. "Well, you aren't human, now are you?"

I can feel the smile forming with his lips pressed against my head. "No. I'm not."

Lifting my chin, I meet his gaze. After everything I've been through lately, I'm worn out, worn down, yet in Cain's presence, a new side of me awakens. I lean in closer and grasp his shirt, fisting it in my hands, suddenly wanting to forget the agony within me. And Cain offers me the solution.

"I've waited to feel your arms around me. To feel safe and adored. It's crazy, I know, but I missed you terribly. And I want you to fuck me, to make me feel so adored, nothing else can touch me. I'm tired of always thinking about how I'm in more danger."

He offers me the most delicious grin, and I love seeing that my words bring him such joy.

His hands fall to my waist, the pressure of his fingers fierce like it takes everything he has to not rip off my clothes right here and claim me on the spot. I might not mind at all, but when he instead takes my hand in his, I suspect he has something else in mind.

"Come with me," is all he says as he gets to his feet, pulling me along. We head up the stairs and right toward his room.

Once inside, he locks the door behind us, and I turn to him, staring at me with utter possessiveness.

"In here, we're forgetting everything out there. It's just us two." He strolls toward me, slowly unbuttoning the buttons at his sleeves before he drags the white shirt up and out from his pants. There is something hypnotic in watching a powerful man like him stroll toward me with purpose. The kind that strips me of all my defenses, one where he won't take no for an answer.

Exactly what I want, still I find myself retreating until the back of my legs hit the bed. My body is so tense with excitement while my heart hammers in my chest.

"Are you wearing anything underneath the pants?" he asks me, slyly.

"Only one way to find out," I encourage him, knowing too well that I've got a thin thong on.

He reaches my side and his hand explores the softness of my thigh, slowly drifting higher to the clasp. It's undone in a flash, the zipper flying down, too.

My breath hitches all the way down to my lungs as I stand before him utterly immobile and gasping for air. It's nearly impossible to breathe when a god stands in front of me with lust in his eyes.

Shoving past the denim material, his fingers trace the edges of the thin fabric, dipping lower and lower between my thighs.

I shudder, and his smile widens.

"There's so much I missed about you, Aria, from the way your body reacts to my touch, to the look in your eyes like you're balancing on the edge of an orgasm and trying so hard to hold on. And how much my body craves every inch of you." His lips are on mine, his kiss powerful and explosive.

My response wedges into my throat as I hold onto him and return the passion, inhaling his rugged, sexy scent, loving the way his tongue pierces the seam of my mouth. All the while, his finger skims the length of my pussy over the drenched fabric of my thong.

I moan against him. What he's doing is going to completely undo me, and I want so much more.

His other hand reaches up and palms my breast through my top, my nipple hardening under his touch, while I'm breathing harder and faster. He knows exactly what he's doing, his finger rubbing me right over my clit, pressing. My legs shake beneath me, unsure how long I can take this.

"Please, Cain," I beg.

He breaks from our kiss. "You're going to destroy me. I knew it from the moment I met you." He leans forward, scooping an arm under my knees and the other behind my back, and lifts me off my feet.

I have my arms around the back of his neck, while my whole body washes over with tingles. I nuzzle my face in the curve of his neck, licking him, loving the slightly salty taste.

He growls under his breath, a sexy sound that belongs to a man in heat, one who won't let anything stand in his way.

"I'm going to take my time with you. Savor you." Lowering me on the bed, he moves to stand near my feet, then reaches down. Fingers grip my pants and wrench them off. Next, and with slower, more tortuous hands, he guides the elastic of my thong down my legs and off.

I shiver at the way he takes in my nakedness with each piece of clothing he peels away from me.

He tosses my shirt and bra somewhere on the floor, then takes my feet and places them on the edge of the bed, my knees bent, before setting his strong palms on them.

"Touch yourself for me," he says so tenderly, there is no way in the world I can ever refuse such a request.

I blink at him first, while he slowly pries open my legs and steps back, taking in all of me.

The look on his face covers me in the most delicious goose-bumps. There's nothing but pure elation in his eyes.

"Don't make me ask twice." He starts unbuttoning his shirt, staring down at me the whole time, while I'm caught between studying the way he slowly reveals a strong chest cut in muscles and angles, and following his command. My hand slithers down my stomach regardless, seeming to have a mind of her own, or maybe it's just that I would do anything to please Cain.

I'm reminded of one of our first intimate moments. The one in the limo during our first outing to Purgatory. So much has changed since then, but I'm still completely lost to him, just as I was then. And so, I push my fingers lower to where I'm incredibly wet, the touch silky smooth. I moan at my simple touch at how swollen and sensitive I am.

He licks his lips, watching my every stroke, at the way I part my inner lips with my fingers, offering him everything that I am.

Yanking his shirt off strong, round shoulders, he proceeds to unbuckle his belt as he toes off his shoes. In seconds, he pushes down his pants, and of course he's going commando. I expect nothing less from him.

When he grabs his cock, it's huge, and he hisses as he tugs it a few times. The thick vein running down the front bulges, and the veins in his neck pulse from how tense and ready he is.

"Oh, yes," I murmur.

I'm so distracted that I don't notice he's glancing at my breasts, then he drops to his knees before me. Large palms push my thighs wider.

"I want to see all of you, every bit that I missed, every inch of you I intend to lick and remind you is mine. To show you that I feel guilty as shit that I let you get taken. To fill my head with nothing but you, to drown in your scent."

His words are magic, and he might as well have sprinkled

enchantment over me because I'm already buzzing with a kind of euphoria I wasn't prepared for.

I want to reply, to say something clever, but all that comes out is a moan, coaxing a laugh from him. Then his mouth is on my pussy, so warm and divine, that I arch my back from the way he clasps his lips over mine. I can easily mistake him for eating a peach, the way his lips and tongue ravage me, leaving nothing untouched. Just like his promise, he is relentless, this powerful demon offering me everything I've craved.

My body seems to burst under his attention, my skin shivering with the building excitement. His finger grazes across the length of my entrance, then he pushes it inside me, and he growls like it does for him as much as it does for me.

Then he pushes in another finger, and let's just say, Cain is anything but small when it comes to anything, including his fingers.

"You're all mine tonight, Aria." His teeth graze the inside of my thighs, nibbling as he pushes in and out of me, fast, and causing my whole body to tremble with the strength behind him fingering me. He leans in and sucks on my drenched pussy, and the way he does that changes something to me, brings forward my climax like a freaking tornado. It rips through me.

I throw my head back to the mattress, my body shuddering like I might burst into flames.

My legs quiver and I'm screaming before I grab a pillow and press it to my face. In it, I unleash my deepest desires.

Next thing I know, the pillow is ripped from my face.

"No hiding. Scream for everyone to hear, for the whole world for all I care. Do you know how fucking sexy you sound when you orgasm?"

He groans as he draws his fingers out of me and replaces them with his tongue.

"Oh, fuck, Cain!" His face is buried between my legs, his hands gripping my ass, lifting it off the bed so he can more easily reach every inch of me. With the heavy breathing and growling sounds he makes, I doubt anything in the world could ever pull him away from me now. He takes all of me, licking what I have to offer, and I'm delusional with desire.

I lie spent, my chest rising and falling fast, watching this incredible man going to town on me. To have someone appreciate my body this much twists me on the inside, makes me feel things for him I never expected. It makes me want to do whatever the hell it takes to keep him by my side for eternity.

I don't even try to make sense of how backward my thoughts are when I have a damn sin demon licking my pussy. My body hums as I float back down from the most insane climax, and when Cain pulls back, his mouth and chin are glistening. He smiles wickedly, licking his lips as though he can't get enough.

"I love seeing you like that," I admit.

"With your juices all over my face?"

I nod. "It's so fucking sexy."

He climbs to his feet. "The only sexy one in this room is you." He presses a knee on the mattress between my legs and lowers his body down over mine, covering me.

Before I can respond, his mouth is on mine, and I taste myself, the strong scent of sex heavy between us, and he reaches under my back, then lifts me a bit higher on the bed. He positions himself between my legs, and he looks at me deeply.

"What would you have done to bring me back from Hell?" I ask, knowing it's stupid, but I want to hear the devotion. Right now I'm craving attention... all of his attention.

"I would've ripped this entire world in half. I would've turned the underworld upside down if it meant getting you back. Nothing will ever get between us again. I swear my life on it."

I smile wickedly, then chuckle, but I won't deny having a man I adore go all cave man over me brings out my primal side. It's raw and addictive.

"Fuck me," I tell him. "Make me forget everything."

His kiss this time is bruising and takes me almost by surprise, showing me how much he has been holding back in controlling himself. How much he's wanted to just bend me over and take me. That thought alone turns me on madly.

He shifts slightly when the tip of his cock pushes against my entrance. Then he kisses me and drives into me. There is no holding back, nothing but the hungry act of claiming me. His mouth swallows my moans, and he's electrifying, licking inside my mouth while his cock thrusts harder and harder. Each slap coaxing a sharp gasp out of my lungs.

My body quivers beneath him as we both fall into a rhythm, me wrapped around him, him burying himself into me, dragging his erection against my walls. I feel every sensation, every touch, and I'm losing my mind.

The reality of what I'm really feeling for Cain is a lot more complicated, a lot more scary, as I don't know where anything between us can end. But what I do know is that, for now, our lives are entwined and there is no escaping imminent danger, so I make the decision that I won't worry about the future between us. Not for now anyway. Focus is how we can survive the present.

My beautiful demon hisses as he drives into me, filling me so completely. It's frightening how much it hurts to think I could have lost him. I don't want to ever feel that sensation of my world growing dimmer. I've lost enough in my life already.

And here I am with him taking me, and I can't help but feel that with him looking into my eyes, kissing me while making me explode, he might be making love to me. This is so much more than sex for him, and I will admit that it feels the same way for me too.

He's pumping in and out of me, and I adore every damn inch of this man. It's only when he kisses me harder that he triggers my own arousal, bringing me to a second orgasm with such ease. I stiffen beneath him, the loud moan a friction against my throat. Sensing I've lost my ability to hold on, his actions become more focused, more determined into faster thrusts, hitting in ways that bring my climax to a newer level.

Bright lights spark behind my eyes as I bellow the most insane pleasure. I thrash beneath him while he grunts, holding onto me, pummeling into me until he pauses and unleashes a thunderous groan from deep inside. One that is just sexy as fuck.

His fingers dig into my shoulders as he pulses inside me, his eyes fluttering backward in his own moment of supreme excitement.

Suddenly his muscles shift and soften, then he lowers his gaze to me. He grabs the back of my head, placing his forehead to mine, both of us battling for breath, our bodies burning up. He tugs me as close to him as possible, his fingers digging into my flesh.

"You are everything to me, Aria. Don't ever doubt my devotion to you. I will destroy and kill anything in my way to reach you."

At his words, my eyes grow a tiny bit misty. I've lived my whole life wanting this kind of devotion, and now I feel like crying that he's giving it to me.

"I'll take everything you give me," I respond, meaning it with every fiber of my being, knowing that the time I've spent with Cain, Dorian, and Elias has been an endless battle. But it's during hardship you see a person's true character, Murray used to say. There aren't a lot of good things he'd offered me in terms of wisdom, but that nugget makes so much sense.

Cain's gaze scans my face, then he smiles so perfectly, I melt beneath him.

"And I'll give you all of me," he answers.

TWELVE

ARIA

The past two days since arriving back from Hell have been uneventful. I shouldn't complain when the three guys insist that I am to take it easy and be waited on for everything, and that includes them coming and spending time with me. They are scared Maverick or Lucifer will return, and in all honesty, that sits in the back of my mind too.

I don't yet know how to regain a sense of normality when I keep looking at my finger where Maverick's ring used to sit. When I sometimes feel Sayah lingering just beneath the surface of my skin, and there's nothing I can do to stop her if she chooses to emerge. Then of course, the big fat white elephant in the room... My kiss with Maverick.

My mind has been drifting to him recently too, to the point where I have to remind myself I did what I had to in order to return home. But what if I'm fooling myself? What if the reason he is constantly on my mind and the feel of his kiss are both signs of something I don't want to admit to myself?

What if I've got a terrible addiction to all things dark, especially demons?

I huff and flop back into my bed, coaxing Cassiel to press his head into my side, grunting under his breath.

I look over at him sitting beside my bed ever so patiently. His head swings to the door and back at me before huffing.

"How can I say no when you look at me with those huge doe eyes?"

Up on my feet, I ruffle the fur on his head then rub his tufted ears, still unable to believe how big he grew on our recent trip to Scotland. More of him to love.

Cassiel makes a mewing sound, staring at the shut door then at me.

"Okay, let's go out."

The moment I open the door, he bolts downstairs and waits for me by the front door. There are several guards there, and with their presence, I stroll into the front yard. For a change, I don't mind being watched if it means no more kidnappings.

I almost laugh at how I used to try everything to escape when I first arrived at the mansion, and now I'm ingrained and don't want to be taken away.

Cassiel sprints across the yard, pouncing across the snow every now and then, before he ducks behind a huge tree and seems to be peeing.

I wrap my arms around myself and realize I should have grabbed a coat as a cold breeze swishes past. Yet the snow glistens beneath the sunlight, sitting perfectly untouched. Well, except for where Cassiel has stamped his footprints. The stone path from the doorway to the road has been swept clean of snow, and I step down, taking in a deep breath of fresh air.

That's when a small shadow swoops overhead, and I crane my head back as a black bird flies nearby, but from the sky a piece of paper cascades toward me.

I snatch it out of the air, not truly surprised by many things these days. Messages falling out of the sky? Oh yeah. Completely normal. I almost laugh hysterically at myself as I unfold the white paper. Of course, there's a good chance it's nothing more than rubbish that the bird was carrying to build its nest...

Except, when the first word I see is my name, written in blue ink, my blood turns as cold as the snow surrounding me.

Aria,

We need to talk. I'm leaving town, but I can't go without seeing you first. I'm returning to my apartment and will be there at 3pm today if you can make it.

I'm sorry for everything.

Joseline

I keep reading the note over and over, but it doesn't change the message. Joseline is leaving, and more than that, if I want to see her again, I have to meet her at her apartment at three.

My mind's made up. I need to see her and find out what's going on. Like, why did she run away from the mansion? Had she gotten herself in more trouble somehow?

I swing back around to head inside when Dorian emerges from the doorway, watching me intently, the bridge of his nose creasing as if sensing my unease.

"What's wrong?"

"What's the time?" I ask, closing the distance between us, and closely behind I feel Cassiel reaching my side.

Dorian collects his phone from his pocket and taps it. "Just a few minutes to three."

"Shit. You need to take me to Joseline's place now." I shove the note in his hand and dart inside to grab a coat from the hallway. Cassiel is on my heels the whole time, most likely thinking we're playing a game.

"You sure that's a smart move?" he asks, and I know his question comes from a place of concern, but so does my insistence to check on the only true friend I've had.

"What if she's really leaving town, running away from everything? I want to see her one last time and make sure she's alright."

"And what if this is a trap?"

"Could be, but why would Lucifer bother luring us there when he can so easily appear at our front door?"

He doesn't argue back. "We're taking Cain and Elias with us."

"Fine by me. Having the whole gang with us is better."

Cassiel mews at me and headbutts my legs like somehow he senses we are all going somewhere. As Dorian darts back into the mansion, I crouch down by my lynx and fluff up the sides of his face. "You want to come for a ride, too? I think you've been spoiled by coming out with us."

He seems to purr against my touch and pushes closer, rubbing himself against my face.

I melt against his soft fur. "Okay, you can come too."

I don't recall how long we've been waiting for Dorian to return, but I'm close to rushing back inside to see what the holdup is when the crunch of tires on snow grabs my attention. Cassiel is already sprinting toward the Town Car before I get a chance to take a step forward.

The back door opens for me, but it's Cassiel who leaps inside, and even from where I'm standing, I can hear Elias bellowing for him to get out.

Laughing to myself, I jog over to them and climb in and shut the door.

Cain sits in the front, Dorian alongside me and near the window, and Cassiel pressed up between Elias's legs.

"Why is the cat in the car?" he asks.

"Same reason all of you are. He's worried. Now please, Holmes, can we go, I'm already late."

Dorian shuffles his arm around my back, drawing me closer to him, while Elias and Cassiel fall into a staring match.

"So, explain to us exactly how you got the note?" Cain asks, twisting his head to look back at us.

I give them a lowdown on everything that happened, which really wasn't much.

"You think it's a raven, like the one that used to belong to Sir Surchion?" Elias asks. "If that bastard has somehow come back from the ashes, I'm going to go ballistic."

"It wasn't a big bird, but more of a sparrow."

Cain's brow furrows and he pulls back into his seat. "Your friend might have just summoned the delivery bird," he finally says.

"That's what I'm thinking, as I don't exactly have a phone, and well, I am guessing she didn't want any of you to know."

Dorian chuckles. "That's where she's mistaken. You're not going anywhere without us."

I press into his side, having zero objections to that.

Cassiel flops his chin down onto Elias's knee and I reach over to pat my adorable lynx. "He really does like you, Elias."

But the brooding demon doesn't respond, and only sits stiff as a board.

It isn't long before we reach the city and are parked right out front of Joseline's apartment. I think of the previous times I was here, at discovering she did dark magic and how it never clicked to me she had lied about it. I'm kicking myself for not realizing the truth before the situation got so out of hand.

As we all climb out of the Town Car, Cassiel spills out and attaches himself to my leg, needing to come with me too, apparently. "Can one of you carry him inside so people don't freak out at seeing him on the loose?" Already I notice a man strolling down the sidewalk, staring at us so intently he walks right into a trash can.

Elias growls and loops an arm over and around Cassiel's torso, then heaves him up to his side. Neither of them looks comfortable, but I'm not about to complain as we all march over to the entryway of the lofty apartment building. I hit the button next to Joseline's name on the panel near the door, which opens almost instantly.

Once inside, Elias drops Cassiel to his feet, and we're all cramming into the elevator.

"So, what's the plan?" I ask.

"What do you mean?" Cain asks.

"Well, you can't all just come into the apartment like my bodyguards. It will freak her out."

"That's exactly what we're doing," Elias responds.

"But what if she wants to tell me something in secret? She won't do it with you three breathing down her neck."

"There's no way we are all just waiting outside the apartment," Dorian adds.

"She has a balcony. Two of you can stand out there and you can look in on us, but we will still have privacy, and another stays outside," I explain, unsure if that will put Joseline at ease to speak openly, but it's a compromise she will have to work with. I'm not exactly in the safe zone myself.

On the fifth floor, I knock on the door, my stomach churning. When it opens, Joseline peers out from behind the ajar door, her eyes wide and on the three demons.

"What are they doing here?" she asks. Her hair is messy, her eyes red like she's been crying, and all I can see on her face is fear.

"They are safe," I explain. "Can we come in?"

That's when her gaze falls to Cassiel by my side, then she opens the door.

I step into the apartment that is still filled with the expensive furniture from my last visit, but there's a heavy feeling of sorrow in the air today.

Cain and Dorian follow, while Elias stands outside the door, pulling it so it's just sitting slightly open.

Dorian makes his way to the balcony, while Cain heads down the hallway and inspects every room.

"There's no one here," Joseline calls out.

I take her hand, which feels so cold to the touch, and draw her to the sofa. She's slow making her way across the floor and limps heavily. When I glance down, I find her right foot casted. Broken.

When she catches me staring, she says, "It was a bit of a jump... when I tried to escape."

Ah.

We both sit.

"So, what's going on? I got your note," I begin.

She is still looking out toward Cain as he re-emerges and joins Dorian out on the balcony, then he pulls the glass door shut. They are both out there, whispering and in our line of sight.

"I made things so much worse," my friend says, drawing my attention to her. She shakes her head. "I-I was desperate and lost my job, and I didn't want to live on the streets. So, I made a stupid decision after I met some local witches who convinced me how easy it would be." Her eyes water, but she blinks the tears away and looks at me. "Your demons are right. It's too dangerous to be around you. I already feel terrible for bringing so much shit to your door. It would be selfish for me to stay."

"You know I don't care about all that. And besides, we can keep you safe. You should stay with us—"

"I can't." She glances out to the balcony and back to me. "I refuse to do any more harm. To you or myself, so I need to leave and make this right. Start fresh somewhere else. Let me have this."

I drag her into my arms and hold her. I remember what Lucifer said about her contract and what's supposed to become of her. Is there any way she can truly outrun that?

According to Lucifer, not unless I join his ranks during the overtaking of Heaven, and that's not something I can do. But I can't tell her all that. Just like I can't judge her for wanting to flee. She wants some control back in her life. Even if it's just for a little while.

"Hindsight is a bitch," I say to her, rubbing her back. "But I might have done the same in your situation. Remember all the things we stole and did growing up just to get ourselves food?"

She pulls back, smiling while wiping her eyes and nodding. "I worry that something is rotten inside me. Now that I've let evil in, maybe it's too late for me."

Wow, if only she really knew about me and the darkness I'm hiding.

Cassiel comes and stands besides us, then lays his chin on my friend's leg.

"Cassiel definitely likes you," I say, and she rubs his head. "Animals can pick up on dark energy and he wouldn't be showing you affection if you were evil."

She just keeps stroking his ears, her chin trembling, and her fear kills me on the inside. We've been through so much together, so to see her so broken makes me want to scoop her up and promise her everything will be alright.

"You know the demons and I will try to help you out of your deal with Maverick." Saying his name brings back my own complications, but I can't let that into my thoughts when this isn't about me. "I don't want you to leave."

A small smile lifts her lips. "I know, but I... I need this."

I take her hand in mine, slightly squeezing it. "I understand," I say. "I don't like it, but I understand what you mean."

"I fucked up so badly." She casts a glance out to the demons who are both watching us with blank expressions, then back at me. "I don't know what else to do, and I can barely sleep from worry and guilt. I hate that my shit spilled over onto you." Her words shake, yet she squares her shoulders, looking more determined than I've seen since arriving at her place.

My chest tightens to see her so lost, but if she feels time away will help, I can't take that chance away from her. "Well... We certainly know how to make a home anywhere," I say bleakly. She nods.

"You gotta do what feels right for you," I go on, "but you've got to keep in touch and keep me posted. Send another bird or whatever."

She smiles at that.

"And please promise me you won't do any more dark magic?"

She hesitates, which only worries me more.

A sort of sadness flares across her face. "I promise I will try my best."

My hand squeezes her slightly again and I lean closer, taking her into my arms. She hugs me back that time, and I can't help but somehow feel like I'm saying farewell to my friend for good. I'm scared for her, for all of us, but we all have to choose our own paths in life too.

"Sorry to be a pain, but I should probably leave," she tells me as she pulls back from our embrace. "My bus comes in fifteen minutes and I can't be late."

"Of course." I swallow the boulder in my throat, unsure how to feel myself.

I wave over to Cain and Dorian to join us, and then open the door for Elias just as Joseline drags a huge backpack down the hallway into the living room, Cassiel by her side, pulling at one of the straps, helping her.

Elias goes to her aid without me asking. "Where's this going?"

"Downstairs please," she says.

"We're heading off then?" Dorian asks.

"Yes, Joseline has a bus to catch." My mouth feels dry, the words like barbed wire on my throat. This is going too quickly, and while she's had time to process this and make her decision, I haven't.

Cain looks at me and I see the dozen questions flare behind his eyes, but to his credit, he doesn't ask them now, clearly feeling the sorrow flooding the room.

Outside the apartment, the air has turned bitter cold and a light curtain of snow is falling. Joseline has the bag on her back, and she's all geared up. She gives me a wonky smile, the kind she'd always give me when she was uncertain. My eyes prick at seeing her like that and I'm not ready to say farewell to her.

She hugs me. "Take care, sweetie, and don't take any shit from anyone."

I laugh as she draws back, but I still hold onto her arms. "Call me once you're ready to return, okay?"

"Aye, aye captain." She gives me a soldier's salute with her hand to the side of her brow, her heels knocking together.

Chuckling, I release my hold on her and she turns away,

hurrying down the sidewalk, dodging people with the huge bag on her back.

My chest starts to feel like it's splitting in half.

Someone's hand slides into mine, and I don't see who it is at first. I'm choking on my own breaths, barely able to keep it together as so much comes crashing down around me. Somehow I manage to make it back to the car in one piece, but the moment we're all pressed in the back like sardines and Cassiel stretches across all our laps, I lose it.

"Are you okay, little rabbit?" Elias asks.

But I can't find my words. Instead, tears pour from my eyes and I hug Cassiel, burying my face against him and crying uncontrollably.

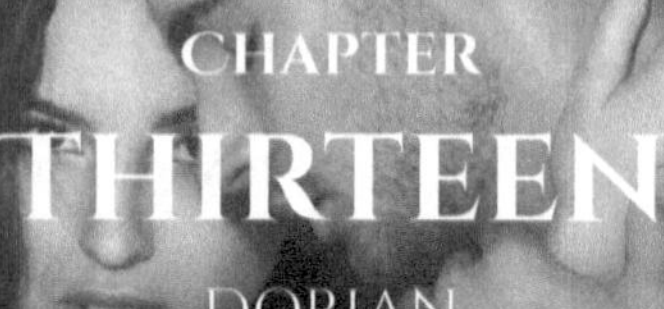

I can't stand seeing her upset. Can't stand it. It tears me up inside.

How did I go from being one of the most renowned bounty hunters in Hell and the king of one-night stands here on Earth, to caring so strongly about one woman that I'm weak when she cries? I'm not sure how I got to this point, but here I am, sitting in the back of the Town Car, Aria partly in my lap, shaking with grief, and all I can think about is how I can take the pain away.

Glancing at Elias and Cain, it's clear they're thinking the same thing, but none of us know what to do or say. We're stiffly silent as Aria cries, only able to offer our presence to comfort her. Elias has her hand in his, while Cain's pretending to keep to himself, but really, I can see his thumb brushing against her thigh between us. It's his way of telling her he's there.

Me? I'm wondering what else I can do. This isn't enough. Aria's been through so much and the hits just keep on coming. We're used to shit like this, but her... I'm not sure how much more she can take before she breaks. I mean, the woman was just kidnapped and dragged to Hell, for fuck's sakes.

Once the tires meet the gravel of our driveway, an idea strikes me. The last time I saw Aria happy—truly happy—was when we were in Scotland, doing touristy things like we were the most normal couple in the world.

I smile, remembering how excited she was to visit the shops, buy souvenirs, and take pictures.

What she needs now is another evening like that. Something simple, almost stupid, but stress-free and distracting.

The Town Car pulls up to the front doors, and Cain and Elias climb out. But when Aria tries to scoot across the back seat to leave, I grab her by the waist and tug her back in. She glances at me, confused.

"You and I have one more stop to make," I say, and shoo Cassiel out next. Cain pauses outside and glances my way, but I give him a knowing look—one that says I can make things right; I just want some time alone with her.

As always, he seems to read my mind and nods. "Come, Elias. We have some things to go over in my office."

Elias, of course, is as clueless as ever. "For the ritual? Or for the vamps?"

Cain's expression blanks. "Both."

"You sure you don't need me?" Aria asks him.

"Not for this," Cain replies quickly. "Go with Dorian." He shuts the door. Elias does on his side as well, cutting us off from the rest of the world. Aria immediately turns to me.

"Where are we going?" she asks.

I punch an address into my phone and pass it to Holmes so he knows where to go. Aria tries to peek at the screen before I can put it in my pocket. "Nah uh uh," I tsk as we start our trip. "It's a surprise."

She frowns at me with adorable pouty lips. "That makes me nervous," she says.

"Nervous? How so?"

"I've had too many surprises with you three demons already. Don't you think?" Despite her efforts to appear unamused, a smile peeks through.

"Touché." I grin.

We drive on in silence. Aria leans a little closer to her window, looking out. I expected her to be more excited about my surprise, but once we get there, that'll change. I hope so, anyway.

With Aria distracted, I pull out my phone and start scrolling through the camera roll. The first picture I see is Aria's beautiful face smiling back at me while posing in a red phone booth. I swipe the screen to find a selfie she insisted we take together with her kissing my cheek and Edinburgh castle in the background. The shock on my face is apparent. She'd surprised me then but, as seen in the next picture, I had surprised her by swooping in and kissing her back.

My chest warms. At the time, I was humoring her desire to do touristy things during our Scotland trip by snapping pictures and shop-hopping, but now I'm looking back and missing the time we'd spent together. Aria's a marvel. She's bewitched me. And I don't think I'll ever delete these.

"What are you looking at?" Aria's voice makes my head snap up. She's staring at me thoughtfully, head tilted.

"You."

She blinks at me in confusion.

I click my screen off and pocket the phone again. Glancing out the window, I see we're nearing the center of Glenside where Christmas decorations light up the Town Square. In the small park, there's a little pop-up shop all strung up with lights and dusted with snow, a community fire pit surrounded by happy kids roasting marshmallows, and an ice-skating rink.

The Christmas holiday is coming fast for these Earth dwellers. As demons, we never celebrated the holiday for obvious reasons, but it doesn't mean we can't take advantage of the perks it brings. Like an impromptu date idea.

"Town Square?" Aria asks as she peeks out her window, too. "Why are we here?"

Holmes stops the car near the park's entrance. I scramble to get out first and beat Aria to her door, which I open for her like a true gentleman should. She eyes me skeptically as she climbs out.

What can I say? I'm a romantic at heart.

I hold my bent elbow for her to take, but she hesitates. "What are you up to?" she asks, scanning me over with those gorgeous dark eyes of hers.

I fake shock and offense. "Can't a demon take his lady out for some innocent fun?"

"'Demon' and 'innocent fun' aren't two things that usually go in the same sentence."

"They do with me," I reply, then snatch her hand and place it in the crook of my elbow. "And besides, maybe I want to show you off to everyone here."

I expect a blush or a shy dismissal, but instead, her gaze stretches out toward the crowded center and her face blanks of all emotion.

Curious... It isn't a reaction I expect from her. Is she really that upset about Joseline? I guess so. But, as I watch her, my stomach flips with worry. Something doesn't quite seem right.

"Aria, my dear, are you alright?" I ask her.

She doesn't answer. Maybe she doesn't hear me.

"Aria?"

"Hm?" She turns slightly to look up at me.

I'm starting to wonder if this date idea was a smart one after all. "Are you feeling okay?"

She blinks slowly, as if coming out of a trance. Then her eyes scan my face, seeing me for the first time. "Oh, yeah. Totally."

I stare at her, not believing a word she's said.

Not meeting my eyes again, she rubs her forehead. "I'm sorry. It's... been a long day."

I sigh. I can't fault her too much. She has been through a great deal. "It's been a long few days for you, really."

"Try weeks." She huffs a laugh, one that sounds forced.

"You're not wrong."

Had her impromptu trip to Hell affected her more than we'd thought? Had something else happened down there that she hadn't told us about?

I am starting to think so.

Now isn't the time to bring it up though, so I nod toward the commotion and urge her forward. "Come on. We're here now. Might as well have some fun."

"I thought demons didn't care for the cold," she says.

It's true. All Hell-dwelling creatures prefer the heat for obvious reasons. "For you, I'll make an exception."

I offer her a smile, but she doesn't seem impressed.

Running out of ideas, I lead her through the little pop-up shops. She keeps quiet the entire way. It's so unlike her, this distance, and soon an unease builds between us. We've never been this way with each other—so cold and formal. That's Cain's thing.

Not mine. Aria's always been a free spirit with me, so the silence irks me.

This definitely isn't what I envisioned for our romantic excursion.

With her hand still planted on my arm, I help weave her through the crowds. Her gaze is trained blankly ahead, and with every passing moment, my worry grows. Something's definitely wrong here.

Ahead of us, I spot the ice rink, busy with adults and children twirling around the circular ring. I steer Aria in that direction.

Believe it or not, being the Romeo I am, I've watched my share of romantic comedies. Ice skating during winter and sharing hot chocolate are right up there with boat rides and walks during sunsets... Girls love shit like this.

Once we get in the long line to rent our skates, Aria turns to me, her pouty mouth turned down in a frown. "Wait. Ice skating?"

"Is that a problem?" I ask.

She doesn't answer at first, chewing on her bottom lip instead. It's a very Aria thing to do, and I smile at the familiarity of it.

"I... I've never ice skated before," she says nervously.

"Really?" But actually, I'm not that surprised. If my knowledge of romances serves me right, the girl doesn't know much about skating and then the guy swoops in and catches her whenever she falls. That's where I come in.

"Had no money growing up, remember?"

"Ah," I begin. "Then, today will be a first for you."

When it's our turn to get our skates, she still looks nervous. We get our sizes, and we sit on one of the benches to lace them up. With hands shaking, she moves slowly.

"Let me help you." I kneel in front of her and finish the ties for her. When I stand again, I take her by the hand. "Don't worry. I won't let you fall," I assure her.

She nods. "Okay."

Together, we wobble our way toward the ice. Other skaters fly past us, expertly gliding along. Even children spin and leap, looking like mini-Olympians.

Aria eyes them, too. "Have you done this before?"

I shrug. "Not exactly."

Her eyes widen. "What?"

"How hard can it be?" I point to a group of ten-year-olds, all holding hands and giggling as they blur past us. "If they can do it, I'm sure I can."

I step onto the ice, and immediately my feet fly out from under me. I windmill my arms, but it's too late—I'm falling. I slam onto my ass. Pain ricochets up my spine and curses fly from my mouth.

There's no way I'm going to be able to walk straight after this. Shit.

When I look up, Aria is laughing. Hysterically. She's bent over, clutching her knees and wheezing. I scowl.

The ice is quickly freezing my butt, so I try to climb back to my feet, but regaining my balance on these skates is near impossible. I'm slipping, my feet going in two opposite directions, and it isn't long before I've fallen again, this time landing on all fours like a dog. Aria continues to laugh, and my annoyance only grows. How can I—a renowned assassin and incubus demon—not be able to do something as simple as stay upright on skates? Frankly, it's embarrassing.

A hand grabs me, and when I peer up, Aria's stopped her fit of laughter and is now trying to help lift me to my feet. I don't know how, but she's managing to at least stay standing on the ice, while I can't even get my feet to follow simple instructions. It's like I'm suddenly a newly born fawn, unable to make my limbs work the right way.

Somehow, she guides me to the wall and I'm able to use it to stand. Breathing hard, I don't make any sudden movements. One little shift and I'm guaranteed to be flat on my ass again.

"Don't you dare tell Elias about this," I grumble, but just speaking makes my knees wobble and I grip onto the wall for support. "I'll never hear the end of it."

I am supposed to be the agile one out of our group. Hell, I can scale a wall or leap across a boiling pit with ease in my demon form. I make fun of Elias daily for being a brute and so ungraceful, yet here I am unable to keep on my feet for more than two minutes. Let alone to skate around the rink.

If he finds out about this, it's over.

Aria snorts a laugh. "I'm not promising anything."

The same group of kids I saw earlier make their way back

around the rink, this time chuckling and pointing at me as they pass. I hiss at them, making them move a little faster.

Little shits.

Ice skating is definitely not as simple as it looks.

"Not so easy, is it?" Aria asks, drawing my attention back to her. She reaches for my hand, but I'm too afraid to pry either of them off the wall. At least she's seeming more like herself now, even if it's at my expense.

"I guess not," I mumble. "But I should've known better. Demons and ice just don't mix."

"Or maybe real life isn't like some cheesy Hallmark movie?"

I stare at her flabbergasted. How in the world did she know—

"Yeah, a blind man could see what you were going for here. Christmas shops? Hot chocolate? Ice skating? What's next? A horse-drawn carriage ride for two? I mean, it's a cute idea, but not my schtick."

I should've known better. Aria isn't like all the other women I tried to wine and dine before bringing them to my bed. It was mostly out of boredom, since I never really needed to convince anyone to have sex with me, but still. She'd seen right through my bullshit from the beginning.

"I just wanted to make you feel better," I say. "You were so upset about your witch friend and I—"

"I get it," she replies, cutting me off. "I definitely haven't laughed that hard in a long time."

I wince as more pain shoots up my spine and my butt cheeks ache from the fall. "Glad to help."

She tugs one of my hands off the wall. "Come on. Let's just go home. Watch a horror movie together and eat some burnt popcorn or something. It's safer."

I smile. "My sore ass thanks you."

With one hand still firmly on the wall for support, she tugs me toward the exit, which is only two steps behind us.

When we're on regular, non-slippery ground again, I turn to her. "I'm sorry this didn't work out as I planned. That's what I get for trying all this sappy romance nonsense. Maybe I should just stick to sex—"

I'm cut off abruptly by her mouth on mine, kissing me sweetly and swiftly. Stepping back, there's a slight smile lifting her lips.

"Thank you, by the way," she whispers, her eyes sparkling in the colorful glow of the Christmas lights above us. How she doesn't know how absolutely beautiful she truly is is beyond me. Staring down at her now, with newly fallen snow clinging to her hair, and her cheeks rosy from the cold, I can't help but think how much this moment now feels like one of those Hallmark movies. Almost magical in the way everything has come together in an imperfectly perfect way.

I find myself leaning in again for another kiss. She meets me halfway, and when our lips touch, the kiss is softer and more tame than any we've shared before. A new and unfamiliar sensation swirls inside me, filling me to the brim and warming me to the core.

When we finally pull away, Aria's face lights up, but there's a bit of mischief there that I recognize as well. "Just so we're clear, I'm all for you sticking strictly to sex, too."

Throwing my head back, my laughter booms. This woman is seriously something else.

I snake my arm around her waist and draw her in close. "Aria, my gorgeous girl, you got yourself a deal."

FOURTEEN

The crisp morning air chills my bones, the snow under my paws icy. Each time I hit the ground with rapid steps, the snow melts instantly from my fiery touch. I'd grown up knowing nothing but fire and brimstone. And I got used to the intensity of the heat, but since being shoved onto Earth, I'd learned to appreciate the varying weather. And winter has grown on me more than I anticipated.

I rush past the dark, dense pines, swerving in and out, leaping over logs. It has been too damn long since I last ran in these woods. And I missed the wind in my fur, racing as if I chased the devil himself.

Bursting out of the forest, I charge over the perfectly untouched snow across the flat landscape. The mansion lays in the distance, surrounded by trees, the driveway leading toward the main gates. Morning sunlight glints against them. The moment reminds of being back in Hell, during a time when Lucifer called for the Grand Chase. A time when newly added souls were released into the woods, and everyone went out hunting them. The more you brought back for Lucifer, the greater the payment from him. It came in the form of souls... everything down there was in that currency. It's what he fed on, what he bargained with.

I used to love those runs, and the prizes I gained I'd always give to Serena. Being a crossroads demon, she was all about trading and selling with humans for theirs. After all, she insisted that they helped her complexion. I used to always think she looked beautiful, except me being such a love-struck fool, I had no idea she was using the souls I gave her to gain favor with Lucifer. All for her greatest betrayal—when she ripped out my heart and reminded me that I was indeed an idiot for ever letting myself fall for her.

I pound my paws into the ground, fury flaring over my body. I hate remembering the past, hate that I can't let it go, hate that every day I'm reminded we are all on Earth because Serena betrayed us and it's how Lucifer found out about us.

Shaking the thoughts away proves difficult today.

I charge faster ahead when a dark shadow catches my attention from near the side of the house. It moves in and out between the overgrown shrubs.

My heart beats faster as I watch the figure, trying to work out what I'm looking at. I keep running, my gaze trained on the shrubs.

Then it leaps out, a large creature dark as the night, fur mangled. It stands on all fours, head low and sniffing the ground.

A chill floods my veins at the sight of a fucking hellhound. In my territory? I growl under my breath, fury bleeding into me.

I knew the drill all too well... A soul needs to be retrieved on Earth and the legion sends the beasts to retrieve them. I'd done my fair share of retrievals when I first joined the forces.

He's here for Aria. To take away what's mine. I know it immediately. And that just isn't going to happen. Aria is my obsession, and there is nothing I wouldn't do for her. Without her I can't breathe, I can't exist, and right now I glare at the thing that came to do her harm.

I spear across the land so fast, the hellhound only hears my approach when it's too late for him. Poor sucker. I slam into him as he turns toward me, the surprise in his wide eyes makes me energized and excited.

He's doing me a favor. Here I've missed the hunt and fights, and this mutt appears to solve my problems. Well, part of them anyway.

He hits the ground, me on top of him, and I lash out, biting right into his throat.

Blood spurts out instantly, so much more than I expected. Well crap, I must have hit a major artery. And I wanted to play with my mouse.

I climb off him and shake myself while the hound bleeds onto the ground. He chokes and gurgles on his own blood.

I stare into his eyes, but I don't recognize this one. There are so many new recruits, it's impossible to keep track of everyone.

It is over quicker than I anticipated, and I sigh at my disappointment. The split second the hellhound stops fighting, he vanishes into thin air, wrenched back into Hell. He'll survive, but the legion master will also punish him for failing. And then more will come... They always do.

Right then, I want to murder Maverick. He may have showed some empathy toward Aria—hell, he'd brought her back to Earth for some reason—but that doesn't stop the need to pummel him into the dirt.

A scream rings through the air, and I jerk my head up, my ears pivot toward the direction of the sound. I'm charging around the back of the house before my next breath.

Aria!

I run at top speed. Careening around the corner of the mansion, I come in direct view of Aria recoiling from another hellhound fucker. They are at least fifty feet from me.

Rage surges through my veins, the anger pummeling into me that the beast thinks it can lay a paw on something that belongs to me.

Just as I lunge toward them, a black shadow bursts out from within Aria. Sayah. The creature. She juts toward the animal, spreading outward like a barricade wall between Aria and the hellhound.

My gaze hones in on the creature who leaps at Sayah, teeth bared, tearing into her form, except it seems to bounce right back off her. I have no clue what the fuck she is, but right now, I love every last dark inch of her shadow freakiness if it keeps my girl protected.

I'm thundering toward them, my heart pounding, lungs sucking in rapid breaths.

Aria's gasp catches my attention. She's pressed up against the house, safe guarded by her shadow, but the hellhound is relentless in its pursuit. Terror bleeds into her expression, which only drives me faster. The beast doesn't even notice me as Sayah grows in size, creating an even larger barricade between Aria and the enemy.

Like the wind, I slam into its side. We both tumble away into a heap of fur, fangs, and debris from the forest floor.

I see nothing but red, fury blinding me to anything but destroying it. We storm into a battle and crash into a tree as the bastard snaps at my front leg, ripping free flesh.

That's it. I'm done playing nice. My thoughts darken, and I lose all control, tearing into its neck and ripping into its throat. Blood splatters everywhere, and its body twitches as the life drains out of it.

I spit out the bloody mess of muscle and tissue just as its limp body disintegrates in front of me. Gone in an instant, and all that remains is a dark spot in the snow.

I twist around. Only Aria stands there, breathing hard. There's no sign of Sayah. As I make my way over, I call back my wolf, my body changing, bones stretching, fur vanishing. I push up on two feet and hurry to her in my human form, naked and splattered with blood. But what else is new?

"Elias," she gasps, and rushes to me. She throws herself against me, her body trembling in fear. Her arms lock around my middle and she presses her face into my chest. "What was that thing?"

"A hellhound," I say. "But you're safe now."

"Hellhound? You mean, like you?"

Thankfully not completely like me, or this confrontation would've been a lot bloodier.

"We got lucky this time," I say instead.

"Where did it come from? Hell? Sayah—she tried to protect me."

"I saw." But what I still don't understand is why? "Is she gone now?"

"I think so..."

She may have been helpful this time, but I still didn't trust the shadow. To be honest, it still freaked me the fuck out.

"Why are they here? Are they after you?"

I shake my head. Hellhounds are sent to drag souls back to Hell. Cain, Dorian, and I are banished. So that only leaves one person.

My stomach clenches. "Not me."

Her eyes widen with surprise. "M-Me?"

I don't reply. I can't. My head is already whirling with the growing danger she is in. We were fools to think Lucifer would ever give her up. It was only a matter of time because he sent his mutts to retrieve her.

I strain my ears, training them to catch any unwelcome sounds. It's not safe for Aria outside anymore.

"I'm not going back into Hell." Her voice shakes, and my heart sinks at hearing her fear.

Oh, the sweet agony I have planned for Maverick for putting her through this torment. I'm going to fucking destroy him. Then Lucifer.

"Let's get you inside."

But she doesn't budge.

Her eyes glisten with tears when she looks up at me, and I run my thumb to catch them from sliding down her cheeks.

"How do you stop hellhounds?" she asks.

"They can only be stopped by Lucifer or by their commander. Hellhounds follow orders. They barely have any thoughts of their own." It is a harsh truth, one I realized when I'd become the head of my own legion. My kind is trained to be killers since childhood. That's all they know. "There'll be more... I'm sure of it."

Aria swallows hard and blinks away her tears. She's been through so much and already dragged into Hell and, as much as I yearned to burst into Hell, that isn't a possibility.

"I promise you that we will find a way to fix this," I say. "And if not, then I'll spend every last breath destroying every beast that comes for you. I promise you with my life."

She holds onto me tight. The wind whistles, blowing through our hair and bringing down more snow, and with it, I feel an ominous sensation I can't shake away.

"How are you feeling?" I ask.

"What do you mean? I was just attacked by a hellhound—"

"No. Well, yes, but that's not what I meant. Dorian said you seemed a bit off yesterday on your date?"

She snorts a laugh. "Date? Is that what it was?"

"Don't tell him that. He may be offended."

Aria finally steps back, her gaze drifting to the mansion and her shoulders sink. "Things just seem to be getting worse and worse. Maybe I'm cursed or something."

"Don't ever say that," I reply sharply. "You are quite the opposite. I've been surrounded by cursed creatures my whole life, and you, my little rabbit, are so perfect, so beautiful, so powerful, that you intimidate others. Lucifer sees it, too. He gravitates toward power…"

Wants to control it. Possess it. Dominate it. But I keep that to myself.

She looks up at me. "And Cain?"

I nod. "If you ask me, I think that's one of the reasons Lucifer never just killed him. He knows Cain is a threat and would rather use him to his advantage." I shrug. "He hasn't always been the demon you see today. Down in the underworld, we are all surrounded by corruption, by greed, by power, and it's easy to lose yourself in it."

"But he's different now."

"He's been fucked over enough times by his family to realize they would never be on his side. That his father would rather burn down Hell before relenting any power. The thing is, Lucifer is already wreaking havoc on many, but everyone's too scared to stand up to him."

"Except Cain, you, and Dorian."

I laugh. When she says it like that, we sound like some kind of hellish superheroes. Martyrs or something. That hadn't been our intention at all. At least, not at first. In the beginning, our motives had been mostly selfish. We wanted power and prestige for ourselves. We wanted to rule Hell. But the more our eyes became open to Lucifer's madness and cruelty, the more we knew something had to be done to remove him from his throne. "We wanted things to change. But Lucifer isn't someone to take any kind of threat lightly."

"He's fucking terrifying. And completely and utterly insane," she admits, and gives me a lopsided grin. "We've gotten ourselves into a huge mess."

"Yes, but out of chaos emerges unimaginable greatness."

She rolls her eyes. "Where the heck did you hear that from?"

"Those are my words, little rabbit. On the outside, I may be ruthless and intimidating, but on the inside, I'm a genius."

She laughs, pushes herself on her toes, and then steals a quick kiss. "A genius, huh?"

"And I may have found that on an inspirational poster somewhere," I admit with a sly grin.

"Now that you mention it, I remember seeing something like that in Purgatory's employee lounge."

Fuck. She'd found out my secret.

We laugh and start making our way back to the front of the house. As we walk through the doors, another loud howl cuts through the early morning silence. Looks like I'm going out hunting today.

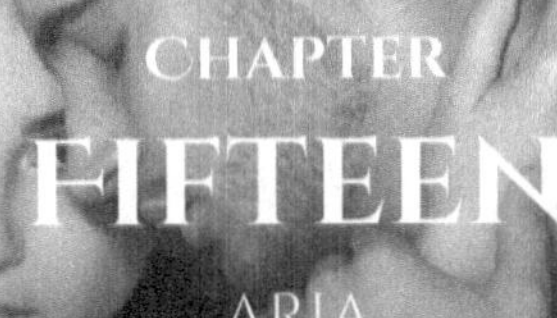

FIFTEEN

ARIA

"Are you sure we should be out here? You know, with hellhounds on my tail and all that," I ask Cain as he opens the Town Car door for me. He's gracious as ever, and for a change he's not wearing a suit, but he still looks delicious. He's got on deep-blue jeans that hug his strong legs, and all the good parts of him—if you know what I mean. Then, to make matters even worse, his button-up midnight blue shirt does nothing to conceal the muscles underneath. He is beyond gorgeous. Just being by his side sends my heart into a thundering race.

"You are safe," he answers with a little smirk. I guess he caught me ogling.

I climb out into a brisk night... Okay, it's so much more than that. It's freezing, and dressed in just hipster jeans and a yellow cotton shirt that sits off my shoulders makes me shiver. But Dorian insisted it was warm inside the bar we're headed to, and I wanted to look good.

"You've got us three with you," Elias responds, standing tall and dressed in all black, blending into the darkness of the parking area. The breeze swishes through his hair, messing it up, giving him that wild-man look, and for a moment, I want to freeze time and just snapshot this perfect image of him. "What could go wrong?" he asks, breaking the perfect illusion.

I almost choke on my breath. "Don't even tempt the universe like that. She has a wicked sense of humor."

Dorian comes up to me, his arm looping around my back, and I press up against him. The moment we touch, my body comes to life, my pulse hitching. I'm super alert of exactly where his hands are, how he feels against me. He always has this effect on me, and I love it. Pressed to him, I close my eyes momentarily and breathe in deeply, a sense of calmness washing over me. My whole life I've been strong, not relying on anyone but myself. It was how I survived in a harsh world. It never occurred to me I wouldn't always have to be that way... that I'd have others in my life who cared for me so much they'd risk their own lives.

"We can't keep hiding," Dorian murmurs. "This is our night out to do what humans do."

The way Dorian says that sounds like we've landed on Mars and are about to join the locals there for a feast. And the funny thing is that I feel more like I belong with the demons than the humans.

When I glance up at Dorian, his eyes glint in the moonlight, and my breath catches at the way he watches me like nothing else exists. If I'm not mistaken, I would almost think they're the ones missing normality more than me.

I take a quick glance behind us to where Elias remains at our rear, scanning the shadows around the parking area for hell-hounds. A shiver races up my spine at the thought of the damned hounds after me to drag me back where I don't belong. Seriously, I couldn't make up this stuff if I tried.

As we start walking away from the parking area, I lift my attention to the double story restaurant that might have once upon a time been a saloon in a cowboy town. It has the wooden front verandah, matching wooden balcony on the next level, and even the swinging doors at the entrance.

Bright lights spill out from the windows as does the sound of laughter and a country song. Up on the balcony railing, the words Daisy's Place glow in bright yellow fluorescent, and when Cain opens the front door, an explosion of voices and music hits us. With it comes smells of beer, peanuts, and roasted meat. There are people everywhere, from the full tables on the right-hand side, the bar across the back, and the pool tables to my left where much of the laughter is coming from.

A young man in a striped apron steps up to Cain and, before we know it, we are all being shown to a round table right in the back near the window. The table is covered in a red and white checkered tablecloth, has four plate settings, and it comes complete with a flickering candle inside a red, glass bowl.

"This is so cute," I say, and quickly take the seat right in the corner with the best view of the entire room.

Before we are even settled down, the waiter brings us complimentary garlic bread and water for the table, then takes our drink order from Dorian for us all.

"I am starved," Elias adds, pouring over the menu that spans over five pages, while chewing on a piece of garlic bread.

Cain and Dorian are studying the place, and I ask them, "Are you two going to try any of the food?" It's not often they eat, unlike Elias.

Both shake their heads, Cain answering, "I'll enjoy the wine though."

Elias nudges me. "Happy for me to order for both of us?"

"For sure," I say, not sure what's on the menu. But in truth, I'll eat anything because tonight is about us all being together rather than the food.

Elias wastes no time in flagging down the waiter. "We'll take everything on this page."

I glance over, convinced he must be pointing to a short page of meals, except he's pointing to a list of at least fifteen dishes.

"Are you sure?" I ask, and the waiter gives a similar quizzical look at Elias.

"Yes, there's four of us at the table." He gives me a look of, trust me, I got this, then ushers the waiter away with the order.

"You weren't kidding when you said you were hungry," I murmur.

"He's a beast," Dorian adds. "I'm pretty sure he might be related to Cain's brother, Valdim, the demon of Gluttony."

Elias barks out laughing, drawing attention from the next table. "Valdim is an asshole, but if you ever want to enjoy the best feast, he is the guy to join. Oh, and bad jokes. He's *full* of them."

"When did you share a meal with him?" Dorian asks.

All I can think is I've only met two of Cain's brother's so far, and it's plenty enough with the chaos they've left in their wake.

"Remember the blood festival when Nix insisted on wearing only his birthday suit and was covered in his victims' blood?" Elias responds, howling. "And how he slipped in front of everyone and landed right on his ass?"

That moment both of them howl in laughter, but I notice Cain isn't joining in. He sits on my other side, and I place a hand on his leg.

"Everything okay?" I ask.

His hand slides over the top of mine, his smile wide. "Most memories I carry of my brothers are tainted by their betrayal, so I don't see the past as easily as them." His gaze lifts to Elias and Dorian exchanging tales of the blood festival, whatever that is. It's funny to hear the amusement in their voices. They truly did enjoy living in Hell.

"I didn't see much while I was in Hell, except one creepy room, but the place was your home, so you must have some good memories too."

His eyes appear darker in the harsh lights overhead, but it's his beautiful smile that I find most appealing. I see the struggle in his expression between loving and hating Hell.

"There are many things I remember fondly, family and friends who are no longer as they once were. At the end of the day, home isn't about a location, but about those you share your life with. Of all people, I'd think you could understand that."

He's right. I can.

"That's pretty deep," I say, leaning closer, and on cue he leans over and steals a kiss. One I'm not necessarily expecting, but I embrace nonetheless. The taste of him sinks into me, and he kisses like he owns me.

"I'm in a sentimental kind of mood," he whispers, while I'm breathing quickly from that one kiss, still holding on and not ready to let him go.

"How about after dinner, I challenge you to a game of pool? Do you know how to play?" I ask him, wanting him to enjoy the night and not let the heaviness of what's happened lately get him down.

"Deal," Cain answers, to which Elias pipes in. "What are we dealing with?"

"That I can kick Cain's butt at a game of pool," I answer.

Dorian's expression beams. "If you really want a challenge, then we'll do a real deal. Beat each one of us, and we'll do a strip tease for you if you win. You lose, and you strip for us."

One of Cain's eyebrows arches at Dorian's suggestion, but he's not saying no either.

"I'm in," Elias states, both of them now looking at Cain.

He drops his attention to me. "A deal's a deal. Do you accept the terms?"

His cheekiness has me smiling at how he tries to be serious but is failing miserably.

"Sure, agreed. What you three don't know is that I used to spend nearly every weekend at the local social club, doing nothing but playing pool. So, this should be fun."

"Should we get out a demon contract for this?" Dorian laughs.

"Nah, the way I see it, there is no loss," Elias replies then turns to me. "We strip, then you will join us very soon afterward."

I break into a fake laugh. "That's not part of the deal. Just you three strip and I watch. The end." I poke my tongue out at him, and I can tell it's killing him to sit across the table from me and not pull me right then into his arms.

But all of that is paused when the waiter arrives with a huge tray filled with dishes. He starts plating them on our table, five meals so far, from fettuccine in white sauce and mushrooms, lasagna, schnitzel, to meatballs and a roast chicken.

It smells divine, but even I doubt we can polish this off, let alone the next tray coming our way.

"I am going to become a balloon after this meal," I say.

"A sexy, stripping balloon," Dorian adds.

I eye him. "That's not really sexy."

He shrugs. "If it's you, it's always sexy."

Elias is already digging into the lasagna, while Cain drinks from his glass of wine.

"Eat up," Cain tells me, "there's more coming." He eyes the next platter, and my eyes bulge out of their sockets. It's so much food that now even nearby tables are staring at us.

"Geez, we look like we've never eaten in our lives. You two better fill up your plates with something, so it doesn't draw attention to the eating machine here," I instruct Cain and Dorian.

Somehow, to my surprise—though it really shouldn't surprise me—Elias makes a massive dent in the dishes, with my small contribution.

And with so much going on, in all honesty, none of us notice the figure approaching our table, until he literally pulls a chair to sit at our table.

It takes me a split second to fully take in who it is and with it comes my heart thundering in my chest.

"M-Maverick," I stutter, my insides turning cold, and I rear back in my seat.

Dorian and Elias jolt to their feet, the seats scraping across the wooden floorboards, and suddenly half the restaurant is staring in our direction.

Maverick grins and something sparkles in his eyes. "There are close to a hundred humans watching us," he says, with a grin in his voice, the implication that they are all in danger clear.

"Sit back down," Cain orders, and while Dorian and Elias hesitate at first, they follow the command.

"What are you doing here?" Cain hisses through clenched teeth.

But Maverick hasn't taken his eyes off me, and under his gaze, I feel a fire erupting within me, along with the feel of his kiss.

When he finally breaks our connection, he leans back in his seat comfortably and twists to face Cain. "I am not the enemy here, Brother. If I was, I wouldn't have released Aria from Hell."

"You put her there," Elias barks, a bit too loud, gripping the edge of the table, looking ready to lunge at Maverick. He, in turn, doesn't even flinch. He's got balls of steel, but then again, living in Hell has got to make you close to fearless.

"As Cain knows, nothing is ever straightforward when it comes to our family."

Cain's gaze doesn't change, not for a second. "What do you want?" he snarls.

"I hold no ulterior motive besides checking on Aria. It's never an easy process for someone with a soul to transition between realms."

Dorian leans in and clenches his jaw left and right. In each of the men, their battle to restrain themselves is palpable. I feel it in the thickening air, in the deathly stares. Even those around us notice as they watch with startled expressions.

Yet Maverick sits relaxed, dressed in a black shirt, open at his throat, the buttons catching the light as if they are made from obsidian stones, his white hair swept off his face, his eyes sharp, and everything about him is jaw-dropping gorgeous. I even notice the table of girls across the room stealing glances at him.

"Stop bullshitting," Dorian throws at him. "We know the truth. You've come to check on why the hellhounds you sent after her haven't done the job yet."

For a moment, I can swear Maverick's face blanches, Dorian's words seeming to take him by surprise. Can it be?

"He's good at acting, I'll give him that," Elias states to the rest of us, his chin pointing to Maverick.

"I had no idea the hounds had been unleashed," he states.

"How could you not?" Cain says. "They are soul collectors. Always have been."

Maverick straightens in his seat, his gaze on me, the pain behind his eyes imploring me to believe him, except I don't know if I can. No matter how much my body reacts around him, that doesn't make him safe or trustworthy.

"Because, Brother, I assumed we would at least have more time. I thought Father didn't know yet. I've—," Maverick starts but then shakes his head, changing his words. "Aria, believe me, I would never endanger you like that."

I lower my gaze while nausea churns in my gut at hearing his pleas with the other three looking on.

"You have no right to talk to her like that. It's time for you to fuck off," Elias states.

A growl comes from Maverick, coaxing my head to jolt up and see the fury on his face, the darkness sweeping over his eyes, stealing all the white. I watch the battle across his expression.

Elias cracks his neck, muscles tense.

"Not here," I say. "For hell's sake, there are innocents in here."

The stalemate between them has me shifting uncomfortably in my seat, and I keep lifting my gaze to the other people enjoying a meal, some with their kids. And little do they know they are sharing the room with four demons straight out of Hell. Yep, this could end up going sideways so fast it's terrifying.

I tremble and lean closer to Dorian. "You need to diffuse this. There are too many humans here."

He doesn't respond right away, but holds his gaze locked on Maverick.

Next thing I know, Elias is hurling himself across the table, plates and food flying in every direction.

A scream rips from my throat from the pure shock as a bowl of fried rice is tossed right into my lap.

Then the commotion erupts like wildfire, spreading across the room.

People are screaming, chairs scraping as everyone frantically tries to get up. But my attention is caught on Elias who slams into Maverick, both of them falling to the floor in an explosion of growls.

Before I can do anything, Dorian's on his feet and hurling himself into the battle too. I can't tell if he's trying to stop them or join in against Maverick because it's all happening too fast.

I'm up too, pulling back, wiping away the rice from my clothes. Cain grabs my arm and tugs me away from the chaos.

"We need to go," he instructs, and we weave amid the throng of chaotic patrons not going anywhere but not moving either. Most are trying to watch the fight. Cain is on a mission, wrenching me to the door, while my heart pounds in my chest.

People are shoving against me, someone stepping on my feet, but I keep glancing over my shoulder. I shift to get a view as security guards now shove their way to reach the brawl.

A thunderous growl blares, seeming to shake the whole bar on its foundations.

Someone screams, the sound of pure terror.

Then Maverick is flying headfirst toward the window, breaking the glass, shattering it into hundreds of pieces that fling everywhere.

People are ducking from the projectile pieces, others are screaming.

Just as Cain draws me to his side, I spot Elias hurling himself through the window and right after Maverick.

"God, he's going to murder him," I cry out, and now I'm shoving myself past people too.

We are spat out of the building from the masses shoving to get out. Dorian is on our heels. I stumble forward onto the front lawn leading to the parking area, and there I spot Elias and Maverick in a ball of anger, punching and growling. Their animalistic instincts are all out of control, and despite Maverick earlier appearing as controlled as the devil, now he is vicious as hell in a battle.

Behind me, Cain is pressing his shoulder on the front door of the bar, locking everyone else inside, while Dorian drags an iron bench to block more people from emerging. And I get it, they need to end this battle without anyone seeing Maverick's wings, or Elias now in hellhound form. Thankfully, the pair have rolled behind a huge line of shrubbery concealing them from those looking through the windows.

I rock on my heels, unsure what I can do to stop the fight. There's so much anger between them. I should feel nothing for Maverick, and I don't, I keep telling myself. Yet, I don't want Elias to murder him.

A bark of laughter comes from Maverick as he hurls Elias right into a sedan. He drops to the ground, leaving behind a huge dent into the rear door. Ouch. I really hope those people have insurance.

"For fuck's sake, is this still going?" Dorian mutters, as if he expected this to be wrapped up in a neat little bow.

Me, I'm tense as an elastic band about to snap. The night breeze whips my hair around my shoulders and ruffles my shirt. It's freezing, yet I'm burning up on the inside with anger and fear, and all kinds of emotions I don't quite understand. Mostly because I shouldn't be enjoying the fact that the two of them are sort of fighting over me.

"Let's finish this," Cain states, patting Dorian on the shoulder, and the two of them rush forward, Dorian releasing a battle cry.

To say I'm not enjoying the show would make me the biggest liar in the world and also a hypocrite.

My pulse is racing, and I'm losing control of what is wrong and right the longer I spend time with demons.

A terrifying growl comes from behind a nearby car to my left, far from the battle.

I flinch at the sound, slowly turning my head in that direction, while my gut hardens because I know what it is before I see it.

Fiery eyes from the pits of hell pierce the darkness. The shadow moves, emerging, revealing itself as a large hellhound as black as the night. Hair mangled and stiff, ears plastered flat against its head in an aggressive manner, the beast prowls toward me.

My heart jackhammers right into my throat and I can't breathe as I recoil right into a shrub.

Panicked, my attempt to call the guys comes out as a gargled sound, sounding like a strangled animal. I hate how weak-ass I feel, how pathetic I am when I should be able to find a way to fight for myself.

My nerves pulse and I can't stop staring at the way the hellhound's upper lip curls over razor-sharp teeth, at the drool seeping from the edges of its mouth.

I frantically grab at the bush behind me, tearing away a branch for a weapon, but come back with a fistful of leaves.

"Cain!" I manage to finally scream, but in that sudden breath I draw on, the beast lunges at me.

My world stops. It turns black with fear, while the edges of my sight feather.

I'm going to pass out.

An unstoppable split second that seems to move into slow motion.

The explosive sound of shouting comes from my right where the guys are, but I can't move, can't think straight.

A sudden blur races past me and crashes right into the hellhound. It comes so fast, so close, that the air swishes right past me with a force that sends me stumbling on my feet.

The cacophony of whimpers and growls pierce the night from the hellhound. It takes me mere moments to work out that Maverick is the one to jump onto the beast. He's on top of the animal that is laying on its side, tongue out, body thrusting to escape. Maverick's knee is against its throat, and he looks up at me.

Blood drips from the cuts on his face, his hair a mess, clothes ripped, yet he doesn't seem to be suffering.

"What—What—" I sputter, unable to form a coherent sentence at the moment.

Maverick winks at me, the kind that melts me on the spot. "See you soon, Aria."

Then he vanishes into thin air right before my eyes, and he's taken the hellhound with him.

Terror lodges in my chest, blinking at the now empty area.

In that exact moment, the door to the restaurant breaks open, the definite sound of wood splintering filling the air.

People are charging out of there, coming in our direction, and they are damn pissed, based on their shouting.

Dorian is at my side. "We gotta go." He wraps his arms around my middle and lifts me off my feet like I weigh nothing. Cain is ahead of us, while Elias sprints toward the car in his hound form.

Once we arrive at the Town Car, Dorian pushes me into the back seat, the rest of them piling in.

"Hit it, Holmes!" Dorian barks and then we're skidding out of there, tossing dust in our wake.

My heart won't stop hammering against my ribcage. I'm still in shock. My body trembles with it. All I can think is that Maverick —*Maverick*—saved me from a hellhound.

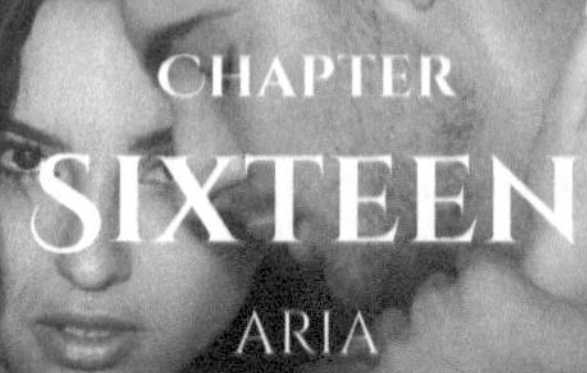

That night, sleep refuses to come. I'm tossing in my bed, Cassiel at my feet snoring away. Cain offered me his bed, as did the others, but I'd insisted I needed some time alone. Now, I'm not so sure.

Maverick refuses to leave my mind. I don't understand his behavior or my own reaction to him. Don't get me wrong, I get it, but the question is why?

In two seconds, I'm on my feet and strolling across the room to the window and staring out into the night. The woods lay still, undisturbed, and there's a darkness that comes with them. Will more hellhounds come for me, or has Maverick finally found a way to stop them? And why would he care to help me anyway?

He knows how I feel for his brother, for Elias and Dorian. I know it, yet somehow my thoughts drift to him.

I keep pacing, needing to get my head straight. There's the ritual coming up. I don't know how to feel about committing my soul to my demons for good. Once I do that, I'll be forever locked in with them. Is that a bad thing, seeing how much they mean to me? But eternity? That is a fucking long time.

I chew on my lower lip, worried, because how can anyone make such a decision?

I exhale another long breath and pad across the wooden floorboards on bare feet. Cassiel hasn't stirred from the end of my bed, and I slip out of my room, unsure if I want to spend the night alone after all.

It isn't long before I find myself standing outside Elias's room, his heavy breathing a comforting sound. I've missed the way he'd wake up in my room during his sleep walking, something he's stopped doing recently, which seems to have coincided with him no longer going out hunting for days at a time. But I miss him, so I slip into his room. He doesn't have much furniture, but his bed is bigger than a king size, that's for sure. The bright moon shines through the windows, giving everything a silvery glow.

He's lying on his back, legs and arms stretched out like a starfish, the bed sheet covering him from his waist down. He's so incredibly powerful and large. I make quick time crossing the room and reach the side of the bed where there seems to be more space. I'm dressed in my pajama pants and a tank top, while I know he's naked, which I don't mind.

Quickly, I climb into bed and under the sheet, then shuffle over to him. I roll onto my side and press my back into the curve of his side, my head resting on his bicep. His body is a furnace to touch, and I press into him, absorbing his heat, while tucking my cold toes under his leg. There's so much warmth, and I close my eyes and smile to myself at how good this feels.

It takes a few moments for him to stir and roll onto his side, before tucking himself around me. His arm slides around my stomach and he draws me closer to him, plastering us together.

"Hey little rabbit," he whispers in my ear, his breath warm. "Everything alright?"

"I couldn't sleep."

He kisses the top of my head. "Anything I can do to help?"

I hear the flirting in his tone, the sexiness in the way he whispers the words, even the twitch of his cock against my ass. Apparently it doesn't take long for him to get horny, even after waking up two seconds ago.

I shuffle in his arms and roll myself around so we're facing each other. His bronze irises seem to glint in the darkness, and he has those gorgeous sleepy bedroom eyes. Everything about him is dreamy. Just being wrapped in his arms and him being naked stirs my own arousal.

"There's so much on my mind, it's hard to quiet the voices."

"You've been through a lot. More than anyone should have to endure."

"Just trying to sort it all out in my mind, you know? But it's a great knotted mess."

He reaches over and tenderly pushes hair off my face. "I used to run in the woods when shit got to be too much. There are some things we can't change, so the best thing is a distraction."

"Did you want to return home that badly?" I ask.

"The opposite. I didn't want to deal with my past, but I also couldn't run away from it and knew it would eventually catch up with me. It was that notion that killed me. Knowing there was nothing I could do but wait. And that is agonizing."

I stare at him, at the way his gaze drifts away, like even now it pains him.

"Cain told me about you performing the ritual with Serena."

His lips thin and he doesn't respond right away. When he does, his voice is dark. "I gave not only my heart but *everything* I had to Serena, and she betrayed me in the worst possible way." He falls silent after that, and now I feel bad for even asking, yet that surge of jealousy pulses. It shouldn't, but I can't help but feel possessive over Elias.

Plus, I'd come here needing company, and now I made him think about his past. I don't push the point. I can only imagine how it must have felt to have someone he cared for hurt him. Though, with the way my own parents treated me, maybe we're similar, having those who were meant to love us reject us.

"It's why I insisted Cain tell you the truth of how much weight the ritual holds. What it'll mean for you," he tells me, his hand on my back, stroking me. "I still feel Serena through the bond, even with her in Hell and me here. It's like a constant itch I can't get rid of. It haunts me."

"Elias, I promise to never hurt you."

His light touch slides over my shoulder and to my lips. He's scanning me and looking deep into my eyes. "You are so pure, Aria, sometimes I worry that being with us will corrupt you."

I arch a brow. "Hello, you are talking to the girl with a freaking monster inside her that even Lucifer doesn't recognize. Not sure I can get more corrupt than that."

He laughs at me, and it makes me lean in and feather a kiss across his warm lips.

"Let me give you something tonight," he offers. "I'm going to eat your sweet pussy, and you'll orgasm so hard you'll be thinking about nothing else but me for the next few days."

"Is that a promise or threat?" I tease, while his words ignite my arousal, and I can't stop myself from smiling.

He rolls over me, nudging me onto my back, and pins me under him. His erection nestles between my legs where he pushes himself closer.

I wriggle, failing miserably at squirming away.

"Are you distracted yet?" he asks.

"Not really." I lie, coaxing a burst of laughter from him.

He slides down my body in no time, his fingers already curling into the elastic of my pants and yanking them down my legs. He kneels back, lifting my feet into the air as he tugs them off me.

Then he pries open my legs, his eyes on me, and he buries his face into my pussy without hesitation. His tongue runs the length of my slick heat, and I tremble with excitement.

I throw my head back, moaning, loving everything about him going down on me. He spreads my legs wide with his hands as he flicks his tongue across me, tasting all of me.

My breathing rushes, and I'm tugging at my nipples as the buildup within me comes so fast. Breathless, I wriggle beneath him.

The sounds he makes are devious, and he does that thing with his tongue where he dips it into me over and over. My hips are grating back and forth against his face, my cries growing louder.

He kisses my pussy before taking me into his mouth and going wild, licking and pulling gently. I thrash beneath him when the climax swallows me.

It hits me hard, and it's the sexiest feeling ever. I'm shuddering, my thighs closing around his head.

Elias never releases me, his mouth licking my wet core, holding onto it like it's a challenge to drive me to insanity with my orgasm. I shake with how incredible my body feels, with how I'm still floating when he finally releases me from his hold. He kneels back, licking his lips before wiping his chin with the back of his hand.

"Fuck me, you are delicious. Sweet and salty and the best kind of candy."

I stare up at him, breathless, my body buzzing and I'm still tingling all over. "You are a god."

He laughs at me, then grabs my hips and turns me onto my side. "I can definitely be that for you, little rabbit." He flops down onto the bed behind me, then pushes one of his legs between mine, parting them.

Only then do I feel the press of his cock sliding against my pussy.

I moan, needing him inside me, and shift my pelvis to welcome him.

He plunges into me, spreading me, and I scream my pleasure this time, the sensation overwhelming me.

With him buried in me up to the hilt, he loops his arms around my middle and presses me to his chest, locking me in place.

"Now, we rest, little rabbit."

"Um, you are still inside of me. Are we not fucking?"

He chuckles. "We will be a bit later, but for now I want to be inside you, to own you, to feel you clamping around me each time you move. And when I can't take it another second, I'll fuck you hard."

I'm pulsing at his words, at the way he is enjoying my body.

"Rest," he tells me.

My heart is close to bursting with how hard it beats, how my desire spikes. He's huge and I can sense him in there, consuming me. He's got me in his arms, yet just having him deep inside me does things I never expected. To have him control me this way is the most captivating torture.

"You're going to kill me," I gasp, my body shifting as he reaches up under my shirt, cupping my breast.

"If that means bringing you to orgasm again and again, then yes," he whispers in my ear. "I want to feel your pussy sucking down on my cock."

"You're not doing a good job of getting me to rest," I respond, moving ever so slightly, this time completely on purpose to get a stir out of him. He's not the only one who can gain control of the situation.

He pinches my nipples and I moan, wriggling more, needing the friction only he can offer.

"Please, Elias, your teasing is so unfair."

He must finally decide he can no longer take it either as his hand falls onto my hip and he pulls out of me.

I protest and pout at him, but his devilish grin tells me this is too much for him. He gets to his knees and roughly grabs my hips, forcing me onto my hands and knees. He kneels between my legs, nudging them wider.

"Is this what you want?" He pushes his cock into me once more, this time with the force of a storm, and he's fucking me madly now.

"Oh hell, this is it... yes!"

He reaches deep within me, hitting hard. My whole body quivers each time he slaps into me. My body flushes with heat, and I'm panting.

That familiar force inside me intensifies just as fast as it had the first time he brought me to orgasm. It surges through me from my toes all the way to my ears. Every inch of me is pulsing with an unbearable need.

"I can feel you tightening. Come for me," he orders.

My head spins with how turned on I am, and with his next thrust into me, my body loses all control.

I throw my head back and scream as my whole core trembles and aches with the most insane climax. Elias growls and pauses while deep inside me, he's throbbing, filling me with his seed. Every part of me convulses, my pussy gripping his cock.

I am convinced that if I tried to stand up now, my knees would buckle from the sensations claiming me.

With a loud groan, he finally pulls out of me and collapses onto the bed, the mattress bouncing beneath me.

"Come here, little rabbit." He collects me by my waist and tugs me against him, now facing one another. We're both breathing quickly, and all that remains between us is the beautiful glow of our orgasms.

He kisses my lips, and I press in against his chest, my palms against his burning hot skin.

"That was the perfect distraction," I murmur.

Elias doesn't respond at first, we both just lie in bed, my eyes growing heavy. Our bodies are tangled together beautifully, and only when I feel myself dozing off do I hear words falling from his lips.

"I'm losing myself to you, and it scares the hell out of me."

SEVENTEEN

In Purgatory, Elias and I sit in our normal place beside the stage. It's a circular booth and set far enough back that we can observe the crowds and employees without being noticed. It's also where we hold most of our meetings. At least, the ones that don't need extreme privacy. There's a back room for those. And for the ones where the guests need a little rough handling? Well, those are taken care of in the basement. For the mess.

This time, we have an appointment with Dalmer and Bechem again, local cartel members who run all the drug dealings in Glenside. The human side of it. And, being more old fashioned in my ways, I prefer to handle our monetary transactions in person instead of direct electronic transfers. Why? For one, there is no paper trail for someone to follow, and two, there's a level of intimidation I want to make sure they leave with. So they know they can't fuck with us, even with them not knowing what we are.

In this business, it's important to have a presence and stay at the top of the food chain. That's the reason I have Elias with me tonight. I've handled Dalmer and Bechem just fine on my own before, but tonight, there's some information I suspect they'll not want to share with us without a little persuasion. And they've never encountered Elias and his quick temper before.

Speaking of the hellhound beside me, he fidgets in his seat, his fingers drumming against his arms as he continues to glance at the club's front door for the two men.

"Patience, Elias," I coax him, and readjust the cuffs of my suit's jacket.

He snorts. "They're late."

I glance at my watch. He's right. It's twelve past nine. Annoyance pinches the back of my neck. All our associates know I'm not someone you want to keep waiting. My time is precious and it's disrespectful.

"If they don't show—"

"They will," I snap, my own aggravation growing. "They know better."

He rolls his shoulders, looking uncomfortable. And my guess is that he is. Elias never likes being cooped up inside any space for too long. That's the wild animal in him.

But tonight, I need him at Purgatory not just for this meeting, but for Aria's safety.

"I wouldn't have asked you here if it wasn't important, but now with hellhounds after Aria, you are the best one of us to protect her. You know your kind."

His yellow eyes slide my way. "You're right."

Of course I am.

Elias nods toward the bar where Aria's picking up a tray of drinks for one of her tables. In a pair of shredded black shorts, fishnet stockings, and a blood red corset, she looks delicious, and it's near impossible not to think about replaying our little Red Room encounter together. Wrapping those slender legs around my neck as she grinds against my face, screaming my name as I devour her.

Unfortunately, I can't indulge tonight. Business has to come first.

But, there is always later...

"Has she seemed off to you at all?" Elias's question breaks my train of thought. "Like Dorian said from the other day? It's like one moment, she's standoffish, then later in the day, she's affectionate."

"No, I haven't. Not besides her being a bit more quiet and reserved, but we all know she's been through a great deal recently."

"She wasn't quiet with me before." He gives me a wolfish grin, and I set my jaw. Suddenly, Elias's gaze flicks to the front of the club and he jumps to his feet. "Finally. Shit."

Following his line of sight, I find the two men we've been waiting to see walking inside. One of the bouncers points our way and Dalmer and Bechem stroll over to us. While I remain sitting, Elias moves to stand beside me, pulling his shoulders back and taking his place as intimidator.

Dalmer is the first to speak when he reaches the table. "Sorry, we're—"

"Late." A growl rumbles in Elias's throat, his lip curling over a sharpened canine.

I throw him a hard glare. He needs to remember these are humans, not ordinaries. They don't know about our world, and I don't feel like unleashing that chaos.

Dalmer and Bechem both find Elias hovering close and his muscles bulging. They immediately step back.

Good.

Neither of them have moved to take a seat yet. They stand rigidly in place.

"We're sorry for keeping you waiting," Dalmer begins, and runs a finger under the collar of his shirt. He has tattoos of thorned roses creeping up his neck and his shaved head. "We had a bit of trouble with this new gang who's trying to move into our territory."

A new gang? Why hadn't I heard about this?

"Call themselves fucking Nightwalkers. They're getting into our business with this new drug. Hush," Bechem adds.

Hush... Where have I heard that before?

That's right. On the radio in the Town Car.

I think back. If I'm remembering correctly, it'd said Hush was a new drug circulating the city and killing humans. Possibly even supernaturals too.

He pulls out his cell phone from his jacket pocket, presses the screen a few times before turning it for us to see. A picture of an upside-down triangle with a cross through its middle. The same one I'd seen on the Queen Ann town home's front door... where the vampires were hiding. "They've been painting these all over town. It's their gang tag. Have you seen it before?"

I glance at Elias. He has recognized the symbol as well.

A new vampire master in Glenside, and a new gang pedaling a hardcore drug at the same time? Not exactly a coincidence.

"Our car was ambushed on our way here," Dalmer says with a grimace. "Blew out the windows of our limo, but we managed to make it out of there. My money's on it being them. Nightwalkers."

"And this drug they're pedaling? What do you know of it?" I ask.

"Only that it's strong as shit. Hella addictive, but the high is said to send you straight to Heaven... *If* you survive it," he replies. "Otherwise, it's sending you to Heaven or Hell for real."

Elias scoffs.

"Has to be some overseas stuff. Maybe from India or some other eastern country." Bechman rubs the stubble darkening his jawline. "We've never seen anything like it. And I've been in this business since I could walk."

Dalmer chimes in again. "We wanted to see if you could help us snuff them out. They're moving into our city and they're doing it fast. I don't know how they were able to get so many members on their side so quickly."

I have a pretty good idea. If the Nightwalkers are tied to the master vamp, Stephan, like I'm assuming, there's no limit to how many children he can create. Especially if he's old and powerful enough. He's building up an army for a hostile takeover. In our town.

There's no way we're going to let that happen.

"We're already looking into it," I say. The relief on the men's faces is instantaneous. "Glenside is ours. And that's how it's going to stay."

They exchange a quick glance with each other and then nod their thanks. They're just about to finally take their seats across from me when Elias throws out an arm, his entire body as rigid as stone. His head tilts up, his eyes trained on the front of the club.

I'd know that stance anywhere. Something's wrong.

My gaze flies to the crowd on the dance floor. "What—" But my sentence is cut off the moment I find five large men shoving their way through the masses, sights set on us. One of them flashes fangs at me.

Vampires. And from the looks of it, they're gearing for a fight.

"Nightwalkers," Elias snarls, confirming my thoughts. Dalmer and Bechem whip around. Spotting them, they pull out their handguns from their hiding spots, but instead of turning them on the Nightwalkers, they spin toward me and Elias.

A shot blares over the music, and I feel the burning pain of the bullet as it embeds into my shoulder. I look down, seeing red bubble up and stain my suit jacket. Rage rises with it, and heat floods every inch of me.

We've been betrayed.

Peering up at the two humans again, I know my demon is peeking through. There is horror reflected on each of their faces.

When I speak, my voice is deeper and more gravely. "You chose the wrong side."

Elias is suddenly behind Bechem and, before he can even turn, Elias grabs the sides of his head and wrenches hard, snapping his neck. He collapses.

Dalmer jerks his weapon toward Elias, and I rush at him, seize him by the throat, and toss him clear across the room. His body slams against one of the black marble columns and he crumbles onto the floor. If he's not dead, he'll be paralyzed for his entire life. There's no way he'll be able to raise a gun again.

People rush out of the way, clearing the area. Some hurry for the exits. With all the commotion, the vampires leap at us. Elias rushes them like an angry bull and takes two down at once. His skin ripples with the need to shift, but he holds his beast back, fighting in his human form instead.

When Dorian, Elias, and I first opened Purgatory, we had agreed to not show our demons unless absolutely necessary, since some of our guests were ordinaries—humans born to or among supernaturals who know of the magical—and had never encountered a Hell-dwelling creature before. Exposing ourselves often could result in fear and ultimately hurt our bottom line.

But even though Elias is wearing skin instead of fur, it doesn't make him any less of a killer. He's just as skilled with his fists as he is with his teeth and claws, and it isn't long before blood soaks the floor and splatters up the walls.

More club-goers dash for the exits. The remaining vamps split as they charge me, two going right while one sprints forward. Fangs bared, he jumps onto a table and then up the wall, moving in a blur of speed. As I track his movements, something sharp pierces into my neck and pain slices into me.

Fuck. One of the bloodsuckers had managed to bury their fangs into my neck.

Roaring, I reach behind me, grab the bastard by the shirt, haul him over my head, and slam him on the ground. He takes a chunk of my neck with him, and white-hot pain blinds me temporarily. I waver on my feet, and before I can right myself again, I'm struck in the side of the head by the other vamp. More blood fills my mouth.

Okay. I've humored these Nightwalkers for too long. It's time to end this.

Slowly, I straighten and roll my neck. My gaze flicks from the vampire on the floor and the one in front of me. The one at my feet has my blood all over his mouth, and the sight has my demon fighting for release. Muscles tensing, my wings stretch under my skin. The blood leaking from my wounds darkens, and I'm struggling to hold the monster back.

Using all my strength, I call my inner fire to my fist and punch it straight into the vamp on the floor's chest. Bones shatter and the heat melts away flesh and muscle. My fingers wrap around his heart and I yank it out. He shudders one last time before slumping. Dead.

My head snaps up to see the other vampire backing up slowly. Even without my wings, I'm sure I'm an intimidating sight, with my eyes as black as ink and lines weaving over my skin. I watch as his confidence drains until only fear remains. I feed off it. Bathe in it. And I lick my lips.

"Oh, how delicious souls taste when absolute terror clings to them," I say, my voice nothing more than a rumble.

He spins, hoping to run, but slams directly into Elias's chest. There's a new gash across his cheek and specks of blood paint his face and clothes.

Elias's eyes spark. "I agree."

Panicking, the young vamp stumbles back but halts the moment he sees me hovering close. He's stuck in between us.

As I step toward him, a high-pitched scream rings out.

Gaze whipping toward the bar, my first thought is Aria and my heart falters. But that's when I see the one missing vampire out of the five chasing Charlotte across the club.

Shit. Looks like we weren't the only targets in this attack.

I look back at Elias and give him a nod. A simple gesture, but one that has everything he needs to know in it.

As I hurry after Charlotte, the audible crack of bone comes from behind me as Elias ends the pathetic Nightwalker's life.

EIGHTEEN

ARIA

A gunshot blares, and the music stops abruptly. I freeze in place, gaze immediately searching for Cain and Elias in the chaos. I find them at the opposite side of the room, Cain with a hole blown out of his shoulder and the blood already welling to the surface.

I drop my tray, panic crawling up my throat. I'm about to rush over to him, but a rough hand seizes me by the arm and yanks me back up and over the bar. I land on my ass, and when I look up, I spot Antonio squatting by me with a finger to his lips. Sting is there, too, huddled near a stack of crates.

Antonio waves to Sting. "Take Aria out the back," he says in a quick whisper. "Get her out of here."

I shake my head frantically. "No, I'm not going anywhere. Cain's—"

"Cain's a big boy. He can take care of himself." He reaches for me again, and I jerk away, my annoyance growing.

"It's your funeral." Antonio crawls over to Sting and they disappear around the bend.

Vicious snarls and hisses rise over the noise, and I get to my feet. Club-goers scatter, heading for the exits. Elias is ripping apart two vampires, while Cain is flipping another over his shoulders. More blood leaks from a missing chunk on his neck.

My veins ice over, and suddenly, I'm shaking all over. I can't stop thinking about how deathly he looked after our big fight with Sir Surchion, and how close I'd come to losing him then. I don't know how I'd ever cope. Pain spikes through me just at the thought.

I feel Sayah rising, her darkness swirling inside me and spreading. My chest squeezes, my breaths coming rapid and uneven, and my head throbs.

It's like whenever I'd hold her back for too long, keeping her dark spirit in instead of releasing her—she becomes too much, like she's consuming me. But unlike those times before, energy bounces within me, and all I want to do is take every single one of the vampires and tear them apart. Limb from limb. Blood spurting everywhere. That dark craving surges through me, deepening with each passing second.

It's a sickening thought, one I *know* is wrong, but I don't care. My voice of reason is growing tinier by the second; it's being swallowed by evilness, too. It's the same conflicting feeling I had while holding the angel blade at Maverick's throat, and again while out with Dorian. The need to kill... The desire to cause someone's death with my own hands... It's there again, this time stronger than ever before. Sayah is taking over.

Even more unnerving? I'm not afraid.

I don't want to fight her. I don't know if I can.

But I'm... excited at the same time.

What is Sayah doing to me?

I don't have too much time to dwell on it, because suddenly Charlotte is sprinting past me and there's a vampire on her heels. Since he's lightning fast, he's on her in seconds, wrapping his arm around her throat from behind and curling his lips over his fangs. She screams.

My gaze darkens, my fury whipping through me like a hurricane. I spy the tray I had dropped on the floor, covered in broken glass from the drinks, and I snatch it.

Not my friend, asshole!

With both hands, I slam it across the back of the vamp's head with all my strength.

ELIAS

I can't believe what I just witnessed. Aria struck a vampire with a serving tray.

Even more surprising is how far he's been thrown from the force of it, skidding across the dancefloor feet away. The tray in Aria's hand has snapped in two.

Fucking hell.

I know the woman has some balls, but vampires are high up on the supernatural power scale because of their speed and strength. Yet, she'd managed to send one clear across the club with one whack.

How is that even possible?

Even Cain is stunned, halting mid-stride as the fallen vamp slides to his feet. Charlotte's rubbing her neck, breathing hard and trying to make sense of what just happened. We all can't seem to come up with a logical explanation.

My small and delicate little rabbit took down a vampire? Now I've seen everything.

That's when I see it. Black wisps of smoke curling around her limbs and orangey-gold light sparking across her skin. It's the same thing that happens whenever Sayah emerges and steals her essence to become more real. More solid.

But there's no Sayah that I can see. Just Aria.

"Ar-Aria?" Charlotte's voice shakes with fear.

Aria's chin lifts her way slowly, and whatever she sees makes her leap back in fear. Aria's muscles are stiff, her movements jerky and unnatural.

Something's definitely not right.

"Aria," Cain calls, a bit more forcefully. It's enough to grab her attention. Her head whips our way, but her gaze is blank, looking through us.

"Aria," he says again more gently. He starts to move closer to her with cautious steps. "Are you okay?"

She doesn't blink. Only stares with those big dark eyes of hers.

A shiver of warning snakes up my spine, and my hackles rise. My hound can sense the new danger standing before us, and it's conflicted whether to fight or submit, since it's coming from his claimed mate... our claimed mate.

Then, the smoke is sucked back into her and the strange light disappears. Aria blinks, the spell seemingly broken. She takes in a sharp breath before her eyes roll back and her knees give out.

Cain's by her side before she can hit the ground, catching her limp body in his arms and clutching her against his chest. Her head lolls to the side, and my chest clenches with dread. I hurry over.

As Cain examines her pale face and feels her neck for a pulse, I bounce on my feet. My fear makes it impossible to stay still.

"She's unconscious but alive," Cain explains, his voice deep and brimming with concern.

In the hundreds of years I've known him, I've rarely seen Cain worried. But it's clear whatever is happening with Aria has shaken him to the core.

"You saw what she did, right?" I ask, eyeing him.

He nods. "It must be the shadow creature inside her. It's getting stronger."

"Shit. It's trying a fucking hostile takeover."

Charlotte steps closer, her brow crinkled with worry. "Shadow creature? What's—"

"Quinn!" Cain beckons to one of Purgatory's guards. A bear-shifter I had recruited when we'd first started the club.

Quinn's hauling the vampire Aria had clocked toward the exit, but he pauses for Cain's instructions.

"When you're done there, I need you to bring Charlotte downstairs."

Charlotte's eyes widen. "Downstairs! But—"

"It's for your safety, Charlotte," he replies, cutting her off again. Not about to question him, she clamps her mouth shut. Usually, the basement here is used for interrogations, prisoner holding, torture, etc., but there are also some private rooms for employees or one of us to stay in if work shifts go on too long. My guess is that he means for her to stay in one of those.

Charlotte looks reluctant about the whole thing, but once she glances at Aria's unmoving form in Cain's arms, she only drops her head and walks over to Quinn.

I peer down at Aria and frown. Lucifer. Hellhounds. Vampires. And now Sayah. Everything's getting more complicated by the second. Not to mention dangerous. How are we going to protect Aria from all this?

"Still think we should let her have a choice in the binding ritual?" Cain asks me with a raised brow.

I grind my teeth. I know what he's referring to. We've already wasted a lot of time waiting on her to give us the okay on something that could protect her from Lucifer. Now we have to add a parasitic shadow spirit to the shit list.

"And what if she says no?" He searches Aria's face and runs a finger down her cheek tenderly. "Are you going to be able to let her die?"

I don't speak. Just the notion of losing her tears me up inside. I refuse to even think about it.

From the way he's looking at her and touching her face, it's clear he's not ready to give her up either.

"Because you know that's what'll happen if she refuses," he goes on, pain in his voice.

"I know, dammit. I know," I snap, anger rising. He's right and I know it. But fuck.

What are we going to do?

NINETEEN

After a long day of doing nothing, especially after the explosion of brutal fighting at Purgatory last night, I am starting to come to a realization.

I am a magnet for danger.

I used to think it was the demons, but now I know it's me.

It's been one chaotic encounter after another, and I seem to be the one constant feature. Chaos loves me. And after the vampire encounters, Sayah's ever-growing influence over me, and my lack of control with everything, it's becoming a bit too much.

Worry whirls in my mind, while emotions twist in my gut from everything.

When I woke up, I was in my bed at the mansion with all three demons hovering over me. I'd blacked out after what'd happened in Purgatory, the last thing I remember is me seeing Charlotte being chased by a vampire and picking up the tray. That's it.

Elias claimed I struck the vamp with it and had somehow sent him flying across the club. At first I thought he'd been exaggerating, but when I noticed the concern furrowed in Cain's brow, I knew he wasn't.

That's when I remembered Sayah's darkness washing over me and the immense power I'd felt. Also, the need for destruction and death. It was overwhelming. Addictive.

It seems like ever since my trip to Hell, she's become stronger.

She is in my head. In my soul, and I don't know how I'm going to beat her. What if she ends up taking over me completely?

I feel out of control.

A crack of thunder roars outside, so loud that the house seems to tremble under its force.

"I love storms," Dorian tells me. We're both in his room, staring outside the enormous windows at the black sky, the heavy rain, and the brilliant flashes of lightning.

"They're perfect for reading," I respond, leaning back against his chest as he holds me close. There's a comfort to being wanted, especially when beneath the calm, I sense the war in my veins. But maybe I've been looking at this wrong and I need to take a new approach. I need to find out everything I can about hellhounds, maybe even Sayah, before things get even more out of control. "Does the library in this mansion happen to have anything on demons and hellhounds?"

Dorian turns me to face him by my waist. "What do you want to know?"

"I hate just sitting around and waiting for the next attack. Maybe there are answers I can find in a book? Something to get rid of at least one of my problems."

The corner of his mouth quirks upward. "You have a hellhound living in this house who can answer everything you need. And after that encounter with Maverick the other night, I am convinced he will put a stop to them returning. None have returned since."

"I know, but what if they come back, or Lucifer re-releases them? And trust me, I've picked Elias's brain. But from everything he tells me, they are unstoppable once sent. The only way to stop them is to brutally slay them. But that only sends them back to Hell anyway." I sigh, frustration billowing under my breastbone. "I hate being vulnerable and I need to guard myself somehow. I can't do it with strength like you, but maybe I can use my wits if I have more knowledge."

He looks at me for a long moment when a resolute look crosses his face. "Alright, then I know exactly the place to take you."

"You do?" I perk up, almost bouncing on my toes. "Not here?"

"There's no guarantee you will find anything new that Elias hasn't told you, but if it will put you at ease, I can take you to the Reverie Bibliotheca. It's an ancient library open only for supernaturals, mostly dealing with customs of different races and histories. But there is a section in the private part about demons." He smirks. "You may even find some things about me!" He wriggles his eyebrows. "Though you've got to take it with a grain of salt, as much of it was written by non-demons, meaning it's exaggerated."

"Now, you've got me curious. Can we go now?"

He glances outside where the storm is hammering into the landscape. "In this storm?"

I'm nodding before he asks. "It will help me calm down."

"Then it's done." His hand slides into mine, our fingers intertwined, and we leave his room.

By the time we tell the others where we're going and we are into the car, I breathe easy. The heavy rains have melted a lot of the snow, and the roads are mostly empty of other cars, but they are also slippery. This encourages Dorian to drive in the middle of the road and avoid the huge puddles on the sides.

In the city, I stare at people running into buildings and stores to avoid the weather, most in business suits, seeing as it's the middle of the workday. We pass by Storm's underpass entrance and follow the road around to the rear, where there are several office buildings all pressed up against each other like giants on either side of the road. Tinted windows, dark walls, and no signs of what's inside.

Dorian swerves into a driveway toward a closed garage gate. He opens his window, allowing in a swirl of cold wind and rain. In haste, he hits the buzzer and speaks to someone on the intercom in a different language.

Moments later, the metal gate rolls upward, and we're gliding indoors, away from the storm.

"Security for a library. Intense," I say, taking in the underground parking area, half filled with cars.

"They have to keep the humans out." He swerves into a parking spot right next to two passages. One has the words Storm above it, the other, Bibliotheca. "You can enter the Storm through here too?"

"Yep, it's just a bit of a long-winded walk, and you've still got to pass through more security."

"Good to know there's another passage."

In minutes, we are heading toward the library, and around the bend we come to a set of black doors made of metal.

Dorian raises his hand and places his palm flat against the surface just above the golden handle, which is in the shape of a wolf's head. Instantly, a red light glows around his hand and fingers. Then in a heartbeat, it flicks to green and a loud click sounds.

"We're in," he says, pushing down on the handle and looking over at me.

"Only certain people are permitted inside?"

He laughs. "Think of it as a library card. You need to register to get in, so if you want, we can get you all signed up?"

"Yes. I would love that."

We stroll through the door and come to a large set of marble steps, the railings made of gold. Gone are the cement walls, replaced with a hallway that might belong in a castle.

Up the stairs, we emerge into a great foyer where on one side is a counter with several people typing on computers, while others are lined up in front of them, I'm guessing to borrow books? Or maybe ask for references?

Dorian takes me in the opposite direction, through an ornate doorway and into an enormous room that takes my breath away.

I gasp with awe.

The long, narrow room stretches outward so far, I can't possibly see where it ends. Every inch of the walls are covered in bookshelves, fitted with ladders on wheels. Running down the middle are wooden writing desks, each with only two chairs and a golden lamp with the lights switched on. There's a grand staircase to the far left that takes you to the next two levels that appear just as immense. I crane my neck up to the ceiling, that is mostly made of glass, light pouring inside, while rain hits the window. Except there's no sound coming from outside.

"Wow, I am sure I just walked into the library from Beauty and the Beast. And you said there was not a lot here. This is humongous."

He laughs softly against the silence. "You should see the libraries back in Hell. They carry texts on every topic in the world. We've had demons get lost in the maze of books and are never seen again."

"That sounds very overwhelming."

"Come this way." He guides me right past the staircase and to the far rear wall, to yet another doorway that leads us to a set of descending stairs. The walls are a luminescent blue and if I look close enough I swear there are fish swimming inside the walls.

Dorian takes me into another room, one laid out the same as the first library room, with the exception of no staircase or window in the ceiling. Burning torches hang off the walls from metal brackets, giving the room a demonic feel. Of course they would keep those books down here. Though it is strange to see a row of computers to my right in a place that seems to have stepped back in time.

Only one other person is in this section, an older man sitting at one of the desks with a dozen books piled up next to him.

"This place looks amazing," I whisper. "Only thing missing is a cup of hot chocolate."

"There are many rules I will break for you, but losing my library privileges isn't one of them. Sorry, gorgeous. I'll get you one on the way home."

"It's good to know you have limitations," I tease him.

He smirks and leads me to the computers. "Alright, let's research and see what we can find for you."

Hours must pass, but it's hard to tell in a room with no windows or clocks. Time stands still here.

My desk is stacked with books. Everything I read on hellhounds mirrors what Elias told me. There is literally no way to stop them once they are unleashed, aside from physically fighting them. So, that sucks, and leaves me disheartened.

Dorian is reclining in a chair across the desk from me, his chin tucked into his chest, and fast asleep. I drag the last book across the table in front of me and sigh. "You better have something new for me." It's leather bound with only a golden pentagram stamped on the front. No words, but it was in the same vicinity of the other hellhound books, so I figured it might contain something.

The hardback book creaks as I pull it open, the print on the pages so tiny, it makes me cross-eyed trying to read it. I flick to the index and scan it for hellhounds or shadow demons, aka Sayah, when another word catches my attention.

Lucifer.

Intrigue has me quickly flipping to the first few pages. Maybe I've been searching for the wrong thing. Maybe I should have focused on the big guy himself.

I scan the paragraphs, passing the usual stuff on him falling from grace, and being imprisoned in Hell, then stop on an interesting passage. One that explains Lucifer had turned the situation to his favor by claiming the underworld as his kingdom. That he grew so powerful that even those in Heaven started to fear him.

He has limitations though, and my attention piques. Leaving Hell is a possibility for him, but only for a limited time with a lot of saved up power. It renders him weak the longer he stays outside, which is why he rarely leaves the kingdom.

I think back to his visit to the mansion, to how swiftly he popped in and out. He had used up his power just to make his presence known.

Refocusing on the text, I keep reading until I pause on the passage about his sons.

I blink at the words, at the list of all seven names and their deadly identity. Of course, Cain is first as the oldest and named as Pride. Then there's Torryn as Wrath, Nix, who I'd met already in Hell, as Lust, Lorcan as Envy, Valdim as Gluttony, who Elias and Dorian had mentioned at the restaurant, Raziel as Sloth, and finally, Maverick as Greed.

It says in the book that each son was created when Lucifer wanted help ruling his dominion. He found a way to rip apart his soul into seven pieces, one for each of his most sinful attributes. Then the deadly sins, and the first demons were born.

Woah. That means Cain is actually the very first demon ever made. That means he must be centuries—no thousands—of years old! I can't even wrap my head around that.

I keep reading, but don't find much else interesting or that can help us. While the demons' origins are interesting, I knew it all already. Cain had explained it to me, but what I still don't understand is what had held Lucifer back from killing him when their uprising failed? Clearly it wasn't any kind of fatherly love.

Lucifer had chosen to banish him, when really, he's crazy enough to slay anyone else on a drop of a dime. There has to be a reason *why*. Something we aren't seeing. But what?

My eyes skim over the words again. *Wanting help to rule his dominion, he found a way to split his soul into seven pieces...*

Split his soul.

Wait a minute.

"Oh shit."

Dorian snaps awake, flinching as he looks around, lost.

"What's? What? What is it? What's wrong?" he barks loud enough that the older man across the room hushes us.

"Read this," I tell him and push the giant book across the table to him. He turns it to face him, and I lean over to point at the important paragraphs before flopping back into my seat.

He reads it and his brows pinch at the center in confusion.

"We knew this already," he says. "The story of the deadly sins isn't really a secret."

"Not that... Think about it, Dorian. Lucifer split his *own* soul into pieces to create his sons. And when one of them rises up against him, he doesn't kill him. That's the ultimate betrayal, and yet he only banishes him to Earth to get him out of the way, when he'll slit anyone else's throat without a second thought."

He waits for me to continue.

"He didn't kill Cain because he *can't* kill him."

His gaze searches my face, his own confusion still apparent.

"Don't you see? If he kills Cain, he kills a part of his own soul. He'd be making himself vulnerable."

I watch the realization cross over his face, and his mouth drops open. "Holy shit."

"Exactly." That means we have an advantage here. He can't touch Cain. Well, kill him anyway. Not without harming himself.

"We need to talk to Cain." Dorian is on his feet, already collecting the books to return to the shelves.

I hurry and grab Dorian's phone that he's left on the table. Flicking the screen on, I pause when I see the picture of the two of us in Scotland as his new phone wallpaper.

A smile creeps across my lips. Oh, my sweet, sweet demon.

As Dorian comes back, I take quick snaps of the important page for Cain and Elias and close the book shut. He takes it and returns to a nearby shelf, then spins me practically off my feet.

"I should've known better." He kisses me, and I can't help myself but kiss him like my life depends on it, our bodies pressed so close, he heats me up in seconds. "You might have just found something we can use against Lucifer."

"When you say it like that, I feel like I need some kind of reward."

His eyebrows arch, and that hypnotic look crosses his eyes. He kisses me again, but it's short lived as the older man in the library clears his throat louder. We both twist our heads to look at him, and he's wriggling his finger at us.

I can't help but giggle under my breath, feeling like I've just been busted kissing a guy under the high school bleachers.

Dorian sets me back on my feet, takes my hand, and we are flying out of there. In no time, we are in his Ferrari and driving back home through the horrid weather.

"I have the best plan for us when we get back," he tells me, cutting me a sexy look when he looks across to me.

"And what's that?"

"After we tell Cain and Elias what we found, we retire to my room. I get the fire roaring and you sit on fur rugs in front of the flames while I bring you a hot chocolate. Of course, you must be completely naked. After that, I will have my way with you."

I laugh at his confidence. "You sure that's how it's going to go?"

"I have no doubts. I will make it happen."

"Well, I admire your determination. You create it and I will be there."

When he turns to look at me quickly, I wink at him, and he howls laughing. "Girl, you know I can't back down from a challenge."

I grin and press my back into my seat, staring outside the side window, at the vicious winds beating into the car, at the puddles of rain, the sludgy snow in the woods we pass. Despite the horrible weather, I am glad we went out. I hope that the information we discovered on Lucifer will benefit us in evading him... somehow.

Dorian's hand is on my thigh, slowly creeping up, his fingers sliding between my thighs. Even through my jeans, I feel the heat of his touch, and it sends a shiver of excitement through me.

The gates to the mansion remain open for our return, and we thread down the path onto the property. Trees shake wildly, and Dorian's getting close to popping open the button on my jeans.

"Hey." I slap his hand. "You said in your room."

"Yeah, well, I lied. I want to touch you here and now." He grabs the top part of my jeans and pulls the zipper open, making my body wobble from his aggression.

His hand is relentless and he's already sliding his fingers down the front of my pants and under my underwear. Of course, I don't go out of my way to stop him because secretly I want everything he promises.

The car jerks to the side, and I grip the door's handle. "Dorian!"

He laughs as he rights the car again and we continue down the driveway. His fingers continue their exploration, despite the dangerous weather and him driving. "You're perfect, Aria, the most beautiful thing I've ever looked at."

He finds the silky heat between my legs, his middle finger plunging deeper, coaxing a moan out of me.

I'm weak, I admit it. How can I say no to him when every fiber in my body craves him?

"You're so wet, so smooth. It's fucking torture to be away from you, and it's been too long since I had you."

"Is that what you want?"

"Yes. I want all of you. To rip the clothes off your gorgeous body, to hear your cries for more, to feel your nipples harden in my mouth as I plunge my cock into you." He's breathless, keeping his eyes on the driveway, bringing us closer to the mansion with one hand on the steering wheel and one in my pants. When he comes to a stop, putting the car in park in the driveway, he pushes a finger deeper into me, and I press my back into my seat, my body humming.

"Sounds like you've been giving this a lot of thought," I murmur.

"You have no clue." I meet his gaze as my breathing speeds up with need, arousal driving me to melt under his touch.

Leaning closer, I grab him by his shirt and kiss him while spreading my legs to give him easier access. Our lips mash, our teeth hitting with the urgency that now drives our pulse.

"You're right," I whisper against his mouth. "These clothes are getting in the way. Pants need to go."

I reach down between us and stroke his heavy cock through his jeans, and he hisses at the way I rub him. We shuffle about as I attempt to push my pants down my hips, unable to believe how brazen I feel to let Dorian take me here where anyone from the mansion could see us.

Lifting my gaze, I look in that direction of the lake that wraps around the property when something catches my attention.

Dorian's lips are on my neck, his finger deep inside me, and I'm moaning, but unable to tear my eyes from the water. Something seems to be shifting across the surface near the bank.

Next thing I see is a huge black figure emerging from the water.

"Jesus Christ, what is that?"

"Don't bring up his name right now, sweetie, and it's my second finger in your sweet pussy that you're feeling."

"No." I wriggle, but he refuses to let go of me. "That out there! Please don't tell me it's a hellhound?"

Dorian stiffens and looks out, quickly pulling his hand out from inside my pants. He stares out to the water. He licks his fingers as if he's uncertain if he'll fuck me first, or deal with whatever the heck that is.

He's blinking, leaning over me for a better look. "Doesn't look like a hellhound."

"Well, maybe it's another Loch Ness shifter," I say.

Dorian pulls back. We're both plastered to the window, staring out past the rain and to the thing hauling itself out of the water. Whatever it is, it's struggling to walk, and it isn't long before it collapses on all fours on the bank of the lake.

"It looks more like the monster from the black lagoon" he says, both of us breathing quicker now.

"Maybe you should go check it out," I suggest.

"In this weather?"

"Will you melt?"

He cuts me a look.

"Aren't you supposed to be a deadly and powerful demon?"

"I am, but I'm also not stupid," he answers and flops back into his seat. "I say we drive back to the mansion and send Elias out there after it."

"Wow. Did you just refer to Elias as your own personal bodyguard?"

He shrugs, throwing the gear into drive. "He is a hellhound and loves the hunt."

We are now rolling slowly down the driveway, closer to where the black creature is stumbling to get onto two feet. Rain pelts everything, water puddles everywhere.

It's only when we are several feet away from the lake monster that it lifts its head and looks at me.

We lock eyes.

I catch my breath and press my face to the window, staring at those familiar eyes, a familiar face, familiar lips.

"Shit, it's Viktor!" I call out, more out of shock than Dorian not being able to hear me.

He slams the brakes, and not that we were going fast, but it still sends me jolting forward since I'm not wearing my seat belt.

"Are you fucking kidding me?" Dorian tears out of the car, and I'm scrambling to follow him, while doing up the zipper of my jeans.

The rain hits me fast, soaking me in seconds, sliding underneath my shirt and down my back with its icy touch. I hiss under my breath while rushing over to him, my shoes hitting puddles, water seeping into them.

"Viktor!" I call out.

Dorian reaches him first, and the master vampire collapses into his arms.

"What the hell was he doing in your lake?"

"Fuck if I know, but we're about to find out."

"He's awake," I state, as Viktor's eyes flicker open. He's sitting on a chair in the middle of the hallway with towels around him from the water he's dripping all over the place.

Cain kneels by his side. "My friend, what happened to you? Everyone's been searching for you."

"How'd you end up in our lake?" Dorian asks directly, while Elias studies the vampire head to toe. Viktor is paler than usual, which says a lot for an undead. His dark hair is plastered to his head, his lips blue, and he's wearing a torn up, black cape with dark clothes underneath.

He coughs and suddenly spews out a mouthful of dirty lake water. I rear back as it splashes everywhere, and I am certain a tiny fish just came out of his mouth too. Eww.

Dorian wrinkles his nose, flicking the splash of water off his pants.

Elias marches out of there quickly and returns moments later with a glass of water. "To clear your throat," he offers, to which Viktor accepts and drinks several mouthfuls.

"My Char," he groans, meaning Charlotte before clearing his throat once more. "Where is she?"

"She's safe," Cain tells him. "But she is worried about you."

"As she should be, obviously. What the heck happened?" Dorian asks.

Viktor straightens in his seat, gaining his composure, and already I see the powerful vampire returning, a darkness sliding behind his eyes. "New vampires entered my territory, so I went to remind them who I was. Except, they knew I was coming. They've been watching us, all of us, including you four, and they jumped me just as I left my home. The fucking bastards anticipated my move." His body shakes, his jaw clenching. "They tossed me into your lake for one purpose." He looks at Cain as he talks, his fingers grabbing the fabric of his drenched black shirt and wrenching it up to reveal a huge wound above his heart. Purple skin surrounds the injury, dark veins sprawling outward under the flesh.

I gasp. "That looks painful."

"It hurts like hell, but once I feed, it will heal." He pauses and lowers his shirt, wincing from the pain. How long had he been in that lake before he woke up? "They wanted me dead so that you, Cain, could find me. They wanted to deliver a message that you are next if you stand in their way."

"Do they even know who Cain is?" Dorian blurts out.

My mind stills on the words that Cain is next, because don't we already have enough on our plate?

"I doubt it. But the fucking weasels missed my heart, so they expect me to be dead."

"And you will use that to your advantage. Get Charlotte and go into hiding. Let them think they have the upper hand, for now," Cain instructs.

"That was my plan as well, but don't be mistaken," Viktor states, his accent swirling around every word. "This new clutch of vampires is dangerous. Nightwalkers, they call themselves."

"Oh, we've already met them," Elias adds. "A few times actually. And gave them a good scare, I think. Well, at least Aria did."

Viktor turns to me with a questionable look.

"Long story," I mumble.

"Even so, I'm sure they haven't given up that easily," he continues. "Their numbers are growing, practically doubling, every day. They know me and my weakness." He glances at me again. "They hurt my Char to get to me."

Sweat breaks out across the back of my neck. I lift my gaze to Cain, finding the corded muscles in his neck tensing.

"And I will rip them apart with my bare hands for daring to enter my territory," he growls, covering me in shivers.

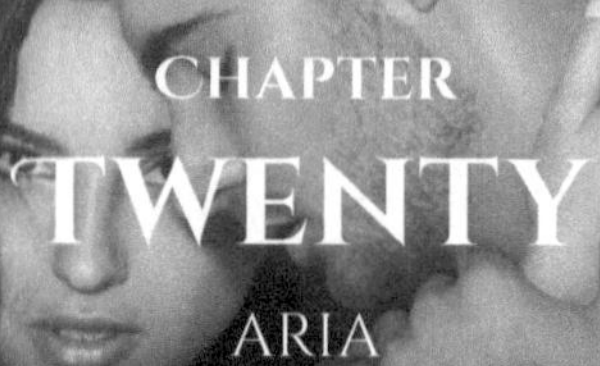

I've actually made up my mind. I'm doing the binding ritual. I can't take much more of this chaos. Hellhounds trying to track me down and drag me back to Hell? Vampire gangs raiding Purgatory, almost killing Viktor, and making it impossible to work and trying to take over the city... It's just too much. Even with the risk of something going wrong, the ritual is the only way to protect not only me, but *all* of us. And the way I see it, we're dead if we don't do it anyway, so I'm willing to take the chance.

Does the whole ritual thing scare me? You bet it does. Growing up, I never saw myself getting married to a human guy, and dating was hard enough when in foster care. I definitely didn't see myself being bound to three demons for all eternity. That was like getting married on steroids. Super steroids. And the entire thing freaks me out a bit.

But, if we can do it right and it can protect me from Lucifer, the vampires, and god knows whatever else is coming down the pike, I'll do it. My only hope is that it'll also be enough to keep me safe from Sayah, too.

Dealing with my unruly shadow spirit is a different kind of issue, one that frightens me the most, if I'm being honest. It's because I don't know what Sayah's fully capable of and I'd rather know my enemy than not.

Ever since I went to Hell, she's seemed stronger. It's like something down there triggered her power and now I can feel her dark influence weaving its way through my soul. Changing me. First, it was when I held the knife to Maverick's throat. I *wanted* to kill him. I *wanted* to slice his throat and play with his blood. Even more fucked up? Just the thought of it had turned me on.

I'd felt her poisoning me again during my date with Dorian. Losing Joseline had upset me a lot, and I think she used my sorrow to wiggle herself into my head again. I'd been able to push her back then, and things were quiet for a while, that is, until the other night in Purgatory with the Nightwalker vamps. Because of her, I'd managed to knock one of them clear across the room before passing out. I didn't possess that kind of strength on my own. It had to be Sayah's doing. It was as if she'd taken me over somehow. And that thought scares the shit out of me.

The last time I'd lost full control of her and blacked out, I had stopped letting her out, keeping all her darkness inside until my body couldn't take it anymore. A police officer had found me on the street, but I had no memory of how I got there or what had happened. The previous twenty-four hours were completely lost to me.

What if her darkness is overtaking me? What if I lose myself to her for good?

It's a terrifying thing to be going through, and one of the reasons I've been keeping to myself mostly. What else am I supposed to do when the woods are infested with hellhounds and work is being infiltrated by drug-dealing vampires?

So, I stay in my room. Every once in a while one of the demons will come to check in on me, but for the most part, it's just me and Cassiel. We've all agreed to do the ritual tonight, and since the full moon is still weeks away, we're performing it using the alternative method. Blood.

Gross, I know, but that's what we have to work with. Especially since Cain says it'll make the magic used during the ceremony even stronger and we need all the help we can get.

I peer down at Cassiel, who's looking up at me with his big eyes with his head on my lap. Sometimes I think he can sense my worrying. He seems to always know.

"Don't look at me like that," I whisper harshly, and readjust myself against my bed's pillows. "If you were me, you'd be freaking out, too."

He lifts his massive head, ears perking up suddenly, and body rigid.

I scratch between his ears. "It's just Sadie, Cass. Our dinner is probably here." I had asked for her to bring my plate to my room, since Elias was out walking the grounds hunting hellhounds, and he's the only one who'll really eat real food with me at the dining table. When he isn't around, like tonight, I'll just take the meal in my room.

I wait for the maid's tiny footsteps or her rap on the door, but when there is none, I hesitate.

Cassiel starts to growl.

My heart skips. My thoughts instantly go to unwanted visitors. Of the Hell variety.

Please, no more hellhounds. I'm becoming a cat person more and more every day.

"What is it, Cass? What do you hear?"

I expect him to turn toward the door, but he doesn't. He only stares at me.

"Uh... Sadie?" I call, my voice trembling with nerves. "Are you there?"

No answer.

Not a good sign.

Cassiel continues to watch me and growl. He climbs onto all fours and lowers his head like he's about to attack.

"Cass..." I say, confused. "It's me. Aria."

Still, he edges closer, a threatening warning rumbling in his throat.

Oh my god. He's lost his mind. He's going to hurt me.

Pulse jumping, I slowly get off the bed and begin backing up toward the door. I don't know what the heck is up with him—Cassiel always protects me—but a close to five-hundred-pound lynx could cause some damage if he wanted to.

Should I scream? Would anyone reach me in time? I doubt it.

As he hops off the bed and continues to stalk closer, my back hits the doorknob. I reach for it, ready to throw the door open and bolt down the hall as fast as I can, but movement on the floor at my feet catches my eye. My gaze drops to see Sayah slinking out of me, stretching and contorting her shape along the ground.

Cassiel's eyes lock onto her and his lips peel back over sharp canines.

He wasn't going to attack me. He had sensed Sayah before I had.

Sayah grows rapidly, and the tether binding us bursts with orange sparks. The strange dancing lights creep up the link until it consumes the massive shadow completely. As her form gains density, icy prickles shoot through my veins. There's no pain this time, and I don't know if that's necessarily a good or bad thing. It seems to confirm my suspicion about her gaining more power while we were in Hell.

Once she's hovering over me, her dark form adjusts and shifts, getting more of a distinct shape. Arms sprout out of the smoke, and legs, a short torso, rounded hips, and... Is that hair? It floats around what seems to be a head, as if this manifested person is in water.

I can't believe my eyes. Sayah is transforming into a human. Or at least is mimicking one's form.

I watch in stunned horror as the wisps of smoke draw in, the sparks die out, and the shadow person in front of me becomes one I recognize.

Skinny legs, wide hips, curved waist, long hair... Sayah has turned into *me*.

Holy fuck.

Her eyes flutter open, and they're the same bright and eerie red they usually are.

I try to step back again, but my back is already pressed up against the door.

The demonic-looking shadow me opens her mouth and a gravelly, unearthly sound comes out.

I'm cemented in place with all my breath trapped in my lungs. Cassiel has put himself between us, snarling so loud, I'm surprised no one else has heard and come to check on me. I'm not lucky that way, I guess.

The creature makes the sound again, but this time, it sounds a bit like my name. Like she's calling to me.

"Sa-Sayah?" Fear has me shaking all over. "Is th-that you?"

Slowly, she dips her head. Even though it's a simple gesture, it's a terrifying thing to behold because she's doing it as a mirrored version of me. But at least she's communicating in a way.

"Why do you look like me?"

"Liiikkkeee meee?"

My blood runs cold. The words may have been drawn out, but I can understand exactly what she's said. "You can talk now?"

Another small tilt of her chin.

I place a hand on Cassiel's head, hoping it'll be enough to calm him down. If Sayah can talk and manifest outside of me without causing me pain, maybe I can get more answers from her.

But, first thing's first. "Why do you look like me?" I ask again, partly scared of the answer.

"Liiikkkeee meee?" she repeats like before.

"Yes, like me. Why did you change your shape to look like me?"

"Ammm youuu."

Goosebumps race over my skin. She didn't just say what I think she said, right? That she *is* me?

As her ruby eyes study me, her head tilts to the side, curious.

"Um... No, you're Sayah. I'm Aria."

"Sayah annnddd Ariaaa the same." Her words are getting clearer now, easier to understand.

"Not exactly," I say. Although I am looking at a creepy-as-fuck replica of myself. "We've always been together. Working together... in a way. You've been living inside me."

Her gaze narrows and something sinister passes over her—*my* —face. "Not for long."

She darts to the side as quick as lightning, but Cassiel moves, too, leaping at her with fangs bared. Because she's more solid than usual, he's able to latch onto her arm.

Pain spikes through my own arm at the same time, making me cry out. Glancing down, I find my shirt torn and blood welling up through the fabric.

Any pain that Sayah feels transfers to me, and damn does this hurt!

To Sayah, it only seems to make her angry. The same ear-splitting sound she spewed before comes blaring out of her mouth, and this time I'm sure someone's heard it. There's commotion downstairs, and it'll be seconds before one, if not all, of the demons will be busting down my door. Problem is, they might still be too late.

Sayah's shape tremors and then spreads out, until she's no longer mimicking me but has turned into a dense black shadow. Her two red eyes remain latched on Cassiel, who still has a grip on her ever-changing form somehow. He swipes his talons at her, but they pass through her middle. For me, though, I feel every inch of his claws slicing into me. Tears spring to my eyes, and I double over in pain.

With another of her piercing roars, Sayah's smoke jerks and whirls and suddenly Cassiel's being launched across the room. To my horror, he flies through the large stained-glass window, the thing shattering into a million pieces, and falls the three stories to the ground.

"Cassiel!" Heart dropping to the pit of my stomach, I hobble over as fast as I can and lean over the ledge. I find him instantly, his large body an unmoving furry mound surrounded by snow. Even with the distance, I can hear him mewing in pain.

He's not dead. Thanks to the snow. But he's hurt. Badly. "Shit! Cassiel! Don't move!"

I need to get to him. I need to help and—

My panicked thoughts are cut off by a shadow stretching over me, creeping up the walls and snuffing out all the light of the room. It's Sayah. I know it is. And who knows what she's going to do. Push me out the window, too? Kill me?

Her looming presence sends shivers down my spine.

"Aria..." She calls to me. Now, her voice sounds almost identical to mine.

I whip around just in time to see her massive, shadowy form filling up most of the space in my room and the door behind her shoot open.

"Aria?" Cain throws himself inside, his gaze rushing over the scene. But before he can do anything, Sayah shrinks and slithers her way back inside me so fast, I am tossed backward, over the broken window's ledge.

I scream.

I'm not falling for long because hands seize both of my arms, and I'm being hauled back into my bedroom just as quick. It happens in a blink of an eye, but when I'm standing on two feet again and the realization that I was almost dead hits me, so does the dizziness. I sway.

Cain's there again, grabbing me and helping me stand straight. He says nothing, but when my gaze focuses enough again to see his worried expression, I know he saw enough of what happened with Sayah.

More than thankful to have him here, I throw myself into his embrace. He wraps his arms around me.

Just then, Dorian comes rushing into the room, out of breath. He takes in the broken window and then me and Cain hugging each other fiercely and his brows knit together.

"Wait, what did I miss?" He spots the blood staining my shirt and he pales. "Shit..."

That's when I remember Cassiel, and my chest clenches with fear and panic. "Oh my god. Cassiel!" I hurry back to the window and peer down. To my surprise, Elias is there, kneeling beside him and stroking his head in a soothing manner. His nakedness tells me he was out roaming the grounds again, searching for hellhounds, but he must've heard Cassiel's cries.

Elias looks up and sees me. "What the fuck happened?" he shouts.

"Is he okay?" That's more important at the moment.

Elias runs his hands over the lynx's back and front legs, examining him in a way only another animal could. There's genuine worry on his face. "It looks like his front leg is broken. This hind one isn't looking too good either, but it may only be sprained. Seems like he landed mostly on this front one."

Acid turns in my stomach. "Will he be okay?"

"He won't be able to walk on it for a while so it can set properly, but yeah. He should be fine."

Cain and Dorian appear on either side of me, looking grave.

"She threw him out the window," I say.

"Who?" Dorian asks.

I glance at Cain. He may have missed that part, but I'm sure he figured it out from context clues. "Sayah."

Dorian's eyes widen.

"I saw her," Cain adds. "When I came in, she had filled this room."

"And that's not all," I reply wearily. "Things with her are even worse than we thought."

Both men turn to me.

"What do you mean?" Cain asks.

I am going to have to explain everything that just happened to them. But first I need to get Cassiel to a vet, and then...

"Cain?" I start. My heart's still thundering behind my ribs.

"Yes?"

I draw in a deep breath and prepare myself for what I'm about to say. I'm terrified, but if it's the only way to possibly stop this living nightmare, so be it. "We need to do the ritual. Tonight."

TWENTY-ONE

I'm standing in the doorway to the backyard of the mansion, hugging my still tender middle. I've been bandaged up, but the pain still lingers. As does the worry. I can't stop thinking about Cassiel. We had to leave him at the vet overnight to be cared for, and even with the vet's and Elias's assurances that he'll be okay, I feel sick about it. On top of that, I have tonight's blood ritual to worry about.

There is no doubt that I'm forced into this situation by Lucifer, by Sayah. And I hate them for doing this to me. I was definitely having a perfect time getting to know the three demons in my own way. And now... well, everything has gone to shit.

The sickle moon in the night sky throws a silvery hue over the yard, the snow glinting brightly under its gaze. Cain is somewhere in the house, and Elias is bringing more sacred soil up from the basement to the yard for the blood ritual. The same soil the three demons were going to use for their trip back into Hell once they tracked down all the relics. I learned that Earth holds magic after dealing with that insane necromancer, Banner, and him storing his magic in a jar. And then all hell broke loose when Cassiel broke the jar.

I shake those memories away. Instead, I'm watching Dorian set up a circular ritual area in the yard, designated by their demon blood. I didn't see them do it, but the bandages on their forearms tell me everything.

Tiki torches, bought from the local hardware store, are spiked into the ground around the area, making everything seem so much more real. I'm trying to imagine how this would have been done back in Hell, and suddenly this yard looks like a picture of butterflies and unicorns.

Soft music plays from behind me, and I turn to Elias, who is carrying a sack of soil over his shoulder and a phone in his other hand playing a soft tune.

"Is that part of the ritual?" I ask.

"Nope. It's to help you calm down." He passes me, steals a quick kiss, then sets the phone down on the back step. He proceeds to pour the soil around the inner circle.

Cain steps alongside me, his hand tenderly against my back. "Are you ready?"

"Not really," I answer.

"I promise it won't hurt, and you might even enjoy it."

"That's not the part I'm worried about. It's what you said before, about this being a danger to us all."

Cain is facing me, his hands on my waist, holding me closer. "We've done everything possible to ensure we don't have too many bumps along the way."

I note he never said everything will be fine, but he's putting on a brave face for me. "So, this is definitely the only option?" I ask for the millionth time.

"There comes a time when taking a risk is the safest course of action. And this is that moment. I will not even entertain the alternative option of the hellhounds dragging you back into Hell for Lucifer."

"I know, but so much has happened and this is still freaking me out. You're right. The alternative is even more terrifying."

He takes my hand and leads me down the steps and onto the lawn, closer to the ritual grounds. My skin ripples in the cold tonight.

"We're ready," Dorian states.

"Alright," Cain says. "Let's begin." There's a strain in his voice, he is anxious, we all are, but no one is letting it show. They are risking everything for me, so I need to find my bravery too.

Easier said than done, but anything is better than becoming Lucifer's puppet, right?

Elias and Dorian start stripping their clothes off, shirts tossed to the ground, pants dropped and shoes removed. Cain remains by my side, while my gaze traces the perfect naked men in front of me. No matter how many times I see them in the nude, it always impresses me, always heats me up. They are spectacular, cut with muscles, their cocks large, and they aren't even hard yet.

"Do you want me to help you undress?" Cain offers, and I glance up to his sincere eyes.

I shake my head. "I can manage."

He gives me his superb smile, then starts disrobing as well, and then there are three of them. So much flesh everywhere I look, and part of me wants to freeze time just so I can admire them. I don't think I've seen all three of them naked at the same time like this.

They are looking at me... Right, it's my turn to undress. I push away the shyness clinging to my skin and unbutton my shirt, then unclip my bra and set them on the step.

Keeping my back to the three of them, I unzip my jeans and undress quickly, feeling their eyes on me, knowing they are taking in every inch of me. I adore them, but being looked at this way can make any girl feel intimidated easily.

I turn to face them, completely naked and my cheeks on fire, while the chill makes me shiver. I resist the urge to cover myself, and instead I stand proud. It's nothing they haven't seen before.

Yet, the way they admire me, their gazes all over my body, you'd think this is a first for them. "You're making me blush." Never in a trillion years would I have imagined myself outside in the nude with three hunks. But stranger things have happened.

Dorian comes up to me, and he's suddenly clutching a hunter's knife. Where had that come from?

"We need some blood, gorgeous. We will all spill blood tonight, paint it on each other's bodies, then we are ready to begin."

I can't get my eyes off the sharp knife.

"I promise it won't hurt." Dorian extends his hand out to me, and despite chewing on my lower lip, I accept his hand.

"I want that wicked mouth," Elias states, which grabs my attention.

"Excuse me?"

"Fine, then I'm claiming her pussy," Dorian adds.

"And I'll gladly claim your beautiful ass," Cain says.

"Is this code for something?" I ask, looking up into the most stunning eyes.

Just then a sharpness bites into my forearm, so unexpected I cry out. "Ouch." I tug my arm, but Dorian isn't releasing me. Blood is bubbling across my forearm where he'd run the blade.

"Ow, that freaking hurts a lot."

Dorian wastes no time cutting open his own arm. I cringe, looking away, unable to bear it, while he doesn't make a sound.

I meet his gaze as he hands the blade to Cain. Dorian runs his fingers over my cut, then begins to rub his blood up my arm. Next, he drags a bloody handprint across his chest, smearing blood all over himself, including two war lines under his eyes.

Rough hands encircle my hips, and when I look over my shoulder, I find Elias there. His touch is suddenly on my ass with a wet, sticky feeling, and I start to understand their earlier comments on which part of my body they're claiming.

The way he rubs me, his fingers exploring every inch of me, ignites my arousal, the deep-felt desire I have for these demons. "I want to suck on your pussy so badly," Dorian whispers to me, which sends a shiver zipping across the heat between my legs.

"Don't say those things now," I murmur in response.

Dorian moves to stand before me, his grin wide.

"He's trying to prepare you, rabbit," Elias says.

My first thought is that I'm being basted like a chicken about to be roasted, and I cringe at the terrible thought.

Dorian is suddenly kneeling before me, his hands on my hips, and he pushes his face against my pussy and takes a deep inhale. Then I forget every single thing. My head tilts back, and I soften under his assault.

My legs tremble under their touches. When his tongue laps out, finding my burning hot core, a cry slips past my lips.

They hold me in place, steading me. "This is completely unfair," I murmur, after which I moan and reach down, my fingers running through Dorian's hair, needing him deeper between my legs.

That's when Cain approaches me as well. It's a strange sensation to see someone I adore watching me as another man eats me out, and another is paying my ass way too much attention. But he doesn't seem to notice. Instead, he swipes the blade over his unwrapped wound, fresh blood bubbling to the surface. He hands the blade to Elias, who's released me from his deliciously sensual kiss.

Cain's expression darkens in a way that promises me pleasure, filling me with excitement. Which is the complete opposite of how I should be feeling before the blood ritual. Maybe that is their intention, to help me lower my inhibitions. Whatever it is, I want more. Cain runs a palm over my cut arm, swiping away the dripping blood, then with his own, he reaches over and cups my breasts, coating them in red.

"You're so beautiful in red," he tells me.

He leans in from my side to kiss me, his tongue piercing my mouth, exploring everything I have to offer.

Dorian and Elias tenderly run their hands all over my body, leaving nothing untouched. I should be shocked that they are smearing me in blood, but their touches feel so incredible, I don't care.

"Tonight, you are ours," Cain whispers against the seam of my mouth, his fingers pinching my hardened nipples, my body shaking with need. He smiles, devouring me with his eyes. "It's time," he declares.

Dorian and Elias pull back from me, and I look down at myself, blood covering every inch, and if anyone walked up on us now they might think I've been murdered. Except, all I feel is the thundering thump of my heart, my clit throbbing at the promise of what's to come.

Cain moves in and tucks an arm under my knees, another under my back, and I'm off my feet. He carries me into the ritual circle. I half expect to feel something the moment he crosses the line, but there's nothing. Part of me screams that I should be terrified, while another part keeps wondering if it will be that bad to be connected with these three demons?

He sets me on my feet in the middle of the circle, the ground soft and cold under my toes.

"What happens now?" I ask.

"You will follow my lead. That's all you need to do. I will

summon the ancient spirit into our bodies, then we will bind our connection, binding us through blood and sex," Cain says.

I blink at him a couple of times. "I'm going to have sex with an ancient spirit inside you?"

Elias grins in the background, while Dorian is shaking his head to tell me that's not the case.

"No, beautiful. The spirit will entwine our souls. The ancient magic will lay witness and then seal our pact."

I nod, though I don't really understand how that technically happens. I guess I'll find out, though that part scares me, not knowing what's going to take place. Something lurches in my stomach, my nerves knotting. I am half tempted to excuse myself. Maybe I need more time to convince myself I can do this.

Except, when Cain, Dorian, and Elias stand around me, their feet sinking into the soil they brought from under the house, I know it's too late. This is for my safety.

I look at each of the men and remind myself I'm doing this because each of them brings me happiness, and that I have no other choice.

"Guess there's no time like the present," I half-joke.

But no one responds. They all close their eyes, and my attention falls to their perfectly chiseled bodies streaked in blood. This all seems surreal, and the cut on my arm stings as a cool breeze swishes past.

Suddenly I feel like I'm a sacrifice, standing out here naked, and all that's missing is the dragon swooping in to claim his prize. Except, I'm no damsel in distress.

Cain lifts his head to the sky, his eyes open and black as ink. He begins to sing words I don't understand, but his tune is catchy and hypnotic. Dorian and Elias soon join him, and who would have known these three could hold a tune and sound amazing. My first thought is picturing them as a rock band and how the girls would swoon over them. They'd be a sensation overnight. But that's not something I can see Cain or Elias enjoying. Dorian, definitely.

Their words grow louder, the air electric, while the hairs on my arms stand on end. Something has shifted in the energy, and fear spikes within me. Gone is the comforting sensation. There's something new lingering in the night.

Cain lowers his head, the song from his lips vanishing. His

expression has changed, a wicked grin splitting his mouth. I won't lie, that look both scares and turns me on, and maybe the problem is me. I'm clearly broken on the inside if I can't discern between lust and fear.

Dorian and Elias fall silent as well, their eyes taking the form of their demons, dark for Dorian and bright yellow wolf eyes for Elias.

They look at me like I'm their prey, their meal. They step into the circle and electricity in the air snaps, replaced with warmth, but there's a sweet smell I can't pinpoint.

Cain doesn't say a word, and I follow his rule to keep quiet, figuring it's part of the ritual. He snakes his fingers through my hair and fists it before tilting my head back. I adore his aggressiveness, his kisses. The passion behind his action melts me on the spot. Everything about him tugs at my heart and wrenches at my stomach. He claims me at that moment, his tongue licking my lips. He makes his way down my neck, and I'm moaning before I know it.

I reach for his powerful shoulders, holding onto him. His skin is burning hot and slippery from the blood on my hands. He dips lower and captures a hardened nipple into his mouth. I cry out and shudder on my feet. I glance over to Dorian and Elias from behind my lashes as they approach me as well.

Desire pulses through me beneath their gazes. They watch with hunger in their eyes while Cain shifts his attention to my other breast. I suck in a breath, feeling no hesitation toward them. For them, I will lose all control.

Cain's mouth leaves my nipples moist and hard, then he straightens in front of me.

His hands fall to my waist, and he draws me against him, his cock so hard and thick. "You are everything to us," he says, his voice deep. "I want to make sure you're ready," he continues. "Turn around, bend over, and hold your ankles."

I blink at him, not sure I heard him correctly. My cheeks burn with a flush, and something about the way he says that makes me nervous. It makes me feel submissive, vulnerable. Maybe that's his intention, and this isn't the time for me to argue, so I do as he demands. I part my legs and bend over, noticing all three of them move to stand behind me for the perfect view.

My heart is beating rapidly as I wrap my fingers around my ankles. The breeze brushing over my ass is like a lover's touch, and I'm shaking with a demanding excitement building within me.

I hear one of them catch their breath at the sight. "Fuck," Dorian murmurs. "You're so fucking beautiful."

"I love your ass up in the air," Elias adds.

But it's Cain who steps up behind me. "I always want to see your sweet pussy like this." This is a new side to him I'm loving.

He runs two fingers over my burning hot core. I tighten all over, moaning at how badly I've been craving his touch. We've been together so many times, and I adore the way he makes love to me. He's always the assertive one, the one who must be in control, and this is exactly what he loves. I can hear it in his voice, in the way he tenderly strokes me, running his fingers across my slick length and all the way up, over my ass.

But when he presses a finger to my clit, rubbing it in small circles, I start trembling, unsure how much longer I can hold myself in this position without falling over. At the same time his thumb pushes into my pussy, while another finger from his other hand slides into my ass.

I'm gasping for air as he works me to the point that my legs are close to giving out.

Dorian and Elias are watching, each of them stroking their cocks, the starvation on their faces palpable.

Cain is relentless. I'm crying out now. "Cain, please, I can't hold on much longer." But before I can even stop myself, I fall forward.

Cain moves like the wind, he catches me in his arms and brings me against his body, my back to his chest, his mouth at my ear. "Did you like that? Showing us all your gorgeous pussy?" He sets me down on my knees.

I shake hard in his embrace, my body humming and so close to the edge, his words not helping one bit.

"Cain," is all I manage, as Dorian steps in front of us, facing me.

"Hey beautiful, are you ready for us all?" he asks so softly, yet the lust in his eyes is eager.

"All?" I ask, knowing exactly what he means despite my shock.

"That's part of the ritual," he explains.

I swallow hard, but the moment his hand falls between my

legs, rubbing the nub of my clit, I lose all ability to think straight. "I want you all," I moan.

"Good girl," Cain says in my ear, his mouth on my neck. Next thing I know, the men are both on their knees, me sandwiched between them.

Elias moves to stand to the side of us, and I look up to meet his eyes. The way he stares at me is filled with admiration, with unbearable desire. He's tall and so large, and at my eye level is his huge cock, and I see clearly now how the puzzle is going to come together.

Before I get a chance to do anything, Cain grips my ass hard, then his fingers are on my backside, a finger slipping into my ass while Dorian fingers my pussy. I spread my legs, wider, maneuvering to straddle Dorian's lap after he sits down.

"That's perfect," Dorian tells me, then steals a kiss. Our mouths tangle, our tongues battle. I'm gripping his strong arms, my cries of pleasure swallowed by him.

Cain's breathing heavily behind me when I feel the tip of his cock replacing his finger in my ass. I stiffen in response. It's not the first time I've been taken from behind, but it is new to have three cocks inside me at once.

Dorian never stops kissing me, distracting me, pumping two fingers into me. I'm losing all control, and the deeper Cain pushes into me, the more my body shudders. "I'm so close to coming," I purr the words. Not how I meant to say them, but I can barely breathe with how fast my heart beats. All I can think about is being claimed. "Please, fuck me hard, make it hurt and make me come."

Arousal overrules all my logic as Dorian pulls his fingers out and positions his tip at my entrance, then he pushes into me as well. I dig my fingers into his shoulders and hold on. The two men are gripping me, slowly thrusting, widening me, fitting inside me.

"You like this?" Cain whispers in my ear.

"Aha," is all I manage as I cry out, with how incredible it feels.

I look over to Elias who's breathing heavily now, and I reach over a hand, wrapping it around his heavy cock.

Who would have thought that having two cocks inside of me would make me so crazy horny that I needed a third? I don't over-think it when my body is humming, when the guys are falling into a rhythm, pushing in and out of me, their hands on my hips and waist, holding me.

My eyes lift to Elias, who stands to our side, his eyes fluttering upward as I palm his erection back and forth a few times. I lower my mouth to his tip and slip it past my lips. He tastes salty and musky, and there's something so captivating and delicious about having him in my mouth. I know that I hold control over him at this moment, and I love it.

I slide him deeper, taking as much as I can, his tip hitting the back of my throat, because there is nothing small about him.

Elias hisses as I lick the underside of his shaft and pump him in and out of my mouth, my lips rightly around him, squeezing him.

"Fuck, fuck, fuck!" he growls.

Behind me Cain groans, while Dorian places his hands on my breasts, tugging on my nipples. All three are fucking me how they want and loving it. My cries are muffled with a cock in my mouth, but the raw primal desire grips me, the hunger and pain these demons cause brings me closer and closer to an explosion.

This is everything I want, and my pussy and ass pulse around them as I know I'm near to coming.

"I love you," Cain snarls behind me.

It takes me moments to register his words, and I want time to think about them longer, to face him when he says them to me. But instead, they're all pumping into me, and I'm sucking on Elias, all of our moans a song of carnal pleasure.

But, fuck... he said he loves me.

Cain breaks into words I don't recognize again, just like before, they are demonic, and it sounds like he's calling to something... to someone.

The more he chants, the more my body tightens like something is wrapping around me. I can't explain it, but the world is starting to blur at the edges of my eyes.

Something is changing within me... doing things to me. Or is this what Cain meant when he said our souls would be meshing together?

In a sudden shudder, I sense Sayah tearing out of me faster than I'd ever seen her do before, like somehow being inside me pained her.

Her shadow hovers over us, and terror runs down my spine. I

shift to release Elias to look over to her, except he places his hand on my head and pushes himself deep into my mouth.

"Don't break the connection," he groans.

Except something feels really wrong... and panic is soaring through me that I've made a mistake.

A deadly mistake.

TWENTY-TWO

I moan against the warm skin of Aria's neck, plunging deeper into her. I grasp onto her waist, my raging erection driving me to go faster. She's so tight, so beautiful, so addictive. She's mine.

It's only when I sense her body tensing that I lift my gaze and immediately I'm staring into the pitch-black figure that is Sayah. She hovers alongside us, towering over us, watching us. When the hell did she slip out?

With us locked into our ritual, to break apart now could mean death or a rejection of the magic, and yet to have this demonic shadow out of Aria makes us all vulnerable.

Elias has his eyes shut, lost in his own world, while Dorian looked over to Sayah almost at the same time as me.

"For fuck's sake, now's not a good time," he growls under his breath.

Sayah's growing, expanding, stretching up the walls of the mansion until she blocks out the moon and cloaks us in a dense shadow. Sensing the change in the air, Elias glances up, and his body turns rigid.

The earth trembles beneath us, and there's a loud boom, like the explosion of gunpowder. I'm struck in the chest by an invisible force and thrown backward, rolling through the snow yards away from the others. When I finally come to a stop, I glance up to see

Aria's gone and Dorian and Elias are being tossed across the grounds, too.

Dread grips me. Would Sayah actually harm Aria, or had she managed to flee back inside the mansion during the commotion? I'd like to say the creature wouldn't, but I had witnessed Aria almost fall out the window to her death because of her, so I'm not taking any chances.

My only hope is that the ritual worked. That way if she truly was in any danger, I'd be able to sense it.

I watch as Dorian's momentum sends him tumbling down a hill. He disappears from view, while Elias slams into a nearby tree hard enough to splinter the wood.

Sayah's monstrous form towers over us, and even though she's nothing more than a thick shadow now, I can somehow feel her rage. She must've been the one to strike us and stop the ritual. She doesn't want us to finish it.

But, since we're all not dead, there's hope we were linked for enough time to cement the magic. But only time will tell.

One of Sayah's black smokey tendrils lashes out, swiping at me. I tuck and roll out of the way just as it thickens to form a massive fist which pounds at the place I'd just been.

My demon snaps fully to the surface, wings spreading wide and Hell's inferno lighting my veins. I throw out my hands, about to unleash the fire, but I stop abruptly, remembering how I'd found Aria early today. Covered in blood and animal scratches and bites —the ones she claimed Cassiel had done to Sayah to protect her.

Fuck... I'd almost forgotten. Aria feels all of Sayah's pain.

And that means we can't destroy her without killing Aria.

Instantly, I scan the night for Elias and Dorian.

There's a blur of movement zigzagging toward Sayah, and in full demon form, Dorian leaps feet into the air, raking his claws across Sayah before landing on his feet on the other side.

Dorian's so focused on taking down what he thinks is our new foe that he doesn't realize what he's actually doing. Hurting Aria, not Sayah.

Just then, a large animal bursts from the woods. Elias in his hellhound form.

My chest clenches with panic. He's going to unknowingly tear Aria apart. They both are.

Elias lunges for the teether binding Sayah to her, mouth open for the kill. I'm already off and running as fast as I can, my feet barely touching the ground as my wings help propel me forward. I collide with him in mid-air, and we land roughly in the snow, rolling over each other.

We come to a stop with him over me, snapping his jaws by my face in annoyance.

I tuck my feet under him and launch him off me. "We can't hurt it," I snap at him. "Anything we do to the shadow affects Aria. You'll end up killing her."

He growls at me, clearly annoyed by my interference.

I love spilling blood as much as the next demon, but not when that blood is from my Aria. I'll take down a thousand hellhounds before I allow that. Including Elias. And I'm sure he'd say the same.

"Remember the bite marks on her arm and the claw marks across her stomach? Those were from when Cassiel attacked it," I explain with urgency. "Do you want to cause her more pain?"

He blinks at me as the realization sinks in and then shakes out his dark fur.

"That's what I thought." I roll out my shoulders, trying to reel back my own demon. This is a delicate situation, one that needs to be handled with gloved hands. We have to think this through first.

"Cock-blocked by a shadow," Dorian says as he strolls up behind me, his silver hair glinting in what little remains of the moonlight. "That's got to be a new one."

Elias begins to pace, huffing out big puffs of hot smoke against the frigid night air.

"If we can't kill Sayah, what the fuck are we supposed to do about her?" Dorian asks the question that's on all our minds.

"Nothing," another voice answers.

All our heads turn into the darkness of the woods. When my youngest brother steps into the dim light dressed in a gray casual suit, I'm instantly filled with hatred and fury. But before I can even step toward him, Elias is pouncing, teeth aimed for Maverick's throat.

He spins at the last minute, unsheathing his hidden daggers at the same time, and as Elias lands and whirls for him again, he holds them up for protection.

"I don't want to hurt you," he says as Elias snarls. Maverick's dark eyes flick my and Dorian's way. "*Any* of you. That's not why I'm here."

"So young and so naive!" Dorian says in a mocking tone. The rune markings across his chest glow brighter. "You know you can't touch us. Not without us killing you."

He rolls his eyes at that. "I'm centuries old—"

"And still a wee demon babe. Still too stupid to know never to come back here."

Elias snarls viciously.

"We won't let you touch Aria, either," I say. "She stays with us."

Bouncing back and forth on his toes and still holding the daggers, his gaze sweeps over us all, seeing the blood and our nakedness. Then something surprising crosses over his face— something I've seen many times on his face. Jealousy.

"You performed the ritual?" he asks, voice dropping. Of course he's put the clues together on his own.

"Oh, watch it now, Mav. Green isn't your color. That's Lorcan's thing," Dorian teases.

Lorcan is the demon of Envy and one of our brothers as well. I expect Maverick to lash out at Dorian for that comment, or at least the young and naive bit. He's always had a complex over being the youngest of us, and Dorian enjoys poking that nerve. But, shockingly, he doesn't comment. Just lets it go.

He lowers his weapons and straightens. His expression smooths over. "I've come here to talk to Aria."

Hearing him utter her name has my temper spiking again. He should've never gotten involved with Lucifer's dealings. He should've kept out of it, like everyone else does, or better yet, grew a backbone while I was gone. Stand up to our batshit father like I did.

Elias takes a threatening step closer, forcing Maverick to shift back. He doesn't raise the daggers again though.

Strange...

I glance over my shoulder to where I know the monstrous Sayah is hovering and Aria is hiding out. Still vulnerable. I have to get to her.

Tired of entertaining my brother and his nonsense any further, I'm about to spin around, when he reaches into his jacket pocket and pulls out a rolled up piece of parchment paper that's singed at the edges.

A demon contract.

My stomach flips, instantly thinking the worst.

"I just want to talk," Maverick says carefully. He holds up his hand. "It's not for Aria—don't worry. It's the contract I own for her witch friend."

"Joseline?" Dorian glances at me, his confusion mirroring my own.

He nods. "I've... decided to terminate it."

"Wait, terminate the witch?" Dorian asks.

Maverick glares at him. "You heard what I said, asshole. The contract's null and void."

I wait for the "But" or his list of his demands, but when they never come, I'm left dumbstruck. I know how demons work; I know how my brother works even more, and they don't do anything without getting something in return. So, what's Maverick's goal here? There has to be something more he wants.

A shadow creeps behind Maverick and when I see the flash of yellow eyes and black fur, I know it's Elias. During the squabbling, it seems he'd managed to sneak up on him. Dorian must've caught sight of him too, but he doesn't hint at it.

"Let me guess," he starts instead. All his focus remains on my brother. "You found the wizard and he gave you a heart?"

Maverick scowls. "You're not funny."

"I'm *hilarious.*"

Moving with as much stealth as a skilled predator, Elias closes the distance, crouched low and not making a sound.

Completely unaware, Maverick goes on, "Look, I know it's hard to believe right now, but I'm not here to fight. Besides the contract, I've also brought a peace offering."

Throwing his head back, Dorian laughs. Almost hysterically. "He talks of peace!"

I wave his offer away. I don't have time for this nonsense. There's a shadow monster waiting for us out of these woods, and I'm not sure where Aria is. If she's in danger or not.

His eyes widen. "You need to listen to me."

Behind him, Elias opens his mouth slowly, jaws about to snap Maverick's leg in half and perform a takedown.

"I may know what Aria is. Or should I say... I may know a way to find out what she is. It can help."

Those words make us all halt. Even Elias.

His gaze locks with mine and he steps back.

"What are you talking about?" I snap, my inner demon making my voice deeper.

Realizing he's captured all our attention, he puts away Joseline's demon contract and pulls out a small, black leather-bound book from the same pocket. He holds it out for me to take.

Glancing between Dorian and Elias first, I snatch it from him. It's light with incredibly old and worn-out pages, all marked with scratchy, almost illegible handwriting. The words are written in reddish-brown ink, and when I flip through and find random blots of the stuff, I realize it's not ink, but blood. Wrapped with a leather cord, it doesn't appear to have anything magical to it, and I don't sense any dark essence while holding it.

So, what could it be?

"What does your diary have anything to do with Aria?" Dorian asks, eyeing the thing in my hand with extreme curiosity.

Maverick shakes his head, mostly in frustration. "It's Lucifer's. He's been quite glued to it lately, and I was able to swipe it off his throne the other day when he'd been pulled away."

I stare down at the book again and flip through the pages. "This is Father's?"

He nods.

Walking over, Dorian peers over my shoulder for a closer look. "*Lucifer's* diary? I never pegged him for the type of guy that kept a little black book."

"What does it say?" Elias stands behind Maverick, now in human skin. He must've changed while we were distracted with the book, and my brother can't get out of his way fast enough.

"I knew you were there the entire time," my brother mumbles, which wins him a hard look from Elias. Turning his attention back to the book, he goes on, "It's written in an old language. One I've never seen before. But he's made notes in Latin in some places."

As he talks, I find a random page and look it over, only to discover he's right. Paired with my father's terrible script, I've never seen these symbols before in my life. Here and there are scribbles of short phrases in Latin, which I can decipher. Most seem to be talking about strengths, locations last seen, defeats, and known weaknesses. Whatever that means.

"And how does this connect to Aria?" I ask.

"I wanted to try and get someone to translate it, but I can't trust anyone in Hell. Not even our brothers." He pauses, the connection to his own betrayal to me apparent. He clears his throat. "But from the pieces I've figured out myself, it seems to be talking about ancient creatures. Ones Father has kept a detailed record of."

"I've read every book written about supernatural creatures and have found none even close to Aria or Sayah." I try thrusting the book back into his hands, but he shoves it back.

"Not like these beasts," he explains. "There's even mention of The Old Ones. Monsters that were around before he was an angel or even made from God's light."

"Well, fuck me," Dorian gasps. "We need to find someone to translate it."

"How do we even know whatever Aria is can be found in there?" Elias asks.

"Why else would Lucifer suddenly be so interested in it again after meeting Aria? For some light reading?" Maverick replies.

Elias grits his teeth and a growl vibrates in his throat. "Watch it, boy."

He opens his mouth to argue back, but I cut him off. "Enough, both of you." And I thought Elias and Dorian were bad. At least they don't actually want to kill each other.

Did I trust Maverick and all he was saying about the book? No. But it was something worth looking into.

And if he is telling the truth, then we can finally find some answers for Aria, and maybe even detach Sayah from her soul for good.

There's a good chance my brother is just fucking with us again, and this is all some kind of complicated trick for Lucifer, but is it worth the risk? I'd say yes. For Aria, it is.

Pulling back my shoulders, I gaze down at Maverick, Greed, and my youngest brother. "And what about you?" I ask him. "If you've stolen this from Lucifer, as you say, then he's bound to find out it's missing sooner rather than later. Especially if he's shown a lot of interest in it recently. And with you missing, he'll be able to put two and two together."

"That's why I'm not going back to Hell this time," he replies. His gaze drifts off to the trees. "I'm staying on Earth."

At first, I think he's joking. Demons *belong* in Hell, after all. None would willingly sacrifice themselves and the bulk of their power to live on Earth. Among humans.

But then I look at the seriousness on his face and his determination to take Lucifer down. It's an expression I so readily wore myself after our banishment.

Something's changed within him. He's done with our father. For good this time.

Before I can think on it a moment longer, a shocking sensation shoots through me, ricocheting up and down and side to side, tickling and hurting me at the same time. It's so strong, I'm momentarily paralyzed, unsure what to even do. And with the odd feeling comes a name. It thrums against my eardrums.

I suck in a sharp breath. "Aria."

Dorian and Elias feel something, too, and we're off and running back toward the mansion in the next second.

Once we make it closer to the mansion, we find Aria standing there, still naked but facing away from us, covered in both her blood and ours.

More surprising? Sayah's gone, and the moon's full light shines down and reflects off the snow all around her. Her pale skin glows, and the hair falling down her back is a dark contrast. She reminds me of a Greek goddess standing there, just waiting to be worshiped, and as tempting as that is, the buzzing of something being wrong through our new bond has us all drawing to an abrupt stop feet away.

As if sensing us, she turns slowly.

What we're faced with has my pulse galloping.

Her eyes are cloudy, milky white staring back at us, and a sinister grin twists her lips.

"Hello there," she says, but the voice coming out of her mouth sounds like a distorted, crackly version of Aria's. Not like it truly belongs to her. And I'm sure it doesn't. "*Again.*"

A violent shiver shakes through the invisible teether that now binds us, meaning the ritual worked, but this only confirms my worst fears.

What we're looking at isn't the Aria we know and care about anymore.

No. This thing is something else entirely.

WHEN HELL FREEZES OVER

SIN DEMONS

There are enemies everywhere... But none as deadly as the one lurking inside me.
Vampire gangs, Lucifer rising, hellhounds on the loose, and an unruly shadow creature hell-bent on taking control... And no, that's not the beginning of a bad joke. It's a nightmare.
And it's my life.
To get to Hell and stop the coming war, we need to find the last three relics and open the gates. But the greatest threat isn't Lucifer. It's the creature who shares my soul.
Hell will freeze over before my demons let me go, but with Sayah's powers and influence growing, I'm not sure anyone can stop my greatest fear from coming true.
I'm losing myself to the darkness.
And scariest of all... I like it.

CHAPTER

ONE

MAVERICK

"The path to paradise begins in Hell."
— Dante Alighieri

I can't believe what I'm seeing.

Aria, the small, meek-looking woman I so easily tricked, is gone. She's not human. Definitely not human, and what stands before us is a creature of immense power. With eyes a cloudy white, wisps of shadowy smoke surrounding her, and sparks of light emitting from her skin, she's quite an unsettling sight.

What the hell is she?

I've seen my share of fucked-up shit in the underworld, but this is new. And from the horrified looks on my brother's, Dorian's, and Elias's faces, I'd say they're just as stumped. And scared. I don't think I've *ever* seen Cain frightened before. Not even by our father, and he's one terrifying S.O.B

"Aria, please," Cain begins, his voice surprisingly calm despite the chaos. He holds up his hands and takes a slow step towards her. "You can't let Sayah take over. You have to fight her—"

The creature's laughter booms, sounding manic against the eerie silence of the night. "You have no idea who you're talking to, demon. She can't control me. Not anymore."

A shiver shoots up my spine at her words. Aria's voice is woven

221

into the shadow creature's, sounding too raspy and strained to truly be hers.

"Well then, who are you?" Dorian shouts back.

Aria's head tilts and her brows pinch in annoyance. "I am the darkness. Ever consuming and never ending. I am the nightmares that keep you up at night. I am the beginning and the end."

"And a bit dramatic..." Dorian whispers under his breath.

Her hand lashes out, and a shadowy tendril shoots from it, wrapping around his middle and lifting him into the air with ease. Aria holds him there, feet above the ground, her eerily white eyes focused on him, and him alone. The symbols across Dorian's chest glow brighter and his long fingers try to rip Sayah's grip from him, but he can't seem to get a good hold.

Cain and Elias take their opportunity to run in opposite directions and loop around, trying to take Aria down from behind.

Still homed in on Dorian, Aria throws her hand out, and the shadow mimics her action. He's tossed yards away, like he's nothing more than a rag doll. He lands with a hard thud in the icy snow. At the same time, Cain and Elias rush her from behind, becoming nothing more than blurs of color in their speed. But somehow, she senses them and whips around, swiping her shadowy arm their way. It nails them both in the stomach and sends them hurtling across the yard, too.

I can't just stand here. Whatever Sayah is, it has Aria trapped inside her somewhere and I need to get her out. Even if that means slicing open the shadow creature and pulling Aria out with my bare hands.

I unsheathe my daggers, aim for the monster's chest, hold my breath, and throw one Sayah's way with deadly accuracy. It whirls through the air, whistling as it flies with incredible speed right for its target.

Again, to my amazement, Sayah's able to track my weapon and snatch it right out of the air by the handle. She holds it there, with the blade pointed at her heart, only centimeters away from piercing the flesh right between her breasts, and lifts her head to meet my gaze.

My cock jerks in response. Shit. This is not the fucking time to be turned on. But there's something so damn sexy about a deadly fight. I don't know how to explain it.

In one fluid motion, she twirls the knife around her wrist like a weapons expert and throws it tip down into the dirt.

I rush at her, my other blade held firmly in my grasp. But she doesn't run. She comes at me, meeting me the rest of the way in seconds. I swing my dagger, but she ducks and twists herself out of harm's way with ease. Using all my speed, I try to swipe at her middle, but she manages to block my attack.

Staring at our crossed arms, I'm stunned. Most demons in Hell can't even match my combat skills, yet here she is, doing so without even breaking a sweat.

She smirks.

My other fist flies, aimed for the side of her face, but she blocks that one as well. Again, I'm dumbfounded, frozen in place from my astonishment.

"Do you want to play together again?" Sayah asks through Aria's lips, and the sound of it grates on my nerves. With every strike, she's able to either stop me or avoid contact, and suddenly we're performing some strangely fluid dance across the grounds, me trying to find an opening to land a hit and her easily evading all my attacks.

"What... do you... mean?" My reply comes in quick gasps while I try and catch my breath.

Spinning, her arm goes out, snakes around my head before snatching my other dagger right out of my grasp. In a flash, the blade is at my throat and her other hand is seizing my arm and wrenching back. The pain in my elbow is immediate from being bent in the wrong direction.

My body stiffens, the sharp edge biting into my flesh enough to draw blood, and I realize she means replaying the moment in Lucifer's throne room. Only she's the one who has me pinned.

An eerie grin splits her lips, and it sends my pulse into overdrive. Even though her eyes have lost their color and are a milky white, I can see the dark intentions behind them. She wants to kill me, but she wants to play with me first.

My cock stiffens to the point of pain, too restricted in my pants. It doesn't help that she's gorgeous, completely naked, and covered in blood. An all too tempting sight. I have to ignore it now, though. I'm all for a little knife-play, but now's not the time for this. Aria's in real danger, and I have to remember this isn't her. Not really. It's

Sayah, the shadow creature; she's got me by the balls. Almost literally.

She pushes my straightened arm even more, causing me to hiss in pain.

"You like that, demon?" she asks and starts to run my own blade up and down my neck. The skin burns, yet the pain not only makes me angrier but hornier. And from her narrowing gaze, she senses it, too. "You like when it hurts."

The moment she loosens her hold on me—even just a little— I'm either going to knock her out or bend her over. Right now, I'm not sure which.

Leaning in close, her lips brush against my cheek when she whispers, "She wants you, you know. I can see her darkest desires. Her most secret thoughts... and she longs for you to fuck her. Hard and raw."

Her words ignite a fire in me, and I'm suddenly sweating all over. Is the creature telling me the truth?

She licks the side of my face, and then murmurs, pleased with what she tastes. "But she's loyal... Loyal to..."

She jerks back, her head whipping to the right. From the corner of my eye, I see Cain sprinting towards us, leathery wings tucked tight to his body and inky-black gaze full of determination and fury.

I take those few seconds of distraction to wrench my free arm up and shove the knife away. Then I duck, twist, releasing my arm from her grasp, and quickly seize her by the wrist to spin her at the same time. Her back slams against me, and I trap her in place with the blade now at her neck. Her bare breasts are soft against my arm, and the curve of her ass presses against my groin. I growl.

Pushing my nose into her hair, I inhale deeply. Hell, she smells so good. Like vanilla and cinnamon and... untamed *power*. It makes my head fog.

Cain halts in front of us, his expression an intimidating mixture of fury and fear. "Don't fucking move," he bellows. His fists glow a fiery red. "You hurt her and you hurt Aria."

"And?" I snap. "We have the creature. What does it matter what happens to Aria? She's just another soul."

He hesitates.

Could it be? My oldest brother actually cares for an earth

woman, and not just because of the dark entity inside her? At first, I thought he might be keeping her around to harness her power, but now... I just don't know.

Hell may just freeze over.

"Let her go, Maverick," he says, pronouncing each word to emphasize the threat behind them. I can see the distrust lingering in his eyes. He's afraid I'll pop out of here and bring her back to Hell.

And maybe I should. Father would be happy about it. He'd even reward me. But is it worth it?

No. Lucifer's admiration only lasts moments before turning into boredom or disgust. I'd learned that the hard way.

I'm done pining for his attention. No more.

If I am going to finally be free of his oppressive hold, I am going to have to kick his ass off the throne. And that means teaming up with my brother and the other two Hell rejects.

I throw the dagger at Cain's feet to show my allegiance, but his gaze only hardens on me.

"Let her go," he repeats as his wings spread wide. The sharp talons at the ends spark in the light of the moon. I spot Dorian rushing over to us, down the hill and toward the yard, and I'm sure that if I turn around, I'd find Elias trying to sneak up from behind me again.

None of them believe that I'm here to help, and I don't blame them. I wouldn't trust me either.

"C-Cain?"

I freeze.

It's coming from Aria. But the voice has lost the shadow creature's inflection. It sounds like her now. Just her.

Cain's eyes widen, and when I glance down at the woman in my arms, the smoke surrounding her is gone, the flickering orange lights extinguished.

Is Sayah gone? Just like that?

Cain's expression softens, his wings folding in and the black veins disappearing from his skin. "Aria..."

Then her entire body goes limp in my arms. Her head rolls to the side. Unconscious.

I lift my gaze to Aria lying in my bed, looking so peaceful. Her breaths are shallow; Sayah's possession took its toll on her body. Everything about Aria is beautiful, yet what lies inside her is terrifying. It took us all off guard and that was our mistake, to not take into account how Sayah would react during the ritual.

My worry comes from an inability to protect Aria.

I move to stand by the bed and brush a loose strand of hair from her forehead.

Voices cleave through the absolute silence, along with heavy footsteps striking the floorboards out in the hallway.

Dorian enters first, his sights set only on Aria and he marches over to her other side. He runs the back of his hand over her cheek, his lips thin, shadows crossing his face. "Fuck, this is bad, and we've been through a lot of shit already. This isn't fair to her."

Elias shoves Maverick into the room, then pushes him down into a seat before tying his wrists behind the chair, and then his ankles together. Neither say a word, but their gazes are on Aria.

A somber, harrowing silence falls over the room once more, and how far away Aria feels from us right now. At how insistent Sayah was that she was now in control.

Memories of what just happened tear through me, refusing to leave me alone.

"What now?" Dorian demands, wrenching me from my thoughts.

"I say we begin with killing Maverick," Elias growls.

"What the fuck did *I* do?" my brother answers. "You three are responsible for the ritual, which brought out that thing from inside her."

"Are you kidding me? This is your damn fault. I bet if you didn't take Aria to Hell, Sayah wouldn't have grown so powerful," Elias persists.

"You can't prove that? Do you even know what *it* is?" Maverick snaps back, disdain on his face.

"Do you, Brother?" I turn on him, my voice like acid, and I close the distance between us. "Because if you do know, that is the best way to save yourself here. Or maybe I'll just feed you to Elias." Anger surges through me. I'm tired of the games.

He's shaking his head. "If I knew, I would have eradicated it back in Hell. But whatever the fuck it is, it's trying to conquer Aria."

A shudder races down my spine, consuming me. I know this, but to have seen it in action, to hear it from my brother who hasn't been around Aria as long as us, fills me with fear.

"Let's not let anger blur our decisions," Dorian says, the calm one among us, which isn't how this story goes. I'm the one in control, except I feel like I *am* losing control. One thread at a time, everything is slipping through my fingers.

Aria.

Command over my territory on Earth.

My goal is to return to Hell and eliminate my cold-hearted father.

But it feels so far out of reach, like I'm losing touch with myself. Aria has distracted me with emotions I never should have felt. Yet, despite that, she is now my priority and if I have to reshuffle my other priorities, so be it. But I can't lose my head in the process or else everything will go to hell.

There's no stopping the onslaught now. We're in the thick of it, and we'll fight our damn way out, even if it means tearing through everyone to get it done.

Sucking in a deep breath, I let go of the tension bunching up my muscles and turn to my men. "Okay, what do we know so far? The ritual definitely worked because we all sensed the connection with Aria. So I doubt anything strange happened there."

"Except for the fact that your ritual aggravated that thing to come out and possess her," Maverick adds, his voice grating on my nerves.

"I'm fully aware of the situation," I growl, not looking at him as I speak. My hands curl into fists. I'm the one in control, but today I'm ready to detonate from the fury burning through me. Refocusing on Dorian and Elias, I continue, "Sayah has grown stronger over the past few weeks, and whatever happened out there, it gave her an opportunity to finally take over. Which begs the question, will Aria be herself when she wakes up, or will we confront Sayah?"

No response from anyone at first. Dorian steps around to stand at the end of the bed. "Sayah is a parasite that's latched onto her, so there is only one way to get rid of it. Exorcising it out."

Maverick clears his throat. "I'm going to agree with pretty-boy over here. At least he's making sense." He glares at Elias.

"Can I throw him out the window now, chair and all?" Elias snarls, his gaze locking on my brother.

I glance over my shoulder at Maverick, and imagine how much pleasure it would give me to see him flying across the room, but I also don't want him out of my sight.

Maverick lifts his head to face me. "Are you willing to risk Aria dying during an exorcism? It could kill her when we don't know what we're dealing with."

"If she's had that thing cursed into her from a young age, it's true. We could end up hurting her rather than helping," Elias suggests. "I've seen it happen. Those bastards are close to impossible to remove from people."

My throat clenches like a fist at the possibilities. Jumbled thoughts crowd in my head, suffocating me, while the urgency of the situation presses down. We don't have time to waste.

Maverick shrugs. "So, what's the plan then, Brother? Wait until she wakes up and kicks all our asses again? Or are you going to try another ritual?" The sneer in his voice leaves me furious.

"The plan is for you to shut the fuck up," Elias snarls, while Dorian sighs heavily.

"Tying her up won't work with Sayah," he says. "So, we need a plan B in case she doesn't wake up as herself."

"Agreed." Maverick steals the words from my lips. "I mean, we all want her back. I can still taste her."

His words seize me, and I wrench my head toward him, fire erupting in my chest. "What did you say?"

The smirk on his face is enough to drive me off the edge. The jolt of anger is instant, scorching hot, and I'm lunging at him before reason settles in my mind.

I crash into him so fast, he's thrown backward, and the chair he's in snaps and breaks beneath our weight.

Two hits to his face, I drive a third to his head because it makes me feel so fucking good to just smash something. The bastard just laughs, pinned beneath me, blood smearing his chin from his busted lip.

His shoulders curl the moment I pause and he headbutts me right in the nose, blood instantly in the back of my throat, catching me off guard.

I get up off him, kneeling beside him and wipe the blood from my nose. The thought of tearing into him bellows in my mind, as do the eager expressions from Dorian and Elias watching us. They're waiting for me to tag them in, to get their chance at Maverick. He's still on his back, hands still tied behind him, but he's smirking.

Something about the look in his eyes, a vulnerability I'd seen once before, wrenched me into a past memory, one where Father had Maverick tied to a chair, torturing him. I knew he'd kill my brother that day. I felt it in the air. I hadn't seen Father that furious before, that dangerous. Something overcame me that day, and I helped my brother. I put myself at risk to aid him. He may piss me off, but I loathe Lucifer a lot more.

That memory remains an unspoken event between us, and now that same expression crosses his face. One where, despite his words and actions, he's asking for help. Why else would he have left Hell and walked out on Father when he knows Lucifer's wrath as well as I do?

I get to my feet and reach down to grab Maverick by his shirt. I yank him to his feet.

"Thanks," he says softly.

I nod and turn back toward Aria and my men, who don't say a word. Family is fucking complicated, and they know it better than me, having seen all the shit with my father and brothers back in Hell.

Our world is falling apart around us, but that doesn't mean I need to fall alongside it.

I crack my neck. "Alright, we need a plan."

"Father's diary mentions Aria's name a lot," Maverick says, his voice no longer carrying the edge of arrogance it had earlier. "When I flipped through it, he had written some notes in Latin I could make out about holy water and theorized its effects on her. It's part of the reason he wants her back, so he can experiment on her, uncover what's inside her."

"So, he's thinking of exorcising her with holy water?" Dorian states the obvious. "Except, holy water doesn't work on demons. That's only in the movies."

"That's because the stuff from churches isn't the real shit," Maverick adds. "From what I've deciphered in the diary, holy water needs a special cross dipped inside it, along with salt, and then blessed with prayer by someone pure of heart. And we all know many priests are far from being pure of heart."

"So, why would Lucifer want to be with Sayah?" Elias asks.

"You're talking about the Lord of Hell," Dorian answers. "What has he always wanted? To grow his power and control everything. Sayah is a new toy for him, and he wants to understand and own it, is my guess."

Dorian isn't wrong. Remnants of my life back in Hell still linger in my mind of all the crap Father pulled, all the deaths, all the anger toward anyone who held a secret from him or threatened his position. Nothing has changed about him. Not a damn thing.

But now he's got Aria in his sights, and that's just not going to work for me.

I stare at Aria for a long moment. "Watch over her. I need to study the diary and see what else I can find in it." I grab Maverick by the shirt. "You're with me."

"Um, what's the deal with Maverick then?" Elias demands, as I turn toward the hallway. "Is he now just staying with us because he said so?"

I twist around to both Dorian and Elias, who stand near Aria's bed, waiting for an explanation. They looked pissed. They hate Maverick as much as me, but what if he's an element we can use? What if he's finally come around and seen the truth of what our father is?

"Can we really trust him?" Dorian asks.

I tighten my hold on my brother. "You're mistaken if you think I trust him, but I'd rather have him by our side than in Lucifer's ear." I look at Maverick. "If you're telling the truth, then we can use another soldier in our war. If not..." I lift my gaze to my two men. "He takes one step out of line, and I give you both permission to take him out."

Maverick stiffens in my grip, but instead of fighting me, he says, "That's fair." His voice is stiff but abiding. "I only want to keep Aria safe and stop Lucifer. So we have a common goal."

Except, a goal without a plan is just a wish...

With Maverick in my hold, we march out into the hallway. I'm determined to find an answer in Father's diary to help us with Sayah so we aren't blind-sided again. And if Maverick proves to be a thorn in my side, I will take him out myself.

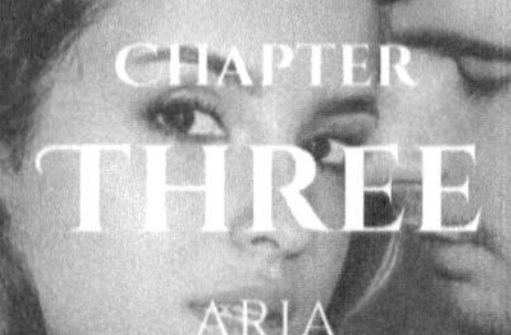

My eyes open suddenly and inhale a loud gasp, as though I've burst free from beneath the water's surface. As if I've been drowning and finally I've found a way to breathe again.

I sit up, finding myself in a large bed. I scan the room... It's Cain's, but I'm alone and there's no sound. The light pours in from the window while snow feathers outside so peacefully.

I don't move, trying to still my racing heart, and think back to the last thing I remember.

Darkness.

Overbearing pressure.

Cold... I remember feeling so cold... and then there was Sayah.

I felt every bit of her taking me over, her grip cruel, squeezing, wrenching me within, anything to suppress me.

My palms grow slick with sweat with the memory and knowledge that I stood no chance. And I received no notice of her rushing out of me. One second, I was blissfully drowning beneath the pleasure of my three lovers, and the next, the monster within me had shown her face. Then things got blurry.

Only snippets of what happened around me stick in my mind, mostly Cain and Maverick facing Sayah, but beyond that I was drowning. Within my head was nothing but my panic and its echo.

The dread that I would forever be trapped inside my head, lost to the world, lost to my men.

My heart thunders harder just at the thought, and I shake so hard that I'm not sure how I'm meant to live with such a thing inside me. She's gotten worse, and I knew my time was running out quickly.

What if I can't stop her... will I disappear forever?

I close my eyes and the room seems to tilt around me. Breaths refuse to come... my entire life I lived with Sayah but I never once believed she was such an ominous being who wanted me out of the way.

The clack of something striking the wooden floorboards erupts in the room, and I open my eyes to Cassiel leaping up on the bed. He's so big, fluffy too, snow dusting his coat, and his two front legs bandaged up, yet he's moving around like he's fine.

"Cass." I throw my arms around him, needing him, wanting to just forget my own horror. He settles in against me, his head in my lap, and he's breathing heavily like he's been running upstairs to see me.

I run my fingers through his thick fur. "I can't tell you how good it is to see you. You scared me half to death when you were thrown out the window." My chest clenches at the memory that almost killed me.

Movement in the doorway draws my attention to Elias, leaning a shoulder on the doorframe, his hands deep in the pockets of his jeans. He's wearing a black hoodie and looks so human. Well, with exception to how ridiculously handsome he is—no mortal could ever look like him with his strength in such ordinary clothes.

But I like him like this. It makes me feel... normal.

The light hits him just the right way, his bronze eyes are especially light today, and that smile almost breaks me. He looks at me as if I'm everything in the world to him, and it's almost terrifying to know that this is what's at risk if I let Sayah win.

"Hey, little rabbit. Good to see you're awake. How are you feeling?" He strolls into the room, his shoulders moving back and forth with his lazy walk. His gaze never leaves me, and behind his eyes I see the agony he's holding back. The pain of seeing me... Was he expecting Sayah to return?

"Get over here," I tell him, needing to touch him, to have him against me.

He's so quiet, which is unlike him when he always has a smart-ass comment to make, especially with Cassiel around. But instead, he takes a seat on the side of the bed and reaches over, ruffling the fur on the lynx's head.

Then he takes me into his arms, abruptly and hard, like it took every ounce of strength he had to not run over to me the moment he stepped into the room.

"I missed you so much," he whispers, his voice breathless.

His hold is perfect. It's everything I crave, so I bury my face into the curve of his neck, his skin so warm, so inviting. And when I inhale his scent, it floods me. Masculine, woodsy, with a hint of wolf. He's everything, and I grip him harder, wanting to bury myself in him.

He rubs my back with one hand, the other on the back of my head, holding me, knowing exactly what I need.

To escape from the horror I've been through.

I'm a complete mess. When I finally come up for air, I lift my head and kiss him, desperate to fill myself with him rather than the monster residing in me.

His lips are gentle, as if he's scared of hurting me, yet his kiss is that of a man who knows how to rekindle my passion with the tenderest of touches.

Our foreheads touch and we stare at each other.

"Cassiel is okay now," I say randomly, and pull back to scratch the little guy still keeping his head on my lap. He's making a purring sound, loving the attention.

"It took a lot of lying and a little threatening to the local zoo's vet, but yeah. He made it out okay." He glances at Cass with a cocky smirk. "I thought cats were supposed to always land on their feet anyway?"

On cue, Cass hisses at him.

I laugh. "Not always. Anyway, it means everything to me that you did." Giving him a lopsided grin earns me a kiss on the nose.

"What about you? How are you feeling?"

"Confused. Lost. Scared. It's ridiculous right, but I've lived with Sayah my entire life, yet the moment she flexes her muscles and shows me her real side, her real intent, I'm all chicken shit."

He cups the side of my face. "You are the strongest person I know, having gone through so much, and you never give up."

I half chuckle. "Seriously, if I could find an exit button right now to just give up on all this crap, I'd be tempted."

He's shaking his head. "I wouldn't let you. I know you too well. You'd hate yourself for it later."

I can't help but smile. "I know you're right, but I hate always being public enemy number one. I need a break."

"How about this? We get through all this shit, then we'll take you anywhere you want. Anywhere. It'll be an Aria-all-request vacation."

I smile and wipe my eyes, before yawning. "Yeah, I'd like that."

"How about you get some more sleep? Cassiel will watch over you and I'll be just outside, alright?" He holds the sides of my face and kisses me softly.

I nod, and as he climbs to his feet to leave, I slide in under the blanket. Cassiel snuggles in beside me, and a heavy sleep already pulls shut my eyes.

WHEN I WAKE UP, there's a calmness in the room, along with a gentle scent of lavender. I crane my head up to see that someone placed a candle in my room, and it smells beautiful. Cassiel is by my side and snores like a beast, but there is no sign of the men. Though my throat is as dry as sandpaper and as rough when I attempt to swallow.

"Don't move," I whisper to Cassiel and slide out of bed, finding myself dressed in one of my long tee-pajamas. This one has a cute orange kitten on the front, one paw hanging off a clothesline with the words, 'Hang in There.'

I laugh to myself, wondering which deadly demon put me in it. My guess is Dorian, since he loves pushing Elias's buttons. Especially when it comes to cats.

And I realize in that moment that I am no longer covered in blood as I had been during the ritual. Which one of the guys won that challenge to clean me up? Though, when I look at my fingernails, there are still traces of red underneath. A shower is a must.

On bare feet, I cross the room and step out into the hallway.

There's no one around and it's quiet, which is reassuring. I love the quiet more and more these days, as it means one thing—no major drama is unfolding.

Once I head downstairs, a whisper of a voice comes from the open basement door. My thoughts go to the three guys, and I want to see them all, my pulse kicking up a notch at the thought of having them surround me. My feet skim the floorboards as I quicken my pace and climb down the creaky wooden steps.

At the bottom, more voices drift down the long hall. It smells like damp earth down here, and that's because of all the bags of dirt lining the way. I remember first finding Elias down here hauling in the stuff and not understanding why. Now knowing that it can help amplify or bind certain magic, it makes sense why the demons would keep it in their home like this. They're always up to something.

I follow the whispers and come upon a room with its door cracked open. Cautiously, I peer inside.

In the middle, Maverick sits back on his heels, his head dropped forward, and he's humming a song to himself. It's a soothing ballad I don't recognize, yet my heart goes out to him, seeing him like this.

Not only are his hands tied behind his back, they're chained to the floor. Blood drips from his mouth and there's a nasty bruise under his eye. A circle of white powder, most likely salt and dirt surrounds him, which I assume are to keep him from vanishing.

I recall him vaguely from last night at the ritual, fighting alongside Cain against Sayah.

Though so much about Maverick leaves me confused. He's an asshole, but he also saved me. I don't trust him, yet when I'm in his presence, my heart thumps in my chest harder. I crave his attention, but I also don't know where his true allegiance lies. I'd seen the way he engaged with Lucifer, the hatred between them, but then again, aren't all demons in Hell similar?

"You can come in," he says, and lifts his head, offering me a saccharine smile. His lower lip is split and blood drips down his chin.

I push open the door and step inside.

"How are you feeling?" he asks me.

"I should be asking you the same question," I respond.

"Just dandy," he responds. "My brother isn't exactly in a trusting mood, so I've been allocated my own room. Like it?" His sarcasm has me smiling at him.

"Why are you really here?" I ask him. "I remember you appearing last night, but then what? Cain captured you and tied you up?"

"It might surprise you to know that I volunteered."

"To be tied up?" I gasp.

He grins. "Not that part. But to stay here. To help you four against Lucifer."

I narrow my gaze on him. "What gives? What do you really want out of it?"

"Can't a guy just finally sort out his shit and realize he's fucked up by choosing the wrong team?"

"A normal guy, maybe. But you? I don't think so."

That overly sweet smile is back. I don't see any ill intent or hidden agenda behind his expression or in his eyes.

Though he might be the world's biggest liar for all I know too.

"Why don't you be a good girl, come over here, and help me out of these chains?" he says, twisting around so I can see his tied-up wrists.

"Not a chance."

We stare at each other, and he pulls a leg out from under him, then pushes himself to his feet, so he's no longer looking up at me. His brown eyes soften, and I find myself staring at him too long, at his lips and remembering how incredible they felt against mine. "I'm not sure if Cain told you, but the contract I held over your friend, Joseline…" He pauses and clears his throat.

"Yeah?" I prod him along.

"It's null and void. I canceled it."

My eyes seem to widen on their own at his words, and I feel myself almost leaning forward. "You did?"

"Take it as a peace offering."

I swallow past my dry throat. "Thank you," I say at once, relieved in all honesty to know Joseline is free from under the demon contract. That means everything to me. Though, I'm still not sure what to make of Maverick or the emotions he rouses within me.

"What made you change your mind?" I ask, struggling to

believe it's all in good faith. Sure, I want that to be the case, don't we all want a world of rainbows and unicorns? But that's just not going to happen. I've fallen for three demons, and I'm letting a fourth get under my skin too because I am a sucker for punishment. But I am also a realist and know that there's motivation behind everyone's decision.

But the creak of floorboards outside the room distracts me and I turn, forgetting my words as Elias steps into the doorway, his brow furrowed at seeing me.

ELIAS

"You had me worried," I say, storming into the room, not even paying attention to Maverick. I pull Aria into my arms, holding her tight. Seriously, when I found her missing from Cain's room, a streak of panic overcame me.

"I was thirsty," she tells me.

"And you ended up in the basement?"

"I heard voices. I thought it was one of you three."

I wave it off. It doesn't matter anyway. "Come, and I'll get you a drink."

But before I can guide her out, Dorian and Cain both enter the room abruptly, suddenly stealing all the space.

"Oh look, we're having a party," Maverick jokes. "Did anyone bring cookies?"

"What are you doing here?" Cain asks Aria. Everyone is ignoring Maverick.

She shrugs. "I was thirsty and on my way to the kitchen, but I heard voices. They led me down here and I found him, expecting you."

"These will be his accommodations while he stays with us," Cain instructs, while Dorian slips out of the room.

"He's staying?" she asks, her mouth kind of half hanging open, while staring at Cain, then over to Maverick, who winks at her.

I narrow my gaze at him, wanting to knock him flat on his back.

"It's complicated, but we're sorting out a solution," Cain says.

"Oh, Brother, can't you ever talk straight. Honey pot, I left Hell and am here to join your little band of demons."

A growl erupts past my throat, my attention locking on Maverick. "Over my dead body. Cain would never—"

"That can be arranged," the asshole replies. Everything about him makes me burn up with fury. One minute he's on Lucifer's side, doing his bidding, the next he's suddenly chummy with us and no longer on the devil's side. Does he think we were born yesterday?

As if he knows what I'm thinking, Maverick holds my stare. Tempting me. He has a way of getting under my skin with a single look. I sometimes wonder how Cain and his six brothers can be so different.

Whispers from Cain and Aria draw my attention, and I twist my head to see that they've moved closer to the door, talking quietly. I lift my head, ears pricked, and I catch the tail end of what they're saying.

"At the ritual, you said you loved me. D-Did you mean it?" she asks, and her words strike me hard.

Love? Cain, Lucifer's very son, had said he loved her? I never thought he was even capable of such an emotion.

How could I have missed it when I was there?

Then again, I was a *bit* preoccupied.

Dorian abruptly strides into the room, carrying a tall glass and pitcher of icy water. He goes over to Aria and pours her a glass, interrupting her and Cain from finishing their chat.

"We'll talk about it later," Cain reassures her as she accepts the drink and gulps it down.

Aria has been on my mind endlessly, and I can't get her out of my thoughts. I crave her, worry for her, want her by my side every second of the damn day.

Shit!

Does that mean that I... Do I... love her too?

"Well, this is a happy reunion," Maverick drones on, drawing me out of my thoughts. "And I see you didn't bring me a glass of water. Incredibly rude. So, are we here to talk about Lucifer's diary again, or are you going to hash out your plans to take over the world?"

"Shut the hell up," Dorian snaps.

"What diary?" Aria asks.

"Maverick stole our father's diary, and I've been trying to decipher it." Cain explains.

"Lucifer's developed quite an obsession with you," Maverick chimes in, which only has Aria's face blanching.

"What does it say? I want to see it," she insists, and I wouldn't expect anything else from my little rabbit.

"I'm still trying to work it out. It's written in a strange language I don't understand."

"That's easy then. We will find someone who can speak that language and get it done." She pushes past Cain and approaches Maverick, standing inches from the line that keeps him locked in. "You must know what language it's written in right?"

But Maverick's shaking his head. "If I did, I would have translated it already."

I step closer to Aria and place my hand on her arm. "There are bits in Latin that talk about testing holy water on you."

"What for?" she asks, her voice almost squeaking with shock. "To eliminate Sayah?"

"Fuck, Elias, why the hell are you scaring her?" Dorian blurts out.

I face him instantly. "She has a right to know everything we do. No more secrets," I reprimand. "That's what got us into so much shit before. We're now a team."

"I can take it," she says. "Elias is right. No more secrets, please."

"Can we talk about translating the diary first, before we bring up any crazy theories? I'd rather know for sure." Dorian glances at Cain. "If none of us can figure it out, then we'll need someone who can. Let's get some help."

"Oh yeah? From who?" I ask.

"Miranda. The seer from the Storm markets," Dorian states. "One thing her gift allows her to do is *see* more from things or people. Maybe she can see past the language barrier and decipher it."

"That sounds like a long shot," I grumble. "And besides, can't she not see anyone Hell-born?"

"This is an object, Elias. Not a person." He taps the side of his head in a gesture for 'think about it.' "It's a loophole."

"Stupid."

"Hey, it's worth a try. I don't see you coming up with anything better."

"You trust this person?" Maverick asks, butting into the conversation again.

When Dorian nods, he turns to me next. I shrug. "She has an extreme love for incense and perfume, but that's really it," I say.

"Dorian is right," Cain starts loudly, regaining all our attention again. "Time is not on our side, so the sooner we know about Lucifer, the better. She deciphers the diary, and we expedite finding the last remaining relics."

"And seeing that we are sharing," Aria states as she fills her glass of water. "A few days ago, when Dorian and I went to the library, I discovered something that might be of interest."

Every eye in the room is now on Aria as she finishes drinking her water and sets the empty glass on a small table near the wall.

"I read that each of Lucifer's seven sons were created when he needed help to rule his dominion, and he found a way to rip apart his soul into those seven pieces and turn them into his sons. One for each of his sinful attributes, hence the first sin demons were born."

"We all know the history lesson." Maverick's head throws back as he laughs.

"Don't you get it?" she asks him, but it's Dorian who steps forward.

"Aria's onto something here. Lucifer wanted to rule his dominion by finding a way to split his soul into seven pieces... He split his *own* soul."

My mind is spinning. "Fuck!" I blurt as it suddenly becomes crystal clear that he used part of himself, meaning he is still connected to his sons.

"Ah, Elias got it."

Maverick let's out an aggravated grunt. "Elaborate."

"When we were kicked out of Hell, Lucifer could have killed Cain—should have killed him—but didn't," he explains.

The look on Maverick's face says he always wondered why that was, too.

Dorian goes on. "If he kills one of you, his sons, he's killing himself."

Aria is nodding. "Exactly."

Cain's forehead furrows. He gets it, and I already see the wheels turn behind his gaze as he processes the information.

"So, that's why he's never killed any of us, even though I swore to Hell he wanted to, and came fucking close some days—he couldn't take us out," Maverick states, excitement in his tone.

I can't believe it myself. Could we really have just found Lucifer's Achilles Heel?

"This explains so much," Cain murmurs to himself mostly. "Along with why he hated us all. He realized he'd weakened himself by making us."

Silence stills the air in the room, and I feel a sense of hope twisting in the pit of my gut. Hope that for the first time in too long, we've found something to our advantage.

Cain turns to the door and glances back at us all. "We're going to the Storm markets now."

The demons are glued to my side as we stroll up to an innocent looking dry-cleaners shop with a small black umbrella painted above the doorknob. The entrance to the magical Storm's markets.

Three of the demons, I should say. Maverick is still being held in the basement tied up.

I hate to leave him there, especially after he helped me when Sayah went rogue, but Cain, Dorian, and Elias aren't budging on this one. Not even an inch.

I mean, I can understand. He did have a knife to my throat. But he didn't blip me back to Hell when he clearly had the chance. And that has to count for something, right?

And he tore up Joseline's soul contract for no reason that I could see. Besides trying to gain our trust. *My* trust. Knowing she's free from it will help me sleep a bit easier, too.

Still, arguing is pointless against beings who've been around for hundreds of years. They've had much more time to perfect their stubbornness.

We just need to go to the markets, talk to the seer, Miranda, and get back home, because we have a trip coming up. A trip that secretly scares me, but it is also a necessity. Should be simple enough, I hope.

The door chimes as Dorian holds it open for all of us, but on the other side, the powerful magic has transported us to what looks to be a cornfield in the middle of west bumble-fuck nowhere. As it always is when I'm confronted by the immense magic of this place, I halt in my tracks and stare. There have to be miles and miles of green stalks. In the distance, I can see the many tents and vendor tables that make up the markets.

Shit. Wrong day to wear a skirt and flats. This is what I get for trying to step out of my comfort zone on a regular, non-work day.

"Where in the world are we?" I ask. The door shuts behind us and becomes a random, floating object in the middle of the field. It reminds me of one of the surrealism paintings I saw during my yearly school trip to the museum.

"Looks like farmland as far as the eye can see. Maybe... Kansas?" Dorian replies. "The markets change on every visit."

"Have you ever even been to Kansas?" Elias asks, as we all walk toward the bustling marketplace, pushing tall stalks out of our way with each step. Elias purposefully pulls a handful back for him to walk through and then lets go, so they smack Dorian in the face.

He whacks them away, grunting. "Really? How mature of you."
Elias only snickers.
Cain's eyebrow raises, unamused, but he lets it go.

As we trudge past the many tables and weave in between supernatural patrons of all kinds, shapes, and sizes, we head to the very back where we know Miranda's tent is located. The sound of birds squawking catches my attention, and I drift off toward a booth with cages stacked high, all filled with small black birds. Are they pets?

That's when I see the sign above the vendor's table. *Messenger Birds.*

Hmm... Like the sparrow Joseline sent me, the one with the message of her leaving town?

"Hello, little lady," the kind-faced saleswoman says. "Near or far, if you have to send a message, these birds can do the job easy-peasy."

I don't even need to turn around to know Dorian, Elias, and Cain are approaching behind me. I can feel their nearness through our bond. Not sure how to describe it, but an overwhelming calm rushes over me knowing that they're nearby.

"How does it work?" I ask the woman behind the table. I'm certainly not a witch by any means. I can't conjure anything like Joseline can.

"Just whisper your message to them and the name of the person you want to receive it, and send them off. Of course, the more information the better. Like an address or town name, but I've seen these tiny birds manage it with only a name. Then poof, they're gone." She snaps her fingers for emphasis.

"Poof? What do you mean?"

"They aren't real birds, Aria," Elias explains. "Just a temporary spell meant to carry the message, and once their job is done, they disappear."

"Exactly." The woman nods. "No feeding or messy clean-up necessary."

I peer up at Cain, who's hovering at my side. As if reading my mind, he sighs and says, "You want to send something to your witch friend."

I nod. "I need to know how she's doing."

"I understand." He peeks up at the saleswoman. "We'll grab one on our way out."

"Thank you." I smile.

"Well then, let's get this over with. I don't like that snake being in our home by himself. Who knows if he's gotten out of those chains and is rubbing his balls all over our pillowcases," Dorian says, meaning Maverick, of course.

Elias gives him a look that says, "What the fuck is wrong with you?" but Dorian only shrugs.

"It's what I would do if I were him," he replies to the unasked question.

Elias grimaces. "I'm... going to throw all my sheets in the wash when we get home. For a completely unrelated reason."

He laughs, and together, we make our way toward Miranda's tent.

The first time I'd met her, she'd saved me from that brutish warlock after Cassiel knocked over his potions. But even with her kind gesture, something didn't sit quite right with me. It could've just been that she was a seer and knew things about me before we'd even met. Or maybe it was something else... I'm not sure.

Come to find out, she's also Dorian's ex.

Now, I know I shouldn't care. We all have a past. But for some reason, as we head for her tent made of brightly colored fabric, strung-up lights, and enchanted by magic, jealousy wiggles its way through me.

How will they act once they're in the same room? Will he remember their time together and want a second chance?

They are ridiculous thoughts—I know—but I can't help myself. Or the sickly feeling twisting my stomach.

Or the anger.

It surprises me how fast it surges forward, like the explosion of water after a dam is released. I imagine myself knocking into one of the floating lanterns that light up the inside of her place, and setting the entire thing of fire. With her inside.

The abruptness of my thoughts stun me. I may have wanted to knock someone out—or two—but never kill. Before my trip to Hell and my confrontation with Maverick, it had never even crossed my mind.

This isn't like me.

Is that because... it *isn't* me? Not really?

Sayah.

She's influencing me again.

A gentle hand brushes my arm, and when I glance up, Cain's there staring down at me with worry in his crystal-blue eyes. "Are you okay, Aria?"

I blink, forcing those murderous thoughts away. I just have to be aware of what she's doing to me, and keep my head leveled. Yeah, that's it. I can't let her take over again. She could end up killing someone. Like one of my demons. And I'll be damned if I let that happen. Shadow spirit or not.

In front of Miranda's tent, everyone stops and watches me closely. I realize I haven't answered Cain's question.

"Uh, yeah. I'm fine." I try to wave it away to really sell it being no big deal, but when Cain's eyes narrow, I know he's seeing right through me.

"If you feel like the shadow might rise again—"

"I'm *fine*," I cut him off, a bit more forcefully than I would've liked. I clear my throat and try to regain myself. "I just want to get this over with. I'm a bit anxious about what's in that diary, you know?"

It's partly true, anyway.

It seems to have worked because Cain nods, pulls back the tent's curtained opening, and gestures for me to step through.

As we all stroll into the enchanted circular space, we're shocked to see Miranda laying across the sitting area in the middle, made up of giant pillows and blankets and rugs. It's like she's been waiting for us to arrive. And maybe she has, being that she's a seer and all.

She stands and walks over to us with the grace of a cat, with that same confident aloofness that they give off, too. Without so much as acknowledging Dorian, Elias, or me, she strides directly up to Cain. As if he's the only other person in the room with her.

"Oh, Cain. Funny, I was just going to call you." A slow, lecherous grin spreads her lips. The way she looks at him, with hard determination captured in her dark eyes, makes anger weave through me again. But Cain's gaze is focused on everywhere but her, and I tell myself I'm just overreacting.

"Call?" Dorian interjects.

She turns his way, unamused. "It's a joke, sweetheart."

"Not a very funny one," Elias grumbles. His voice sounds funny through his pinched nose.

"Don't think about it too hard. You might hurt yourself." Then Miranda puts all her attention back on Cain. Holding out her hand, she says, "The diary, please."

He pauses. No one had mentioned Lucifer's diary to her yet, of course.

"Do you want me to decipher it or not?" She waves her waiting hand impatiently. "Hand it over then."

Reaching into his jacket, he pulls out the small black leather book. "And you're sure you can translate it?" he asks.

"Let's hope so, for all your sakes."

"And before you ask about payment," Dorian begins, but doesn't get to finish.

"Payment? Oh, I'll just add it to your running tab." Eyes still locked on Cain, she throws him a wink while running a finger down the pages of the book. Suggestively.

Rage seizes my body. It paralyzes me for a moment. It's not Dorian she's after. It's Cain. And I don't know if that's worse. It's certainly not better.

She opens the book, licks her finger, and starts thumbing through the pages, murmuring to herself. "Hmm... It'll take me some time, but I'm sure I can get a chunk of it done. The important parts."

"Perfect. That's all we need," Dorian replies.

With a flick of her wrist she snaps the book shut. "Now, since we were talking about tabs and payment and whatnot, I think it's time to discuss the terms?"

Dorian rolls his eyes. "You finally figured out what you want?"

She snaps her gaze his way, annoyance flaring behind it. "I've always known," she says sharply, "but good things come to those who wait. And now's the time to talk about it."

Cain's as rigid as a statue beside me. It's clear he hadn't expected this part of the conversation yet.

"What are your terms then?" he replies through clenched teeth.

"It's simple really." She turns away and starts walking around the circular room, swinging her hips and pushing past any of the brightly colored drapes in her way. Drawing it out.

Next to me, Cain vibrates with his repressed anger. His blue eyes begin to darken.

Once she gets fully across the room, she stops and turns. "I want Hell, of course."

Elias steps back, as if her words just struck him square in the chest. Dorians bursts out laughing, hysterically, and bends over, bracing himself on a nearby column. I don't know what to think. What does that even mean? She wants Hell. As in, she wants to own it? Rule? Surely she can't be serious.

Like a predator stalking its prey, Miranda never looks away from Cain as she makes her way back to us again. Completely ignoring me and everyone else, she strolls right up to him, presses her breasts against his chest, and tilts her chin up to look at him.

"I want to rule," she whispers, glancing at his mouth. "With you."

My hand shoots out before I can register it, clamping around her throat. The fury hits after, flooding me to the brim and making me squeeze so hard, her eyes bulge.

She stumbles back, and still holding her firmly, I step in front of Cain, watching the way she sputters and gasps for her next breath and loving every second of it. I've about had enough of her trying to make moves on him. Now she says she wants to rule Hell with him? I don't think so.

Cain's mine, bitch. Mine.

No one moves to stop me. Not even when Miranda claws at my arm to try and make me let go. Her long nails drag across my skin, leaving lines of red, some deep enough to draw blood, but I don't care. The stinging is *nothing* compared to the look of pure terror in her eyes.

Me. Little ol' me about to end her pathetic life.

Didn't see *that one coming, did you?*

"We... had a... deal," she manages to croak out.

"Fuck your deal," I snap back.

"She's right, though," Dorian pipes in from behind me. "A demon deal signed in blood. It's unbreakable."

"Can't... kill me..." Miranda wheezes.

"It's in the deal that we can't kill her," Dorian continues to explain.

"Well, I didn't agree to anything, so that doesn't apply to me." The hatred whirling inside me is untamable. Her face is beginning to turn blue, the veins in her eyes more prominent as I crush that snarky attitude right out of her.

"She's got a point there," Elias chimes in.

Perfect.

"Aria." It's Cain. Surprisingly, his voice is calm and it washes over me, easing the tension gripping my muscles. "Let her go."

Wait, he wants me not to kill her? But the contract—

I pause. There's no way he's actually going to give her what she wants, right? That he's going to rule Hell with her?

"Aria," he tries again, still gentle. "This isn't you. It's Sayah."

I glance at him over my shoulder and see the worry on his face. Looking back at Miranda and the desperate look in her eyes, I wonder if he's right this time. Is it really Sayah's darkness seeping into me, or is this my own rage, my own jealousy, finally set free? It feels like my own. It's too hard to tell anymore where Sayah ends and I begin...

And that thought alone has me releasing Miranda. She drops to the ground, clutching her throat and sucking in air.

When I feel Cain's hand rest between my shoulder blades, I

jerk away and move towards Elias, near the tent's entrance, my lethal anger still buzzing inside me.

None of the demons move to comfort me again, and this time, I'm thankful. I just want to be left alone.

Looking grave, Cain turns back to Miranda, who's still rubbing her bruised throat and trying to regain her breath. "Lucifer has the throne, so your side of the deal cannot be fulfilled," he states matter-of-factly.

"Yes, for now." Miranda's voice is scratchy when she replies. "But you have plans to overthrow him, do you not?"

"I may have wanted the throne at some point, but not anymore. It's more important that Lucifer is stripped of his power."

Slowly, and on wobbly legs, she raises to stand. "Ah, that may be true, but as his heir, that'll automatically make you next to wear the crown. And that's where my side of the deal comes in. I want to be at your side. As queen."

In my mind flash images of those red, pointed nails trailing down Cain's bare chest. The two of them wrapped in each other's arms, her head thrown back in ecstasy as he plows his cock into her, over and over. I can hear his grunts of pleasure in my ears.

Rage explodes within me again, driving me forward, wanting to sock her straight in that pretty little face of hers. But Elias's arm juts out, stopping me from moving any further.

"We're obviously not going to let that happen," Elias whispers, mostly to me, but Miranda hears it too because she replies quickly.

"You don't have much of a choice." She throws a glare my way. "That's my payment for helping you find this little wench and for translating Lucifer's diary. That's it."

Everyone looks at Cain, waiting for him to reject it. Lash out. Curse her off. Something. But instead, he grunts, "Very well," and spins on his heel to trudge toward the exit. When he passes me, he doesn't even glance my way, just throws the curtains back and disappears into the busy marketplace again.

I turn to Dorian and Elias. Both of them look just as confused as I do. Before we leave, I glance at Miranda and find that she's grinning from ear to ear. Our eyes lock and I can see the spark of triumph behind them.

She thinks she's won. She thinks Cain's chosen her, and maybe he has.

But that doesn't mean I'm going to let him go. Not without a fight.

The ride home is quiet. Tense.

Questions hover in the cramped space between us, but as I suspect, no one is brave enough to speak them aloud. They're all wondering what I'm thinking. How am I going to get out of this one? Honestly, I'm not sure yet.

Miranda may have played innocent in the beginning, but she knew what she'd wanted from me from the start. She wants Lucifer's throne, and she sees being my queen as the only way to get it.

Problem is, I don't want it. Nor do I want anything to do with her.

I glance in the back seat where Aria, Dorian, and Elias are all squeezed in together. Instead of taking her usual spot in the middle, Aria's chosen the one end seat, as far away from me as possible. I suspect that's on purpose. Her irritation toward me is palpable. I saw the betrayal in her eyes when we left Miranda's tent. But I couldn't offer her an answer then. I couldn't give one to any of them. Especially in front of Miranda.

But I am going to figure this out. It's just one more thing to add to my long fucked-up list of things to remedy, but I refuse to be used in someone else's power play. I didn't let my father do it, and I'm certainly not going to let her, even with how clever she *thinks* she is with using our deals against us.

I'll have to speak to Aria once we get home and explain what's to come. After seeing Sayah almost make another appearance today in Storm's markets and how easily Aria almost killed Miranda, I'll have to be careful. She's incredibly fragile now, teetering on the thin edge of control, and the last thing I want to do is be the one to send her hurtling over that cliff and into the abyss.

When the Town Car pulls around our circle driveway and stops in front of the mansion's front door, Aria's the first to get out and march into the house, not even bothering to wait for any of us. As the rest of us watch her go, Dorian turns to me.

"She was kind of scary back there, don't you think?" he mutters, meaning when Aria almost choked the life out of Miranda before our eyes.

"Scary, but incredibly hot," Elias adds with a smirk. "Seeing her take charge like that, go all protective-mode..." He licks his lips, his thoughts clearly traveling somewhere dirty.

But he's not wrong. I was shocked to see her immense speed and strength at first, but then realizing she felt threatened by Miranda and refusing to let her have me—it sent shockwaves of desire through me.

I had to remind myself that it wasn't her, though. It's Sayah. And the shadow's ability to so easily manipulate Aria's thoughts and actions now is disturbing. I'm terrified we'll lose her completely to the monster, and I hate that I don't know how to spot it.

That's why we need Miranda to tell us what's in Lucifer's notes. It's the only thing we have to help us on this matter, so let the seer think she's getting what she wants. For now.

When we enter the house, I see the fluff of Cassiel's tail disappear down the hall toward the library, and if I were to guess, that's where Aria has gone. Either to the library or into the room to visit my brother.

Dorian places the messenger bird he bought for Aria on the way out of Storm's markets on a nearby table before heading upstairs.

"Where are you going?" Elias huffs.

"Shower. I don't know why, but every time I go to those

markets, I feel like I have to scrub myself afterwards." He shivers for emphasis. "Filthy place."

"And I think you have some corn stalk in your hair," Elias says, pointing.

"What?" He runs his fingers through it multiple times to check, but of course, there's nothing there. When he realizes Elias is just fucking with him, he glares. "You little shit."

"I may be a lot of things, but *little* isn't one of them."

Shaking my head, I stride after Aria and Cassiel.

"Cain." Elias's call stops me, and I turn. "Are you planning on telling us what that was all about?"

Dorian leans over the banister, eager to hear my answer. But I don't have one for them right now.

"I need to talk to Aria first," I say instead. "Then I'll come find you and we'll discuss what happens next."

"With the Nightwalkers?" Elias asks.

"What about Maverick?" Dorian adds.

"*All* of it," I say through gritted teeth. "We'll discuss it all. But I need to get to Aria first."

Dorian continues up the stairs, while Elias heads for the kitchen, probably for one of his many midday pre-meals before lunch.

Spinning back around, I head down the hall and pause once I get to the basement door. I'm about to open it to see if she's gone downstairs, when I feel the familiar vibrations of her soul through our link at the other end of the corridor.

She's in the library.

Inside, I find her sitting on the chaise lounge with a law book in hand. The sight of it makes me smile. She really wasted no time.

"You're not going to find anything in there," I say, and gesture to the regular law textbook. "Demon contracts are a lot more complicated than the ones humans sign."

Without looking up, she slams the book closed, gets up, and shoves it back on the shelf, all her movements stiff, jerky, and full of anger. Cassiel pops his head up from his place on the rug, watching as Aria scans the spines for something else to read, before stretching, yawning, and walking out.

"They don't make reference books about Hell dealings. Otherwise everyone would be able to find a way out of them."

Still, she doesn't respond or even look at me.

I move closer. "Aria…"

Nothing. She continues to pull out books and check their covers before putting them back.

I reach for her hand, but she yanks it away, dropping the book she'd been taking out, and whirls on me. "What?" she barks, fury flaming in her eyes.

"Have you heard anything I've said?"

"I have to do *something*," she bites back. "Someone does."

Her words stun me. "What do you mean?"

"I have to do something because you aren't."

"That's not true."

"You're just going to ride off on your black-winged stallion into the hellish sunset with her and never even think about me again."

Stallion? Sunset?

I almost laugh at the absurdity of it all, but when I see the real pain in her expression, I hold back.

As she reaches for another book on the shelf, I snatch her hand. I need to get her attention; I need to tell her how I feel about her. The truth.

When she tries to jerk it away again, I spin her and press it over her head. My body hovers over her, towering over her much smaller frame, and she lets out a little gasp in surprise.

"Let go of me," she says.

"No," I whisper. "I won't."

She grunts in annoyance and tries to tug herself free.

"You need to listen to me," I tell her more forcefully. She keeps squirming and tries to avoid my gaze. I hold her firm. "Aria, listen to me."

"No!"

I remember a time when she feared me. When I would make her quake with both terror and desire. Sometimes, the demon in me misses those days, but as she glares at me with fire in her eyes, the same kind of hunger I'd felt for her then rises within me with even more force. I enjoy the challenge. The push back. The resistance.

I like the game.

Because I always win.

My other hand grabs her by the chin, and I force her to look me in the eye. "Aria, I don't want Miranda."

At that, she stops resisting, and her body sags. The hurt and betrayal she's been feeling really shine through as she peers up at me, and my heart aches. Does she really think I care nothing for her at all? Have I not made my feelings for her clear enough? I guess not.

This is all still so new to me. What I feel for Aria—what I confessed during the ritual—is something I thought demons could never feel. Something I thought *I* was incapable of feeling. Until she came into our lives.

"I don't want her," I repeat, just to make sure she hears the truth. Really hear it. "I have no desire to either rule Hell or have her as my queen. None."

She's quiet as the words sink in, but in her silence, I find myself rambling on.

"I want you, Aria. You. And only you. I don't know what else I have to do to—"

She kisses me, hard and fast, cutting off my words. I'm momentarily paralyzed as my mind catches up with what's happening, and in those milliseconds, she pushes up on her tiptoes and sweeps her tongue into my mouth to deepen the kiss.

Instinctually, my body presses her harder against the shelves, the need to have her more than this shooting through me like a lightning bolt. The hand that was holding her in place now snakes into her hair, tangling with her curls. I use it to wrench her head back.

Sucking in a sharp breath, her mouth opens and I capture her bottom lip between my teeth.

"Is that all you wanted to hear?" I breathe against her mouth. "That I want you?"

"And only me."

"It's true," I say. I press a kiss on her jaw. "Only you. Forever."

"Then show me."

A growl rumbles up my throat. That's what I want to hear. "Gladly."

Without wasting any more time, I reach up her skirt, find the seam of the nylon stockings between her legs, hook my finger in and yank. The material splits and tears easily down the middle.

No panties?

Perfect.

I'm not surprised to find her already wet and ready for me, and the demon in me loves it even more. Spreading her slick folds, I slip one finger inside her.

"Ahh…" She squirms against me, her mouth still hovering close to mine. Another finger in, and she's panting with need. I pump them into her fast, without remorse, knowing that she loves when I fuck her like this with my fingers. A little prelude of what's next.

And when she comes, I'm going to kiss her, taste her passion and drink down her ecstasy. Then, before she can even catch her breath, I'm going to drive myself into her. Over and over, until she's too weak to move and she's begging me to stop.

Still pressing her against the shelves, I feel her body tensing and her legs trembling, barely able to hold her up anymore.

"Come for me, Aria," I command. "Come for me, and then I'm going to fuck you so hard, you'll never have to question how I feel about you again."

With a small adjustment of my fingers, I find her sweet spot and she instantly comes undone in my arms. Screaming. Shaking. And I watch her lose herself to my touch, knowing deep down, this is what I want for all eternity. Her. No one else.

I withdraw from her and quickly undo my own pants. She got her hands on them, rushing to pull them off. Seizing her by the thighs, her skirt bunches up and I lift her up to wrap those sexy legs around my waist.

"Cain," she begs, and as always, the sound has my control teetering. Liquid fire shoots through my veins as the demon rises, and my vision sharpens.

As her orgasm rages through her, I push into her tightness, grunting as her muscles clench around me.

Fucking hell, she feels so good.

With her back against the bookshelves, I drive my cock into her. A sweet mixture of pleasure and pain flashes across her face, and the books above us rattle in their place. I bury my face into her neck as she clutches the back of my dress shirt as if she's holding on for dear life. Maybe she is because I'm not slowing. I ram into her with so much force, the walls tremble and books rain down all around us.

I throw up an arm to protect her, and when her legs clamp around my hips, I know she's about to come again. Problem is, I can feel my own climax nearing, and if she reaches her peak, I surely will, too.

I slide myself out of her and set her feet on the ground, immediately winning myself a death glare from her.

I'm about to tell her not to worry—we're not done yet—but she grabs me roughly by the front of my shirt and jerks it down, taking me along with it.

Fuck. She's strong.

Somehow, I'm on my back, the fallen books digging uncomfortably into my spine, with her standing over me and a pleased grin on her face.

My heart pounds. This isn't like her first attempt in the Red Room. She's confident and so incredibly hot when she takes charge. My head's spinning with desire, but as I sit up and try to grab for her, she presses her foot into my chest and shoves me back down.

I may be in trouble. This woman has managed to get me, the first son of Lucifer, on my back. Literally and figuratively.

Emotionally as well.

Just then, she lowers herself on top of me and eases me inside her again. I grit my teeth. "Aria... Fuck..."

"My turn," she says, and I never thought two words could affect me so much. She begins to move up and down, sliding me in and out of her slickness and taking full control. Locking gazes with me, she picks up her pace.

I grip her hips, lifting my own in time to meet her thrust for thrust. The sounds of our bodies slapping together fills the room, and my entire body tightens. I'm not going to be able to hold back any longer if we keep this up.

She fists my shirt as she rides me, and I growl.

"Do you love me, Cain?" she rasps out as we move in perfect time together. She blinks down at me with those long, dark lashes that can hypnotize the strongest man.

"I do."

Like when I said it the first time, during the ritual, there's no hesitance or regret. Only truth. I can't deny it any longer. What I feel for her can't be anything else.

Aria is everything to me. And I'll do whatever it takes to have her by my side.

"I want to hear you say it," she says. "Say it."

My grip tightens on her, and we both speed up to a frantic pace. "I love you, Aria."

Throwing her head back, she screams as her climax sends her soaring. That delicious tingling shoots down my spine. Her muscles are tightening around me in all the right ways, and it's only seconds before I'm coming right along with her, unable to hold back anymore.

Breathing hard and with sweat slicking her brow, she collapses onto my chest. I'm full of so much relief and happiness, despite all the danger surrounding us, that I wrap my arms around her small frame and hold her there against me until everything calms.

We stay like that for a while, quiet and still, just listening to our rapid breaths until they return to a normal pattern.

Aria's voice is soft when she speaks again. "Cain?"

"Yes?"

"Why didn't you let me kill Miranda?" she asks. "It would've freed you from the contract."

Not really what I want to be talking about after some really good sex, but okay.

I sigh. "Because, my love, it wasn't you doing it. I was afraid that if I let you take her life, it'd be something you'd regret for the rest of yours."

"What if you're wrong, Cain? What if it was me all along? What if this rage and darkness I've been feeling isn't Sayah at all? What if it's actually me?"

"It's not. I know you, and that wasn't you."

She glances up at me, eyes big with concern as they search my face. "But do you really? Because I'm starting to think I don't even know myself."

I push myself up onto my elbows, and she pulls back to look at me.

"I do," I say, and brush a loose strand of hair behind her shoulder. "I'll figure another way out of Miranda's deal. I will. There's always a loophole in these contracts in the demon's favor. I just need to find it and exploit it."

Aria seems satisfied with that answer and leans into me again, causing me to lay down once more. She shifts to take the place against my side, settling under my arm, and I can't help but think how perfectly her body fits there.

"Cain?" she calls to me again, her hand resting over my heart.

I glance down at her and give her a small smile. "Yes, Aria."

"I... I love you, too."

CHAPTER

SIX

MAVERICK

Above me, the ceiling quakes, causing dirt and dust to shower down on me. I snort and shake out my hair, trying to get all of it out of my face and mouth.

I can hear Aria's cries and my brother's grunts as he fucks her brains out one floor above me, and a concoction of anger, jealousy, and hunger ravages through me.

Fuck Cain. He doesn't know how good he has it.

He's been on earth for a century, living it up, building an empire, completely free of Father's psychotic tendencies, when he was supposed to be banished. Punished.

Yet, my other brothers and I were in Hell, doing everything we could just to survive. It doesn't seem fair.

The old support beams above me rattle, the booming of their bodies banging against the wall becoming faster, their moans becoming louder, and I grit my teeth. That should be *me* fucking her. *Me.* I could tame that darkness within her, give her the kind of pleasure she craves. Something that hurts in the best possible way.

But will Cain ever accept me into the life he's made here? Will Aria? That is the ultimate question, now isn't it?

Glancing around the dark room, at the circle of fresh soil and salt around me, I'd say so far the answer to that is no.

I just needed to convince them that I'm willing to be in it for the long haul. *If* they'll have me.

Lucky for Cain, I hate Lucifer more than I hate him. And lucky for Aria, I don't hate her. Yet.

Tugging on my ties, the chains rattle. I yank them a little harder, but with the demon circle dampening my powers, there's no way I'll be able to break out of them. Or blip myself free.

But the downside to these traps is that they're very fragile. Just one little gush of wind or brush of the foot to break the circle...

I scoot myself down and stretch out my legs and arms as far as they can go. Shit. Even pointing my shoes, I'm still too short to reach the edge. Looks like this is about to get painful.

The sounds of sex on the floor above keep on.

Perfect. It'll drown out any noise I make down here.

At least my brother is good for something.

I keep stretching, my muscles straining, burning. But I clench my teeth, embracing the pain, and wait until I hear the audible pop of my shoulders dislocating.

"Fuck!" That shit hurts, but it does the trick. I'm able to slide down far enough for the toe of my shoe to brush away some of the circle's salt and dirt, and instantly, the pressure of the magic suppressing me eases.

I blink and reappear on my feet, the chains and ties off me.

My arms hang lifelessly at my side.

Damn. When was the last time I fed? I can't remember. Maybe when I'd drained that guy who'd been working for Cain, in the Missouri swamps.

That was a long fucking time ago.

That's going to slow down the healing process for sure.

Oh well. At least I'm free.

I stride to the door, but before I can step through, my brother's broad shoulders fill the frame, blocking me. I hadn't even heard his little fuck fest come to an end.

Icy gaze on me, he steps toward me, forcing me to shift backward, further into the room again.

"You're a skillful escape artist, I'll give you that," he says, expression as still as stone.

Out of all of us, it's amazing how much he looks like Father. In facial structure. In presence, down to his hair color. His demon. Both of them radiate dominance and power, command respect and authority, just by walking into a room. While I, being the last of my brothers to be pulled from Lucifer's soul, is almost his opposite. White hair, silver winged demon... The only thing we share is the sin that binds us. Greed—the need to always want *more* and never be satisfied with what we're given.

I look Cain over, noticing his wrinkled and untucked dress shirt with the top buttons missing and mussed hair. My chest pinches with jealousy.

"You didn't need to stop on my account," I say, gesturing to his disheveled state. "Sounded like you were having a hell of a good time up there."

His body tenses. Is he surprised I was able to hear them? Because I'm sure half of Vermont got an earful. They weren't exactly keeping it hush-hush.

"If you're planning on staying here, I suggest you get used to it," he replies.

Get used to it? I want to indulge.

"You're obsessed with her," I say, eyeing him.

Another step toward me. "I love her."

His words strike me like a blow, and I actually stumble backward, almost tripping over my own feet.

Unable to find my voice, I stare at him for a long moment, wondering if maybe I'd misheard him. But no. He'd said it. The "L" word. *Love.*

Hysterical laughter bubbles up my throat. I try to hold it back, but I can't help it; it explodes from me, and I laugh so hard I can't catch my breath. Soon, I'm coughing and hacking and wheezing all at the same time.

"I'm s-sorry, but did you say—" I manage between gasps.

His eyes narrow.

"You're joking!"

But there's not a hint of humor on his face.

I stop abruptly and stand. "You're not joking." Finally, the tugging and pulling of my body starting to heal itself starts. My fingers tingle as feeling returns to them. "But that's impossible."

"There may have been a time when it was, but not anymore," he says.

"But you're—I'm—we're—"

"Demons, yes."

"Lucifer's sons," I reply, my voice rising. "Pulled from his own soul. And we both know that bastard's incapable of feeling anything close to... *that.*"

"We aren't Father," he says, but then eyes me. "At least, I'm not."

"I'm most certainly not that psychopath."

"Which only furthers my point. Who's to say we can't have lives of our own? The way we want to live them. Love who we want..."

I lean back on my heels. I *still* can't believe what he's telling me. My brother had never shown interest in another person, let alone care for them.

Love? Forget it.

"Shit. That must've been some really good sex," I mumble. "Maybe I can take a spin next?"

He's in front of me in a flash, eyes black, veins lining his skin, and wings spread wide. What's left of his shirt hangs torn in half down his arms. He doesn't lay a hand on me though. Only stands over me, a threatening rumble in his throat.

"You stay the fuck away from her," he snarls. His voice is always deeper and thunderous in this state.

I meet his gaze head on. My own demon tries to rear up, not liking being challenged. "What are you going to do, Cain? Huh? Kill me? Go on, do it. Maybe you're more like Father than you think." But as my wings unfurl, pain ricochets through every muscle, paralyzing me, and I'm forced to reel them back in. I can't help it; my body trembles from weakness.

Dammit. I hate having to submit to him, but between the magical drain of the demon circle and my lack of souls recently, I have no other choice.

To my surprise, Cain eases back a little and his inky gaze searches me. "How long has it been since you've eaten?" he asks.

"Who cares?" I snap. More pain bites up my arms as things take their time realigning and connecting.

Stepping back, he opens his mouth to reply, but another voice interjects instead.

"What is this now?" It's Dorian, and he strolls into the room with his usual stupid, confident smirk on his face and wet hair. Like he'd just come from swimming or a shower. "Are we having a pissing contest among brothers? Oh! Maybe we're measuring dicks to see who is bigger?" He starts undoing his skin-tight pants.

"Fuck no. Keep that shit where it belongs," I say.

"You say that because you know I'd win."

"Yeah, yeah. We all know about incubi and the mess that's below the belt."

"It's a two for one special."

I don't even know what to say to that, so I leave it alone and glance at my brother again. He's shaking off his demon, and it snaps back fast and without a fight.

When his wings fold back in, he looks back at my dislocated shoulders and lifeless arms. "You realize you'll have to go back in the circle."

"And you realize that I'll find a way out again, right?" I reply. "I only stayed there as long as I did to show you all I'm obeying your rules and can be trusted."

"Yet you escaped," Cain says blandly.

"He escaped?" Dorian repeats, voice rising in disbelief. "How? The circle—"

"Apparently it wasn't drawn big enough," Cain finishes. He gestures to the spot where I was able to break the dirt with my shoe.

He glances between me and the circle, as if he can't believe I'd found a way out of it. "Well shit."

The sudden *blarrriingggggg* of a cellphone rings, and Cain pulls it out of his pocket, clicks the button, and puts it to his ear with blurring speed.

"Yes," he says into the receiver.

There's a muffled voice on the other end, not loud enough for me to make out. This is where having a hellhound's ear would be handy.

His expression never changes as he listens to the caller and only responds with "Mhm" and "I understand" and "Immediately" before pressing *end* and putting the phone away again.

"Well?" Dorian presses before I can. "What was that all about?"

"Our team has located another relic," he replies. I don't know how he does it, but his face is a mask of stone.

"Wait, isn't that a good thing? Haven't you been looking for the harp's pieces?" I ask.

"Yes, but after your stunt with one of the last ones we went to find, we have to be overly cautious."

Dorian blows out a breath. "You think this could be a set up?"

"From me?" I throw out.

Cain shakes his head. "From Lucifer."

I guess that's possible. He may not be able to get out of Hell easily, but he could always get one of our other brothers to set traps for him. He had recruited me.

"What's our next step then?" Dorian asks.

Cain's silent for a long moment, thinking.

"Elias, Aria, and I will go to Brazil to retrieve the relic," he instructs after some time. "Dorian, you'll stay here and make sure our house, our club, and our city is protected from those Night-walkers. And from..." He glances my way. "Other unwelcomed guests."

Ouch. Low blow.

"And Nightwalkers are?" I clench and unclench my fists, biting back the pain that still lingers as the healing continues at a slower than normal rate.

"Vampires who're trying to encroach into our territory," my brother explains.

"Shit, you've been busy up here."

"You have no idea," Dorian mumbles, before swinging his attention back to Cain. "So, I have to stay here and babysit is what you're saying."

"I'm trusting you to stay behind."

He sighs. "Fine. I don't know why Elias gets to have all the fun."

As if summoned from thin air, Elias appears at the door, completely naked, looking a bit frazzled for a hellhound.

Cain steps toward him. "What's wrong?"

Elias's tattoos and scars that mark up his torso are on full display, and blood matts his long hair. His skin ripples across his chest and his muscles bulge as he shakes off what's left of his hell-hound form.

"Two more hellhounds stalking our property line," he huffs as he tries to catch his breath. "These fuckers gave me more of a chase."

I may not be able to stand Elias, but the hellhound is the best at what he does. There's a reason why he was moved up and commanding his own legion at an early age. He's a killing machine.

"Congratulations?" Dorian slow claps for him. "Did you come down here just to gloat?"

His head tilts as he tries to remember his purpose for barging in. "No, actually." He turns to Cain. "On my way back, I ran into someone else."

Everyone waits for him to finish.

"Viktor."

Dorian and Cain exchange confused looks.

"Isn't he supposed to be in hiding?" Dorian asks.

"He's in the foyer waiting for you." Elias nods toward Cain. "He wants to discuss the Nightwalker problem. Insists he can't just sit around and wait. He wants revenge."

"I don't blame him," Dorian replies. "So what now? What about the relic?"

Everyone looks to Cain for the final word.

Pulling back his shoulders, he addresses the room. "Everything still carries on as planned. Elias and I will stay here to handle the hellhounds and the vampire problems. Dorian, you and Aria will go to Brazil and follow the search team's directions to find the other part of Azrael's harp."

"I want to go," I pipe in. "I can help."

"Abso-fucking-lutely not," Elias answers before Cain can.

"Not a fucking chance," Dorian adds for good measure.

"I'm useful. I know the way Lucifer plots. If this is another trap, I'll be able to sniff it out before anyone else," I say.

Cain only stares at me, not saying a damn thing. It doesn't help that it's near impossible to guess what he's thinking. He's harder to figure out than Lucifer's book.

"I want a piece of this," I confess. "I want to live on this plane, make this city our own little slice of Hell. But mostly, I want to be free of Father once and for all." I'm hoping I can persuade him that I'm not a threat. At least, not anymore. "It's why I haven't just popped out of here. And you know I've had plenty of opportunities once I broke the circle. But I didn't."

Still, he says nothing. My insides tighten with worry. What if he rejects me? After everything I've done to him, his friends, and Aria, I wouldn't be surprised if he did.

"I stayed. Because this is where I want to be," I go on.

"Fine," he says suddenly.

"Wait, you want him to go?" Dorian croaks out, eyes wide with disbelief. "Why the fuck should *he* go anywhere besides pitched off a cliff."

"I get it. He's joking." Elias barks a laugh. "He's got to be joking."

But not a hint of humor can be found in Cain's expression.

"Cain..." Dorian starts cautiously. "I don't think this is a good idea."

Cain whirls on me suddenly, causing me to leap back. Fire burns in his eyes. "This is your last and only chance to prove what you say is true, *Brother*." He emphasizes the last word on purpose. "Show us your allegiance and help retrieve the relic so we can get back to Hell and take down our father."

I nod, but inside, I'm buzzing with excitement. "Understood."

Get me the fuck out of this basement.

Then, he starts walking toward the door but stops and places a hand on Dorian's shoulder. "If he steps one inch out of line... kill him."

Dorian glances over at me and grins wide. "With pleasure."

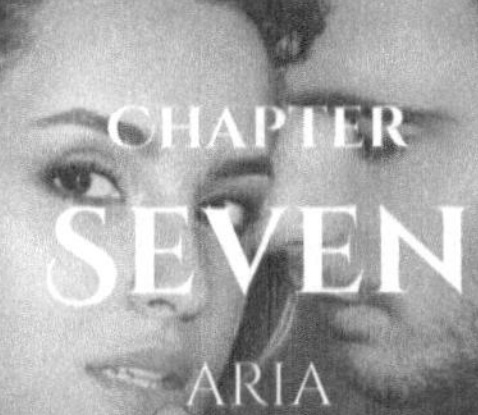

CHAPTER

SEVEN

ARIA

The snow cascades outside the Town Car. It's twilight and all the streetlights are on, almost giving the town a wonderland feel with the snow. Except, it's all an illusion. This world is run by supernatural creatures, and the things that go bump in the night are real. I should know—I'm living with three of them.

Three of us are headed to the airport, and I'm not sure any of us are ready for a mission in Brazil, in the Amazon Rainforest, but if one of the relics is there, well then, that's where we'll go.

Dorian sits between Maverick and I, his arm wrapped around my back. There's hardly been talk since we left home, so this is going to be an interesting trip.

"Have you been to the Amazon Rainforests before?" I ask them, mainly to break the silence.

Dorian shakes his head. "It'll be my first time. Though, I have always wanted to go there under different circumstances."

"Doesn't interest me," Maverick states. "There are piranhas and all kinds of shit that want to kill you."

"You're mistaking it for Australia," Dorian corrects him.

"Don't think so. There are insects in the Amazon that crawl up your dick and plant eggs in there."

Dorian stiffens against me, drawing his legs together. My mouth might have dropped open; and that's not something I'd

269

expect from Maverick. Maybe he's a lot more spooked out about the trip than he first let on. Or he's been hanging out with Elias too long.

"Bullshit," Dorian barks.

Maverick shrugs. "I dare you to go for a swim in the water once we get there."

When no one answers, I giggle to myself. "Let's all plan to not go into the water, how does that sound?"

"You should be more worried about the anacondas," Dorian pipes up. "They're man eaters down there."

"Well, lucky for us, we're not men," Maverick answers.

I glance out the window as they continue their chest beating of what creatures they won't be afraid of. I suspect they'd both scream like a girl if they fell into the river.

A police car, its siren blaring, shoots right past us, and I press my face to the window to see what's going on up ahead.

Moments later as we race up the road, a lot of flashing red and blue sirens are clustered near the end of a residential street. It's too dark to fully make out what is going on.

Dorian leans against me, staring outside too. "What's going on?"

"No idea."

In a flash, something dark darts right across the street with the flashing cop cars. Fast enough that those on the road would have missed it.

"Did you see that? What was it?" I ask.

"Looked like a vamp to me," Dorian answers. "Freaking fanged bastards."

"Really? Could be a hellhound," Maverick interjects, his words covering me in chills.

"Why'd you have to say that?" I blurt.

Dorian growls and shoves him into his seat. "Seriously. If we encounter a hellhound, you are responsible for kicking its ass. It's your fault they're here anyway."

"I have no problem with that," he boasts.

Dorian has his phone out and is calling Cain by the looks of it. As the phone rings, he turns to Maverick. "Let's set ground rules for this trip. I'm in charge. You do anything to piss me off or hurt

Aria, and I'll finish you. And you don't do anything without asking me permission."

"Dorian," Cain's voice is loud enough for us to hear. "What's wrong?"

"On the edge of downtown, something's gone on. I saw a vampire and the human authorities are involved."

He falls silent, listening, though I can't make out the murmur of Cain's voice.

"Sounds like a plan. Bye." Dorian hangs up, then tucks away his phone.

"What's he going to do?" I ask.

"Him and Ramos are going vampire tracking tonight, starting with that street back there."

Ah, the albino dhampir with the ninja skills. He'll definitely be good in a fight.

"Elias is still hunting down hellhounds on our property?" I ask, and he nods.

The car falls quiet once more, and I'm staring out the window, feeling strangely sad about leaving behind Cain and Elias. Especially after Cain and I confessed our love for each other. I understand why they stayed behind, but I wish they could have joined us as well.

When we turn off on the exit ramp toward the airport, my stomach clenches with excitement and nerves. I have no idea what to expect, and if our past experience of relic hunting is anything to go by, we're in for one hell of a ride.

THE BREEZE SWISHES over my face and through my hair, the air fresh and crisp. We're in Brazil, on the Amazon River, and since we boarded the open vessel I've been hanging practically out from my seat, taking in the surroundings, in awe.

This tropical rainforest is how I might have pictured Eden. Lush green trees and plants, so densely packed together along the river's edges that there is no way of seeing what lays beyond. It explains why there are so many howler monkeys swinging in the branches, unleashing loud whooping barking sounds. It's the only way to move about in this place.

"Everything wants to kill you out here," the boat charter guy had told us. Even traveling with two demons, we agreed not to go off by ourselves and take any chances.

The murky water ripples as we carve our way across the river. The longer we are out here, the longer I'm certain that I don't want to spend too much time in this wilderness.

I turn in my seat to find Maverick and Dorian sitting at the back of the charter boat, talking almost normally. I can only imagine they have quite a history, having both grown up in Hell. Despite missing Elias, it makes more sense that he's not here, or else Maverick would already be pitched into the river. Or out of the airplane.

I completely adore the big hellhound, but his short temper can be problematic in such situations.

I shuffle out of my seat and make my way past the two rows of seats and flop down next to Dorian, our legs touching. We're all wearing long pants and boots to avoid creepy crawlies.

"You guys talking about going for a skinny dip later on?" I glance to the murky water and back at them, laughing.

Neither of them jump at the chance, but only give me a deadpan look.

"I'm only kidding," I say. "How much farther?"

Maverick tells me, "It might be a while."

It should be easy, I keep telling myself. We disembark wherever Dorian gave the driver instructions based on Cain's lead, and I just have to track down the relic, right? Except, we've been on this boat for over two hours, and I have yet to see a break in the thick woodland and foliage to allow anyone to penetrate it.

I lounge back in the seat, Dorian stretches out his arm behind me, and I enjoy the sun beating down on us. There is no cover on the boat, just a few rows of seats and the captain at the front, steering us amid the serpentine channel. And it's just us in the boat. Guess it's not tourist season.

By midday, I lean forward and look across to Dorian and Maverick, both lounging in the seats, their eyes shut, sunbathing like lizards.

"Hey, this is taking a long time, don't you think? What if it takes us just as long to find the relic? I don't fancy spending a night out here, unless there's a hidden five-star hotel behind all this tangled forest."

Dorian pries one eye open. "We aren't spending the night here. It'll be alright." His arm around my middle shuffles me toward him, pressing our sides together. He's scorching hot. It's too much and I'm on my feet, going to the supply of drinks and snacks in the cooler. I grab two bottles of water and toss them at the guys. Dorian catches both, as Maverick hasn't even stirred.

Does he miss Hell so much that being in the sun has rendered him into a sloth?

When Dorian shoves the bottle at him, he groans and straightens in his seat. I guzzle down half my bottle, then grab some of the premade sandwiches, figuring I might as well eat to keep occupied.

On my last bite, the boat starts taking a sharp turn right, and I sway in my seat. We're following the curve of the river, then careening down an adjacent waterway that takes us off the beaten track... or water track I should say.

It's a narrower passage, the trees hanging lower over us, the sun faded.

I glance around at how close the branches are, to the point that I can reach out to touch them, which I resist. I've seen the movie *Anaconda* where they are on a boat like this in the Amazon, and let's just say that beast decides to make the people his meals.

Geez, I've let the guys get into my head.

When we slow down, I raise my head and see that we're pulling into a muddy bank where the forest opens up to a track, a hidden doorway like we're in Narnia.

Nerves dance in my stomach.

"This is it," Maverick calls out as if he's finally woken up.

I'm grabbing my backpack and stuffing a few more bottles of water and snacks into there, figuring it might be a gift in case we meet any locals. The charter guy had told us that a small indigenous tribe lives out in this part of the woods, so I figure I can use food as a bargaining tool if needed.

Once the boat pulls up as close as possible, the driver, an older man with deeply sun-tanned skin and pitch-black hair, looks our way.

"Two hours," he says, showing us two fingers in case we didn't understand his words. "I will return in two hours; don't be late."

I want to ask him about traveling at nighttime across the river, which unsettles me, but I keep it to myself. Instead, I let Dorian usher me to the edge. He climbs out first, hoping into ankle-deep water, while I'm frantically threading my arms through the backpack.

"I'll carry you," he tells me, and I don't waste a moment, but climb over the edge of the vessel. He swoops me into his arms. We cross the water quickly and the splash of water behind me confirms Maverick is right on our heels.

My feet hit the soft soil, and I feel a heavy heat across my back as if the forest itself is exhaling.

Almost instantly, the three of us are standing by the water's edge, watching the boat glide away, the man apparently scheduled to pick up a group of trekkers from farther down the river and take them to another point.

Once he's out of sight, we all turn to the forest. And it's overwhelming. Everything is enormous, crowded, and there are so many strange noises that I can't tell if it's coming from bugs, birds, or monkeys. Maybe something worse.

"Okay, where to?" Maverick looks at me.

"Now, Aria does her thing," Dorian says, his hand sliding across on my lower back. "We have two hours. So we stay on the track, and we move fast."

Maverick's gaze falls on me. "Aria's...thing?"

Dorian presses his lips together, instantly regretting letting it slip.

Oh well. It's not like him knowing is going to change anything. If he's truly on our side, then great. And if not, Lucifer wants me anyway, so it doesn't matter.

"I can sense magical objects," I begin, glancing Dorian's way to see if he'll stop me. He doesn't. "Through my toe."

Maverick blinks, as if waiting for something more, but when I don't go on, he bursts out laughing. He clutches his chest, head thrown back, his body shaking from the force of it.

"Okay, okay. It's not *that* funny," I say.

He doesn't stop, and my annoyance grows.

"Hey!" I smack him in the shoulder, and only then does he start to settle down.

Wiping tears from his eyes—yes, actual tears—he says, "Fuck, that was a good one. Hilarious!"

"She's not joking," Dorian pipes in with a straight face.

Maverick glances between us, disbelief still on his face. "I'm sorry but what? You're trying to tell me that your...*toe*...lets you track relics?"

"The darker the magic latched onto them, the better," I reply.

"This is absurd."

"It's how we've been able to find the other harp relics so far," Dorian explains. "It's quite a nifty trick."

"Wow, okay then." Maverick rubs his forehead. "So that's why we brought her on this trip."

My eyes widen. "You thought I shouldn't come?"

"To the wild Amazon? Honestly, no."

Well, that stings, but if I am being honest, this wouldn't be the first place I'd pick to vacation to.

"Can we just start moving?" Dorian smacks his neck. "I'm already getting eaten alive by mosquitos."

"What a wuss." Maverick shakes his head.

I nudge them both forward. "Let's be focused. No bitch fighting."

We make our way into the woods, following the worn track. They close in behind me. Shrubs and greenery spill over into our path, while the ground is littered with dried leaves. I'm scanning the ground to avoid stepping on a snake, while looking around for anything to drop out of the trees.

But I need to calm the hell down before I go into a panic attack as my head swings in every direction, and my breaths are racing.

Sweat drips down my back, and I pull my hair up into a ponytail with the elastic from around my wrist.

We're tracking for a decent half an hour, when the tune of a soft song finds me.

I pause, and Dorian runs right into my back. "Sorry, babe."

"Do you hear that?" I ask, turning on the spot, determining the direction of the sound.

Both of them have their heads raised. "A panther's cry perhaps?" Maverick suggests.

"No, it's a song, almost like a lullaby. You know, the kind made by those wind-up jewelry boxes. It sounds exactly like that."

It's coming from my right, and when I turn in that direction, the song seems to grow louder. Something feather-soft curls in my chest, and suddenly, I'm cutting right across the deluge of plants, stomping on vegetation, needing to find the source of the music.

Someone snatches my arm, strong fingers pausing me in my track. I turn to face a worried Maverick.

"No leaving the path." He tugs me back out of the jungle, and I shake my head, clearing it of the music that seems to haunt me, to call me.

"I think it's the relic," I say, but neither Dorian nor Maverick are forcing me to go chase it down.

"We follow the track and see if it gets stronger as we keep going," Dorian instructs.

Of course, I know they're right, but for a moment there, the determination to go to the song overcame me. Just as it had when I tracked the first relic in the basement of the demons' mansion. If all goes well, we can find it fast and be out of this rainforest.

I scratch my arm for the hundredth time, convinced bugs are eating me alive.

We keep on moving, the shadows growing murkier, the heat intense, and the strangest sounds come out of this forest. Except, my attention homes in on the music that lures me forward with fast steps.

We step around a gigantic tree that has to be a few hundred years old and emerge into an open area free of greenery. The ground is well worn, and further ahead the land opens up to reveal a cluster of homes made of flimsy wood. They sit on stilts, taking them off the ground a decent three feet, the roofs pointed and made of dried leaves and what looks like straw.

"Whoa, we found the tribe," Maverick states, brushing right past me and going in first.

Fine by me. If he wants to be the first to be potentially attacked by trespassing into a tribe's home, then he can be my guest.

Except the stillness sends a shiver up my spine.

"Where is everyone?" I ask Dorian.

"Maybe they abandoned the place."

"Why?"

Dorian takes my hand in his, and he guides me in behind Maverick.

There are no people.

No movement.

Except the music, it's stronger here, and with it a slight tingle starts at the tip of my toe. "I feel it," I admit. "The relic is close. Let's find it so we get out of here, as it's creepy as hell with no one around."

Unease consumes me with each step, shadows shifting in the woods circling the tribe village.

A sudden blurry figure flashes in my peripheral vision, and I'm not the only one who sees it, as all three of us twist in its direction. All that's left is a rustling of shrubs and palm-like plants, as if someone had indeed burst right past them.

My heart is thundering wondering what it could be.

When a brutal howling sound echoes around us, I flinch. It's quickly followed by more howls, all so savage sounding, like they're declaring war. And we are the enemy.

"Shit, what is that?" I murmur.

Dorian and Maverick close in around me, their backs to me, each scanning the village for anything.

My heart thunders in my chest, and I twist around on the spot, trying to find something, see something. "Are we being hunted?"

Another flash of movement, directly across the open field. And that time the image is clear... a dark tanned man in black shorts, which tells me they have definitely been in contact with people before, is running at full tilt across the land, gripping a long spear over his shoulder.

And just like that, he vanishes into the woods.

"Okay, that was strange right?" I ask.

"Must be a tradition to scare away newcomers," Maverick says. "We need to look as unthreatening as possible."

"Not like we have any weapons on us," I say.

"Shhh," Dorian interrupts.

The music is louder here, my toe's still vibrating, so we are in the right place. All we need now is to overcome the fearful locals.

"You, shh," Maverick bickers back, and I would roll my eyes if we weren't in danger. Well, that guy had been carrying a weapon, and to them, we entered their territory.

"Let's make an offering to show them we come in peace? My sandwiches."

Dorian and Maverick both scoff at my suggestion in unison.

"Wow, you two have suddenly turned into jerks. What are your ideas?"

But when a sudden explosion of howls comes again, I lift my head to the dozen tribespeople bursting out of the forest.

A small cry slips past my lips, and I'm recoiling.

Terror clings to my lungs. I'm struggling to breathe.

The locals are rushing toward us with weapons ready, except that's when I notice others are running toward one another and clash into a brawl. They're fighting amongst themselves.

Of course, the worst-case scenario comes to mind. Half the group wants us dead and the other doesn't? Please don't let them be cannibals. I don't even know if they exist in this region, but right now I'm too terrified to think straight.

"We fight them," Maverick says, pushing the sleeves of his shirt up.

"No, you can't hurt them. We're the intruders." I'm determined to not be the reason a tribe in the rainforest is eliminated.

I grab the back of his shirt and wrench him backward with me, Dorian by my side.

"She's right. Don't be such a dick, Maverick. You're good at running away, so that's what we do."

Maverick swings toward Dorian, both of them standing toe-to-toe, nostrils flaring, the testosterone off the charts.

But we are in the middle of a battle and men with long spears are coming our way. I can't help but wonder if those sharp tips are dipped in poison.

"Run," I bellow, and turn to run out of there, the buffoons can deal with their own crap if they want to have an argument in the middle of a battle.

But they are on my heels just as quick, breathing heavily.

I can't think where to go, but when I swing back down the track we'd come, it's blocked by two men with spears arguing with one another. Instinct has me swinging in the opposite direction, shoving my way into the shrubland, darting past branches and lofty trees, plants tearing at my pants, but I don't stop, not while the tribesmen are howling with anger right behind us.

With Viktor's unexpected visit to our house, Cain took the evening to discuss the Nightwalkers at Purgatory with him. He even brought Ramos for back up, just in case more vamps crashed into the club and wreaked havoc again. And, you know, since I'm busy with my own shit.

I've been left to guard our home. While we wait for Dorian, Maverick, and Aria to return from their trip, I'm responsible for keeping our property hellhound free. Like cockroaches, they're relentless. They'll keep coming until they get their claim. So I'm on pest control duty 24/7. Even been sleeping outside. When I can sleep at all, that is.

I don't mind, though. I was missing the fun of the hunt and chase, and now I got that in spades.

As I trot along the lake's edge, the blood from the last hellhound I'd mangled still damp in my fur, a touch of sulfur rides the passing breeze, and I swing my head in that direction.

Another one. Has to be.

I'm off and sprinting north, through the dense forest and muddy terrain. It's the dead of winter and the freezing temperatures can't touch me through my thick black fur, but it still nips at my nose. I think of the days when I was still a youngling, taking commands from another, and running all across this plane to find damned souls and bring them back to Hell. It's how I'd originally met Serena. Being a crossroads demon, she was always on Earth to make deals with unsuspecting humans.

Most supernaturals were wise enough to stay away from her kind, but humans? They were easy targets, especially when they got desperate enough. And finding the most pathetic and needy ones was her specialty.

I guess you could say I could've fallen into that category, too. She had played me for a sap. A love-sick puppy.

Like every time I remember Serena's betrayal, my blood runs hot and rage consumes me. Not just for what she did, but for my own stupidity. I speed up my pace, chasing down the scent all hell-beings leave when they first pop into this world, wanting to tear into something. To release these feelings. To taste blood.

I'm closing in, and to my surprise, the creature isn't running away or charging toward me, like most will do once hearing me coming. And I made sure to be noisy on purpose—I like the chase—but from the lack of sound or change in scent, it seems like the hound is staying put. Just waiting for me.

He wants a stand off? Fine. Doesn't bother me any. The cocky ones are usually the ones to die the fastest, and it's not like he can hide from me and try a sneak attack. I've already pinned his location.

He's a sitting duck.

Spotting a shadow in between trees, I leap through the brush and land on the other side, in the middle of a small clearing. And what stands before me isn't a hellhound.

Hell, it isn't even a man. It's a woman.

And not just any woman, either.

Blonde hair styled in an asymmetrical bob, piercing green eyes, leather motorcycle jacket, torn jeans, and a smirk that says, *Yep, it's me...*

Serena?

Speak of the motherfucking devil.

She gives me a little wave. "Hello again, Elias."

It's been so long since I've seen her, I've almost forgotten how smooth and enticing her voice is.

I recall my hound, pushing him back so my human form can step forward. He tries to protest, not ready to be caged, but I can't talk to her in this state. I give him another firm nudge, and he relents, and within seconds, I'm standing on two legs again, with the bitter cold biting into my bare skin.

I stand there for a moment, completely dumbstruck with what to say or do. I haven't seen her in a hundred years—since that night she ripped my heart out and betrayed us. The hound in me is confused, too. With the ritual's bond still linking us, it's not sure whether to kill or sit.

When I finally find my voice again, I decide to just go with the obvious. "What the fuck are you doing here?"

Her gaze roams me over from head to toe, and her green eyes spark when they linger on my groin. I take a step back.

"Believe it or not, I came to check on you," she says, and crosses her arms. "Hell's been buzzing about you three again. Seems you've found something Lucifer deems interesting."

The name "Lucifer" on her lips has my jaw clenching. Of course she would know all about him and his *interests*. She's been working as one of his lackeys to gain his favor.

"Get away from here," I snap. "This is my territory."

She rolls her eyes. "Hounds and their *territory*. What did you do? Pee on all the trees?"

I clench my jaw so hard, pain shoots through my temples.

"So...What have you been doing up here?" she asks. "Missing me?"

"Quite the opposite," I reply.

"Oh, Elias. Don't be like that." She walks over and places a hand on my cheek. I don't know why, but I let her. And when she smiles tenderly at me, my heart begins to race again, like it used to whenever I'd see her. After all this time, after all she's done, there's still a part of me that cares about her.

And I hate it.

Something cold flashes behind her gaze, despite the warm smile lifting her lips. "You've always been such a good boy for me, Elias. So loyal. Loving. Obedient."

I huff. "You've described a dog. A pet."

"And maybe you were like a pet to me," she says with false sweetness. "Maybe I just wanted something to train, something to follow me around."

"I loved you." My entire body is trembling now with the conflicting needs, to either rip her to shreds or fall apart at her feet, warring through me. Her betrayal destroyed me, left a gaping hole in my heart.

Her hand drops from my face. "That was your mistake. Demons aren't capable of love."

I snarl. "Yes they are. We love fiercely. Dangerously. Brutally. With fangs, fur, wings, and claws. With all the darkness in our souls."

"Are you a poet now?" She laughs, and the sound that once brought me joy now grates on my nerves. "You've grown soft, Elias!"

"Fuck you."

"Don't tell me you really believe in that garbage."

"I did." But then Aria's beautiful face rises in my mind, and warmth spreads through me, drowning out some of the pain. "I still do."

"Then you are a fool."

Rage rockets through me, and my beast rears up. Throwing my head back, I roar so loud, the trees quake and nesting birds launch themselves into the air. Her heart is as black as Lucifer's. Why hadn't I seen it sooner? She's incapable of feeling anything besides her own thirst for power.

Serena doesn't even flinch, which only angers me more.

"You won't hurt me. I know you won't," she says smugly.

"Are you sure about that? A lot has changed in the last hundred years." Which is more than true. A lot has changed just within these last few months. Ever since Aria came into our lives.

With a growl rumbling in my chest, I take a giant step toward her. That makes her shift back, and there's actual fear in her eyes. As a crossroads demon, she doesn't have any outstanding powers like incubus or the sin demons do. If I wanted to, I could kill her on this plane. Easily.

And right now, I want to.

"This is your last warning. Leave. Now."

She doesn't move.

Man, this woman is really testing my limits.

I take another threatening step.

She shrinks back. "Fine, I'll go," she says, holding up her hands in surrender. "I think that was enough time anyway."

I lean back onto my heels and stare at her in confusion. "Enough time? For what?"

A howl tears through the night, and icy cold dread shoots down my spine. That's just not any wolf's howl. It's from my kind. A hellhound.

And it's coming from a mile southeast of here. From the mansion.

Shit.

That's why Serena is here. To distract me long enough to let the hounds reach our home.

Glancing one last time at the woman I once loved, I find her grinning broadly, pleased with herself. But as much as I want to slash that smile off her face, I'm off and running back the way I came, changing into my animal again mid-stride, and then picking up speed once all four paws hit the dirt.

CAIN

IN THE BASEMENT OF PURGATORY, in one of the meeting rooms, I sit at the long table with Ramos to my right and Viktor taking the seat at the far end. Charlotte's here, too, sitting on the master vampire's lap, and I'd be lying if I said seeing them together doesn't affect me. The way she looks at him with such admiration and love, with her arms wrapped around his neck and her head on his shoulder makes me miss my Aria fiercely. I wish I could have joined her on the trip, but these Nightwalkers are getting too bold for my liking.

"I want to thank you again for keeping my Char safe while I was...indisposed," Viktor says, with his thick accent. "I don't want them alive a second longer, knowing what they did to her."

Of course, after bringing Viktor here and reuniting him with Charlotte, he was furious when he discovered what the Nightwalkers had done to her while he was gone. It had made him even more determined to slaughter them all. And I didn't blame him. If anyone had done that to Aria... well, I wouldn't sleep a wink until I ripped every single one of those bloodsuckers' hearts out with my bare hands.

Love has definitely made me even more crazed. And I wasn't exactly sane to start with.

"I understand," I say. "Charlotte has been with us for a long time. She's like family to us."

"Do you have a plan? Stephan has infiltrated my clan. Turned some of my most loyal men against me. There's no one to trust anymore."

"Stephan is turning everyone and anyone he can to increase his numbers, but as you and I both know, young vamps can only do so much. They're clumsy, sloppy, weak. He has the soldiers but not the army."

Viktor nods.

"We were able to extract some information from the vampires we found in the Queen Anne Townhomes. That's how we discovered who was behind this mess, so my assumption is that these baby vamps aren't exactly loyal to their master yet. If we capture one, we may be able to extract information that could be useful to us," I go on, and glance at Ramos. He's no stranger to our interrogation...practices, having participated in many of them himself. "If we find out where his nest is, or even where they're storing this new drug, Hush, then we can rally our allies and get ready for a full-on attack."

"No survivors," Viktor says, and slams his fist onto the table, making the thing rattle.

"Exactly."

Ramos stands, ready to go. Viktor lets Charlotte down and is raising to his feet when I hold out a hand to stop him.

"We don't want Stephan to know you're still alive," I tell him. "It may be wiser for you to stay here, enjoy your time with Charlotte. Ramos and I will do the hunting."

His gaze flicks Charlotte's way and a smirk lifts his lips. She winks at him.

"But you will be bringing the vamp here, yes?" he asks.

It doesn't take a genius to know what he's implying. He wants in on the action, and that's something I have no problem allowing.

"For the messy part? Yes."

Darkness slides behind his eyes, and his fangs push past his top lip. "Perfect."

TRACKING down and capturing one of the Nightwalker vamps is easier than expected. After Dorian's call on their way to the airport, all we had to do was follow the sirens. Ramos and I were able to pick one off in the industrial part of town, right before the highway exit ramp. A man in his mid forties who was scoping the area for new customers.

We dropped him off at Purgatory, and Ramos made him "comfortable" in the basement. Before I left, I told Ramos to do what he must to get him to talk, maybe even invite Viktor to get a few jabs in. As long as they kept him alive, I didn't care much what they did. But with Ramos's more...unique skills, I had no doubt we would be getting an answer fairly soon.

Exhausted, I have Holmes drive me home. As I walk through the front door, I check my phone for any calls or messages, but the screen is blank.

I'm not sure what I expected. Maybe a text from Dorian saying, "Oops. Had to off your brother. Didn't even make it to the airport."

And honestly, I wouldn't be surprised.

Laughing to myself, I look up and stop dead at what's before me. The carpet is torn to shreds, mud and blood paint the walls and floors, and deep scratches mark up the staircase. The entry table—which we had *just* replaced—is splintered in pieces again, the messenger bird's cage we'd bought Aria at the marketplace crushed and empty.

It looks like there's been a wild animal running amok through here. Maybe two.

My stomach tightens into a knot, but before I can call to Elias, he suddenly appears at the top of the second landing, covered in blood and completely naked.

"What happened here?" I snap, glancing into the parlor to see the couches torn up and the books all ripped apart, too. Fuck me. No one better have touched my office.

Elias hurdles himself over the railing, falls the two floors, and hits the ground in a crouch. When he straightens, I see worry etched deep on his brow. Something obviously happened while I was gone.

"Hellhounds," he growls. All the blood, scratches, and wreckage make sense now. "They tore up the entire place. Our rooms. The parlor. The dining room."

"My office?"

"I haven't gotten a chance to see the total damage yet, but so far it looks pretty bad."

It sure does. Especially from where I'm standing. "They must've been looking for Aria."

"Or the relics," he points out, which I hadn't even considered. It's a pretty good assumption though, and more than likely a right one, since Lucifer doesn't want us back in Hell. Send his hounds to bring Aria and the relics back to him.

"Thank fuck Aria wasn't here," he goes on. "That could've been really bad."

I don't even want to think about it. "And the hounds?"

"Dead. All of them."

"How many?"

"Four."

"Four?" Anger prickles up and down my arms. How the fuck did four hellhounds get into our home? It was Elias's job to keep them away. What the hell has he been doing all this time? Hunting rabbits? "And where were you?"

"A mile up north chasing…" He glances away. "…something else."

What is that supposed to mean?

"Cut the crap, Elias. How did four hellhounds get into this house?"

He runs a hand over his face and lets out an exasperated sigh. "Serena," he mutters on the exhale, and I'm unsure I've actually heard him right.

"I'm sorry, but did you say Serena?"

He nods. "The one and only. Yep. She popped up north of here, near our property line, and used the opportunity to distract me so that Lucifer's four mutts could sneak in here and trash the place."

Looks like her loyalties have remained the same. She's still one of Lucifer's groupies. I doubt she ever cared about Elias at all.

"You said you were chasing her… Please don't tell me you fucked her," I say. He may have said he learned his lesson when it came to her, but I don't know. He had fallen for her lies hard before.

He blanches. "What? No!"

"Good."

"I did almost kill her, though."

"I wish you had." I scan the foyer again, taking in all the damage. All our furniture, the walls, stairs, decor... All of it is going to have to be either fixed or replaced. Sighing, I rub the place between my brows where a terrible migraine is brewing. "Please tell me they didn't touch the relics."

"That was the first thing I checked. Still safe in your room."

Relief washes over me. At least there's that.

"And where's the lynx?" I ask, thinking how devastated Aria would be if anything else happened to him.

"Cassiel? Good question. He didn't come out to help when the hounds were here. I just assumed he was hiding under a bed somewhere, like a coward."

"If he's hurt..." I start but Elias is already nodding, understanding where I'm going with this.

"It'll break Aria's heart."

"Exactly."

A crash sounds down the hallway, near the rear of the mansion, and my heart drops. Elias and I stare at each other, the same thought passing between us.

More hellhounds.

Another loud thud, this time like something heavy falling over. A chair?

Not waiting a second more, we rush down the corridor, toward the loud sounds of destruction. We burst into the library to see not a hellhound but Cassiel balancing his massive body on the end of the chaise, surrounded by upturned tables and broken glass. He swats the air where a small black bird circles, just out of reach. The messenger bird.

"Are you shitting me?" Elias snorts. "He's just a giant pussy cat."

He walks over, and when the bird swoops low, he snatches it out of the air with one hand. Cassiel growls at him, and he snarls back, flashing sharp canines. Gingerly, he passes me the bird, which I hold in my enclosed hands. Its wings beat against my palms.

Even though the thing isn't real, the magic is fragile enough to snuff out with the slightest pressure of my closed fists. I think about how bad things could've been today—how close we could've been to losing Aria or the relics only because we glanced away for a millisecond.

There's too much at stake now. Too much riding on us succeeding in this. Not just for us, but for every soul out there.

If Lucifer succeeds in his plan to take down Heaven, well then, he could flex his muscles—one little squeeze of his hands—and all of earth, every human, every supernatural, would be at his mercy.

Crushed.

A day like this one could never happen again. No more slip ups. Because the next one could very well be our last.

I'm running crazily through the Amazon Rainforest, panic squeezing my lungs.

Strong arms grab me around my waist and I'm off my feet in seconds.

I cry out, batting away the hands gripping me, when a familiar voice floats in my ears. "Slow down, Aria." Maverick's breath is warm on my neck, his hold protective. "We've lost the tribe. They're no longer chasing us."

Gasping for air, I twist my head around to find that he's correct. Dorian is behind him, glancing back the way we came too, but we're alone. We are standing in the middle of the rainforest, practically swallowed by the greenery.

Maverick lowers me to my feet, but his arm remains tightly looped around my waist, holding me close.

"Okay, we need to regroup," I say. "What the hell just happened? Did anyone else notice that they were fighting among themselves as well? Perhaps we walked in on a tribe argument?"

"More like a war," Dorian adds. "Those spears are meant to kill."

"Maybe we should have fought them," Maverick says.

"Bad idea," I say. "We need to get back into the village without being attacked to retrieve the relic. It's in there, so attacking them is the opposite of what we need right now." Though, truth be told, the idea of just charging in there and taking the relic hums in the back of my mind too.

"What if they know what we came for?" Dorian asks.

"You're being paranoid," Maverick barks back. "They want Aria for themselves. Did you see any signs of females?"

I want to argue with them, but part of me starts to wonder if both of them are right. I don't even have the logic to reason why, but it feels right. Like these tribespeople are against us somehow.

"Okay, so what's the plan then? We sneak in and track it down?" I'm talking fast, my gaze swinging left and right. I know I'm buzzing on adrenaline, I feel it humming in my veins. I also don't feel completely right, as if something's twisted in my mind and I can't see beyond it. I keep praying it isn't Sayah, except, it feels different and I can't work it out.

"How are we going to do that?" Dorian asks. "They are everywhere and now we've lost our element of surprise."

"Have you gotten sloppy in your hunting since leaving Hell?" Maverick taunts.

"Fuck off. I'll run circles around you."

I rub my temples as the two go at it again, their fuses so short, anything sets them off. I get it, as I feel that way too, like I want to scream. And the realization comes to me fast that there's another element at play here that's influencing us.

Instead, I take a deep inhale, pushing aside the storm inside me, and place a hand on each of the guys' arms.

"Enough. Don't you feel it? Something's in the air. It makes us all angry and paranoid. It has to be what's affecting the tribesmen as well."

They look at me, neither responding right away, like my words take a bit to filter through the fog in their thoughts.

Dorian nods first and reaches over to take my hand in his. "I think you're right. We gotta stay focused."

Maverick's heaving for breath, his gaze on where Dorian holds me, where his thumb strokes the inside of my wrist.

"I know what this is," Maverick mutters. "You just want Aria for yourself and want to separate us, don't you?" He shoves a hand into Dorian's chest, sending him back a few steps.

Before I can even find the strength to put him in his place, Dorian releases me and leaps at Maverick. They both hit the ground and are rolling around like madmen, punching and fighting.

"Seriously, are you idiots? There are snakes, venomous spiders, fire ants, and so much more crawling all over the place. Get the hell up."

Not that they are listening to me, and I'm convinced at this rate, we will end up spending the night in the woods, then we'll die after being swarmed by all the deadly insects in this place. And eaten alive.

I find a stick on the ground and grab it before poking the two guys in the back and legs, who seem to be on a different level of existence. I huff with frustration, then pull out a bottle of water from my backpack and splash it all over them.

Their growls and attention swing my way, that has done the trick.

"Can you two stop fucking around and focus for two seconds?"

I feel the sting of my shoulder blades burrowing into my muscles at how tense they're making me. Realization resigning in their eyes, the duo climb to their feet, brushing off the debris from their clothes and hair. The blood from their split lips and cuts from their punches will heal soon enough I guess, but I don't care right now as I'm seconds from hitting them myself.

"We are not the enemy," I implore them.

They nod in unison, when I catch movement over Maverick's shoulder.

My heart nearly stops at the sight of the world's biggest centipede crawling up and over his shoulder, and holy shit, it's long and fat. I'm sure I've read these things are venomous and eat snakes.

"Maverick, whatever you do, don't move," I say.

Dorian rears back from him instantly, and of course Maverick does the opposite.

He's shifting around, moving. "What is it?"

The centipede is scrambling down his chest, making its way between the buttons of his shirt. Maverick might have screeched as he flicked the thing, which then comes flying towards Dorian and I.

I scream and throw myself out of the way, while Dorian

catches the thing like he's superman and tosses it into the woods. He shakes his head at us. "Babies."

"I wasn't scared," Maverick says, trying to look over his shoulders for more bugs, turning on the spot like a dog attempting to catch his tail.

"Well, I sure as heck was. New rule. Anyone gets a creature on them, don't freaking fling it at me, understand?"

We're all just standing there, I'm flustered as fuck, but I need to calm down.

"Let's set a plan," Dorian begins, his voice semi-normal, and please let it remain that way. "We go in calmly, maybe offer them your sandwiches, and I will use my mojo to reassure them we are safe. As I do that, you and Maverick go and collect the relic."

I nod because I don't see how else we can do this.

"Alright, I'm ready for this. How much time do we have until the boat comes back?" Maverick asks.

Dorian pulls out my phone and gasps. "Shit, forty minutes. How the hell did we lose so much time?"

"We gotta do this fast then," I say.

"And please, fight the urge to be paranoid and fight," I instruct them, to which they both agree, though proof will be in the pudding I guess.

We make our way back through the dense woodland, and I have no idea how we came so far and hadn't been bitten by something. Now that we're moving closer to the path, everything catches my attention, from the bright green snake curled up in a branch, the tarantula with a bird in its mouth, the bugs...I have never seen so many insects in my life. I'm surprised anyone can live here.

Dorian pauses as we reach the edge of the track, and farther down to our right lays the opening into the village. Unlike last time, the dozen men are now standing around, arguing in a language I don't understand, two are beating each other up.

"Hand over the sandwiches and water," Dorian orders. "Once I've got their attention, you two sneak around the back and do your thing."

"Deal," Maverick confirms, and he's eyes are on me with a ravenous look that sort of scares and turns me on. Why is he so weird sometimes?

Dorian grabs hold of the offerings and he takes off toward the village in a split second. Upon reaching the flat land, he slows and puts his hands in the air, with the food in his grip, I guess trying to look as harmless as possible. Which might be hard, considering the locals are lucky if they reach his chest in height, and are nowhere near as broad as him.

They turn on him, their spears pointed, but he doesn't flinch or back away. Instead, he talks to them. It's too far to hear them, but part of me swears he's speaking a combination of English and Portuguese. I lean forward, needing to hear his words, know what he's saying. For all I know, he could be ratting us out, telling them exactly where we are, so he can grab the relic first and look like the hero in all of this.

Maverick's in my ear, his hands on my waist, distracting me. "You ready to do this?" he whispers.

I turn my head to meet his gaze, and there's something almost obsessive in his eyes, like he's been waiting for the moment to have me all to himself. Of course, I might be imagining it all, as I still feel the heated call of the relic, the faint hum of the song, all while thoughts of paranoia swarm my mind like gnats.

It's almost like I'm suffocating on these overwhelming feelings.

Maverick grabs my hand, and we run in a roundabout trek around the village to avoid being seen. I can't even think about the fact that we're moving so quickly through a forest filled with all kinds of creatures, and I'm pretty certain this is the wrong thing to do.

I mean, sure Maverick doesn't care since he's a demon and things out there can't kill him, even if he did freak out over a centipede.

Branches swipe across my face, my hair caught in the plants we shove past, and I'm getting tangled in vines. Maverick is having none of it and like a knight in shining armor, is ripping at the plants attempting to wrap themselves around me.

"Do you want me to carry you?" he asks, sincerely.

While I entertained the notion, I doubt that would help our cause in moving swiftly, or from having things touch me. That is impossible.

"I'm fine," I whisper. "Let's just move quickly."

Maverick is next to me as we make haste.

"This jungle reminds me of the hunting grounds back home. It's fuming hot, plants and vines everywhere, and filled with monsters. Cain and I would go hunting there long ago," he whispers.

I never got the impression from Cain that he did much with his brothers, but then again, they've been around for an insane amount of time, so it would make sense that they had.

"What happened between you two?" I ask quietly as we push past the foliage.

"Time. Hell drama. Lucifer. Thing about my father is that he's a jealous bastard. When any of his sons got along, he saw it as a threat and drove them apart with lies. Because, you see, if any of us grew close, it might mean we could conspire against him."

"He's a psychopath." Just hearing the stories made me loathe Lucifer even more, which is hard considering I already want to see him dead.

"And so much more," Maverick answers.

Trampling onward, we soon find ourselves in the woods facing the rear of the huts. With no one in sight, Maverick and I move out silently, and sprint across the open ground to hide behind one of the homes. Our backs press to the huts, my heart pounding in my ears. His side presses so close to mine that I feel the heat he radiates like a furnace.

The hum of the song from earlier grows in volume in my ears. My toe is also buzzing uncontrollably in my boot. "The relic is near."

From our position, Dorian's voice reaches us from where he stands in the main village area.

"I am like a god," he says to the locals, in English this time. "The gods you pray to, that is me."

I roll my eyes while Maverick makes a fake choking sound. He leans in, whispering, "I just want to go out there and knock him flat to the ground. Then we'll see who the god is."

"Don't you dare," I hiss, snatching his arm, though I can't deny that hearing Dorian bragging does have my hackles rising.

Focus on the relic, I repeat to myself.

Maverick nods, except I don't believe him.

Not wasting another moment, I drag him around the curve of

the hut we're near. I peer out from the corner and find the tribesmen all looking up at Dorian as if believing his words. There are no other people around.

Where are the women and children?

I can't make out what Dorian is saying, but a man with facial markings stands before him, his hand weaving up and down as if describing a wave or a snake or hell knows what. Then he points to the sky. They are still talking about gods is my bet, maybe challenging Dorian.

Maverick is pressed up against me, his growl rolling through his chest, vibrating against my back. When I look at him over my shoulder, his eyes are locked on Dorian and the men. He's like a territorial wolf, ready to attack his prey.

"What's the bet, he's going to sell us out? I think it's just us two from here," he whispers. "We get the relic and leave him behind."

For a moment, I consider his words, when I catch myself, and scold myself for even thinking of such a thing.

"Shut the hell up and pull yourself together." I swear, we need as much distance from this relic as possible because it's the only reason to explain why I feel like I've got a split personality all of a sudden, except for the fact that we have to find it first and take it with us back home.

Maverick's hands are on my ass and he squeezes it. I flinch and turn, before shoving a hand to his throat. "What the hell are you doing?" I hiss.

But his eyes are milky, and he's not himself. Just like back in the woods, he's losing his mind fast.

Crap. I shove him to the back of the hut, and then slap him hard across the face. Yeah a bit over the top, but hell, I can't have him go haywire. "Pull your shit together."

Fire burns in his eyes, and next thing I know, he's throwing himself at me, and our mouths clash. It's explosive and scorching and so fucking hot that I forget myself. That hungry, devious side of me screams for him, to bring him over to my side, so if Dorian does turn against him, we are stronger together. I kiss him back with desperation, loving the way he tastes, the way he holds me like nothing can tear us apart.

Desire sparks within me, an arousal I've desperately held for Maverick whether I want to admit it or not, I crave him insanely.

I want this...I want him...I want him to have all of me.

He groans against me, his body pinning me to the back of the hut, his erection between us. His hands are on my breasts, squeezing, and he swallows my moans. I wrap a leg around his hip, practically climbing him like a tree, every inch of me begging him to claim me this very moment.

I whimper as his hand slides between my thighs, teasing me as he slowly drags his fingers over my aching pussy, only the fabric of my pants between us.

"Fuck," he growls in my mouth. "I'm going to taste you."

There's a sudden explosion of Dorian's laughter in the distance that breaks us apart, and we're both gasping for air.

Maverick's eyes cut toward the front of the hut where Dorian is still bragging. He snarls, fury morphing his expression, and before I can even clear the fog from my head and remind myself we're derailing and failing badly, he darts between two homes, directly for Dorian.

"Shit!"

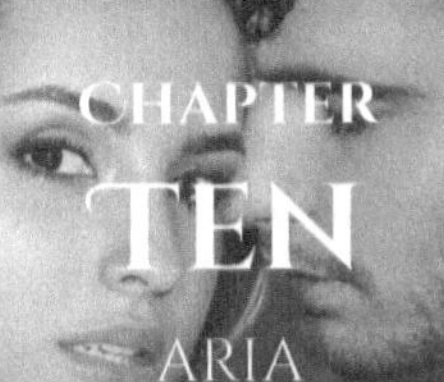

I'm gasping for air myself, stumbling to find my footing after Maverick's kiss...it left me completely destroyed. And as dumb as it sounds, I want more.

Except, my head isn't right, and I fear I'm being delusional.

Maverick and Dorian are falling apart around me, and I'm not doing any better. We're all going to kill each other, I feel it, and that's if the natives don't do it first.

"Focus, Aria. What are you here for, again?" I'm rocking on my feet. "Relic. Hell, we need to find the relic in this village, except, we are in so much trouble."

The sound of Maverick's voice booms along with Dorians from in front of the huts, but I can't make out their words.

So, I choose to leave them behind and move quickly while I have a fraction of my brain in working order. The sting of rejection that he left me, that he will now partner up with Dorian against me flares, but I fight the jealousy, the paranoia.

Focus. Focus. Focus.

My buzzing toe brings me to a hut right at the end of the village. The building is larger than the others, with a pointier roof.

I hurry up the creaky steps that resemble a small ladder to reach the front porch, when I notice none of the men are even remotely looking my way. I do catch Maverick and Dorian in an argument, their hands thrown in the air, their chests puffed out. Seriously, I can't even try to make sense of anything when my insides feel twisted like I've been morphed into a pretzel.

The doorway to the hut is dark and covered by hanging strips of long grass.

I know this is the right place. My toe is going berserk, the song wailing in my ears, and on the inside my chest is on fire.

With soft steps, I part the grass doorway, then slide inside. That's all this hut is, just one huge room. There are close to twenty people in here already, all women and children by the looks of it, but they are on their knees and bowing forward, murmuring things I don't comprehend. They are all facing the front of the room, seeming to be worshipping a small, golden statue positioned on a wooden pedestal.

I blink through the darkness, waiting for my eyes to adjust from the bright light outside to see things clearer.

Without a shadow of doubt, I know instantly that the golden object they are worshipping is the relic. It doesn't take an expert to work out that thing is affecting these people. To the point that they consider it godly.

Sticking to the wall, I inch forward to get a better view of the item, my pulse racing.

How the heck do I get that thing out of here, anyway? I doubt they'll let me skip away with their god under my arm. Maybe I ought to bring Dorian in here so he can claim to be their god instead. While I had mocked him, it may not be such a bad idea.

On the bright side, the more I shuffle up in slow motion, the clearer the object comes into view. I'm staring at a golden snake coiled in on itself with its diamond-shaped head sticking out from the middle with the brightest emerald eyes. It's beautiful for sure. Where in the world did these people find the relic anyway?

I shift to turn around, when the floorboard creaks under me.

Panic freezes me on the spot, and everyone's head snaps up, their eyes on me. I might just pass out. Their looks are confused, and who could blame them? They are praying and just found a completely strange, city person in their place of worship.

"Hi," I say stupidly, while awkwardly waving my hand.

But my chance to make a bigger fool of myself is stolen by the sudden explosive sound of shouting coming from outside. I flinch in my boots, and even the women and children are up on their feet, scrambling to the door, pouring outside in a flash flood.

I'm swaying on my feet, my gaze swinging from them exiting to the relic they've left completely abandoned. Every inch of me is trembling, but there's no time to waste. I run across the room and grab the golden snake, which is the size of a small chihuahua, and won't fit in any of my pockets, but holy shit, it weighs a ton. It must be made of pure gold because my arms are about to break off.

Shuffling off my bag from my shoulders, I unzip it and shove the snake in there, except when I drop it in, it falls all the way through the base, tearing a hole in the fabric of my bag.

Plonk.

The relic hits the floorboards.

Oh, fuck off!

I'm seething with anger. Seeing I have nothing of real value in the bag, I dump it and pick up the statue then glance around, but there's nothing else in the room for me to use to carry it. I dart right outside onto the wooden veranda. All the women and children are down in the center of the village with the men, and they're surrounding something...

I step to the end of the veranda and I gasp at the sight.

Dorian and Maverick are each tied up to a thick branch at their backs, and the men are building a mountain of broken branches at their feet. They're going to burn them? Why the fuck are they just staying there, shouting at each other, still arguing?

Carefully, I step down the ladder while juggling the golden snake that keeps threatening to slip out of my grasp.

I have half a mind to just leave them behind because for all I know, they tried to tell the locals about me stealing the relic which caused them to be tied up in the first place.

The snake hums in my arms in tune with the lullaby in my ear, while the fire of paranoia bubbles in my chest.

Leave them, that's what I should do.

A sudden loud honk blares in the distance, and the familiar sound cuts through my thoughts.

The boat. Oh, shit.

The charter guy has returned, and there is no way in the world that I am being left behind in this place to go mad.

I rush right past the cluster of people seeming to cheer their newly captured victims. Once I'm closer to the path that brought us to the village and against my better judgment, I unleash a loud whistle, gaining everyone's attention.

Seconds are all it takes and all eyes are on me.

The tribesmen instantly see what's in my arms and swing in my direction, their spears pointed at me, promising death.

"Pare," I call out, one of only two words I know in Portugese. One being stop, and the other is cócegas, meaning tickle, and that isn't going to work now, is it. Joseline had taught me a few of the words she'd learned from taking language at school and those were all that stuck with me.

Raising the golden snake over my head as if to show I'll throw it and break it, I realize what a terrible mistake that is. My arms are trembling horribly.

"Pare," I yell again, the tribespeople pausing while the women and children have fallen to their knees in my direction praying to the snake. My heart goes out to these poor people, fooled by the magic of this object. Just like Dorian and Maverick, seemingly made to forget that they are freaking demons and mere rope can't hold them captive.

They are both looking at me strangely, like they are trying to work out what I'm doing.

"The boat is here, free yourself or I'm leaving without you," I yell at them.

As if my words actually ring some common sense in their relic-influenced brains, they writhe and thrust against their restraints. They break out of them like the Hulk, and those around them back away. Smart move.

"Please, we need to leave now," I insist, already recoiling, but the few tribal men in front of me haven't taken their attention off the snake in my hands. I lower it because my muscles are screaming and cradle it against my chest instead.

Dorian is shaking his head, and I see the same battle across Maverick's face.

"Focus," I call out. "We got the relic, and we need to go."

When one of the spear-wielding men turns to Dorian, screaming for him to get back, he moves as swiftly as the wind, snatching the weapon from the man's grip and snapping it in half over his knee.

And well, let's just say, that has the rest of the men swinging in his direction with aggressive stances and war cries on their lips.

But when another honk of the boat comes, panic digs its claws into me.

"Run," Maverick says. "Get to the boat, and don't you dare leave without us."

I spin on my heels and clumsily run down the dirt track through the woods the way we came. The relic is a bitch to carry, but when I glance back, there are half a dozen women chasing after me, their grassy dresses flap in every direction, revealing they are completely naked underneath.

Except, it's their panic-stricken expressions that worry me. They'll do anything to get back their god, so I run faster. The way back seems so much farther than I remember, and it feels like I'm running forever.

My lungs burn, my arms are on fire, and my heart is drumming.

The boat soon comes into view, and he's already starting to pull away from the shore.

"Wait!" I scream. "Please wait, I'm here. We're coming."

The driver's head turns in my direction, and he must see the mob on my heels as his eyes widen to the size of orbs.

Everything in me is thrumming, the shudder in my chest unstoppable.

Our boat driver has hopped out of the boat and is coming right toward me, grasping a gun. Next thing, he points it into the sky and shoots.

The sound is ear-piercing, my ears ringing louder than the relics' song. I hunch forward and dart right past him, taking a look behind me.

Those chasing me have ceased chasing me, but they aren't retreating. They are staring at me taking what they believe belongs to them. I hate doing this, the pain painted on their face leaves me feeling like shit. But this relic isn't their god, or anyone's, and if left with them, how long before they turn on one another?

Once I reach the water's edge, I spot Dorian and Maverick sprinting toward us so fast, the women barely notice them zipping past. They're by my side in seconds, and our driver is rushing to the boat.

"Get in," he yells at us. "I don't know what you did, but I don't want to kill anyone today."

I gasp for air, breaths see-sawing in and out of my chest. My gaze swings from Maverick to Dorian. "What do we do? This relic seems to have a large radius. We can't take this back through the city or even on the boat for long before it starts influencing the driver."

"Cover it with soil," Maverick suggests. "The earth should safeguard its power, even if for a bit."

"How can you be sure?" I ask, doing exactly what he says regardless. The soil from the water is muddy, and I use it to frantically coat as much mud on the snake as possible, covering its eyes, and in that exact moment, a sense of heaviness slips off my shoulders.

"Do you feel that?" I say, glancing up at the men.

"It's done." Maverick tears off his shirt, revealing a sculpted chest that has me staring at him a bit too long, and he wraps the relic in it.

Dorian snatches me into his arms and I'm on the boat in seconds. We all are, standing there, filthy, breathing heavily, and terror leaching through me at how badly that could have really turned out. The tribespeople crowd near to watch us leave, and I wish them all the best to find happiness once more from the demonic relic that only brought chaos to their doorsteps.

"I'm not even going to ask," the driver says, steering us out of the tight channel and onto the main Amazon River, back the way we'd come.

"Best you don't," Dorian says.

The three of us are sitting in the back seat, and I'm stunned at what we just went through. "For the next relic, I vote Elias and Cain go to fetch it without us," I suggest.

"Fuck yes," Maverick answers. "I still can't make sense of the things I was feeling back there, you know. I mean, to be honest, they're still lingering in the back of my head like a cobweb of that angry, possessive sensation, but I completely lost control in the village."

"Yes, you both did."

Maverick arches an eyebrow, his hair unruly and dirt covers his cheeks. "Says the girl who kissed me like she might rip off my clothes despite the danger."

My mouth drops open. "Excuse me, you attacked me."

"Wait up," Dorian says, his voice deepening. "You two kissed while I was trying to save our asses? And since when is there kissing going on between you?" His hands are on me, and he tugs me against him possessively, which I completely adore.

Maverick bursts out laughing. "Is that the time you were telling everyone you were a god?"

I can't hold it back and I'm giggling at him. "That part was hilarious, not to mention both of you letting yourselves get tied up like roast chickens. What the hell did you two do?"

Dorian cuts Maverick a sharp look. "This idiot levitated himself off the ground."

"I had them convinced until you lunged at me."

I'm still laughing, collapsed back into the seat, enjoying the cool breeze, never wanting to do that again. Maybe I'm laughing so much because of the serious danger we were in. "You two lost control big time."

"No one is to ever talk about what happened here, deal?" Dorian asks, his wrists still raw and pink from where he'd been tied up.

"Deal," Maverick states, and now both of them are glaring my way.

"Elias would love to hear how you both almost became kebabs."

When their glares only intensify, I huff. "Chill out, I won't say a word. I swear it."

"Good," Dorian says. "Now, I have an important question for you."

"Yeah, and what's that?" I ask.

"Who's the better kisser between us? It's me isn't it?"

Maverick barks out a forceful laugh, and it seems the relic isn't fully out of their system.

"That's something I'll never tell." I'd rather tease them and not cause competition because, before I know it, this will filter back to Elias and he will demand it's him. That's what happens when dealing with so many egos.

I laugh and kick back, smiling, because for the past two hours, it felt as though I'd been run through a meat grinder, and now I just want to catch my breath. And if these two don't stop staring at me like I'm some kind of candy, I might very well have to announce that I pick neither as my ideal kisser.

The cab driver comes to a quick halt halfway down the driveway of our mansion. There are half a dozen trucks parked in front of us, and then there are men in brown uniforms everywhere carrying boxes and furniture into the house. Is that a couch?

"What's going on?" I lean forward from the back seat. "Did Cain and Elias decide to move out while we were gone?"

Maverick laughs. "I wouldn't put it past them."

"They wouldn't." I'm already climbing out of the cab, worry burrowing through me. I hurry across the snow-covered grounds, the cold biting into my flesh, mostly because I left my coat in the cab. But I need to know what is going on, to make sure Cain and Elias are alright.

I rush up the front steps and Elias pulls open the door at the same time that I reach for the handle.

"Aria!" His eyes widen, and he's got me in his arms before I can even say hi. I'm wrapped in his strong arms, our mouths finding each other. The kiss is hungry but short as he has me on my feet in seconds. "We had no idea you were back already. No one contacted us. How did it go?"

"Yeah, Dorian's phone went dead back in Brazil, and it's not like Maverick or I have one, but the mission was a success." I grin. "But is there something we should know?" I glance at the trucks behind me. Add to that, the hallway is barren of furniture, the walls sport gaps in them, and someone is plastering and filling as we speak. "Was there a war in here?"

"Excuse me," a man says from behind me, and Elias takes my hands, drawing me out of the doorway. Two workmen shuffle through the double doors carrying a bed.

"Close to it," Elias says. "We've had a hellhound incident. Fucking furballs broke in and destroyed the place, searching for you or the relics. Probably both."

"Shit! Did you and Cain get injured?"

He shakes his head. "Boss man is in his office setting things up after the hounds tore it apart. He's pissed. But I told him it's the perfect chance to redecorate the mansion with new furniture." He's talking fast...the nervous kind. The attack rattled him whether he tries to put on a brave face or not. We definitely need to trade war stories once we settle down.

But my head is too blurred to think logically, when my thoughts fly to what would have happened if I'd been here at the time of the attack. Then panic strikes.

"Crap! Cassiel? Please tell me he's okay?"

"He's in your room, little rabbit. Slept during the whole ordeal and not a whisker was harmed."

I'm already darting up the stairs to my room, needing to see him for myself. Passing more furniture deliverers, I sprint right into my room to find it empty. Everything is gone.

Except for Cassiel, who sits on his belly in the middle of the room, his tail swishing from side to side, his eyes glued on the small cage with the magical messenger bird Cain had bought for me from the Storm markets.

I dart over to him and loop my arms around his neck, but he doesn't even look my way. "Did you even miss me?" I kiss the top of his head and pull back on my heels, scratching his back, which he loves. "It seems I missed quite the craziness here. But I'm super glad you, Cain, and Elias are all safe. That's what matters."

"Fascinating. The cat comes before me?" Cain's deep voice says from the doorway behind me.

A smile curls my lips, and my heart is in my throat. I'm on my feet, flying in his direction. I crash into him and he's stumbling back into the hallway, not expecting me to come at him so fast.

He's got me in his arms, my legs curled around his waist, and we're kissing. I feel dirty at how quickly I jump him, when a workman can walk in on us at any moment. But in truth, I couldn't care less when I've been desperate to be back home with my men.

Cain's hands are on my ass, squeezing.

"I've missed you," I whisper against his lips as he turns around and has me pinned to the wall, pressing into me with his hard body.

I whimper when his finger slides to the fire between my legs, his forehead against mine, and his breathing heavy. "I want to strip you down now, spread your legs, and fuck you."

His breath is on my face, and I'm moaning against him, a shiver of excitement racing over my body.

He gently kisses me again, finding my tongue and sucking on it. I rub my hips against his erection pressing between my thighs, gasping with pleasure.

His teeth nibble on my lower lip, pulling it, the intensity in his eyes overcome with desire. "You make me so hard," he growls, pushing his hips against me, the hunger in his eyes deepening.

I wrap my arms around his neck. "So, what are you going to do about it?" I tease, when he slides a hand down between our bodies and pushes under the band of my jeans and underwear.

He grins wickedly, and I moan as he slides two fingers into me, curling them to find that exact spot that drives me insane.

"Oh, hell." My hips rock to meet his thrusts, our kisses wild and chaotic, matching the racing adrenaline bursting inside me.

"Is this what you had in mind?" he growls, and captures my lips again while he keeps fingering me ferociously.

I shiver against him, completely falling apart at his touch, writhing as he drags his mouth down to my neck where he licks me. "I love how you taste, how you smell. I never want you gone from me again for so long. Never."

His movements are aggressive, fast, and I'm drowning in arousal. I'm clawing his shoulders to hold on as I've lost all ability to control my body. Cain owns me, he does as he pleases, and I just moan, losing grip on reality.

Rocking back and forth on his fingers, his teeth find the sweet flesh just above my collarbone, and the moment he bites down, I scream from the orgasm that tears through me.

Cain never ceases his fingering, his biting, until I beg for mercy.

His eyes are completely black when he looks up at me, and I see that he lost himself too, and I fucking love that about him. With a blink, his eyes are back to normal, then he takes his hand out of my pants.

"I'm guessing you missed me too?" I laugh and get to my feet, my knees wobbly at first.

"You have no idea."

Only then do I realize we've had an unexpected observer.

One of the delivery men stood at the end of the hall near the staircase, his mouth and eyes wide open, and the box he was carrying lay discarded by his feet.

"Leave," Cain growls at the man, who flinches and scrambles down the steps. Then he turns to me. "I never asked. How did the trip go?"

"We got the relic is all that matters, and Dorian thinks it's the intestines since it resembles a snake."

He's nodding, smiling with that perfect grin. "Should I ask what that means?"

"Best you don't."

His phone rings from his pocket, drawing his attention from me, and I want to toss the thing out the window. I've missed him and Elias like crazy and I want nothing more than to be in their arms.

Cain collects the phone and looks at the screen, his brow pinching. "I've got to take this. I'll be back though. I want to hear everything." He hurries down the hallway and downstairs, and I enter my room where I find Cassiel, still obsessed with the bird. My breaths are still racing from how intense things got there, but I'm not surprised in the slightest. My relationship with the demons in my life has taken on a life of its own.

When a knock comes at the door, I'm greeted by two delivery guys carrying what looks like my new bed. I know instantly that I need to get out of their way.

"I'll let you guys set up, I'm heading out," I tell them, then rush over to collect the small cage with the bird. Cassiel instantly rushes after me, sniffing at the little black sparrow. I don't stop until we're in the backyard. I sit on the porch steps and stare out into the woods in the distance. Cassiel plonks down beside me while I cradle the cage in my lap.

The little creature looks real with the little chirps it makes, even its eyes move about, and seeing the house is chaotic, this is the perfect time to use this spell.

I open the cage and collect the sparrow into my hand. It doesn't fight me, and at my touch, it feels feathery but soft on the inside, like if I squished it too much, my fingers would go right through it.

Cassiel props his chin on my shoulder, intrigued by the bird way too much. I take a deep breath, and say, "I have no idea if this is going to work, but I'm gonna try. Hey Joseline, it's me Aria. Great news, Maverick has canceled your contract, so your soul is free, girl. No demon owns you. Anyway, I miss you terribly, and please—"

The bird flinches in my grasp, and it's twitching in my hand, so I unfurl my fingers. Then it flutters its wings wide and takes off. Cassiel lunges after it, but I snap my arms around his neck, and hold him back. "Nope, that's not for you."

Guess there is a limit on the length of the message. I lift my neck and watch the little thing disappear into the distance. Cassiel plonks back down next to me, both of us bathing in the sunlight, and I wish I could hear Joseline's voice and make sure she's doing alright.

DORIAN

CAIN CAUGHT me up on the shit that had gone down in the mansion over the last few days, leaving me furious. We're dealing with enough shit from Lucifer without having these bastard vampires causing havoc in our town.

In hindsight, we should have spilled their blood the moment we got a whiff of their intrusion on our territory. But we fucked up and let the opportunity slip as we dealt with more pressing issues —Hellhounds, Sayah, not losing Aria.

So, now I stroll right into Purgatory at Cain's command to get intel out of the vamp with my incubus power. Ramos and Viktor hadn't had much success it seems, and I have no doubt those two excel at torture, which tells me these bloodsuckers are more afraid of upsetting their new master vampire, Stephan. Cain told me to do this fast, so that's the plan.

The club is quiet during the day, but still operates for business clientele who love to share a drink and lap dance over their lunch breaks.

I amble my way down into the basement of Purgatory to find a vamp half slumped over in the iron chair he's tied to.

On my approach, his head snaps up, fangs bared. The fucker is bruised and bleeding, one eye closed shut from how puffy it is. I feel no remorse for this ass. He looks like he could be in his forties in human years, short dark hair, huge bent nose, and lips that are all cracked. He's on the thinner side, but when it comes to vampires size doesn't matter as much, as they are all fucking strong. The undead seem to have that ability in natural abundance.

He hisses at my approach, writhing and fighting the chains restraining his arms and legs.

"I have a feeling you're going to tell me everything I ask," I tell him.

He huffs and spits out blood on the concrete floor between us. "Try your hardest. You're not going to scare me, so save your breath. It won't last once we take over Glenside and everyone in it."

I walk around him, circling him, knowing this will be so easy... too easy, and really I'm not beyond having some fun. I hate anyone who threatens me or those close to me. And right now I'm just pissed that I'm wasting my time with this prick instead of being back at the mansion with Aria.

Circling around him once more, I slap a hand to the top of his head and fist his hair, wrenching his head back. He stares at me upside down, and that's when I unfurl the demonic magic that makes me who I really am.

His eyes widen as he takes in the dark horns that curve out from the top of my head, at the intricate tattoos weaving across my flesh, but I see his attention homes in on the blue runes in my skin that awaken my incubus power.

"How you feeling?" I ask, grinning.

"What the fuck are you, man?"

I grab the knife from my belt and place the blade against his neck. No words are needed because the terror on his face is all I need. The knife bites into his flesh as I swipe it across his throat, just deep enough that it bleeds him, but not enough to kill him. Not yet anyway.

He bucks in the seat, thrusting against my hold on his head. I release his head, then move to stand in front of him. Blood drips from his neck and onto his clothes, and he's hissing at me, the cold-blooded monster showing its true form.

Crouching down, I flick the blade in my hand. "Demons don't need weapons to kill, did you know that? We do well enough ourselves, though it's messy. Flesh torn, bones snapped, all while you're alive. That's the thing about us, we love to watch the terror in our victims' eyes."

I don't give him a chance to respond, but jam the blade right in that sensitive spot between his thigh and groin. I smile as I draw it back, blood spurting everywhere.

His screams bleed into the darkness around us and I close my eyes, bathing in them. There's something almost soothing about terrified screams. While I preferred not to get my hands dirty back in Hell, I never passed up the chance to make the worst of the worst suffer. That's the thing about Hell...many feed on fear, and the sweet, sickly sensation that slithers over me from this vamp brings back memories of ancient times. Of the blood, massacres, the battles, the fun we'd have. From a young age, Cain and I hunted, and once we brought Elias into our pack, he took it to a brand-new level of torment.

I won't deny, I do miss some of those old days. But now, I take pleasure in slow torture, which fits with seeking information.

When his screams are stifled and morph into sobs, I close in and grab his tongue from his mouth, a disgusting pale thing, then I grab the knife again.

He whimpers, his eyes drowning in terror, and when the stink of piss hits me, I look down to see he's wet his pants.

Fuck.

He's trying to say something, so I release that slimy thing he calls a tongue and wipe my hand down my pants.

I stare him in the eyes, and I call on my persuasion ability when I talk to him, needing him to open up before he bleeds out too much and becomes hysterical, like vamps have been known to do.

"You will tell me everything I need to know." I push out with my power, letting it coat my words.

"I'll talk." He's nodding his head like one of those bobbing dolls, his face streaked with blood and tears.

"Of course you will. What the hell is Stephan up to?"

He's whimpering, and it's pathetic really, how much I see him fighting my ability. Except he's never going to win.

I point the bloodied tip of the blade to his groin and press down, just in case he forgets who's in charge here. I don't give a shit what big bad monster you are, no man wants his cock hacked and sliced, even if it grows back.

"Don't make me ask again."

He's shaking terribly, and starts mumbling, "C-Cookies."

"Come again?" Seriously, he fucks with me and I'm finishing him now.

"T-The abandoned cookie factory down t-town." He's practically convulsing, fighting himself to shut the hell up. This is so much fun.

"What about it?"

"Hush. It's where Stephan keeps the Hush."

The drug that the news has been talking about with humans overdosing and dying, and I've heard similar stories of supernaturals.

"Why?" I press him.

"Money," he yells. "For fuck's sake, I've told you everything."

I somehow doubt that.

"Try again," I growl, tired of this game, and heavy power seeps from my words.

He falls silent in response and looks at me like he's gone comatose, then he speaks. "H-He's gonna kill you all and those who don't die from Hush will be turned."

I'm on my feet and wipe my blade on the shoulder of his shirt before tucking it into the back of my belt. So, Stephan's making himself an army, while building his wealth, and then like any dictator, he'll spread his takeover across the country, the world. It's what I would do too, if I was a sadistic bastard. But those days are way behind me.

"Y-You gonna let me go now?" He's shaking, bleeding worse, and I'm tired of looking at his damn face.

"Sure, I'll give you the freedom you seek." I undo the chains keeping him locked to the chair, and rip them off his ankles, but leave his hands tied behind his back. "Now, you're going to be a good boy, aren't you?"

He is desperately nodding, and doesn't even move to run.

I grab him by the hair and drag him up the stairs. He's stumbling behind me, crying out. Thing is, while he's in my influence, he stands no chance to think for himself.

The few customers in the club glance our way, including Antonio from the bar, but this is a rather regular image seen in Purgatory. Us taking out the trash. I rip open the doors into the foyer and then the main door.

The vamp is backpedaling now. He's screaming for help, but no one's coming to his aid.

I heave him forward and kick him right into direct sunlight.

He howls instantly, and rushes back toward us, but I slam the door shut in his face. And my last image of him is his body already disintegrating into ash. Seconds later, I reopen the door to a small pile of dust on our doorstep.

Well, that definitely feels better. One vamp down, dozens to go.

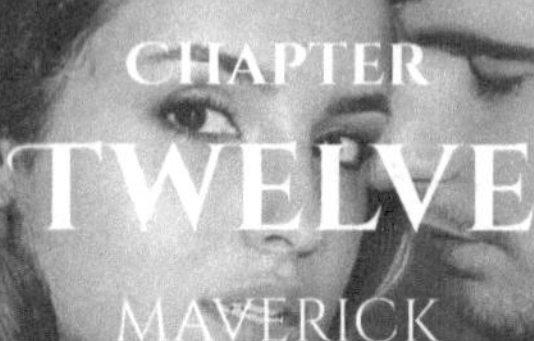

I stand at the edge of my room, staring down the crudely painted target I made and hung up on the opposite wall to practice on. Well, I say *my* room loosely. Since when we'd come back from Brazil, I'd found Cain had set up a single bed and dresser for me in the basement room they'd locked me up in.

How sweet of my brother, right?

It was hardly close to the extravagance I lived in back in Hell, but it would do. Besides, I didn't mind the dark and damp, almost dungeon-like atmosphere. I've slept in worse.

Retrieving the intestine relic has granted me other liberties, such as allowing me my daggers, so I've been passing the time sharpening them and brushing up on my combat skills, just in case they're needed in the final showdown with Lucifer.

Or anyone else who feels like testing me.

With only a quick glance at the target, I throw one of them with a flick of my wrist. It sails across the room and its blade embeds perfectly in the bull's-eye.

I laugh to myself. It's almost *too* easy.

Closing my eyes, I chuck the other dagger. The door creaks open the same time I hear the thud of the blade making contact with the target, and I look up to see Aria's head peering inside, staring at my dagger only inches away from her face with complete and utter terror.

Slowly, she pushes the door open more, her cheeks deathly pale and her hands trembling. "That was a little too close for comfort," she says, and swallows when she glances at the daggers again. She's wearing a white sweater that swoops down one shoulder and exposes the creamy skin of her collarbone and cleavage. The tight black leggings may not reveal any flesh, but I can make out every curve of her tantalizing body. Her thighs. Her ass.

Even though there's no secrecy to her—I've seen her naked, after all—my muscles tighten at the potential of getting a look at it all again.

I walk over, getting close enough to brush by her, and rip the daggers out of the wood. Just the brief contact with her sends my pulse skipping. It's unnerving and invigorating at the same time. I never thought anyone could affect me this way, especially a female.

"I wasn't expecting any visitors," I say, strolling across the room again and taking my position like before.

She quickly moves away from the target, closer to my bed. "I can go...if you want."

"No." The word flies from my mouth faster than my brain can realize it, and I quickly clear my throat and regather myself. My grip on the blades' handles tightens. "I'm not doing much anyway. Just practicing my way around a knife or two."

She glances back at the wooden plank, marked up with all my past throws. Mostly in the middle circle. "I can see that," she replies. "I was almost your new target."

"Believe me. If I wanted to hit you, I would have. I never miss."

She eyes me. "Right..."

"Is there a reason you're down here?" Holding up each blade, I pretend to examine their edges, running my thumb along them to test for sharpness until the pinch of pain and the swell of blood on my skin gives me the answer.

"Can you teach me?"

Her question throws me off kilter. "Uh, excuse me?"

"Can you teach me," she repeats a bit louder, "you know, to use a weapon like you."

Interesting...

Definitely not what I expect from her, but I am learning quickly that Aria is full of surprises. And this one I rather like.

I run my bleeding thumb over my bottom lip and then chase it with my tongue. Her gaze watches my every move with intrigue. Studying me.

I confuse her.

Excite her.

Good.

I want to do all that to her, plus so much more.

I want to test her limits.

Fuck her.

Taste her need.

Hurt her in the best kind of ways.

But as much as I long to explore those things, there's one big problem blocking my way.

My brother. Cain.

He's obviously smitten with her, and I'd heard his threat to leave her alone loud and clear. If I ever want to escape Lucifer's tyranny and make my own little piece of Hell on earth, then I need to stay on his good side. Gain his trust. Follow his rules.

And playing around with Aria clearly isn't going to gain me any of those things.

But boy, would it be fun.

"You want to learn how to fight?" I ask her, wondering what her true motives could be. She's so small, young. If it weren't for her shadow, she wouldn't be able to defend herself much.

Maybe that's the point.

She nods. "Whenever we're attacked, I have to run or watch from the sidelines as the guys take the lead, and I'm tired of it. I don't want to be rescued anymore. I don't want to be scared—" She stops abruptly and clamps her mouth shut. I suspect she's just revealed something to me she wished she hadn't, and when a blush kisses her cheeks, that guess is confirmed.

"Being afraid isn't a weakness, Aria," I say. "All emotions can be harnessed, learned from and used to your advantage."

"How do you know that?"

"It's my business to know," I reply.

"Oh, that's right. You can manipulate emotions."

"I wouldn't say manipulate. That sounds like I'm doing something wrong. I simply amplify or repress the ones that are already there."

She rolls her eyes. "Same thing."

"I don't think so."

"Whatever helps you sleep at night, Maverick," she says.

Arguing with her is pointless, so I turn and place my daggers on the dresser.

"Look, let's try this again." Aria begins and comes up behind me. "Please show me how to defend myself. You're the only one who can."

I don't know why, but hearing her say the word "please" has desire stirring. Fuck, what I would do to hear her begging to taste my cock while on her knees. To wrap one of my brother's stupid ties around her neck and use it to force myself so far down her throat that she chokes and gags but still can't get enough.

I shake the poisonous thoughts from latching onto me. Tragically, I have to be good. At least until Lucifer is defeated and the power shifts to us. Then I can say fuck Cain and do whatever I want.

But that isn't now.

"Ask one of your demons upstairs," I bite out. "I'm sure Cain would show you if you asked."

Aria glances away. "He'll never let me touch a weapon. Let alone fight with one," she murmurs. "He's too afraid I'll break."

I huff a laugh at that.

"Besides, I don't think I've ever seen Cain, Dorian, or Elias using a weapon before. Just you."

Also true. My brothers—well, most demons—use their brute strength or abilities when facing down an opponent. Weapons are seen as a sign of weakness. But not to me. I fight smarter, not harder. Living with six older sin demon brothers and one crazy as fuck father has taught me that.

I see no shame in using my daggers. I see strategy.

This may be a way for me to spend more time with her. Not break any rules, technically, but annoy my brother in the process.

Snatching my daggers again, I turn around with a smirk. "You know what? I think that may be able to be arranged."

She grins at me and bounces on her toes. "Okay, what's first?"

I answer by pushing one of my dagger's handle into her hand.

Gripping it loosely, she pales. "Uh...Shouldn't we start without the daggers first? Maybe work on stance or balance or something?"

"My brother's paranoia's gotten into your head I see." I laugh. "If you're going to be learning to fight from me, then that's just what we're going to do. Learn while fighting."

"Can't I get hurt?"

"Of course you can. Either of us can. That's half the fun." I hold up my dagger and point the tip at her. Hesitantly, she mimics me, but I can already see her hand quivering. Despite her obvious fear, she holds her chin up as she faces me down.

Oh boy. I'm going to enjoy this.

I lurch forward and swing my blade, causing her to leap back with a squeal. I come at her again, jabbing right, but she dances out of the way.

"Are you *trying* to kill me?" she gasps as I slice the air, trying to catch a piece of pretty unmarked flesh.

"Not kill. Only maim a little."

Backpedaling, she continues to dodge my attacks. Her back slams against the wooden target, and when she realizes she's trapped herself, panic flashes across her face. "Maverick!"

I aim for her shoulder, adjust my grip on the handle, and stab out. She drops at the last minute and the sharp tip embeds into the wood instead.

"You can't run forever," I say, as she hurries under my arm. Grunting, I rip out the dagger, spin, and something silver flashes before my eyes.

I feel the burning sting on my cheek before my brain can register what's happened. Aria's holding up her blade and red glistens on the edge. Blood.

My blood.

My fingers fly to my cheek, and when I pull back, they're covered in blood, too.

Shit. She's drawn first blood.

Shocked and slightly amused, I look up at her to find that she's smiling. There's a devilish gleam in her eye, too. The same one I'd seen when we'd faced off in front of Lucifer, and again the night Sayah took over.

It may be the shadow creature's influence this time; it may not be. There's no way to really know. But one thing's for sure, seeing that familiar darkness slide behind her gaze, the one I can recognize in myself, it makes my cock hard as a rock.

"You like to see me bleed, don't you?" I ask her, my voice deepening as my arousal grows. "You want to make me hurt?"

At first, she hesitates. But then, her gaze slides to the dagger with my blood dripping down it's blade and a pleased smirk lifts her lips.

Oh, yes...

Lunging toward me, she swipes at me again, her movements increasing in speed tenfold. I dash to the side, and lash out with my own, but she twists and throws out her weapon to meet mine. Our daggers clash.

"You lied to me," she says, sliding the knife up and down mine. It makes an ear-splitting sound ring out, and chills race up and down my spine. It's as if she knows what she's doing to me. Teasing me. Pushing the boundaries of my control.

"You made me trust you." Her dark eyes are locked on mine. "Put your ring on my finger."

"Don't forget I dragged you to Hell," I tack on.

She stomps on my foot with her heel, and pain bounces through me. I grunt, but I see her next attack coming, so when she swipes at me again, I shift and find my opening. This time, my weapon finds skin.

She stumbles back, bumping into the dresser, more shocked than anything. It's just a small cut, nothing serious, but her dagger drops from her hand and she peers down at the delicate crimson line across her right breast.

My mouth parches at the sight of it, and suddenly it's all I can focus on. All I can think about.

She's breathing rapidly, and with every rise and fall of her chest, my heart pumps a little faster. I'm moving closer to her before I know it, sliding my hand behind her back, and pulling her body against mine. She doesn't fight me at all. Doesn't even say a word as I dip my head and run my tongue across the curve of her breast, along the cut, and tasting salt and copper.

Still, she doesn't stop me.

It's so easy to become enveloped in her intoxicating scent. This close to her, I can see the sheen of sweat gleaming on her skin. Her pulse thumping in her neck, her throat as she tries desperately to swallow.

Fucking hell, I want more of her.

As I lift my head, our eyes meet again, and I find hers hooded with the same lustful hunger I feel. In that instant, she grabs the sides of my face and crushes her mouth against mine.

There's no saving me now. I'm drowning in her very essence, unable to come up for air. She kisses me fiercely, her fingers raking up into my hair and tugging me closer as our tongues wrestle for dominance.

During the madness, she pulls my bottom lip between her teeth and bites down hard. Blood coats my tongue, but it only seems to fuel the raging fire within her and the kiss grows more wild.

My one hand glides up her back, grabs a fistful of her hair, and yanks her head back. She cries out, but not in pain. And when I run my tongue up the curve of her throat, that cry turns to a delicious moan that sets me on edge.

"This is going to hurt," I warn her, my voice husky with my own deranged need.

"Doesn't everything with you?" she snarls back, and I yank her head back again to prove it true.

When she glances down at me, there's conflict warring over her face—she wants to hate me; she thinks this is wrong, but she can't stop herself. Deep down, she's loving it.

Just like me.

And I...I need *more*.

This may be a mistake, but I'm too far gone now. Suddenly, I don't care about any of Cain's warnings or threats. I'm going to fuck Aria. I'm going to make it hurt. I'm going to help her release some of those darker desires she's kept buried. To hell with the consequences.

Taking my dagger, I draw another thin cut across her collarbone—just slicing through the surface of her skin. She hisses as she draws in a sharp breath, but like before, I trace it with my tongue then nip the end with my teeth.

Her hand finds the hard bulge of my cock through my pants and rubs me through the material. I clench my jaw.

Yes. More.

I make another small nick on her shoulder and press my mouth against it, sucking and swirling my tongue along the wound.

Her body trembles against my lips. "Ah...Maverick..."

I usually like to take my time when it comes to sex. Draw out the pleasure as much as I can, but hearing my name on her lips like that makes me want to rip off my pants and those leggings she's wearing and plunge into her with no remorse. Until those moans turn into full-on screams and we're both riding on that thin edge of ecstasy and torment.

And that's just what I am going to do.

When I reach for my fly, the sound of footsteps echo down the hall. I hesitate.

As if waking from a trance, Aria abruptly puts her palms against my chest and shoves me back just as the door to my room swings open.

"What the fuck!" In seconds, I take in the scene before me.

Aria looks startled, blood seeping from the cuts on her shoulder and collarbone, her white sweater torn and stained red. Her eyes are wide in that doe-in-headlights kind of way a victim freezes when they are terrified.

Maverick stands near her, blood drops on his lips and at the corner of his mouth.

The air is thick with the scent of arousal, and that cuts me to the bone. All I can picture in my mind is Maverick forcing himself on Aria, hurting her like the beast he is. I see her face now, twisted and terrified, her screams covered by his hand.

I'm shaking, absolutely livid that he took advantage of her like that.

Fire burns through me, my anger like kerosine.

A howl tears from my throat, and I curl my hands into fits, eyeing Maverick warily. Everything inside me roars, the blade of guilt spearing into my heart that I didn't find them earlier, before he hurt her.

His mouth is moving, as is Aria's, but I don't hear a thing. My heart is thumping in my ear, my mouth-watering for his blood. I need to hear his cries.

I fly at Maverick and bowl into him.

He hits the floor hard with me on top of him, and I'm seething as I slam fist after fist into his face for daring to hurt my little rabbit.

The bastard fights back, of course he does, but I barely register the punches he delivers, not when my speed is unmatched by him.

The sounds of screams coming behind me are followed by Aria grabbing at my shirt and trying to pull me back.

I grunt, needing to finish this asshole first. He never should have come to our home. Fuck, Cain knows better, except he has a soft spot he refuses to admit. And it's going to get Aria killed.

My jaws clenches as I pummel into Maverick and growl in his face. He catches me under the chin with a sharp jab, giving him just enough time to shove his fists into my chest, sending me back.

The slippery prick rolls rapidly out from under me, and Aria is there in my face, shoving a hand into my shoulder.

"Stop!" she's bellowing in my face, her eyes watery, while the rush of my heart hammers in my ears louder.

The fuck! "You care for this monster who attacked you?" Maybe I had it wrong, and the slimy bastard didn't just attack her. No, he tricked her into believing he cared, into some made up shit to get into her pants.

Next thing I know, a heavy weight crashes into my back, and his razor sharp fangs pierce into the back of my shoulder.

"You sonofabitch," I shout, and twist around with enhanced hellhound speed, but the thing is, Maverick might not be as big as me but he's a sin demon. Those asses are just as powerful, just as strong, and that means they come complete with ammunition. For Maverick, it's fangs, horns, and spiny wings.

I shove him off me, and he stumbles backward a few steps.

He's heaving for breath, blood streaked across his cheek and chin, dripping onto his shirt. Everything about seeing him this way makes me beyond happy. But what I find interesting is that he isn't running away like he normally does. He's standing toe-to-toe with me, and ready to fight.

Maybe he isn't the weasel I'd always seen him as.

Aria's yelling at us to stop, but when I see the grin on Maverick's face, enjoying the fact he got a rouse out of me, I lose the sliver of calm that found me.

"You are nothing but ego, dog-boy," he drawls.

Before I can say anything, I'm flying across the room at him and slam him into the wall, then headbutt him, needing to wipe the stupid grin off his face.

"You were saying," I snarl in his face.

Except, Aria is there, slapping and punching us both to stop. "Get out of here," I yell. "Before he attacks you again."

Maverick, the snake he is, clips his bony fist right into my nose in that same moment. Stars dance in my vision, the pain is a bitch, and blood drips over my lips and chin. He's fucking broken it. The world spins for a second. I stumble backward, shaking my head, but that isn't going to work.

Aria's pushing her hands against Maverick's chest, trying to shove him out of the room, and maybe the dickhead should listen to her. I reach up and snap my broken nose back into place, my eyes watering from the fucking pain. But it subsides just as quickly, and I wipe the dripping blood.

"It's time you left, Aria," I tell her. "This is something I should have done a long time ago."

She whips around to face me, fury narrowing her gaze, her small hands balled up. "Will you get your damn head out of your ass, both of you, and fucking stop!"

"He's going to be sorry for touching you, for tricking you, trying to rape you."

She stills, staring utterly surprised. "What are you talking about? You think I'm that stupid? That I'd let him trick me?"

"He's done it before!"

She stills, staring at me in disbelief.

Maverick wipes the blood from the open gash across his brow. "Maybe we should start again?" he suggests. And I fucking hate him for sounding so calm when I'm shaking with anger, with confusion.

Aria lets out a sound of pure frustration, throwing her arms into the air. "Why must everything be a fight with demons? He was..." She pauses and glances over to Maverick. "Teaching me how to fight."

My head swims with her words, trying to make sense of what she just said.

Then a wave of rejection flares over me. I turn toward her and take her hand in mine. "Why didn't you come to me? I would teach you anything you want, little rabbit. I've been a warrior my entire life."

She doesn't respond right away, but I still smell arousal in the air. There's no denying that, if she is telling the truth, what I'm smelling is her willing attraction toward him. Is that why she asked him for training tips? It had nothing to do with who's the strongest warrior, but an excuse to get closer to him. What the hell happened in Brazil to make her want more of Maverick?

What am I missing?

"So, the cuts on your shoulder and...?" My gaze dips to the one that slides down beneath her collarbone, blood staining the fabric of her white sweater.

"Fighting wounds," Maverick answers and steps past us, standing behind Aria, like somehow he's now her protector. Over my dead body.

Aria glances over to the floor near the door, where a blade rests. She goes to collect it. "I've got hellhounds on my heels, and I love that you all protect me, but I need to be able to defend myself better, too. I can't always rely on you four to be around."

Four. So she counts Maverick in the mix now?

I reach a hand out to her. "Let's go get your cuts cleaned and bandaged."

There's no hesitation in her taking my hand, but when she looks over to Maverick, jealousy claws through me. I accepted long ago that Cain and Dorian will share her, but I'm struggling with Maverick, considering I still don't trust the bastard. But I'm left curious...what does she see in him that I'm missing?

Unexchanged words float between them, then she lowers her head and we walk out of Maverick's room. I shut the door, locking it behind us.

She rips her hand from me once we leave the basement and are upstairs in the hallway. She turns on me, clearly pissed at me. "Do you really think I'm that stupid?"

"It's not you I don't trust," I tell her truthfully.

"Then at least have faith knowing that I wouldn't risk myself by going to see Maverick if I thought him dangerous."

I bite my tongue, knowing I shouldn't say anything, but

keeping quiet has never been my strong point. "Like I said, it's not your judgment I question, little rabbit. You seem to forget who Maverick really is. He's the demon who sold out Cain to Lucifer, who lied to you about being an angel, who kidnapped you and took you into Hell. How can you be sure this isn't another game? The asshole has been around for too fucking long, has experienced so much. So don't you think it's strange he is suddenly the good guy?"

She stiffens in front of me, the fury on her face reddening her cheeks. "And what about you? And Cain and Dorian? None of you started out *good*." She air-quotes the word 'good' with her hands. "But you changed, so why can't Maverick?"

I understand her frustration. Hell, it bleeds into my veins. "Because it took us centuries to get to this stage. Not overnight."

The angry expression doesn't leave her face, but only then do I notice her hands shaking by her side. Just as quick, her face pales, and a different kind of terror encases her. I know the look instantly, and she looks at me with a pleading desperation.

"Sayah," she breathes the name, and I rush to her, collecting her in my arms in a panic.

I don't waste a second and rush with her outside into the cold. It's the first thing that comes to mind...to cool her down, to help calm the anger she's feeling, which would be fueled with heat.

She trembles terribly when I set her down in the yard covered in perfect white snow.

"Deep breaths," I tell her. "You're in charge, Aria."

She's nodding but scrunching up her nose as she shuts her eyes —clearly her battle is within her. And I realize now how careful we need to be about setting off Aria's emotions as they seem to be a trigger for Sayah to gain control. Or is it that she feeds off them, giving her strength to emerge?

I swear under my breath for being so fucking stupid and not shutting my big fat mouth about her and Maverick. For pushing her when that's the last thing she needs.

I've got her in my arms, holding her closer, her body tense as hell.

"Listen to my voice, Aria," I say. "Focus on staying strong because you are in charge of your body, and not Sayah."

Her eyes flip open, and I stare at the war waging behind them, the tragedy, the ache, the darkness. There's so much to Aria we still don't understand, and I hate that it makes her vulnerable, that it leaves us on the sideline when I want nothing more than to reach into there and rip Sayah to shreds.

Her lip curls into a sneer, and my heart plummets that she might be losing the battle. Panic has me throwing Aria over my shoulder and rushing her into the house, directly to Cain's room where he'd had her in his bed. Last I remembered, there were ropes still in the room. I had to tie her down just in case... Something I should have done initially, but alarm bells have a way of fogging my brain when all I care about is helping Aria.

I burst open Cain's bedroom with a kick and rush inside as Aria's voice calls me, "Elias, please put me down."

Cautious, I eye the coiled rope near the window, so I move to the side of the bed near it and set her down there.

I'm still gripping her arms, and stare into her eyes, needing to see for myself it's not Sayah. Eyes are the window into someone's soul, and that's one thing Sayah can't hide from us when she takes over Aria. Well, not to mention her going psycho and wanting us dead. It's not my first rodeo show.

Aria flops down on the bed, sitting there gasping for breath like she's run a marathon. It's like I can physically see the tension bleeding out of her as color returns to her cheeks.

"I don't know how long I can keep doing this," she whispers, her voice still shaky, and her hand holds onto my arm tightly.

I draw her into my arms, her cheek pressed to my chest, and I never want to let her go. The urge to keep her with me forever is unbearable.

It's only when the floorboards creak in the hallway that I look up to find Cain standing in the doorway of his bedroom, his eyebrow arching, wondering why we're in his bedroom no doubt.

Aria shifts around to look at Cain, but she doesn't move from my arms.

Cain is quick to lower his attention to the cuts on her shoulder and around her collarbone, the blood staining her sweater.

"What happened?" He steps inside quickly.

"Had a scare with Sayah almost showing up," she says. "I don't think it's going to stop, or that I can keep holding her at bay. She is getting so much stronger."

"Is the screaming match downstairs what led to Sayah coming out?"

I nod once, and it's clear Cain is clued up on most of what led us to this point. The rest I'll fill him in later.

Silence falls between us, and Cain stands close now, reaching over to wipe his thumb over the blood smear from her jawline. Trepidation deepens his expression and furrows his brow.

"We can't wait around for an answer anymore," he says. "This is getting worse."

Aria shakes in my arms, and I want nothing more than to press her against me, to make her forget the crap following her.

"What do you suggest?" I ask.

"Maybe this is a good time to go and visit your mother, Aria, and see if she knows anything more about Sayah. Something we've missed," Cain suggests.

She tenses in my embrace and untangles herself from my arms. "Wait, you know where my mother is?"

He nods, and something crosses his face as he realizes he's revealed a secret he's been keeping from her. Shit, this isn't going to go well.

Clearing his throat, he says, "I managed to track down the residential home for the mentally unstable where she's being kept."

I'm holding still, knowing Aria well enough to understand this news won't go down well with her. It's why I didn't agree with Cain in holding back information from her.

She's staring at him, her eyes glistening, but when I reach out to her, her body is tightening up. Those aren't happy tears. "How long have you known?" Her voice is deep and her shoulders bunch up.

"A short while. The time hasn't been right for me to tell you with everything going on."

She's trembling. I collect her into my arms again. "Let's all keep calm," I say, directly staring at Cain, who understands my concern instantly, as she exhales loudly. But she shoves against me and pushes herself to her feet, confronting Cain head on.

"A...while?" she repeats. "Why the hell didn't you tell me this earlier?"

Cain stiffens, his lips thinning, but I watch the war raging behind his eyes—not wanting to hurt Aria while defending his actions. "Would it have made any difference? At the time, we didn't consider Sayah a danger, and things have now escalated fast."

"Yes, it makes a difference to me," she snaps back. "You don't own me! And you have no right to keep such information from me. Do you know how long I've wanted to find my mother?" Her voice trembles, and my chest tightens.

I hold back the urge to correct her that in fact she does belong to us now. We're locked in from our blood ritual for eternity, but that's not going to help anyone. Except make her as pissed at me. And I sort of like the notion of him being in her bad graces. More for me.

"Aria, please. My decisions are never made with the intention to hurt you. Quite the opposite." He stretches out a hand to her, but she doesn't take it.

"What else are you holding from me?" she demands.

He exhales loudly, his nostrils flaring. "I found her name. Victoria Dawson."

Aria falls quiet and wipes her tears with the back of her hand. The hurt on her face kills me, and it feels like she's going to burst into inconsolable crying any moment now, and I want to throttle Cain for doing this to her.

"I-I c-can't believe you," she stutters. "All this time, I could have gone and seen her, but you let me believe she was lost to me. How could you do that?"

He steps toward her. "Aria—"

"Don't," she growls. The darkness in her tone has me shooting to my feet. My thoughts fly to Sayah making an appearance any second now.

The same resolve must have crossed Cain's mind, as he lowers his arm and doesn't push her. His eyes darken as he watches her though, expecting the worst. He's not the kind that takes defeat well, but he knows the danger simmering inside Aria.

"Maybe it's time we went and visited your mom," I suggest, to defuse the situation.

Silence.

She finally twists around to face me, her cheeks red, her eyes brimming with tears. "Yes please. Just us two, okay?"

"Of course, little rabbit." This time, when I pull her close, she melts against me.

My gaze locks with Cain's, and there's fire in his eyes. Without a word, he storms out of the room. Well, that went to hell.

I finally get to go on one of these trips with Aria alone, and where are we going? A mental hospital in Illinois.

Quaint.

Oh, it's to visit her mother—the mother who abandoned her and sent an evil shadow creature to kill her father.

Romantic, right?

And that's the shadow that's attached to her soul and who's trying to take her over.

Perfect.

As our Uber driver parks in front of Clover Hill Mental Wellness Center, I grunt and shift uncomfortably in the front seat. Since I don't drive and Aria can't, Dorian made sure to arrange a service to pick us up at the airport.

How do I know it was Dorian who did it and not Cain?

It's a mini cooper that picked us up.

The entire hour and a half ride, my knees were smashed against the windshield, and my back aches terribly. So, the moment we're parked, I throw the door open and un-pretzel myself to get out. The entire car teeters and groans as I do, and I silently curse Dorian. He's going to pay for this one.

After stretching my back until it cracks, I open Aria's door and help her out of the back seat. I can feel the driver staring at me the entire time, probably wondering how I'd managed to fit my massive self into such a small car. Honestly, I don't even have an answer to that one.

"Give us an hour or so," I tell him.

"No problem, chief," he says with a nod, and speeds off to circle the lot for a spot to park.

Chief? Okay. Weird. But I've definitely been called worse.

As we step up to the glass front doors to the psychiatric hospital, Aria grows tense beside me. It doesn't take the bond between us to know she's panicking on the inside about this meeting. And I don't blame her.

"She's just a woman," I whisper, as she stares unmoving at the doors. "Practically a stranger."

She glances up at me, worry etched into her beautiful face. "I know…" But her voice cracks, some of her fear leaking through.

I slip my hand over hers. "I'll be with you the entire time."

A small smile flickers across her lips, and she nods once. I walk over to the intercom with Aria at my side and press the call button. The speaker crackles and a high-pitched female voice answers.

"Yes?"

"Er—hi." I stare into the camera lens pointed my way. "We're here to see a Victoria Dawson?"

"You're visiting her?" She sounds surprised. Guess mommy dearest doesn't get visitors often.

"I'm her daughter…" Aria pipes up next to me, and pushes onto her tiptoes to get into the camera's frame.

Only the crackling of the speaker answers for a while.

I'm about to ask if she's still there, when the loud buzzer sounds, then there's a click of the door opening. I push the door for her and we walk inside to a waiting room with a few chairs, large double doors, and a visitor's window where a woman in a white nurse's uniform is waiting for us.

Aria strolls up to it first.

"You're here to see Dawson?" the nurse asks her.

"Y-Yes. I think so." Aria's voice shakes with an abundance of nerves.

"Do you have any ID?"

The window is on the short side, so I bend down so the nurse can see me. Instantly, her eyes grow wide and she steps back. It's the typical initial reaction I get from most humans, so I'm used to it. "I believe someone called for us ahead of time. Cain. He should have sorted everything out for us."

And by "sorted out," I really mean he donated a large sum of money to the facility if they let me and Aria in, no questions asked.

Aria snorts at the mention of Cain's name, unimpressed and still ticked off at him for not telling her about her mother sooner. Maybe it's because he finally seemed to have a breakthrough with her only to have this happen, but I feel a bit bad for him. He's only doing what he thinks is best for her, even if it's a bit skewed.

Another one of the nurses hurries out from the back and shoves the other to the side. "Yes, yes!" She shoos her coworker away, leans closer to the window, and lowers her voice. "You can come right through to the back. She's on the third floor. Room 310."

Perfect. I love when things are this easy.

She presses a button on the desk and a loud buzzer sounds again. The large mechanical doors swing open for us and we go through. Before us is a set of elevators, and when I push the button to go up, Aria starts to rock on her feet.

"Still nervous?" I ask her as we both watch the numbers on top of the elevators count down to the ground floor. The right one dings and, once the doors roll open, we step inside.

"Yeah, but mostly still furious at Cain for hiding this from me for so long." She jams the third floor button with a scowl. "I could've been here months ago. Asked her about myself or my dad or—whatever—instead of wasting all this time wondering. Searching. Worrying."

We start to ascend, and although she's not looking at me and staring straight ahead, I can see her anger reflected against the metal elevator doors.

Man, Cain really fucked up.

When I get that ominous tingle through the magical link between us, I also suspect Sayah has something to do with her rage at him as well. She seems to like amplifying all Aria's emotions—that's when it's the easiest for her to take over, or so it seems.

"You know...he probably thought you didn't want to know any more about your mother. That's why he kept it from you," I try to reason out, trying to think like Cain does. "He did say you were pretty upset about finding out you were abandoned during your trip to the closed-down hospital. Maybe he didn't want to upset you more."

Her head whips my way and anger flares in her eyes. "Are you defending him?" She snaps the question at me like a whip.

"Defending? No, I wouldn't say that. I'm just trying to understand."

"He should've told me," she says and crosses her arms. "I'm beyond tired of the lies, the coverups. But what else am I supposed to expect from a demon?"

Well, shit. That's a punch below the belt.

The elevator dings again as we reach our floor. Once the doors open, we're greeted by a long hallway with more metal doors and sterile white walls.

Not very homey of a place, is it?

We walk in silence, passing a nurses' station and a few empty gurney beds lined up against the wall. The entire place is way too cold and reeks of alcohol, urine, and latex. Eventually, we come to a door labeled 310. Aria stops dead in her tracks, the anger she felt before quickly draining out and leaving only the heavy worry, fear, and uncertainty she'd felt before.

She rubs the backs of her arms and glances over at me again. "Elias?"

"Hm?"

"I-I don't even know what I'm going to say. We're meeting each other for the first time. She won't even recognize me."

"You can start with hi, I would think," I say with a short laugh.

"This isn't funny."

"What did you want me to say? That you should walk in there and start with, 'Hey ma! It's me, Aria. That's right. The daughter you latched an evil dark entity to? Sound familiar?' Is that what you want from me?"

She swallows roughly. "I feel so sick...like I need to throw up."

I turn to her and grab both her shoulders, forcing her to face me. "Aria, listen to me. The pressure you feel, you're putting on yourself. This woman may be your mother by blood, but blood doesn't determine family. Look at Cain, Dorian, and me. Not real brothers, but I trust them with my life."

She nods weakly.

"Victoria Dawson can only get to you if you let her," I go on. "And you shouldn't let her. She's just another person—someone that might be able to offer you the closure you need."

Aria presses her lips into a thin line, and I can see pending tears gathering in her eyes, but she manages to hold them at bay. I can't stand to see her torn up like this.

"If you really don't want to do this..."

"I do," she answers quickly, but when she reaches for the door, she pauses. "You won't leave me, right?"

"I'll be with you the entire time."

"Okay." Then, taking a deep breath, she grabs the handle and pulls the door open.

ARIA

The first thing I notice is how quiet and still the room is. No sounds. No movement. Not even from the bed where the woman who's supposed to be my mom lays.

I focus on her face, how pale she is, with sunken cheeks and gray greasy hair. It's hard to see any similarities between us when she looks so sickly and aged. She definitely doesn't look like she has the strength to summon an evil entity, or like the psycho bitch my father described. But a lot of time had passed since then, and like Elias had said, she is a stranger.

When Elias's hand presses into my lower back, I realize I haven't moved from the doorway. I step further inside.

Still, my mother doesn't move. It barely looks like she's breathing.

I glance over my shoulder at Elias.

"She must be heavily sedated," he whispers. "I'm not sure we'll be getting any information out of her."

I think he's right. It looks like this trip was for nothing.

Defeated, I shuffle back to the door.

"Is it time for my medication again?" a frail voice calls out.

I freeze on the spot, my breath catching in my lungs.

"Nurse?"

Elias grabs my shoulders and helps me turn around. My mother is pushing herself up in the bed, skinny arms quaking, and licking her dry lips. When her gaze dances over me, it doesn't hesitate. Only passes over me. And why wouldn't it? She wouldn't recognize me. I was a newborn when she'd dropped me off at the hospital and left forever.

I don't know what I was expecting, but my heart pounds frantically against my ribs.

Then she sees the massive, brooding man behind me and she frowns. "I won't fight this time," she says. "Please don't restrain me. I won't fight."

Restrain?

They'd actually tie her down?

My heart aches and I'm not sure why. I shouldn't have any feelings for this woman.

"We're not nurses." Elias speaks while I'm still finding my voice. "We're just here to ask you a couple of questions."

She blinks in confusion.

Elias steps in front of me to take the lead. He makes sure to keep his voice calm and gentle. "Around eighteen years ago, your husband was killed—"

"Not my husband," she shoots back. Her stare turns cold. "Thank god I never married that lying, cheating bastard."

Take aback by her intense reaction, Elias glances at me. But I'm lost for words. Not being married isn't a big thing—people have babies out of wedlock all the time. But what strikes me the most is how quick her anger is. Plus, what she's said is eerily similar to what Liam had told me, too.

"The world's a better place with him gone," she says. Her entire body is shaking, her hatred for the man pouring through her. "But he deserved more for what he did to me."

I peer around Elias. "What did he do?"

Victoria looks at me. "Unspeakable things. Horrible things..." Her voice breaks, and she glances away as if the memories are too painful for her to remember. "He was a monster."

Something in her wounded expression, the way her shoulders curl forward, and the pain lacing her voice all resonate with me. I'd been through my share of fucked-up shit in the foster care homes I stayed in. Foster siblings or caretakers who were too handsy or had sick fetishes taking advantage of scared little girls. And I recognize the look of a broken woman in her, along with the fierce anger that arises with it.

Could my father have lied?

He is in Hell after all…

But Sayah admitted to killing him, so what gives?

The only way I'm going to get the information I need is to ask for it.

I draw in a deep breath. "You…had a daughter? Is that true?"

She hesitates, and the lines around her mouth deepen as she frowns. "I did," she says. "The most beautiful baby girl."

Of course, I know the answer to this question, but I have to ask it anyway. "What happened to her?"

Her gaze dances between Elias and me. Unsure. "I…had to give her up for adoption."

It hurts even when she says it, and tears begin to prickle in my eyes.

Elias steps forward to take the reins of the conversation again. And right now especially, I'm so thankful for him. "Was it because of Liam Cross?" he asks. "Did he make you?"

She shakes her head meekly. "No, not him. But it wasn't safe."

"What do you mean?" he presses.

She stops suddenly and bites the side of her cheek.

"You can tell us," Elias goes on gently. "We're here to help you."

Still, she looks over us with uncertainty and distrust. And I don't blame her. But there has to be a reason she ended up in this place. And that Sayah came into my life. I need to know more.

"Where did you say you're from?" she asks.

Oh shit. We hadn't even thought up a good lie to explain why we were here asking her such personal things. What are we even going to say?

But, as smooth as butter, Elias rolls out his lie. "We're part of the board of directors," he says without so much as a second's delay. "Some patients have been selected as improved or rehabilitated enough to return to everyday society, and you were one of the few chosen. We just need you to answer some basic questions to the best of your knowledge, so we can make our decision. Can you do that for us?"

I stare at him, stunned. Quick thinking and spinning lies? Those are things I expect of Cain. Even Dorian. But Elias? Guess he's been hanging out with the other two a little too long. They're starting to rub off on him.

The lie seems to work, though, because Victoria sniffs once and nods. "Okay, but this is going to sound crazy." She looks at the door behind us.

"Trust us. Nothing is too crazy," he assures her.

Again, she glances past us at the door, as if she's expecting someone to come bursting in at any moment. When no one does, she goes on, voice low. "As I said before, Liam was an asshole. He abused me. Beat me badly. The only reason we had a kid was because he forced himself on me one night when he was piss-drunk. I would fight him sometimes, but he was too strong, you know? And the beatings that came after were always worse if I tried to defend myself. So, most times, I just...let it happen."

My throat dries.

No wonder my father is in Hell.

"He wanted me to terminate, but I refused. Even though the pregnancy was a bit of a shock, I wanted to be a mom. And I knew I could do it without him. But when I refused to get rid of the baby, things got more scary. *He* got more scary. Outbursts and stalking. Stole from me. Planted drugs in my apartment, you name it. Anything he could do to make my life miserable. I needed a way to protect myself and my daughter. The law obviously wasn't helping me any. He had a buddy on the police force, and I swear he was helping him out behind the scenes so I became desperate...

"One night, after work, I knew Liam would've set up some chaos waiting for me at home, so to delay it a little longer, I stopped in this antique bookstore. I was close to my due date and my anxiety was through the roof. But I stumbled across this old book about occult magic. Dark stuff. Scary stuff. But there was a spell to 'rid you of your earthly demons' and, like I said...I was desperate."

"You performed a spell?" I say, listening intently and hanging on her every word.

She huffs a laugh. "Sounds crazy right? I told you it would."

Elias gestures for her to continue. She does.

"That night, I performed the spell. At least, I think I did. The book was so old, a lot of the words were faded and hard to read. I did what I thought it said, and as expected, nothing came from it.

At least not that night. I ended up having my baby girl two days later. For once in my life, I was happy. Truly, truly happy." Tears glisten in her eyes, and my chest clenches. I'd been so wrong to think she'd never wanted me. So, so, wrong.

"With Liam, happy moments never last long, and the day I came home with Aria, he was there waiting for me. He attacked me." Her voice begins to rise as the words tumble out of her mouth in a rush, and her body shakes. "He tried ripping her out of my arms and punched me in the face, broke my nose and fractured my eye socket. I blacked out. I must've. I don't remember much else except that when I came to, I was laying on the ground with Aria next to me, screaming. And this massive black shadow was hovering over Liam's dead body."

Shadow.

As if being summoned, Sayah stirs inside me. I feel her slithering around my mind, like she's waking from a deep sleep. Her icy cold influence washes over me, covering me in goosebumps.

"Elias..." I breathe as panic crawls up my throat.

His head whips my way, and whatever he sees has his eyes widening in fear. He seizes me by the arm and jerks me towards him, but it can't stop the darkness sliding out of me, making my shadow grow along the tile floor and change size and shape.

Victoria scrambles back in bed, her face contorted in absolute terror. Her screams fill my ears, but Sayah is already lifting off the ground and filling the small space of the room.

Sayah, no! Come back!

My pleas go unanswered. She continues to stretch and grow, her ruby-red eyes shining my mother's way. Is she going to try and kill her, too?

Rushed footsteps come from outside the door, and it is thrown open. In a blink, Sayah zips back into me as four female nurses in white uniforms hurry to Victoria's bedside. She thrashes, pointing at me, and screams while the nurses struggle to hold her down. One holds a needle, one I'm sure is full with some kind of sedative.

"We gotta go." Elias is shoving me out the door and into the hallway. More nurses run past us to get into the room. We use the chaos as our cover and slip down the emergency staircase to the first floor. By the time we get to the large metal doors, Elias is practically carrying me. He dashes us out of the building and through the parking lot. The waiting mini cooper's engine starts up and Elias heads towards it.

Sayah spins inside me, restless. Wanting out. Even when Elias places me in the back of the car, I can feel the frigidness of her touch grabbing onto me and starting to pull me down.

"Elias…" I gasp. Head whirling, my vision darkens, and I try desperately to stay afloat.

"Hold out a little longer, okay?" he says, and shoves his massive body into the front seat.

"What's going on?" the driver asks, picking up on his urgency. "Is she sick?"

"Hotel. Now." Elias growls like the half animal he is, making the guy—a human—yelp in fear. The cooper's wheels peel out as we speed out of the parking lot and onto the main road.

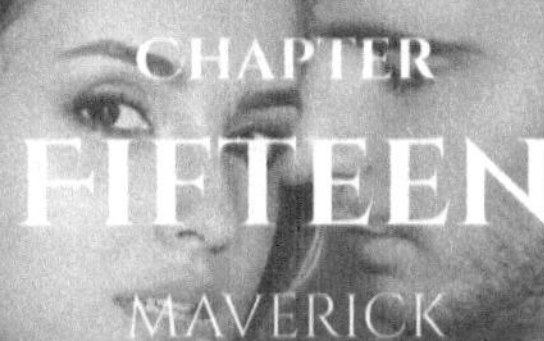

If there's one thing I hate about my brother Cain...well in truth there are plenty of things but one to focus on now, it's that when he wants you locked up, he does a fucking fine job of it. Back in Hell, he'd do Father's dirty work and sometimes that involved securing one of us sin demons until Lucifer was ready to deal with us. Cain would use anything he found around, be it vines or a curse. Whatever got the job done, right?

I grab the handle to the basement door and tug. It opens a sliver only. "Oh, fuck you!" I wrench on the thing, but it's like trying to haul a wagon of fat-ass hellhounds. I glance out into the hallway through the thin gap and find a line of salt and earth running along the floor, and it's clear it's the spell keeping me locked down here. "Fucking ass." Of course Cain would make it impossible for me to break out this time. Crouching down, I take a deep inhale and blow a long breath, hoping to dislodge the salt and soil.

Nothing.

No chance of breaking the line from my distance.

Shit!

The huge cat in the house comes to mind and how he could scuff the dirt to release me. I have no idea if he'll come like a dog, but I'm not beyond trying anything right now.

I give a low whistle. "Here, kitty kitty. Got a treat for you." Okay, that sounds creepy, but I don't stop.

After fifteen minutes of calling, the familiar click-clacking sound of nails hit the floors. Around the corner, the lynx appears, and it approaches, sniffing.

"That's right, come closer, kitty." I make small kissy sounds, as I hear cats seem to respond well to them.

Sniffing the line of salt and soil, the cat stops, not far from the door, then lifts its head at me. "Now come closer," I say with the sweetest voice I can find. "Drag those huge fluffy paws over the line."

Instead, the thing looks at me as if understanding what I'm up to. And as quickly as he came, he turns and pads his way out of here.

"Wait, no, come back, you stupid cat!" I growl under my breath, and it vanishes around the corner. "Fine," I yell out. "Go choke on a furball."

Huffing, I turn back to the basement and resume my pacing.

The thing is, I didn't leave one prison in Hell to come to another on earth.

I drop onto the bed and groan. Apparently, helping my brother equates to locking me back up like a dog. Even that furball gets treated better than me.

Of course, sitting around doing nothing has my thoughts drifting to Aria. She's constantly on my mind, and I can picture her standing in front of me. Five-foot-five, long black hair, pouty tempting lips, and huge vulnerable eyes that scream 'I need saving.' She may not know it, but that look drives men nuts, and just like my brother and those two idiots who follow him around, it's close to impossible to resist such a beauty. Now, add on to that her toned legs, a curvy ass, and perky breasts, and I'm drowning in her presence.

I need to taste her, bite her, draw blood. Fuck, the distance between us is infuriating. But my cock is hard just thinking of her. The taste of her blood and skin is still on my tongue, her intoxicating scent in my nostrils. I've been aching for release since we came together, and I need her.

My fly is down before I can even think straight, and my cock jerks to attention at the thought of her.

My hand wraps around my dick and I palm the thick, heavy flesh as I tilt my head back. I pump it slowly up and down at first, my eyes closed as I imagine it's Aria's mouth. I'm so fucking hyped, so wired, that my heart bangs in my chest from the blood diving south.

Working faster, I picture Aria with that gorgeous body naked, her determination to play my blood games ripe as she grips a blade. In a quick swipe of her flesh above her breasts, she stares at me, and I take all of her in. The drops of blood rolling down her tits, following the perfect curve of them, and how delicately they drip from her gorgeous little erect nipples.

"Fuck," I groan, pumping faster.

Lines of blood run down her body, the red so striking against her pale flesh. They follow the sexy-as-hell curves and find her sweet pussy.

My body twitches. I'm restless, starved for her. I can still hear her moaning and gasping when I licked her wounds.

Each breath I take comes out ragged and my pulse pounds as I picture her climbing onto me, straddling my lap like the good girl she is. I draw in a deep breath and still smell her, that honeyed, mouth-watering scent that is all her.

I grunt with pleasure as I imagine her sitting down on me, my cock plunging into her wet pussy, and the cries she'd make already drive me to insanity. I jerk my dick faster, and I'm reaching the point of no return.

In my head, I hear her screaming out her orgasm, panting as I never stop fucking her.

I'm growling deeply, stroking harder, doing a shit imitation of how Aria would feel. Every muscle in my body tense and builds as my own orgasm bursts through me. My cock stiffens in my hand, my balls tightening as ropes of cum spew from the head. I groan, wanting to spill into her, fill her, the climax rocking through me for what feels like eternity. My dick keeps pumping out ropes of thick cum that spill down my hand as I keep thinking of her.

Finally, when I'm finished, I'm breathing heavy, free of the arousal over Aria that refuses to let up. But for how long? I wipe myself up with one of the bed's pillows and chuck it onto the floor.

Even after spilling my seed, her face remains pinned to the

forefront of my mind, those striking dark eyes, her wicked grin like she knows the effect she has over me.

"Fuck," I mutter to myself. "What am I doing?" I'm now starting to better understand why my brother is so addicted to Aria. She's a storm that bursts into your life and once she's got a hold of you, fuck... She'll have no mercy on your heart.

CAIN

While Elias and Aria are away in Illinois, Dorian and I decide to follow our captive Nightwalker's lead and head over to the older part of the city.

Choosing an old cookie factory isn't the most stereotypical place for a vampire hideaway, but that's the point, isn't it? Choose a place that's the least expected. And in this case, the vamps picked an abandoned building that once made Aunt Ida's famous snicker-doodle cookies.

The moment we step out of Dorian's Ferrari and step into the dark lot, we're hit with the tantalizing scents of sugar, cinnamon, and ginger. Along with some more unpleasant ones, like gasoline and sitting water. The factory is a massive square building with almost every window broken and boarded up, and graffiti deco-rating the walls. Among the scribbled spray-painted nonsense is the mark of the Nightwalkers—an upside-down triangle with a cross in it—painted small just above one of the loading dock garage doors in the back.

"This is definitely the place," Dorian says, when he spots the symbol as well. "Are we sure we even want to wait for Viktor to do this thing?"

"I made him a promise I'd let him get the revenge he craves. Especially for what they did to Charlotte."

He sighs. "You're right. If it were Aria, I'd want a piece of that vengeance pie, too."

Aria...Just her name stirs emotions in me that I'm still having a hard time sorting out. I love her. Fiercely. And the intensity of it worries me. My list of enemies is vast and deadly beyond imagina-tion. As proven time and time again, my love could kill her.

And I can't forget how pissed she is at me for not telling her about her mother. The pain in her eyes. As if I'd betrayed her. It's been eating at me since they left.

I want her back. Plain and simple. But I know how much this trip means to her. She needs the closure, so I'll finish our little problem with the Nightwalkers and welcome the distraction for now. Then, when she gets back, I'll have to find a way to mend my mistake. Flowers or chocolate...or whatever it is women of this realm like.

I'll have to ask Dorian.

"Let's just hope Viktor gets here sooner rather than later. I don't trust your brother in our house alone." He peeks at me to see if I've been listening, which I haven't. He snorts and slaps a hand on my shoulder to shake me out of my thoughts. "Cain, come on, relax. Loosen up some. We're about to get our hands dirty. Rip some vampire heads off. You love this stuff."

Normally he's right. I do. But there's too much shit going on in our lives for me to truly enjoy it like I used to. I just want it over with to move on to the next thing; I just want Aria safe. From everything.

If that means from me, too, so be it.

"She'll get over it," Dorian goes on. "You did it to protect her."

"Every time I try to protect her, I end up hurting her anyway, it seems."

"Women are complicated creatures. It doesn't help that Aria's even more so than most." He offers me a sympathetic smile, and in that moment, I'm thankful to have him by my side through all this chaos. He's proven to be a good ally and an even better friend. A brother to me—a *true* one. Unlike whatever creature resides in our basement at the moment.

Behind Dorian, the shadows shift, drawing my attention. Noticing my change, Dorian spins around just as Viktor strides out of the darkness. As if he's walked out of the pages of an old-style romance novel, he's wearing a flowy white cotton shirt that's open wide at the neck and tight black pants. His dark hair is even slicked back, but there's murder in his eyes. He wants blood to be spilled tonight. And lots of it.

"About time you showed up," Dorian says and waves him over.

Ignoring his quip, Viktor examines the run-down factory. "We're sure this is where the Nightwalkers are hiding?"

"Their nest? No—" I begin, which makes him scowl.

"Then why the fuck are we here?"

"From what I got out of the vamp we had in lockdown, this is where they're storing their Hush. This is where the money is coming in and out of," Dorian explains, but by the look on Viktor's face, he's not happy with that answer either.

"I don't care about drugs or money," he snaps. "I want Stephan's head."

I nod, making sure to keep my voice low. "And we understand that. But one of the reasons his gang has been able to expand rapidly like it has is because of the money backing them up." It's something I learned quickly after coming onto this plane. Money equals power; it is a simple concept to see, and that would be anyone's focus when trying to rule over a city. Increase the money flow coming in. "Kink the pipe, stop the water flow, cripple the town."

Tilting his head, Viktor stares at me in confusion.

"Here, let me help you out." Dorian chuckles. "Cain likes to speak in tongues sometimes. He means to say that by taking away their money, we'll be weakening them from the inside."

"But—"

"You want to slaughter them all. We know," Dorian cuts him off.

"Believe us. This will help get rid of the Nightwalkers completely. Just dethroning Stephan will only do so much. His followers can keep up his work without him," I explain.

Viktor considers my words for a while. Then, with his tense muscles easing, he says. "Like cutting off the head of a hydra. Only to have more grow in its place."

Now he got it. Metaphor and all. "That's right."

"Besides, any Nightwalkers inside we'll let you have."

He agrees, even if he doesn't like the less bloody plan.

"Don't worry," I say. "This is only the first step."

"I trust you," he replies and dips his chin Dorian's way. "Even for demons, you've always been fair to me and my coven."

"Your alliance is one we need and appreciate." I glance back at the loading dock and the door with the painted symbol above it. Then Dorian and I lock eyes. He's thinking the same thing I am. It's time to get this night moving before we draw too much attention to ourselves.

We walk to the door, which has a heavy padlock on the latch. Easy enough to break, so I grab and wrench it. It pops off. As I chuck it to the side, Dorian takes the lever and lifts the garage door slowly. The rusty metal whines loudly against the silence, and if anyone is hiding out inside, they'd know to come running.

To our surprise, no one comes running as we step inside. Oddly enough, we're greeted with only more stillness.

"Are you sure this is the place?" Viktor asks in an impatient whisper.

"Dorian's gift never fails," I reply as I scan the large open warehouse. Besides us, the only things occupying the space are abandoned confectionery machines, sacks upon sacks of sugar and flour, and boxes stacked with Aunt Ida's cookie logo. "This is where the vampire's Hush should be."

"And you'd think there'd be some of the fuckers guarding the place," Dorian chimes in as he circles the places. "But there's not an undead soul here."

He's right. This Stephan bastard has some balls. That, or he isn't afraid of us, and that only enrages me more.

But no one is as furious as Viktor. Throwing his head back, he roars, spit flying and eyes turning a bloodshot red. He throws himself at the boxes and starts tearing through them. Cookies fly in all directions. Then he shoves over one of the large mixing machines, the massive weight of it shaking the ground.

"He's on a rampage," Dorian says as he comes to my side. "Should we stop him?"

I shake my head. "It's not the bloodshed we promised him yet, but Stephan will know we were here either way. It's better if we leave him an important message."

"Got it. Then I'll let him have his fun."

We watch as Viktor destroys everything in his path and shouts at the emptiness.

"I won't rest until every one of you are nothing more than ash in the wind!" he yells, seizes a hundred-pound sack of sugar, and chucks it across the room like it weighs nothing. He reaches for another. "STEPHAN, YOU COWARD! FACE ME YOURSELF!"

This time, when he chucks the bag, it tears midair, spilling a purple crystalized substance all over the floor.

He stops.

That definitely doesn't look like any cookie ingredients to me.

Walking over, Dorian crouches and touches the stuff. He examines it between his fingers. "I know we're still new when it comes to most earthly things, but I've never seen purple sugar before."

"Me neither." I glance over at Viktor. He's temper tantrum proved more helpful than we thought.

"Looks like we've found their Hush." He rises to stand again. "Now what?"

There's a sharp sound and a burst of cold air. Water splashes across my face, and I look up to see Viktor hanging from the rafters, holding a broken pipe. Water gushes out of it all over the sacks of hidden drugs, soaking it all. As the Hush rapidly dissolves, a river of purple flows toward the center floor drain in the middle of the factory.

Pounds of drugs, all washed away.

Thousands, possibly millions of dollars, gone.

We wanted to get Stephan's attention.

There's no doubt he'll be listening now.

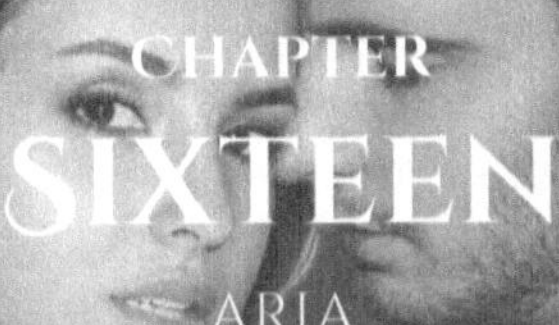

I wake up to a weight pressing into my chest. My lungs struggle to suck in enough oxygen, and my head whirls.

What the heck happened?

It's hard to remember through the stabbing pains in my chest and the fogginess in my brain, so instead, I take in the room where I am.

I'm in a large bed, covered in white linens. Like a hospital or a hotel. No, not a hospital. The mattress and pillows are too comfortable to be from a hospital. A hotel then. Yeah, that sounds right. There's a dresser in front of me with a flatscreen television and mirror, a lamp, and a small eating nook with a table and two chairs.

Once I see my reflection staring back at me in the mirror, I quickly avert my eyes. I'm a hot mess. Hair sticking out of my ponytail, eyeliner smudged across my cheeks, lips dried and pale.

Gah! I look like I've been out of it for hours.

Movement through the closed balcony doors catches my eye, and Elias's gruff voice slips through the cracks. Not enough for me to make out the words, but from his urgency and annoyed, frantic movements, I'm guessing he's talking about me. And more than likely, to Cain.

The memory of the mental hospital and everything that

happened with my mother starts to come back into focus. I've learned a lot on this trip.

For one, my dad was a lying bastard. He was the one who had made my mother's life a living hell and then wanted to get rid of me before I was even born. She'd only been trying to protect me and, out of desperation, sought out dark magic to do it. Apparently, Sayah attaching herself to me had been a complete fluke. An accident. Sayah had done what my mother had asked and killed Liam, but what she'd seen left her mentally unstable and in the hospital.

Am I any closer to knowing what Sayah is and how to stop her? No.

But I do know the reason she's around. And that I wasn't completely unloved and unwanted like I thought I was. That makes a world of difference. To me, at least. My mother had loved me so much, she was willing to do anything to keep us safe. Things just hadn't turned out the way she'd hoped they would.

The creak of the balcony doors opening steals back my attention, and when I look up, Elias is trudging back into the room. When he sees me awake, he stops and a smile breaks across his face.

"Rise and shine, sleeping beauty," he says.

I kick off the blankets and scoot to the edge of the bed. "Who were you talking to out there?"

"Cain."

Knew it.

"I had to tell him about everything that happened. He's a bit worried about you."

Again, I'm not surprised. But right now I'm still peeved at him for not telling me about my mother. If I'd known sooner, I could've made this trip, asked my questions, and gotten some closure a lot earlier than now.

He wants to protect me? From what?

I'm starting to wonder if he's just afraid of losing me. Which is stupid. He's given me chances to go—I've had plenty of opportunities—and I've stayed. I'm in way too deep with these demons. I care too much. I'd even dare to say I...*love* them.

"We're all a bit worried about you," Elias confesses, running a hand through his long hair. "Back in the Uber, I thought—" He stops himself and glances away.

Guilt tumbles inside me. Elias can be a big brute and fearless, so whenever he shows these moments of sweetness, it strikes me right through the heart.

I walk over and place my hand on his thick upper arm. "What's happening with Sayah scares the shit out of me, too. But right now, I'm okay."

He glances down at me, worry creasing his brow.

"I hope you're not beating yourself up about it. Nothing about this is your fault."

He heaves a big sigh. "I've made it my life to serve, fight, and protect the ones I love. But when the enemy isn't...well, *here* here, I don't know what to do. How am I supposed to protect you from yourself?"

"That's a good question. One I don't have an answer for," I say.

Turning, he strides back out to the balcony and leans over the metal railing. The sun presses against him, and when the breeze picks up, it blows through his hair and kicks up the white curtains.

I bite my bottom lip and wonder if it's best to follow him or give him his space. When things get tough for Elias, or he gets too much in his head, he goes for a run through the forest. Or a hunt. But in a hotel, in the middle of a city, there's not many places for him to go to unwind. Besides out on the balcony.

After a few seconds, I decide to join him and slowly come up to his side. Placing my elbows against the metal, I lean over like he is and draw in lungfuls of cold, wet air. It must've rained while I was asleep because the streets and sidewalks below are littered with puddles

We stay like that for a while, looking out and not speaking at all. Just watching cars zoom by five stories below us.

"You know..." I begin, peeking over at him.

His brows rise. "Hmm?"

"I'm pretty sure you made that poor Uber driver wet his pants before," I say with a chuckle. "The way you screamed at him to get driving."

He shrugs but a smile teases his lips. "That's okay. I'll leave him a good review."

"I think he deserves it. A big tip maybe, too."

"Probably right." There's a soft buzzing sound, and Elias pulls out his cellphone from the pocket of his sweats. He frowns.

"Cain again?" I ask.

"Yeah, he's booked us an earlier flight home."

"And you're upset? I thought you'd be jumping to get out of the city and back to the woods."

"You're right. I am," he begins, gaze stretching out to the noisy streets again. "But I was hoping for more time away with you."

I hesitate as tingles spread all over my body. I know *exactly* what he means. My heart seems to know, too, because it thumps faster with excitement and anticipation.

Swallowing, I reply, "Well, how much time do we have?"

He glances at his phone again for the time before putting it away. "A little more than three hours."

"Ah."

"Not nearly enough time for all the things I want to do to you."

Every part of me tightens at his words, and my mind instantly jumps to a very unholy, unclean place. With Elias, I know the possibilities are endless, but one thing's for certain. We're going to be exhausted, sore, and gasping for breath by the end of it.

My favorite.

Even though my throat is drying at the thoughts running rampant through my mind, I put on my best calm and coy act and blink up at him. "And what did you have in mind?"

To my surprise, he drops to the ground and flips over so that his shoulders are pressed against the railing's bars and his long legs are spread out. This massive hunk of a man is half-sprawled out across the balcony floor. Confused, I only stare at him.

"First, I'm going to need you to do me a favor, little rabbit," he says with that devilish gleam in his amber eyes.

"Oh? And what's that?"

"I'm going to need you to sit that delicious pussy over here. On my face."

His dirty words and cocky attitude light a fire in me, and when he tacks on one of his famous animalistic growls, I almost turn to mush on the spot. I'm not even sure I'm breathing anymore, let alone thinking straight, and he hasn't even laid a finger on me yet.

"Well?"

It's tempting... And would be a hell of a lot of fun, but before I can do anything, a car honk blares in the distance, reminding me that we're very exposed up here. Anyone walking by or in a neighboring building could see.

"Let's move this inside," I say and walk towards the open doors. But Elias snatches my wrist and pulls me back to him.

"No. Here. Now."

"But everyone can see—"

"And?" he snaps. "Do I look like I give a fuck?"

He grabs my thighs and tugs my leg over him. I'm still wearing my dress from my visit to my mom, so when he shimmies himself lower, his face is right where it needs to be to make his request a reality. The grip he has on my legs strengthens, and when he peers up at me, he looks like a starving man now confronted with a feast.

Like he's going to devour me.

I tremble.

He seizes the hem of my dress and wrenches it up, exposing all of me to the city around us. "Now come here." I don't move; don't need to. He yanks me forward, perfectly positioning himself between my legs, and leaving me to do nothing but grip the railing for dear life as his fingers pull aside my thong and his tongue dives into my heat.

No warning. No more sexy talk. Just him lapping at my sex like he can't get enough.

Suddenly, I don't care who can see us. I'm lost in the pleasure sweeping through me, of his rough hands digging into my ass cheeks as he makes a feast of me. When his masterful tongue stops its rampage and concentrates on my clit, my vision fogs. Bolts of electricity shoot through every nerve ending, and it isn't long before I'm panting, my hands clutching the railing for dear life as my muscles tighten in the most delicious way.

My orgasm slams into me, turning my legs to jelly, but Elias isn't letting up. Instead, as he licks my all too sensitive nub, he spreads my ass, runs a finger along my slit, up my backside, and presses against the tight little hole back there.

I tense automatically, but with more teasing flicks and sucks on my clit, I'm soon relaxing and pressing myself against his finger.

He growls against me, sending vibrations through my core. My hips begin to move on their own, grinding against his mouth.

Loving the sounds coming from him. He's enjoying this as much as I am, and that only manages to turn me on even more.

Another finger pushes into my back entrance, but the shock of it is soon replaced by the mounting pleasure as I increase my speed.

I'm not even sure he can breathe okay down there with how aggressively I'm riding his face, but at the moment, I don't care. The climax I'm chasing is explosive, and I'm too close to stop now.

His fingers move slowly, pumping in and out of my ass, and the sensations clashing inside me are too much. This time, when I reach my peak, I cry out, and then quickly bite my lip to hold it in. Don't need someone calling the cops because there's a woman screaming on the fifth floor.

Elias's hold on me shifts back to my hips and he lowers me onto his lap, where he's already yanked down his sweats and pulled himself free. The hard silky length of him rubs up against my sex, the heat of him burning me up from the inside out. From his tongue and my intense need for him, I'm already dripping wet.

"There's just something about fucking you with a dress on," he says, his voice heavy with desire. "It drives me fucking crazy."

"Easy access." I slide onto him easily and groan as his full length buries itself deep inside.

His eyes shine a little brighter when he stares at me. "Exactly."

Elias is no little man in any way, especially when it comes to his cock. The sheer size of him should hurt me, but he's always so careful when he moves, so particular with how he holds me and positions himself, that having sex with him is never anything less than mind-blowing.

And this time's no different.

He never lets go of my hips, but instead, uses his hold to take full control of the pace and how deep and shallow he thrusts. He's testing me. Making sure I can handle him before going full force, and I dig my nails into his shoulders and arch my back to give him my answer.

That's all he needs. With another growl vibrating in his throat, he pounds into me and hits my inner wall each time. It hurts, but in the good kind of way that has my eyes rolling back and me whimpering for more. When he kisses me, his tongue is as relentless and aggressive as it had been on me before, and I'm drowning in the feeling of him all around me. Inside me. Overwhelming me. Controlling me. Dominating me.

I love every fucking minute of it.

"Fuck, Aria," he gasps between strokes. "I can't get enough of you."

"Good thing you don't have to try."

Something passes over his face, a hesitance and a question lingering behind his eyes, but before I can ask about it, he lifts me off him, puts me on my feet before getting up himself. Then, he spins me around and pushes my stomach up against the chilly metal of the balcony's railing.

My gaze zeros in on the city street below and my stomach somersaults at just how high we are. "Uh...Elias?"

When I glance over my shoulder at him, he's spitting into his hand and lathering up his cock with it, pumping it over and over in his fist. The gesture should disgust me, but for some reason, it only excites me more. Heat prickles along my skin.

"What-what are you doing?" I rasp.

"What does it look like I'm doing? I'm going to take that sweet ass of yours."

His words make me squirm.

He presses one hand into my lower back, forcing me to lean over the railing even more, and my heart pounds with a mixture of lust and fear. One false move and I'll tumble over this thing. To my death.

"Elias..." I call to him again. I'm not so sure about this.

He captures my gaze with his. "Do you trust me?" he asks.

That's a silly question.

"Yes, but—"

"Then shush." He grabs my wrist and jerks it behind me enough to make me yelp in surprise. With my dress already pushed up to my waist, I feel his cock running up and down my ass crack as if asking for permission.

"You're going to have to bend over more, or this is going to hurt," he whispers.

"But if I lean over any more..."

"You won't fall," he assures me. "Don't worry."

That's easy for him to say. He's not the one dangling over a balcony right now, facing a huge drop.

Still, I do as he says and lean over a little more.

His tip pushes into my tightness, and I suck in a sharp breath at the spike of pain that always comes in the beginning. Slowly, carefully, he goes deeper, and the initial pain is replaced by nothing but sweet, sweet bliss.

"Oh yeah," he practically howls. If no one had heard us yet, there's no doubt they have now. "That's what I'm fucking talking about."

He throws his head back and closes his eyes. With one hand still holding my wrist behind my back and the other spreading my butt cheek to help him fit, he begins to draw in and out of me. Gently at first, like always, to test my comfort.

But slow and steady rarely does it for me, so when my own need to kick things up a notch takes over, I reach between my legs, find his balls, and begin to massage them. His entire body tightens.

"Aria." There's a warning in his tone.

"Fuck me, Elias. I'm not risking my life here for nothing."

He chuckles softly. "I love a woman who knows what she wants." He readjusts himself behind me, pressing his chest against my back, and grabbing my breasts. Then, he rams into me so hard, I scream.

"Is that what you want?" His voice rumbles by my ear. He thrusts into me again, hard, and again I cry out. "Me to fuck you like this? This hard?"

Fuck. His filthy mouth paired with the rough and risky sex is driving me wild.

Another merciless thrust, one that steals my next breath away.

"Huh? What was that? I can't hear you, little rabbit."

He slams into me again.

"Y-Yes! Yes! Just like that." I can barely get the words out, but by some miracle, I do. Thank god his arm is around me, otherwise I might collapse from the sheer intensity of the pleasure spinning through me.

"Would you like more?" he asks. His hot breath spills down my neck, causing goosebumps to rise.

I nod, and with that, Elias pulls back slightly. He spits again, but this time, he rubs his wet fingers up and down my ass before inserting himself again. The whole thing makes me feel dirty and sexy and horny at the same time.

When I look over my shoulder again, he's smirking wickedly at me.

"Hold on," is all he says before plummeting into me. Over and over. Each time going deeper until I'm sure I've managed to fit all of him inside me somehow. Colors explode before my eyes, and I'm gripping the railing so tight, my knuckles turn white.

He fucks my ass with no remorse now, and with each thrust, the bolts holding the metal bars together groan and whine from his forcefulness.

There's a familiar pressure building, and I know if he keeps this up, I'm going to come for a third time. I just don't know if my body —or this balcony's railing—can take it.

Guess we're going to find out because within milliseconds, I come undone. Another scream rips from my throat, but I'm quickly silenced by Elias's hand as it clamps over my mouth. I yell into his palm instead, everything shattering into a million pieces, and he crashes into me a few more times before every muscle of his tightens and relaxes in a final release.

Together, we lower ourselves onto the cold floor, me cradled in his lap and his arms coming around me to hold me close. We sit in silence for a while, just listening to the booms of our racing hearts, our stagnant breathing, and the loud noises of the city going on all around us.

Finally, when I find a way to string more than a few thoughts together, I lick my dry lips and say, "So, do you think anyone saw us?"

He peers down at me with brows furrowed. "Absolutely. And whoever didn't *see* us certainly *heard* us."

I slap him in the chest, and he kisses the top of my head.

"It's okay, little rabbit. We gave them quite a show. One to be jealous of."

At one time, I would've been embarrassed at what we'd just did, but now...now it doesn't bother me at all.

When I look up at him again, I see that same hesitance as before wrinkling his forehead. Something's on his mind. Something more than just the heart-stopping sex we just had. But he's struggling to tell me.

"What is it, Elias?" I ask him, a bit worried about the answer. If it's bothering him this much, it can't be good, right?

"Hmm? What do you mean?"

"There's something you've been wanting to say to me. I can see it in your eyes."

He stares at me, mouth agape, shocked I've figured him out. But he doesn't deny it. Instead, he sighs and presses me tighter against him. "The other day...I heard you talking to Cain."

Not exactly sure where he's going with this, I wait for him to continue.

"Did he really tell you he loved you?"

Oh.

Shit.

"Uh, yeah. He did."

"Did you say it back?"

I pause. "Yes, I did."

He glances away for a long moment, his thoughts drifting.

Now I'm even more curious. "Is that a problem?"

"What?" He shakes his head. "No, no. I'm just surprised is all."

"Surprised?"

"Yeah. I never thought Cain was capable of any feelings like that. Especially not love."

Where is he going with this? "Do you think he lied to me or something?"

"No! Shit." He runs a hand over his face. "I'm really fucking this up."

"Why don't you just come out and say it then. I'm not sure what this has to do with Cain at all."

"It doesn't," he replies. "Not really."

"Then tell me, Elias. Tell me."

He pales. It's the first time I've ever seen him so confused and weak. And by what? Knowing Cain and I said I love you to each other? I don't understand.

His gaze searches my face, but I don't know what he's looking for.

"Elias..." I begin and touch his cheek. He leans into my palm "What's going on?"

He draws in a deep breath. "I asked about Cain because, well, I'm pretty sure I love you too."

I let his confession sink in. Let the truth seep into the empti-ness I've carried so long in my heart and fill up the holes. Like when Cain told me the same thing, my chest warms and I'm overcome with happiness. So much so that tears prickle the corners of my eyes.

Aria, the orphan who grew up having no one, now has two demons to love forever. It's no fairytale, by any means, but it's more than I could've asked for.

I realize then that I haven't said anything, and Elias is watching me intently, hanging on by a thread for my response. And of course he would, after what his bitch of an ex put him through. No wonder he was terrified to tell me.

To ease his fears, I tilt my head up and press my mouth against his for a sweeter than usual kiss.

When I pull away, I meet his golden hellhound eyes and say the words I feel in my very soul and the ones I know he's been dying to hear. "I love you, Elias."

Elated, he jumps to stand, pulling me up with him. He kisses me again, and the passion he puts behind it makes my head whirl. When he finally lets me go, I become aware of the wetness trailing down my legs from all the seed he'd spilled inside me.

"You sure know how to make a mess," I say lightheartedly. "I need a shower."

He laughs. "I don't know. I kind of like seeing you covered in me. It marks you as mine."

I roll my eyes. That's an animal for you.

He slides an arm under my knees and scoops me up like a bride ready to cross the threshold after her wedding day.

"What in the world are you doing?"

"You wanted a shower, didn't you, little rabbit?" He grins.

"Well, yeah but I didn't think I needed company."

"Saves water that way." There's a mischievous gleam in his eye as he carries me into the hotel room and heads for the shower. "And besides, we still have about two hours and ten minutes to go before our flight. We can get clean and we'll still have plenty of time to..."

My pulse speeds up.

Oh boy. When it comes to Elias, it looks like this little rabbit is going to have to turn into the Energizer Bunny.

SEVENTEEN

I'm not sure how much time has passed in this void they call a basement. Ten minutes. Ten hours. Ten years.

When a scuffing sound comes from the far corner of the room, I jerk my attention in that direction.

A figure stands in the shadows, green eyes glowing, and I know instantly who it is.

"What do you want, Nix?" I growl.

He steps out of the dark, his brows narrowing, and he's staring at me with a grin. He's taking in the dingy room, wrinkling his nose while strolling closer. The tee he's wearing is at least two sizes too small and it pulls taut across his chest and biceps, not to mention riding up his stomach. As always, he's in jeans. His arms up to his elbows are painted in blood, droplets hitting to the floor on his way toward me.

"You escaped a blood bath?" I ask, well aware that his sudden arrival must have been impromptu.

He pauses in front of me, then sniffs the air and glances at the door I left ajar. His lips curl upward at the edges, and fuck, his smugness pisses me off. He knows instantly that I'm trapped down here. That's the thing about my brother, Nix. Despite being the sin demon of lust, he notices every tiny little thing.

"What'd you do to piss off Cain?" he asks, circling the room. After my little stint with Aria, Cain was pissed. Hell knows what that green-eyed hellhound told him, but I didn't give a fuck when what blossomed between Aria and I can't be undone. The wicked spark I discovered within her awoke the beast in me, and now I will make her mine. The complication of the other three men in her life should be a fun obstacle to deal with. The way I see it, this can go a couple of ways. They accept I am not leaving her, or I take her for myself. A decision that still hangs heavily on my mind, seeing I don't have anywhere to take her without Cain on my heels. For now, anyway.

I shrug. "When isn't Cain in a pissy mood?"

He laughs. "Man, Hell sucks worse than before with you gone."

"What's Father said?"

"He's quiet. Really quiet, and you know when he gets like that, it's fucking bad. Overheard him talking to Torryn how you'll pay for betraying him."

Maybe I should be scared, but how much more terrified can I get when I've been living with the devil my entire life? He's been torturing me endlessly, so the distance we have between us is a vacation for me. "He threatens to kill everyone," I say. "And is Torryn the new favorite son now? Guess with Father's crappy mood, why not talk to the demon of Wrath, both of them can be constantly seething anyway."

"You laugh, but this is different, brother. He knows things you've done, and Lucifer will not be played."

I lick my lips as my thoughts swing to the diary I stole from him. Of course he'd know, and of course he'd suspect me. I knew that the moment I grabbed it and tucked it under my shirt. A sick feeling rises through me, except I can't change what's done. Cain's been tossed out of Hell for betraying Father, and he's made a life for himself out here. So I can too.

Nix steps back and glances at the door of the basement then back at me. "I could help you get out. What do I get for helping you?"

I stuff my hands into the pockets of my jeans. "Nothing. You still owe me one for killing that cross-road demon so you could sell his souls to buy that little red-haired woman for your pleasure."

"She was my servant," he corrects me.

"Servant. Sex slave. Is there a difference?"

"That was a long time ago, brother." His nostrils are flaring as he folds his arms across his chest, the fabric of his black T-shirt crawling farther up his stomach. "And you can't talk. You think I can't tell that the scrumptious little thing you brought to hell has you tripping over your feet? What is so special about this girl that two of my brothers are willing to risk everything? Is her cunt made of gold?"

"Shut your fucking mouth," I growl. "If you're going to help, then do it, otherwise fuck off out of here. Or have you forgotten how deals work? I do you a favor, and you pay back when I call it in."

Except, the way he's staring at me, I can tell he *wants* something from me too. But trusting him is a mistake I won't make. He might be my closest brother, but that doesn't mean I would trust my life in his hands. Far from it, but sometimes it's the whole better-the-devil-you-know. And it couldn't be truer in our case.

"Are we doing this, or what?" I ask him, my voice darkening, glancing down at the blood on his hands dripping over his clothes. "By the looks of it, you've got somewhere to return to."

"Nothing that can't wait. I'm helping out Lorcan in the torture cellars and just needed some escape from all his moaning about not being allowed to hunt, as Father's put a ban on it for now. And I'm that bored and going bat-shit crazy that I'm visiting him."

I lift my gaze to the bruise on the side of his neck. It's faint and it won't last long. We heal fast, but the only person capable of leaving such marks on a sin demon in Hell is our father.

"What did you need help with?" I ask, and curse myself instantly for asking. I must be getting soft by living here on earth, but it's hard to ignore the same signs of abuse I received regularly.

He strides around the room. "Tell me what you find in Father's diary."

I freeze, staring at Nix, trying to see through him and if his words are a direct order from Lucifer.

When I don't respond, Nix turns to me. "I used to sneak into his quarters and take a sneak peek into his diary, but fuck if I could work out what it said. Not like I could ask anyone without it getting back to him, you know."

"I don't have it."

"That's not what Father told Torryn."

My shoulders curl forward, an ache racing through me like a

spear had been plunged right through my chest. I shouldn't be surprised by his revelation, but I had hoped Lucifer wouldn't be onto me that quickly.

"I'm on your side, Brother," Nix tells me. Except, I don't fucking believe a word he says.

"Get me out of this room," I command with steel in my voice.

Nix drops his arms by his side, his fingers splayed. "All I want is a shield against him. Like you and Cain have; there is only so much you can take of torture. How long before he locks us all up, or throws us out of Hell, or shit knows what?"

A soft groan rolls in my chest. I'm familiar with how Nix plays his games, how he uses pity to get his victims. You'd think with his power of lust, he'd gain who he wanted with ease, except all my brothers are predators who loved to hunt. But if Nix has any intention of reporting this to Lucifer, then I have every intention to keep my enemy close.

So, I nod once, giving him hope where there is none. My alarm bells are off the charts. I might have just made a grave mistake, but too late for regrets. That's why there's a saying in Hell that one should hug their enemies, so you know how big to dig the hole for their graves.

Nix claps me on the shoulder. "Good, now let's get you out of here, shall we?"

While he goes to the door, I can't stop the dread churning in my gut. A flicker of fear lingers at the back of my mind...not for me, but Aria.

Nix pushes the door open, which does resist him, and he scuffs his foot across the mark, creating a gap in the salt and soil. Of course Cain would have created a protection barrier personalized to only affect me. What a prick!

"Done," Nix calls out, glancing back at me. "I'll be speaking with you soon, brother." Then he fades and vanishes in a blink.

It irks me that he visited, but at least it served two purposes. One, it let me know Lucifer knew about the diary, meaning we had to keep our guards up. Me specifically. Two, I'm free from this dull basement and I can track down my girl.

I step out into the quiet hallway and make my way upstairs just as Elias storms outside into the yard. I wait for him to vanish from sight, then I turn up the steps quickly and make my way to the upper levels of the mansion.

ARIA

I RUN a comb through my wet hair as I stroll back into my bedroom after *another* much needed steaming hot shower. Since arriving back home from Illinois with Elias, I've been exhausted. My thoughts are on overdrive after finally speaking with my mother, discovering how much of a douche my father was, and despite all of that, Elias knew exactly how to put a smile on my face afterward.

I still tingle all over as I think back to the things Elias did with his tongue on the hotel's balcony. That guy never ceases to amaze me with what he does to me, leaving me constantly craving him. Even now, I can't forget how his hands felt all over my body, how he pounded into me, over and over. I already miss him, feeling partly empty with him not by my side.

When we first met, he scared the hell out of me, but now everything about him fills me with arousal and admiration. Funny how initial perceptions of people can be so wrong. I put the comb down on my bedside table and search for my socks as there's a chill in the air. It's then that Cassiel trots into the room like he's a show pony.

"Where have you been?"

He responds with a half groaning sound, then hops up on my bed and lays on his belly, his front legs stretched out in front of him and his chin propped over them. But his eyes follow me around the room. With all the new furniture in the room and having salvaged my clothes, everything is all over the place. Finally, I track my underwear and pants at the bottom of the chest of draws and hop around the room to pull them on. Then I begin sorting through the huge bag of clothing I still haven't put away.

I hit the power button on the radio and start folding to the dance song that is playing.

It's only when I'm tucking my underwear into the draw that I notice someone standing in the doorway.

I glance up and lock eyes with Maverick, eyes widening appreciatively at me. Hastily, I toss the panties inside and slam shut the drawer with my hip.

"Aren't you supposed to be in the basement?"

He pushes forward, strutting his stuff, and well, he is freaking gorgeous in every aspect. Those strong shoulders, biceps that make me want to curl up against them, and kissable lips, that I recall all too well how they taste. "Is that really where you want me to be, or here with you?"

He sweeps right past me, his arm sweeping across my stomach as he crosses the room. His touch leaves me tingling, and I turn to find him chuckling as he's staring out the window.

"It's not about what I want, but where Cain believes you are safest," I answer.

He turns and lounges against the wall, arms folded across his chest. "Safe for me, or the rest of you?" There's something almost antagonizing about his tone, and I'm not sure why but it irks me. Perhaps it's all the bullshit we've been facing lately, or that I had been craving some alone time.

"I was thinking this might be a good time to pick up from where we left off down in the basement." He casually unfolds his arms and collects a blade from the back of his jeans. Standing there, he spins the knife in his hand effortlessly.

I'd be lying if I say the temptation of his offer doesn't linger on my thoughts. The memory of the excitement he brought out in me, the impulse to play dirty, the exhilaration of cutting him excited me. I don't quite understand it, but even now, my gut buzzes with the adrenaline of what we did.

Except what came afterward with Elias and him was an explosion I don't ever want to experience again. I swore he was going to kill Maverick, and I was powerless to stop him. I'm shaking remembering how hard I screamed and beat my fists into them with no effect.

I've just found happiness with three demons, and of course I go and find myself drawn to a fourth who's bringing chaos to our lives. Maybe the mistake is mine for letting myself go there with Maverick, with believing anything could happen.

"It's not a good idea," I answer. "If Elias catches you again, he'll murder you this time. And I'm exhausted from the fights. I just want you all to get the hell along."

With a final spin of the blade, he tucks it into the back of his belt. "You really think it's that easy? Elias is a mutt and has hated me since forever. Dorian is a wannabe sin demon, so my hopes are on making peace with my brother. He's the one who calls the shots here, but that will take time."

My shoulders rear back, and I hate the way he speaks of the men who destroy me with their love, and I won't let anyone talk shit about them.

I grind my jaw as fire licks across my skin, and my words come flying out. "No wonder Elias wants to rip you apart. Maybe it's better if he does find us together, and then I'll be sure to grab myself some popcorn and enjoy him beating your ass instead of making him stop."

His eyes narrow and his face goes still, as he watches me with serious eyes. "Want to give it a try yourself? You and me. Take this anger you have out on me and let's move past this point."

My insides tremble. "You want to know what I really think?"

"Be brutally honest. I can take it." Darkness sweeps over his gaze, and if I look too close into them, I am convinced I'll find the darkest pits of Hell.

"Deep down inside, you're lonely and want to make peace with the guys desperately. You see how hard they've fought after being tossed out of Hell, and now you wish you would have joined them instead of taking Lucifer's side. But your ego stands in the way of just being honest and admitting you made mistakes."

He arches a brow. "My ego isn't that big. Do you even know Dorian?"

I roll my eyes. "Your head is so inflated, I'm surprised you even fit into this mansion."

He chuckles, the sound forced and fake.

"And you want to know my truth?" he replies.

I brace myself, expecting the venom as I see it swimming across his expression.

"You are terrified of how much you crave the darkness. From me, from Sayah. Because if you accepted it, then you'd have to admit that maybe you're not so innocent. Maybe it's not Sayah who's been making you think these terrible things."

I stare at him as fury climbs through me at his words. Something in my chest soars with anger. "What the hell is that supposed to mean?"

He pushes off the wall and strides across the room. "You've been living with that thing inside you most of your life. You don't think that she might have shaped who you've become as a person?" He reaches my side and takes hold of my chin, lifting it, forcing me to look into those deep brown eyes. "I accept what I am, Aria. That inside me flows a river of darkness that drives me to hunt, to fuck, to take what I want. What about you?"

Everything about him annoys me, and I hate his words. I shove his hand away. "You don't know what you're talking about."

He laughs and strolls out of my room. The strike of his heavy boots on the floorboards fades as he heads downstairs.

Panic surges in me, that part of what he said is right. What if the attraction I have toward these demons, toward Maverick's darker side, is because even without Sayah, I've become something dark myself?

DORIAN

"Well, that didn't turn out how I'd pictured it," I say, crashing down on the couch in the parlor. The blaze in the fireplace crawls over my freezing body. Even though I've been on Earth for what feels like forever, the cold is still something I haven't fully acclimated to.

"It turned out better than we could have planned." Cain rubs his hands by the flames. "You checked on Maverick?"

I nod. "He was asleep on the bed down in the basement." I had noticed the salt and soil ring looked slightly thinner in one part, which could have been the cat if it went down there to explore. I fixed it up regardless.

Thumping steps coming from the hallway has me glancing over my shoulder to the parlor doorway.

Elias appears, all serious and stiff. "We have a visitor."

I laugh beneath my breath at how much he reminds me of a butler, but before I can mock him, Miranda steps into the room with a small bag under her arm.

I stiffen in my seat, curious why she's here.

She's wearing black riding pants over her long legs and a cream knitted sweater. Something about her looks...normal. I'm used to seeing her in a witchy dress or wearing crystals. No one would ever suspect she's a powerful seer looking like she's just come in from a round of Polo.

She only has eyes for Cain, not even acknowledging Elias and I as she goes to stand by the small table in the middle of the room. Cain moves to join her, and I recall the tense conversation in her tent when we dropped off the diary. I hurry to my feet and stroll over to join the pair, as does Elias.

This woman has been playing us from the beginning, her sights and claws aimed at Cain, wanting a spot right by his side, ruling over Hell. Fuck, she has balls to set her sights that high, but to also think she could control a deranged place like the underworld, well, she has to be partly crazy.

"Is it done?" His words are direct.

She nods. "It's fully deciphered," she tells him.

Sure, Miranda and I had a thing way back when, even if I left her high and dry. But I have always appreciated her directness, and right now I want to hug her. Fuck, she got Lucifer's deepest secrets from his diary all translated.

"What's it say?" I ask.

Her gaze remains glued to Cain. She's lucky Aria isn't with us now, or she might have ripped out Miranda's eyeballs for staring lecherously at Cain.

I'm sure Miranda isn't really that into him, but more into his power. The energy radiating off her isn't a command of arousal, not like Aria. With Miranda, this is strategic and calculated, and I wouldn't be surprised if her plan involved gaining favor with Cain to get to the throne, then stabbing him in the back.

Elias has his hands on the table, leaning forward, catching Miranda's glare.

"Give us space. Don't you have something better to do, like fetch a stick?" she taunts, snapping her attention back to Cain.

"There's plenty of space," I reply, standing across the table from Elias, and he grins my way. "Now, talk. What did you find?"

She still grips onto the diary, holding it close to her chest now. "You remember our terms, right, Cain?"

Shadows slither over our commander's face, his eyes darkening, but he hasn't shifted over into his demon form either. He's in control, like he always is. But the air might as well be molasses from how thick it's become.

And I love every second of it...the tension, the uncertainty, the games. There are many things I don't miss about Hell, but watching others play their political games was something of a favorite pastime for me.

"I never go back on my word. Now, what did you find?" Cain's words are sharp and clipped, carving through the tension. It's clear he hates the situation, but what's the human saying about the captain going down with the ship? Part of me wonders if that's his backup plan, should things ever reach that stage and Miranda forces him to fulfill his end of the bargain. Except, Aria would never let it happen...she would murder Miranda, that I have no doubts about. My girl is a hellfire, and maybe that's what Cain is counting on.

Now that is something I don't plan on missing.

We're all silent, watching Miranda, waiting.

She grins, taking her time to lower the diary from her chest and slowly opening it, flicking through the pages before she shuts it and slides it across the table to Cain.

He grabs it quickly and checks it, then looks up at her. "Where's the translation?"

Miranda taps her temple. "I figured you were in a rush and didn't want me to waste weeks typing everything up, especially based on my findings."

"And that is?" I usher her to speak. This drawing out bullshit and waiting has me itching to force her into speaking. But I also don't want a seer on my ass.

"Are you going to tell us, or is that going to take a few weeks too?" Elias asks through clenched teeth.

Miranda huffs, put out by having to deal with minions like Elias and myself. Fucking arrogant bitch.

"In all honesty, the majority of the stuff in there were ramblings," she began. "Repeating the same stuff over and over. He was basically using it as a notepad to collect information on types of creatures. A few things in Latin about holy water, but not much else. Think of it as a monster manual." She laughs, but no one is laughing with her and then she quiets down. "Tough crowd."

I stare at her, wanting to remind her that when she showed her claws at our last visit, she made it very clear where she stood with us. And it sure as fuck wasn't on any friendly levels. "Is there anything in there mentioning Aria?"

"Once only, and it was a title to an empty page. But you know what I think?" she asks, sucking in a deep breath. "To me, the rest of the diary almost read like a list of possibilities, like he was writing down his thoughts on what she could be."

"What makes you say that?" Cain asks, his narrowing gaze piercing into Miranda.

"Well, for one thing, there were a lot of pages where he'd scribbled origins and features of a monster, but then crossed them out. They were ridiculous ones, like shifters for example. Even I could have told him that's not what's going on with the girl."

"And the ones not crossed out?" I prod, feeling like we're having to pull the answers from her excruciatingly slowly.

"They were varied. One was a Shadow Caster."

"That wouldn't be it," Cain interrupts. "Those things produce regular shadows, not living ones. And they can't possess anyone."

"Exactly," she agrees with him, then shuffles the chair back to sit down, making herself comfortable. The three of us follow suit. "He listed a fallen angel as a possibility, with only a few features and lots of scribbles that made no sense. "There were quite a few things like Shades, Wraith, and even Nightmares, which I don't know much about, but again, he only made notes of their features that could relate to Aria I assume."

"It sounds like he has no fucking idea," Elias mutters the obvious.

"He doesn't know enough about Sayah to determine the best match with the monsters," Cain answers, then glances over to Miranda. "I'd like the typed-up translation sent to me by next week for me to study."

Cain knew Sayah better than Lucifer, so he might find something in his notes to help control Aria that the devil himself had missed.

"It's a research journal, really," she tells us. "And it comes with no conclusion. Just random thoughts and information he's discovered."

"Well, guess it's something," Elias says, leaning back in his chair. "Not sure it's information worth dying over, but that's your brother's problem, not ours." He's looking over at Cain, who doesn't answer. By the distance in his eyes, I'm guessing he hadn't even heard what Elias said.

"Anything else?" he asks suddenly.

"Yes," she admits. "It's not a lot, but toward the back of the book there are notes that talk about torturing someone to extract their soul, or maybe in this case, whatever is inside Aria. It doesn't mention her, but what else could he be talking about?"

I straighten in my chair and my chest tightens, my sudden catch of breath fills the room.

"He really is a depraved soul, isn't he?" she answers, her mouth thinning. "There is no discovery on those pages aside from his own thoughts on torturing someone. I'll let you read those when I supply the full transcript."

That's not what I want to hear, and I tense, my hands by my side curling into fists. It shouldn't surprise me that Lucifer would turn to torture. It's his go-to with everyone.

Miranda's on her feet. "Well, that's all I found. There's nothing else, but just because it doesn't give you the answer you seek, it doesn't change our deal."

Cain's brow furrows but he doesn't argue the point. "Walk with me. I'll show you to the door."

Once they leave, I look over to Elias, who's tense as hell, his shoulders curled forward like he carries the world on them.

"He can't get his hands on her," he says. "We've both seen Lucifer's tortures in action, and no one comes out of them alive. Look how fucked up the sin demons are, all because of him. If he gets hold of Aria, he'll break her and she'll never come back. We'll lose her forever."

I swallow hard and drag a hand through my hair. My chest aches with his words because he's right. If we let that sonofabitch get his claws into Aria, then we've lost everything.

EIGHTEEN

ARIA

My eyes fly open at the sound of a thud by the door.

Night cloaks my room and I stare at the door, slightly ajar, still lying in bed silently, trying to hear the sound again. If someone is in my room, then I want them to think I'm sleeping...at least for now.

When nothing comes for a long pause, that feels more like fifteen minutes, I crane my head up gently to see Cassiel isn't on the bed with me. And I'm certain I know what woke me up...him jumping out of bed.

I breathe easy, hating that I've become so jumpy lately. I seriously need to chill. Taking a deep inhale, I flop my head back down onto the pillow and wonder if one of the guys would be awake.

Closing my eyes, I settle in and let sleep take me.

The floorboards groan, and I roll onto my back, my eyes opening groggily, and I wait for Cassiel to hop back up and settle down. Instead, a blur comes toward me from the corner of my eye so fast, I know it can't possibly be Cassiel.

I flinch to get up, but a heavy weight crashes into me, shoving me back to the bed. What the fuck? I fling my arms to get up, but it's so huge, so heavy.

The cold bite of a blade is suddenly at my throat. "Quiet down, dark one."

"W-Who the hell are you?" I'm stiff in bed, terrified to move. One slip of the blade, and I'll bleed out all over my bed sheets.

And really, dark one?

Talk about the pot calling the kettle black.

The fuckwit is straddling me, and like a mountain he towers over me. All I see in the dark is the silvery glint of his eyes.

"Who I am is of no consequence. It took me a long time to finally track you down."

My mind is buzzing and I'm rolling through all the sin demons in my mind wondering who the hell this one is. Clearly not Nix. But that doesn't stop the furious quiver that runs through me at being attacked in my bed at night.

"So, which one are you?" I ask brazenly, even if my life hangs in the balance. But if there's one thing I know about demons, it's that they love to talk, especially about themselves. "So, the hellhounds have failed and you're the backup? You know that means you are just one step up from those hounds according to Lucifer."

"Don't you dare speak his name in my presence!" he hollers, his whole body shuddering, and that pinch of the blade pushes harder against my skin. I press myself into the bed, as if willing myself to slide right through the mattress. The glow of his eyes intensifies, and shit, but this guy is freaking me out.

"Okay, chill. We all have daddy issues."

"Listen carefully. You are *The First*, and I care not for your love of Hell or your decision to become Lucifer's concubine, but—"

"Um, excuse me, but let's back up a bit. There is no concubine happening with that sadistic asshole. Ever. I mean, is that what he told you?" Geez, I really don't need the psychopath who rules Hell to suddenly decide he is going to claim me. That would be the worst scenario in this entire damned world. In that circumstance, I'd purposefully allow Sayah to take me over just so she could have a go at him. And knowing my luck, she'd love his brand of bat-shit crazy.

But the beast on top of me hasn't shifted or loosened his blade from my throat.

"What do you mean, I'm The First? Like, I'm your first mission and it's the first time you've been allowed out to play?"

"You talk too much."

"And you haven't killed me yet, so what do you really want?"

He lifts his head, laughing, the sound terrifying and exactly what I'd expect from a serial killer finding out he just got away with the perfect murder. The moonlight hits his face, revealing the grinning sneer painted on his face. "You are like the rest of them, even if you don't know it yet."

"Like who? Your hellish brothers?"

His head lowers, the darkness stealing his features once more. "I can't exactly deny that. My brothers are frustratingly annoying," he hisses.

"That's putting it mildly. More like arrogant asses."

His head tilts to the side, studying me for a long pause. "Are you ready to die, fiend?"

"Well, no, the answer is no to that. And why am I the fiend when you're the one from the pits of the most depraved place in the universe...*Hell*." Everything about this dude feels like the opposite of the spawn of Lucifer. He's asking me if I want to die, and there's no lecherous flirting. What am I missing?

He flinches at my response, his shoulders curving forward. "Do not insult me."

The blade presses to my neck harder, and I freeze, a quiver rushing down my spine.

"Look please, you don't have to do this. Let's talk about it, hash it out, anything."

"Oh, but I do. This is my mission."

Mission?

The light to the room flicks on and blinding light burns my eyes. I squint just as the blade eases from my neck. The bulky thing on top of me groans, shading his eyes with an arm.

I squirm and shove his hand with the blade away from me, which fails miserably. Shit, is this guy made of steel?

"Gabriel!" Cain growls as Dorian and Elias burst into the room behind him. "What the fuck are you doing here?"

My mind is reeling at the name Gabriel. There are no sin demons by that name. The only Gabriel I've heard of is...I gasp. No fucking way! There is no way in the world the man on top of me is...

"Please don't tell me an archangel is trying to kill me," I say, getting really tired of being everyone's punching bag.

No, it can't be. Angels are our protectors and do good deeds. It has to be another demon with a similar name.

I blink to clear my vision and slowly the man on top of me comes into view. I gape at the sight in front of me. The guy is glowing. It's the only way to describe it.

Soft curls the color of sunshine frame his strong face, all sharp jawline and cheekbone, prominent nose, and those pillow-like red lips. There's something almost cherub-like to this man, and then there's his piercing silvery eyes that hold that same glow.

I don't even have to ask because there is no way this man is a demon.

Shit!

"Now Heaven's involved?" We're in so much trouble.

"This isn't your business," Gabriel orders, the angry glower on his face deepening as he glares at Cain. "I am here to slay the dark one."

I fake cough, though on the inside, I'm trembling. "You have me mistaken for someone else."

Here I always assumed angels would have voices of...well, of angels. Except, that's not the case with Gabriel. His voice is gravelly, like he's just finished chewing on a bag rocks. Damn, he's huge, and incredibly intimidating. Guess he'd have to be if his task is to keep humans protected from demons. All those images I've seen of angels are misleading.

They're painted as vulnerable, almost fragile, while this guy looks like he's made of two quarterbacks, his muscles bulging against the sleeves of his white tunic.

My men don't look impressed. "It's very much my business," Cain growls, his shoulders rising as he steps forward. "She is ours, bound by blood. She is not yours to take. Whatever reason you have for being here comes to me." A growl rolls out of his throat, Dorian and Elias on either side of him. They're a terrifying fighting machine when together like this.

In a blink, Cain's eyes darken, as do the veins under his skin.

I swallow hard.

Three demons against an angel, and I'm in the middle of it. Not good.

I'm sort of terrified to have them fight. And it has nothing to do with the whole good-versus-evil thing. All the men are large and powerful, but I suspect Gabriel here can unleash some terrifying holy shit against them. And I don't want my demons hurt.

"Umm, how about you get off me before you squish me to death, and we talk about this misunderstanding over some coffee?"

Gabriel glances down at me, his eyebrow arching like I made a stupid joke. Wow, he has no sense of humor.

Suddenly, he shifts and climbs off me smoothly like he's well versed in getting off victims he's knifed to death while they sleep. I move to get up when his hand grabs me by the shoulder and forces me to my feet. Searing pain shots down my arm at how hard he grips me, and I wince.

"Ouch. You don't need to jab your fingers through my bones."

He releases me and turns to Cain.

"Sin Demon of Pride, exiled Son of Lucifer, speak," he demands.

Wow, that's quite the title there.

"Your conflict isn't with us." Cain steps forward, his chin high. Nothing scares him. Hell, I freaking adore him and love seeing him so powered up.

It's probably not the best thing to be thinking about, considering the situation.

"*She* is our concern," Gabriel states. "And you know it, son of Lucifer. She is The First and needs to be vanquished."

I blink at him, my mind catching up with his words, realizing he must be referring to Sayah as The First. "Wait a second...I need to be vanquished?"

My earlier levity evaporates instantly.

When no one responds and my guys look as confused as me, Gabriel breaks out into one of his over-dramatic laughs, and even places a hand to his chest for extra effect. "Oh, you have surprised me today, demon."

I am so confused right now, my gaze swinging between the angel and demons. "Did I miss something?"

His eyes widen as he glances around the room. "None of you know, do you?" he continues. "How can this be?"

"If you're going to keep talking in circles, get the fuck out of our house," Elias says.

But Cain lifts a hand to silence him, studying the angel. "Enlighten us."

"You are harboring a Leviathan creature in your midst, a ticking time bomb for all angels and demons, for all humanity, and you've been protecting her."

Did he just call me a Leviathan creature? "What the fuck is that?"

Gabriel swings toward me swiftly and has his hand around my throat, squeezing.

Panic spears through me, and I claw at his hand.

"It's a filthy creature. The very first monsters God created. You were a mistake, an abomination, and I was ordered to clean up the mess. I did my job, eradicated the beasts, but one got away."

In a flash, Cain is at our side, his fist colliding right into the angel's head, unlodging him from me. I tumble backward, tripping over my own feet. But I fall right into Dorian's arms, who's there to catch me in a flash.

The battle with Cain and Gabriel sets off like an explosion, moving so fast I can't see where one begins and another ends.

My heart is thundering in my chest, and I turn to Dorian. "I don't really understand what a Leviathan is, but it's bad, isn't it?"

He nods and pulls me to my feet, and brutal fear trembles through me now. I've wanted to know for so long what Sayah is, but now I take it back. If it's brought down the wrath of an angel who wants to kill me, I'm literally in the worst-case scenario of what could happen.

Gabriel is hurled into a wall, leaving a gaping indent.

Cain zips over to him in a blur and grips him by the throat. His demon is out, black wings spread, the claws tipping the ends curling in toward Gabriel. "Neither of us will win if we keep fighting, you know this. You need to understand there is a greater danger on Heaven's doorstep, and Aria might be the only thing that can help all of us. Now back the fuck down!"

Gabriel's nose wrinkles in disgust, then he shoves a fist into Cain's chest, sending him reeling back. "Speak then, demon."

They face each other, each of them tall and formidable.

Dorian and Elias are on either side of me, holding me close, ready to fight to keep me safe, and my heart beats for them. They are everything to me. But I'm seriously scared right now.

"Lucifer is set to unleash war and overtake Heaven, killing as many angels in the process as possible. He believes he needs Sayah...I mean, the Leviathan creature as the weapon that will aid him."

Gabriel's chest puffs out and he's exhaling loudly. "Then we strike down the monster now, just as I had intended."

"Except, she is *our* weapon to stop him. He won't see it coming."

There's something not reassuring about them talking about me as if I'm not even in the room. From the intensity of their words, the power radiating from the two powerhouses, they both seem to have forgotten they aren't alone in my bedroom.

"Explain!" Gabriel barks, folding his arms over his beefed-up chest. "How will you do this?"

Cain doesn't miss a beat. "We are ironing out those details, but when it comes to Lucifer, we are all on the same side. We need to stop him."

"So, what is stopping you from dethroning him right now?"

Cain runs a hand through his dark hair. "We haven't found the last two relics for Azrael's harp to give us entry back into Hell."

Gabriel watches him intensely, then glances over to me, leaving me covered in goosebumps. How is it possible that an angel scares me more than a demon? Except, as Cain said, he's on our side. Well, except for Sayah...the first creature God created. Fuck, that sounds horrible and she's inside me. No wonder she wants to take me over. And here I was, suspecting the entire time that she might be some kind of demonic beast or curse.

Except, she originated from Heaven.

Does that make me God's mistake, or weapon? I really prefer to be neither, in all honesty.

"If she really is a Leviathan, as you claim, then she is the only one who can dissolve Lucifer's plan and bring him to an end," Cain goes on.

Gabriel hasn't said anything for a short while, but has his eyes shut like he's decided to take a brief mediation. When they flick open I flinch, and did I mention the guy freaks me out?

He finally speaks. "Since I was the one to destroy the harp and scatter it's pieces, I will reveal the location of the last two parts for you to dethrone Lucifer. You fail, and I will personally hunt you down, Cain, and your demons, smothering you into oblivion."

Cain doesn't seem disturbed by the threat. He's standing tall, staring directly at Gabriel, but then again, he's always had the best poker face.

"Deal," he states.

Gabriel shifts closer to him, talking to Cain, but his hushed words are undecipherable.

Cain gives a nod, and the two break apart.

"What will you do with Aria?" Dorian asks out loud. "She's free and in our care." He states this as a matter of fact.

Gabriel twists in my direction, his gaze burrowing into me.

No word.

No expression.

No movement.

He's a goddamn freak and reminds me more and more of serial killers with their laser focus on their prey.

In a flash, he pops out of existence, a whirlwind blowing against us while half a dozen white feathers swirl through the room.

Cassiel suddenly appears from who knows where and lunges to catch the feathers with his huge paw, batting at them as they fall.

"We're in so much shit, aren't we?" I ask.

But no one answers. Elias pulls me to his chest and I press into him, waiting to be wrapped up and whisked away.

Cain moves to stand in front of me, his hand on my cheek so tenderly that my next breath hitches all the way to my lungs. The passion in his eyes is everything to me.

"This might actually work in our favor. We have Gabriel on our side for now," Cain states. "We are going to speed things up. We have my father to dethrone. And now we know where to go next."

Absolutely nothing about what he just said has put me at ease. Especially the fact that Gabriel never answered the question about what he plans to do to me. "But what about what Gabriel called me. Leviathan. Someone please tell me more about what the heck that is. It's freaking me out."

Cain sighs, and I already know I'm going to hate his answer. "They are rare and never encountered. All I've seen about them are what's in the Bible, and since it was written by man, it's not very reliable. It basically says all Gabriel gave us—one of God's first creations that he accidently made too powerful and had to destroy."

"Great."

"At least now, we have a name for Sayah," he says in an attempt to make it sound better.

I want to believe that what we've just discovered is a good thing, but then why is there apprehension flashing in Cain's eyes?

Our first stop is Iceland. To the Kirkjufell mountain to be exact.

According to Gabriel, this is where the harp's foot is located, while the last piece resides at the bottom of the Atlantic Ocean. So, while Aria and I hopped on the next flight across the world, I had ordered the closest of our search teams to charter a boat and retrieve the skull.

I would've asked Dorian and Elias to go, but with the Nightwalker and hellhound problems still looming over us, they're of better use at the mansion and Purgatory. Plus I don't trust leaving Maverick home alone still. Even if he seems to be keeping to his promises for now. I know my brother, and he's like Houdini, the way he can break out of all my restraints. Magical and non.

As the tour guide drives us through the icy and rocky terrain, I find myself staring at Aria again. She sits next to me, gazing lazily out the window, and much like the plane ride here, she's spoken very little to me. Despite my poor attempts to strike up a conversation, she's remained cold and distant.

I sigh, remembering how not long ago I'd put such a gap between us on purpose. It'd taken time, but we'd gotten past that and opened up to each other. So why did it feel like we were back to square one? Why were we ignoring each other, waiting for one of us to bend our stubborn ways and apologize?

She doesn't need chocolates or flowers, like Dorian suggested. I need to just talk to her. Explain everything—why I did what I did. She needs to know that I only have her in mind.

Sucking in a deep breath, I open my mouth to say something, but her excited squeal cuts me off. Pressing her cheek to the window, she points outside where the sky is ablaze with neon greens and yellows, colors flashing and moving as if they're alive.

I let out all my breath, entranced by the sight myself. I've never seen something so amazing. Especially on earth. "The aurora borealis..."

She glances over her shoulder at me. "The northern lights?"

"Mhmm." I never thought earth could offer anything so breathtakingly beautiful. Until I met Aria, of course. And now, being here, watching two of the most magnificent wonders this world has to offer at the same time, I'm practically speechless. In awe.

"I feel it," Aria says suddenly, jarring me out of my daydreaming.

"Feel what?"

She glances at the driver, who is undoubtedly human, and lowers her voice. "My toe..."

Ah. She's feeling the dark magic of the harp's relic. Perfect. "That means we're in the right place."

The car bumps along the dirt road until we reach a chained-off area with signs saying to keep out. The driver throws it in park and shuts off the engine. "This is as far as we can go," he says.

"It's far enough." I throw open the door and on the other side, Aria does the same.

"No one's allowed past the chains. It's too dangerous of a climb," the man begins.

"We'll be fine," I call to his rolled down window and join Aria at the rear of the car. When I drape my arm around her, she side-eyes me. "Just a bit of...romantic sightseeing."

She snorts a laugh.

"We'll be back in a few minutes," I tell him, and guide Aria past the chains before he can say anything more. My hope is that this will be a quick venture, certainly less eventful than the time we'd gone to Missouri on Maverick's wild-goose chase.

The land is frozen over and slippery. Aria clutches my arm as her shoes slip and slide. She struggles to stand, let alone walk up the steep mountain. If I didn't need her gift to tell us where the foot relic is hidden, I'd make her stay in the car.

"Do you hear anything yet?" I ask her.

She shivers against me but nods. "A high whistling, I think. Like a flute. But I'm not sure if it's the relic or the wind whistling past my ears."

"And your toe?"

"It's twitching like mad. I think it wants us to keep climbing."

I sigh. "Of course it does." I secure my grip on her waist as we round the back of the mountain. Slowly. Very slowly. At this rate, we'll make it to the top by dawn. "Would you be opposed to me flying us to the top?"

She grimaces. "What about the driver? Won't he see?"

"The mountain will be blocking us mostly, and I'll stay close to it. The darkness should help as well."

Still, she looks unsure.

"Even if the human did spot us, I doubt he'd believe his own eyes," I assure her. "Humans have a way of convincing themselves of things to ease their fears."

"That's true. People see what they want to believe."

"Precisely"

She nods, giving me the okay, and I press her body against mine as my demon bursts out of me. My wings tear through my shirt and jacket, hellfire spinning through my veins, and wasting no time, I push off the ground. Aria's arms clutch me around the neck as we ascend, and I make sure to keep as close to the mountain as I possibly can, even with the wind pounding into us.

Peeking her head out, she points to the very top.

The moment we touch ground again, my demon shrinks away and my wings fold in. I roll my shoulders to ease the discomfort restraining my monster always brings.

Aria stops at the crest, and her face falls.

"What is it?"

"Do you feel that?" she asks. "The ground? It feels like it's...pulsing."

I glance around us but see no signs of movement. Feel nothing too. "Pulsing?"

"Maybe breathing? I'm not sure how to explain it. But it feels like the mountain's alive under my feet."

"It must be the relic."

She nods. "My toe agrees. Although, the flute has stopped." Her gaze drops. "How are we going to get the thing if it's under layers of ice and rock?"

Not a problem. I wave for her to step back and summon the demon part of me again but concentrate the raging fire inside me to my enclosed fists. They glow an orangey red. Crouching low, I position myself over the rock and punch down with all my strength and power. Sharp pieces of earth and ice fly out in all directions, causing Aria to leap back a little further. I do it again and again, pain ricocheting up my arm but getting deeper each time.

"Keep going," Aria says. "I can hear the music again. You're almost there."

Another three hits and the rock breaks away to a hollow cavern. Air rushes out at us, hitting me in the face and smelling like decay and stagnant water. Carefully, I reach inside.

Once my fingers brush against something solid and icy cold, I seize it and wrench it out of the hole. Under the lights of the aurora borealis, I can just make out the wrinkly gray scaly skin and clawed toes of a creature's foot. Not human-like at all. No, this thing looks to be from some animal.

As I examine the thing in my hand, green light flashes before my eyes, stunning me. I hear Aria gasp somewhere close by, but I can't see anything past the brightness.

I'm blind.

ARIA

MY EYES BURN against the harsh green light. I can't see Cain; I don't even know if he's still on the mountain with me. Or if *I'm* on the mountain, for that matter. There's no way for me to know when I can't see a damn thing past my nose.

Dark forms begin to take shape in the distance, and I blink rapidly to help them come into focus. The lights shift and dim, and gradually the shadowy blobs gain more of a form—human forms —until the scene before me becomes clear.

I'm standing in the middle of a large room, medieval in style but made up of black polished marble and draped in red and gold. There's a colossal stone fireplace, one I remember, and a dais set up with an altar and throne fit for a king.

A king of Hell, that is.

My breath freezes in my lungs. I'm in Lucifer's castle again.

How the fuck did I get down here? And where's Cain?

I glance around desperately, wondering if the foot relic managed to transport us somehow, but when I see Cain, he's crawling up the few steps, clothes torn as if he'd just been in a vicious battle, and blood painting every inch of him. His wings are out, his black veins decorating his skin, and I can feel acid burning its way up my throat. He's hurt. Badly. I want to run to him, but my feet are somehow glued in place. I don't have any control over my body.

"Cain!" I try to yell, but my voice is trapped inside me, too. Panic surges forward. Is it Sayah again? It must be. She's taken me over again, and I'm powerless to regain my control.

That's when I notice that he's trying to get to another person who's laying on the other side of the throne. With silvery white hair and equally pale skin...

I gasp, my heart thundering. Maverick.

He's on his back, clutching his stomach, which has been torn open and is bleeding profusely.

But he'll heal, right? We're in Hell, and demons are immortal here. It should only hurt like a bitch for a bit, but he should be okay.

When Cain reaches him, he lifts his hand and the candlelight around the room glints on something metal in his hand.

A dagger.

And not just any dagger. An angel blade.

Cain's going to plunge it into his brother's heart.

"No!"

But it's no use. They can't hear me.

"I'm sorry, brother..." he whispers, pain lacing his voice.

To my horror, Cain does exactly as I predicted and stabs Maverick straight through the chest. My head fills with my screams, but none of them leave my mouth. I can only watch as Maverick's body jerks before going completely still. Dead.

Oh my god...

I can't even process what's happening. And when Cain grips the blade again, points it to himself, and raises it again, my brain completely fogs over. One of my greatest fears is about to play out before my very eyes, and there's nothing I can do to stop it. He's about to kill himself too.

Cain's black eyes flick my way and automatically change to their beautiful crystal blues. This time there's a great deal of sadness reflected in them as he looks at me, but not a hint of remorse, telling me he knows what he's doing. He just wishes he didn't have to.

My heart twists. *"Please. Don't."* I beg him silently, hoping somehow he knows what I'm thinking. But it's clear in his expression that he's made up his mind.

The moment he thrusts the angel blade through his chest, I lurch forward with all my strength and somehow my feet are able to leave the floor. The neon green lights flare again, blinding me, and suddenly, I'm sliding on slippery ground, my sneakers unable to get a grip. Disoriented, I windmill my arms and grasp for balance, but it does nothing. I feel myself falling.

"Aria!"

Strong hands seize me and wrench me back. Colors burst in front of my eyes as the strange light fades away, and once I can see again, Cain's face is there, as perfect as can be, but creased with worry. No blood. No wounds. Just my demon prince breathing hard and holding onto me like he's afraid to let me go.

When my gaze drifts to the right, I see why. I almost fell down the side of Mount Kirkjufell.

I leap forward, slamming into his chest, and he wraps his arms fully around me. I can barely feel the fear of almost dying myself when all I can see is the image of him killing Maverick and then himself playing over and over in my head. As vividly as if I was there in Lucifer's throne room.

I can't hold back the tears that come rushing forward, or the sobs as they wrack through my chest.

Cain tightens his hold on me, and his fingers begin to comb

through my hair. "You saw it too, didn't you?" he whispers against the top of my head.

I squeeze my eyes. At that point, I couldn't even form words if I tried.

"It has to be from the relic," he goes on gently. "Some kind of... moment of fear or something."

I peer up at him. As I struggle to regain my composure, my voice cracks. "But you were holding it. Not me."

His head tilts in thought. "You're right. And killing my brother isn't a fear of mine."

"How about killing yourself?"

"A fear? No."

"Then what the heck was that? And how did I see it, too?"

"My guess is that it has something to do with the link between us now," he explains. "The magic was able to transfer through the bond we share."

On cue, Cain's cellphone rings. He pulls it out of his pants pocket and glances at the screen and says, "It's Dorian," before holding it to his ear.

"Yes?"

"What the fuck was that?" I hear Dorian saying.

Stepping back, I put a little space between us but make sure it's not too much with so much ice underneath me.

"So you saw it as well." Cain nods my way to say this only confirmed his theory.

Dorian goes on loudly. "Bright green light? Popping into Lucifer's throne room? You offing your brother and then—"

"Yes, yes. *That.*"

"What the fuck, Cain?" Now there's concern in his tone. Of course there is. He just witnessed his closest friend stab himself to death. "Is there something you want to tell me?"

"We found the foot," he says, and then clarifies. "The relic. I believe whatever we saw was part of its dark power, and it transfers through our bond. Aria saw it, too, and I'm guessing Elias will be calling me next to say the same thing."

There's a tense moment of silence on the other end of the phone before Dorian speaks again. This time, in a lowered voice. "You don't think that was a flash into the future, do you?"

The thought sinks like a boulder in the pit of my stomach. "A flash into the future? What? That's actually going to happen?"

"I'm not saying that," he replies in his normal overly calm manner. "We won't be able to tell if that's what it is until..."

"Until you run an angel blade through your heart." My voice is rising; I can't help it.

Cain's about to take a step toward me but then remembers he's still on the phone with Dorian and hangs up without saying good-bye. He pockets the phone and then reaches out to me.

"Aria, please."

The sorrow in his eyes reminds me too much of what I saw in the vision—or whatever it was—and my chest squeezes.

"Can I..." He lets out a breath, almost annoyed at himself. "Can I...hold you a little longer?"

His question throws me off guard. It's so unlike him to ask such a thing, but after what we've just seen, how can I say no? It feels like my insides are shaking, and all I want is for him to hold me close and tell me he'd never do something that insane. No matter what the relic says.

I close the distance between us and welcome his embrace again. He squeezes me a little tighter this time, but I don't care. It's the comfort I need right now.

Drawing in his cologne and fiery scent, I let it wash over me and calm my raging nerves. Above us, the northern lights have vanished, leaving only an inky-black sky dotted with stars. It's almost as if the relic was causing the magical light show. And maybe it was. When it comes to these relics, nothing much surprises me anymore.

We stay locked together like that for a while. Saying nothing, only enjoying each other's company and warmth. Whatever anger I'd felt towards him before about my mother is gone now. Long gone. And there's only the pain and absolute grief that comes with possibly losing him again. It engulfs me.

I want to ask him if he's been planning on doing what I'd witnessed in the vision, if it really was a glimpse into the future, but I'm almost too terrified of the answer to ask it. I rather not think about it ever again.

I love him so much it hurts. Physically *hurts* to think that he won't be with me anymore. I never thought I'd ever feel like this towards anyone, especially a demon.

But I do.

After more time passes, Cain finally releases me and steps back. Then he shrugs off what's left of his torn jacket and uses it to pick up the foot relic without touching it again. To our relief, no more bright lights flash or haunting images appear.

Wings unfurling, he's about to grab me around the waist to fly us off the mountain when his phone rings again. Sighing, he takes it out of his pocket and answers it without even looking at the screen.

Through the speaker, a familiar deep voice booms, "What the fuck—"

"Yes, Elias. I know."

CHAPTER

TWENTY

DORIAN

Elias and I are still rattled by the vision.

I mean, how could we not be? We just witnessed our closest friend sacrifice himself in the middle of Lucifer's throne room. And for what? I'm not sure. But I have a sneaking suspicion it has something to do with what Aria and I discovered in Storm's library about Lucifer and his son's souls being connected.

It may have been just a faulty flash of something not real, a way to spook us as part of the relic's magic. Or it could be something more. A peek into a future event, and that's where my fears lie. Knowing Cain for as long as I have, I wouldn't put it past him either, so you bet your ass the moment he and Aria walked through the front door from their trip to Iceland, I waved Aria up the stairs to sleep off the trip and steered Cain right into the parlor to talk more, one-on-one.

The second I assure we're alone, I whirl on him. Before I can even get a word out, he holds up his hand.

"Where's Elias," he asks, voice as emotionless as stone.

"Hellhound duty," I say dismissively. I know he's avoiding the inevitable conversation, but he can't hide from me. He paces in front of the fireplace and I cut around the couch to stop him. "Cain."

He frowns.

"Please don't tell me what we saw was a vision of the future," I say. "Don't tell me you are planning anything crazy like that."

He glances down at his jacket in his hands, and it's then I realize that it's wrapped around something. Most likely the relic.

His silence irks me. He's not answering my very simple question, and that's not a good sign.

"Cain..."

"I don't know," he replies finally and draws in a deep breath.

But that's not good enough for me. "What do you mean you don't know? How do you *not* know whether or not you're planning on killing yourself? That's what I'd consider a big fucking thing and not something you're on the fence about."

Sighing, he runs his fingers over the jacket before looking up at me again. "I've been thinking..."

"Uh oh. Never a good sign."

"Listen to me," he begins again more sharply, "if what you and Aria discovered is true, and my soul is somehow linked to Lucifer, then there may be a way to weaken him."

"You mean by killing yourself." I can't believe what I'm hearing here. "And your brothers."

He nods. "The more of us that die, the weaker he'll be. And then you and Elias can take him out. For good."

I blanche. He isn't serious; he can't be. "Look, I know Miranda is a handful, but there has to be another way to get out of the demon contract than offing yourself."

He's deathly quiet. Not a flicker of humor on his face.

"What I'm *trying* to say is, abso-fucking-lutely not. You're out of your damn mind if you think I'll let you kill yourself."

"Do you want to take Lucifer off the throne?"

"That's a fucking stupid question."

"Then this may be the only way."

"I severely doubt that," I snap. "Why do you have such a death wish all of a sudden? We've done everything to survive. Fought, scraped, and clawed to stay alive, and you want to just end it? Just like that?"

He doesn't respond, only continues to stare at me grimly.

I clasp my hand on his shoulder and lock gazes with him. "Cain, listen to me. I told you I'd follow you to the end of time, and I will. I'll do whatever you ask of me. Hell, I'll spike an angel blade through Maverick myself. Even Lorcan. Or Val. Fuck, even—"

"I get it." He cuts me off as a small smile curls his lips.

"Sorry." Got a little too excited at the thought of killing those ass-wipes. "You get the point. But the one thing I'll never do is let you die. Never. It's nonnegotiable."

He pats the arm on his shoulder. "You're a good friend, Dorian. I'd be lost without you."

"Ain't that a true statement," I scoff and step back. "Now, I'm guessing what you're holding there isn't just a pile of dirty laundry?"

He nods. "I need to put it with the others in my room."

"I'm supposed to be giving Elias a break for a few hours. I've convinced him to finally take a shower. Although the stink may be what's keeping the hounds at bay."

Another crack of a smirk, but he hides it well. "And Maverick?"

"Still in his hidey hole in the basement. Throwing knives at your portrait or something."

"Good, that means the magic's holding," he says.

"For now, yeah, but you and I both know he's an escape artist."

"Not if he's trying to prove his loyalty to us."

I don't know about that. I don't trust Maverick at all. He's scheming down there. I'm sure of it.

"Go relieve Elias of his guard duty," he says. "I'm sure he'll want to talk to me too."

I watch him walk out of the parlor and up the stairs before heading down the hall and out the back door myself. Right away, I spot Elias huffing it up the hill toward the mansion. When he sees me, he rolls his eyes.

"You were supposed to meet me a half an hour ago," he barks in annoyance.

"Cain and Aria are home."

His eyes widen. "I need to talk to—"

"He's waiting for you," I say. "In his room."

He pushes past me and heads inside.

"Don't forget to bathe!" I shout to his back. "You smell like a barn."

He holds up a middle finger before slamming the door behind him.

Turning back toward the dark woods, I make my way down the hill and head for the lake at the edge of the property. As I pull off my shirt and chuck it into the brush, I release my demon form and let the hellish power race through me. It warms my skin, chasing away the bitter winter cold. Part of me wishes I'd run into a hellhound tonight, just so I can stretch out these wound-up muscles and get the chaos and destruction my demon craves. But the other part of me wants a smooth and easy stroll so I can get it over with and pay my sweet little Aria a visit tonight before she goes to bed.

When I reach the lake, I gaze upon the silvery ice coating the top and shimmering in the moonlight. It's almost poetic. Especially how a light haze clings to the frozen ground and among the trees on the opposite side.

Sights like this you could never get in Hell. This peacefulness. This ghostly glow and calm. It's...dare I say...*heavenly?*

The crunch of my footsteps in the snow coupled with whistling of the wind are the only sounds in the night. I don't know how long I've been out here or how many times I've walked around the mansion surveying the land for anything suspicious, but when I reach the lake once more, the chill starts to seep into my bones. I don't have fur; I'm not made for this type of work, so it looks like it's time for Elias to switch with me again. Hopefully the dog took his bath.

As I'm about to make my way back to the mansion, a low hum vibrates in the distance, somewhere behind me. I stop dead in my tracks.

Another sound, louder this time, and I realize it's not a hum, but a growl, and every hair on my arms stands on end. I spin around to see a pair of glowing yellow eyes through the haze, staring at me from across the lake.

Then another pair.

And another.

Until every shadowy place between the trees is shining with predators' eyes. Hellhounds.

There aren't a few of them, but dozens, and that's only from what I can see. Fear spikes through me, and their snarls and growls rip through the silence.

Fuck. It's an ambush.

ELIAS

TERROR WEAVES through the invisible bond that connects all of us, and simultaneously my hound senses approaching danger.

Dorian. Shit. He's in trouble.

I rush out of the shower butt-ass naked and head into the hall, only to find Cain there, his face reflecting the worry I feel. He'd sensed it too.

A clatter of footsteps, and Aria hurries down the stairs. "Something's wrong. Dorian—"

"We know." Cain's already flying down the remaining steps to the first floor.

I take the easier route and leap over the railing. "We're under attack."

"Aria, you stay here. Go to the basement with Maverick. He'll protect you," he orders.

As much as I don't like the idea of Maverick anywhere near Aria, she should be safer with him than alone if our enemy gets past us. It's a risk, but one we need to take.

"What? No!"

"Stay. Here." He grinds out each word before dashing out the front doors. It's not up for negotiation, and I can't stand up for her this time. Cain's right. If Hell's come back to play, it's too dangerous for her.

I glance at her one last time and growl, "Go downstairs," then sprint for the back door, releasing my beast mid-stride.

The moment I burst into the frigid night, I spy Dorian running up the hill toward me and the army of giant wolves thundering after him, too big to be from this plane.

Really? I leave for ten minutes and this is what happens.

They must've been hiding and waiting for me to leave so they could make their move. Dammit. I should've known better than to let Dorian's pestering get to me. And besides, I didn't smell *that* bad.

A shadow swoops down from the skies, and suddenly fire erupts, blazing through the darkness and knocking several of the hellhounds out of the line. Cain's wings beat against the wind as he drops low, pick up one of the massive animals, and shoots back into the air with it. The hellhounds snaps its powerful jaws at him, but Cain spins and uses his momentum to launch the thing across the grounds. Squealing, it disappears somewhere far off past the trees.

I thunder down the hill, my beast wanting blood and nothing less. Dorian halts suddenly, drops to his knee, and turns his arched back to me. I'm confused for a second, but then I realize he's created a ramp for me to jump off.

Smart, I'll give him that.

I rush for him. Once my paws hit his back, he thrusts himself to his feet to give me even more lift. I sail through the air, the wind cutting through my fur, and when I land, my claws sink into the flesh of two hounds. We roll together, and during the tussle one of them manages to latch its teeth into my hindquarters. Pain slices into me and I lash out, fangs gnashing at anything I can get ahold of. I get the soft underbelly of one and tear. Warm blood fills my mouth. The other hound lets me go and I buck my wounded leg back, nailing it in the eye.

When I look up again, Cain is flying low and circling the pack, throwing balls of fire into the chaos. Dorian's joined in too, his silver hair and glowing rune tattoos like a beacon in the darkness. He jumps and dodges any animal who gets too close, using his long nails to rip through muscle and flesh.

But there's too many of them. As many as we take down, there's still a herd of hellhounds sprinting for the manor. We can't get them all.

"Don't let them reach the house!" Cain shouts. He sends a blaze of hellfire, creating a temporary wall that makes the hounds stop. But with so much snow around us, the flames are quickly extinguished, the creatures on the move again.

Shit. He's right. We can't let them get to the mansion!

Heart hammering against my ribs, I speed back up the hill, clamp my jaws on one of their legs, and drag them back down to me. Tearing into its jugular, it dies, and I lurch for the next one.

There's still too many of them. And they're almost at the back door. Some even break off and around to the front in a divide-and-conquer maneuver.

We're in deep shit here.

I take down another hound, but a dozen more are still racing ahead of me. Only feet away from barging their way in.

Glancing over my shoulder, I find Dorian's too occupied taking down the lot by the tree line, and Cain's following the group heading for the driveway and trying to stop them from busting through on the front doors.

We've failed.

MAVERICK

THERE'S a thunder of footsteps upstairs. More dust and who knows what else rains down on me as I lounge on the bed and I leap up, sputtering and coughing.

Fuck this room. Fuck the basement. I was getting tired of spending my time down here while Cain and his Brady Bunch lived nice and comfy in their rooms above.

Fucking ridiculous.

Of course, I could leave this room whenever I felt like it. The little smudge in the demon trap circle is still there, since the reinforcement job Dorian did was half-assed. He missed a spot. And it seems Aria has kept my visit to her a secret, so, really, the only thing keeping me in the room is me.

And my need to get on Cain's good side and defeat our father once and for all.

Although, I will admit, it is getting rather boring.

Where's the excitement? Where's the danger? The action? My brother's been swimming in it lately, and I want a piece of that pie.

"Maverick!" Aria's fear-filled shriek comes from somewhere upstairs. "Maverick!"

My stomach instantly drops and before I know it, I'm high-tailing it up the steps to meet her in the foyer. Alone.

I glance around. Something's not right here. I can sense trouble nearby, see the fear in her eyes...but why is she alone?

"We're under attack," she says in a rush. "I'm not sure by what, but from all the commotion outside, I'd say it's not going well."

A symphony of growls, animalistic snarls, and all too familiar sounds of fighting erupt outside, getting louder by the second. Closer.

Uh oh. Looks like the boys are having a hard time winning this one.

"Hellhounds," Aria says. "Has to be."

"Where the fuck is Elias? Can't he control his kind?"

"Something must be wrong. They're all out there, and I can feel their panic through the bond."

"The hounds must be closing in." I glance around the room, looking for some kind of weapon we might be able to use if it comes down to it. There's a shield with two crossed swords hanging on the wall near the staircase—a priceless antique, no doubt—and I rip them down.

I had asked for excitement, hadn't I?

"What are you doing?" Aria asks, eyes wide.

"Getting us something to defend ourselves," I tell her.

More terrible sounds come from outside, and shadows move outside the windows. I push one of the sword's handles into her hands. It's heavier than she expects, and she struggles to lift it. "Time for you to put those fighting skills I taught you to good use."

"Skills you taught me?" Her voice rises. "We only ever had one lesson. Barely a lesson at all."

"Time to put whatever you know to work."

With two hands gripping the sword, she manages to lift it to a fighting stance. Well, sort of. I take the other sword and hold it in a firm grip. I also have my daggers strapped to my belt, just in case they're needed, too. I'm more accurate with them anyway.

More shadows pass in front of the windows, closer to the front door. Then a blaze of fire and light.

Has to be Cain. My brother is the only one of us seven who had the ability to control hellfire.

Better go out the back then.

"Let's go." I spin and, together, we run down the hall. I kick the door open, and we leap into the snow and right into the middle of the insanity.

Hellhounds as big as cars are scattered throughout the grounds, with Dorian doing his best to battle them off at the tree line. Fresh claw marks tear across his chest, bleeding profusely, but they don't seem to slow him down. He's fast enough to bounce around most attacks and snap the animals' necks before they even know where to lunge.

The main carnage is coming from just yards in front of us, where a massive black hellhound is bulldozing into the ones charging at us, throwing them left and right. Blood spurts as its powerful jaws tear into necks and stomachs—really anywhere it can reach—and paints all the wintery whiteness with crimson.

"Elias," Aria gasps beside me, confirming my guess that the one ramming into the crowd like a bull is the big oaf.

But despite his outdated fighting style and Dorian's quickness, there are too many hounds for them to take on and a few are slipping through. If Cain's dealing with his own problems at the front of the house, that means we're the last defense back here.

"They want the relics. We can't let them get into the house," Aria says, widening her stance and lifting her sword. Even with all the danger surrounding us, I can't help but marvel at how incredibly sexy she looks with the weapon in her hand and the look of determination on her face. She may be scared, but she's not going to back down either. Not when it comes to defending what's hers.

"Relics? I'm more worried about them getting to you." The words slip out before I've realized what I've said, and she side-eyes me. I quickly come up with a clever explanation. "Cain will kill me if you get hurt again."

One of the hounds break out of the scuffle with Elias and head for us. Quickly stepping in front of Aria, I swipe my sword and cut the beast down. Easy enough.

Two more race towards us, and I grab my daggers with one hand and unleash them. They spin through the air and nail the fuckers right in the middle of their foreheads. They drop instantly. Dead.

With a slight flick of my wrists, the daggers fly backwards and find my hand again.

Aria stares at me in disbelief. "That's a nifty trick," she says.

"What?" I chuckle, loving the impressed and stunned look on her face. I show her the crystals along the handle, which are laced with some heavy-duty magic. A special gift I got from a warlock whose soul I had in contract. "I wasn't going to tell you all my secrets."

From over her shoulder, I see a hound rounding the corner from the front of the house, coming at Aria full force. Its eyes glow yellow when it spots her, and my lungs squeeze in panic. I try to move in front of her, but sharp teeth sink into my calf at the same time and pull me to the ground. Twisting, I see another pair of amber eyes latched onto me as one of the beasts bites into my leg.

Pain hits me like a semi-truck, and my vision goes black for a second.

Fuck, that hurts!

Lifting my hand, I realize I dropped my sword during my fall, and it's become lost somewhere in the snow. That's when the hound decides to shake its head, tearing muscle away from bone. I roar with anger.

Screw the sword. I'm better with my daggers anyway.

Grabbing them both in my one palm, I plunge them into the creature's eyes. It squeals, bucking, and rears back but lets me go. My victory is short lived, though, because another hellhound wants to take its place and comes at me.

My leg is a bloody mess of skin and tissue, and I know standing, let alone running, is going to hurt like the dickens, if possible at all. But I'm a sitting duck otherwise. I can't just lay here.

As I call my daggers back, the hell-thing pounces. Right before it lands, there's a glint of silver that comes down with it.

As its full weight lands on top of me, I feel the warmth of its blood seeping into my clothes. But I hadn't been the one to stab it and end its wretched life.

Then I see Aria standing over me. Her sword's blade is coated in red, she's breathing hard and her shoulders are shaking.

Holy shit. She killed it. She saved me.

She blinks, and that's when I notice the eerie white film over her eyes. It's starting to fade back to their naturally brown color, but it was definitely there. I'd seen it with my own two eyes.

The shadow creature wants to come out and play.

I know I should be worried, and part of me is, but another part —the darker, twisted part—is incredibly turned on.

When I shove the dead hound off me, Aria offers her hand. I don't need it, but I take it anyway and let her help me up.

"You okay?" she asks.

She *sounds* like Aria. No weird mingling of her and Sayah's voice yet.

"Yeah, are *you*?" I press back.

She nods slowly, slightly unsure. But that hunger for death lingers on her face. Especially when she turns back to the chaos raging before us. Sayah wants more blood, more destruction, and letting her have it could make Aria go fully dark again, like the other night after the ritual. We could lose her.

"What are you doing? Get Aria inside!" Cain flies overhead, his huge, bat-like wings blocking out the light of the moon. More hellhounds thunder up the hillside, and Cain throws another stream of fire at them to try and hold them off.

"Inside!" he bellows. "Now!"

I whip around to Aria. "Come on. We'll barricade the door." I grab her by the arm, and her head jerks toward me, her movements too stiff.

"They need our help," she snaps. There's an odd rumble lacing her voice now. A twist of the dark entity within her coming to the surface.

Uh oh. We may be too late.

I tug her back, but her feet don't move. They're planted in place.

"They're big boys," I tell her. "They can handle it themselves."

Her hands whip out, making me jump back, and the earth begins to quake under our feet. A warning zips up my spine.

I may be no Cain, and sensing darkness isn't really my thing, but evilness is radiating off Aria in dense waves. So much so that I can feel it even from where I'm standing.

"Aria!" Cain shouts, voice full of fear. "Don't let Sayah control you. Fight her. You have to fight her."

She ignores him and flicks her wrists. A shadow shoots from the ground straight into the air, creating a dark wall in front of us that rises like an opaque skyscraper. I can't do anything but gape at it, shocked and thoroughly impressed.

"Ar-Aria," I try instead. "Cain's right. You can't let this thing rule your life. You can control it."

Arms still out, her fully white gaze flicks my way. The venom in her stare makes me shift back. The hellhounds smash into the makeshift wall at full speed to try and break through. The audible crack of their necks breaking comes next, and Aria's mouth ticks up in a wicked smile.

She's loving this.

I love death and carnage as much as the next demon, but this is a little freaky. Even I can admit it.

Cautiously, I approach her. "Aria…I know you're in there."

"She knows her place, demon! And you'd be wise to as well," Sayah barks back. It's Aria's lips moving but their mingled voices coming out.

Another flick of her wrist, and another tall shadow wall appears at the bottom of the hill. The ground trembles again, and suddenly both walls begin to move toward each other, pushing any hellhounds or demons that were in between to the center. And I say demons because Elias and Dorian are in that mess, and now they're being shoved along with the rest. Cain shoots upward to escape being crushed by the rapidly moving walls, but Elias and Dorian are having a hard time running for the ends with so many hellhounds in the way. They're being tossed about and trampled as the walls slide closer and closer to each other.

They're going to be crushed.

"Aria!" Cain shouts down to us, but of course she's not listening. Her mouth is split into a full-on grin now.

What do I do? Do I take her out? That may save Dorian and Elias, but it'll hurt her. I grip my daggers. Is there any other option at this point?

"Aria, listen to me. You can control Sayah. You can. You've been doing it your entire life, and you can do it now." My words tumble out in a rush, but Dorian and Elias only have seconds before being flattened into demon pancakes. "She's working off your fear. Off your insecurities." I should know. My power allows me to do the same.

Wait, shit. My power.

Without another thought, I slap my hand against Aria's shoulder, dive into her and Sayah's tangled and chaotic emotions, and shift through until I find Aria's confidence. It's small, fragile, and overwhelmed with so many other negative feelings surrounding Sayah, but I yank it out and fill her with enough ego to make Elias jealous.

Aria blinks and her outstretched hands begin to waver.

Sayah's losing her grip.

My hand stays firmly on her. "If you don't push Sayah's ass out now, you're going to kill Dorian and Elias. Shove that shadowy bitch back in her hole."

The shadow walls flicker, and I watch the transformation on

her face. Her eyes lose the milky whiteness, and her features soften. Her shoulders slump, and the walls start to slow down.

"That's it, Aria. Sayah can't survive without you. You can call the shots. You have the strength to do it."

Again, the walls flicker in and out. Dorian and Elias rush for the exits on opposite sides, leaping over hellhounds and fighting their way out. Finally, they make it out just as the two sides speed up again and collide in a huge plume of smoke. Every hellhound trapped inside? Gone. Poof. Smashed into oblivion.

Elias shifts back into his human form, and he and Dorian look at each other, breathing hard and bleeding from their battle wounds. That was fucking close.

Aria's knees buckle and she goes down, but I quickly grab her and pull her against me. Her head tilts up, her gaze roaming my face.

"Thank you," she whispers.

I snort a laugh to cover the worry, fear, and regret warring inside me. As much as I don't want to admit it, I hate seeing her this way. So weak. "Thank you? For what? You did all the work."

Cain lands in front of us with a loud thud. His wings fold in, and as he looks Aria over, he frowns. "Are you okay?"

She tries to nod, but she's too weak to even do that. Cain moves and takes her from me, cradling her in his arms. When he looks up at me, anger and uncertainty pass over his face. But, to my surprise, there's relief there, too.

"Thank you," he says, with a firm dip of his chin.

My brother...thanking me. I never thought I'd see the day.

Then, without another word, he turns and walks Aria inside the house. Elias and Dorian stride past me, Elias with a slight limp, and follow Cain inside. They keep the door open for me to come in, too.

Before I do, I gaze out onto the mansion's acres of land and try to absorb everything that just happened. Hellhounds, Sayah, the incredible and terrifying powers Aria possesses... Adrenaline still pumps through my veins, and I'm having a hard time settling down. Now we know for sure there's a way for her to control them. Not sure how exactly, but at least we know there's a way.

And that makes all the difference.

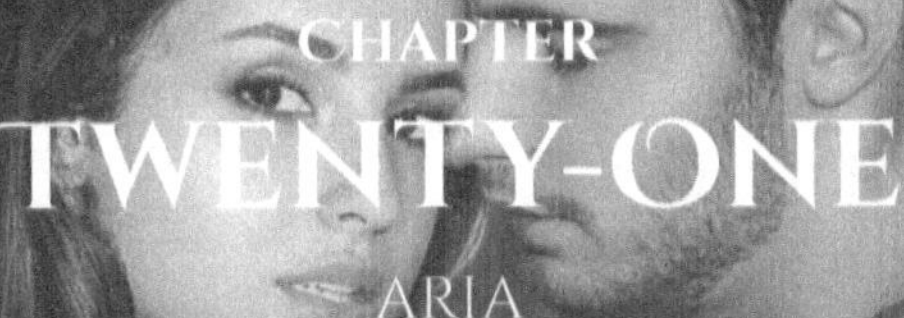

Morning light drenches my bedroom, and outside the woods are peaceful. Not a creature stirs. Who would have thought that last night this was the scene of a bloody battle with hellhounds...with Sayah?

Not me. But I am starting to learn that I shouldn't be surprised anymore by the things that happen in my life.

A leviathan. One of the first things God ever made. Before angels? Before demons?

I've seen Sayah's immense power. I can understand why God wanted to snuff all of them out. They must've been too powerful. But somehow, Sayah got away and hid for centuries. Hell, millenia. Until she latched herself to me.

There's so much more I want to know about her, now that I have a name for what she is. But that'll be a job for another day. There's still so much I'm unpacking.

I shake my head and drag myself into the bathroom, stripping down on my way.

The hot shower sprays over my head, steaming water rushing down my shoulders and body. I close my eyes and tilt my head up at the hot stream, washing away all the aches, the worries...I want them all gone.

Is it too much to have a day where I'm not being hunted down? *Today, I will be lucky!*

I laugh to myself, otherwise I'll end up crying at how fast things got out of control yesterday and how quickly Sayah came over me. On the bright side, I seemed to gain some control over her, so I'm going to take the small wins where I can.

I grab the soap and lather my body until I resemble the marshmallow man from *Ghostbusters*, then let the hot water roll down my body, creating a pool of suds around my feet. The stress from the day threatens to wrap me up like an anaconda squeezing the life out of me. And maybe that's been my problem. I'm overthinking things.

Look at Elias and Dorian. They don't seem to care about most problems and deal with them as they come. I need to be more like them.

The swishing sound of the shower door sliding open has me snapping open my eyes.

Speak of the devil…Dorian is sticking his head inside, smirking, his eyes narrowing in on my breasts. "Hey beautiful."

I instantly smile back. Something about him just melts away the tension, and butterflies burst through my stomach, beating their little wings.

"You feel like having sex?" he asks bluntly.

I can't help but burst out laughing at how candid he asks the question. It's only when he pushes open the steamed-up shower door that I see he means every word. He's stark naked, his heavy cock already erect.

I narrow my gaze at him. "How long have you been watching me?"

"Wouldn't you like to know. Now, is that a yes?"

I step back in the large shower that easily accommodates two people. "How can I possibly say no to your crazy-butt-naked-ass? As you're practically in here already."

He chuckles and steps inside, only to make way for Cain stepping in behind him, also naked.

My eyes might have bulged out of their sockets, like one of those ridiculous cartoons.

"Oh, did I forget to mention I meant both Cain and I?" Dorian remarks, then loops an arm around my waist and tugs me up against him, his cock cradled between my ass cheeks, which he purposefully rubs against me. He holds me tight as my sin demon climbs in to join us.

"It might be a tight squeeze," I say, watching Cain step in sideways before sliding the door shut and moving under the spray of water, his cock just as hard and erect. Water splashes down his body, his muscles bulging, and I'm utterly mesmerized how beautiful and sexy this man is.

"That's what we're hoping," Dorian whispers in my ear.

I do that thing where I'm half rolling my eyes, and half laughing at his terrible pun.

Cain is facing me, dripping wet, the wounds he gained from yesterday's fight sealed, but they still blush red and look painful. He cups my face and says, "Do you feel like being shared?"

I'm unable to really find my words. I've been with Elias and Dorian at the same time, but Cain...he's always been more of a lone wolf.

"We figured you could use some pampering," Dorian tells me, while I'm still lost in Cain's eyes, in the seduction flaring over his face.

"Oh, I see," I finally say, and clear my throat. "So does this session come with a foot massage afterward?"

Cain moves even closer to me, and now I'm sandwiched between both men, their rock-hard erections against me, and I'm gasping for air suddenly.

His gaze roams over me before he leans in and kisses me with the kind of passion that weakens my knees. Dorian has his mouth on my neck, his hands on my ass.

"I'm going to fuck you until you scream, gorgeous," Dorian whispers in my ear, while Cain licks my lips.

"She won't have a chance to scream," Cain teases, looking me in the eyes, promising me all the filthy things I can't get enough of.

Right now, I am having trouble focusing on anything but my men and how quickly things have escalated. They weren't kidding when they said they want to have sex, like, *now*.

"We've come to the conclusion that we haven't been showing you enough attention," Cain tells me.

"You two have been conspiring about having sex with me?" I gasp the words, as it's especially hard to concentrate with Dorian's tongue running the length of my neck and his fingers sliding across the crack of my ass. My chest flames with how hot I'm feeling, how hard my heart is beating. I'm soaking wet and aching, and I'm not talking about the spray of water splashing over us.

Cain smirks with a wickedly evil grin. There isn't much room to move in the shower, but we're managing perfectly well.

"We are going to make you ours over and over," Dorian breathes in my ear while Cain runs his hands down my breasts, follows the curve of my waist and down my legs. When his fingers sweep back up on the inside of my thighs, I moan.

I'm tingling all over with how feather-soft his hands feel.

He finds my pussy with his fingers and teases my swollen folds. His lips press to a hardened nipple and he sweeps it into his mouth, devouring me.

I moan, arching my back, clawing at Cain's strong, round shoulders to hold myself upright.

"I adore your body," Dorian says gruffly against the soft skin behind my ear, and there's something dark and erotic behind his words. The heat inside me sparks alight into a bonfire, and my skin pricks with goosebumps. Every inch of me grows extra sensitive to every touch, every stroke of my skin, every kiss.

When I look over my shoulder at him, his eyes are partly glazed over, like he's so lost to arousal, there is no coming back. And I know he's using his incubus power on us all, heightening the already inflamed arousal between us.

The sensations are suddenly so much more erotic, their moans sexy, the way they tease me primal and raw.

Dorian suddenly pushes his finger into my ass unceremoniously and without warming.

I moan louder at the unexpected flare of sharp pain that quickly morphs into the most exhilarating sensation.

Cain moves onto my other breast, his two fingers now pushing into my pussy.

The sounds pouring from my mouth, the cries of pleasure, are the most delicious sounds I'm certain I've ever made. I'm floating, unsure how much of this is me and how much is Dorian's influence, but my core is tightening and I need more.

"You keep making all those sounds and you'll have Elias joining us," Dorian warns, except I'd welcome him. Well, he may not fit into the shower with us, but there is no way I'd exclude my huge sexy hellhound.

My hands are threading through Cain's hair as his tongue flicks over my nipple. These gorgeous, dangerous men are driving me mad with lust.

Cain releases me with a popping sound and straightens... though he keeps his fingers deep inside me, fingering me, while Dorian does the same from the rear.

I'm barely standing upright with how much my body hums.

The moment is just absolutely perfect.

I am being turned on by two gorgeous hunks, and my body burns up, while the water pours down our bodies. Why haven't we had sex in the shower before? This is sexy as hell.

Cain pulls back his fingers and puts them into his mouth, savoring me. "You are so beautiful and perfect."

His words mesmerize me and I lean in against his chest. My hands slide down his rock-hard chest to where my fingers brush over his heavy cock.

Dorian pulls out from my ass and has his hands on my hips. "I want you bent over," he demands.

I glance up at Cain, completely smitten by him. How did I get so lucky?

"I would do as he asks," Cain teases me, but the lust behind his eyes carries him to a place of explosive pleasures. I palm his cock, stroking him up and down quickly now, which only has him groaning. And I love the way he looks like this.

Completely under my influence.

Dorian has his mouth on my ear, a hand on my breast, squeezing. "I need you, beautiful."

I twist my head around and our mouths meet, our kiss made of hungry arousal, of unbridled need. His teeth scrape my lower lip and a growl rolls from his throat.

"Fuck! You're made for me...for us!" He pulls back, stepping to press his back to the wall, then runs a hand down my spine, forcing me to bend forward.

Cain steps back almost instantly, falling into rhythm with Dorian's instructions. And I take that as my cue to bring Cain the kind of pleasure he serves to me. Leaning down, I slip the tip of his cock into my mouth.

He growls, his hands fisting my hair in a dominating manner

that has me buzzing with excitement. I love being dominated and I won't deny it.

Dorian rubs the tip of his cock across the soaking wet folds. I part my legs to give him more room, to accommodate us in this tight space.

He pushes into me and a moan escapes my throat as he grips my hips, his fingers digging into me.

I slid my lips lower over Cain's erection, loving his musky, salty taste.

Dorian pushes deeper into me, building his momentum, rougher, quicker. His greedy hands adjust his grip and he's rocking in and out of me, our fiery flesh slapping.

The three of us quickly fall into a pattern of fucking and sucking, our groans escalating.

I hungrily run my tongue along the base of Cain's dick and cup his tight balls with my hand, my other resting against his thigh to stop myself from falling over.

In that moment of raw ecstasy, I forget everything. I shiver as these men bring me to the ultimate state of euphoria, and I want to give back just as much. My mouth works over Cain's erection, needing him to lose himself just like the buzz claiming my body.

Dorian's growling, plunging into me, while his fingers tease over my clit. I'm shuddering under the explosive climax pushing me over the edge, I never saw it coming. It erupts through me so fast, that my pussy clenches tight around Dorian. I'm groaning, shaking.

"Fuck!" Cain snarls in response, as if my orgasm has set off a chain effect. His cock stiffens in my mouth and he's pumping his seed into me. I swallow everything he gives me.

Dorian is fucking me wildly and groaning. Suddenly, he's twitching and pulsing his own climax into me. The sounds he makes are so damn sexy. Thick, sticky cum fills me from both ends, while I'm floating on air, unable to get enough.

I have no idea how I'm even still standing, seeing I can no longer feel my body. I'm breathless and release Cain, coming up for air. Licking my lips, I swallow what's in my mouth. Dorian collects me into his arms, my back pressed to his chest, while he's still buried deep inside me.

He's growling in my ear, his dick pulsing still, his hot seed seeping down the inside of my thighs at how hard he's come.

Cain watches me, smiling. "I love watching you get fucked."

And I can't help it, but hearing him say that turns me on so much. My pussy squeezes, clamping down on Dorian. He howls behind me, while I reach over to Cain's growing erection.

"It's your turn to take me," I purr. "I want more. Please."

His lips pull into a wicked grin and he closes in against me. "Aria, my love, I'll give you the world if you ask for it."

<hr>

Cassiel bumps into my leg as we both emerge from my bedroom at the same time. I ruffle the fur on his head and he groans at me.

"Hey, *you* shoved out at the same time as me." He rushes up ahead of me, and I shake my head at how pushy he's become, like he thinks he owns the house.

A thunderous wind howls and the mansion creaks as it's battered by the snowstorm raging outside. I went to sleep early last night, and I am certain I could sleep for twenty-four more hours.

After the recent events I'm embracing a calm day, considering there is still the last relic for us to hunt down. But today I want no end-of-world problems. My e-reader is in hand, and I have every intention of crashing in front of the fire downstairs to curl up with a good story.

Sadie is coming up the stairs, her head up and eyes wide at seeing me approach. She smiles at me warmly, and I find myself doing the same. She's wearing her long black frock with the white apron looking every part the maid.

"Miss, Cain requests your presence down in the dining room for lunch."

"Luckily, I was headed in that direction," I say, jokingly. The girl smiles shyly and nods, then heads down the stairs. Cassiel races down, thinking she is racing him. I giggle to myself as he practically bowls her over to reach the bottom of the steps first.

Sadie straightens and pats down her dress, seeming slightly perturbed.

"Sorry, Sadie. He's a bit stir-crazy being stuck in the house."

"It's fine," she says, tight-lipped, then sweeps her hand toward the dining room for me to proceed. The double doors are shut, which is unusual, but maybe they are keeping the room warm. The demons aren't particularly fond of the freezing cold.

Sadie has already left so I step forward, then pull open the doors.

I'm instantly bombarded by so many visuals cues and colors that I'm unsure where to look first.

A giant Christmas tree towers in one corner, the tip bent at an angle from being too tall to fit into the room, and every branch is blinking with ornaments and lights. A mountain of food and a plump turkey adorn the long table. Then there are the greeting cards hanging from ropes strung across the room. Oh, and the oversized red ribbons plastered to the walls. Bowls spilling over with Hershey's Kisses chocolates all through the room, and for some reason there are red Coca-Cola cans and bottles everywhere. Like, I'm even talking about an actual crate in the far corner with the bubbly stuff. What is that about?

I turn on the spot, loving the room, and I'm smiling like a crazy person that my demons remembered Christmas. I love the festive colors, the roast turkey has me salivating, and everything they did is just adorable. Though I want to know what is with all the soft drinks.

So much has happened that it never occurred to me that it's Christmas Day. In all honesty, most years I ignored the day, hating that I had no real family to celebrate it with. Murray would go out with his buddies to play poker.

But this is...everything. My throat chokes up that they made this for me.

It feels like I've just walked into a room where Santa might have exploded and all his cheery goodness has splattered over the room.

When a soft version of the song "Carol of the Bells" starts playing from a speaker in the room, I look around for the guys, but the room's empty. I step inside, blown away at the creation, when someone clears their throat from behind me.

I twist around instantly, and my mouth might have just fallen open.

Cain strides into the room dressed up in a Santa suit. I am not sure if I should be laughing or strip down naked for him. He's wearing baggy red pants very low on his hips, revealing those V-dips at his hips that make girls go silly, and his red Santa coat sits open, revealing a bare chest beneath. Ripped muscles are all I can stare at.

A half-strangled moan falls from my lips at the sight of this delicious hunk. Sweet hell! Does he want me to eat the food or him?

From either side of the doorway, Dorian and Elias emerge, each of them dressed in a polar bear onesie, complete with hood and ears.

My heart might have just melted into a puddle by my feet. And seeing these powerful men dressed like that for me destroys me.

I half laugh, half start crying like a baby. Geez, I feel stupid for overreacting and probably looking like a mad person as I wipe away the tears.

All three guys surround me quickly, Cain taking me into his arms. "What's wrong, Aria?"

"Told you we should have brought in real polar bears," Dorian states.

"And have it maul your ass," Elias answers. "My vote was for those beastly Clydesdales from the Budweiser ads. Then we could have gone on a ride."

"In the snowstorm?" Dorian barks back.

I'm watching them, laughing, while more tears run down my face.

Cain is looking at me with a confused expression. "I'm not sure what we did wrong to upset you so much," he says.

I'm shaking my head as I say, "You did everything right. These are happy tears." I have my hands plastered against his solid chest, his skin is on fire, and there are so many emotions vying for attention inside me. From the ache in my chest that they did this for me, to wanting to study every inch of my men in their costumes, and then the notion of finding out if Santa Claus goes commando play heavily on my mind.

"Y-You did all this for me." I hiccup my next inhale as my throat thickens some more.

Cain wipes away the tears from my cheeks with his thumbs as he cups my face. "I would bring Krampus himself to kneel before you, if that would bring a smile to your face."

Tears slide out from the corners of my eyes, not at the notion of him bringing anti-Santa to me, but that I know without doubt that he would if I asked him to.

"Why are you crying?" Elias asks genuinely.

"You all remembered Christmas while I completely forgot about it." Who exactly is the real demon in this room, anyway? I break from Cain's embrace and turn on the spot to face the room. "This is perfect. I mean I don't fully understand the giant bows or the crate of cola, but I love it." Turning to face my three demons, I smile softly. "And what I love more is that you made this happen, and you even dressed up."

"We are here for you," Cain says.

Dorian crosses the room to the tree, bends over to collect something, then strolls back with a small wrapped gift in his hands. "You've got something to wear too." He's grinning especially wickedly. All three of them are, as a matter of fact.

"Wow, you got me a gift. Thank you. I didn't know or I would have got something for you all too."

"Open it," Dorian insists, more concerned with my reaction to the gift.

Curiosity has me ripping off the green wrapping paper and I pull back the lid to the black box. I peer down at the red silk and lace folded within pink tissue paper. I pick up the piece of clothing as Dorian collects the box from my hand. I'm holding onto a sexy, one-piece lacy bodice that really doesn't conceal much at all. It is mostly made with thin white lace that sparkles like it's been woven from diamonds, and a few well-positioned red streaks of ribbon to cover vital parts. Thin shoulder straps, a low V-neck, and the bikini line looks like it might reach my armpits. This is extravagant and so revealing that it almost makes me blush.

I glance up at the guys, who stare at me like they're wolves. "This is beautiful. Extremely revealing, but just stunning."

"Will you put it on?" Elias asks mischievously, their gazes already devouring me.

They're nodding and I'm laughing almost hysterically now because I shouldn't be surprised it's what they want. "You know what, after lunch, you got yourself a deal."

If there's one thing that never gets old, it's the delicious look on my men's faces that show me how turned on they are by just thinking of me. That stuff does things to a girl, like how my nipples harden instantly, and when I squeeze my legs together, heat flares between my thighs.

Lust sweeps over their gazes, and I fold up the gift and place it back into the box in Dorian's hands. He sets it aside like it's a precious crown. On the inside, I'm giddy with anticipation at seeing how they'll react to me dressed in it, along with exactly what's going to come right afterward.

That's when Cassiel suddenly bursts into the room, half knocking into the back of Elias's legs. He wobbles, arms thrown outward to balance himself, while I laugh.

Cassiel is already at the food, front paws up on the table and he's got his nose in the bowl of gravy, splashing it everywhere.

"Cass," I call out and we all rush over to stop him in some chaotic crazy moment of pulling a full-grown lynx from delicious gravy.

He growls at the guys grabbing him, and they back up, then he shoves his nose back in there.

I can't stop laughing in all honesty. "Just let him have the gravy." I'm gripping my middle, unable to stop laughing at how crazy Cassiel looks, but it's his first Christmas too.

The rest of us take a seat at the table. Cain at the head, Dorian by my side, and Elias across from me. Cassiel is at the other end across from Cain, slurping away.

Cain does the honor and carves the turkey, and I'm still tingling all over to think that the first time I've ever felt so completely content and at home is when I am sharing Christmas with three demons and a lynx. Who would have thought? And that's when my thoughts travel to Maverick.

"Should we invite Maverick to enjoy Christmas lunch, too?"

"No," all three say in unison. Okay, well that's a unanimous decision.

"Saw him settled down in the basement," Dorian confirms. "He looks content."

I want to push back at his comment, but I also don't want lunch to end up in another fight between the guys.

With my plate filled with turkey, roast potatoes, and greens, I dig in. Elias has the turkey leg in his hand and he's eating it like a beastly king sitting on a throne.

Dorian and Cain are enjoying their wine, watching me.

"I've never had a real family, and Murray avoided Christmas, so you guys doing this for me means everything. Thank you. But I gotta know...what's with the ribbons and years supply of Coke?" That's when I spy a pile of toy boxes for Hess trucks near the tree. "And are we donating toys to kids later on?"

Dorian strains to look around and follow my line of sight to the trucks.

"These are all the things humans enjoy at Christmas," Cain tells me. "For years, we've seen the human television ads push the same things every year, and we wanted it perfect for you. The huge ribbons are always on cars at Christmas, which I assume is a good luck thing. Though it does surprise me that so many people buy their significant other a car for Christmas."

"And there are constant ads with Santa and his polar bears drinking Coke. They are what humans seem to enjoy," Dorian says.

"Hmm well—"

"Told you the bear costumes were too much," Elias says, smacking his lips with a mouthful of turkey. "I could have just shifted forms."

"Really?" Dorian answers. "Is that so you in your hellhound form and the lynx can both fight over the gravy?" He bursts out chuckling.

"I didn't mean full transformation, but to show a bit of our real selves."

"I don't mind either option," I reply instantly, which is completely true. I take a bite of a roast potato, then sit back, chewing, and stare at them. Hell, I love everything about these men.

The way they squabble always makes me laugh.

They might have come from the underworld, but they aren't above showing the kind of affection I never expected from demons. And they adore me more than anything. They barely let me out of their sight, they protect me with their lives, and I feel like I can talk to them about anything. The whole being sexy as sin goes without saying. These three devour my body and own every inch of me.

Sometimes they are so loving and kind to me that it makes me want to cry.

I keep eating as the conversation turns to a polar bear shifter they knew in Hell, and I'm mesmerized. Cain reaches over and places a hand on mine.

"Happy Christmas," he says, and my heart is close to breaking at how adorable he is. I can't even bring myself to correct him that it's *Merry* Christmas. I just smile and soak up everything he tells me, wanting this moment to last for eternity.

That's when I realize that in truth, I can no longer live without my men. I need them.

TWENTY-TWO

ARIA

Goosebumps cover my bare skin, but nothing compares to the fire pulsing between my thighs. I'm not exactly naked, but looking down at myself in the skimpy, sexy bodice from the demons, I might as well be. The strip of red ribbon barely covers my nipples, then between my thighs it's just a strip of fabric that leaves nothing to the imagination. And from behind, I am practically butt-naked.

My face is on fire, yet my mind fills with filthy images of what the guys will do to me, the porn-star kind of naughtiness that has me burning up.

Butterflies tingle in my gut in anticipation, and just thinking about it already has my pussy soaking wet.

Down girl!

A soft knock at the door to the bathroom has me flinching. Geez, why is it so hot in here?

"Won't be long," I reply.

"Okay, babe," Dorian replies, and I can hear his eagerness from just those two words. Seconds later, he's back. "Just in case you need any help getting dressed, I'm here for you."

"Ha, I don't think so. You can wait and be surprised like everyone else."

I turn back to the mirror and am almost shocked at the girl

416

staring back at me. Okay, girl is not an accurate word. More like sex-kitten bomb. Who would have thought that a lacy ensemble could completely change the way I look and even how I feel about myself?

I grab the headband that came with the outfit. I slip it on and stare at the cute little reindeer antlers. How this outfit is in any way meant to resemble a reindeer is beyond me, but I'm willing to play along. It's Christmas after all.

I take a deep breath and reach for the door handle. "You got this. You're going to go out there confident and get fucked by Santa and his two polar bears." I roll my eyes at how bad that sounds. Yet, the thrill of their promise flares over me.

Outside in the hallway, there's no sign of Dorian. Whispers from the guys float from the parlor, so with a quick look left and right to make sure Sadie and Ramos aren't around to see me, I dart forward. The floor is freezing against my feet.

My heart is thumping so loudly that I fear I might pass out. Then I pause in the doorway, my face flushed, but I tell myself nothing I do right now would turn off the guys. Not dressed like the reindeer queen of all sin.

I drape an arm against the doorframe, half leaning against it, staring at the guys with their backs to me.

"Is this a bad time?" I purr, putting on my best sexy voice.

They turn around at the same time and Elias trips over his own feet as he tries to move around the couch.

I grin devilishly, bathing in the lustful looks, at the way their eyes devour me...all of me.

Cain has his Santa jacket off, standing only in his red pants, with a pressing erection tenting them. Dorian and Elias are almost gobsmacked, which isn't like them at all.

I laugh at their reactions.

"Fuck me!" Dorian growls, coming toward me as he peels away the onesie to sit very low on his hips, revealing a sculpted body, lines of muscles. My sights are locked on the peek of dark hair skimming to the fabric over his groin, and I'm suddenly breathing heavily.

My nipples harden at the sight and his powerful arm loops around my waist, hauling me against him. His erection presses against my stomach and his lips lock to mine, his tongue plunging into my mouth. There is no ceremonial dance. Dorian is horny and he's going to take what he wants.

DORIAN

ARIA MOANS out loud against my mouth and I lose my mind seeing her dressed up this way. She's fucking beautiful.

When I first saw her in the doorway covered in strips of fabric, my cock hardened so fast it made me dizzy.

That insanely hot image is forever imprinted on my mind.

The curve of her breasts and her tight nipples poking the red ribbon covering them, her hour-glass figure, the length of her sexy legs. But I can't get the image of her sweet pussy out of my mind. I don't want to. That sliver of fabric just barely covers her slit, the soft outer lips of her shaven pussy exposed.

Fuck!

I press her against me, deep throating her with my tongue, my cock already leaking pre-cum from how much I need to fuck her, and hard.

I'm a damn incubus, but with Aria, I'm losing all control.

Her hand slides down the front of my onesie pants, her small hand wrapping around my swollen cock. I'm so fucking huge and thick, and to feel the softness of her touch, the eagerness of how she squeezes me, undoes me.

I growl as she pumps her hand up and down my shaft.

Our brows are touching and we're looking into each other's eyes. Everything about her makes my body react, and I slide the strap off her shoulder easily, the fabric rolling down and revealing a gorgeous breast, tipped with the pinkest of nipples. I reach over and cup it, then knead it.

"You are everything to me," I groan, barely able to catch my breath from her touch. "And go harder. That's it, gorgeous."

She's making that delicious moaning sound again, the one that lingers on my mind long after I'm finished with her.

Fuck!

Footsteps sound upstairs, from one of the maids no doubt, but it's enough to draw Aria from my embrace. Her hand releases my cock and I growl, needing her touch back. She glances over her shoulder, and I sidestep past her to slam the rolling pocket doors shut.

Aria's licking her lips and staring from me to Cain and Elias, who both look ravenous. Cain has his hand down his pants, stroking himself. He doesn't make a move toward her, just watches.

She strolls past me and goes toward Elias, swinging her hips, and from behind her the view is spectacular. That luscious ass moving with each step is perfection.

She is too much. I'm going to fucking lose it today and nothing will be enough until I sink my cock into her.

ELIAS

THE SIGHT of those perfect tits have my balls tightening. Slowly, my little rabbit prowls toward me. She knows exactly what she's doing...when the fuck did she become such a temptress?

When she looks at me there's only raw hunger behind her eyes, and my hellhound rises to the occasion. He wants to come out and play. I sniff the air, drawing in her sex. Fuck, I'm barely holding it together.

"This is how I want you...naked and wet for me."

She almost misses a step at my words, and I adore the faint blush of pink on her cheeks. Every inch of her turns me on. My breath catches in my throat and I take her into my arms, my hands falling to the back of her thighs. She's off her feet in moments and wrapped around my waist, just how she should be.

She fists the ridiculous polar bear outfit and pulls herself closer, finding my lips. Her kisses are the sweetest candy, but when she bites down on my lower lip, I snarl in response. My cock twitches at the pain, at the fucking agony that I'm not slamming into her yet.

Cain and Dorian are near, they're watching, but my focus is on my Aria.

She's mine.

Every inch of her I own.

I walk her over to the table as those delicious lips glide over to my ear. Her breath is warm and like a feather tracing over my skin.

The fire inside me roars to claim her and remind her she is ours...
and only ours.

"Tell me how much you want to suck on my pussy," she whispers in my ear.

My vision blurs at how fast my blood jolts down to my cock at
her words. All I can smell is her sweet nectar, so to hear her teasing
me breaks me. There's only so much a man can take.

I lower her carefully onto her back on the table, her legs still
spread and on either side of my hips.

Dorian and Cain are there, watching, stroking their cocks.
Their eyes are only on Aria, and that's my focus.

"You are spectacular," I say. "But it's time we unwrapped our
present."

"Do it," Dorian groans.

I want every inch of her.

I peel back the strap from her other shoulder, releasing the
other breast, and she gasps quietly, staring at each of us. My eyes
move to the softness of her stomach as I slide the fabric over the
curve of her hips. She raises them as I tug on the lace, and she
raises her legs into the air for me. In slow motion, I drag the lace to
her ankles and slip it past each of her gorgeous little feet, which I
kiss.

Cain is growling, his impatience as harrowing as mine, but we
have all day and night. An eternity to enjoy Aria...so for the first
time, I want to take it slow and savor every part of her.

"Elias..." she purrs, squeezing her breasts and pinching her
nipples. My cock hurts at how desperately I need release.

I pry open her legs wide and run my fingers lower on the inside
of her thighs.

She trembles under my touch.

My gaze lowers, and her pink little pussy is glistening with
excitement, her inner thighs so wet from how turned on she is.

Dorian and Cain are on either side of me, their heaving breaths
loud like beasts. Aria spreads open for us, moaning as her hand
slides down between the valley of her breasts, over her stomach
and to her fiery core.

She's stroking herself, rubbing her clit.

My body tenses and I drop to my knees, pushing her hand

away and pressing my face between her thighs. She's so wet, her scent intoxicating. A growl snarls possessively in my throat.

I take her into my mouth, rolling my tongue over the soft folds of her pussy. Her moans escalate, her hips rocking, pushing herself against me.

I love when she's so turned on she shoves her pussy into my face. I'm an animal and devour all of her, the wet licking sounds only escalating. I lose myself eating her and let myself get carried away as her hips rock and her moans intensify.

Her body tenses and I know she's close. I want her screaming but not yet. So I break away and lick my lips. "It's not time."

She cranes her head up toward us, her cheeks flushed, her eyes lost in arousal. "Are you kidding me...why are you stopping? Please keep going."

I laugh, getting to my feet. "I love it when you beg."

CAIN

She is a goddess.

Soft curves, perky breasts, an unparalleled beauty. She's so much smaller than the three of us, yet she has us all eating out of her hands.

Her lips pout at Elias holding out on her, and when he moves aside, glancing my way, I take my position between my love's legs.

"Cain, please don't make me wait."

"I love you like this." The words roll from my lips as my fingers glide down her thighs.

She's nodding, her gorgeous breasts bouncing from the gesture. "Uh-huh. Now are you going to do something about it?"

I slide my fingers down her swollen pussy and press two thick fingers into her wet softness. She moans and tilts her head back, her chest rising with burning arousal.

"Yes. Yes!"

Dorian and Elias are breathing loudly, their gazes locked on our girl. The things she does to us is unimaginable. She's curled herself around our hearts and there is no escaping her hold.

I pump into her furiously, her hips rocking, her pussy sucking down on my fingers, her eagerness so fucking beautiful.

An abrupt knock comes from the doors to the parlor.

I growl and Elias snaps at the intruder, "Leave us."

But the persistent knocking comes again. "Cain, I apologize for interrupting. Please, I must speak with you urgently." The hoarse voice tells me it's Ramos, and the tightness in his tone tells me something's wrong. He knows better than to interrupt me unless the reason is dire.

Groaning, I pull my fingers from Aria. Her disappointed moans are blades to my heart.

"What-What's going on?" She blinks up at me.

I lean over her and kiss her, then whisper, "I'm not finished with you. Don't go anywhere, my love."

I cross the room, feeling disgruntled at the interruption. I'd promised myself today would involve nothing but spoiling Aria, giving her anything she wants. And that doesn't include work getting in the way.

Swiftly, I step out into the hallway, pulling the doors shut behind me. Ramos is sanding there, bouncing on his feet anxiously. The dhampir is usually calm and relaxed, no matter the situation, so the fact that he can barely stay still has worry spinning through me.

"What is it?" I ask him.

The air around him is charged though with tension, and the bitter cold air is blowing into the mansion from the front doors being wide open. He must've burst in here, frantic. He doesn't even acknowledge my nakedness in front of him.

My anxiety ticks up a notch.

He licks his lips before he answers, "The Nightwalkers have taken over Purgatory."

I stare at him, unsure if I've even heard him right. "Excuse me?"

"Their master and his followers barged in, kicked out the customers, and locked down the place," he goes on, his words picking up speed in urgency. "They say they own it now."

Laughter bubbles up my throat.

This vampire clearly has a death wish. Did he really think he could just waltz into my club, put down his flag, and claim it as his own? That's not how things work around here.

What an idiotic and amateur mistake. One he will end up paying for with his life.

I built that club from the ground up. *I* did the work to make it what it is today. It's one of the things that propelled us to the top. And no one—*no one*—is going to take it from me. Especially some new-age vampire with an entitlement complex.

It's laughable that he'd even try.

But I did have other people to think about. Like Antonio, Sting, and the rest of my employees. "What's happened to the staff?" I ask.

"They've been tied and locked up for now, but from their talks, it sounds like they have plans to either turn or feed on them."

The amusement within me dies and is replaced by anger. Stephan wants to make a meal of my people? I don't think so.

"Were you there?"

He nods. "They tried tying me up like the others, but I was able to get away."

He means he used his special skills with pressure points to knock out his assailant.

"And what of Viktor and Charlotte?"

"Gone. They had left before the attack."

Getting into more trouble, no doubt.

I'm about to head out the door, where I see the Town Car and Holmes waiting for me, but then realize I'm still only partly clothed. I turn abruptly and race up the stairs. When my demon begins to push out of me, I let it, my wings bursting out of my back and my vision darkening.

"My Lord, what would you like me to do?" Ramos calls from below.

On the landing, I spin abruptly, and he jumps back at the sight of me transformed. "Tell the others." My deepened voice echoes off the walls. "Get them to Purgatory. We finish this tonight."

I bound up the rest of the stairs, push into my room, and quickly change my pants. Seconds later, I throw open the balcony doors and step outside. My wings stretch out and beat against the wind.

I had a feeling Stephan was going to retaliate after Viktor decimated his Hush supply, but going after Purgatory? He's going to regret this.

My black heart pounds with brutal hatred as my wings carry

me higher. I speed toward the edge of the city, right toward Purgatory, knowing Elias and Dorian won't be far behind.

As the treetops and dirty roads give way to blacktop and highrises, I notice billowing black smoke in the distance filling the night sky. The air reeks of fire, reminding me of Hell, and as I swoop down lower, the immense heat coming from below scalds my face. Red and orange flames consume one of the corner lots.

But not just any lot.

It's Purgatory.

And it's been set ablaze.

TWENTY-THREE

Everything I have worked for. Years of my life, money, time and energy. Gone. Up in smoke.

I stumble through my landing, unable to take my eyes off the inferno raging through the building, practically swallowing it whole.

I had put my heart and soul into this club; I'd built an empire from the ground up. And now, all I can do is watch as it burns.

Sorrow grips me unlike anything I've ever felt before. I'm paralyzed with it, only able to stare at the flames and know there's no way I'll be able to salvage anything, even when the human fire department comes.

I don't know how long I'm frozen there, but when I hear the frantic pounding of wings and the scratching of nails on pavement, I know I'm no longer alone.

"Shit..." It's Maverick. He must've flown here.

Although he hadn't been one of the people I'd wanted Ramos to tell to come, I don't mind him being here.

"What the fuck happened?" he asks, strolling up to my side.

I don't answer.

The violent and painful sounds of bones breaking and realigning come on my other side and soon Elias stands at his full height, completely naked.

He glances at me, waiting for the next command. When I don't give any, he says, "What do you want us to do?"

Tires screech in the distance, and suddenly light floods the parking lot as the Town Car whips around the corner. No Holmes driving this time. It's Dorian behind the wheel, driving like a madman, and the moment he throws the car in park across three parking spots, he flings open his door.

"Fuck me," he mumbles, the bright colors of the fire dancing off his face.

Now dressed for the freezing weather, Aria and Ramos get out next, and for some reason, seeing the devastation on Aria's face almost undoes me. Purgatory may have started just as a way to keep her busy while she was under our contract, but it had turned into much more for her, too. A second home. A place where she had some freedom and could be with friends. I can see the grief and torment clear on her face.

"Cain," Elias repeats, a little louder this time, "what do you want us to do? The fire department will be here in minutes."

That's when I remember that Ramos had mentioned Antonio and the others being tied up somewhere inside.

"Ramos, you and Elias run inside and see if any of our staff members are still in there," I order, and without even a flicker of hesitation, they both rush into the building.

Aria steps forward, her face contorted with fear.

"They'll be fine." Dorian places a hand on her shoulder. "Remember, we're made from hellfire, and Ramos is too smart to die."

But despite his somewhat comforting words, she still seems unsure.

We all wait, every second feeling like hours. It's impossible to hear anything beyond the fierce hissing and crackling of the flames. When neither Ramos or Elias return, my concern begins to grow. It shouldn't be taking this long.

This blaze has reached a dangerous level. Even for Hell creatures. Let's not forget that we're weaker on this plane; we can die.

That's it. I need to go in and get them. I pull my wings back into my body and trudge toward Purgatory, the heat and smoke intense enough to make my eyes water.

"No, Cain!" Aria shouts behind me.

I have to. I can't just leave them in there.

But just before I reach the threshold, the roof folds in and collapses, causing an explosion of hot air and flames so large, every window shatters and pieces of ash and wood and glass fly everywhere. Throwing my arms over my face, I'm pushed backwards from the power of the blast, my bare feet sliding across the pavement.

Aria's screams fill my ears, followed by Dorian's curses. Panicked, I rush toward the fire again, this time with Dorian on my heels, but a massive shadow suddenly darkens out the light and a black hellhound bounds out of the wreckage, five people clinging onto its back. Ramos appears next, stumbling out and shielding his face. He drops to the ground and I rush over, dragging him further away from the club in case of another collapse. He's coughing and hacking, his eyes bloodshot.

Despite his weakened state, he pats my arm, a silent way to tell me thank you and he'll be okay.

Rising to my feet, I look across the lot to see Elias dropping off the five very shaken up Purgatory employees, Antonio and Sting among them. Aria is there, checking them all over for any life-threatening burns or wounds. Besides being rattled and a bit knocked around, they seem okay.

"Good job, you big oaf," Dorian teases, swatting at the smoke that radiates off Elias's fur. He snorts at him in response.

"What's a-matter, demons? Afraid of a little fire? Isn't that, like, your thing?" A male's voice floats down from somewhere above us, somewhere hidden behind all the thick smoke. Laughter rises, and instantly the sadness of losing my club is gone. Replaced only with immeasurable rage.

I unfurl my wings, ready to take to the sky and find who's speaking, but the smoke parts as a man leaps through and lands in a perfect crouch before me. Slowly, he rises, and I realize I was wrong to call him a man. He's too young. Barely looks over twenty-five with short buzzed hair, a wide nose, and a clean shaven face. A boy.

His mouth splits in a cocky grin, fangs on display, as he saunters across the parking lot. "No hard feelings, I hope," he says as he closes the distance between us. He hooks a thumb toward Purgatory still engulfed in flames behind him. "You took something very important from me, so I had to take something from you. Fair is fair."

Dorian comes to my side and snorts a laugh. "Wait, you're Stephan? *You*?"

When the vampire bows, Dorian's laughter bursts out of him. "This is a joke. It's a joke. It has to be. Are we on one of those stupid reality shows? Where's the camera?"

Something he said must've struck a nerve because Stephan's confidence seems to waver. "You've lost, old man." He spits the last words as if it's an insult. "It's time for a new generation to rule this town."

Elias steps up to my left and growls, lips curled over sharp teeth.

"What's with these millennials?" Dorian teases. "Always think the world owes them something, and that they can just take what isn't theirs."

Maverick shouts from somewhere behind us, "What's a millennial?"

"Hell if I know. I just hear it used a lot."

Unamused, Stephan rolls his eyes. "You're pathetic. Really," he says. "And if you're hoping for the fire department or police to swing by, I wouldn't."

That means he has his hands in both, influencing them behind the scenes. He's even extended his reach to the human side of Glenside. Not just the supernatural.

Fury pumps through my veins like molten lava.

"Maverick, Aria, get Antonio and the others somewhere safe," I order, my eyes never leaving Stephan. The thundering of hurried footsteps tells me they have no problem doing so.

Good.

My wings stretch out, my demon growing restless with this pointless back and forth. I want blood. I want revenge. And no prepubescent little vampire child is going to stop me from getting just that.

Stephan looks at his nails, seeming bored with this whole thing, and I don't know what irks me more. His nonchalance or the fact that he's still able to breathe, let alone talk. "Before we kick this party off and things get bloody, I have a proposal for you."

I grit my teeth. Now he's just toying with us. "A proposal."

He raises his hands. "Hear me out. I know deals are usually your biz but I got one you'll want to hear."

Dorian glances at me. "Did he just say biz?"

"Not interested," I bark. My nerves are running low.

"Yeah, take that proposal and shove it up your *biz*," Dorian shouts back.

"You've run this city for a long time," Stephan goes on, ignoring him. "You obviously know what you're doing. It's only because of that I'm offering you a place on my team. To become my ally, not my enemy."

Elias snarls, spit flying.

"That's 'fuck you' in dog language, if you couldn't get that from the context clues."

"Took the words right out of my mouth," I push through my clenched teeth. "This city is ours. Always has been. Always will be."

"It's a shame you feel that way." Stephan flicks his fingers and more vampires drop from the smoke. Behind us. All around us, until we're completely surrounded by them. They bare their fangs at us.

I look from Elias on my left to Dorian on my right, whose horns curl back on his head, nails grow into claws, and runes glow underneath his shirt. They're bouncing on their tiptoes, ready for the fight.

"Like old times?" Dorian asks, a wicked smile on his face.

I nod. "No survivors."

Head tilting up, Elias lets out a mighty howl, and then the three of us are tearing off in opposite directions.

ARIA

I RUN WITH ANTONIO, Sting, and the other crew members of Purgatory down the dark street when a warning of danger wiggles up my spine. I stop in my tracks when I realize it's not from me or Sayah, but from the tether that binds me and my demons together. Something's wrong.

I glance up and spot danger leaping from the tops of buildings, heading back in the direction we'd just come. To Purgatory.

More vampires.

Oh shit. Stephan's brought back up. And from the looks of it, he brought an entire army.

Fear churns in my gut. The last time Cain, Dorian, and Elias had been up against vast numbers like this, they'd almost been beaten.

They're going to need help.

Maverick notices I've stopped and skids to a halt. "What are you doing? We have to get everyone out of here."

"They know that. They don't need us anymore." I switch directions and start running back toward Purgatory. It's not long before Maverick's beside me, keeping up with my strides.

"We were given orders, you know," he says.

"Oh, that's right. I forgot. You are all about following orders from someone else, regardless of the consequences. You did it with your father."

His eyes widen. He's stunned by my words, but I don't fucking care. If my demons need me, that's where I'm going to be.

He's quiet for a bit, still running at my side. Then, he says, "Fine, then I'm coming with you."

That's a bit obvious now but okay.

"And you're going to need this." He unsheathes the sword at his hip. During all the madness of Ramos telling us what was going down at Purgatory and us all rushing over here, I hadn't even noticed Maverick had it. Slowing down, he passes it to me. It isn't until the weapon is in my hand that I realize it's the same sword from our fight with the hellhounds.

"You brought this?" I ask, turning it in my hand.

"You did pretty well with it before." He shrugs. "Besides, you *never* want to go into a vamp fight empty handed."

"Right."

He nods toward the next street where the club's raging fire is still lighting up the night. "Let's go."

We pick up our pace again. I'm no expert swordsman by any means, but I did feel a little safer with a weapon to battle vampires with than nothing at all. Especially since Sayah is such a wildcard nowadays. Calling her for help could lead to disaster.

When we make it to the empty parking lot, we're halted by the sight before us. Bodies litter the ground. Even though most of the snow's been plowed into mounds, everything—from the pavement to the benches and parking meters—is painted red with blood.

In the background, the fire rages on, providing light on a very dark scene. Elias is ripping out a vampire's entrails and throwing them across the ground while Dorian claws his way through a crowd of them, impaling one with his taloned fingers and launching him across the way.

Cain's in the air, holding two vamps by the neck and then flying full speed into a neighboring building to crush their skulls against the stone. I hear the crack from all the way down here, and it makes me nauseous just to think about, so I try not to.

"There!" Maverick calls and points to the closest rooftops. The shadows I'd seen before are hopping closer to the brawl.

Panic seizes me. "We have to stop them!"

"Here, hold on!" Maverick scoops his hands under my arms and before I know it I'm being lifted into the air. His wings aren't as strong or large as Cain's but he's able to fly me onto one of the rooftops with no problems.

The moment our feet touch the rooftop, the vampires veer in our direction, coming at us in a maddening rush from the shadows.

My skin crawls at the sheer number of vampires, my grip tight on the sword.

Maverick unleashes a war cry and charges, moving with unimaginable speed. Pulling out his daggers from his belt, he throws them through the air with deadly precision and takes out two vamps in one go. With a flick of his wrist, the blades are sailing back into his hands, only for him to cut down three more vampires.

I've seen Dorian, Elias, and Cain fight many times, but Maverick is almost beautiful in the way he skillfully uses all parts of his body to fight with his weapons. Whatever it takes to finish off the enemy—and he's good at it too.

At the sight of carnage, Sayah rises up, wanting a piece of the action. I can feel her darkness seeping into my muscles and clogging my veins. But, as I learned during the hellhound attack, her presence helps me, makes me stronger, faster. I can use her to my advantage...

If only I could control her.

I'd managed to keep her from taking full control of me before, but that was with Maverick's help. He'd been able to bring out confidence in me, more than I'd felt before on my own. Would we be able to do it again if things got too out of hand?

I don't have time to think any more about it because a vamp lands in front of me from somewhere above. It's a woman with a short blond bob and a pink cardigan sweater. If it weren't for the red staining her teeth and rapidly healing bruise under her eye, I'd swear she was a PTA mom or running some soccer fundraiser. Not a bloodthirsty creature of the night.

Stephan was turning housewives too?

I raise my sword and she hisses loudly, fangs flashing. She pounces and I swing the weapon. In a blur of speed, she dodges my blow and comes at me again. A warning zips up my left side—a warning from Sayah—and I spin sharply, whirling my blade. It slices the vamp clean through her middle. She blinks, stunned, before her top half separates from her bottom, and she drops.

Sayah rejoices at the death, and my excitement grows. Maybe I can do this after all.

The thud of another enemy landing nearby has me whipping around, sword slicing through the air. I move only on instinct, and when warm blood splashes over my face and chest, I know I've delivered another fatal blow. A smile tugs at the corner of my lips.

I'm enjoying this. Maybe a bit too much.

The vampire stumbles backward, clutching his neck. I fall into my attack, bring the sword down into the center of his chest. I watch the life drain from his eyes, and something inside me ignites with excitement.

When I yank it back out, I kick him for good measure.

Someone grabs my hair and pulls it hard. I cry out, pain shooting through my skull and making my eyes water. My assailant tugs it back again, jerking me into his chest. His arms come around me, and his rancid breath spills over the side of my face.

"Hmmm, you're a fiery one," he purrs in my ear. "I wonder if you taste as good as you figh—"

There's a swoosh of air and a flare of pain at the top of my ear, and suddenly, the vamp's arms loosen on me. I jump away from him to see Maverick's daggers embedded in his forehead. Shuffling back, his eyes cross as he tries to look at it.

Another whoosh as Maverick's other dagger whizzes past me and nails him in the heart.

In a flash, Maverick is at my side. I touch my stinging ear, and when I glance at my fingers, they're glistening with blood.

"Shit!" I gasp.

"Sorry about your ear," he says with a playful wink.

"Just a scratch. Could've been much worse." I lift my weapon again and swing it toward the next bloodsucker coming at me, while Maverick darts into battle.

He calls over his shoulder, "The heart. Remember to aim for the heart for a sure kill."

The heart. Right.

This time, I grip the sword with two hands, heave the hilt back, and charge. I ram it into the first vamp who spins in my direction, and I drive it hard into his chest, getting it as close to his heart as possible.

When the thing convulses, eyes widening, blood dribbling from the corners of his mouth, I figure I've done right.

Pushing a foot up against his leg, I heave the sword out of him. He collapses to the ground in a heap. Boots slap the floor behind me, and I whip around to the oncoming monster. I charge forward and lash out my weapon, taking him out.

Maybe it's the adrenaline of not dying, or having Maverick close to me destroying these vampires, but I am feeling more confident than I ever imagined myself to be with a sword.

Cain soars overhead and uses his wings to push a huge gust of wind across the rooftop. The vamps lose their footing and are thrown back, some rolling off the roof and plunging to the ground below.

I look up, happy to see Cain unharmed, when a dark figure climbing up a neighboring fire escape catches my eye.

"Cain!" I scream, just as Stephan leaps through the smoky haze and lands on one of his wings, dragging it down. Unable to wrench it free, he spirals out of control and together, they tumble through the air. Cain's punching and clawing at any piece of Stephan he can grab, but Stephan's grip stays ironclad. I run to the edge of the rooftop, drop onto my knees, and watch as they fall straight for Purgatory and the fire.

My heart stops beating, terror paralyzing every inch of me. Just before the flames can swallow them up, Elias in hellhound form appears out of nowhere and leaps across the inferno, knocking both men out of harm's way.

The three of them land in a dark alley, out of my line of sight, but from the vicious snarls and sounds of fighting that follow, it's safe to say they have things handled.

"Aria!"

At the sound of Dorian's voice, I spin on my heel and drop to the ground as another one of the Nightwalkers swings something at me. It isn't until he tries to swing it down that I realize it's a lead pipe. My hands jut out in reflex, his blow meeting my sword instead.

He snarls at me, fangs out, and leans into his weapon. Inside me, Sayah's hold on me increases, and my mind starts to drift. She wants to take over me; she wants control.

But I can't let her have it. But without it, I may die.

Dorian appears behind the vamp in a blink of an eye and taps on his shoulder. "Um, excuse me."

Confused, he glances over his shoulder, and that's when Dorian slashes him across the face with his long nails. It isn't enough to kill him, obviously, but he does pull away the pipe and lashes out Dorian's way with it. He dodges it effortlessly. Sways left then right, back and down. With the gashes across his face already closing, the vamp growls in frustration.

"Okay, you're right. Enough playing around," Dorian says. When he swipes the pole at him again, Dorian grabs it and rips it out of his hand so fast, both the vamp and I are stunned. Then he stabs the thing directly through his chest.

The vamp sputters, blood bubbling out of his mouth, before dropping like a sack of potatoes.

Dorian steps on the corpse to get to me and offers me his hand. He helps me stand. "You're not too bad with that thing," he says, nodding toward the sword.

I smile. "Thanks."

"Oy! Dorian!" Maverick calls from the opposite end of the roof.

He's leaning over the edge and peering down at the street below. "Looks like we're getting a second wave!"

Dorian and I rush over and follow his gaze to see even *more* Nightwalkers coming to join the fight.

"Holy fuck. How many of these fuckers did this high school dropout make?"

"Looks like another fifty or so," Maverick answers, even though the question was clearly rhetorical.

"He couldn't just stay in his mom's basement and be addicted to internet porn like the rest of this generation?"

Maverick wipes the blood splatter from his forehead with the back of his hand. "Is that what you did as a kid?"

"I fucking wish," he says, then jump onto a nearby drainpipe and begins to climb down. "Keep her safe," he barks Maverick's way.

"She's pretty capable of taking care of herself, if you haven't noticed," he shouts after him. Glancing up at me, he offers me a smile and butterflies flutter awake in my stomach. At least someone believes in me.

A loud battle cry shakes the night. Maverick and I exchange puzzled looks before gazing back down. Out of the shadows comes a man dressed in a gold chest plate and leather skirt. With his dark hair and tanned skin, he looks like he just stepped out of a time machine from ancient Rome.

"What the fuck is that?" Maverick asks in disbelief.

I only know one tall, dark, and handsome vampire like that. I laugh. "That's Viktor."

He throws his head back and lets out another warrior shriek. The darkness behind him shifts and moves and suddenly, more vamps rush out, spilling into the parking lot and clashing head on with Stephan's horde. It looks like he's brought some friends from other covens.

"He brought the cavalry," Maverick says. "But why is he dressed like..."

"I wouldn't ask," I reply.

"Gotcha." After twirling his daggers in his hands, he sheathes them in his belt. "Well, hopefully that means all this can be over with faster."

Taking in the space around us, I notice the rooftop is scattered with dead bodies, mostly Maverick's handiwork. "You didn't have fun?" I ask him, because it sure looks like he did.

He smirks as his answer.

The savage sound of screams and death from down below has us both leaning over the roof's edge again. Down below, the lot and the remains of Purgatory are a chaotic mess. They look like a swarming nest of ants from up here, spreading out over the land, consuming everything in their path.

There are so many vampires against my demons, and from the looks of it what Maverick and I did up here has barely made a dent. My stomach drops.

"Stay here," Maverick commands, and before I can argue, he jumps off the building, wings out, and glides right into the heart of battle.

"Maverick! Wait!" But he doesn't hear me and vanishes into the masses to combat the enemy.

This is insane.

I thought the hellhounds were bad, but this is an all-out war. How many casualties will be caused by this? Will my demons survive?

My heart twists. There needs to be another way to end this bloodbath. A sure way.

The shrill wind blows past me, tossing up my hair, and rising goosebumps on my arms. My skin tingles, and I realize the chill rushing around me isn't natural. It's supernatural.

Sayah.

Across the rooftop, my shadow wiggles and grows and Sayah leaks out of me. At first, my pulse races with fear—I know what she's capable of, after all. She's a leviathan, a monster, and she wants to use me like her puppet to do whatever she wants.

But then, I remember fighting the hellhounds and Maverick's encouraging words. He'd said Sayah *needs* me. I don't need her. And that's the key, isn't it? She's protected me all these years in a symbiotic relationship. But we're more than that.

I've controlled her before, when I thought she was my friend. Then, when I saw how strong she really was, I deemed her my enemy. Maybe I've been looking at this all wrong.

It's not her versus me. Her power is mine, and what's mine is hers. If I'm weak, she'll step all over me. But if I call the shots, she'll have to listen.

We're...one.

Can this work?

I draw a deep breath in through my nose and try to draw on that confidence I'd felt under Maverick's touch. It's not as easy to find within myself like when he did it, but I repeat to myself that I can do this. Like with the sword, like with finding the relics and outsmarting the necromancer, and escaping the dragon, I keep surprising myself. And I can do this too.

I am a survivor. It's what I've always been. But this time, I am going to be more than that.

I'm going to be the ruler of my own destiny. And no one—not a demon, a leviathan, not even Lucifer himself—is going to tell me otherwise.

This is my life, and I'm taking back the reins.

Power surges through me, unlike anything I've ever felt before. Wind rushes all around me in a mini tornado, throwing up my hair and through my clothes. I feel strong, invincible, immortal, and it's not Sayah doing it to me; it's me. I'm in control.

I drop my sword. It clatters to the ground, but I don't care. Hopefully I won't be needing it anymore.

Slowly, I lift my hand and Sayah's shadow mimics my movements and lifts from the ground. She stands tall before me, like a ghostly stretched-out version of myself.

Sayah is a force alone, but I wonder how far I can take it.

I continue to lift my hand even more, and to my surprise, every shadow on the rooftop darkens and grows before peeling off the ground to stand freely on their own, too. Like miniature Sayahs, complete with glowing red eyes and all. Their opaque forms float closer to me as if waiting for my next command.

Holy shit. This is absolutely terrifying. A nightmare in the making.

But I can't be scared. Right now, they're obeying me, and I can use them to end this battle with the Nightwalkers once and for all.

I ball my raised hand into a tight fist.

Shadows? I call to them mentally, like I used to do with Sayah. Hearing my command, they all perk up. *It's time.*

Their red eyes shine brighter, and then they're off, zigzagging down the building and weaving in and out of Viktor's men. One by one, they seek out Stephan's vampires, covering them in their shadowy essence, engulfing them, until nothing remains. Once they move on to the next, there's nothing left of the vampire before. Not a trace. They've been completely swallowed up by their darkness.

I watch with a mix of horror and excitement as Sayah and the others take out the Nightwalkers with little effort. I spot Cain, Dorian, and Elias among the crowd, watching the whole thing unfold but unsure what to do about it. When Cain lifts his head and sees me standing on the roof, he leaps into the air.

His wounded wing doesn't go unnoticed by me, especially since he has a hard time directing himself to land on the roof. He misses the edge and slips, causing my heart to skip a beat. I rush over to the side to see him still there, only holding onto the bricks.

One good heave up, and he's over the top. The moment he stands, I throw myself into his arms. He pulls me close and tucks in his wings.

"It's still you..." he murmurs against my head.

I tilt my head up to him and find his baby blues staring down at me. "Who did you think it'd be? The Queen of England?"

"But...the leviathan..." He glances over his shoulder at the scene below, where my shadows are doing a good job cleaning up the place and fewer Nightwalkers litter the parking lot. Some are even fleeing now after seeing what they can do.

"I think I'm getting the hang of this now," I say, but his gaze is searching my face, looking for any signs of Sayah controlling me.

"Your eyes are still white, but you sound like my Aria."

"That's because I *am* your Aria."

Still unsure, he continues to stare at me.

I let out a nervous laugh. "Cain, it's me. Really."

He waits another long moment before asking, "Then how did you summon more creatures?"

"I'm not quite sure exactly... But I realized that I have the ability to control them. And Sayah. Thanks to Maverick."

"Maverick?"

I nod. "Yeah, he helped me see that I don't need Sayah. She needs me. And she was only able to take me over because I was letting her. If I'm the one calling the shots and believing in myself, she has to listen to me. I mean, I think so anyway. It seems to be working so far."

He glances down again. "I'd say so. But I think you should call them back to you now."

His words surprise me. "Call them back? But why? They haven't taken out all the Nightwalkers yet."

"They've done their job more than efficiently," he says. "Most of Stephan's coven was only under his command because of their allegiance to him for turning them. Now that he's gone, Viktor can take over again as Glenside's master vampire and reform his coven."

"He's dead?" I ask eagerly. After all the shit that vamp's put us through, it does give me some sick satisfaction to know he's done for. I just wish I could've been the one to do it myself. Or with the shadows.

"Yes, he's dead," Cain confirms. "So you can recall the creatures. The fight is over. We've won."

Problem is, I don't want to stop them. The energy buzzing inside me is intoxicating, and the thought of me being the reason all those bloodsuckers are dead...it fills me with pride.

Little Miss Aria, now able to kill so many without so much as lifting a finger. Or sword.

Little Miss Aria, no longer needing to cower or run or need protecting.

I have power, *real* power now. I can fight back.

"Aria..." A warning rumbles in Cain's throat as he shifts toward me.

"But your club... They destroyed it. And what about your wing? They all deserve to die," I try to reason with him.

"I'll heal with time. And my club is replaceable. You're not."

"But I'm fine," I tell him. "Better than fine, actually. See?"

He keeps walking toward me, making me shuffle backward. "It's done," he says. "Call the monsters back."

Everything inside me is saying no. Don't do it. Every one of those bloodsuckers deserves the horrible death coming to them. But the way Cain's looking at me, like I'm becoming the enemy instead of his love, has me rethinking everything.

He's right. I don't want to go too far either and sink into that dark mindset Sayah can put me in. I need to be aware and find the balance.

Like before, I lift my hand and find the power inside me that is attached to Sayah.

Return. Your job is done.

On command, Sayah zips up the side of the building with the other shadows in tow. Cain and I watch as the others take their rightful spots and become the rooftop's natural shadows once again.

Once Sayah shrinks back into me and my normal shadow returns, the power radiating off me ceases and Cain smiles.

"There she is. Aria. My love." He wraps me in his arms again and leans down for a kiss. It's sweet and gentle and everything I need to calm the adrenaline still rushing through me. It helps douse the fiery need for more death and destruction.

Once he pulls away, I whisper, "Thanks for keeping me from losing my way."

"Anytime." Then he glances around the rooftop and concern wrinkles his forehead. "With my wing, I'm not sure it's safe for me to get us both down from here. Dorian may have to carry you..."

Chuckling, I hook my thumb toward the rooftop access door. "Or we could always just take the stairs."

He laughs, his eyes sparking with amusement.

"Walk down stairs to the ground floor? You mean like normal people?" he says as we walk toward the access door.

He's a prince of Hell. I'm a leviathan—whatever that really means—and shoot shadows out of my body, and we just finished killing an army of vampires together. What about any of this is normal?

"Yeah, sure. *Normal.*"

Whatever the fuck that means.

I COLLAPSE into the back seat of the Town Car, completely exhausted, but my pulse is buzzing. Cain is in the front, while Elias and Maverick climb into the back snug seat with me and Dorian drives.

It's a tight squeeze, but we manage. There's no argument from anyone, we just make it work, like somehow after what happened, it's become clear we are not the enemy to each other. Maverick is more *us* now then he's ever been.

We're all splattered in blood, covered in wounds and cuts, clothes torn, but we're smiling.

"Fuck Stephan and those vamps," Elias growls. "My little rabbit, you demolished so many. Fuck, do you know how sexy and terrifying that was to watch?"

I can't stop smiling, which is odd, feeling such satisfaction after leaving a bloody war zone. But for the first time ever, a sense of belonging and satisfaction flares over me. For the first time, I don't feel like the freak I've always been.

"You were mesmerizing," Dorian adds and glances at me from the rearview mirror. "You controlled Sayah again."

I'm beaming on the inside. I catch Cain watching me from the front seat with a proud look on his face. Is it strange to love bathing in their acceptance and compliments?

"It's thanks to Maverick for showing me how to control her, really." I lean forward, glancing over to him, grinning at him. Adoring how damn sexy he looks with blood over him. All my men mean everything to me, and right now, I'm including him in that lot.

Every demon turns to look at Maverick, who shrugs nonchalantly. "It's nothing."

Dorian chuckles. "Maybe you're not all that bad."

I roll my eyes at his attempt at a compliment, but Maverick smirks at that. "Maybe."

"So, what's next?" Elias asks.

"Nothing," I say in unison with Dorian.

"I want a damn break from all the end-of-world stuff," I admit truthfully. "At least for a day or so, especially since we never finished celebrating Christmas completely."

"What happens during Christmas?" Maverick asks.

"For you," Elias answers hastily. "Absolutely nothing."

I giggle to myself at his possessiveness, adoring when they go all macho. These demons are mine. There are no take-backsies. I'll fight tooth and nail to hold onto them as they do for me. Now when it comes to Maverick...it's still a work in progress, but I have a feeling he'll be the decent guy he's showing himself to be of late.

I lean back against Elias and just enjoy the peacefulness for a change. I know there's a big mess waiting for me with Gabriel and the showdown with Lucifer. I also still want to find out more about Leviathan, if I can. But that can all wait until later.

Once we pull up in front of the mansion, we all peel out of the Town Car and stumble into the mansion.

"I'm going to sleep for a week straight," I joke, though in truth, I crave it so badly. Along with foot massages and breakfast in bed.

Cain is already dragging himself into the parlor, Dorian behind him, and they're dripping blood over everything.

"Hot shower and food," Elias responds, and loops his arm around my waist, drawing me toward the parlor. I'm guessing we're going to chat about what happened first.

I glance back to Maverick, who's already strolling away and down toward the basement instead of joining us.

"Maybe he needs another room. The basement is so doom and gloom," I suggest, to which Elias grumbles but he doesn't outright say no either. I smile to myself, knowing that as much as Maverick is growing on me, he's slowly gaining acceptance by my three lovers as well.

Inside the parlor, I make my way toward the fireplace. The warmth of the blaze against my skin is like heaven

On my next breath, the hairs on my arms lift.

A current of power races down my spine. But with it comes the tingling in my toe...the power I feel when I'm near the relics, when they are activated.

I freeze and glance at the three men at the same time they ice over too. "Did you feel that?" I ask.

They're nodding. "What the fuck now?" Elias growls.

"Magic!" Cain answers, his face panicked.

My stomach knots because we barely got home and it started again?

"Fuck, now?" Dorian snarls.

"My toe," I gasp out, the sensation dancing heavily across all my toes now. "The relics," I barely say, when the three demons rush out of the room.

I'm on their heels, and we're flying directly into Cain's room.

There's soil strewn everywhere like someone's been tossing earth in here, covering every piece of furniture.

"What the heck happened here?" I ask.

Cain darts across the room and throws open the closet door. Then he drops down to his knees in front of a latch door in the floorboards that's already open. There are piles of dirt all around the closet, like someone's been digging for a bone.

And I know instantly it's where he's been stashing the relics. The earth keeps their power at bay.

My blood turns to ice as I close in and find the gaping hole empty of relics. Cain is digging furiously through the soil with his bare hands.

"Fuck!" he roars, and rears back on his heels. When he lifts his gaze, there is a look on his face I never thought I'd see, and I want it gone because it doesn't belong to him.

Defeat.

"They're gone. All the fucking relics are gone!"

My heart thunders and terror wrenches through me.

"You are fucking kidding me!" Dorian's pushing forward, needing to check for himself.

"How? Who?" I ask.

Elias's thunderous growl has me turning toward him as he tears out of the room.

My knees are trembling as I stumble closer to the closet, and my wide eyes greet Cain as he gets to his feet.

There are no words I can find to ease the ache of what they've all lost. What we've all lost...our chance to eradicate Lucifer from our lives.

Shock hits me hard, and I'm stumbling backward as the world stands still for those few moments.

Cain's face reddens with fury, and Dorian is digging through the earth desperately. But it's true. There's nothing there. Someone's stolen the relics.

Movement rushes across my back, and I twist around to Elias bursting into the room. His livid, his eyes on fire, and his hands fisting.

"Maverick's gone," he snarls breathlessly. "The fucking weasel is nowhere in the mansion. He took the relics!"

Dorian scrambles to his feet as a rush of breath expels past his lips. "That sonofabitch! I'm going to rip his spine out with my bare hands, then feed it back to him."

Cain doesn't move, doesn't say a word. He's shaking with rage, and his silence is terrifying. I can't even begin to know how it feels to have his brother betray him this way.

But this disaster destroys everything we've been working toward.

I can't catch my breath as only darkness sweeps over me, stealing the earlier hope I'd been clinging to. Stealing everything.

Maverick...what the fuck have you done.

HELL ON EARTH
SIN DEMONS

The journey's been Hell... but it's time to give the devil his due.

This is it. This is where it all ends.

It's me, my shadow, and my demons against Lucifer.

With the relics stolen, the only way to get them is to go back into the hellfire--back to Hell where Lucifer awaits. Defeating him may mean making the ultimate sacrifice, but even with so much at stake, I don't know if I can.

Things heated up fast with Cain, Elias, and Dorian, and now Maverick, but I'd sell my soul a hundred times to keep them as mine. Forever.

What if that's impossible?

There's so much danger ahead of us, but I'll bring Hell on earth to save the ones I love. I just wonder that when all's said and done, who will be the one wearing the unholy crown?

CHAPTER

ONE

CAIN

"Speak of the devil and he appears."
—Anonymous

The absolute fury that's clashing inside me is unlike anything I've ever felt before.

Every inch of me is trembling with it. I can barely see straight. The monster inside me rips at my core, wanting out. Wanting more blood. Wanting death for those who wronged me.

I tear past everyone and throw open the balcony doors. Aria tries to move toward me, but Dorian quickly snatches her and pulls her back. He knows me too well to know that when I get like this, I'm like a tornado, taking down anyone in my path. I'm uncontrollable, and it's not safe for anyone to be by me right now. Aria included.

Once the frigid air of the night hits me, my wings explode from my back, the transformation into my demon too fast for even my human side to process, and pain ricochets through me. It's easy to ignore it, though. Especially with so much adrenaline and hellfire pumping through my veins.

The roar I unleash booms across the quiet landscape. Animals flee from their resting places and birds take off for the skies. Not only did I lose my club tonight, I lost six of the seven pieces of

Azrael's harp, and any chance of us returning to Hell along with them.

Why? All because of my fuckwit of a brother.

He conned me. He convinced us all that he was on our side and wanted to help, only to swipe the relics once our backs were turned and make a run for it.

I should have known better. I should have never allowed him into our home. I should've slaughtered him the moment he showed up. But he knew I was distracted—between what was happening with Aria, the vampires, and the hellhounds—he took full advantage of my overwhelmed mind.

He fucked us all over.

The big question is, what do we do now?

It's more than likely Maverick took the relics back to Hell, and that's the one place we can't go. Retrieving them is impossible.

We may have won with the Nightwalkers and getting our city back, but we've lost so much more.

As my fury boils me alive, another roar raises up my throat. Maverick's lucky I can't go to Hell. I'd rip him from the underworld and peel off his skin with my bare hands. Death is too quick and easy for him. I'd prolong the suffering; he deserves nothing less. Lucifer may be the king of torture, but I'm going to temporarily take the title from him, just for Maverick's sake.

He's going to wish I'd let Father kill him that day. I'll make sure of it.

Stopping abruptly, I sense the change in the air before I see it. That strange skitter in the atmosphere, like time is holding its breath, and what follows is never good.

Whipping around, I notice the ripple of the air in the center of my bedroom. Then the big exhale and pop through the very fabric of time and space as the archangel Gabriel appears in its place.

Dorian yanks Aria farther back, while Elias protectively steps in front of them both. Gritting my teeth, I quickly hurry inside, only to have the hulk of an angel whirl on me first, eyes blazing with an ancient hatred I'll never understand. He looks over my leather wings and black-lined skin, and his lip curls in disgust.

When he spins again and finds Aria, his body stiffens and the grip on his sword tightens.

He wants to kill her—and the Leviathan inside her—more

than anything. I can see it in his stance. She represents God's mistake, and he's dying to eradicate her because of it. Me, Elias, and Dorian are the only things standing in his way.

Well, besides the need to stop Lucifer. But I have no doubt that if one of us blinks, all sense will go out the window and he'll kill her in an instant. And that's something I'll never let happen.

"Gabriel!" I shout, gaining his attention once again. I recall my demon for the moment but keep it close, to appear less threatening. "No one summoned you here."

"You can't just pop in here whenever you feel like it," Dorian adds. "You may be wearing a dress, but you're no fairy godmother."

Gabriel glances down at his tunic and sneers.

"Get out of our home," I tack on, in case it wasn't clear enough. "Or we'll make you."

The cold bastard ignores the threat and lifts his nose at us instead. Unbothered. As if he's staring down three cockroaches instead of three powerful demons. If he wasn't carrying an angel blade—or sword in his case—I would have made good on my word right away. But God-made and blessed weapons are the only ones that can kill any creature. Maybe even God himself, if anyone ever got mad enough at him. It's why they're rare and only archangels have them. How Lucifer got ahold of a dagger before he fell is unknown to me.

"Son of Lucifer. Sin Demon. I would not have come to your..." his lip curls up in obvious disgust, "*home*...if it were without purpose."

"Well, spill it then, Gabe. We got shit to do, places to be," Dorian snaps.

Gabriel waves his sword Dorian's way, and Aria stiffens nervously. "Do not call me that."

"What? Gabe?" Dorian laughs. "It's just a nickname, man. Relax."

The archangel clenches his teeth. "I am not a Gabe. Nor am I a man. So I will not *relax*, as you say. One purpose has brought me to Earth and one purpose only. And that is to find out if you Hell-vermin have obtained the rest of Azrael's harp." He turns to me again. "So, tell me, Son of Lucifer, what news do you bring me?"

Elias's breathing picks up and his nostrils flare as his anger builds. The skin across his face and arms ripple as the power of the shift crawls through him. It's not such a smart move to call a hellhound a rodent. I'm surprised he's kept it together this far.

I have to defuse the situation before it gets out of hand and we have another issue that we don't need.

"We found the foot and the intestine," I interject and step closer, which isn't a lie. We had hunted down and collected the two pieces of the harp. I just don't think he needs to know that they, along with the other four parts, were taken from us.

Gabriel's head tilts and disbelief washes over his face. Did he honestly not think we could do it? Must have.

Bastard.

"And the skull?" he asks.

I clench my teeth. Even though I know it's in Mexico, that doesn't mean it'll be an easy piece to retrieve. "We're working on it."

"You have all the locations," he says. "There is no excuse."

"I don't know if you saw while you were sitting on your golden pedestal on cloud nine, but we had a little vampire problem to deal with here. And all Lucifer's hellhounds," Dorian says.

"Hellhounds will be the least of your worries," Gabriel replies, which wins him a guttural growl from Elias. "That's not a threat from me, you wretched creature," he spits. "Lucifer will be sending other legions next to retrieve the Dark One. Demons. Shades. Whatever will do his bidding."

Aria glances at each of us, the worry clear on her face, and I know Gabriel's right. Now that he has the relics, there will be no way for us to get to Aria if he does steal her from us.

"Retrieve the skull," he says, gaze sweeping over the room. "Hell is coming." And with that, Gabriel pops out of existence right before our eyes.

The room falls into a thick silence, one heavy with all the doubts and fears we don't want to utter out loud. After battling vampires and losing the relics to Maverick, we're finally coming down from the high of the fight, and rock bottom isn't looking very welcoming.

"Who pissed in his Cheerios this morning?" Dorian says to break the stillness. "I swear, he needs to get laid. Can angels even have sex?"

"Dorian..." Aria whispers and touches his arm. "Not the time."

He holds up his hands in surrender. "All I'm saying is that it's no wonder Lucifer fell from Heaven. They all have giant sticks up their asses."

Aria looks at me with her mouth tugged down into a hard frown. "Cain, why did you lie to him? Why didn't you tell him about Maverick? Maybe he could've helped us—"

"It would've only worsened things," Elias answers for me. "We don't need Gabriel's wrath on us now."

"But what he said...about Hell coming. What are we going to do?" Aria asks.

Every eye turns to me for guidance, but this time I have nothing to offer them. Nothing that can ease our situation, fix what's been broken, or save what was lost. For once, I have no ideas. No answers to give them all or reassuring words. None.

My chest clenches as the weight of what's happened grips me fully.

We are in deeper shit than ever before.

And we're running out of time.

The mattress bows slightly beneath me as if someone is climbing into bed with me. Fear spikes inside me, until I realize it's probably Elias. It's been too long since he made his way into my bed during the night, and I've missed waking up to find him beside me.

The blanket tugs and pulls behind me as he slides under, and he's doing a terrible job at not causing the whole bed to creak. I smile to myself.

A strong arm loops around my stomach and roughly pulls me back against his solid body, followed by a growl that rumbles in his chest. I squirm in his arms, loving how I'm already feeling wet from such an aggressive gesture.

"Hey sexy," I whisper and arch my body, pushing my ass back against him to tease him. Seeing as he just woke me up, he owes me to help me go back to sleep.

"Felt like some company?" I purr when he doesn't respond.

His cock twitches and hardens as his voice caresses my ear. "Right there, that feels so good!"

I stiffen. Wait! It's not Elias. And I don't move at first, instinctually knowing the danger I'm in.

A squeak leaves my throat, "Maverick! What the fuck!"

I shove my hands against his arm to dislodge myself, but his grip tightens, forcing me to be caged in against his hard body.

And not to mention his erection is pressing right up between my ass cheeks, and I'm wearing my thin pajamas. I feel every inch of him pressed to me, even though I can feel he's wearing clothes too.

My earlier boldness dissolves in moments, replaced with a rising anger.

"But we were having fun," he says, his voice carrying a dangerous edge. "Or were you imagining me as one of your demon lovers? Who was it? Can't be Cain since he doesn't seem the type to practically hump you. Maybe Dorian, but no, this has Elias written all over it."

"Let me go before I scream and wake the whole damn house."

"First, I want you to listen to me."

I clench my teeth. "Why? So you can spin a lie about how you vanished with our relics? How you played me like a fool while you pretended you cared." My pulse is racing now, and it has nothing to do with his body glued to mine.

"Aria, I would never—"

"You really hurt me, Maverick. And I feel like an idiot now thanks to you." I hate that tears sting my eyes as the weight of what he really took from me feels like someone is crushing my heart. I realize how much I had let Maverick into my life, how much I truly started to like him. And to have him return is like a blade to my chest, reminding me of his betrayal.

But with those emotions tearing through me, a familiar sensation rises within me, one that comes so fast. In seconds, Sayah pulls out of me. She's darker than the night, her eyes blinking.

Maverick's breath catches, and his grip around my middle loosens. I take the chance and roll away from him, then scramble clumsily out of my bed and right over Cassiel, who doesn't move a muscle and keeps on snoring.

I roll my eyes at the lynx.

Hopping out of bed, I quickly cross the room and hit the light, turning around to face him. Sayah is hovering over him, and with a single thought of, *Sayah come back to me*, she zips into me. There's something rewarding about gaining that sense of control over her once more, to have her listen and not be terrified of my own shadow.

But my attention now falls on Maverick again.

I don't want any surprises, plus I feel safer being near the open door and with Sayah at my fingertips.

"Clever trick. And you've proved your point." Maverick pushes out from under the blankets and stands. I grin when I realize I've startled him.

He's dressed in all black...tight jeans that do nothing to conceal his boner, a V-neck tee that's tight across his strong chest, and combat boots. This guy is powerful and gorgeous, and he's going to destroy me if I'm not careful. Everything about him screams dangerous. There's wildness behind his gaze when he studies me.

"You couldn't help yourself, could you?" I insist. "Just be honest with me for a change and admit you're working with Lucifer."

He runs a hand through his light hair, his eyes lowering momentarily as a painful expression sweeps over his face. "My whole life I was told to make a call on whose side I'd be on. My father's or my own, which meant going directly against Lucifer, so there really wasn't a choice after all." He lifts his head. "Everything was an illusion. My brothers and I have always been captives in Hell. Except we've got more privileges, but a prison is still a prison."

"Why are you telling me this?"

He's shaking his head. "Because, for the first time in my life, I made a call on whose side I'm on. I want to escape Lucifer's oppression. On your side, on Cain's side." He takes a step closer, and I recoil, my heels hitting the wall. "No more second guessing, and I'm not willing to sacrifice myself anymore for him. Believe me when I say, I didn't take Azrael's relics."

"So, what? They just vanished at the same time you did?" I roll my eyes, not sure why he thinks I'm an idiot.

"I know who took them, which is where I've been." He's closed the distance between us completely and he stands in front of me, a hand poised against the wall over my shoulder. He looks down at me, his heavy breath washes over my face, and I can't stop myself from looking at those lips, remembering how they felt against me. His mouth presses into a tight smile, and I kick myself how even in this circumstance I'm admiring him, how my chest pushes toward him instinctually. *Down girl. He could be the enemy.*

It's really impossible to tell if he's lying and about to eat me like the big bad wolf in Little Red Riding Hood, or if he's being genuine.

My gaze moves from those tempting lips to his sharp eyes as I consider my next move. Run and call the others, or give him the benefit of the doubt.

"I've never said I was the good guy, Aria, or that sometimes my heart doesn't feel as black as the darkest pits of Hell, but around you, I'm different. I crave the high of making you smile, to touch you so you'll moan. The sounds you make drive me wild, and I don't think you have a clue what you've done to me."

"Is that supposed to convince me you're innocent?" I don't know what's still holding me back from shoving him off me, and the thing is, Maverick knows exactly how he affects me, which is why he's come to me first, why he's flirting this way.

Sure, everything about this demon sends my pulse into a frenzy, but that doesn't make him safe now, does it?

"They're just words," I answer. "Demons lie all the time. It's one of your specialties."

"And how would you know that?"

"It's a known fact."

He leans in closer, and I press my back to the wall. "Maybe people change. Cain's my brother, and you've given him a chance after he bought your soul."

"Good for you in doing your research, but it's not that straightforward. And I've had enough of this game." I shove my hands against his chest, pushing him off me. "The fact is, you took the relics, and you're an asshole for everything you did to me."

He stands several feet away, and I've decided I'm no longer going to fall for his tricks. I can't stand his persistent lies. I want more than anything to believe him, but everything points to him taking the relics, lying to us. Cain hasn't trusted him from the beginning, but it was me who fell prey to his charm. Now I'm burdened with my mistakes and the awful ache that I let myself fall for someone like him.

I should have known better. Dammit. Taking in quick breaths, in and out, my pulse is on fire with anger.

I turn fast and head out of my room and down the hallway, cloaked in the night's embrace.

Footsteps strike the floorboards behind me. "Aria, please, you need to believe me. I am on your side. After everything, do you really think I'd betray you?"

He snatches my wrist and roughly forces me to face him, but as I stumble around I lash out and slap him across the face.

"You don't get another chance to hurt me," I croak, surprised I can even speak straight with how much I'm trembling with anger.

He stiffens from my strike but doesn't release my hand. He instead lifts my palm and places it on his chest. "You broke me from the first moment we met, but I hadn't known it at the time. You've become my obsession and I can't get you out of my head. When I close my eyes, I only see you, I hear your voice, I can't stop smelling that gorgeous scent you have. It's unbearable being away from you. Aria, do you think I'd risk losing someone as special as you for some fucking relics?"

"I...I don't know what to think." I yank my hand free and stumble back a few steps, my pulse jackhammering in my chest. His words wreak havoc with my head, with my heart.

He lets out a frustrated sound as he stares at me sharply. "I returned to Hell to chase my brother, Lorcan. He took the relics. I'll die trying to help you. Anything you want, I'll give you, because in my heart, I claimed you as mine from the first time we met."

Before I can respond, a terrifying growl floods the hallway from behind me. The hairs on my arms raise when a sudden whoosh of air rushes right past me.

One second, Maverick stands in front of me, and the next, someone slams into him, sending him sideways. The bangs and growls sound like an earthquake is tearing down the mansion.

I know instantly that it's Cain tearing into Maverick. Brother against brother.

My stomach shouldn't ache at seeing them battle, but it does. I'm trying to make sense of what Maverick told me. Why would he return if he got what he wanted, to rub it in my face? It sure seems like something he'd do, except something just doesn't feel right.

I rush down the hallway after them. The pair are tossing each other into walls, leaving gaping holes. Paintings drop from the walls. It's chaos.

Cain is fighting as his full demon with his wings out. So is Maverick, and there's something almost beautiful about watching these powerful, dark beings battle. Only the light from my room behind me illuminates the fight, their shadows like monstrous puppets twisted in their own battle along the walls.

Maverick is suddenly thrown into the air where he slams into the ceiling. His silver feathered wings sweep against the chandelier, sending the entire thing to the ground. It falls to the floor with a tremendous crash, and the crystals break off and fling like projectiles.

I duck and cover my head, when a large hand sweeps over me, and someone covers me with their body. Dorian, I smell his cologne instantly.

"Stay behind me," he says.

I lift my head to Dorian and Elias, who are now by my side, watching. Neither of them interrupt.

The look in Elias's gaze is filled with blood lust, with hatred.

But my mind swirls with Maverick's excuses about Lorcan taking the relics. With Gabriel's insistence, the knowledge that Lucifer and his demons would do anything to get the relics.

My head hurts and my gut churns while working out who to believe.

Cain's clawed wings slice through the air before slashing Maverick across the chest, his other fist colliding into his face. Maverick stumbles backward, his blood splashing the wall, and he glances my way for a brief moment as he catches his footing. It's enough for me to see a harrowing look in his eyes, of him pleading for me to believe him.

"You couldn't pay enough for ring-side viewing of such a fight," Elias brags, grinning wildly.

Dorian isn't any better with how enchanted he is by the battle. And sure, I won't deny that seeing Cain fight is spectacular. He moves like the dark, barely noticeable until he's savagely mauled you.

But the longer I watch, the more I know this isn't the solution. It's not going to help us.

"Stop," I call out suddenly, and I'm pushing forward when Dorian snatches my arm.

"That's not going to happen," he tells me. "This is long overdue."

"And then what? He kills Maverick! We need to grill him, and he told me Lorcan stole the relics."

Elias barks a laugh. "He'll say anything to not be blamed."

"Then why did he return?" I ask hurriedly, as another thunderous bang comes from Maverick slamming Cain to the ground in what I can only describe as a wrestling flip over his shoulder.

"Gorgeous," Dorian says, still holding onto my arm. "He came to take you back to Lucifer."

His words just add to my tangled thoughts, though I can't help but wonder if that were the case, why did he waste time trying to tell me otherwise? Why not snatch me while I sleep and kidnap me?

My throat tightens like someone has punched me, and all I can think is what if he is telling the truth?

I yank my arm free from Dorian and scream, "Cain, you need to stop, please!"

In the exact same moment that Cain looks up at me, two things happen simultaneously. Maverick drives a fist right into his face, sending Cain falling backward, and Dorian snatches me off my feet and swings me away from the fight.

"Put me the hell down," I yell, slapping his arms.

"Calm down. You don't get it, do you?" he growls in my ear, then finally puts me down.

The sounds and grunts of the battle escalate.

I look up at Dorian. "What do you mean?"

"This fight has been long overdue. They won't kill each other; in Hell, this is how shit is settled."

I'm breathing heavily. "So, they're not going to kill each other?"

"Not if Maverick accepts his defeat."

I flinch in response as I doubt Maverick is the kind to ever give in. "And if he doesn't, Cain will take him out?"

He shrugs, which doesn't put me at ease.

"This is just crazy. It would be easier if we just talked."

Dorian half chuckles like that's the most ludicrous idea in the world. "You see, Maverick bowing to Cain is also an admission that he's on his side and not Lucifer's. And that's done with battle and drawing blood. Without it, how can we believe him?"

"And what if he's lying?" I huff as frustration pinches along my shoulder blades. Of course, demons only settle things barbarically.

It doesn't help that my heart is trying to leap out of my chest, leaving me feeling dark and trembling.

Dorian's fingers skim under my chin, tilting my head back. I stare into his darkening eyes as he grins. Something about him is different...it's not like before, where he'd never stop me. Maybe I need to let my demons do what they have to do. Even if I don't agree with it.

It isn't Cain I'm worried about. It's finding out that perhaps Maverick has been lying this entire time and I'm about to find out the truth.

I DON'T KNOW how long Cain and Maverick have been fighting, but it feels like eternity.

The sounds of war rattling the house abruptly ends.

Without warning, Maverick comes sliding out of the haze of dust, on his back, and pauses feet away from us, bleeding and bruised. He winces as he starts to push up.

Cain leaps toward Maverick, his black wings like shadows curling in on either side of him. He lands with a thud by his brother's side. Then he moves lightning fast, and his hand strikes out gripping a blade, and presses it to Maverick's throat. Blood starts to trickle out.

My heart seizes. "Cain, no!" I choke out the desperate words.

His head snaps up, and my eyes connect with his black stare, dark veins standing out beneath his skin.

"Please, Cain," I say.

He pauses for a long moment, holding my gaze, then abruptly draws back, a heavy growl rolling past his throat. He cracks his neck and, in a heartbeat, his demon slides back into him. Clothes torn, bleeding, and his lip ripped open, but there's no pain on his face. He'll quickly heal the wounds he's gained—it's what demons do, after all—but what I find in his gaze is something else. Something that brings a flare of worry through me.

He looks down to Maverick. "Do you yield and vow allegiance to me?"

Maverick groans and pushes himself up into a sitting position and wipes blood dripping from the cut under his eye. He heaves for breath, his chest rising and falling with the strain. The silence drags, and Cain's nostrils flare with what I imagine is impatience.

"I won't ask again, Brother," he growls.

Maverick gets to his feet, and glances at me momentarily, a tiny grin at the corner of his mouth. "Yes," he finally says, looking at me, then swings his attention back to Cain. "I give my allegiance equally to you and Aria."

Confusion washes over me. To me? "What does that mean?" I murmur.

Cain huffs, his hands curling into fists.

"It's my right," Maverick states, lifting his chin.

Cain doesn't look at me but anger crosses his face.

"Fine, have it your way," Cain finally says and brushes past Maverick. He pauses in front of me, pushing a stray strand of hair from my face. "Aria, if anyone ever hurt you, including my brothers, I'd make them regret it."

I blink at him, confusion heavy in my chest. "W-what does that allegiance really mean?"

"It means I don't trust Maverick's intentions. To put it in simple terms, it also means that he considers you his superior as much as he does me."

My thoughts are spiraling out of control and too many things are happening at once. I glance over to Maverick, who watches me with a strange expression.

"Aria, I would give you the world, but when it comes to demons, every deal ends up twisted to somehow benefit them."

"Maverick, can we talk?" I ask, to which he nods.

"Elias, stay close to Aria," Cain orders, glancing over his shoulder at him, then he swings his attention back to me. His brow furrows and annoyance dances across his features. "Come down to the parlor with Maverick once you're ready."

Him and Dorian head downstairs, leaving behind an air of tension. I'm partly surprised that Cain isn't locking Maverick up, but I guess if allegiance has been given, technically Maverick is free.

Elias gives me a lopsided grin as he approaches me. His hands clasp around my waist and he leans in close, whispering in my ear, "Aria, I hold you in my heart and love every inch of your body. No matter what happens around us, you can always trust in knowing

I will be there for you, to catch you, to lift you, anything you need."

It is strange that his words make me want to cry…happy tears of course, but who would have thought demons experienced such deep emotions.

I hug him and bury my face into his chest, loving the way he smells so masculine and woodsy. "Love you too, Elias."

Maverick is clapping, which has Elias tensing. "Give me a moment, Elias."

He takes a few steps deeper into the hallway to where I can still see him.

Maverick lifts his head at my approach, and there's a glint to his eyes. If I thought Cain had been badly battered, Maverick is devastatingly so. Blood drips from the cuts across his arms and chest, from the gash over an eye, but he's not wincing or moaning from pain.

I step over the debris, noting the broken paintings and statues, and pass the chandelier that has somehow ended up half sticking out of a wall, like someone used it as a weapon.

A dark look flashes across Maverick's face, and he wipes the blood dripping down his chin.

"Why did you give me allegiance? I don't get it," I say.

He's staring at Elias over my shoulder, and I look back to find my gorgeous hellhound leaning a shoulder against the wall, arms folded over his chest and one leg crossed over the other at the ankles. His gaze never leaves us.

He gives me a sexy wink, which makes my heart flutter.

"You can trust me," Maverick says, and I turn back around to where he's running a hand through his white hair, the intensity in his eyes softening my knees. This man…this demon, is stunning. Even bleeding and beaten, he takes my breath away. Strong jawline stained by blood, scruffy and delicious, despite his frown —he's the level of handsome that would stop any girl in their tracks. "And I trust *you* to do the right thing."

"Sure, whatever that means," I murmur.

"Cain and I have never seen eye to eye, and despite me vowing my allegiance to him he'll never completely lend credence to what I have to offer. And when things go bad, I will be the first to be blamed until I can show him I am a man of my word. So, I've given you power over me to stop him from ever taking me out, should he decide to do so."

His confession surprises me. It's not what I expect from him, but it reveals how deep the distrust between these sin brothers are. And it's incredibly difficult to ignore that his true intentions no longer side with Lucifer.

"So, you're saying I have control over you now, right?" I tilt my head to the side, wanting to take control of the situation. After what he told me, the deal he made with Cain, I want to give him the benefit of the doubt and believe him.

The corners of his lips curl upward. "Does that turn you on?"

Elias clears his throat from behind me. "Are you ready to head downstairs?"

There is an edge to Maverick that has always intrigued me, aroused me. It also scares me a bit, but then again, my demons aren't exactly safe either.

Maverick lifts his head, his lips curving into a grin. "Let's go."

I find myself giving him a smile back in response. "Are you sure you don't need to be patched up or something?"

His gaze meets mine. "You want to play doctor?"

Elias is suddenly strolling alongside me, and his arm goes around my waist in a possessive gesture. My cheeks flush with warmth.

"The only playing you will do is with me," he growls, and I can't help but snicker a laugh.

Maverick mock-coughs, "Jealous-ass."

When we reach the parlor, Maverick wastes no time and strides across the room like he owns the place. He carries himself very similarly to Cain...full of bravado and arrogant confidence. Must be a sin demon thing.

"To put it simply," he begins, while the rest of us gravitate to the couch in front of the fire, "Lorcan broke into your bedroom, Brother, and took the relics. I spotted him when it was too late, rushing out of your room and mansion. I chased the bastard because you know Lorcan. He's a fucking slippery ass and fucking fast too, but he's always up to something bad."

"Lorcan is a two-faced prick," Dorian adds, then falls quiet. Seems someone's had an encounter with this demon.

"That he is," Maverick continues. "So, I chased him down to a mountain entrance that led to Hell, and like a serpent, he vanished inside."

I swallow hard at the thought that Lucifer may now have the relics. Well, not all of them as one is still outstanding, but still... We are so fucked right now.

Maverick's mouth presses into a thin line. "There is one way to find the relics quickly, but it's risky." He glances over to me, as do the others.

My stomach hardens as the realization hits me too. He's implying that I will be the one to track down the relics in Hell.

Cain roars and is on his feet. "Over my dead body. There is no fucking way Aria is going back into Hell!"

THREE

CAIN

I've been thinking long and hard about my brother's proposition and what it means for us all.

Do I trust him fully?

Absolutely not.

But I have to trust in Aria. I have to believe she's capable of protecting herself and making the right decisions.

On the other hand, Hell isn't like Earth, and during her last visit, she only got a glimpse of the insanity that lays beyond the veil. If she goes—I won't sugarcoat it—I'm terrified for her. She'll be easy pickings for Lucifer without me, Dorian, or Elias there. Even with Maverick there, he can only do so much.

And that's why I won't let her go. I can't.

But the relics...

I pace across my room, past the closed balcony doors, and glance at the two drained corpses at the foot of my bed. Ramos will be up soon to dispose of them, and although I feel more powerful after devouring their souls, I'm just as anxious and riled up as before. Nothing's changed.

I want another way to fix this. At the same time, I want to keep Aria safe, but the three of us can't pass through Hell's gate without Azrael's harp. How else are we going to get the pieces back?

My head pounds. How long have I been up here, going over the same questions and winding up with the same answers? Must be hours now. There doesn't seem to be any other way.

I'm going to have to let Aria go.

It kills me. Truly. But if Maverick is right, and it is Lorcan who snuck into our home and took the relics, well...the Demon of Envy isn't an easy one to catch. While Maverick's slippery, Lorcan's fast, and he'd be the next one on the list of demons pining for Father's attention and favor.

Rubbing the worry lines across my forehead, I sigh heavily. When will my brother learn? Lucifer doesn't care about any of them. Not a single soul in the underworld. I'm not even sure he cares for his own. He's using whatever and whoever he can to get what he wants. That's all we are to him. Pawns in his game.

Then there's Maverick. He may have pledged his allegiance to not only me, but Aria as well, but again... They could be just words. It's near impossible to know for sure.

He cares about her—I can see it whenever he's near her—but he doesn't know how to explore those feelings yet, and that's what troubles me. Any hesitance or weakness will be used by Lucifer. I need to be certain he'll protect Aria at all costs while in Hell. Whatever that takes.

I think back to the dream I had while teetering on the edge of death before Aria, the necromancer, and the others brought me back to life. Aria covered in blood, eyes black as my demons', with Lucifer's crown upon her head. What else could it mean other than her becoming queen and ruling Lucifer's kingdom? But, was it a premonition or just a fever dream? I have no idea.

And then there was the vision we all shared after I touched the foot. Us in Lucifer's throne room while I ran an angel blade through Maverick and then myself. Again—was it a flash into the future or something else? Hard to say, but it did get me thinking about how this war would end for me. Maybe for all of the sin demons.

Shaking my head, I stop and peer out the glass doors. The gray sky is darkening again outside, signaling the end to another day.

I'd been right; I've been confined to my room and my thoughts for too long.

It's about time I go and find my Aria to tell her I've thought things over and changed my mind. We need the relics, and we need her to get them.

Twisting my father's ring around my finger, I wonder if there's a way we'll all come out of this infernal war alive.

Because, if I'm being honest with myself—truly honest—I'd have to say I doubt it very much.

ARIA

That discussion didn't go over too well.

Cain is absolutely against me returning to Hell.

To make matters worse, Dorian and Elias were soon to follow.

"You go," Dorian snaps at Maverick, crossing his arms over his broad chest. "I think it'll be an excellent way to prove your loyalty to us. Go and bring the relics back."

"If it was that easy, I would've done it already, don't you think?" Maverick scoffs. "I can't believe I'm saying this, but I need Aria's magic pinky toe to sniff them out."

"No." One word, but the way Cain says it makes it slice through the room like the swing of a sword. A final blow.

"Do you have any other ideas? How else are we supposed—"

"NO." This time, Cain's demon emerges to really drive it home, voice deepening and black veins crawling from his eyes and all. Maverick clamps his mouth shut, and that was the end of the conversation.

But as we dispersed and went on with our day, I couldn't help but think about what Maverick was proposing.

Go back to Hell. Me? Right into the lion's den where the lion was waiting to eat me, or in this metaphor, Lucifer? Just thinking about it scares the shit out of me, but I also think he's right. Since Cain, Dorian, and Elias are still banned and unable to use the gate, that only leaves Maverick and me to get the relics. There's no other way to get the demons into Hell to take down Lucifer. They are stuck on Earth without them.

How am I going to tell Cain that, though? He's made up his mind, and there seems to be no changing it.

Maybe I just need to let him stew for a bit. Let it rest and then revisit it later, once he's calmed down. But privately, with just me and him. That way his malice towards Maverick won't leak into his decision.

In the meantime, I want to know more. More about me and Sayah and what lies ahead for the both of us.

What is a Leviathan exactly, and what does it mean for me, since I'm living with one inside me? Now that it seems I'm learning how to control Sayah and use her power to my advantage, I want to make sure it won't be short-lived. I can't have her taking over again and wreaking havoc. I have to stay in control.

And that means I have to do some research.

I head to the library.

Yes, I know Cain already devoured every possible book in this place looking for an answer to the mystery of what I am, but that was back when Sayah didn't have an identity. Now she does.

But, as I spend hours combing the shelves, I quickly discover that Cain was also right about another thing—Leviathans are ancient creatures without many records. The only thing I can manage to find is, ironically, in a Bible Cain keeps on a shelf in his office.

A demon with a Bible? The irony is just too much. Shouldn't it burst into flames or something? Should *I* for touching it? I don't know how this works.

Sitting at Cain's desk, I plop the thick book down and sit at his chair. The last time I was here, I'd snuck in to search for information about the hospital where I was born, only to be found by Cain and *taught a lesson* in the best kind of way. That felt like years ago, not weeks. It's crazy to believe how different we both were then. And how different we are now...

All I wanted to do was leave and have my shitty life back with Joseline. And now, I couldn't imagine a day without my three demons.

Opening the thick cover, I start to comb through the pages blindly. I'm lucky it's in English and not Latin, but the words are so small and I really don't feel like reading through all of this which I'm just skimming rather than concentrating like I should. I do this for a while, turning a page, glancing over the small print, then going to the next. Until I spot the word I'm looking for in the center of the page.

Leviathan.

Bingo.

Stopping, I lean forward and lick my lips. Here we go.

I read—really read this time—the sentence.

In that day the Lord will punish Leviathan the fleeing serpent,
With His fierce and great and mighty sword,
Even Leviathan the twisted serpent;
And He will kill the dragon who lives in the sea.

Well, fuck. That's not what I want to see.

Fierce and great and mighty sword?

I think of the angel blade Gabriel wants to run through my gut and swallow hard. That part may be a little true, but fleeing serpent? Sea dragon? I don't think so. Whoever wrote this thought a Leviathan was a big fish or something. Living with Sayah my entire life, I can tell them firsthand that's not even close. A powerful shadowy ghost thingy, yeah, but no Loch Ness Monster here.

I already met one of those and he's in Scotland. Where he should be.

I flip through a few more pages, seeing no more references to the word I need, and sigh. As I shut the book, I look up to see Cain standing in the doorway, leaning his shoulder against the frame in the most casual way—for him, at least—a smirk playing across his lips.

"At it again, I see," he says, and I can tell by the lustful gleam in his eye that he's thinking back to our sexcapade in this office, on his desk, and against the window. Just like I was.

"Just trying to cover all my bases." I pick up the Bible to show him. "Why do you even have this in here? You're a demon."

"I am aware," he replies and walks over to the desk. "But it's also a part of our history, too."

I'm not sure I'm buying that one. It must show on my face because he follows up with, "You ever hear the saying, 'know thy enemy'?"

"Come on."

He chuckles. "Would you believe that I read it for entertainment, then?"

"Now that I believe," I say.

He picks up the massive book with one hand and holds it up to examine it. "I'll never understand why so many people worship a book written by a few dirty old men who knew nothing about God or Heaven or Hell. Just stories."

"Like fanfiction."

He glances at me, confused. "Fanfiction?"

"You don't know what fanfiction is?" I ask.

He shakes his head.

"Of course you don't." A centuries old demon knowing what character shipping or slash fiction is? I should've known better. "Maybe I'll explain it another day."

But he's unsatisfied with that answer. "Is it when people make up stories for their own amusement?"

Okay... Maybe he did understand. "And those stories become more popular than the original. Yep."

"Ah, then yes. You're right. This is like fanfiction." He tosses the book back onto the desk. "Useless really."

"I was just hoping I could find something else about...about me."

He holds out his hand, and I find myself reaching for it without a second thought. He guides me around the desk and brings my hand to his lips for a sweet kiss.

"Aria, my love, what else do you want to know?" His voice is as tender as his lips.

I blink, a bit dumbstruck by his sudden shift in demeanor. Especially when the last time I'd seen him, he was fuming just at the idea of me returning to Hell with Maverick.

"I...uh... Well, you know. Just what being a Leviathan really means? What can I expect?"

"You've lived with Sayah inside you for your entire life. I don't think anyone knows more about what you are than you do," he replies and stares deeply into my eyes.

Heat crawls across my face. How can this demon still make me blush like a schoolgirl from a single look? I don't understand it.

"You know she has a mind of her own. And if I'm not careful—"

He runs his hands along my arms and draws me in closer. "I don't want you to think like that, Aria. You showed that you're fully capable of controlling Sayah during our fights with the hell-hounds and the Nightwalkers. It's as if you both aren't two enti-ties, but one. Someone just needs to take the lead, and when you do, you're stronger than any of us combined. Stronger than Gabriel. Even Lucifer."

"Let's not get ahead of ourselves," I tsk.

His serious facade cracks as another smile peeks through. "I saw it for myself."

As I peer up at his handsome face, I see nothing but his admiration and love reflecting back at me, and my chest warms. God, I love this man—this demon. There's no other way for me to describe it other than love.

"You know, you're starting to sound a lot like your brother," I tease but immediately regret it because the change in his posture is sudden and drastic. His muscles stiffen, his eyes flash a shade darker, and his hands fall away from me.

Ah, shit. Why did I have to mention Maverick?

I want to kick myself for being so stupid.

Read the room, Aria. Geez.

When I try to step toward him, he shifts back, his lips pressing into a hard line.

Then he does something else unexpected. He slides off his ring, the one with the dark red—practically black—stone from his father, and holds it out for me to take. I only stare at it in confusion.

"What do you want me to do with this?" I ask.

He holds it up high, pinched between his two fingers. "It's for you to wear."

Instinctively, my hand shoots to the necklace he'd given me at the beginning of this hell-of-a-relationship with his signature emblem. A single wing. I still wear it everyday.

"You already gave me this," I tell him.

Cain grabs my wrist, presses the ring into my palm, and closes my fingers around it.

"But I can't take that from you. It's... It's..." I stammer.

His gaze bores into mine. "You're going to need it."

"I don't under—" But then it clicks, and I look up at him in disbelief. "Wait."

He nods. "As much as it kills me to say this, Maverick was right. You have to go back to Hell with him and retrieve the relics. And I..." He sighs heavily. "I have to let you go."

I don't know why, but those few words make my heart clench.

Why? Because I know Cain, and I know this wasn't an easy decision for him. I wouldn't be surprised to find out that he'd agonized over it, obsessed over it, all night and day. From the moment Maverick had returned.

A part of me wonders if what he's saying has another meaning, too. About giving me more freedom and letting go.

"Like Maverick's, it'll help you cross over," he goes on, and I can't help but notice the hint of sadness in his tone. "It should keep your soul safe while you are there, but that means keeping it on always. No matter what anyone tells you, you must keep it on. If you remove it, even for a second, you will be lost to us forever."

I remember from last time, but it still makes me shiver. He wants the warning to sink in. "Don't worry. It'll stay on me the entire time I'm there. It'll be like you're with me."

"Good." The small smile is back. The one that makes my heart flutter. "If it were up to me, I'd always be with you."

Hell, I love when he says stuff like that. It gives me goosebumps; I don't know why. Maybe because he rarely expresses himself like this.

I slip the ring onto my finger. It's heavier than Maverick's and takes up more space, but it's Cain's and I love it for that reason alone. When I hold it up, the dark stone catches the light and gives me a peek at his blood red center.

"It's no engagement ring, but it'll do." I chuckle.

His brow arches. "Engagement ring?"

Ah, shit. Probably shouldn't have said that.

"It was a joke," I say, swatting away his question.

"Would you...want an engagement ring?" he asks, which throws me for a loop.

"What? No! Well, I don't know. Maybe someday." I'm babbling, of course. "The binding ritual was hard enough for me to agree to. I never really thought about marriage or anything like that before. Not with my shitty life growing up. I rarely had a steady boyfriend, let alone..." I pause, my words trailing off as I look up at him. He's watching me intently again, taking in my every word.

"Three demons."

"Uh...yeah. That."

"I see," he says.

"Not saying that's a bad thing," I quickly recover, "because it's not. Not at all. I'm all for being with whoever makes a person the happiest. No judgment here."

"I'll have to remember that."

Rubbing my lips together, I glance away, a bit embarrassed I even confessed such a thing.

Silence stretches between us as we're both lost in our own thoughts but, after a while, Cain slides his hand in mine, his finger finding the ring right away. He rubs the stone.

"A ring here does look good on you," he muses, and I blush. "I can always respect ritual and tradition, and if I remember correctly, a human marriage is supposed to end in a very specific way."

Oh, I think I know where this is going, but I ask the question anyway. "And what's that?"

His eyes darken a shade. "Consummation."

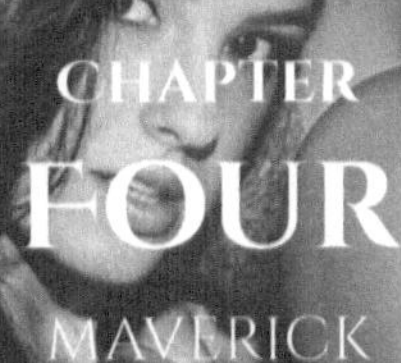

CHAPTER
FOUR

MAVERICK

I have no idea what I'm doing here, or why Cain insisted I come to Dorian's bedroom.

As expected, the place reeks of sex, sweat, and who knows what else. It makes me gag just thinking about what vile things happened on this very couch I'm sitting on—why is it so sticky?

Fuck, the demon's disgusting.

Across from the large party-size bed, there's a rack of *toys*, if you know what I mean. Whips, ropes, chains, handcuffs, straps, paddles, feathers, *appendages*.

My eyes widen. I know we all have our kinks, and Dorian's power thrives off pleasure, but damn. The guy needs a hobby.

I really shouldn't talk though. My sexual needs are...a bit on the dark side. But at least I clean up after myself.

But what I still don't understand is why I'm here. What game are my brother, Dorian, and Elias playing at? Especially after the incident with Lorcan and the relics, I doubt they trust me fully. No matter how many times I swear allegiance to Cain or promise my commitment to their cause, it doesn't seem to be enough, so what-ever this foolishness is, I hope it's the last thing I have to do.

The door opens and the three demons plus Aria walk in. Her large dark eyes find me immediately, and I can't help the smirk curling the corner of my lips. She quickly glances away, back to Cain, who is guiding her to Dorian's bed with their linked hands.

His claims about loving Aria float back to me, and I clench my teeth. I don't know why it annoys me so much that the idiot thinks he's been struck by Cupid's arrow, but it does.

"So?" I start, that annoyance leaking into my tone. "What's this all about?"

Dorian smiles wickedly, like he's holding some secret he can't wait for me to figure out, because he knows I'll hate the answer. He and Elias stand on opposite sides of the massive bed and start taking off their clothes.

What the fuck?

Aria seems just as confused. "Uh, Cain. What's going on?"

"Do you remember us talking about humans and their wedding rituals?" he explains.

She nods. "The wedding night."

"Consummation. Yes."

She glances at the bed, at Dorian and Elias, who are both now naked, and then me. "Wait, now?" Her voice rises with nervousness. "But Maverick—"

Cain pulls her into him and crushes his mouth against hers in a possessive kiss. My insides twist into a tight knot as Aria melts against him, instantly lost to his hunger for her, his desire.

He breaks away for only a second to whisper against her lips, "If my brother wants to be a part of this cause, then he is going to have to know his place."

He's challenging me. I see it now.

That's what this is. A power move.

The three of them plan to fuck Aria and make me watch so it's clear who she belongs to and to make sure I know that she's off limits.

The fucking bastard.

Anger spikes. I already promised my loyalty to him. I don't need to be here for this and be humiliated.

I push to my feet. "This is fucking stupid," I bite out. "There's no way I'm sitting here while you...while you..."

"Ah, but you don't have a choice," Dorian interjects.

"You leave, you're deemed the enemy," Elias adds, and his hard gaze lights with murderous intentions. "Which means, all bets are off."

Meaning, they plan to kill me.

A quick look at Aria proves that she's unsure about this, too, but I'm not one to fold from a threat. If my brother wants to play his stupid games, fine. I'll play. I'm tired of being seen as a lesser demon because of my age or rank.

It's just sex.

If they want to fuck her, go for it. Fuck her. I don't give a shit.

Unlike them, she means nothing to me. I'm a demon—not some love-drunk fool. Never will be.

I drop back on the couch and make sure to look as bored as possible. "Let's make this quick, then. We got shit to do."

Cain touches Aria's chin, turning her head so that he can resume kissing her. His tongue sweeps into her mouth, and when his hands start to peel away her clothes, she lets him without hesitation.

It's like she's hypnotized by him. Entranced. And it isn't long before she's standing there in just thin black-lace panties with her creamy breasts on full display. His fingers tangle in her hair and wrench her head back, and she groans from the pleasure and pain.

I know all too well how much she loves pain. I got to see a taste of it myself a few times, especially during our little knife fight in the basement. The cuts, the taste of her blood on my tongue... Like me, pain turns her on.

As she slowly gets to her knees, Cain's fingers stay locked in her hair, holding her in place. Face to the stiff bulge in his pants, she licks her lips and my own body tenses, knowing exactly what's going to happen next. My own cock twitches, and I curse myself for feeling anything but disgust or indifference.

She undoes his belt and tugs his pants down. When his dick springs free, she grabs it eagerly and presses her lips to its hardened tip. Her tongue swirls around it, her eyes lifted the entire time to Cain's, who watches her with a mixture of admiration and starvation. Using his hold in her hair, he pushes her down more so that his cock disappears past her lips.

She takes it all without hesitation, squeezing his balls at the same time. And when he yanks her off, saliva drips from the side of her mouth.

Holy fuck, that's hot.

He does it again, pushing her mouth down, all the way to the base. This time, he tilts his hips, and I can see a bulge growing at the center of her throat. That makes her gag, and Cain jerks her off him just as fast but she pouts, wanting more.

My pulse speeds up, and to my own surprise, my demon stirs. It wants out. More importantly, it wants to be in Cain's place, fucking her throat, making her plead for me to do it harder.

Without waiting for permission, Aria leans forward and takes him back into her mouth, devouring him. Her head bobs, her tongue lapping at him, the sound of her sucking and slurping filling the room. Cain's head rolls back, his ecstasy clear, while Elias and Dorian both watch everything unfold from the sidelines, palming their own dicks and patiently waiting their turns.

Itching to touch myself, too, I clench my fists against my thighs.

Again, Cain yanks Aria off him, but then he forces her head in my direction. Our eyes lock, and sweat starts to slide down my back. She's so incredibly sexy on her knees, lips parted and breasts out, her eyes hooded with lust.

"How do I taste, my love?" Cain asks, his voice husky with need.

Eyes still glued to mine, she whimpers and the sound sends shockwaves straight to my cock. I'm so hard now, sitting is uncomfortable. But I do my best to keep how much this is affecting me off my expression.

"Tell my brother how much you love it when I fuck your throat, Aria," he says.

"I do," she pants. Her breasts swing with every movement. "I love it."

I can see that.

"Do you want more?" he presses and glances at me, gauging my reaction. He's testing me. He's trying to rile me up and see if I walk out, but I won't let that happen.

She nods her answer.

"Beg for it," he commands.

Still looking at me, she says, "Please... Cain." She swallows roughly. "Fuck my throat."

He answers her by grabbing her under her arms, lifting her off her feet, and throwing her onto the bed. Like wild animals, Elias and Dorian take that as their cue and descend on her. Dorian flops onto his back, upside down, and pulls her body over his.

A quick snap and her panties are torn off and tossed away. Like a ravenous beast, he starts to devour her pussy, making her cry out. Elias moves toward her rear, spitting on his hand like a savage, and lubing himself up with it. He then presses his two fingers into her ass crack, and she gasps.

Lifting his shirt over his head, Cain takes his place in front of her, his cock at full attention and positioned right in front of her mouth.

She peers up at him through long, dark lashes, and he runs a finger up her throat to her chin. A smirk lifts his lips. "My sweet, sweet Aria," he whispers. "I don't think he heard you. Say it again. Louder."

She's panting now, her back arching as Dorian grips her legs and sucks on her clit. The hellhound continues to finger her while stroking himself.

She's close to coming. I can tell. And my jealousy and arousal are starting to outweigh my need to win this challenge of Cain's. Even more, I hate that it's even affecting me at all. It shouldn't be, but no matter how many times I tell myself that, I can't ignore the raw desire spinning inside me.

My hand slides to the erection straining against my jeans. I begin to rub myself, imagining myself getting ready to fuck her tight little pussy. Or that delectable mouth of hers. I want to hear *my* name on her lips. Hear her beg for *me* to give her what she craves.

"I... I..." She can barely get the words out. When Elias removes his fingers and rubs the tip of his length along her crack instead, she moans, "Oh fuck."

"Come on, Aria," Cain coaxes. "Say it. Look at Maverick and say it."

Her dreamy gaze flicks my way again. In that moment, so lost and free of any fear or worry, she's the most beautiful woman I've ever seen. My heart thunders, and I stroke myself even faster through the tight fabric, loving the way the friction burns.

"Fuck me…" she says in a weak voice. Since she's looking at me on Cain's orders, it's almost as if I'm the one she's speaking to, and just the thought has me holding my breath. "Fuck me, please."

Fucking shit. I don't think I can do this.

It takes all my strength not to leap to my feet, shove one of them out of the way, and take their place.

As if working in perfect sync with each other, Cain, Dorian, and Elias readjust themselves and do exactly what she asked for. Elias stands on his tiptoes and pushes into her tight ass, groaning, while Dorian continues to eat her out. Slurping. Sucking. Until she's screaming.

Every time Elias rams into her from behind, she's thrown forward. Cain takes the opportunity to hold her head with two hands and thrust himself deeper into her mouth. They all fuck her mercilessly, and she takes it all, moaning loudly.

I feel my own body tensing, getting closer to release. It's not the real thing, but my imagination is doing a hell of a job by itself.

Cain pulls back for a moment, and without missing a beat, her head drops to Dorian's erection, taking him into her mouth and tasting him from base to tip.

"Ssssshit," he hisses, clearly not expecting it.

Cain steps away, letting his friends have their moment—Elias speeding up so that her ass slaps against him with every thrust. Aria uses both her hands and her mouth on Dorian beneath her, pumping, licking, teasing.

Suddenly, Aria cries out, her entire body tensing as the orgasm explodes through her. Dorian reaches down and keeps her head in place, thrusting his hips up to fuck her mouth through it, and she lets his cock mute her screams. He lets out one last thrust and grunt with his own release, before sagging into the mattress, and simultaneously Elias slams into her two more times to flood her with his seed.

This time, when Cain steps forward, his demon is released. Huge leathery wings tucked into his back, marble-like skin lined with dark veins, and inky black eyes. A figure of power and darkness, he steps closer to the bed. Dorian and Elias move away to give him space.

Another power move. By bringing forth his demon and taking

her like this, he's saying he's the strongest. The one in charge. In hellhound terms, the alpha.

He might not want to hear it, but it's a very Lucifer thing to do.

With a confidant strut, he walks around the bed, grabs Aria by the ankles, and rolls her onto her back. Then he crawls over her, his wings and her legs spreading wide.

Without warning or mercy, he thrusts into her. Hard. The entire bed shakes and the headboard slams against the wall.

Boom.

My demon rears up again, and jealousy replaces all the earlier desire, followed by fury. My spine prickles as my own wings push against my skin, wanting to tear through.

I don't know why, but seeing him fuck her to oblivion as his demon hits me harder than watching it in his human form.

Maybe because, like he's said before, there's something more to this than sex. He *loves* her, and she loves him for what he truly is.

And he wants me to see that.

He rams into her again.

Boom goes the headboard against the wall.

She cries out.

I can't stand it. I can't even look. My gaze drops to the floor, but I can hear it—the crash of the headboard every time he thrusts.

Boom. Boom. Boom.

Faster. Faster.

Plaster falls from the new hole quickly forming in the wall.

I'm getting flashbacks of hearing similar sounds from above the rafters and the dust raining down on me when I was in the basement, which only fuels my anger.

Boom. Boom.

"Fuck, Cain! Fuck!"

I jump to my feet. Every inch of me is shaking with rage, and if I don't leave now I may do something even worse. Something I'd regret that could ruin everything.

Fuck this. I really don't care if Elias hunts me down and kills me, at this point. I'm out.

Heading straight for the door, I refuse to look back. I'm sure Cain, Dorian, and Elias are loving my weakness.

Even when I slam the door shut behind me, I can hear the thudding of the bed against the wall. Mocking me. Calling me out.

As I trudge down the hall, I'm surprised neither Elias or Dorian come after me to drag me back.

I guess there's no need. Cain has gotten what he wants in the end... For me to obey and learn my place among their demon trio.

Which is at the bottom.

The same ranking I was in Hell.

Problem is, it's not where I fucking want to be.

ARIA

THIS IS IT. The moment I've dreaded since I escaped Hell's fiery clutches last time.

I swore I'd never go back, yet here I am, standing at the base of the mountain that is supposed to be a hidden gate to Hell, holding a flashlight in the dark.

Cain, Dorian, and Elias stand behind me, the collective tension between them pulsing through our invisible link. It only heightens my anxiety, too. It also reminds me that while Maverick and I are in Hell, I'll lose contact with my demons, even with the bond between us. The magic is too weak to reach across the planes, and that's worrisome in itself.

Not like they would be able to come down and rescue me if I was in trouble anyway. But still...

I guess I am just going to have to rely on Maverick.

Speak of the devil—or one of his sons, I should say—Maverick steps up to my side and rolls his shoulders and neck like he's about to head into a fight. And maybe we are. I don't know.

"Have the ring on?" he asks, glancing at my crossed arms that I have wrapped across my chest to keep out the cold. It has to be below thirty degrees and there's snow on the ground, but I'm only in leggings and a sweater, and he's in jeans and a button-down. Definitely not dressed for this weather.

I pull out my hand to show him Cain's ring on my finger. "Got it."

"I don't have to tell you to never take it off, right."

I narrow my eyes at him, feeling so tense I might burst. "I know the deal."

"Good. Because I won't have Cain skinning me alive because you decided to be stupid and got your soul lost forever."

I clench my teeth. Maverick has a knack for getting under your skin, and it seems I am no exception. It's no wonder Elias wants to punch him in the face ninety-nine percent of the time.

"Maverick." Cain's voice rumbles across the darkness, but the warning rings clear in his tone.

"Yeah, yeah. I know."

I don't understand where all this attitude came from. He seemed to be enjoying himself quite a bit during Cain, Dorian, Elias, and my group session last night. Well, in the beginning. The next time I was able to glance over, he looked miffed. And then when we had... you know, finished, he'd stormed out. I guess he wasn't happy watching me with the three demons.

"You are to go to Hell, retrieve the relics from Lorcan, and come back. Nothing more. But Aria is always—"

"My first priority," he sing-songs as if Cain's repeated this very phrase to him a million times. "Don't worry your pretty little head about it, big Brother. She'll be safe with me."

Dorian and Elias exchange looks that say they still aren't so sure about this arrangement. I'm not so sure about it either.

Without warning, Maverick snatches my left hand and tugs me toward the mountain's rocky face. My pulse races, and I glance over my shoulder at my three demons standing in front of Dorian's Ferrari, the bright headlights casting them in shadows. Despite that, I can still see the worry and fear etched on each of their faces. Especially Cain's. He's wound so tight, he looks like he might just leap forward, seize me, and wrench me back to them after changing his mind.

Part of me wishes he would, but he doesn't. He only stares at me, lips pressed into a thin line, the internal war he's fighting clear in his eyes.

I don't want to leave them.

I hope to god I'm coming back.

At that moment, Maverick and I pass through the rock, the mountain swallowing us whole and engulfing us in blackness. I lose sight of everything, and the air becomes so thick, I can barely take another breath.

I lose sense of Maverick's touch, even though I can vaguely feel him tugging me along, but it's like we're moving through sludge. Slowly. Agonizingly so. And I wonder if we'll ever get to the other side.

It feels like forever but eventually the immense pressure eases and I can feel Maverick's firm grip on my hand again. The darkness gives way to a blaze of colors, making me squint.

Then comes the heat.

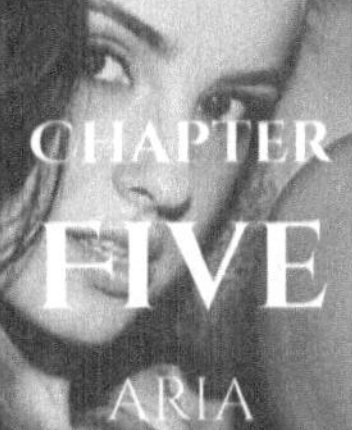

An oppressive heat bears down on me like someone's smothering me in a woolly blanket. How can it be so hot in a place with no sun, where there is permanent cloud cover?

But with the way my feet overheat with each step, I have my answer. It's coming from underground, like we're walking on a blazing fire that roars beneath us.

Maverick and I are moving quickly down a dingy alleyway between two buildings made of black stone. Something drips sluggishly down their surface, and because of the sulfur stench in the air it reeks. I don't want to know what the gooey stuff collecting in puddles on the sidewalk is.

"Where are we exactly in Hell?" I ask, feeling I have to keep my voice down to not attract attention.

"Outskirts of the city," he replies, not giving me more. Someone's still in a pissy mood. I glance behind us to where we'd been spat out after entering Hell from the gates. At the end of the alley lies an adjacent road peppered with trees, though I'm not sure if they can be called that. They have no leaves, the branches are gnarly, and even the ground looks like it's been scorched by flames.

We pause at the corner as Maverick peeks out on either side. I turn Cain's ring on my finger over and over, partially terrified that it's not going to mask my human side from the demonic beasts living here. The metal feels cool against my fingers despite me perspiring.

"All clear," Maverick mutters and turns around. "We're heading to Lorcan's place, and I'm hoping you can detect if the relics are anywhere near without us having to go inside."

He takes my wrist and hauls me alongside him roughly, then we're moving out from the alleyway.

"Hey." I tug my arm back. "Not so rough."

His hand loops around my waist and pulls me against him instead.

I cut him a glare.

"Relax," he whispers, which only makes me elbow him in the ribs. But his grip is like iron, and he turns on me swiftly, towering over me, and I can swear his eyes are darkening. "Listen, Aria. My brother's ring can only protect you so much. But you don't exactly look like you belong here with your deer-in-the-headlights look. I mean, I should have given you some scratches or something. Maybe take off your shirt so you look the part of my whore."

My mouth falls open with utter shock as a wicked grin spreads over his lips. "Over my dead body."

"We need to play the part. It's just a few gropes between us."

I'm not sure if I want to laugh at him or slap him. He's definitely enjoying this and making the most of it by being the ultimate asshole. "Well, let's make one thing straight. I am not taking my top off for any demons."

"Oh yeah? You didn't really follow that rule before in Dorian's room."

My face flames. What a freaking prick!

"How about I'm the one whoring you out? I prefer that role-play," I suggest.

He barks a laugh, throwing his head back like that would never happen, which infuriates me further.

"Okay, stop cackling like a hyena."

"You forget one little detail, Aria. Everyone knows me down here, and the Greed Demon is *not* a prostitute."

I grind my teeth. "Fine, I'll play the damn part, but let's just get this shit done fast."

"Eager, huh?" He laughs again.

I exhale, trying to ignore my rapidly growing irritation, then glance around to see where we are. It's an empty street lined with black stone buildings, each dilapidated with broken windows, some sporting holes in the walls, and one is even covered in that transparent goo. But considering a woman—who could have just walked out of *The Grudge* movie—steps out of a front door and is holding hands with a miniature version of the kraken, well, I'm guessing this is a residential part of town.

"Let's move," Maverick growls under his breath, his hand slapping my ass, grabbing it, and not letting go. I'm plastered to his side regardless.

"You're a real dickhead today," I hiss under my breath.

"Only today?"

Thankfully we're on the opposite sidewalk of the terrifying woman and her child, but they're watching us like they'll fly in our direction and rip my face off any second.

I try to keep my head low as we hurry down the street. Once we pass them, I glance back to find the little kid staring at me. He knows something is up.

"See, that wasn't so bad," Maverick says as he turns me down the next street which has more homes, but right at the end stands a tremendous castle. Not even sure I can call it that.

It's like a medieval cathedral with a pointy tower so lofty, it might very well be touching the clouds. It's made of black and gray stone, dark windows, and surprisingly the front yard is perfectly cared for. A long driveway with manicured shrubs in the front. They're trimmed in the shape of... I squint to get a better look. Yep, I'm right. It's people being tortured, one looks like a person on their knees with their head by their side, another is lying on a bed of spikes.

Just lovely!

"I'm getting major Freddy Kruger and Edward Scissorhands vibes here," I mumble.

"Who are they? Kings from your land? Exes?"

I almost choke on my next breath. "Ha, no! They are fictional characters from old movies that my friend and I would watch growing up."

"The witch," he answers, and I nod.

"Yeah, the one who you tried to steal the soul from."

"Hey, I ripped up that contract."

True. "*Anyway,* what I was trying to say is that those movies have this same Gothic, creepy feel to them too."

"Good, then you're familiar. This should feel like home." He drags me forward by my arm.

We power-walk the rest of the way. I catch the movement of curtains in the homes we pass, the crack of doors.

Upon reaching the building, I'm still utterly mesmerized by this weird-ass castle. "So, Lorcan lives here, you say?"

"Can't you see the lofty tower? That screams insecurity. The prick had to make sure his house was the tallest in the land. One time, Valdim started building a worshipping church—as he called it—with the intention to make it taller than Lorcan's. It mysteriously burned down two days later."

"So, which sin demon is Valdim again?"

"Gluttony."

I nod, remembering. "There's definitely no love lost between all the brothers."

Maverick shrugs and guides me outside the edge of the home, keeping the broken fence between us and the castle. "It's how Father brought us up. He's always encouraged hatred and competition between us."

"Yeah, but if you got along, you might all turn on him. It makes sense. Have you guys fight each other instead. It makes you weaker."

He stares at me, impressed. "Exactly."

We quickly march past the house, hoping we can get the relics and the heck out of here. On our walk, I'm finding more of those disturbing shrubs around the lawn.

"Feel anything with your toe?" Maverick asks.

"Not a thing."

His mouth thins, and he yanks me forward again. We circle the entire building, which turns out to be not as big as I first thought.

And aside from sweating in my shoes, my toes don't react at all.

When I shake my head at Maverick, he sighs. "Well that fucking sucks. Maybe we should go inside?"

"If I can't feel it here, then I doubt the relics are here."

He looks over at the house again. "Fuck. This was meant to be a fast job. In and out, then you're back with your precious Cain."

Of course he'd bring up Cain again. The sibling rivalry between these two is getting annoying fast.

"Oh, sorry to disappoint," I begin. "Trust me, this is the last place I want to be stuck with you."

He ignores me.

"So, where would a jealous prick hide his stash?" I ask, staring at Lorcan's castle.

"Good question," he replies.

"Would he give them to Lucifer, you think?"

"Maybe, but I doubt it. He won't hand them over until he's sure it's going to benefit him majorly, so he'll be assessing all his options first."

"So, then what? We trail through Hell until my toe reacts?"

"That's our backup plan. For now, let's go to my place. I need to get you dressed in something more suitable that won't attract unwanted attention, then we might pay Lorcan's lover a visit. He tells him everything."

MAVERICK

"THE DARK DECOR is an interesting touch. I thought it was just your bedroom, but you've gone with the theme all over your house," Aria says, turning on the spot, and taking in the third dining room. I have six of them, but this one has always been my favorite, which may be due to the arched windows that look out on the Scorched Woods. I don't have many windows through the rest of the house; I like to keep my privacy from my family, but sometimes even I crave light.

Aria walks along the dark stone walls, circling the room. Part of me wishes she'd stop talking. I'm still fuming after watching her with Cain and his two demon nitwits. It shouldn't fuck with my head as much as it does, but each time I remember the scene, it's like poison bleeding into every fiber of my being.

I hate that Aria has made me care when I shouldn't give a fuck.

She pauses in front of a painting above the fireplace and draws my attention. "What's this about?"

I glance up at the image of me riding a two headed fire-breathing horse. I frown, as I unfortunately remember the day too easily.

"Get on the fucking fire-horse," Father bellows, even though I'm standing right next to him, so now my ears are ringing with his voice. I can smell the whiskey on his breath, fury vibrating through his body, and he's clenching his fists.

One of the maids had once told me that parents were meant to protect, love, and cherish you. Of course, she had been a recently dead human forced into labor for Lucifer, but her words have always stuck with me. For a long time, I waited for Father to treat me that way, but when all I received were beatings and ridicule, I learned quickly that the maid's words were a delusion.

Demons like me don't get happy endings. We receive endless punishment for merely existing.

The animal neighs, shaking its heads and digging the acrid ground with its front hoof. It gives a sudden snort and flames shoot from its nostrils.

I flinch back but Father shoves me forward. "Don't you dare embarrass me. Grow some fucking balls."

I pause within striking range of the animal's flames and turn on Father. "Why the fuck do I need to take an image with this thing? They spit poison and hate being ridden."

"And you, my son, need to change your reputation from a weak-ass sin demon, to one everyone will be terrified of."

I blink at him, my entire body tensing while rage burns through me. I loathe everything about him, and how all he cares about is others' perception of him.

"Now, get on that fucking horse and look like you've conquered the beast for the painting. Or I'll get the thing to burn the flesh off your bones over and over until you do as I say."

And that's the truth right there, isn't it? At the core, Father only cares about how I make him look. At the end of the day, he never cares about me.

He waves for his marble soldiers to come for me, and the horse rears up in their presence, hating them. The scorching heat of the animal's fire strikes my back, and I start bellowing. Then my world goes dark.

I exhale loudly, driving the memory away. The only reason I keep the hellish painting is as a reminder of who Father is and the devil I'm dealing with. To never become complacent around him or believe he'll ever have my back. No matter his promises, he's a snake.

Aria's by the long mahogany table now, staring at the bowl filled with black grapes. "They're edible," I tell her.

She laughs. "You think I was born yesterday? There's no way I'm trusting anything in Hell."

She's smart then. She shouldn't trust anything Hell-made. Including me.

"They are probably the equivalent of the pomegranate seeds that got Persephone stuck with Hades in the myths," she adds.

"You know that stuff's not real?"

She shrugs. "And for a long time, I had no idea Sin Demons or Archangels or Leviathans existed, but here we are."

A loud bang at the window sounds and she jumps in fright. Growling under my breath, I turn and wonder what the fuck it is.

All manner of creatures roam these woods, but surprisingly, the person standing outside my window is my brother, Nix. A different kind of psycho.

I roll my eyes. "Go home," I yell at him, unsure if he can even hear me. "No one wants you here."

He's nodding and pointing at the only secret entry that I have that I was stupid enough to show him on a drunken night. It was meant to be used as an escape route if anyone decided to ambush me in my own home, cloaked by magic, but now he thinks he can use it to pop over whenever he wants.

He marches in that direction.

"Shit, he's coming in here?" Aria murmurs.

My shoulders tense. "Looks like it."

Maybe it won't be all bad. Nix is known to be one nosey SOB, and usually knows all the gossip in Hell. He might know where Lorcan has been stashing things lately.

Aria nervously licks her lips as she stands behind one of the tall black chairs.

Nix struts into the room, his long dark hair fluttering over his shoulders, those sharp eyes finding Aria instantly. He's dressed in a black double-breasted jacket with glinting red buttons that run from his throat to his waist.

His tongue flicks over the small smudge of blood at the corner of his mouth and he smiles wickedly. Looks like he's just come in from a grand feast. Maybe with Father.

Nix never misses the opportunity to stick his nose in my business—or anyone's business for that matter. Father's no different.

"Oh, Brother. Why do you never tell me when you're having fun so I can join?" He purrs for effect and drifts to the opposite side of the table from Aria. "Hello again, beautiful, mysterious human. Or do we have a better name now for what you are?"

"Hey to you too, demon," she responds cheekily.

"What do you want, Nix?" I growl, my patience thinning by the second.

He swings in my direction and rubs his fingers along his baby-smooth jawline. "You've been gone for so long, is all. I've missed you."

I snort. "Liar. Why are you sneaking around my home?"

He grabs one of the chairs from the table and flops down before crossing one leg, placing his ankle across his thigh. "You're the one who's been gone all this time. Playing house with Cain and his…" He glances at Aria and reevaluates his next word. "*Plaything*. And now you're suddenly back. Call me curious."

"You're a drama queen."

"Yes, I am. I'll admit that. But how else is one supposed to occupy his time? Torturing, hunting, and fucking can only satisfy me so much." He clicks his tongue. "Besides, what I really want to know is what is *she* doing back here? A human with a soul returning to Hell? Is the place really growing on you, sweetheart?"

Aria rolls her eyes.

"We have a job to do," I say, and hope that'll be enough to quench his thirst for information. Of course, it doesn't.

He leans forward, hands on the table, eager for me to go on. "A job, you say? For Cain?"

"For us all. Will you just drop it?"

"Does that include me as well?" he asks, genuinely interested now. "Have you discovered something helpful in Lucifer's diary?"

Ah, shit. I had forgotten I'd agreed to tell him what was in the thing after we'd translated it as payment for getting me out of Cain's demon trap.

"Yes and no," I say vaguely. "The diary was useless. Only

contained the scribbled descriptions of creatures he suspected Aria to be."

His eyes narrow. "So then, what's the helpful part that you found out?"

"We found out how to take down Lucifer," Aria says bluntly.

I curse. That's definitely not something we want circulating down here. Especially while we're looking for the relics.

Nix's eyes glow a brighter shade of green. "Oh?"

"Aria," I warn. "Shut your mouth."

"Come on now, Brother. That's no way to speak to a lady. Go on, Aria. Tell me."

Her gaze flicks between us, debating. Then, she lifts her chin. "We're supposed to be getting your brothers all on our side anyway. How can we do that if we don't tell them what we know?"

I pause, taken off guard. That's a damn good point, but still. It's safer the fewer people know—while we're searching for the relics, at least.

"Our job is to get the relics back. That's it. When Cain, Dorian, and Elias get down here, they can handle that part." And the mess that I'm sure will follow.

"Relics?" Nix's head perks up. "They're gone?"

"They were stolen," Aria explains.

Nix rakes his fingers through his hair, his normally confident expression faltering. "He did it, didn't he? Lorcan."

"You knew?" My eyes widen.

"He's been talking about it for a bit now, going up there and taking them so that Cain can't return. He's delusional, thinking he'll be next for the throne, but if Cain returns, that screws up the plan for him."

"Why didn't you say anything to me?" I press.

"I didn't because I didn't think he'd actually go through with it. Honestly," he says, "you know Lorcan. He talks a lot of shit but rarely does anything about it."

"Yeah, well, he did something. I chased him out of the house, but that fucker is fast," I reply.

Nix gets to his feet and meanders in front of the dark fireplace. A click of his fingers, and it ignites, roaring to life, flames licking the black stone in the hearth.

"Whatever it is you're planning, I want in," he says.

Call me a pessimist, but I don't trust him. "Fuck no," I snap.

"Maverick!" Aria gasps.

"We can't mess this up," I tell her. "It's our only chance at it."

His expression pinches as he takes a step closer. "That hurts, Brother. You know as well as me that Hell is breaking us down, bit by bit, until we'll be nothing but one of Father's fucked-up marble soldiers. I can't live an eternity like that. Cain couldn't, and neither can you. If you and Cain are cooking up a way out of Father's clutches, I want to help."

For a moment, I almost feel pity for him, until I remember who I'm dealing with. He was one of the ones on board with Cain, Elias, and Dorian's coup attempt the first time, but then bailed when things got nasty. How am I supposed to know if he'll do that again?

But, to be fair, I hadn't been much help to them back then either.

Things are different now.

"I want in on the action. Let me help," Nix repeats, with a pathetically sad smile.

A familiar ache deepens in my chest, brought on by the desperate look in his face. I've been in his position, so I'm familiar with the overburdening terror of being stuck with Lucifer, knowing he has your balls in a vice and there isn't a thing you can do to change the fact.

"Fine, but the first step is getting the relics back from Lorcan. That's objective numero uno," I finally answer.

His eyes light up. "I can definitely help with that. I hate the fuckwit, so tell me what you have planned."

I glance over to Aria, who's watching us intently.

"We need to know where Lorcan's lover boy is," I tell him.

He steps back. "You're going after *him*?"

"He'll know where Lorcan's stashed the relics. It's the only way we find out without drawing attention to what we're doing."

"Okay, I think I can manage that. He's a slippery one but very predictable."

"So you know where he is?"

"I know where he could be. But, of course, that information will come at a price."

Annoyance prickles up my neck. "Your payment is having your freedom from Lucifer," I grind out.

He gives me a deadpan look. "That will take time, if we can manage it at all. If we don't, I need to be thinking about a plan B for myself, another way out. That'll require a lot of power. And a lot of souls."

My souls? "You're joking."

"Another option is to let me have a taste of the human girl."

Fury comes over me and instinct kicks in. I throw my fist out, slamming it right into his face. Damn, that felt good.

Nix stumbles backward, blood dripping from his nose. He wipes it with the back of his hand, blood streaking his cheek.

"Fuck you, Maverick," he barks. "If I knew we were going to fight, I would have worn my battle clothes. This is my good suit." He scrunches up his face in disgust as he looks down at his jacket splattered with blood.

"If you keep wasting my time, then you can go fuck right off."

He heaves his next breath, his eyes squinting, and a harried look crosses his face. "Fine then. I'll settle for your demon contracts. All your pending souls. It's a fair exchange."

"What? No!" He wants me to hand over all the contracts I've made with humans, the ones whose souls now belong to me?

No way.

Nix watches me, tapping his toe on my stone floor, hands across his chest, and the temptation to hit him again grows within me.

"That's my final offer," he says. "Plus, I just saw Lorcan this morning. He told me where Lucifer's expected to be, so you'll need me to avoid him too."

When I lock eyes with Aria, she half shrugs. Of course, she doesn't understand how valuable souls are down here. Their life-force sustains us, gives us strength, so they're used as currency too.

I worked hard for mine, and to just give them up...

"Do you really need all those souls now?" Aria asks me.

"Yeah, do you, Maverick? With your new life on Earth, having them is a bit pointless," Nix tacks on.

As much as I hate to admit it, they're right. If I'm starting my life anew, do I really need all those souls?

"Fine, you have a deal," I answer reluctantly.

"Perfect!" Nix claps, then looks at me with a smug grin, revealing hundreds of tiny sharp teeth—part of his true demon form that people rarely get to see. It reminds me of who I'm working with here.

I really hope I don't regret this. I swallow the lump in my throat. "Get us to Lorcan's lover. Help us avoid Lucifer and any of our brothers, and then Aria and I will do the rest."

Nix doesn't respond right away, but his eyes drift upward as if pondering my plan. He gives a sudden clap. "I know exactly where we can find that information, and you'll need my help. But first, we need something more appropriate for Aria to wear so she blends in and doesn't draw attention. We need her demon-fied!"

Aria releases a small gasp, drawing our attention, and the fear on her face is plain as day.

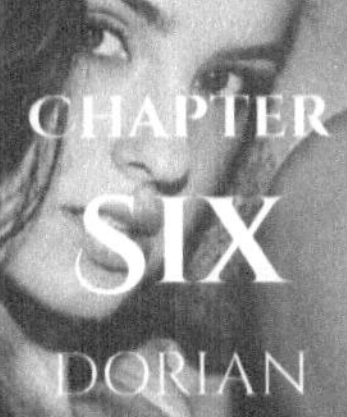

E lias and I step out of my Ferrari to find Cain exactly where I knew he'd be—standing outside the empty lot where our club Purgatory once sat. Since Stephan and the Nightwalker vamps set it aflame, nothing was salvageable. The little that was left standing had to be bulldozed but, of course, Cain refuses to give up on it. In typical Cain fashion, he's determined to resurrect the club from the grave and make it bigger and better than before.

We don't *need* the money it makes; we have plenty to continue our cushy lifestyle until the end of time. We don't *need* to use it for our reputation; it speaks for itself. So, why bother?

Cain won't say so, but I know him well enough to know the real reason. Something was taken from him, so he's going to come back tenfold. Sometimes the best revenge is success, even if that means rising from the ashes after a defeat. Literally, in this case.

So, since Aria went off with Maverick back to Hell, Cain's been keeping himself busy by overseeing the plans of Purgatory's rebuild.

He's standing cross-armed on the sidewalk, watching the construction crane lift a steel beam into the air, while the crewmen bark orders at each other as they work.

I glance over at the space next to Purgatory, where an old office building has been reduced to rubble, and pieces of it are finally starting to be moved by a backhoe.

Before I can say anything, Elias asks the question as we come to Cain's side. "What happened to the neighbors?"

Cain doesn't even look at us, only tilts his chin up. "I paid them well."

"We're expanding," I conclude. Again, not surprised.

He nods.

As the crane swings the beam to the top of the building's frame to start a second story, I realize that not only is he expanding Purgatory out, he's going up with it, too. "And two floors?"

Another subtle nod, and then he changes the subject. "Have you found anything out from Jamal?"

Jamal is the leader of one of our search teams located in Mexico where Gabriel placed the final relic to Azrael's harp. Cain tasked us with contacting him and making sure he found it.

Unfortunately, we had also come here to deliver bad news.

Elias glances at me with raised brows. It is his signal for me to break the news. I sigh. "So...we got ahold of him. He found that the coordinates Gabe gave us ended up being on top of the ruins of a temple. An Aztec temple. One that's long been excavated, turned tourist attraction..."

The muscles in Cain's jaw harden, but his expression remains smooth and unreadable.

"But—" Elias chimes in, "We found that it's a part of a traveling museum exhibit."

"Exhibit," Cain repeats stiffly. "Museum."

"Yeah. It's been on display at the British Museum for decades, but recently, it's been moved to New York City."

"Our plane is booked," I cut in. "We leave in an hour. You can stay if—"

"No, we'll all go," he says shortly.

"What about Purgatory?" Elias asks.

"It'll still be here when we get back," he explains. "And Gabriel wants us to retrieve the relics. No one else."

I clap Cain on the back. "Okay! Guys trip! Like the good ol' days!"

That gets a quirk of a smile across his lips. With my hand on his shoulder, I guide him back to my car, but Elias stays behind, looking less than pleased.

"What is it, big boy?" I call over to him.

Slowly, he makes his way over to us. "I'm not a fan of the city for obvious reasons."

I laugh at the absurdity of that. "But we're in a city. Right now."

He grumbles, "Glenside is small. New York City is a different animal entirely."

He's not wrong there.

"What museum are we going to?" Cain asks as he opens the car door and climbs into the back.

I take my place in the driver's seat, while Elias begrudgingly squeezes into shotgun. "The biggest one they got. The American Museum of National History."

As I turn the key in the ignition, my gaze flicks to Cain in the rearview mirror. He's peering out the window at the active construction. As if sensing my stare, he turns to meet my eyes in the reflection.

I know what he's thinking. Fixing Purgatory is just one check-mark on a very, very long and very dangerous to-do list.

"So, how are we doing this? Ambush? B&E after dark? The traditional distraction with some sticky fingers? Oh, or my favorite —murderous rampage?" Elias is practically salivating at the thought of how we're swiping the relic from this museum.

When neither of us answer, Elias glances between us in annoyance. "Is anyone going to tell me what the plan is? There is a plan, right?"

Cain shushes him sharply and takes the lead as we make our way through the throng of people and the many displays. The place is bustling with activity. Families, couples, older folks...and all on a weekday.

As we walk along, we pass a security guard who's dressed like a police officer, and is packing like one. Both a gun and a taser are strapped to his belt.

I tense. Not out of fear; more out of confusion and apprehension. Why does a security guard in a museum need a gun? I know we're in New York City, but damn. Is stealing artifacts such a common thing around here that they need to be locked and loaded? It doesn't help that we're here to do that very thing, *and* his gaze is locked on us as we cross the room.

Cain must've seen the same detail I did because he says in a harsh whisper, "Enough. We don't want to draw any unneeded attention to ourselves." His eyes flick the guard's way again, but at least it doesn't seem like he's following us as we enter the next room.

"I don't know if you noticed, Cain, but Elias is the size of a tree and I'm ungodly handsome. We stick out."

Elias snorts at the comment about me—of course. Jealous.

"At least tell me how we're planning on finding the skull." Elias makes sure to lower his tone this time, but we're practically bumping into people with every step. No matter how quietly he whispers, someone's bound to hear if he continues. And he does. "Without Aria to track it down—"

Cain stops short, spins, and points to a sign directly above our heads that reads "Ancient Civilizations."

Glancing around, Elias realizes where we are. We're surrounded by exhibits about Egyptian pharaohs, golden and sculpted artifacts, and mummies of all shapes and sizes. Actual mummies, too. Not replicas.

The skull was found in Aztec ruins, so if Jamal was right and it was shipped here, this section of the museum is where it will be.

"Cain, did you forget?" I tease. "Elias can't read."

"Fuck off," Elias grumbles, his shoulders growing rigid with anger.

It's not my fault he makes it too easy to piss him off, and I enjoy poking the bear. Or hellhound, I should say.

Ignoring us, Cain takes the lead and weaves through the crowd to a section labeled "The Aztec People."

Elias looks extremely uncomfortable with so many people around, and he tries to move quickly without bumping into anyone. There's a scale model of an Aztec temple, a few broken pieces of pottery, beaded necklaces, and...

A skull.

My pulse switches into overdrive as I spot it in a long glass case, surrounded by the other bits and pieces the archaeologists must've found during their dig. If you've seen a skull—and boy have I—you've seen them all, and this one could be counted among the rest. The only difference I can see right out of the gate is in its size. This one is larger than the average human skull. But there is a good chance its owner wasn't exactly human, either.

Fascinating stuff for any other history buff, I'm sure, but we're here for one thing and one thing only.

As we stand in front of the relic, I notice the little plaque next to it labeled "Unknown Man - Date Unknown" and huff. Why even put the sign there if it offers no information at all?

But I digress.

"Okay," Elias begins impatiently. He's bouncing side to side, eyes locked on the last piece of Azrael's harp right in front of us. "How are we doing this?"

I glance at Cain. Surely he has an idea. He always does.

His attention is pinned on the skull, too, and I know it's because he's itching to get to Hell. More specifically, to get to Aria. But he doesn't move or say anything as his brain works out a plan.

Peering down, I see Elias's fist clenching, and a thread of trepidation shoots down my spine. I know what he's thinking; I've seen that look on him before. He wants to take the quickest way to the relic, and that'd mean punching a hole through the display and stealing it, launching all the bells and whistles.

Although I appreciate the enthusiasm, it'd only make our job a lot harder. Especially the escape. This entire place could lock down. With one armed security guard, there is bound to be more, and that'd mean taking out whoever is in our way.

My follow-up thought is: why do I care?

A good question, considering I'm a demon and nothing should get between me and what I want. But Aria's voice is in my head, coaxing me to think about this another way. Avoid innocent deaths, and even though she's not here, my gorgeous girl is impossible to ignore.

I sigh and quickly scan the area for another way to solve this rapidly escalating problem. Smashing the glass and running is out of the question, so we have to be clever about this.

Lucky for us, clever is my specialty. Just like getting people to do what I want with a simple command.

Ah, yes, that's it!

Just then, a woman in pointed heels, a pencil skirt, and frilly blouse comes walking out of a nearby employees only door. There's a lanyard around her neck, one I'm sure would say something official about her working here.

Perfect. Just what I need.

I slide by Cain and Elias and make my way over to her.

"Dorian..." Elias starts to call, but Cain holds up a hand to stop him. He trusts me enough to know I can get this done.

Moving fast, I weave in between the many families, couples, and strollers, and manage to catch up to the woman I need. "Excuse me." I touch her arm, drawing her to a stop while using my power to push through our connection. "I need your help. There's something in that display case back there that needs to be taken out."

Her dimpled chin lifts as she looks at my hand on her arm and then meets my eyes. Her pupils shrink as my power slithers over her, taking control.

"I-I'm not sure what you mean," she stammers.

"Give me that skull in the display case," I command.

Her spine straightens automatically, the magic sinking its claws in and gaining full rule over her mind and body.

As she strides by me, I notice her lanyard says "Senior Museum Curator." So really, she's a pretty fucking important person. She pulls out a few keys from her pocket and finds the one she needs for the display.

Before she slides the key into the lock, her gaze finds Elias and Cain and apprehension passes over her face.

"Who...are you?" she asks.

Ah, shit. I forgot to add on the "Don't ask questions" part after my initial command. But luckily, a lie forms swiftly in my head.

"There was a mistake in the transfer of the exhibit. This piece needs to be returned to the British Museum, and me and my coworkers are here to take it back across the pond." I push more power into my voice. "That is what you'll tell anyone who asks about what we're doing here or why the skull is missing."

Did that cover all my bases?

Wait.

"Oh, and walk us out of here through the back, won't you,

lovely? My big friend here has a thing about large crowds." I slap Elias on the shoulder for good measure, but he jerks away.

"Y-Yes, of course."

I grin. Easy. Cake. And not a drop of blood spilled.

But then, when I look at Cain, he's pinching the bridge of his nose and shaking his head.

"What?" I whisper. "Took me a second, but I saved it."

"Barely," Elias snorts a laugh.

"Hey, you wanted a murderous rampage. This is easier. Cleaner."

"Yeah, and less fun."

"Dorian. Elias," Cain snaps our way as the woman opens the glass and carefully pulls the skull from its shelf. I hadn't even noticed before, but it was laying on a scarf or blanket of some kind. Gingerly, the curator wraps it up, careful not to touch it, before passing it over to me.

"You must be careful," she warns us, her gaze deadly serious. "A lot of people think it's cursed."

Her words take me off guard and, not sure how to react, I laugh nervously. Cursed? She has no idea. As a part of Azrael's harp, cursed might not be the right word for it, but it does hold some extremely powerful and concentrated dark magic.

The curator's expression hardens. "This is not a ghost story, I assure you. Bad luck follows anyone who handles it. The worker who unpacked it from storage committed suicide the following day. We've had employees quit, go missing... Even the British Museum had similar problems..."

I peer down at the skull.

Yep. Sounded like relic magic to me. But suicides and missing people? That sounds a bit more intense than just some bad luck.

"We'll make sure to handle it with care," Cain assures her. I pass the skull to him, and he holds it close but with careful fingers. If it's anything like the foot or the heart, direct contact could unleash the magic it holds.

The crackle of a walkie-talkie radio sounds, and I glance over my shoulder to see the security guard we'd pass earlier head straight our way.

"Shit."

Elias spots him next. "If we want to keep this clean, we have to go."

I whip back to the curator and touch her arm again. My magic surges. "Lead us out the back. And make it quick. We're going to be late for our scheduled flight back to England."

Blankness washes over her face and she nods. With my power of compulsion, she has no other choice but to obey. Taking the lanyard from her neck, she strolls to the employee door she'd come out of before, swipes the card, and holds it open for us to walk through. "This way, please."

We push our way inside and come face to face with a long stretch of hallway and many closed doors. Rooms for employees to take breaks or hold meetings, if I were to guess. Once we're cut off from the loud noises and many museum goers, we're drenched in a heavy silence. The curator's heels click against the titled floor as she crosses the hall and opens another locked door. This one has cold air rushing out of it and is clocked in darkness.

Like before, we follow her inside.

"Fuck." Elias gasps, looking around the massive warehouse-like storage room.

It's set up with shelves that rise close to two stories tall, all filled with priceless items on pallets, crates, and in bubble wrap. The smells of mold and dust saturate the air.

It's like Costco for history nerds in here.

Speaking of... I glance at Cain. He's looking up and down the shelves, lips parted in awe.

Well, what do you know? The demon may have just found his heaven.

"Hey, you may want to wipe the drool from your chin," I say, nudging him playfully with my elbow.

Unamused, he clamps his mouth shut.

"I know what you're getting for Christmas next year." I waggle my brows at him. "All access backstage passes to this place, compliments of my powers of persuasion."

When the sound of a metal door unlatching and opening echoes across the vast room, we all spin to see the curator at the end of the aisle, pushing the exit door open and waiting for us. At the same time, the security lock from the hallway clicks and foot-steps approach the warehouse door.

"The guard," Elias barks, saying all our collective thoughts out loud.

"Let's go." Cain hurries away, and we follow at his heels.

As we rush past the curator again and step outside, I say with vigor, "Close the door and make an excuse to anyone who asks about the skull being gone. Tell them you don't know which way we went."

My power invades her senses, fogging over her own thoughts, and she hastily closes the door behind her. We walk down a set of cement steps into an alley that's full of more pallets and crates, these all empty, but we keep moving out of the empty back lot and towards more of the chaotic hustle and bustle of New York City.

As much as we hate the crowds, my power can only do so much; the woman can tell him what I instructed her to, but whether or not the guard believes it... That's a different story. The three of us know we're better off hiding among the masses, disappearing into the ebb and flow of people on the sidewalks enjoying the snow and left-over Christmas decorations adorning the streets.

"I *hate* running away," Elias grumbles. "Hellhounds weren't meant to run from a challenge. Especially a human. It's degrading."

He means his ego more than his hellhound.

"There's a time for everything, so keep up."

Spotting our car and driver looping around the corner, we head for it. Police sirens blare in the distance, and my chest tightens.

Looks like the nice curator lady wasn't convincing enough.

Even though this mission was rather easy, and we didn't have to dive into an active volcano, cross a frozen tundra, or fight off deadly Amazon village people, I don't want to be arrested either. Not how I want to spend my time.

We hop into the car and Cain gives the driver directions to go straight to the airport. No stops. We speed off.

Good thing too, because the streets light up blue and red behind us as police motorcycles and squad cars drive up and park in front of the museum.

"Cain," I begin, feeling a bit uneasy. He turns in the front passenger seat, the skull relic still wrapped in his lap. "Should we be... worried? They're sure to have cameras..."

"I'll handle it," is all he says, and those three words ease my worries. We've been in a lot of shit over our century on Earth. Hell, we've been getting into a lot of shit since... forever. I don't know how Cain does it, but he manages to get us out of trouble every time. So, when he says he'll handle it, I know he will.

"Does anyone think this went a little *too* easy for us?" Elias asks, scratching at the stubble across his jaw. "No Black Castle of doom or Indiana Jones-like booby-traps."

At least I'm not the only one thinking it.

"Maybe we finally got some good luck on our side?" I shrug.

"Famous last words."

"Hey, I'm trying to be positive here. We've been through so much shit lately—"

"Lately? Try the last hundred years."

I'm about to argue but then realize he's right. "Yeah, so we deserve something to go right for once."

He rolls his eyes like a disgruntled teen. "At least we got the skull. Let's just hope Maverick and Aria are having luck finding the other relics."

Cain's muscles tense. He hates this helpless feeling a bit more than the rest of us.

I reach over his seat and touch his shoulder. When his hard gaze flicks my way, it softens a tinge.

"She'll come back to us soon," I whisper, in an attempt to comfort him. And, if I'm being honest, myself as well.

Closing his eyes, he dips his chin in a nod and draws in a deep breath. "Yes. I know." Then, his jaw sets and when he opens them again, his eyes are black. "Or I'll take this entire world to Hell with me."

"I feel ridiculous."

As I look down at myself, my stomach clenches. I'm wearing a jumpsuit with spaghetti straps and plunging V-neck. Completely transparent and all Nix's idea.

Good thing I wore a black bra and thong, but my entire backside is still on display. I'm pretty much in my birthday suit with all the see-through lace. Didn't know demon fashion could double as stripclub-chique.

"Got you some kick-ass boots that should fit," Nix announces, like he's doing me a favor. He drops the combat boots by my feet.

"Oh, thanks. They'll go great with the fuck-me-now outfit, drawing the attention of all the monstrous demons who want to kill me. Are you sure you know what you're doing?" I glance over to Maverick. "I think he's setting me up as bait."

Maverick stands up from the dining table and approaches me. He circles me, studying me like a predator.

"You'll be fine. Your tits are covered."

"Are you kidding me?" I grip my hips. "Look at me. I might as well be naked."

"Will you go naked?" Nix butts in. "I mean, I did propose it to Maverick but he said you wouldn't go for it."

"Fuck no is the right answer!" I snap.

"Then let's get a move on," Nix orders, already making his way across the room to the doorway he entered earlier. "Lorcan's lover is a fickle thing and doesn't like visitors in the afternoon."

"Wouldn't it make more sense that only you go?" I suggest. "You get the info and then let us know."

"Ha, I wish. He hates us sin demons, and last time I was alone in a room with him, he tried to skewer me with his chandelier."

"Wow, great. Who the heck is this demon?" I ask. "I never want to see him alone, ever."

Nix laughs wickedly. "He'll eat you on the spot if you do. We go as a team and stick together."

"Oh shit," I say, really not wanting to do this now.

"And what makes you think he'll talk?" Mavericks asks. "Seriously Nix, if you take us on one of your insane goose chases, *I'm* going to spear my claws through your heart."

"You're always so dramatic, Mav." He waves at the air between them as if he's swatting a fly. "Come on, let's go."

"Don't call me that," he snaps back.

Nix faces both of us. "Look, I have something he wants, and for it, he'll tell us anything. Now, move your fucking asses."

Maverick falls in line next to me and we head out as I lean in closer and ask, "Do we want to know what he's offering Lorcan's lover?"

"Nope. Not at all."

With Cain's ring still on my finger, and me in the company of two sin demons, no creature comes near us. If anything, I look like a hooker accompanying two men, and we're heading back to their place for a devious time. And while I initially thought my outfit might grab attention, I had it wrong. No one is even looking at me.

We're sticking to the suburban streets, which aren't too different from some of the run-down cities on Earth. Tall buildings, derelict houses, trash everywhere, steam gushing out from the cracks in the road. That's if you ignore the lofty black castles in the distance and the charred mountains surrounding us.

A man in a pinstripe suit strolls toward us, dragging a huge tail behind him. When he passes, I glance back to see the back of his pants are cut to allow the monstrous scaly tail to drag behind him. I'm not even going to ask.

But he doesn't bat an eye at us. So, flimsy, transparent fashion is the norm in Hell, apparently. The only good thing about it is that it keeps me cool, seeing as it's stinking hot in this place.

"We've been walking for ages," I groan. "Don't you have a carriage pulled by demonic horses we could use or something? You are sin demons for Hell's sake. I mean, why do you have roads when I haven't seen one car yet?"

They both cut a sharp glance at me, eyes narrowing, and for the first time I start to see a familiarity in their faces. Then they're howling with laughter.

"You've been watching too many movies, sweetheart," Maverick murmurs. "And the roads are only for Lucifer to use when he's in the mood."

"It's not far," Nix adds, still chuckling to himself. "Carriage. That's fucking classic."

"Whatever," I groan.

After what feels like an eternity later, we finally turn down a side alley that reeks of death. I cover my mouth and nose with my hand and hurry after the brothers, stepping over puddles of more goo. It's disgusting.

Finally, Nix pauses in front of a narrow, two-story building where the front lawn had been burned to a crisp. A dead tree stands out front with animal skeletons hanging from the branches.

A thought strikes me. "Wait, can't Nix just shapeshift into Lorcan and talk to his lover? Get the info we need that way?"

"Ah, yes, that would be easier wouldn't it," Nix replies, sounding somewhat impressed I thought of it. "But unfortunately, I've tried to fool him before—you know, for a bit of fun—but they've been together so long, he's able to see right through the guise."

"Just means we're going to have to do this the hard way," Maverick adds in.

Hard way? Not sure I like the sound of that.

Nix knocks on the black door, and my stomach hardens in anticipation.

Maverick's glued to my side.

The door opens slowly, the hinges squeaking.

At the entrance stands a man, taller than me, and on the

thinner side. Every inch of him is dark maroon, including his horns, which are curled back around his ears. Gold upside-down crosses dangle from his earlobes, and his expression is scrunched up in confusion at Nix.

"Sweet Lucifer, what do you want?" He glares over to Maverick and me, then scans the rest of the street. "Two sin demons in one visit. What are the neighbors going to say?" He snorts, and I can't tell if that's a laugh or an angry gesture. There's smoke coming out of his nostrils. "Is Lorcan with you?"

"It's just us," Nix answers. "I have something you want, and in exchange, I need a favor."

"Like I told you the last time you thought we could be friends." He rolls his eyes, his upper lip curling over fangs. "Go fuck up shit elsewhere. I'm not interested."

He goes to shut the door, but Nix kicks his foot out, blocking it.

"Irnonoch, are you really going to say no to *this*?" Nix stuffs his hand into his pocket, and I shift to get a better look at what he's offering.

Nix takes out an old-fashioned bronze key in his hand, waving it.

Irnoni…Inoch—fuck it, I'm calling the red demon Irno—gasps, his mouth hanging open.

"Is that what I think it is? Because if you're fucking with me, Nix, this time I will carve your heart out and eat it in front of you."

"Ouch," Maverick mumbles under his breath.

"What's so special about the key?" I whisper back, only to have him shush me.

"We got a deal then?" Nix counters, his chest puffed out.

"Come in. Don't touch anything and leave your germs all over it," he sneers, more smoke floating out from his flaring nostrils, and swings open the door.

If Lorcan's lover is this aggressive and terrifying, what the heck is Lorcan like?

Nix steps inside and waves for us to follow. With Maverick's hand on my lower back, I head in next. "Thanks," I say as I pass Irno, but he only leans in and sniffs me.

"You're a strange looking thing, and so pale, but you have a decent ass," he mutters to me.

I glance back and smile. "This is all natural." I grip my hips. "Men love ass." And I cringe hard on the inside, regretting instantly opening my mouth. I sound like a demon whore.

Shut up, Aria.

Irno huffs, snorting in the process. "Whatever, let's just do this quickly." He brushes right past me, nudging me into the wall in the process.

Maverick is quick to snatch me into his arms and steady me. His breath streams across my neck, his chin propped on my shoulder. "Best you don't engage. Lorcan may be the Sin Demon of Envy, but Irnonoch is jealousy incarnate."

Straightening myself, I walk down the long corridor. It's dark in here and we seem to walk for a long time, until we finally swing left into a dimly lit room.

We pass black stone walls and ceiling. There's a glossy chandelier with large fanged teeth hanging from it where there should be crystals, and a long wooden bench with spikes on the seat. Piece of furniture or medieval torture device? Take your pick.

"Take a seat," the demon sneers my way, then glances over at the spiky seat.

Is he joking?

"I'm fine. I love standing." I square my shoulders and attempt to look as comfortable as possible in a room that has my skin crawling.

"Suit yourself. Only being hospitable so you can rest your big ass."

Big ass? Bastard. I stiffen while Maverick sidles closer to me. "Don't let him get into your head. Plus, you have the most stunning ass."

I can't even deal with that right now.

The demon turns on Nix. "Okay, what do you want in exchange for it?" He juts out a red hand, palm up, long claws curling at the tips of his fingers. He's eyeing the key in Nix's grasp.

"I need to know Lorcan's hiding location. Where he hides his most precious possessions."

Irno barks a laugh, then lashes out and seizes Nix by the neck. He slams him up against the wall, and I flinch into Maverick.

"Are you mocking me? You come into my house thinking I will

betray my lover?" He's squeezing Nix's neck so hard that I'm certain I just heard bones crack.

"He can't respond if you're choking him," I suggest.

Nix hisses at his attacker, his hand punching the demon in the face. It's enough to make him release him. That's when I notice scales materializing over Irno's skin.

Eww, he's a reptilian demon?

Maverick watches the two demons crouch low, appearing amused. "Are they going to fight?" I whisper to him

"Maybe. It's just an ordinary gesture when you visit someone to show your strength."

I tense up. "This is normal behavior?"

He grins at me. "You don't have such social etiquettes on Earth?"

"Yeah, bringing your host a bottle of wine perhaps, not choking and punching them in the face."

He looks confused. "That's strange."

I would almost laugh if I wasn't watching two demons in a power struggle. And, just as quickly as it started, the demons both stand, agreeing to a stalemate.

Nix straightens his jacket and lifts his gaze, still gripping the key like everything is normal. "I'm offering you your own castle, Irnonoch. No more living like a peasant with all the other wannabes in this part of the city." He lifts the key once more, and the fiery torches on the wall glint off the metal. "This is the key to the Castle of Souls, the most haunted building in Hell."

Irno has his arms folded across his chest, his lower lip between his teeth. He's blinking a lot too.

"And, did I mention, it's the second tallest building in Hell, with a direct view across the Field of Death, to Lorcan's castle? Do you really want him to keep lording over you that he owns a castle?"

Irno lowers his arms by his side, his chin rising, and huffs. "What is so important that you need from Lorcan?"

"He took something from me," Maverick states and steps forward, speaking strongly. "Nix is helping me retrieve it. We only want to retrieve what belongs to me."

Irno taps a talon on his chin. "So, you're saying I will own the Castle of Souls, all deeds given to me?"

"Exactly," Nix answers.

"And just so we make it clear, there will be no taking it back."

"Absolutely not." Nix grins widely. With a snap of his fingers, a puff of smoke erupts from his hand, along with a scroll. He hands it to Irno. "Sign this with blood, and it's yours."

Thick tension fills the air, but when Irno snatches the scroll greedily, I can't help but smile.

Instead, I wait, just like Maverick and Nix, in complete silence, as Irno unravels the scroll and reads it. From what I can see over his shoulder, the writing is tiny and there's a lot of it.

After what feels like an eternity, Irno cuts the tip of his index finger and uses the black blood to sign the contract.

"Done!" he snarls and thrusts out the rolled-up scroll at Nix. "Now, hand me the key!"

"Once you tell us Lorcan's hiding spot." Nix stands tall, shoulders squared, and I get the impression that if he really wanted to, he'd smite this demon in seconds. But he doesn't, which means he must hold some care for his brother Lorcan.

"Fine, but you didn't hear this from me." Irno lowers his voice.

"Absolutely not," Nix replies, green eyes shining with excitement.

Irno's lips pinch tight and he hisses the words. "In Lucifer's whorehouse. Behind the skull mirror. I hate it when he goes there."

"I know where that is," Maverick answers, and I cut him a narrow gaze, which he doesn't notice. Who else goes to this whorehouse? Did Cain visit it when he lived here?

I'm still trying make sense of what he just said, when Maverick asks, "Why the fuck would he hide anything in there?"

"Because Lucifer still visits the place. Lorcan tells me it's the most guarded place, and as a sin demon, he has free access to go in anytime."

I want to call bullshit on behalf of Irno, because if Lorcan is hiding things in the whorehouse, it sounds like the perfect excuse to go there without him. Poor Irno, but that's none of my business.

MAVERICK

THE WALK to the whorehouse takes longer than I anticipated.

With Aria by my side, we stroll through the open gates to Father's spectacular fuck-mansion.

Nix lingers with the guards behind us, laughing and distracting them, while I keep my head low and get Aria onto the grounds. She flinches at any sound, and her eyes are huge, swinging left and right across the manicured land surrounding us. Statues pepper the lawn in all manner of debauchery.

One statue is of a woman who is lifted off the ground by two men, while a third kneels and has his head buried between her thighs, devouring her. Another is of a man bent over, and a woman taking him from behind, while a huge horned demon claims her in the ass.

I used to love coming here to study the pieces of art, until I learned these were actual humans and demons who had managed to piss off Lucifer. So, his punishment was to place them in an eternal frozen state on the brink of ultimate pleasure... but never gaining the release they crave. Now that is fucking Hell.

"Are you okay?" I look down to Aria, who's studying a demonic goat with a hard-on chasing a girl who's running away, her clothes mid-way falling off her, her face in a panicked scream.

"I'm scared to ask what kind of whorehouse this is," she says.

"Anything goes here. Father built it to fulfill his every desire."

"And for sin demons too?" She arches a thin eyebrow at me, her voice croaky, like she doesn't want to hear the truth but still asks the question.

"Yes, you are correct. I won't lie, all my brothers and I have frequented the mansion many times, but we have also been around for a long time. Personally, I haven't visited the place in years."

When she doesn't respond, and there is unspoken tension between us, I focus on what I can control. Our mission. "You'll be my escort once we enter—just follow our lead so we can get out fast."

"Trust me, I want to get in and out of here as fast as possible too." She licks her lips nervously and turns her attention back to the dark building with lofty, arched windows, stone walls, and a pointy roof. *Three stories of depravity*, Irnonoch once called the mansion. And he wasn't wrong. The things I've seen within those walls would make even a demon blush.

Nix catches up to us, strolling alongside me. "Fuck me, but it's been a while. Last time I came here, Father had brought in those sirens from the pits of Hell. I remember they were so fucking horny, that we—"

I jab him in the ribs, which makes him groan, then he looks over to Aria who's watching with huge eyes, listening intently.

"Umm, yeah, I gave them a good fuck. The end." He smacks his lips, making a popping sound.

"Why'd you give one of your castles away to Irnonoch to help us?" I ask him, out of curiosity and to change the topic.

Nix shrugs and stuffs his hands into the pockets of his dress pants. "I can't do a good deed to help my brother?"

I laugh and roll my eyes. "Don't mock me, Nix. Everything you do is to benefit you."

Nix doesn't respond right away as we make our way toward the mansion down the long, winding path. Aria fiddles with Cain's ring, twisting it around her finger.

"I want in," Nix finally answers. "And for you and Cain to see I'm serious about this. So, if I have to give away all my castles, I'll do it."

"Yet you were quick to take my souls," I remind him.

"That's different, Brother. I needed to make sure you were serious about working with me."

"Do demons ever just help people out of the goodness of their hearts, instead of making everything a deal?" Aria asks.

"Think you just answered your own question there, luv," Nix says. "Goodness and heart don't go with demons."

"Don't agree with you there," she rebuts, and I know she's referring to Cain. My brother has changed a lot since he was kicked out of Hell. He's settled down, more in control of his rage, and he's found love with a human girl. When I look at Aria, I can't blame him. She's fucking gorgeous and brings something out in me that makes me want to be a better demon.

But then I can only picture him buried deep inside her, forcing me to watch. I have no issues with watching...but only if I can also join. Not to have them just prove a fucking point.

We head up the front steps, and as we reach the doorway I swing my arm around Aria's waist. Nix stands on her other side. I wrap my knuckles on the door.

It opens in moments, and we're greeted by Chyd, the mansion butler. He's an old human with no soul after he ended up down here for killing half a dozen women.

"Masters." He bows his head at me. "It has been a long time since you have enjoyed our establishment."

"Yes," I respond and walk inside, taking Aria with me. Chyd steps aside, eyeing her carefully.

"Is the lady a new guest?" he promptly asks.

"She's mine," I growl and grab her ass, to which she flinches against me.

He reels back a few steps, bowing his head. "Of course."

Nix falls behind us and takes Chyd aside, which I can only assume means he's going to buy his silence about us being here.

Aria makes a small gasping sound as she lifts her head and takes in the grandeur of the entrance hall—the marble, the golden chandeliers, the paintings on the wall of males and females naked, posing in sensual positions. The sweeping staircase curling up to the next floor, railings made of pure gold, the windows tinted with a faint blue, casting everything with its hue.

"It's not what I expected," she murmurs.

"For Hell?" I answer and guide her quickly up the stairs along the red rug.

"Just for the house being what it is." She's busy studying a painting of a woman with heavy tits bound in rope, and when she glances my way, there's a light blush to her cheeks.

Fuck me, but that's a beautiful color on her.

Footsteps strike the floor behind us, and I glance back to find Nix marching to catch up with us.

He gives me a wink, which I take as him having dealt with Chyd.

In silence, we hurry down a dimly lit hallway, then take the next set of steps to the third floor, where we finally come to a stop in front of ornate black doors that reach the ceiling.

"What's in there?" Aria whispers.

"Lucifer's fuck room," Nix answers. "Are you excited to see it?"

She scrunches up her nose. "Not in this lifetime."

Nix snorts a laugh, and I push open the doors. Bright light from the window drenches the oversized four-poster bed that is completely black and made to fit at least twenty people. It swallows most of the space in the room. The carpet is pitch black, as are the walls, the only color coming from the arched windows.

Aria rushes ahead of us, turning on the spot, her mouth hanging open almost in awe. "My toe is tingling. They're in here."

"Toe?" Nix asks.

"Don't ask," I snap in response. I wouldn't even know how to explain it if I tried.

Nix strides across the room and throws himself on the bed, and I can only imagine how much fucking has taken place there. Knowing it is all with Father, I avoid touching anything.

Aria screams, and I literally jump in my boots, then twist to find her staring into the skull mirror. I let out a long breath.

The thing is, the actual mirror is a simple long piece the length of her body, with a black decorative frame. Except, it's not the design that gives it that name. But its reflection.

"What the fuck!" she cries out, running her hand over her face, her head and body shown as a skeletal form dressed in her lacy number. Hollow eyes stare back at her, her bony jawline moves as she opens her mouth then closes it.

She glances over at me. "What the hell is this thing?"

"It's an illusion," I say, stepping closer, except I fucking hate the thing. It freaks me out to look at myself in skeleton form.

"It's one of Father's fetishes," Nix pipes in. "He likes to watch himself *boning* someone while looking like that." He waits, clearly hoping we'd get his joke and laugh. But when I only snort, he climbs off the bed to stand next to Aria, both of them now looking ghastly.

"This is just some freaky shit," Aria replies, striking different poses regardless.

I step behind the mirror, figuring the relics have got to be back here somewhere. Lorcan would have hidden them somewhere out of sight. But there's nothing obvious, so I peer around the tiny space. Except, all I can see is the flat back of the oval mirror and its clawed feet. The relics are too large to conceal anywhere behind it.

"Fucking shit," I snarl. "If Irnonoch lied to us, I am going to murder him."

Aria and Nix pop their heads around the mirror and look at me.

"They've gotta be here," she suggests. "My toe is going crazy right in this spot."

"Well, unless they're invisible, I don't see where they could be hidden."

She steps around with me, as does Nix, and that's not helping us one bit. We can barely move now, caged by the mirror and wall behind us.

"It has to be here," she insists, her brow furrowing, scanning the floor and the mirror. On either side of us, there's nothing. "I feel them. They should be here."

"You keep saying that," I insist.

Nix shrugs and steps out from behind the mirror, while I suck in a deep breath. I can't fail at this. I made a promise to Cain, to Aria. Though, after his asshole act, part of me would love to make him suffer somehow. But that means harming Aria...and while I'm still pissed, I have other ideas of how I'd prefer to bring her pain.

The door opens abruptly, and I jut my head up, shoving Aria behind me because I expect it to be Father. She hits the wall or something in the process, because a creak sounds. But my gaze is locked on Chyd rushing into the room, his breath racing, and panic scribbled across his face.

"Lucifer has arrived at the manor," he gasps with terror. "You must leave his room immediately."

"Fuck!" Nix races across the room to Chyd.

My lungs freeze, and I whip around, reaching for Aria. "We leave now!"

Except my hand swings through the air because Aria isn't standing, she's crouching down and her hand is half buried in an open compartment in the wall.

"Is it there?" I whisper and kneel down as she draws out a black box with a metal lock on the front. She holds it easily in two hands and looks at me with a smile.

"This is it. I can hear its song now. This box is holding back their power." She shuts the secret compartment and scrambles to her feet.

I get to my feet. "Good, now we need to get the fuck out of here."

Nix is by the doorway, waving for us to follow.

Aria tucks the box under her arm, and we run, my pulse thundering in my veins. Her smile has faded, and now a dark fear crawls over her face.

At the doorway, I peek my head out, and see it's clear. "We can't go the way we came, so we head out the back way."

"Agreed," Nix whispers, and Aria tenses against me.

We rush outside, shutting the door behind us, then I swing left, in the opposite direction of the staircase.

Aria stays close, not making a sound, while Nix lingers behind us as a kind of protection. He knows as well as I that if Father finds Aria, we'll both be punished for sneaking a human into his whorehouse. Not to mention what he'll do to her.

Voices rise from behind us. Aria stumbles on the rug as she tries to look back. I catch her while she clings onto the box of relics.

Shadows appear at the top of the steps.

We're exposed, and the end of the hall for our exit is too far away.

Nix looks at me with horror, and panic slams into me. I glance around and spot a door several feet from us. I flick my hand at him and we all scramble inside like the devil is on our heels.

I shut the door hastily, my breaths ragged, and I place my ear to the door to listen for sounds.

Aria suddenly gasps, drawing my attention to the room, and I sigh because of course I had to pick this room of all places.

Three bodies hang from the ceiling by their ankles. They're not dead...nothing truly dies in Hell unless Lucifer makes it so.

Nope, this is the storage room for his play toys when he's in the mood for fucking something close to death. Truly, Father is a vile creature.

I collect Aria by the waist and twist her toward me, my chest clenching. "Don't look, sweetheart. I hate that you even have to see this filth," I whisper.

She clutches onto that box and nods, while Nix is beneath a woman, staring at her face. They're all out of it, placed under a sleeping spell until Father has use of them.

When I place my ear back against the door, the loud thumping of footfalls sounds near...too fucking near, like they're coming this way. As though they've walked right past the bedroom.

Shit. Shit.

I swing around, my gaze whipping across the room, and I settle on our only option. A chute door in the wall.

"They're coming this way," I growl, to which Aria's face whitens.

"Fuck," Nix mouths, but I've snatched Aria's arm and we're speeding across the long room to the back corner. I pull open the silver chute door.

"Are you fucking kidding me?" Nix hisses, standing in front of the window. "We go this way."

"And then what? Have him watch me fly away with Aria in my arms and you crash to the lawn down below?" I whisper. Nix isn't like me and Cain. We were the only brothers to get the perk of wings.

To hell with that. I don't even wait. I just collect Aria into my arms.

"Are you sure about this?" She's trembling in my arms as I push her feet-first into the chute. "I don't want to die here."

"Oh, Aria, I would throw myself onto a blade before I let anything touch you. Trust me." As angry as I still am, this is about saving all our lives.

She looks at me for a short pause, like she's still determining if she can trust me, but then she nods. And I nudge down into the chute that dips diagonally from the room. Her small squeal has my heart squeezing.

Footfalls stop at the door. My stomach hits the floor, and Nix literally flies right past me and into the chute, head first. I throw myself in there too, grabbing the latch and shutting it just as I hear the door swinging open.

Putrid air rushes past me as I slide down in pitch darkness. Next thing I know, I'm freefalling and, out of instinct, my wings snap out, beating them just once to glide down to my feet.

The basement around us is dimly lit, and we're alone.

Nix groans, clutching his shoulder. "I think it's best if we split up for a bit," he says. "So Father doesn't think we're up to something." He dusts off his clothes.

My gaze swings to Aria, who's kneeling in front of the box that's snapped open from her fall.

"Shit," she grumbles, quickly placing the relics back into the box and shutting it. I cross the space between us in two long strides.

"What is it now?"

She glances up at me, blinking like she's lost. "There are only three pieces in here. Where the hell are the others?"

"That fucking *sonofabitch*!"

The second we walk through the mansion's door, I head straight for my office with the wrapped skull still tucked under my arm. Dorian and Elias follow close behind.

"We can't hide it in your bedroom again," Dorian says as we enter the library. "Lorcan knows that hiding spot."

He's only stating things I already know. "I'm aware."

My bedroom and the basement are the safest places in the house, and since both places were breached, I'd rather keep it close to me for protection. And since I'm either here or at Purgatory, and the club is temporarily out of commission, this is where I will be spending most of my time while waiting for Aria to return. This is where I'll store the skull.

After striding inside, I place the skull on my desk, pull back my chair, and kneel before it. Dorian comes in and leans over to watch while Elias stands in the doorway, arms crossed. I wrench open the drawer and feel around the inside for the secret latch at the back. Moving around the other items in there blindly—a stapler, pens, some ink pads and stamps—I find the small groove in the wood and push it. There's a small pop and a panel opens underneath the desk.

"Woah, that's impressive. Is that where you hide your diary?" Dorian asks, and I glare his way. "What? Your father has one."

I ignore him and reach into the compartment. There are a few important papers in there, such as the deeds for our properties, some spells I've acquired over the years from some powerful spell-casters, etc., but luckily, there's still enough room for the skull.

The sound of soft, heavy paws signals the entrance of Cass, the tiny lynx kitten turned massive domestic house cat, thanks to Aria's attachment to the creature and an unknown magical potion. Like any feline, Cass is curious and, at times, a menace.

On cue, he jumps onto my desk, the wood creaking under his enormous weight. To our horror, he swats at the skull, sending it flying off the edge.

"No!"

Dorian tries to grab it, but he's a millisecond too slow.

Panic surges as I watch the last piece of Azrael's harp plummet to the ground. If it shatters, that means the end of our chances of getting back to Hell.

Suddenly, Elias is there and snatches the relic right before it meets the floor.

I release my held breath and rise from under the desk.

"Fuck, that was close," Dorian snarls.

Narrowing my eyes at Cass, he responds by growling at me. I growl back even louder, and the lynx hops down and leisurely strolls out of the office, bushy tail swiping side to side.

"Good catch, man. Those fast animal reflexes really came in—" Dorian stops abruptly. When I look over at him, I realize why.

Elias is standing there with the skull sitting on his bare, open palm. The scarf covering it must've fallen off during the drop, and he is frozen in place, eyes wide and mouth slightly agape.

"Oh no." Dorian and I move closer. "Elias..."

When he doesn't respond, Dorian looks at me, fear clear on his face. "The magic has him. He's been rendered catatonic. How do we get him back? What do we do?"

During his rushed questions, a flare of power zaps across our bond, taking us off guard.

"D-Did you feel that?" he asks and rubs his arms.

Goosebumps rise on my arms, horror rising as the realization crashes down on me. "It's like it was with the foot relic. Because of the bond, it's going to affect us all."

"Shit, Cain! What do we—"

Another surge shoots through the magic tie, but this time

Dorian stiffens in place, the same blank and lost expression as Elias.

Fuck. I've lost him too.

That only leaves me.

I have to get that skull out of Elias's hands.

Moving as fast as I can, I grab the scarf and hurry around the desk. I reach for the relic just as another wave of magic hits me, striking me like a hammer to the head, and everything goes black.

I BLINK. At least, I believe I do. I can feel the brush of my eyelashes against my cheeks every time I do it. But I can't see anything. Even with my demon's advanced eyesight, I can't seem to penetrate the darkness.

Where am I?

My entire body tingles with static electricity, almost to numbness, and even though I command my limbs to move, I can't tell if they're actually doing as they're told.

Elias? Dorian? I call into the abyss, but like my sight, the words are swallowed up by the void. I hear them echoing in my head, but they never touch my ears.

I remember the moments before I arrived here. Cassiel knocking the final relic off the desk, Elias catching it, and the magic radiating across our bond and freezing first him, and then Dorian.

It must've gotten me too.

That's what this must be. I've been captured by the skull's dark magic.

My feet touch solid ground, and instantly the numbness dissipates. The darkness lifts, and I find myself surrounded by stone walls, wet with condensation. The air reeks of mildew, sulfur, decay, and fear, and I recognize the place instantly.

I was a frequent visitor of Lucifer's torture rooms in the lower levels of his castle. Ever since my conception, he'd bring me down here to brag about his handy work and preach about it being my responsibility to oversee the torture of captured souls. And I was damn good at my job, too. Unquestionably so.

The screams of the damned penetrate the walls, begging for a death that can never really come. I take in the heavy feelings of despair, desperation, and pain saturating the air. There was a time when I got nothing but sick satisfaction out of being here, but things are different now. *I'm* different, even if part of me gets excited over the idea of reliving this part of my life again.

But the other part of me knows better. I am under the skull's dark charms. This isn't real—it can't be. I'm still banned from Hell. So then...what is the relic trying to show me? Is it like the foot? A possible flash into the future or the past?

A moan comes from the shadowy center of the room, and I hesitate. I didn't know someone was in here with me.

"Hello...?" I step closer slowly, allowing my vision to adjust to the darker spots. There's a metal table there, similar to an autopsy table, and even under the matted dark hair and dry blood painted across pale skin, I can tell it's a female. She's naked and seems to be unconscious, which isn't an uncommon occurrence for the torture rooms, but what takes me by surprise is the glimmer of gold around the woman's neck.

My heart hammers, trepidation prickling up my spine.

No. No. It can't be.

Terror seizes me, my breaths speeding up.

It can't be her. It can't.

With shaky hands, I reach out and gently brush the hair away.

The single wing pendant...

Aria.

My mind blanks. Her face is bruised and swollen, almost unrecognizably so. But I know it's her; I can feel it in my very soul. My Aria. My love.

"No... Aria... Wake up. Please." She doesn't stir. Not even when I brush my knuckle across her cheek, avoiding the nasty gash marking it. Her lip is split too, and she's so thin and pale... Like she's been down for days. Weeks.

"Aria, p-please." My voice trembles. "It's me, Cain. I'm here. If you can hear me, please open your eyes. Move. Something."

She looks dead, and just the thought has me panicking. Souls can't die down here, but then why can't I feel her through our bond? There's nothing there. Just emptiness.

I have so many questions; they bombard me, torture me. How

did she get down here? Did Lucifer capture her? Where's Maverick? Did he betray us?

Then comes the anger. It rips out of me, snapping my demon to the forefront. So much fury and grief whirl within me, all I can think about is finding whoever did this and unleashing hell on them. My wings whip out, filling up the entire room.

"Put those puny things away. You'll poke an eye out."

Every muscle in my body tightens at the familiar smug voice.

Father.

Folding in my wings, I whirl on him and cross the room in two great strides, my rage fueling me.

He doesn't even flinch, which only angers me more.

"You did this!" I roar.

His black brows knit together. He stares at me and then huffs a laugh. "What is this? Some kind of joke?"

My insides tremble, and I'm doing all I can not to punch a hole through his chest or let the thought of Aria being gone sink in and cause me to collapse onto the ground.

"My son, I'm only here to admire your work. As you asked."

My...work?

He walks around me to the table, where Aria's unmoving body lays still. My chest clenches. "Don't touch her!"

Rubbing his chin, he circles her, his hungry gaze roaming over her body. My stomach tightens as more anger tumbles through me.

"She is quite the specimen, isn't she? I'm a bit envious you got to play with her," he says as he continues to walk around the table and look her over like a hungry predator. I have no idea what he's talking about, but seeing Aria practically unconscious in front of me tears apart my soul.

"Although, I'm surprised you chose to have her unconscious and not begging you to stop. I know how much you like to hear them beg."

My fists clench as heat rushes over my skin. Unable to contain it any longer, my hellfire ignites.

"Shut your fucking mouth," I snap.

"I don't understand why you're getting so upset," he says calmly. "You're doing good work down here. Why can't you take the compliment?"

Good work?

"You think I did this?"

"Who else? None of your other brothers have the precision, patience, and skill of torture like you do, Cain. Why do you think I picked you? You get it from me."

"I'm nothing like you."

Again, his gaze sweeps over Aria. "Oh, but you are. Just. Like. Me."

Terror claws up my throat. I know what he's implying. He's saying I did this to her. I hurt her, tortured her close to death.

Impossible.

I would never.

Would I?

I step back, chest heaving.

Extinguishing my hellfire, I lift my hands to see that they're covered in blood. Her blood.

No...I...I wouldn't. Not Aria.

Not her.

My knees give out and I collapse.

No!

DORIAN

HANDS SLIDE ACROSS MY TORSO. One, two, four... They run along my shoulders, down my arms, across my waist. Teasing. Stroking. Making every hair on my body stand on end.

Power sizzles across my flesh. My power. And it's growing rapidly by the second.

As the sexual intensity around me heightens, I'm charged, like a battery struck by a lightning bolt. As an incubus, this is what we live for.

It's been a long time since I've felt such power, bathed in it, relished in it. When I finally open my eyes, I am temporarily blinded by the kaleidoscope of colors dazzling me—part of my power manifesting as it gains strength. There is so much red, the coloring for the highest level of lust a person can feel, that I'm drowning in it, dizzy from the euphoria it leaves me with. I can hardly think straight.

I try to grip onto any solid thought that I can find. Like... Where am I?

It's a good start, but when one of the hands dips past my waist to stroke my cock, I push my head back into the pillows and lose myself to the delicious sensations crashing into me. There's heat—someone's breath, I realize—whispering across my cock's tip. A warm tongue circles around one of my balls and then draws it into their mouth, sucking gently, and I'm struck dumb on the spot.

I can't make sense of it still, but while part of me is drunk on both the magic and the sex, another part wants me to refuse it. To rip myself away and see this as wrong. But the demon in me growls with a vicious need to fuck and feed, so I let these strangers do whatever they please, leaving me to become more lost in the fog.

Weight presses into me as someone straddles my waist. Lips press onto mine for a scorching kiss that sends bolts of desire straight to my cock. Nails rake through my hair and pleasure-filled moans fill my ears.

Unable to resist, I find the person's hips and help slide them down where I want to feel them most. They begin to rub themselves against my raging hard erection. Teeth nip my shoulder, and the deadly combination of pain and pleasure is almost too much to bear.

A voice in the back of my head keeps telling me to stop. This is wrong. But, fuck, it feels so good.

Over all the panting, grunting, and moaning, I barely make out the creak of a door opening.

Another person to join the party?

"Dorian?"

That voice. The pain in my name.

Oh shit. Aria!

Realization spears through me, and as if cold water had been thrown on me, I'm thrown out of my sex-crazed stupor. When I sit up, I find that I'm in bed—my bed—with four women. Naked women.

Oh no.

Everything stops.

"Aria... It's not what you—" But I stop myself, because it is *exactly* what it looks like, isn't it? But I don't know how I got into this situation. I don't know how this even happened.

As I spiral down from cloud nine, I crash and burn, my body sluggish, my limbs feeling like a ton of dead weight. I can't even move in the bed to get out of it, and boy do I try. I want to run to her, hold her, and plead for forgiveness, but my body doesn't respond.

The look of immense pain and betrayal on Aria's face murders me.

I did that.

She trusted me, and I hurt her beyond repair.

I destroyed her after I swore to her I would never. That she was the only one my heart and body needed.

"Aria... Please. I'm sorry..." I don't know what else to say. Nothing is good enough.

Tears glisten in her eyes, angry ones, and her body grows taut. "I shouldn't have expected anything less from a sex demon." She spits the last word like it's poison on her tongue, then she spins and storms out of the room.

Stomach plummeting, I use all my strength to haul myself out of bed, but it's no use. I'm paralyzed until my power balances out again.

All I can do is watch her walk away and disappear down the hallway, and I know, deep down, I've lost her forever.

Hands glide up my chest again, pushing me back into the pillows.

"Get off me," I shout, as the women begin to kiss my stomach, neck, and legs. "No! Stop!" But I'm helpless, unable to move or fight.

"Leave me alone!"

My power flares again, building and building the more they caress me, their fingers exploring every inch, and their kisses becoming more demanding on my flesh. Different shades of red dye-out my vision, and it's not long before I'm lost to the intoxicating feeling of the moment.

It's like a drug, and I'm an addict.

After all, like Aria said, I'm a sex demon. An incubus. I'm a slave to my baser urges. Nothing more. That makes me a glutton for sex and the power it gives me. I can't control myself, and that means I can't commit myself to only one person; I can't truly love someone.

My eyes sting with tears, and the stabbing in my chest is immeasurable.

I love her. I know I do.

I love her.

And now she's gone.

Forever.

ELIAS

WHEN I HIT something solid underneath me, I land on all fours and start running. The frigid wind whistles past my ears, combs through my fur, and stings my nose, and when my eyes finally catch up with the rest of my senses, the blur of the forest rushes by me.

I don't know how I got here. The last thing I remember is being in Cain's office, looking for a place to store the last of Azrael's relics, but somehow, I've made it to the woods.

Strange... Things aren't adding up.

But, before I can think harder on it, I burst into a clearing and spot the last person I expected to see standing in the same place I'd found her the first time. Serena.

Like last time, I skid to a halt, changing mid-stride into my human form. She has some balls, showing up here again after what she did with the hellhounds breaking into our house. Her cocky smile never wavers though. Has she come here to gloat?

Anger whips through me. I don't think I have an ounce of love left for her. All that love has turned to pure hatred, and I have no problem keeping good on my promise and strangling her where she stands. Our bond be damned. I'll do it.

As I trudge over to her, her face changes before my eyes. Dark eyes, equally dark hair, an innocent face, but a look that says she's hardly an angel.

Aria.

My Aria.

I shake my head, confusion making me stumble. How could I have thought she was Serena?

Am I losing my mind?

"Elias," she says, and the voice belongs to Aria. A smile

brightens her entire face. "You've been out here for days. Are you going to come back inside?"

My heart beats a little faster, like it always does when I'm around her. "Do you miss me?" I tease.

She chuckles. "I was just wondering if I'm going to have to build you a doghouse outside or something."

What a little shit.

I hurry over, wrap my arms around her, and lift her off the ground.

"Hey!" she shrieks, laughing.

She weighs practically nothing, so I spin her around for good measure.

"Elias! Stop! I'm getting dizzy!" But she giggles and throws her arms and head back, giving in. I keep spinning us, around and around.

"Elias! Let me down."

This time, the voice speaking doesn't sound like Aria.

Confused, I slow down.

"Fuck! Enough, Elias! It isn't funny."

No, definitely not Aria.

I stop abruptly and let go. Serena stumbles back, angrily readjusting her jacket and brushing down her hair.

"You never know when to stop," she snaps.

"Serena?" I stare at her, dumbfounded. I was just holding Aria; I know I was.

"What's with you?" She glares at me. "It's not funny."

What the fuck is happening?

I scan the clearing and sniff the air. I don't know *what* I'm looking for, but I can't help but feel like someone is trying to play some kind of fucked-up trick on me.

When I don't see or smell anyone lurking in the shadows, I turn back to Serena. "What are you doing here?"

"Just wanted to see how much you're fucking up your life." She smirks, and my hellhound bristles.

"Fuck you," I growl. "I told you I'd kill you the moment you stepped foot in my territory again."

"So, then why haven't you?" She holds out her arms, challenging me. "Here I am. Still very much alive."

My hellhound shoves against my restraint, wanting out, and at this point I may just let him. Why haven't I ripped her apart?

I can't answer that.

Not wanting to even deal with her and her nonsense, I spin on my heel and march away. If this is another one of her tricks to distract me, it's better to ignore her. I'll send Cain to finish her off later if she's still trespassing. He'll be more than happy to do what I can't.

"Oh? Is that it?" she shouts to my turned back. "You're just going to leave? Walk away like the pussy you are?"

A mighty roar rips from my throat and I whirl around again, fury blazing, only to almost bump into Aria standing there, right in front of me.

"Shit!"

"Sorry..." she mumbles bashfully. "I thought it was impossible to sneak up on you with you hellhound senses."

I look across the clearing where Serena had just been, only to find it empty. When I glance back down at Aria, her brows are pinched in worry. Her gaze searches my face, and her hand comes up and touches my cheek.

"Elias, are you okay? You're scaring me a bit."

Terrified she'll switch on me again, I pull her into my arms and bury my face into her neck. I inhale deeply, taking in her unique smell, the one my animal recognizes and loves. The one that I know is mine.

She hugs me back just as hard, and I relish the way her body presses into mine.

An excruciating sharpness jabs into the center of my chest, paralyzing me and making me backpedal. Looking down, I see a dagger handle, its blade embedded into my chest.

Rapidly, I lose feeling in my arms and legs, and my knees buckle under my weight. I crumple, my mind a fog from the pain. She pierced my heart.

Rolling into the fetal position in the snow, warm blood covers me, but I'm cold. Too cold. And suddenly I'm so tired, I can barely keep my eyes open. My vision blurs, but I can see someone standing over me. A dark figure among the white winter background.

"Ser-Serena?" I croak out. It has to be her. She must've been using some kind of spell to change her identity.

But as she crouches closer to me and her form comes more into focus, it's Aria's beautiful face smiling down at me. Not Serena.

I can't believe it.

"You're an idiot," she spits with venom. "You actually believed I cared about you?"

I can't believe what I'm hearing. The words sound like Serena's, but the voice and person saying them is Aria.

"Cain and Dorian were right. They said you're the weakest of them. That you'd be easy to kill. I just didn't think it'd be *that* easy. Pathetic really."

Cain? Dorian?

But they are my brothers. They wouldn't plot against me.

The pain is overwhelming. Every inhale feels like there's glass in my lungs. But I don't know what's more debilitating—being stabbed in the heart or Aria's deadly confession.

Keeping my eyes open takes much more effort than it should, but I refuse to die easily. "I don't know who you are, but you aren't my little rabbit. She loves me, and I love her."

Throwing her head back, she barks a laugh. "Will you die for her then?" She kicks me hard in the side, making me grunt.

"Yes, and I'd kill for her," I begin, my voice cracking from the pain. "I'd destroy worlds for her. Raise Hell for her. But you aren't her."

As the words flow from my lips, the pain in my chest ebbs and breathing becomes less of a chore. I'm not sure how, but I keep going. "I don't know who you are, but you aren't Aria."

Her eyes widen, and when I follow her gaze, I realize the dagger is gone from my chest. Even the wound is healed over.

I touch it just to make sure.

Yep, nothing. The blood's gone, too.

It has to be a hallucination or some other kind of magic.

I knew it.

I start to get up, the weakness slowly draining from my limbs. Racking my brain, I try to think back to what I was doing before running and winding up here.

On my feet, I search the clearing for anything amiss, or for something to trigger a memory. When my gaze lands on Aria again, she backs up with a look of panicked horror on her face. I wobble on my feet but square my shoulders as I walk toward her.

"Who are you?" I demand.

"I-I don't know what you mean."

"You're not Aria," I say, and the words make me stronger. "This isn't real. Where am I? Where're Cain and Dorian?"

At the mention of their names, I get a flash of an image of Dorian, Cain, and I in Cain's office. Then Cass knocking over the skull and...

Wait a fucking minute. The skull.

That's what this is. The relic's magic.

"It's the relic!" I shout at the sky, and as if triggering something, the scenery around me spins, taking the impostor Aria with it.

MY EYES FLY OPEN.

Breathing quickly, I take in the room—the desk, the office's Victorian style decor, filled bookshelves, giant paintings of mythical battles...

Yep. This is definitely Cain's office.

To my left is Dorian, and in front of me is Cain, both suspended in time and locked mid-pose. Cain's holding the scarf, and by his frantic look, he had been hit with the skull's magic just before reaching me.

I snatch the scarf from him, wrap the relic up, and put it on the desk. The moment it's out of my hands, both Dorian and Cain snap out of their trance. They gasp for air as if they'd been holding their breath for hours.

"Holy shit. What happened?" Dorian half-chokes.

Cain's gaze jumps all over the room, unsure if the magic's truly been broken. When he spots the skull, his tight muscles ease.

"The relic... We got trapped in its darkness," he says and swallows uneasily. "I... I was in Hell. In Lucifer's torture rooms. I had... hurt Aria."

Oh shit.

"Aria had stabbed me in the heart," I explain. "At first she was

Serena, but then she changed to Aria, and told me she never cared about me."

"Stabbing you and saying that shit to you? That has Serena all over it," Dorian replies and runs a shaky hand through his hair.

"And you?" Cain asks him wearily. "What did the relic make you see?"

Dorian hesitates, his gaze dropping to the floor.

"Let's hear it," I tell him.

He sighs heavily. "Just me... in an orgy."

I blink. "Excuse me?"

He holds up a hand so he can finish. "And then Aria walked in. The look on her face... I had ripped her heart out."

I don't know. It seems like Dorian got the best one of us three, but the heavy regret and distress on his face says otherwise.

He glances at Cain. "That may have been me at one time in my life, but after we found her, I..."

"I know what you mean," Cain finishes for him.

"The look on her face, Cain... It damn near killed me." Pain strains his voice. "Not being able to control myself like that, hurting her like that, it's one of my biggest fears."

"Mine as well," Cain says. "In mine, my father was praising me for being like him and torturing her close to death."

"Sounds like the relic gave us all nightmares," I suggest.

Staring at the skull, Cain shakes his head. "Not nightmares. It showed us our greatest fears."

Dorian's eyes widen. "Fuck, I think you're right."

Making the same mistake I had with Serena and being literally and figuratively stabbed in the heart classifies as my greatest fear.

Yep. Checks out.

"Now we understand why those museum employees thought it was cursed and went loco bananas," Dorian says.

Cain nods, then picks up the skull, careful to touch only the scarf, and places it in the secret compartment under his desk.

"One thing I don't quite understand though," Dorian begins when Cain remerges, "how did we manage to break free of it?"

"I think I was the one who did it somehow," I admit. "I was able to see through the magic's ruse, and once I realized it wasn't real, I was able to snap out of it."

"It's lucky you did, otherwise who knows how long we would've been stuck in our own fears," Cain says.

Dorian squeezes me on the shoulders and shakes me. "Go Elias! I'm so proud."

I shrug his hold away, and he bursts into a fit of laughter.

Just then, Cass strolls back into the office, and jumps on the computer chair. Like always, he's got an air of smugness to him whenever Aria's not around, almost like he's proud of knocking over the skull and sending us into a fear spiral.

The fucking furball.

To my surprise, Dorian glares at him. He's always been on the sweeter side to Cass than me or Cain, but right now, he looks like he wants to throttle him.

"Guys, let's all take a moment to realize that we—three of the most powerful and handsome demons Hell's ever created—were almost killed because of a fucking cat."

Cass responds by lifting up his leg and licking the underside of his fur. Not a care in the world.

Why did we think getting the relics back would be that easy?

I never met the demon, but Lorcan's a sin demon—he's smart enough to know someone may come looking for the relics, and if he can't stash them in seven different places all over the world like Gabriel did, then he's going to do what he can to make it difficult.

That means hiding them separately as much as he can.

Maverick is fuming and cursing out his older brother so fast, it sounds like he's speaking in tongues. Rightfully so. But we need to worry about getting out of this basement, especially now that Lucifer's mucking about upstairs.

"We need to get out of here," I say, searching the darkness for a way out. I spot a small, barred window two feet above us, a strip of Hell's red sky beyond it. If we manage to take out the bars somehow, we can shimmy our way through. "There. Do you think either of you take out the bars?"

"Easy." Maverick steps up and uses his wings to lift himself off the ground. With one hard yank, the entire grate comes off, and he tosses it to the side.

"Age before beauty," Nix says and throws me a wink over his shoulder.

Maverick rolls his eyes. "Just scout the yard and let us know if it's clear."

"Right." He leaps up, grabs onto the window, and pulls himself out with ease. Then, he scrambles to his feet and disappears.

Maverick and I exchange looks.

A tense moment passes by.

"You don't think he'd leave us, do you?" I ask.

"We're demons, so yes, I do."

When there's still no sign of Nix, I curse.

"Should've known better than to trust him," Maverick groans.

"And you should know that I like to keep you on your toes, Brother." Nix's face appears in the window. "The yard is clear now. But I'm sure we don't have much time. Let's go."

Maverick's hands are suddenly on my waist, and I'm rising toward the window, where Nix's waiting hands are. When I'm close enough, he seizes me and yanks, while Maverick shoves me from behind, palms full of my ass.

I can't help but think he'll be teasing me about this later. When we're not in serious trouble.

Relic box in hand, I flop onto the grass at Nix's perfectly polished shoes but quickly hop to my feet and wait for Maverick to follow. He folds his wings back into his back and hauls himself through.

He stands and shakes the ash and god knows what else out of his silvery blond hair. With a hasty look around, he snatches me by the hand and starts to tug me down the path at a brisk pace. Nix stays close behind, glancing over his shoulder every now and then to check if we're being followed. Luckily, we aren't.

Once we're far enough away, Lucifer's whorehouse nothing more than a blip in the distance, Maverick whirls on me. "So, we only got three," he says, running a hand down his face as he thinks. "Only three..."

Is there an echo here?

"Yes. Only three," I repeat.

"Which three? Did you see?" Nix asks eagerly.

"The eye, hair, and heart—because they've been connected," I reply.

"Connected?" Maverick asks and starts to lead us back toward Hell City.

"Um, yeah. The hair and eye accidentally connected before I was kidnapped by a werewolf biker gang. And I guess the heart locked on during our tumble down the chute."

Nix clears his throat. "Excuse me. Did you say werewolf biker gang?"

"They called themselves the Full Mooners."

"You're kidding," Maverick says, close to laughter.

"Can't make this shit up if I tried."

Nix's brows shoot up in surprise. "I guess Earth is more exciting than I thought."

I want to say that when it comes to my life, it's a three-ring circus, but I refrain. Our mission was a success for the most part. We may not have gotten all the relics back, but we have three. Hopefully there is only one more stop for the others and we can hightail it back home to the living plane. All the sulfur and close encounters are making my stomach hurt.

After some time, we reach Maverick's castle, if you would call it that. As we approach the massive building, Nix stops and starts to walk back the way we came.

"This is where we part, my dears. It'll be too suspicious if we're together for too long," he says, saluting us. "I'll ask around and see what I can find about the other relics. I'll come back when I can."

I give him a short wave, and Maverick guides me around the back of the house to his secret entrance. He opens the door for us to step inside, and I ask, "Does he do that all the time? Just pop in and out like that?"

"Yes, he does it to everyone. It's kind of his thing." As we walk along the corridor, he unbuttons the cuffs of his shirt and begins to roll up the sleeves to his elbows. I try not to stare at the way his muscles flex or how the simple clothing change makes him look even more sexy than he already does.

My mouth's suddenly dry. "He seems to have taken a special kind of liking to you though."

He side-eyes me and his lips quirk up at the corner. "He's probably the closest brother I have."

"But you don't trust him?"

"Nope."

How weird.

"You can't trust anyone here," he goes on. "Sometimes, not even yourself."

What the heck does that mean? Probably best if I don't ask.

Instead, I say, "Do you think he's going to snitch on us being here and hunting for relics?"

We begin to climb a grand staircase to an upper floor. "There's a good possibility. But do I think he'll tell? No. Not right away at least. Not when I've promised him all my soul contracts in exchange for his help."

Even he doesn't sound certain, and that makes me nervous.

"So, what do we do now?" I ask and hold up the box. He takes it from me and goes over to a large grandfather clock in the hallway. Like everything else is this damn place it's black but with what look like tree roots weaving through the other pieces of wood and brass. When he presents it with the relics box, the roots slither away from the face, as if they are alive, and reveal a hollow opening inside. He slides the box inside and the roots crawl back into place, perfectly concealing it from view.

"Woah," I gasp.

That gets a chuckle out of him. "Lorcan's not the only one good at hiding things. This entire place is full of secrets."

After seeing what the fireplace in my old room could do, I believe that a hundred percent.

"*Now*," he says with emphasis to circle back to my original question, "we're going to get some rest. Tomorrow, we will go and hunt down the other relics."

"Rest? You mean sleep?" I glance around to find a window, but there barely are any in this place. "How do you know when it's night here?"

"Night doesn't exist in Hell," he replies smartly. "It's one smoky, burning red sky forever and ever. But our bodies know when it's time to shut down, and mine is saying I need to feed and regroup if I want to be strong enough for what's ahead."

"Hopefully nothing crazy," I whisper, my heart beating a little fast.

"Aria, this is Hell. Or did you forget?" He turns and strides down the hall again, forcing me to run to catch up. We walk along in silence for some time, and when he stops in front of a door without warning, I almost bump into his back.

"You can stay in here," he says and opens the door for me.

Stepping inside, I'm shocked to find it's not the same one he'd imprisoned me in last time. This one is full of paintings, some displayed on the walls and some on easels half-finished. They range in size, color, and subject, but all of them are extremely detailed. Even more surprising is that this room has huge glass doors leading out to a balcony and, with the curtains drawn back, light floods inside.

There's a modest size bed, a couch, a few bookshelves, and paint-splattered canvases haphazardly stacked on the floor.

I'm in complete awe. It actually looks somewhat...normal.

For a medieval doom castle, that is.

Maverick hovers in the doorway, unrolling and rerolling his sleeve, but now almost as if he's fidgeting. "I'll try to find some... edible food for you to eat. Although I can't promise anything. It's been a while since I've been home, and as I'm sure you know, demons rarely eat regular food."

I wave his offer away, my gaze still dancing over all the paintings decorating the walls. Most of the hanging space is gone; every inch is covered with a framed masterpiece.

They're all renditions of earthly things, too. A swan in a lake surrounded by a lush meadow, two horses running across a grassy plain, spindly trees covered in snow with the full moon shining through the clouds...

Then a thought hits me. "Wait...did you paint all these?"

"Hm?"

I turn to face him fully. "All of these. Did you paint them?"

His gaze drops like he's wondering if he should tell me the truth or not. But then he nods. "I did."

I don't know what to say.

"As you know, demons have eternity to waste, so I've taken up a few hobbies to keep me sane." He's trying to brush it off like it's no big deal, but I'm still having a hard time believing it. These paintings aren't just 'meh, okay.' They're actually good. Really good. Like...should be hanging up in some exhibit or museum, good.

"Hunting, killing, fighting..." he goes on, rattling off his list.

"And the arts apparently."

He shrugs. "When I would go to Earth to see you or do Lucifer's bidding, I'd see some interesting things. And I wanted to remember them."

I stare at him, wondering who the hell he really is.

"I'll wake you in a few hours," he says, taking the door handle. "Sleep well."

When the door shuts and the lock clicks, silence overtakes the room. I take another full look around, still marveling at the secret talent Maverick possesses. It makes me wonder if Cain knows about it, or Nix. It definitely doesn't seem like he wants to boast about it, even though he should. The attention to detail and coloring are amazing. Lifelike.

That's when my gaze comes across something interesting in one of the paintings. It's of a woman standing in a fog, part of her face obscured by it, her dark hair wet and stuck to her face. The half of her that you can see is dripping wet, and even though only one eye is visible, her gaze pierces you.

I get closer, familiarity striking me.

Is that supposed to be...me?

And the haziness surrounding me... Is that meant to be the hot springs Maverick had taken me too? Where we'd kissed back when I'd thought he was an angel.

Holy shit! It is!

Another painting, not too far off, is of a woman laying on a large four-poster bed and colored as if the viewer is peeking in through a stained-glass window.

Like my bedroom's window at the mansion.

I glance to one of the unfinished canvases on an easel and see myself there too, half-painted. A dark womanly figure against a white, snowy background.

"When I would go to Earth to see you or do Lucifer's bidding, I'd see some interesting things. And I wanted to remember them," he'd said.

Interesting things, like me?

I should be weirded out that he was stalking me for so long, watching me from the shadows, but my stomach tightens for a different reason. Flattery? I'm not sure. But the fact that it doesn't freak me out only confirms how fucked up I am.

It's so hard to peg Maverick down. He's a wildcard, and I never know what he's going to do.

Shaking my head, I cross the room and climb into the bed. The mattress is surprisingly soft, and once my head hits the pillow, the exhaustion really sinks its claws into me. Even with the constant wails of Hell creatures outside the castle, it doesn't take long to drift off to sleep.

***

THE BOOMING KNOCK echoes through the stone walls, amplifying the sound. I leap up in bed, my heart hammering.

We've been found out! Lucifer knows!

My mind is going a mile a minute, nausea and panic rolling in the pit of my stomach.

The bedroom door shoots open and Maverick stands on the other side, eyes wide with terror. I'm off the bed and rushing over to him in a flash.

"Someone's here," he says in a harsh whisper.

"Who is it? Nix?"

He shakes his head. "Nix never knocks. This is someone else."

My heart is hammering against my ribs. "What do we do? What if it's Lucifer?"

He pauses. Obviously all of these thoughts have been going through his head as well. "Stay here. Do not leave this room. Whatever happens to me," he commands.

"Whatever happens to you? What the fuck are you talking about, Maverick?" Does he think the person behind that door means to hurt him?

His voice booms. "I'm not kidding, Aria. Fucking stay here. If things get bad, get yourself out. Go to the gate."

I can barely process what he's implying before he spins and hurries down the hall and jumps down the staircase. Seconds later, the echoing creak of the big front doors opening breaks the eerie silence.

My entire body tenses, bracing for the worse.

"What the fuck are you doing here?" Maverick sounds angry, not scared, but I'm not sure if that's better or worse.

"Hello to you, too."

It's a woman's voice. One I don't recognize.

"I said fuck off," Maverick growls.

Whoever it is, he doesn't want them around.

"Cool it, Mav. I can't just stop in for a visit?"

"No."

"Come on, I just want to chat."

"When was the last time I saw you, Serena? Over a century ago? And now you just want to pop in for a *chat*?"

Wait, Serena? Elias's bitch of an ex, Serena?

Fury scorches through my veins, and my feet are walking me toward the voices before my brain can register what's happening. But I need to see this bitch; I need to know who betrayed my demons and broke my hellhound's heart.

When I reach the landing, I lean over the railing to get a clear look of her through the sliver of open door. Blonde hair cut in a sharp bob, emerald-green eyes, and dressed head to toe in motor-cycle chic.

She's gorgeous, of course, with a badass edge that I'll never have. Super skinny, long legs, and a model's height.

So, naturally, I hate her.

When Maverick tries to slam the door in her face, she grabs it and shoves it open a little more. "There's been a lot of talk throughout Hell that you were back. Chyd said you visited your father's whorehouse of all places," she begins, trying to grab his interest.

"Needed to release some frustration," he replies blandly.

"I had money on Cain killing you while you were up there." A smirk twists her ruby-painted lips.

The mention of Cain has Maverick's shoulders stiffening. "Yeah, well, he didn't."

"Lucky you," she says. "You know Lucifer's ticked you weren't able to bring back more information about the shadow girl. I'd expect a visit soon, if I were you."

Fear weaves up my spine. There goes our cover. Or Maverick's. But if Lucifer comes to see him, there's no doubt I'll be figured out, too.

He must be considering the same thing because he says, "Well, I better start preparing. Thanks for the warning."

Again, he tries to close the door and she shoves it to keep it open. "One more thing," she says, and my annoyance prickles across my skin. I can feel my temperature rising along with it. "Did you see Elias? How's he doing?"

Hearing his name on her lips sends my anger spiraling and Sayah darting to the surface. Silently telling her to wait in case I need her, I practically fly down the steps, Serena's gaze quickly finding me, and her cocky smile wavers. Maverick's expression is a mixture of fear and aggravation, but I ignore it.

"Oh, Mav, you didn't tell me you had a lady friend over," she purrs, and for some reason, the way she says the nickname even grates on my nerves.

"I visited the whorehouse. What do you think I did there? Check out some library books?"

His comment doesn't even touch me. Neither does the fact that she's looking down at me like I'm below her in every way, with her lip curled up in disgust. Like I am nothing more than one of Hell's sex slaves.

I'm breathing hard, my body shaking with rage, unable to think about anything else but the pain she put Elias through, how she ripped out his heart and stomped on it repeatedly.

"You totally could've gotten someone prettier, Mav," Serena says, out of the corner of her mouth. "This one looks like she was crossbred with a horse."

"Why don't you go lick Lucifer's balls some more? After all that time in the whorehouse, I'm sure they'll need a good cleaning." The words fly from my lips, my voice not even sounding like mine.

But there, I said it. And I'm not taking it back.

Serena leans forward, eyes narrowing. "Excuse me?"

"That's what you're good at, isn't it? Doing Lucifer's dirty work?"

She glances at Maverick, the shock clear on her face. "Are you going to let this slug in fishnets talk to me like that?"

He cocks a brow. "But is she wrong?"

She scoffs and then points a long fingernail in my face. "Listen here, you little trollop—"

My fist shoots out and connects with the side of her face before she can finish her sentence. Something tells me Sayah put some strength behind it, because it sends Serena stumbling backwards, tripping down the front steps, and holding the side of her cheek, which is now bleeding and split open. I look down at my hand and see Cain's ring glistening with blood.

I smile.

Who knew this thing would come in handy in more than one way?

Serena looks up, cursing, but Maverick's fast to shut the door and lock it this time.

An apology hovers on my tongue, but Maverick holds a finger to his lips to silence me before moving to a peep hole in the door and looking through. When he confirms she's gone, he turns back to me.

"You know that was really fucking stupid, right?" he bites out. "You could've been found out."

"I know. I know," I reply, looking at my bloody ring again. Even though I know all that, I still don't regret it. "But damn, did it feel good."

I expect him to bagger me more, but instead, his mouth twitches as if he's holding back a smile. "Serena deserves much worse, but socking her like you did is a good start."

Oh, well then, I'm glad he approves.

Unfortunately, his mild cheeriness doesn't last long. "Bad news is that her visit means we're in a lot of trouble. Now that word's out that I'm back in Hell, she's right that Lucifer is going to want to meet with me."

"So, what does that mean?" I ask as worry wiggles its way through me.

"It means time's gotten cut shorter. And we can't stay here. It's the first place he'll come."

That's not good.

"Any ideas?"

He pauses, thinking.

After a long moment, he says, "One…"

One is better than nothing, right? "Whatever it is, let's do it. I'm in."

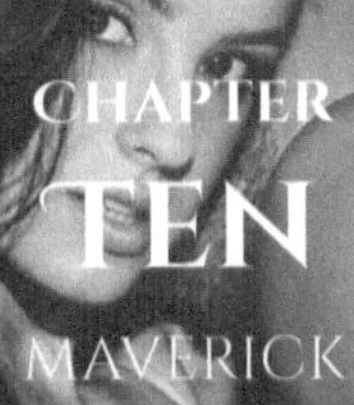

"This place is safe, you say?" Aria asks as she cautiously steps through the door. We walk into the palace's empty foyer, our steps echoing loudly in the silence.

"Yes. No one comes here. It's been abandoned and some think it's cursed, so it should be left alone. Lucifer won't check for me here." The sweltering heat is unbearable today. Father must be pissed—the demons working underground always torture twice the number of souls when he's in a foul mood to attempt to cheer him, and as a result, everyone suffers.

A hellish gnat swarms around me, a pesky thing with six fangs, and I swat it out of my face. Another side-effect of increased heat.

Aria glances over her shoulder at me, gaze narrow. "Like a witch's curse?"

"It's not hexed. But rumors spread like wildfire in Hell, and many of these fake tales are cast out intentionally." I shut the door behind me and lock it.

She studies me carefully. "So, you've made yourself a safe house where no one would find you? Clever."

"Don't sound so surprised," I respond. "I may be the big bad demon in the room, but I'm not a fucking monster. Now, keep going straight ahead, past the staircase," I growl.

Her eyes flare with defiance, but instead of snapping back, she turns away from me, and I follow her deep into the main room.

"I see you're still in your shitty mood," she mumbles.

I bite my tongue hard at the fact that we're here after her confrontation with Serena. The coppery tang of blood coats my tongue. With it comes a fire that scores my chest while my mind fills with images of Aria being fucked in front of me by my brother, and me being unable to join in. It's been on my mind endlessly and it's driving me nuts.

Cain can be such a bastard when he's jealous. I nearly lost my mind watching them...

I stuff my hands into the pockets of my pants and trail close behind her, my gaze on her tight body, her curvy ass in her lace jumpsuit, and dark hair I'm craving to wrap around my fist as I fuck her. My cock twitches at the thought.

The thing about Cain's stunt is that it made me jealous as fuck, and the image is imprinted in my mind of her body, her curves, her moans, her scent. It's all stuck in my head, torturing me.

She pauses a few steps ahead and tilts her head up to take in the monstrous main room. The walls shine like polished black glass, and our distorted reflections stare back at us as we move. Even the flooring has the same translucent, ice-like effect, and every one of our steps echoes against the suffocating silence of the place. It speaks volumes to who my brother was when he lived here.

Broody. Arrogant. A recluse.

"Wow. I thought your other house was over the top. This is the epitome of a bachelor pad for a serial killer. Did this home once belong to Lucifer?"

"Father has never lived here," I say, which is true. She doesn't need to know who did. Not yet, anyway.

That'll be my little secret.

I turn to take in the vaulted ceilings, the space lacking any furniture. Everything in the room guides your sight to a set of elevated steps against the far wall, traveling to a black throne.

Two pillars flank it on either side, and a lofty wall embedded with skulls rises up from behind the seat. There's a window located over the throne, casting bright light from above giving the impression that whoever sits in the spot is somehow divine.

I roll my eyes. I've always hated this fucking eyesore.

Aria's staring at the seat, then looks at me, and back again.

"This is so you." She waves her hand toward the throne as if anyone could ever miss it. "Very over-indulgent."

I bristle, squaring my shoulders. "What's that supposed to mean?"

"You're a sin demon, right? Figure it out." She turns from me abruptly and walks deeper into the room.

I exhale an exasperated breath. "I'm surprised you think so little of sin demons. Especially since your loverboy, Cain, is one," I snap, strolling toward the doorway leading into the hall. "Guess now that you've let him fuck you, he's no longer a horrible demon like the rest of us."

"You asshole!" she bellows, her jawline clenched when I grin back at her. Oh yeah, that got her all riled up.

"Such language." I tsk and keep striding across the room, loving that I've roused her anger.

Her footsteps strike the hard floor, her breath quick. "You've been in such a pissy mood ever since we arrived in Hell. I'm sorry you didn't like what you saw with Cain and me. That's your problem, isn't it? But don't take your family issues out on me." She's shaking, but her expression is firm, and it seems she's not finished.

But I don't give her the chance. I grab her arm and haul her with me into the hall and up the grand staircase.

"What the hell? Let me go, Maverick," she warns.

"You think I'm an asshole, then fine, I'll be that asshole for you."

My jaw ticks as I grind my back teeth. I wrench her to a door that I kick open, and then shove her inside.

She rips free from my hand, stumbling. The room is dark with barely anything visible except for the light pouring in behind me from the hall.

"What is this room? What the hell are you doing?" Panic streaks her face.

As anger flares over me, she glares my way.

"You want to know the truth? I am fucking livid at the stunt Cain pulled. He knows what you mean to me."

Her expression softens. "Yeah, and what's that?"

I huff and step inside, shutting the door behind us with my foot, encasing us in darkness. Good thing the dark is my friend.

"If you can't work it out for yourself, then there is no conversation to be had," I snarl, while an excitement rises in me at watching her stumble about blindly. Her arms are out in front of her, waving about, trying to find a wall or something.

"Seriously, Maverick. You're really starting to piss me off."

"Welcome to the club." I step toward her, and my hand falls to the blade I keep in my boot. There's something just so delectable about the scent of her fear, to see her frantically trying to find the door. Something in me wants to make her hurt.

I sneak up behind her and blow a breath into her hair.

She snaps around and I slide out of her reach. "Fuck you. I don't like this game," she yells.

"Yeah, and I didn't like being the observer either."

She swings in my direction, following my voice, so I sweep to my left, but not before I nick her on the arm and across her cheek with my blade. I want so much more, but that's coming.

Her cry is music to my ears.

"What the fuck is wrong with you? Did you just cut me?"

"Does it feel good? Figured we could have our own party. How does that sound?"

"Like you're a lunatic."

"Then it's safe to say you like them crazy."

"You're such a prick today. Boohoo, you got blue balls and now you're being a baby. But if you want me to play along while you keep being an ass, then fine. Make it a fair playing field. I need light." Even in the dark, I see her gripping her knife.

With a smile, I silently move across the room to the window covered in a cloth. I rip it off, light stealing the dark, my eyes momentarily blinded...just as something zips past my head. A sharp bite of metal grazes my ear. I hear the dull thump of it striking something behind me, and I twist around to see a knife embedded in the wall.

Savage.

"I adore how volatile you are." But I'll admit, underestimating her might be my undoing. I touch my ear and my fingers come back with blood.

She lifts her chin confidently and grins. "You're not the only one with surprises." Just as she grins my way, I hurl my blade for that pretty little face.

She ducks, a gasp on her lips, but then swings around just as fast and lunges for the weapon I threw at her.

I snatch the one near the window while she scrambles up on the bed and leaps at me, releasing a war cry.

Be still my heart and cock—which just hardened—at the beautiful sight. That brief pause is all it takes for this gorgeous creature to crash into me, shoving me to the ground, my blade falling from my grasp. She straddles me and something sharp pierces my shoulder.

I wince.

"Oh, oopsy." She acts coy as I glance at the blade sticking in the meaty part of my shoulder. It's not deep but stings nonetheless.

She starts to shift off me, but I snatch her hips and rock my erection against the heat burning between her thighs.

For a moment, she moans, her eyelids fluttering upward, but just as quick, she slaps me across the face.

Not that it hurt, but it catches me off guard long enough for her to lunge off me.

"Clever," I say as I yank the knife out of my shoulder with a groan, blood drenching my shirt and dripping down my chest and arm.

I twist back up on my feet. "You're good. Must have had a hell of a teacher teaching you to use knives."

She snorts a fake laugh. "He was mediocre. Too busy being caught up in his own petty jealousy to really focus."

I arch a brow. "Petty?" I blow out a breath. "Is that so?"

She comes at me, my pulse racing at her insult, my chest bursting to prove her wrong. All the while, my cock pulses because seeing her in fight mode, makes me fucking wild for her.

At the last second I swing out of her path, snatch her hand with the blade, swing her around to face me, then drive her backward.

I lean toward her face. "Maybe the problem is you weren't paying attention and were too busy flirting with your teacher, wishing he'd just fuck you already."

She gasps, the sound of my obsession. Her ass hits the bed and she rips her wrist from my grasp.

Swiftly, I snatch her by the back of her neck, holding my knife to her throat.

Just as quick, the cold steel of her weapon presses to the base of mine.

"Stalemate," she coos, though she's frozen on the spot, her chest rising and falling quickly. The cut on her cheek pebbles with blood, and it looks spectacular on her.

My hold on her nape never relents, and I push forward, the bite of her blade razor sharp against my skin. "If you intend to cut me, then do it."

She trembles. "Y-You're always so dramatic."

I inhale deeply, taking in her perspiration, her fear, and the sweet scent of her arousal that would drive any man to insanity. Nudging my knee between her thighs, I force them farther apart and push myself between them.

"It's tempting, isn't it?" I whisper. "One swipe, and my throat is sliced. Is that what you want?" I press my bent leg forward a bit more, my thigh wedged between hers, her heat flooding through the fabric of my pants. I wriggle my leg slightly to make sure she feels me. "Or do you prefer this?"

"Seems you're projecting your own fantasies on me," she mutters, her chin high, but lust swims behind her gaze. She's not fooling anyone.

"Then why is your pussy so hot and drenched?"

Her eyes narrow on me with hatred, and she bites the side of her lip when I rub her once more. *Fuck me.* My cock is throbbing.

Aria sets my pulse on fire with her body and that wicked look, like she wants to fuck me, then murder me, in that order. She's the kind of woman that any man would desire. I can see why she's reduced my brother to a love-struck mess.

"I'm not afraid of you," she says brazenly.

"Good," I reply and release the back of her neck, but she doesn't go anywhere while I have the length of my blade pressing into her throat. "I hate pushovers. I want a fighter." Lowering my free hand to her waist, I grab a fistful of the lace jumpsuit, my nails extending into claws, and I tear the fabric roughly off her, shredding the material.

She cries out, and I glance down to where I've accidentally cut her across her hip. "Oops." I grin deviously.

"You're a real bastard, you know."

"And I love it when you flirt with me." I tear more of the material from her, leaving a gaping hole across her middle and lap, her skin so tempting. The black thong needs to go. "I prefer this look on you."

I reach down and hook a claw into the elastic of her underwear.

Her free hand is on mine, nails digging into skin, her glare warning me.

"Don't think about it," she raises her voice.

"Oh, I've thought of nothing but having your pussy bare so I can see exactly how much I'm turning you on." Before I can even give her the chance to respond, I flick my claw, slicing through the elastic and her underwear pulls apart at her hip.

"Bastard!" Her eyes grow wider.

"You know you love it."

Sharpness cuts across into my throat, and I know she's sliced skin. Her bulging gaze says it all. Her hold softens as the warm trickle of blood rolls down my neck and under my shirt.

I smirk, loving the sensation of my cock swelling, while the sting on my neck hums as if it has a heartbeat of its own.

"Did it feel good to cut me?" I retract my claws. My normal fingers now crawl higher up her thigh, and this time she's not pushing me away. I skirt across her bikini line, and the temptation to shove her down and bite into her, fuck her, is unbearable.

Except, this isn't just about me, now is it?

She gasps while spreading her legs for me shamelessly.

I push aside the rest of the torn fabric of her underwear and run my fingers across her slit. She's so wet, so beautiful, it undoes me. Her eyes flutter upward as I spread her lips with my fingers and plunge two into her warmth.

My dick strains for release.

"This doesn't change how angry I am at you," she promises, as a trickle of blood rolls down her cheek and onto her neck. The urge to lean in and lick it grows by the second.

"Aria, I am the one angry, not the other way around." I finger her faster, and it takes her moments to look at me. She watches me as if barely holding herself together. It's exactly how I've always wanted to see her... on the verge of losing control, me the one who pushes her over the edge.

"And now I will hurt you in the most delicious way," I promise.

Her mouth curls into a smile that begs for more.

I pull out of her, much to her protesting moans, and I wrap my free arm around her lower back, holding her in place. She reaches for my pants. A hard tug of her fingers at my pants and zipper, then she has them dropping down to my feet.

There are still blades at each other's throat, and I sure as fuck won't be the first to put mine down. I've seen the savagery in her gaze, and as much as I'd love her to cut me rougher, to make me feel the biting agony of steel on flesh, I want something else first.

She palms my cock, and I hiss as I step closer.

"That's it, gorgeous."

"Maybe you should let go of your blade," she suggests. "It'll be easier."

"You'd like that wouldn't you."

She shrugs with an adorable grin. But the hunger coursing through my veins is killing me. The desperation to finally have this girl all for myself is becoming too much.

I push her hand away and guide my cock to her swollen pussy, my mind thrashing with hunger. She lifts her legs, spreads them wider, rocking her hips, and I push into her.

She cries out, her breaths quickening, her free hand on my arm, and I drive deeper into her while staring into those gorgeous dark eyes. Her pussy sucks down on my dick, squeezing, wanting more.

"Is this better?" I ask, my voice breathy.

Neither of us have relented on lowering the blades. I push against the one in her hand, and feel her softly pulling back. She doesn't want to hurt me, so I lower my blade and set it to the bed next to us.

But she holds hers still, and I reach up to grab her arm. "If you wanted to kill me, you'd have done it already." I push her hand aside and the knife tumbles from her gasp and onto the floor.

Then I push myself closer, slamming my cock harder into her tight cunt, and our mouths clash. We kiss like hungry wolves, lips and tongue, her hands yanking on my shirt.

I wrench the fabric up and over my head, then grab her hips and lift her ass off the bed with ease, ramming into her harder.

She moans, her fingers digging into my arms as her legs curl around my hips. At this stage, I'm only interested in fucking her, not caring what clothes I'm wearing. But hers... oh, they need to go, and fast.

I tear at them with one hand as she holds onto me, the sound of material ripping echoing around us. The whole time she's groaning, rocking her sweet hips to meet each slap.

"Drag me to the dark side, Maverick." She lets go of me and falls onto her back on the bed, her legs still strangling my waist. She's slowly peeling away the shred of her clothes, her bra sliding off.

Her breasts bounce with each thrust, and she's tugging on those perky nipples, her back arching, her cries fucking beautiful.

"You're going to ruin me," I growl.

I reach over and collect my knife, pausing my assault on her tight body, my cock deeply rammed into her.

She cranes her head up to look at me with an arched brow, finding me holding the weapon. "Maverick."

She tenses against me, I set a hand on her chest, pushing her back down. "Relax."

Then I place the flat side of the blade across her stomach and she flinches at its coldness. She's frozen in place, her skin covered in goosebumps.

"You like this?" I move the cold metal under her collarbone and she moans as I trace the valley between her tits with the dull side of the knife. I pick up my pace of fucking her once again, pulling and pushing into her. Her lips curl up with her moans, her gaze lost in arousal.

Then, I make a tiny incision just over her left breast.

She flinches and cries out, her eyes huge, while blood beads instantly. "What the heck?"

The drop races around her breast and runs down the middle, leaving a red path across such perfect skin.

"It's beautiful," I say, then I lean forward and run the flat of my tongue over the wound, licking up her blood. Coppery, slightly warm, and sweet. An excited shiver runs down my spine. "This is how I want you. Naked, spread for me, and covered in blood."

She blinks at me, drawing her full lower lip between her teeth, then reaches over to cup the sides of my head. She draws me down on top of her.

"My turn," she purrs.

Her mouth latches onto my bleeding shoulder where she'd stabbed me earlier, her tongue lapping at the blood. My cock hardens, my balls constrict, and I hammer into her hard, my world spiraling around this girl... This human.

When she releases my shoulder and peers up at me, she licks the blood from her lips like I've given her the most incredible gift. Part of me twitches, and I tighten my hold on my hilt as I place it across my other shoulder, relishing in its cool touch.

I take a fast swipe across the skin, the sting deep. But the way she stares at the blood is worth it. I bury myself in up to my balls and groan, so damn close to the edge.

She's so tight, so fucking amazing.

She wipes her hand across my cut and comes back with blood dripping from her fingers. With a grin, she smears it across her tits.

"Don't stop fucking me," she orders.

And I don't hesitate to plow into her, thrusting so hard the entire bed rocks with us. I drop the blade to the floor and lower myself over her once more, the sticky wetness of blood gluing us together. Our mouths crash together, like this is where we are meant to be, bound to each other.

I flash her a smile and jackhammer into her tight core as I reach down between us, two fingers rubbing on her adorable little clit.

It's only seconds before she stiffens under me, her eyes squeezed shut, a scream singing on her lips.

Her expression is beautiful as she orgasms, but the way she's constricting my dick, she unleashes my own climax. Together we're writhing, bellowing, drowning in the most insane orgasms.

"Fuck, keep squeezing my cock. Take it all."

I don't know how long we've been lost to our bodies, but when I finally come up for air, I'm staring into the deepest eyes. At the most stunning smile. Her body painted in blood.

"I've underestimated you," she breathes heavily.

"Yeah, how so?"

"Here I thought you brought me to a creepy Gothic castle, but instead, this room, this bed, is starting to grow on me. It actually feels comfortable." She stretches her arms out on either side of her, throwing her head back on the blanket. "And hell, you can fuck well." She almost blushes, and the sight has my dick swelling again.

I lean forward, covering her body with mine and pressing my lips against hers. "As they say, best for last."

She smirks while I pull out of her and stand up. I hadn't expected to feel such a strong draw to her, or how much I wish we could curl up and stay in this bedroom for a week so I could fuck her brains out.

My gaze dips to her swollen lips between her thighs, at my seed starting to seep out of her. The sight is glorious.

"Now this is the kind of fucking you should use to measure every other that will follow." I grin and lick my lips.

She blinks at me, seeming stunned at my words.

I pull my mouth into a harsh smile, then yank up my pants.

"Why are you looking at me with that strange smile?" she asks, propping herself up on her elbows and closing her legs.

Collecting both our blades, I can't stop staring at her naked. "I find it adorable that you like this room. Maybe it's because it belongs to Cain. And I just fucked you in his bed."

Her eyes narrow with that earlier feisty fire I'm used to. "Wait, what? This is his home? And you had sex with me here on purpose, just to spite him? You bastard."

I smirk. "That's where you're wrong. I've been aching to fuck you. It just so happened that our first time was in Cain's aban-doned home."

And I can't wait to rub it in his stupid, arrogant face. It may be even better than the sex.

For an abandoned palace, Cain's residence still has all the amenities: running water, power, and a lack of spider-webs. But I did discover he has a walk-in closet with all manner of clothing, like I'd walked into Macy's. Men's and women's clothing, shoes, jewelry.

I don't know if I should be worried that Cain is secretly a cross-dresser or that he kept these in his home for all the women he picked up in Hell.

Except the Cain who lived here and sat in that intimidating throne downstairs is not the same man back on Earth waiting for me.

I get dressed in the most modest thing I can find. Leather pants, that must be one size too small and a black tank top that creeps up over my stomach.

Running my fingers through my wet hair after the hot shower, I head back into Cain's bedroom, where I find Maverick lounging back on the bed with eyes closed and hands behind his head. His legs are crossed at the ankles, and he's freshly dressed in black pants and a button-up shirt.

I'm still annoyed at him for not telling me this is Cain's place, but I'm so used to the brothers being competitive that it doesn't surprise me.

When Maverick cracks his eyes open, he pushes up to sit on the side of the bed. He eyes me head to toe. "You look ready to go into battle."

"Maybe I am." I slide up next to him and flop down onto the mattress. "To kick your ass again for lying to me."

A devious smile spreads his lips. "I never lied to you. I just withheld information."

"Tomayto, tomahto."

He shakes his head. "What's that mean?"

"It means you're splitting hairs and making excuses. It's the same thing."

He twists around to look at me, his leg bent between us. "I wanted to see your reaction to the castle without knowing who owned it, so it was the truth."

I roll my eyes hard. Why don't I believe him? "So, have you got all the jealousy out of your system?" I ask.

He shrugs, locking gazes with me. "I may need more time with you to make up my mind."

"I think you got your moment to stick it to Cain, which is plenty enough."

He watches me intently. "Do you still not realize what you do to me? How much I want to be with you?"

Everything about Maverick screams gorgeous and dangerous, and he brought something out of me that I never knew I liked... knife play, tasting his blood, letting me see the beauty in darkness.

Does the desire he stirs within me stem from Sayah, or is it purely me craving dark things? I don't want to think too deeply on it because I don't know if I'll like the answers I find.

I shouldn't be embarrassed after what we just did in Cain's bedroom, but talking about feelings has me blushing. Go figure.

Maverick smirks in acknowledgment. He knows how I feel, even if I struggle to admit it. Loving three demons took me a while to accept, and now to find myself falling just as hard for a fourth— Cain's brother of all demons too—well, my brain and heart are having trouble keeping up.

"So, where to next? We need to find the rest of the relics and head back home."

He studies me for a long pause, and I can't help but wonder if he's pondering my words. I realize what I implied, *our* home.

"While you showered, I flew back to Irnonoch and threatened

to take his new castle from him if he didn't spill more on Lorcan and his other hidey-hole."

"And?" I get to my feet and tug down on my pants, since they bunched up and are strangling my lady V.

His eyes follow my hands and he goes silent.

"Focus," I say.

"Right." He raises his gaze to meet mine. "Lorcan had gone to the hellhound ring just yesterday. It's not a place he'd ever visit. Father goes there often, but not my brother. So, that's strange, right? And I know the guy who runs the joint. So that's our next stop."

"Okay. What the heck is a hellhound ring?" It doesn't sound good.

"I'm assuming Elias told you hellhounds are used as soul collectors from Earth. The hellhound ring is a fighting pit and tavern in one. It's where the furry bastards congregate and bid on the winners."

"Okay, well that sounds like a fun place," I say sarcastically.

"And we should head there before it gets too late."

With new determination, I nod and look down at Cain's ring on my finger. "You think this will be enough to keep me concealed?"

"It has so far. Though your clothes are rather bland, which might draw attention."

I sigh. "There must be something I can throw over the top of this for dramatic effect. If we're going to a hellhound tavern, I don't want to draw attention."

"I'll find something." He doesn't look concerned. Instead, he takes my hand in his and leads me out of the bedroom. Worry curls in my gut. All I can think about are all those hellhounds that had been sent after me on Earth, how terrifying and feral they'd been.

A HOT BREEZE swishes past us, tugging at my hair and the black cape I now wear over my sexy demon ensemble. After our run in with Serena, I thought more coverage was needed in case we ran into anyone else familiar down here. And for my own sanity, honestly, since I still don't feel completely comfortable wearing clothes this... *tight.*

"This is it," Maverick states.

I glance up at the words above a door of a stone building—'The Ring' painted in red. And I swallow the boulder clogging my throat

"Anything I should know before we go inside?" I ask, just as a beefy man struts past us, grunting with each breath, and—shit—he's three times my size. "Geez. I'm going to die in there," I mumble under my breath.

Maverick grins. "You'll be fine with me. Just stay close, and like before, you're my escort. All you need to focus on is picking up on the relics in there."

I nod, and he takes my hand in his, then we stride into the establishment. The moment I step inside, my toe gives a faint twitch. Yep...we're on the right path.

It's dark inside, stuffy too, and it's hard to tell what I'm looking at first. The dark ambience unnerves me. But the deeper we walk in, the more my eyes adjust, and the more my toe buzzes.

"This is definitely the right place," I whisper to Maverick.

"Perfect." His arm loops around my back and he hauls me tightly against him, as if he wants to make it clear he owns me. And I'm perfectly okay with that when a huge monster of a bald man leers in my direction, his grin revealing missing front teeth.

I cringe hard on the inside.

Then I swing my attention to an empty boxing ring in the middle of the enormous room. Around the edges of the crowd are tables and chairs, half filled with demons. Both male and female by the looks of it. Though, to be honest, I try my hardest not to stare and draw attention. Against the back wall to our right stands a bar that stretches the width of the room. Several bartenders are serving drinks to the masses pushing to get served.

There's no music playing, just the loud hum of voices, growls, and laughter.

Maverick looks over to me, his eyes shining from the spotlights over the stage. "We're going to walk around, and you can tell me if there's one location that has your toe going crazier than others."

"Sounds good." And we're off, doing the round. Me keeping my eyes low, Maverick, holding me tightly. I feel gazes on me, studying me. It doesn't take long before sweat pools between my breasts.

A shadow falls over us, and Maverick unleashes a thunderous growl, to which the demon with pointy horns backs away. Then we keep on walking. This place is feral, demons establishing dominance by means of growling. Another reason shivers keep racing down my spine.

After a round, Maverick pauses and looks at me, expectedly.

"Nothing. No matter where we are in the room."

He sighs heavily, then guides us to an empty table at the edge of the room. "Stay here, I'll be back."

I grab his arms. "Wait, you're leaving me alone?"

"Just getting us some drinks so we don't look so suspicious. You've already drawn the attention of several mutts. Let's fit in." He unpeels my fingers from around his wrist. "Won't be long."

I take a seat quickly and lick my lips, hating how uncomfortable this tavern makes me feel. I let my gaze roam the room, and notice two men looking my way, their stares dark, shadows over their faces. The other females in the room are dressed like the men...in heavy leather pants and jackets, lots of buckles and weapons on their belts. It would have made more sense to dress like them rather than like a fucked-up mix between an escort and a magician.

Shit.

Part of me can't help but wonder if this had been Elias when he lived in Hell. Partying, fighting, bidding for jobs...

Someone suddenly sits in front of me, a bulky man with muscles rippling down his arms. "You are a small thing. I might break you, and that excites me. I'm the strongest hellhound in here, and I will destroy them all if you want me to."

"Um, okay?" I look over my shoulder to Maverick, who's chuckling with one of the bartenders. I clench my teeth, glaring at him to get his ass back here.

A loud bang on the table has me jumping in my seat, and I turn back around to the brute with squinty eyes and a huge jaw.

"I understand," he growls. "You need more proof that I am the toughest. Leave it to me." He shoots to his feet, sending the whole table rocking. I grab hold of it so it doesn't topple over as the guy takes several steps to the next table and grabs the first guy by the throat. He lifts him out of his chair so fast I gasp.

With ease, he slams him onto the table in some swift wrestler move, and with his second hand, he twists his head hard. I hear his neck snap.

A small cry slips from my throat, and I shuffle back in my seat. The others at that table scramble away. Then the beefster glances at me, head high, with an awkward smile that shows way too many sharp teeth. It's like he's waiting for me to confirm he's the toughest.

Fuck. Fuck. Fuck.

When the hellhound sneers, I freeze. But instead, he whips away from me and stalks deeper into the crowd, leaving a trail of screams and dead bodies.

Fuck me.

Sayah's lingering just below the surface, nudging me to release her so she can show this hellhound a good time her way. While that's the opposite of keeping a low profile, I'm tempted to do it if that gorilla comes back my way.

I slip out of my seat and get up, bumping right into Maverick. He's not even carrying any drinks.

"Shit, we need the hell out here," I whisper. "Why'd you leave me alone? I told you not to." Shaking, I glance out over the room just as the beast tosses two men off him.

"Is that you're doing?" Maverick states, not looking the tiniest bit concerned.

"Shut up unless you want your neck snapped too," I snarl and fist his shirt. "We gotta leave, now!"

"Well, lucky for you, I know where Lorcan might have hidden the relics."

I can't stop staring at the hellhound, my heart pounding in my chest like a storm. "As long as it's far from here."

"Come with me," Maverick says, his hand in mine, and we move quickly toward the door next to the bar.

A terrifying growl comes from behind us and I flinch, twisting around and half expecting that monster to be chasing after us.

But instead, he's in the boxing ring, beating his chest. Oh, shit!

I shove past the door with Maverick and shut it behind us. I can't calm my breathing.

"It's okay," Maverick reassures me. "I could have taken him."

"Really? He is double your size and he killed six hellhounds out there in just a few seconds. And I'm not like one of you. He could have killed me for real."

Maverick leads me down a long passage, right past the kitchen, and then we're rushing down the steps. "Brinkus didn't want to kill you. He wanted to fuck you."

His response has me stiffening, but he doesn't relent and keeps hauling me down the dusty steps. "Wait a second. You know that crazy beast out there?"

"Not personally. But here's always here, trying to pick up any girl when she's alone. He's an insecure bastard."

"You dickhead," I cry out. "You knew he'd try to pick me up and you left me to him?"

He chuckles. "Hey, I needed to get the eyes off us, and now everyone up there is entertained by his theatrics."

I'm shaking, unsure how to feel, but I want to strangle Maverick. "You're a real prick sometimes, you know that? It wouldn't have hurt to let me in on the plan."

He shrugs. "Yeah, I suppose, but then you would have given it away. You don't exactly have a great poker face. Your emotions are so easy to spot. So it had to look real."

Once we reach the bottom of the steps, I kick him in the shin. "Ow."

"Don't ever use me as bait again." Then I turn to really take in where we are, considering my toe is going berserk. "Okay, relics are definitely in here."

The basement resembles an endless maze with several passages spearing out from the main room. Darkness yawns from within each opening.

"It worked out, didn't it?" Maverick states. "We found the relics."

"Yeah, by taking a risk. What if he kidnapped me while you were too busy blabbering with the bar guy?"

"Don't worry. I had an eye on you the whole time."

I exhale loudly and stomp away from him. Following my twitching toe, I stop in front of the first tunnel to my right and it responds by going even crazier in my shoe. "Okay, it's down there." I point into the pitch black. "Do you have a flashlight?"

He swoops toward me. "I'll go first. I have great night vision." Then he slips inside, and the darkness swallows him.

"Hey, wait for me." I rush in behind him, and I can't see a damn thing.

I pat the wall and move swiftly, when suddenly there's a hand on my breast, squeezing. "Hmm. Mine," Maverick whispers.

"Stop fucking around," I snap, pushing his hand off me.

Next thing I know, he snatches me by the waist and lifts me off my feet, pinning me back to the wall. His breath is on my face.

"Doesn't the dark just make you want to fuck?"

"Not really."

"It does for me." His mouth is suddenly on mine, our lips crushed. I should shove him off me, but call me weak. I kiss him back, adoring the way he takes me with such possessiveness, how he licks my mouth, attentive to my needs.

My pulse races for a very different reason now.

His mouth is at my ear. "Just give me the word and I'll strip you, lick that sweet pussy of yours, and fuck you until you scream for me to stop."

My stomach jumps at the thought of him going down on me here of all places. I chew on my lower lip, hating and loving how easily he's broken me.

When I don't respond quick enough, he releases me and I collapse back against the wall. The tingle of nerves pulse between my thighs. A kiss and a few words render me completely flustered.

Goddamn him.

My chest rises and falls quickly as his hand trails down the side of face. "Your choice."

The magnetic pull between us is unbearable, but the constant hum of my toe brings an air of logic into the decision.

"Relics," I breathe, then clear my throat. "We focus on the relics; no distractions."

He chuckles. "If that's your preference. Not that we can't do both if you change your mind." He pulls my hand into his and we move swiftly through the darkness.

A faint orange glow appears up ahead. We pick up speed, soon emerging into a cavern where the walls and ceiling are carved out of stone.

My toe is in a frenzy. We're in the right spot, and I veer to the left where I sense my toe pulling me.

There are wooden boxes all over the room, most filled with

bottles, so I guess this is where they stash their liquor, or whatever they drink. Human blood? Baby tears? Something gross, I'm sure.

Maverick is on my heels as I close in on several empty crates. With haste, I move them out of my way. And behind them, we discover one wooden crate with black fabric covering it.

"What do we have here?" Maverick quickly pulls it away and lifts out a black box. It's identical to the one we found in Lucifer's whorehouse. He hands it to me. "Want to do the honor and check if the rest of the relics are all in there?"

I turn and pull open the latch. It isn't locked. At once, the overwhelming buzz of their power swarms over me. It's intense and has me swaying, so I take a quick look. Three items are all there—from what Cain told me, they are the spine, intestine, and foot of the harp. I shut the box with a thud and the energy fades.

Their intensity is crazy. I can't even begin to imagine what this box is made of to contain all their power.

"All there. Let's collect the others from your place and get back to Earth." I tuck the box under my arm, and we practically run out of the basement.

"As much as I like being back in Hell, part of me misses Earth," Maverick mutters as we race up the steps.

"Maybe because it's awful down here."

"Yeah, perhaps." His voice is almost strangled, and part of me feels bad for saying that about the only home he's known most his life.

Once we emerge into the main tavern, my senses snap to high alert. The entire room is in chaos. Half the patrons are at the tables, and the other half are in a brawl. No bouncers are kicking them out, so I'm guessing this is a normal event.

I'm frantically scanning the room for that brutish hellhound, while Maverick drags me toward the exit, when a filthy growl erupts from in front of us from the shadows.

I lurch backward, Maverick does the same, taken off guard by the lunatic hellhound lunging in front of us. He has half a dozen mates on either side of him, all staring at us.

"Do you see now why using me as bait was a shit idea?" I hiss.

"Yeah, hindsight is a bitch," he says quietly, then pushes me behind me. He steps forward, shoulders broad, a growl rolling within his chest.

"What business do you have with me, mutt?" Maverick booms, drawing the attention of those nearby.

Great idea. Insult the big demon.

"You don't scare me," the hellhound snarls. "I've been wanting to sharpen my teeth on one of you asswipe sin demons."

The demon has barely finished his insult when Maverick lunges at him, his horns and wings out. Someone screams, and I'm pretty sure it's the hellhound. They slam into a table, bringing it and those sitting at it down.

Utter chaos breaks out. I can't tell who's who, but there's blood spurting and something just got thrown across the room...oh shit, is that someone's tail?

"Maverick!" I call out, hugging the box under my arm, worried for him as two of the brute's buddies have jumped into the battle.

But the others have turned toward me, leering over my body.

One of them slurs, "Slut, want to show me your whore pocket? You can sit on my fuckstick."

"Eww. And your pickup lines are shit," I blurt, while my mind races with a way to get away from them and get out with Maverick intact.

In a flash, the big beast with a long biker's beard comes at me fast. I swing away from him, but he seizes my cape with his meaty hand. I desperately tug at the ties around my neck to loosen it.

I leap out from his reach and twist around as he tosses the cape to the ground.

"Where will you run to?" He mocks me with a disgusting grin.

"Only one reason a soulless person like you comes here," his friend mutters. "To be fucked, and you haven't had a real demon until you've had a hellhound, or three, in you." He barks, his buddies joining him.

I roll my eyes at how cringe-worthy they are.

"Sure, whatever you say, Tweedle Dee, but one of my boyfriends is a hellhound, so how about you three go fuck yourselves elsewhere." I don't even know where my brazen confidence comes from, but I've had enough.

Another demon is suddenly thrown across the room from the battle, then Maverick slams into the back of the huge hellhounds in front of me. They all crash forward, and he rolls off them, and comes to me. He's in bad shape. Bleeding and coughing up blood, his shirt ripped to shreds. His wings are retracted. So much for sin demons having any kind of authority in Hell. Yet he smiles like this is a walk in the park.

Behind him, half a dozen demons make their way in our direction.

Panic hits me hard, and I tremble.

"I'll be fine," Maverick slurs.

"Are you so sure?" But as the hellhounds descend upon us on all fronts, terror rattles me.

The monsters shove one another to be first to get to us...to me.

The pounding of my heartbeat in my ears is all I can hear.

So, I do the only thing I can...I reach deep within me and my lips curl with the command. "Sayah, come out."

There's no hesitation. She rushes out as though she's been lingering, waiting for my call. Like suddenly she only follows my command.

Her dark shadow rears, extending taller than any of the hellhounds in the room, rising up before us like a monstrous horse.

There are so many of them now. Fifteen, maybe twenty. But her presence doesn't seem to scare them.

A howl bleeds into the background, and suddenly the demons are charging toward us.

"Sayah," I call out as Maverick drags me behind him.

Immediately, her dark shadow snaps outward in a circle, slamming into each beast, throwing them off their feet and onto their asses. She completely excludes Maverick, which tells me she knows he's with me. She watches everything, after all.

I grab Maverick by the arm but he's too busy gawking at the sight of Sayah.

"We need to leave," I yell.

At my words, Sayah retracts and carves a path for us toward the door, knocking out anyone in our path like a wrecking ball.

We rush past the hellhounds groaning on the floor, and as we pass the dickhead with the beard, I can't help myself. "Fucking cocknose. There's a new word for your vocabulary."

We shoot forward, lunging toward the exit, when I glance back to ensure no one follows.

That's when I see him... Lucifer.

His steely gaze slips over me, his mouth twisted in hatred.

My blood runs cold.

Hell, why is he everywhere?

He's watching us, taking a step after us.

Terror squeezes my chest and I can't breathe, so I do the first thing that comes to mind. I unleash Sayah at him. "Stop him," I command.

She rushes toward him like a giant black mass.

"Move your ass," Maverick yells behind me, pulling me by the arm to leave the tavern.

Sayah throws herself at Lucifer, and she must have caught him off guard, because one second he's coming for us, the next he's flying across the room. He crashes down in the boxing ring.

The room explodes with growls and bellowing shouts.

"Sayah, back to me," I call out, and I'm already running outside on the street with Maverick as she zips back into me so fast, I barely sense her sliding within me. There's no resistance from her and I can't thank her enough at this moment.

The echo of howls fills the tavern behind us, escalating.

"Fuck." Maverick's wings snap out from his back, and he sweeps me into his arms. We're suddenly airborne, the wind crashing into us, and I wrap an arm around Maverick's neck, the other clutching the box of relics.

Down below, demons spill out of the building.

"We need to go get the other relics, then head to Earth urgently," I say.

"I know. Now, hold on." He picks up incredible speed and we're suddenly shooting through the air so fast I can barely take a breath.

My heart clenches, and I squeeze my eyes shut, praying with everything that we get home before Lucifer can grab us.

Morning light bursts past the horizon, painting the inky black sky a brighter shade of gray. I sprint through the forest on four paws and circle around the mountains, like I've done every night since Aria and Maverick left for Hell. Just in case they decide to pop up during the late hours of night.

I pass Hell's gate, which has no signs of the door opening. Not even a hint of sulfur in the air, so with dawn approaching, I decide to turn around and hightail it back home.

As I swing around to change directions, the sound of rock grating against rock splits the silence and the strong caress of magic strokes my fur. I stop just as molten cracks split the mountainside and slowly melt away.

Sulfur is the first scent to assault my senses, and then the unmistakable smell of my mate. Aria.

My hellhound instantly rejoices at her return, and I tilt my nose to the sky and let out a loud howl.

Aria stumbles through the gate first, gasping for breath, eyes wild with panic. Maverick soon follows, and the moment he passes through, he glances over his shoulder to watch the rocks reform and seal shut.

Sensing the tension and fear between them, I command the power of the change into my bones and within seconds, I'm standing on two feet again, buck naked in the snow.

The moment Aria spots me, she runs over and leaps into my arms. Squeezing her tight, I lift her off the ground, inhaling her sweet, sweet scent.

"Holy shit, I missed you," I say, swinging her around.

"Ditto." She presses her lips against mine for a much needed kiss. My hunger for her ignites instantly, and I sweep my tongue into her mouth.

Maverick clears his throat to cut our make-out session short. Aria and I break apart. "Sorry to interrupt this little seven minutes in heaven, but we need to get out of here. The devil's on our tail."

My heart falters, and I drop Aria onto her feet. That's when I realize she's holding a box.

The relics. Has to be. "Wait, Lucifer?" I ask, realizing the severity of the situation.

"No, the fucking Easter Bunny. Yes, Lucifer." Maverick's silvery wings snap out of his back and he grabs Aria around the waist. "Let's move it!"

He leaps into the air as I race back toward the mansion, shifting mid-way to increase my speed. When I reach the tree line and spot the lights of the house on top of the hill, I change back. I see Maverick and Aria touching down and hurrying through the back doors.

I follow them inside.

"Isn't Lucifer bound to Hell? I thought he couldn't leave often," Aria says, still breathless as Maverick tugs her along.

"You want to risk this being one of those times he can?" he replies.

At the sound of footsteps and voices, Cain and Dorian pop their heads out of the library. Seeing Aria, their eyes light up with relief.

"You're back." Dorian beams.

Cain's gaze drops to the box in her hands. "Was it successful?"

"Yes, yes. Hi, hello. We're here. We have the relics, but the excitement's not over," Maverick explains quickly as he pulls Aria deeper into the room.

Cain's face turns serious. "What's wrong?"

"Lucifer and his demons were chasing us in Hell. We barely made it to Maverick's place for the rest of the relics and then out of there," Aria says.

"So, if Father isn't on his way for an unexpected visit, then there's no doubt he'll be sending friends to knock on your door." Finally, Maverick lets go of Aria. Walking to one of the tall windows, he peers out.

Dorian heads over to his side and looks out, too. "We need to protect ourselves. Cain?"

"Then we'll prepare for a fight," he says. "I don't believe Father will be strong enough to pass through the gate a second time, but he'll send legions."

"Is there an echo in here?" Maverick huffs.

"Wait," Aria chimes in. "What about Gabriel?"

"The angel? What about him?" Dorian answers.

"Can't he do something to help? This is his problem, too."

"She's right," Cain replies. "We have the relics. He needs to help protect them if he wants us to keep Lucifer out of Heaven."

"Well then, summon the halo-wearing ballerina," Maverick snaps. His attitude is really getting on my nerves.

Cain tilts his head up to the ceiling, and when he speaks, his voice booms with power and command. "Gabriel, archangel. Appear."

The air around us charges with electricity and grows heavy, like the feeling right before a huge thunderstorm. There's a flash of light that burns my eyeballs and dries my mouth, but when my vision adjusts, Gabriel is standing in the center of the library, hand on the hilt of his sword and massive wings spread wide. His menacing gaze sweeps over all of us but lands on Aria last. Seeing her makes his lip curl in a silent snarl.

A warning rolls over the animal in me and my muscles tense. My hellhound can sense the danger, and I immediately cross the room and become a barricade in front of Aria. His desire to end her burns in his stare, and I have no doubt the angel would kill her the moment we looked away.

Cain knows it too, because he shifts closer to us and addresses Gabriel to reclaim his attention. "Gabriel, I summoned you here because we have retrieved the relics."

That makes him turn to Cain fully and his brows lift in surprise. "You possess all seven pieces of Azrael's harp, then?"

"We do."

His mouth peels back, exposing perfectly white and straight teeth. Too perfect. Serial killer perfect.

Aria steps back, while I hear Maverick breathe "Holy shit" nearby. And I don't blame them. It may be a smile, but it's eerie as hell.

"It seems you're good for something, son of Lucifer," Gabriel goes on. "You must pass through the gates, enter Hell, and defeat the Hell king immediately."

Cain only shakes his head, appearing bored more than anything else—his specialty. "We need to rest and feed to be at our strongest before doing this herculean task. We will go tomorrow."

"Tomorrow?" he repeats, his voice gaining volume with his anger. He's about to argue further, but Cain stays in control of the conversation.

"If we are to win, we need to be at our best. We get only one chance at this."

Slowly, Gabriel's shoulders ease and he leans back on his heels. His hand even falls away from his sword. "Fine then, demon. Tomorrow. But why summon me now?"

I catch movement at the corner of my eye and glance over to see Maverick bouncing on his toes. He's dying to say something, to put in his two-cents, but he's also trying to be respectful of Cain's position. It's something I had a hard time learning myself when joining him and Dorian. I'd gone from a commander of a hell-hound army, Alpha, to taking orders from someone else. But that's the way our dynamic works best, so even I have to sit back sometimes.

Realistically, the fact that Maverick's even attempting to let Cain lead says a lot in itself, doesn't it? I definitely didn't expect him to comply—not this soon at least.

"It was with purpose," Cain explains. He pauses, glances at the angel's expanded wings and waits. Finally, getting the hint, Gabriel folds them against his back. "Lucifer knows Aria and my brother were in Hell. It won't be long before he discovers why, and he knows exactly where to send his legions to find us. Here."

It takes a moment, but as the words sink in, realization passes over his face.

"We are asking for your protection. I have this house warded by magic, but you and I both know it can only do so much. We need something stronger."

He looks over us all one by one again. It's obvious he's debating whether it's worth helping us or not.

I'll tell you what, the moment this is all over, if he ever shows his ugly angel mug here again, I'll spare him the torture and fight him myself. Then we can really see who's stronger—a soldier of Heaven or of Hell.

After some time, he says, "I can shield the house in Heaven's light. No one, Hell-made or Earth-born, will be able to get in or out during that time."

"But then how are we going to get to the gates?" Aria quips behind me.

His piercing stare latches onto her again, and his hatred seems to radiate from him. "I will relinquish the light at midnight. Then, the danger will resume and it will be up to you to make it to the gates alive. I will not be able to assist any further."

Not be able to, or just doesn't want to? I'm thinking the latter.

"That'll be plenty of time," Cain says, to steal his attention away from Aria once more. "We can work with that."

Gabriel nods once, pulls his shoulders back, and steps more toward the middle of the library. Then, pulling out his sword, he holds it straight above his head. The air becomes charged with power, making every hair on my arms stand on end. White light swirls around the blade and shoots through the ceilings, cloaking us all in brightness. My skin prickles and burns as if I've been laying in the summer sun all day, and that's from inside the light bubble. I can't even imagine what it'd be like to touch the outer edge. As demons, we'd probably get zapped into oblivion.

Maverick rushes over to the window and peers outside again. "It's lit up like the Fourth of July out there," he says. "Nothing's getting past that."

Cain turns back to the angel. "Thank you."

Gabriel sheaths his sword. "Don't make me regret this alliance, demons." Then, he pops out of existence with another blaze of light.

I grunt and rub my eyes furiously to stop the itching and burning. "Fucking angel."

"He has a serious attitude problem," Dorian says. "But at least he was good for something this time."

"Do you really think this light shield thingy is going to keep out whatever Lucifer is trying to throw at us?" Aria asks.

"We have to hope so," Cain answers. That's really all we can do.

Then Cain holds out his hand to her, which she accepts with a small smile, and he leads her over to the couch to sit. "Now, tell me, my love. I want to know everything that happened in Hell."

She tenses slightly, but it doesn't go unnoticed by me.

"We all do," I say and throw myself onto the chaise. "And now that we have some time..."

Dorian perches himself on the back of it. "I see Maverick has you wearing the latest Hell-whore-chic."

At the mention of his name, Maverick glances over his shoulder and snarls. "She had to blend in."

"Riiiighhhttt." Dorian winks. "But go on, gorgeous. Story time."

With everyone's eyes watching and waiting, she draws in a deep breath and then starts weaving the adventures that the three of us missed out on in Hell. Nix, the close encounter in Lucifer's whorehouse, the run in and much-deserved punch with Serena—which is my favorite part for obvious reasons—and the fight at The Ring...

When she ends, her gaze passes over each of us to gauge our responses. I'm just glad she's home, in all honesty. My hound hates being away from her for so long. And her punching Serena? Icing on the cake. I don't know why, but just the thought of it has my cock hardening. My little rabbit defending me, wanting to fight for me... It's hot as hell.

Dorian's lost in his thoughts, tapping his chin, while Cain's silently processing it all. I'm sure there were some parts to her story he didn't like, especially how close they came to being caught by Lucifer not once, but twice, and maybe even his other brother Nix's involvement, but after all that, Maverick had done what he'd asked. Aria is safe, and we have the relics now. Even I have to give him credit for that.

"The most important thing is we got the relics back," Aria says, finishing. "All of them. And you said you found the last one?"

Cain nods. "We have the skull, it is true."

Her face scrunches in disgust. "Of course it's a skull. Of course."

"Azrael wasn't the type to make it into something desirable, like a pair of fuzzy bunny slippers." Dorian laughs.

She smiles at his stupid joke. "He should have."

"Maybe you should write him a strongly worded letter."

"Maybe I will."

Maverick snorts, unimpressed with their banter.

Get in line, buddy. Can't escape it.

"Can we focus here?" Maverick snaps in annoyance. "We have everything to build the harp and get you into Hell, but we need to figure out what we're doing once we get there."

Aria presses her lips together and tries to look more serious. "He's right," she says, but another chuckle slips out. She covers it up with a cough. "We need a plan. Even with the five of us and Sayah, I'm not sure we can take Lucifer down."

"I know. That was one of our mistakes the first time," Cain says. "We thought we could do it on our own."

"And any back-up we did have bailed. The people want to be free of him, but their fear outweighs anything else," Dorian adds.

"We have Nix," Aria says and turns to Maverick. "He's proved himself so far. Right, Maverick?"

He dips his head in a subtle yes.

Aria continues, "So, what about the other sin demons? What if we can recruit more to our side? We'd said before that the brothers are all pieces of Lucifer, and killing them would make him weaker—"

"In theory," Cain reminds us.

"Yes, true. But that also means you're stronger together. If all the sin demons work as one, your collective power equals his," he says.

"Holy shit. She may have something there," I reply, glancing around the room.

Unimpressed, Maverick rolls his eyes. "You forget one teeny-tiny, important detail. Our brothers are complete and utter assholes."

"But we got Nix to help," Aria says.

"Yeah, but Nix is a kitten compared to the others."

"I wouldn't go that far," Dorian replies. "Every sin demon is a hellion of their own right. I think we can get some others on board with this. Valdim would be my next ask. And I can see Raziel being down for a little payback."

Val is a glutton of all things—including revenge, and Lucifer's done some shit things to Raz in the past. He hates his father as much as we do.

"Yeah? But what about Lorcan? He stole the relics from you. You think he's just going to agree? Just like that?" Maverick throws his hands in the air, exasperated. "Come on, Cain. You know better than all of us. There's no way Lorcan will agree to any of this."

Cain, though, doesn't say anything. Only stares, too lost in his own thoughts to give an answer.

"Don't forget Torryn," I chime in. "He's the most stubborn one out of all of you."

"But he loves a fight," Dorian quips.

Very true. "That he does."

"We just need to word it a certain way to all of them. You know, tell them what they want to hear, kiss three-horned babies, *schmooze*." Dorian waggles his eyebrows in a suggestive way.

"Schmooze." Aria laughs. "What is this? Politics?"

"Pretty much the same idea," Dorian replies and then looks at Cain. Like usual, something silent seems to pass between them, but this time, I have a pretty good idea what they're both thinking. Maybe it's the magic linking us or maybe I've finally gotten on their same level of friendship, but I'm almost positive they're both thinking about Cain's vision after grabbing the foot relic and his idea of killing the sin demons to make Lucifer weaker.

Of course, none of us want to do that. Dorian and I flat out refused to even acknowledge it as an option, but Cain's willing to do whatever it takes to boot Lucifer off the throne. And if that means making the relic's premonition come true... Well, he doesn't care.

Personally, now that we have this other idea on the table of uniting the brothers instead, I'm liking it more and more.

"Cain, what do you think?" Aria asks him, breaking the silence. "Do you think it's possible? Getting all your brothers together?"

He pauses as he contemplates his next words. We all wait because it's near impossible to ever read his expression or know what is going on in that head of his.

After a long moment, he says, "It's worth trying."

That's good enough for me, Aria, and Dorian. Maverick, though, looks a bit dumbstruck. He wants to say something more —I can see him itching to argue his point more—but he backs down, deciding against it.

Well, would you look at that? The kid's finally getting it. He must've realized the other option wouldn't end well for him either.

CAIN

I BEGIN TO UNDRESS, unbuttoning my dress shirt and glancing at my reflection in the standing mirror. I look worn—even I notice it— like I'm holding the weight of the world on my shoulders.

And maybe I am. Heaven and Hell certainly depend on us winning this fight. There's no doubt Lucifer will be coming for the living plane too, if he's to succeed in his plans.

This is critical.

I may have appeared calm on the outside, but Aria and Maverick's return, coupled with the sudden danger we were in, rattled me. Even now, I can see the shadows of Lucifer's Hell creatures stalking the perimeter of the bubble Gabriel put us in, and I wonder if it'll crumble at any moment. My hope is that Gabriel's loyalty to the cause and his god is stronger than his hatred of us. It's all I can do at the moment.

Although I instructed everyone to rest before we face down the hellions and use Azrael's harp at the gate, I won't be taking my own advice tonight. With my chaotic thoughts running amok, sleep would be impossible.

We need to feed to gain strength for what's ahead, but with the light shield, no one can get in or out of the mansion. It's not ideal, but we'll work with what we have. We have no other choice.

Soft footsteps outside my room make me pause. It's Aria. I can feel her presence through our link before anything else. She's like an extension of me now. Parts of one entity. We are all.

"Cain?" Her timid voice has me looking up. I can see her reflection in the mirror hovering in my partly open door. "C-Can I talk to you for a minute?"

Her look of worry doesn't go unnoticed by me, so I wave her inside. She steps in.

"Close the door," I whisper, and she obeys. But she continues to stay close to it, almost afraid of coming any closer to me.

The hideous memory of her laying in Lucifer's torture rooms, cut up and bloodied by my own hand, comes to mind, and nausea rolls through me. I quickly cross the room and wrap my arms around her. To my relief, she presses into me, burying her face into my chest, and I relish in the feel of her close to me again.

I would *never* hurt her. Never.

Damn that skull and what it made me see. There's no doubt in my mind its dark power made me, Dorian, and Elias live through our deepest fears—mine still haunts me. It may very well haunt me forever.

We stay like that for a while, holding each other, saying nothing. And this time, when Aria tilts her head up to look at me, a smile touches her lips.

"I missed you," she says.

"I've missed you, too."

"Would you say...you've missed me like hell?" Her smile widens at her poor attempt at a joke, and I feel my own mouth lifting at the corners.

"You're spending too much time with Dorian. His poor sense of humor is starting to rub off on you." I chuckle.

She steps back and shrugs. "Maybe so, but you didn't answer the question."

Ah, she's going to make me say it. "Like Heaven, Hell, and everything in between."

"Good." That seems to satisfy her. For now. "I'm not interrupting anything, am I?" She starts to walk across the room but stops at the mirror I'd just been in front of and glances at herself in the demon getup. Her nose scrunches.

"No. I was getting ready to relax before midnight."

"You mean obsess over what we need to do until midnight," she corrects me.

I can't even argue. She knows me too well.

"Yes," I confess with a sigh. "Exactly that."

She touches her arm and glances at the floor. There's something she wants to tell me—I know it—so I wait.

"Cain... I..." she begins, the words not seeming to come.

I come to stand behind her and run my hands down her arms. She glances at me through the reflection.

"What is it, my love? You can talk to me," I encourage.

"Promise you won't be mad."

Never a good sign.

My stomach flips with worry. It's clearly something that's been troubling her. Maybe something that happened in Hell that she didn't want the others to know, and that worries me even more. Does it involve my brother? It must. Did he harm her in some way? If so...

I tell myself to settle down. My thoughts are running away from me again.

I keep it all off my expression and reply, "I will say I'll listen first and process before reacting."

Her troubled look says she doesn't care for that answer, but it's all I can give. Which she knows. Instead, she lets out a breath.

"Okay... So...in Hell, Maverick took me to your home. Well, your old home. The black castle."

My spine stiffens. That is certainly not what I expected her to say.

I don't know what Maverick's motives were when showing her my castle, but when I assess her face, it still weighs heavy with fear and uncertainty.

"I haven't been there in a century," I explain. After being banished, I missed the place I called home, but recently it hasn't even crossed my mind. I could even dare to say I've forgotten about it. "I'm not the same demon I was when I lived there."

"You're right. Your style has definitely changed." She gestures to my mahogany four-poster bed with deep blue curtains and gold accents. Dorian likes to tease me for my love of nineteenth century decor, but it's the century we first walked onto the living plane and established ourselves anew, so I have a fondness for it.

"Is this really about my style preferences, Aria?" I ask her. I can't imagine that it is.

She shakes her head. "No, of course not. I didn't know it was your place. Maverick kept that from me when we..." She trails off and meets my eyes in the mirror.

I hear the next words loud and clear; she doesn't need to speak them. She and Maverick fucked.

To my own surprise and credit, no anger stirs. Why? I'm not really sure. I suppose it's because I expected it in a way. Maverick did pledge his loyalty to me *and* Aria after our tussle in the hall, which means he'll do anything for her as well. She is his master.

At first, this confused me, but then I realized it's simply Maverick's way of saying he cares about her. More than he wants to admit it. To me and himself.

The "picking my house to do it in" was his attempt at revenge for making him watch us fuck her earlier. His last jab at me. Does it bother me? A little, but like I told Aria, I've moved on from that part of my life. Our house in Glenside feels more like home.

When I meet Aria's gaze again, I realize I haven't replied and she's been waiting anxiously.

"You're mad. I knew you'd be. Don't kill Maverick. He didn't force me to do anything. I wanted to, too. Cain, please. I'm really sorry. I'm—"

"Do you care about him?" I cut off her ramblings.

Not expecting the question, she blinks at me.

"Do you care about Maverick?" I repeat.

Her large brown eyes lock with mine. "I do."

Said with such certainty. Such truth.

I sigh. "Then that's all I need to know."

She spins and peers up at me in disbelief. "Really?"

I rub my thumb down her cheek and over her upper lip and then her lower. "If you truly care for him, then I will not get in the way of your happiness. He will be welcomed here."

As my words take their time to sink in, she continues to stare at me.

I keep tracing her beautiful mouth, watching the way her tongue presses against her teeth in anticipation. My muscles tense with the sudden urge to kiss her, to claim her again as my own.

"It's about time I let go of my past and look to my future." This time, my voice comes out huskier and full of need. "One I hope you will be a part of forever."

"Cain..." she breathes.

I can't stand it anymore. The distance between us feels too great. I lean forward and taste her lips for myself. She instantly pushes up onto her tiptoes and deepens the kiss, her tongue wrestling with mine. My body vibrates with hunger, my demon's reaction to her closeness immediate and too powerful to ignore. As it snaps to the surface, my wings shred through my shirt and hellfire ignites under my skin.

I pull away briefly so I can peer at her beautiful face. Desire sparks in her eyes, even with me in my demon form, and my pulse picks up speed. I love seeing her this way, hungry for me. The real me. I don't have to hide who I am when I'm with her.

"You are my world, Aria. My everything," I say.

"I don't think I'll ever get tired of you talking like that," she whispers.

Good, because as an immortal, she is going to hear it for the rest of eternity.

"Stay with me tonight," I tell her.

I don't want to dwell on what's waiting for us in Hell anymore, and you help me forget.

She replies by tilting her head up and kissing me again. Her entire body presses against me, and I can feel Sayah's power hovering close to the surface. Our coupled darkness makes goosebumps rise on my skin, and the energy passing between us ups the urgency tenfold.

Kissing her hard, my wings fold in around us, caging us in and drowning us in shadows. I grab the waistline of her tight pants. One hard rip and they're in two pieces dropping to the floor. At the same time, she's tugging off her top, unable to get it off fast enough. My hands are on her gorgeous breasts, nipples between my fingers, and I pinch them just a bit so she moans.

She's so petite against me, and yet so fierce.

I shrug off the shreds of fabric left of my own shirt and yank my belt out of the loops of my pants.

A sharp nip of pain shocks me temporarily, and I realize she's bitten my lip. When the metallic twang of blood hits my tongue, my demon roars.

Fuck the foreplay.

I'm desperate as I inhale her delicious smell, run my hands over her perfect body. And the way her soul calls to mine... I can't resist. I had intended to take my time with her, but I can't wait a second longer. I need to bury myself inside her.

The moment my wings open up, I toss her onto the bed and flip her onto her stomach by her ankles. That curvy ass calls to me, and I lean over, then take a mock bite. She winces, and I love the sounds she makes.

Pulling myself back up, I run my large hand over her ass, and she shivers under my touch with her need.

"Get on your knees," I demand with a growl. I want to consume every inch of her. Everything about her is so soft and delicious that I can't keep my hands off her.

She obeys, lifting her ass into the air, giving me a perfect view. Her pussy is glistening wet, just begging to be devoured. My cock strains to plunge into her.

"Beautiful." I grip her ass cheeks, spread them wider. I bury my face in her, opening my mouth, covering her clit, giving her firm strokes of my tongue. Tasting. Savoring. Teasing. I can't seem to get enough.

"Cain," she breathes my name, begging for more. Her body trembles against me, but my fingers dig in to hold her in place. There is nothing in the world that can explain the exhilaration of having my face buried in between the thighs of the most gorgeous girl. My girl. My love.

"You're so perfect," I say and lap at her clit.

Her body shudders, her back bowing as her orgasm starts to crest.

"Come for me, Aria. I'm going to fuck you through it." I turn my attention to her swollen clit and suck on it mercilessly. Her body rides the orgasm, and I never let her go.

She cries out. "Fuck! Cain!"

"Mmmmm..."

"Fuck! Fuck! Fuck!"

She grips handfuls of the comforter as she hits that delicious high, and I quickly reposition myself behind her. There's no time to fully undress, and my pants are wet from leaking, so I yank them down and then push the head of my cock into her pussy.

I sense her tensing against me at my girth. "Let me in, beautiful." I kiss her neck and shoulder, sensing her relaxing.

And I push into her, her body squeezing me.

"Shit, you're tight." I suck in a sharp breath as her muscles clamp down on me the deeper I go, but the demon in me wants more. He wants the pleasure to come with pain.

I slam into her so hard, she collapses on the bed. She's too weak to hold herself up anymore, but that doesn't stop me. I slide my arm under her waist to help tilt her ass up and ram into her again until she screams.

Then I lower my body over her, never relenting as I fuck her. I nuzzle her neck and whisper, "This is how I want you, so I can control you, fuck you, love you."

Her response comes in the form of a moan as I drive into her, picking up speed. Together, our bodies slide against one another, igniting a fiery friction that could burn the world if we let it.

She's so swollen and needy. I absolutely adore her this way.

She pushes her hips back and forth as much as being pinned under me allows her. The sounds she makes are so fucking sweet. So primal at the same time.

"Cain!" she gasps, barely catching her breath, and yet I know she demands more.

With a growl, I keep thrusting into her, burying myself deep, to the hilt. Her cries fill the room entirely. I fell hard for Aria from the first time I saw her, and fucking her is beyond my wildest dreams. I bounce against her ass, making her cry out for more.

"I'm close again," she says, her hips rocking to meet each slap as I plunge deep into her. "Make me yours."

Every inch of me is on fire, my balls tight, and I rush to the edge myself.

I growl. "Oh, fuck!"

She tenses suddenly, howling her scream, which in turns triggers my own climax. My dick throbs inside of her and stars dance behind my eyes as everything shatters and realigns.

She thrashes under me, her pussy squeezing around me, sucking on me. The fire between her thighs is an inferno. We're both breathing heavily.

When I finally slow down, I pull out of her and crash down on the bed next to her. I wrap her in my arms, her heartbeat still thumping wildly.

We're both gasping for air.

Hell, that was everything I needed.

She turns her head over her shoulder to look at me.

"You fuck like a demon possessed, you know that?" She presses her ass against me, and if she keeps wiggling that way, she won't see me coming.

My wings fold back into my spine. "Is that a problem?" I ask.

"Do I look like I'm complaining?"

I laugh as a wave of exhilaration flares over me. She curls against me, and I spoon behind her.

"Might be a good idea to get some sleep with what's coming up," I suggest.

"Mhmm..."

After a while, she whispers, "Cain..." but when I look down at her, she's sleeping. I hear her heavy breathing.

She's dreaming of me. Of us.

Completely beautiful.

I wish more than anything I could freeze this moment in time and keep her safe in my arms for all eternity.

We stand just outside the back doors of the mansion, the Heaven's light shield over our house still in place but gradually dimming the closer the seconds creep to midnight. Just beyond the brightness, hundreds of shadows of Lucifer's Hell creatures twist and pace restlessly, waiting for their chance to pounce.

We're going to be cutting this close.

My gaze passes over the group. Everyone's attention is pinned on the danger in front of us, a look of determination on their faces. Dorian is crouched low, horns curling out of his silvery hair and symbols glowing across his bare chest. Elias has already changed into his hound form and is snarling at the monsters beyond the barrier. Maverick and I both have our demons freed, our wings spread, and our charges in hand that we are to guard with our lives. Maverick will fly with Aria out of harm's way to the mountain, while I'm to bring the box with all the relics to the gate.

"Are we all ready?" I ask.

Dorian glances at the watch on his wrist. "We better be. T-minus thirty seconds."

The light shield continues to dim, the magic waning in and out. I begin to count down silently.

20…

19…

18…

I glance at my brother. Aria turns and wraps her arms around his neck. He hoists her legs around his waist and holds her close. When he glances at me, surprisingly, I see no hint of smugness in his expression. Only understanding and certainty.

He's ready to get this done just as much as I am.

10…

9…

8…

7…

The barricade flickers, and the yellow eyes from Lucifer's hellhounds shine menacingly. There are demons among them this time. Known as imps, they're lowly, spindly creatures that look more like giant spiders mixed with rabid, hairless dogs than anything else. Hideous things with unhinged mouths and scaly gray skin. They're known for not being the brightest, so they aren't the best in most missions, but since they like to kill and not think, they add bulk to an army where it's needed.

"Shit, he sent the imps," Dorian says.

"Stick to the plan," I order. "Nothing changes."

Maverick's wings begin to beat against the air, lifting him and Aria off the ground.

"Lucy, baby, we're coming home!" Dorian lets out a battle cry.

3…

2…

1…

The second Heaven's light extinguishes, the monsters charge.

I leap into the air and hop off the backs of two hellhounds. Jaws snap my way. I twist just as the talons of one of Lucifer's imps slash the air. I dodge it, barely, the pointed tips slice the surface of my skin.

Dammit, maybe I should've worn a shirt.

Oh well. If I learned anything from Elias, it's that women dig scars, so maybe some more battle wounds will get Aria in a tizzy.

Not that I need any help in that department.

The whoosh of wings beating against the wind sounds, and as two dark shadows pass over me, I peek up to see Maverick, Aria, and Cain flying above the trees. According to Cain's plan, it's my and Elias's job to lead the hellions away from the mountain so that they can safely put the harp together and open the gate.

So, in other words, we're the bait.

Elias's shadowy form moves left, bulldozing through more imp creatures and tearing out the throat of other hellhounds. When we have a somewhat clear enough path, we zigzag through the masses. I let out another battle cry and Elias howls, tongue lopping out of his mouth in excitement, as we rush toward the driveway and gravel road leading to town, as far away from the mountain as possible. Luckily they follow, and only a few hell-hounds break off to chase Cain, Maverick, and Aria's shadows.

As long as we got most of them off their tail, that's what matters. I have no doubt Cain can handle the stragglers.

The next question is, how are we going to shake all these monsters and get back to them in time to step through the gate?

Elias seems to have an idea. He's leading us closer to the main road where cars and trucks are zooming past, their headlights cutting through the pitch blackness.

Oh! I see where this is going.

He picks up speed, and so do I.

We're going to have to time this just right for it to work.

I see the beams of light growing brighter from the distance, hear the rolling of eighteen tires and the rumble of a diesel engine getting closer. Louder.

Together, we dash into the middle of the main highway, the hounds and imps right on our asses. A horn blares, so loud my ears pop, the bright lights of a semi-truck blinding us. I hold my breath as Elias and I jump for the ditch on the other side of the road, and then there's the boom of the collision. The tires are still screeching and I can smell rubber burning from the driver's attempt to hit the brakes on time.

Black blood smears across the ground and paints the truck's hood, but the creatures themselves have disintegrated with their death.

A fast and terrible way to go. But efficient.

I glance at Elias and he gives me a satisfied snort.

The truck blocks our view of the other side of the street, but from the shadows moving underneath, it's a good guess the surviving hellhounds and imps are retreating back to the house. Or worse—to the gates.

"We need a shortcut," I say.

Elias's ears perk up and his snout whips to the right. He knows the way.

He's off and running, a speck of darkness against the wintery backdrop. I push my demon hard to keep up with him, sprinting further up the road then down into a small ravine with a partly frozen creek running underneath a bridge.

We follow the curves of the water, trying our best not to freeze our feet—or paws, in Elias's case—and when he finally guides us out, I can see the rocky face of the mountain through the naked trees. We've come up on the opposite side of it.

The echo of fighting sounds from not far off, accompanied by the snarls of attacking hellhounds, and we're off and running towards the commotion.

A blaze of hellfire ignites the night, the heat smacking me in the face even at this distance. And a dark figure zooms in and out of the shadows, swallowing up hounds and imps, like a phantom of death.

Rounding the mountain, the scene unfolds in front of Hell's hidden entrance. Cain is in full fight mode, ripping apart imps with his bare hands, spearing them with his taloned wings, and blazing any approaching hellhounds with his inferno powers.

Maverick is kneeling in front of all the relics, scrambling to get them connected before any of Lucifer's monsters descend.

The most amazing sight is Aria, who is standing in front of him, hands out, black tendrils shooting from her feet and across the white snow. Each line connects to a mini Sayah, each zooming in and out of the trees and bushes, taking out anything in their path. An imp will be there one second and then swallowed up by one of the shadow monsters in a blink.

Utterly horrifying.

I catch movement out of the corner of my eye. One of Aria's Sayahs and it's coming right for me.

My stomach plummets.

Aw, fuck. I can't fight a shadow.

"Sayah, no!" Aria's voice booms. "Back."

Right before it engulfs me, it shifts right, just missing me, and zips back into Aria.

That was too fucking close.

Elias has joined the fight, helping Cain take out the rest of the creatures. I hurry over to Aria and Maverick.

"Sorry about that," Aria says sheepishly. "She didn't know who you were in the woods. And when she's given free rein to kill...well..."

"Explanations later," Maverick snaps, then waves for me to join him. "Make yourself useful and help me get this thing together."

I drop to my knees beside him. "What do you have done so far?"

He gestures wildly to the pieces, all scattered except for the eye, hair, and heart, which had bonded previously with Aria.

"So, nothing," I say dryly.

"Look, asshole, I'm trying here, but they aren't sticking for me."

"Sticking."

"You know, connecting."

"Please tell me you aren't touching them with your bare hands," I say.

"Of course fucking not." Then he clamps his mouth shut. "Well...yeah actually." He points to the intestine or "snake." The one that made us all panicky as hell in the Amazon.

"No wonder you're spazzing." I glance around, looking for something to grab the relics with without having their dark magic affect me. I'd use my shirt like before, but I voted to skip it for this trip.

I start to undo my pants.

"Woah, buddy. Not the time or place," Maverick says.

"I don't see you coming up with any ideas. We need to get them together, but we can't touch them."

"I told you. That doesn't matter. The intestine wouldn't even connect when I handled it. It's like something's missing. A key or something."

"Or glue?" I huff a laugh.

"This isn't fucking funny," he bites out. He points to the heart, eye, and hair. "How did you get these to stick together?"

I hesitate. "We didn't."

"Will you two stop bickering like an old married couple?" Aria chimes in, gaze still focused on the other mini shadows helping Cain and Elias fight.

Aria. That's right. She was the one who linked the other three. During her tussle with the werewolves and Sir Surchion.

Shit.

"Aria!"

Her head whips our way.

"You need to be the one to link the relics and form the harp!"

Her brows pinch. "Me?"

Maverick grabs her shirt and yanks her to the ground with us. Every tendril and Sayah creature wiggles back to her and disappears into her actual shadow.

"We need you to do whatever you did before," he growls, annoyance growing.

"I-I didn't do anything really. They just...clicked together," she replies.

"Well, do that again."

Reaching out, her expression falters, unsure.

Then she sits back on her heels and whispers, "Sayah."

Instantly, the shadow re-emerges, this time at full size and mimicking Aria's shape.

"Do you think you can put these relics together to form Azrael's harp?"

"How is this shadow going to know what Azrael's harp—" Maverick's cut off by Sayah darting over the relics, moving them in a blur of speed, and aligning them. They begin to vibrate, gradually shifting closer and closer. Sparks fly and pop, like a damn firework display, and we leap back to dodge the rogue cinders.

I push Aria back and Maverick protects his face, but the moment all the relics connect, a wave of magic explodes outward, making us all stumble back and fall onto our asses in the snow. Even Cain and Elias lose their footing as the harp's power cascades over the earth in a massive wave. The pungent scent of sulfur wafts through the air, strong enough to make a person gag.

When I peer at the ground again, a small harp of tarnished gold lays there with all the relics in place. Like some kind of morbid and grotesque trophy. The skull sits at the very top, mouth open as if it'd been paused mid-scream. Inside, the eye sits, and the water from Styxx's river shines bright inside the jeweled orb. The hair, heart, and intestine have been unwound and pulled tight at the strings, the spine arched as the back of the piece, and the foot as the base.

Then Sayah retracts back into Aria, and we both stare at Maverick.

"You were saying?" she teases.

"That's your smarter-than-average shadow," he mumbles.

"Leviathan, remember? Sayah's been around since the beginning of time or some shit," I reply and stand, wiping the snow and ice from my pants.

I help Aria to her feet, too, and Maverick follows.

Cain and Elias walk over, Elias now on two legs instead of four, and both of them covered in Hell-creature blood.

"Who's going to play the thing?" Elias asks, wiping his bloody face with the back of his hand.

"*Play* it?" Aria asks.

"It's the only way to open the gates," Cain replies.

"But what if it backfires?" Aria glances at him nervously.

"She's right. If each relic held its own curse, I can't imagine the impact they all have together," I say.

"Ask the Leviathan again," Maverick suggests. "The relics don't seem to affect her."

Aria closes her eyes briefly and draws in a deep breath. When she opens them again, she looks concerned. "She's refusing to come out."

"What! Tell her to get her shit together and—" Maverick shouts.

"Maverick," Cain warns, and he shuts it.

"Yeah, didn't you just see Sayah suck up all those hellhounds? I wouldn't piss her off," Elias says.

"I'll play it." Cain pulls his shoulders back, taking control of the situation, as usual. "Hopefully the darkness won't be too overpowering for me."

Aria's eyes widen. She doesn't like the sound of that plan. "Hopefully?"

"I'll do it," I offer. "What's a little more excitement after tonight?"

"Fuck it. Give it to me." Elias steps forward.

Aria reaches for it first. "No, I'll do it."

"No!" We all yell in unison, but that doesn't stop her. She's about to swipe it when Maverick grabs it first. He strokes the strings a few times, a terrible thudding sound coming from each of them.

No one moves. We wait, gazes dancing over Maverick and then the spot in the mountain's face where the gate is supposed to open.

When nothing changes, Maverick holds out the harp and frowns. "Did we do something wrong?"

"Maybe it needs to be tuned?" I suggest. "It did sound a bit...dead."

But then again, how much music can a bunch of body parts make?

The ground shudders beneath our feet. We all freeze in place.

"You all felt that too, right?" Aria squeaks.

Another quake, followed by a low rumbling sound.

Maverick looks around wildly. "What the fuck?"

Another rumble, louder this time.

"That sounds like...drums," Elias says.

Then the ground opens up beneath our feet and music erupts from the earth—an eerie but melodic tune with a choir of voices singing an ancient language even I don't understand. The music hums across my very being, and my bones rattle under my skin.

Aria covers her ears, and Cain quickly pulls her against his chest.

Damn, was this the type of music Aria's been hearing when searching for the relics? It's hauntingly beautiful but way, way too loud.

"Look!" Maverick shouts, pointing to the mountain, where cracks of glowing magma line the rocks. "It's opening!"

Slowly, the stones melt away to reveal a massive cave, cloaked in darkness.

Holy shit. This is it.

After a hundred years, we're going home.

Suddenly, a powerful wind pushes past us, strong enough to lift our feet off the ground. Cain holds Aria tighter while we all lock our knees, trying to fight against it. But it's no use. It's drawing us closer to the gate.

"We're being sucked in!" Maverick tries to yell over the deafening music. I read his lips more than hear him.

Do we fight it? Do we let it take us? I have no idea.

I glance at Cain for guidance, but he's more concerned about Aria. He's wrapped his wings around her to protect her, but it makes the pull of the magic too great for him to withstand.

A second later, the wind swoops them off their feet and they both spin through the air, plunging toward the gate at a deadly speed. The moment they pass through the entrance, they disappear behind the veil of darkness, and panic crawls up my throat.

Fuck!

Maverick's next. He's lifted off the ground and flies into the cave feet first, the harp still in hand.

The only ones left, Elias and I exchange fearful looks.

What do we do?

Then certainty passes over his face and I understand what he's thinking. If one of us goes, we all go. We're in this together. Until the end.

At the same time, we jump into the air and let the forceful current take us, too.

My ass hits something so hard my teeth rattle in my mouth. Pain laces up my spine, and I let out a loud oomph.

The ground. I hit the ground.

Looking up, I see I'm surrounded by tall grass in every direction.

I push to my feet, rubbing my aching butt cheeks. Is it possible to break your ass? Because I just might have.

The sharp scent of rotting flesh assaults my nose, making my eyes water, and when I look above me, red streaks burn across the sky, as if it's made of smoldering embers.

Yep. Definitely in Hell.

Some things I could never forget.

But where in Hell am I?

I spin in place, seeing nothing but rolling hills of more and more of this high grass.

Dorian's head pops up on my right, not too far away. Like me, he looks around to search our surroundings. "Where are the others?" he asks, brushing off dirt from his arms and chest.

"No idea." I scan the hills, seeing nothing again at first, but then I spot three dark figures sprinting right for us, the grass swaying behind them as if moved by the breeze.

Dorian follows my gaze and squints his eyes. "There they are.

They must've spotted us, because they are running like bats out of Hell." He chuckles to himself at his stupid joke.

As Cain, Aria, and Maverick get closer, their fearful expressions become clearer, and my pulse gallops with the sudden sense of danger. They're not running toward us; they're running *from* something.

Dorian must notice it too because he freezes and says, "What the—oh shit!"

"What?" I gasp.

"Griyns!"

Griyns...Why is it not ringing a bell? But Dorian's hopping on his toes, ready to bolt out of there.

I peer across the hill at Cain, Aria, and Maverick again, who are closing the distance between us rapidly, and then the strange wave of the grass behind them.

But that's not from a breeze. The air is dense and stiff here.

Dorian doesn't waste any more time and makes a run for it too.

The field behind him moves frantically now, narrowing in a funnel right behind the gang.

"Run!" Maverick's yelling like a big baby, holding onto the harp. He's a damn sin demon. They all sprint right past me. But I'm pissed that we are being chased by these small critters, screaming scared.

"For fuck's sake!" I growl, storming forward in the long grasses, having had enough. These freakish griyns have always annoyed the shit out of me. I clench and unclench my fists, ready to fight.

The grass around me sways wildly, clear where the suckers are.

"Elias, you idiot, just run. Stop being a hero," Dorian calls over his shoulder.

"Yeah, yeah," I crow back, and then I lunge, snatching one of the shitheads by the back of the neck. It's a scrawny thing, with pale, sagging skin, like those animals humans call monkeys. Except it has no hair.

The griyn wriggles ferociously in my grip, hissing at me, sharp teeth bared and used to slice the skin off their victims. It's their delicacy, and revulsion fills me at the sight of them. It's not the way these naked things look that bothers me. I'm more than used to hideous forms in Hell, but that they attack anyone. Even their own kind when they get hungry enough. Fucking vermin. Zero loyalty.

I grab its head in my other hand, then swiftly snap its neck, then dump the creature to the ground. It's been too long since I've really gone hunted, so I shake myself, unleash a howl from my hellhound deep inside and attack.

One after the other, I tear them apart with my bare hands, with my teeth. They're so small compared to me...only a foot in height, but their numbers are where their danger comes into play. I carve my way through them...they come at me in pairs, snapping out of the grasses where they hide, but I'm just as fast.

I've broken so many necks, and still there are more creatures.

Snatching one in each hand, I squeeze the life out of their necks, their screeches piercing the air, when something sharp bites in the back of my leg.

I groan and look over my shoulder. One is latched onto my calf, biting me, and I kick it off with my other foot. The high grasses in front of me sway like a stormy ocean, undulating savagely right toward me.

There are so many of them...the reality hits me like a hammer to the chest.

I've never seen so many of them together, and I've hunted in these fields before.

Crap. Maybe confronting them had been a mistake. They normally attack in small groups...half a dozen or so.

"Well, aren't you all a bunch of fuckers!" I toss their dead friends toward them and swing left, sprinting out of their way.

Dorian's yelling something at me from a distance, and I look up to him waving his hand as if I can't see his fat ass.

My mind races. That one bite in the back of my leg still stings like a bitch.

Aria's calling me too, and I glance back to find the grass has gone dead still...too still.

I don't stop, my chest is pumping, and I dart toward the crew, figuring I'd taken down enough.

The piercing bite of small teeth comes fast at my ankles, then so many more I lose count.

I growl and turn to shake them off, but before I can even make a move, a ball of them crashes into the back of my legs, sending me forward, and I fall, the ground racing up to my face.

Goddamn fucking weasels. There is no way I'm going to die at the hands of these hairless monkeys.

DORIAN

ARIA SCREAMS at the top of her lungs at Elias being yanked under.

One minute, Elias is tossing dead griyns into the air like he's a fucking juggler, the next he drops and he's dragged away.

"Of course the idiot got himself taken," I snarl, giving the spot he stood seconds earlier a glare. So much for keeping a low profile.

"Let them have him if he's going to do something so ridiculous," Maverick mutters under his breath. "Better yet, why doesn't he just go to Father's front door and declare you're all back? Damn him."

"We need to help him." Aria turns and sprints after Elias, pushing through the tall grass that swallows her up to her waist.

"Aria," Cain calls out, going after her, but she's not stopping.

So now, we're all busting our asses running through infested grass, and I'm not in the mood to have my skin razed off and eaten in front of me as I pass out.

Suddenly Aria yelps and she falls into the grass. Then she's gone.

"Fuck no!" My heart beats hard and fury bleeds through me. I thunder faster, all of us frantically searching for her where we'd seen her last, pushing grass aside, yelling for her.

"Aria! Scream so we can follow," Maverick calls out, clutching the harp while pushing the grass out of his way.

When her cry comes from across the field, not too far from where Elias had fallen, we charge in that direction.

The grass shakes viciously around us now. My skin crawls, but I'm too damn scared for Aria to give a shit about what happens to me. Unlike us, she'll die out here.

Cain's wings spread out and he takes flight, blotting us in his shadow. He flies low, then he dive-bombs to the ground as if he's spotted something. Aria?

An explosion of grunts and hisses are all that we hear. I swing in that direction and glance over to Maverick, who wears just as much determination on his face as I have pumping through my veins.

But without warning, his drops and all I see are his flailing arms before he vanishes beneath the greenery. I lunge after him, but he's gone, along with his gurgled yelp.

Shit.

Fear coils deep in the pit of my gut knowing that if we all fall here, that's it. All those years of effort to find the relics, to not die at Lucifer's hands, are wasted if we lose Aria. Everything will be undone by some freaky skin-eating demons.

Anger burns through me at the thought, and I lunge toward a sound, only to find Cain wrenching Elias up by the arm. He's bleeding and covered in scratches, his clothes ripped, but he's growling for retribution like the hellhound he is.

The ground around us is littered with dead griyns.

"Where the hell is Aria?" I scan the area but she's nowhere, and my gut twists in on itself.

Another scream, this time sounding like Maverick. Seriously, he better not have lost the harp.

"Aria!" I yell and stare out across the field, catching movement up ahead in the grass.

I throw myself that way, my demon spilling out, horns and claws. I lunge and drop down on three of the little shits, which I shred to pieces, blood splashing everywhere. Their squealing hisses attract more of the fiends that rush toward me. And I go ape shit on them, tired of this crap.

Moving with lightning speed, I demolish every single creature that comes to me. When all I'm left with are dead carcasses and me splattered in their blood, I rise to my feet.

Sucking in scorching hot air into my chest, I scan the enormous field and find myself completely alone. My lungs are on fire as dread strikes. They're all gone!

"Aria? Cain? Elias?" Where the fuck are they?

I know, deep down, we are in huge trouble now.

I spear back through the field to where Cain and Elias had been last. Of course they're not there, and my mind blanks.

The grass is swishing in every direction when Aria's scream reaches me. She's farther to my left, and I sprint like a mad man.

I gulp. "I'm coming."

For the space of a heartbeat, time seems to stand still. My pulse pounds in my ears, while the weight of the situation drives down on me, drowning me.

Maybe ten feet from me, Aria bursts up from the field with a fierce battle cry on her lips, a creature in her grasp and bites all over her arms.

Sayah emerges from her chest, stretching outward. Her shadow is so immense, it's intimidating. Even to a demon like me.

And in a flash, Sayah surges outward across the field, flittering past me then vanishing down into the long brush. She spreads across the whole field, being in all places at once with unbreakable speed.

The sharp squeal of hisses and cries taint the air in seconds, the sound deafening. It confirms that there are so many more of those bastards than any of us realized.

Slowly, Cain and Maverick climb to their feet nearby, followed by Elias, stumbling and looking like they'd been run over by a truck. But they're alive. And by some miracle, Maverick is still clutching the harp.

"Aria." I take quick steps to her side and she drops the dead griyn, then wipes her hands on her shirt.

"Talk about the worst welcome party back into Hell." She half laughs, while I reach over and wipe the drop of blood rolling over her cheek from a cut.

Then I collect her into my arms, a slight tremble within me is a reminder of how close I came to losing her. "You belong to me, Aria. And I would have died if anything happened to you."

She cradles her cheek against my chest for a moment, then pulls back. "I feel the same way. And that's why I had to run for Elias. Each one of you mean the world to me. I won't ever pick one over the other, so I just need everyone on board to protect one another." She almost sounds pissed that we didn't stop Elias from pulling his dumbass stunt.

I kiss the top of her head and swallow my words. They aren't for her. I also remind myself of promises I'd made—that we'd all share her. Even when Elias does stupid crap that endangers us all. "I know and agree."

Her laughter is like music, even in a macabre field with us both splashed in blood.

"By the way, you're glowing." She points at my chest.

I look down to where my incubus runes beam a bright blue through my clothes. "Always happens during battle."

"I like the look on you." Her grin is wicked and she traces a hand over my collarbone.

"Sounds like you want a private showing?"

She laughs even louder and turns to the others, who are just now joining us. We're all together again, alive, even if bitten and bruised.

Aria throws herself at Elias. My initial reaction is that she'd slug him one for being an idiot, but instead she hugs him. I don't like that it disappoints me.

"We're a team now," she reprimands him with her stern voice. "No hero stuff, okay? We fight or run together."

He offers her a lopsided grin, which I am guessing is his attempt at being coy about apologizing.

"Can I punch him now?" Maverick pipes in.

"Fuck, first time you've said something I agree with," I mutter, and a sense of triumph flares through me that it's not just me wanting to smash my fist into Elias's face.

Except he's rolling his eyes, chuckling. "Can't believe you're so jealous."

I stiffen when Cain steps forward and collects her from Elias, showing us his possessiveness.

"Aria's right. We're a team. Sometimes we'll fuck up, but we help each other, no matter what."

"Fine," I finally admit. "Now can we get the hell out of here."

"About fucking time. Follow me, we're heading to Torryn's."

Good news, Cain and Torryn don't have a broken relationship. Bad news, him and I never see eye to eye. I'm all about love and the art of fucking, but that bastard flies off the handle at the smallest thing.

Let's hope Cain can tame the Sin Demon of Wrath.

ARIA

THE STREETS ARE BUSY, unlike anything I've seen before in Hell. Plus, we are now in Hell City, a decrepit place with high-rises and demons running all over the place.

We stick to the alleyways, which stink so bad I can't stop gagging from the putrid smells.

Maverick is leading the way, with Dorian close behind him. Cain is at my side, and Elias is at my rear. We don't exchange any words, just Maverick pointing which direction to take. He's leading us through the intricate web of a city filled with demons in an attempt to avoid us all being identified.

Cain would be the first to be spotted, as he's the most well-known, especially after being expelled from Hell.

I look over to him where he stares straight ahead with a focused gaze. I want to ask him what it feels like to be back home and if there's any nostalgia at seeing a place like this again. Or has it been so long since he'd moved to Earth that nothing feels familiar anymore?

I keep my mouth shut for now though. We'll have time for that later, if we all survive this crazy mission.

At the end of the alley, we wait in the shadows for slug-like demons to make their way across the road, each dragging black sacks with something that's writhing frantically inside. I don't even want to know what's in there.

I must have winced because Cain slides his hand into mine and squeezes slightly. When I meet his gorgeous blue eyes, his lips pull into a tight smile and he mouths, 'We'll be alright.'

I want to say I believe him, but we're in Hell and wanted by Lucifer.

Maverick waves us on and we sprint across the road and into another alley. We move with speed and I lose count of how many turns and stops we take.

Finally, we emerge from a back street into one empty home and there is an explosion of woods across the road. They're packed in tight too, branches twisted, trunks growing at weird angles, and vines coiled around everything.

"Please don't tell me we're going in there?" I whisper.

Maverick's looking my way, raising an eyebrow as though he wants to say yes, but restrains himself. "Not quite."

"We're here," Cain states, and takes the lead with Maverick.

Elias and Dorian fall in by my side, while I glance behind us to the dark, stone walls of the buildings with no windows. Wherever we are, it's isolated.

"This place is fucking creepy," I murmur under my breath.

"Torryn is not a fan of people, yet he wants to live close to Hell City. So, he's carved himself a small paradise," Dorian explains.

"This is the farthest thing from paradise."

"Can't agree more," Elias adds, then takes my elbow and has us rushing to catch up with the others.

Maverick and Cain have stopped on a narrow sidewalk, facing the woods, and only then do I notice it...

Realization flashes over my mind. There's a black door within the forest in front of us, and it's attached to a house swallowed by trees and vines sporting huge thorns.

The whole explosion of forest is an actual mansion...a monstrous castle. Except it's concealed so well, entangled by trees, that it's impossible to see at first.

The front door opens and a huge man stands in the doorway.

"What in the name of all things Lucifer is going on here!" The man stares at all of us. He's large, equal in height and width to Elias, and his upper lip must have once been half torn off and never grew back. I can see the top row of his teeth when he closes his mouth. His eyes are similar to Cain's when he's furious. With his short-cropped dark hair, his cargo pants, and black tee, he reminds me of a soldier.

"Torryn." Cain strolls toward his brother. Sin Demon of Wrath. Despite his title, I don't see an angry demon in front of me yet. Someone more annoyed than anything at having visitors.

"Cain!" His shoulders rear back and he seems lost for words, his face shocked.

"Brother," Cain says and slaps his shoulder. "We have lots to talk about but not a lot of time."

"We do." He turns to wave Cain into the house. We go to follow, but he stops in front of us to make the rest of us halt. His pleasant expression quickly morphs into one of hatred. And when his dark gaze hones in on Dorian, it increases tenfold. "You step a foot in my home, and I'll break every bone in your body."

"Got it," Dorian responds sharply, and I don't make a move to enter his home either. Maverick marches inside.

When Torryn lifts his chin at Elias for him to join them, he states, "I need the fresh air."

"Suit yourself." His eyes land on me, and he studies me for a long time. "Human...you wear Cain's ring, but I can still sense you. I won't ask. If you are with Cain, then I give him the benefit of the doubt."

I swallow the lump in my throat and watch him go inside, shutting the door behind him. As much as curiosity has me wanting to go into his forest home, it also petrifies me. Part of me pictures the walls adorned in the heads of all the creatures he's butchered. The demon has that savage hunter vibe going for him.

"What the hell was that about?" I spin toward Dorian.

He shrugs nonchalantly. "You steal someone's woman five hundred years ago, and he still holds onto the grudge."

Elias raises an eyebrow at Dorian. "Well, you did use your powers to seduce his wife."

"Oh, that's bad," I mumble.

"I was in a different head space then," he groans, his brow furrowing. "I did a lot of shit that I'm not proud of, but the past is just that...the past. So, what's going on with Maverick then?" Dorian asks, and part of me wonders if this is distracting us from talking about his shady past.

Elias is staring at me just as intently, and I'm not surprised. With so much happening, I haven't had the chance to talk to them as I had with Cain.

"I'm guessing Cain told you about Maverick and me?"

"Bits and pieces," Dorian answers curtly.

I reach over and take each of their hands in mine. "I didn't expect this to happen, but Maverick's wriggled into my heart. Yeah, I know he's also been a jerk to us in the past. He's lied and done some unforgivable shit, but I believe he's changing. He wants to fight against Lucifer, wants to be close to his brother. And we've grown closer, too. Bonded."

They both watch me, almost incredulously, as if they aren't ready to accept this.

"Don't look so shocked. He's actually a surprisingly decent guy. Did you know he paints beautiful portraits? He makes me laugh, and there's just something about him that awakens me, just like you two and Cain do. I don't even know how to explain it, but it feels right in my heart."

"He does not paint," Elias mutters.

"See, you don't even know him properly, yet you hate him."

"When someone behaves like a monster, then they usually are a monster," Dorian says.

"I understand you've all had a bad history with him, but people change. Look at you two and Cain. Maybe Maverick was that way because of how Lucifer and others treated him. And not all monsters do monstrous things." I arch a brow at Dorian.

His lips thin, while Elias just watches me.

"Look, I know this is going to take time. All I ask is give him the benefit of the doubt for me, please? I honestly believe he is a man with a huge heart, and he's let me see enough of it that I am drawn to him."

It doesn't surprise me that neither reply right away. So, I go and sit on a log near the edge of the woods near the doorway, both men soon follow and take a spot next to me.

"I don't know what else you want me to say," I add.

"That you won't fall for any more demons because sharing you is hard enough," Dorian says.

"I know, and I promise that if we can just survive Hell, literally, we can be a huge happy family. And I'll have all the time in the world for us to do more things together."

"I want to also hear that he is shit at sex," Elias says.

I burst out laughing, because my memories of Maverick only spike my arousal. When Elias doesn't smile, I say, "Oh, you were being serious."

He sits back. "I've seen his dick once, and it doesn't compare to mine."

"Or my two," Dorian contributes, both of them staring ahead at the black stone building, seeming content for now to know they are better than Maverick.

Well, who would have thought that my conversation with two powerful demons on jealousy would come down to dick size.

I lay my hands on both of theirs. "All I care about is that I have you all by my side."

They shuffle closer and hold me, and I melt against them. I still couldn't believe that after my foster father sold me to pay his debt, the very demons who owned me now loved me.

I never used to believe in truly happy endings because they don't happen to people like me. But look at me now. I am so close that I might actually believe in such fairy tales. If we survive, that is...

"So, what do you think is going on there?" I ask.

"Three sin demons together...hmm," Elias says. "Definitely lots of chest puffing and ego stroking."

"Or maybe getting into a fight. Nothing would surprise me," Dorian adds.

I don't know how long we wait outside, but I'm sweltering in the heat. When the sound of laughter comes from the open door, we all leap to our feet as the three brothers emerge. Cain and Torryn exchange a few quiet words, then Cain and Maverick stroll in our direction.

"So?" I ask. "Is he joining our cause?"

Cain nods. "He was easy to convince, seeing that just last week Lucifer took away his legion of demons. Torryn is pissed, and he wants revenge against Father." The smile on his face is warm, and I'd go as far as to say that bonding with one of his brothers might be exactly what he needs after being away from Hell for so long.

"Fabulous. Where to next?" I turn to Cain, knowing that while this brother seems easy, I doubt the others will be so cooperative.

"Raziel. But first, we change our clothes. He won't appreciate us turning up like we've walked out of a war zone. As the Sin Demon of Sloth, he is very particular about respect from others, and we need him on our side."

I groan internally. Great. This should be fun.

CHAPTER

FIFTEEN

I watch Cain as everyone pours into his castle. The way he looks around makes him almost appear out of place in his own home. As we all enter the grand room, he glances over to the throne and a shadow crosses his expression, like the sight pains him.

I can't begin to imagine how it must feel for him to return to Hell after so long.

Maverick, Dorian, and Elias make their way upstairs, chatting like this is normal for them. They don't seem to be as bothered by their return to Hell like Cain is.

"How are you holding up?" I approach him.

His earlier expression morphs into a more confident one, the kind where he conceals the truth of his feelings. "I'm fine."

"Cain," I say with more force. "Don't lie to me. You can talk to me about anything. You haven't been home in such a long time, so this has to be strange for you. It's understandable."

He takes in the dark room once more, a frown appearing and revealing the truth. He feels lost here. In his old home.

"I'm a stranger in my own castle." His words are pained, and they clench at my heart. "This place used to be one of Hell's crown jewels. It used to give me such pride. But not anymore.

He glances at me, gauging my expression, and when I wait for him to go on, he does. "I've been gone for so long... Yet I thought that once I returned I could pick up from where I left off. Like my banishment never happened. But now that I'm back, I can't help but feel out of place."

A sense of pity spreads through me, hearing the uncertainty in his voice. Of course, I'd never let him know that. He's too proud to ever accept my pity, but it shows me just how much humanity has affected him during his time on Earth.

"Just give it time," I say. "A century away is a long time. You've just gotten used to Earth."

"I didn't care for it until you came into our lives. You've changed everything. Me included."

"That's what I like to hear," I tease and hug him hard.

He lowers his face and his lips graze mine, igniting my arousal like he always does, but he remains tense against me. "Our time here is dangerous. Lucifer won't give up once he discovers we're back," he whispers against my mouth. "And no matter how things turn out, my priority is keeping you safe."

Well, talk about a mood killer. My shoulders sag. I guess this is the part where I am supposed to agree with him, except I can't make such promises. We've come so far. I won't stop fighting by his side.

"But what if you're in danger?" I ask, remembering that terrible vision I saw of him sacrificing himself and Maverick. "I don't want to lose you either. Or any of the guys upstairs."

"I know you don't." Of course he doesn't offer me any promises I want to hear, like nothing will happen to him or no one's going to die. He can't, not when danger is all around us.

He wraps an arm around my waist and guides me to the staircase in the hallway. "I'd give you a grand tour of the place, but you've probably seen it all."

"Nope, not even close, but I got the gist of how monstrous it is on my first visit."

He laughs, throwing his head back, and I adore how he sounds. There's something comforting, reminding me of being home. And that's when it hits me too...that I've grown so close to my men that my home is where they are.

Up on the next floor, I make my way into one of the several bathrooms, leaving the others in a main common room with couches and golden statues.

Washed and dried, I wrap a towel around myself and rush on bare feet right into Cain's walk-in wardrobe. I make a beeline for the back corner where I found the leather pants last time. Not sure if I want to deal with demons in a skirt.

If I've learned anything from my trip to Hell, it's to never let Nix and Maverick pick out outfits for me again.

Racks of clothes surround me in every color, and across the back are shelves of shoes and accessories. I reach for the drawer filled with women's underwear, some still brand-new by the look of them. I pluck out a simple, black thong. No bras, but the one I wore from home will do.

I drop the towel and it falls to my feet just as the whoosh of the door shutting sounds. I flinch around, grasping my underwear to my chest.

Of course I'm completely naked.

And he's nude too, drying his hair with a towel. But now, he's frozen mid-action, and his cock twitches as it hardens. I won't lie... the sight does have me staring longer than I should, bringing with it a surge of fire deep between my thighs.

His gaze roams over my body as his mouth curls into a devious grin. "Came to check on you," he says in a husky voice as he strolls toward me.

"Is that what you call it?" I exaggerate my stare down his body and back up.

"If you want to touch it, you just have to ask, my little rabbit." He palms his dick a few times, his eyes rolling backward at his touch, then they lower onto me. They're glazed over, and a grin spreads across his face, wider than before.

He stands before me, so tall, so huge, and my libido twists into lustful knots. We're so close now, I feel the edge of his cock against my lower stomach.

"I missed you so much," he says, running a hand down my arm. "I missed your laugh, tasting you, fucking you, the way you scream when I make you come."

I stare at his lips and think about how much I want them on mine. His touch and words set off all kinds of explosions throughout my body.

I reach down and wrap my fingers around his beastly cock. He's so big, so hard. He growls, and I love when he does that.

"Is this what you missed?" I pump my hand up and down his shaft, and a shuddery breath slips past his lips.

"You have no idea." Suddenly, I'm in his arms, and he's groaning against my mouth. He kisses me savagely, and my breath hitches.

Running my hands to the back of his head, I fist his hair, holding on while I curl my legs around his hips like a vice, hooking my ankles just under his ass. I kiss him back just as hard, my lips already feeling bruised.

With one hand on my ass, his other shoves aside clothes hanging from the metal frame, tossing some of them to the ground.

My back hits the cool wall between clothes, and he's nipping on my lower lip, then sucking on my tongue, keeping me caged by his body.

"You have no idea how hard I resisted fucking you the moment you got back." His hand is on my breast, and he lowers his mouth to a nipple, slipping it into his mouth.

In seconds, his cock is pushing into me. I stiffen and adjust, preparing to take him. He lets go of my breast and kisses me again, hungrily. His hands fall to my hips, and he lowers me down to the hilt.

I arch my back, loving how big he is, but he never stops kissing me. Then he begins his rhythm, quickly picking up speed.

It's a wild ride, and I know he's not holding back. This is my Elias when he's been starved for too long, and I love when he gets this way. It leaves me feeling adored and wanted.

My heart slams inside my chest the faster he takes me. I desperately kiss him harder, taking his tongue into my mouth. A spark of electricity buzzes across my body, my pussy throbbing with each thrust.

I moan, but when he pauses and pulls out of me, the sound coming from my mouth is one of protest.

"What the hell, Elias. I was so close."

"Good," he growls, his amber-colored eyes flashing. "That's what I like to hear." He steps back and lowers me to my feet, then takes me by my hand to the middle of the room where he turns me to face away from him.

"On your back," he commands, his hands pushing down on my shoulders.

When I follow his instructions and glance up at him, his eyes are blazing brightly.

"I dreamt about you while you were gone. I woke up with such a hard-on, I was in fucking pain."

"Well then, the more reason you should get back to fucking me."

He chuckles and runs his hands from behind my knees to my ankles, drawing my legs straight into the air. Grabbing my feet, he spreads me wider, and I feel him settling in place.

"Fuck, your pussy is glorious. So wet and swollen." This time, there's no ceremonial preparation, he just slams into me so hard and fast, my entire body convulses. I might be going cross-eyed at how furiously he thrusts into me. He nips at my foot as he holds on.

I'm completely coming apart, chasing my breaths.

"You are so beautiful," he snarls, and this is him really fucking me. A man with a desperate hunger who holds nothing back.

He breathes harshly and I moan louder, sweating, rocking back and forth with his motion. My breasts bounce from each thrust, and he eyes them hungrily.

Labored exhales rush past my lips. He's going to kill me. My head falls back, and I'm moaning his name. "Elias." Every inch of me is taut, and the wave of climax slams into me so fast, I lose myself.

I scream as an orgasm rips through me. My body trembles with the most incredible pleasure.

Elias bellows his own explosion, and I feel him pulsing inside me, flooding me. My head goes slightly hazy with how high I'm floating. He shudders against me, and I peer up at him, loving the way he looks when he's coming.

He notices me watching, and a sexy smirk teases his lips.

"That was exactly what I needed," I say as he lowers my legs onto the floor.

He rubs his closed fist across his chest and blows over it. "I'll be your de-stressing fuck-man anytime."

I laugh and he groans as I squeeze his cock with my pussy.

"Seriously, if you keep doing that, we're going another two rounds." He slaps the curve of my ass.

"Hey," I gasp breathlessly.

That's when he sits back and pulls out of me. As I sit up, he spreads his legs and draws me closer. His skin is clammy like mine, and when I look up at him, he kisses me tenderly.

I press my breasts against his chest, wanting so much more of this gorgeous demon.

The ache between my thighs is delicious and reminds me of what we'd just done... It always happens after he fucks me.

I'm breathing hard again, and when he breaks our kiss, my lips feel full and sore, while my head still buzzes. I'll never get enough.

Our brows are touching, and my mind is racing with so much going on. "Do you think we'll survive going up against Lucifer?"

"We have to," he answers instantly, without hesitation. "I never thought I'd find love again. At this point, I'm not sure I ever had it in the first place—but then I found you."

I blink at him, and I might be on the verge of tearing up.

I press myself against him and kiss him slowly, wanting nothing more than to show him that he never has to doubt how I feel about him. About us.

I open the door to Cain's castle and stroll through with Nix not far behind me. The moment he steps inside, his wide-eyed gaze sweeps across the onyx floors and high vaulted ceilings.

"It's been so long since I've been here," he mumbles to himself. "I forgot how dramatic it was."

"You mean melodramatic," I correct.

"No, dear Brother, that's your home."

I snort at that. "No, that's *you*."

He grins. "Guilty."

I start to walk down the hall, toward the throne room where the others are waiting, but when I glance over my shoulder, I notice Nix has stayed behind.

"Are you coming?" I ask him.

He pauses, still taking in the room, but there's a frown weighing down his expression.

"What is it?" I hiss, my irritation growing. "Why are you just standing around?"

He waits another second before replying. "Why did Cain ask me here again?"

Not understanding where this is going I stare at him, dumbfounded. "Cain needs information on Raziel, and you have dirt on all our brothers."

He says nothing.

"You said you wanted to join the cause, right? Help anyway you can?"

"Yes, I do. But..."

"But what?"

"Do you think he's still pissed at me for leaving him for the sharks the last time?"

What the fuck is he getting at here? "Sharks?"

"Father," he says dryly.

Oh. He's worried about Cain's motives for summoning him here now. Especially after he abandoned the cause last time they'd attempted their coup. He's afraid he wants revenge.

A justified thought, I think. I'd be wondering the same thing if I were in his shoes.

"Is he still pissed?" he whispers. "I let Lorcan get in my head, and my fear outweighed my loyalty. But not this time. I'll stand by his side until the end."

"Good."

Nix and I snap our gazes up to the very top of the staircase landing where Cain stands, dressed in a slim-fitting suit—black on black—his hair slicked back to emphasize the sharp lines of his face. He's looking more like the son of Lucifer now than when we left the living plane.

I guess some old habits die hard.

"Cain." To my surprise, Nix bows his head as Cain leisurely walks down one of the two curved staircases. "Welcome home."

Cain says nothing as he crosses the room. His shoes click loudly against the polished floor, and somehow, he's able to take full command of the space just by being there.

He goes straight up to Nix, and for a tense moment, I wonder if he really is going to punish him for the past.

His narrow blue-eyed gaze roams over him, and a boulder of worry sinks in my gut.

If he does decide to hurt him, there's nothing I can do, is there? My allegiance is with Cain.

But then, Cain does the unthinkable and grabs Nix by the arms in a welcoming embrace. A pleased smile stretches his lips. "It's nice to see you again. *Brother.*"

Nix still hesitates, unsure if he can trust him, but when he realizes Cain's welcome is genuine, he beams. "Glad to see you, too. Back where you belong."

Cain's smile falters a bit at the last comment, but he quickly turns and gestures for us all to follow him into the throne room. Before we even get inside, the voices of Elias, Aria, and Dorian echo to us in the hall. When we enter, everyone goes silent, and Elias's and Dorian's hateful glares pinpoint on Nix.

He glances at me for help, but all I can do is shrug.

"Cain is one thing. Dorian and Elias are another," I mutter. "They might not be as forgiving."

"We have a common goal," Cain begins, overhearing us. "And to achieve it, we need to work together."

"Unlike last time," Elias growls.

"Yeah, when *some* of us were too chickenshit to stick around when it mattered," Dorian tacks on.

Nix holds up his hands as a sign of surrender. "I hear you. And I'm incredibly sorry. Won't happen again."

"So, you've grown balls in the last hundred years?" Elias says.

"Big, big hairy ones," Nix quips, without missing a beat. "Like yours."

He huffs a laugh. "We'll see about that."

Aria steps forward in an attempt to calm some of the rising tension. "Nix is here to help us now. That's what matters."

"Right," I add. "He's been keeping tabs on everyone while you've been away from Hell. And he knows what Raziel's most recent rules are. If we want to have any chance of converting him to our side, we need to know what we're in for."

"Wait, rules?" Aria glances between us in confusion.

"Raziel may be the Sin Demon of Sloth, but he expects everyone else not to be. All visitors must comply to his rules as a form of respect, however ridiculous they may be," Cain explains.

"And they change almost every week. Sometimes every day, if he's particularly bored," Nix says.

"Like, as his entertainment?" Aria asks. "He wants us to be his dancing monkeys?"

Nix thinks about her question then nods. "I'm not sure what that means, but it does sound right."

"And what if we refuse?"

"It's the hole for us," Dorian answers. "He still has it, doesn't he?"

"Absolutely. It's the hole and an eternity of servitude. You'll be forced to be his *dancing monkey* forever," Nix says.

She gasps. "A slave! That's unethical."

"That's Hell, sweetheart." He smiles.

"So, what's his ridiculous requirements for today?" Dorian asks and crosses his arms.

"White," Nix replies.

Dorian balks. "Wearing white? In Hell? Talk about there being slim pickings."

"Oh, that's the easy part," he goes on. "We all have to talk in hypophora."

"Excuse me?"

"That's the spirit."

Dorian clamps his mouth shut and glances around the room. Everyone but Cain looks confused as hell, including me.

"Cut the shit, Nix. What does that mean?" I demand.

"Talking in the form of a question," Cain explains.

"Wait, like in *Jeopardy*?" Aria asks. When no one responds, she goes on, "You know...the game show?"

"Is this another human thing?" Nix whispers my way.

"I think so."

"Ah, yes then. Like that—whatever that is. But always. Anything that comes out of your mouth has to be in the form of a question."

"What the actual fuck?" Elias snaps, his anger growing. "Is he out of his damn mind?"

"You're doing quite well so far," Nix chuckles.

"And if we refuse or mess up, we're done for." Aria's fearful gaze flicks to Cain.

"Then I will do the talking," Cain replies with a stiff nod. His mind has been made up for a while; he was just waiting on when to say it aloud. "We need Raziel on our side, so we must follow his rules, but I will not risk any of you because of it. I will do the interacting."

Nix claps his hands together loudly, the sharp sound bouncing off the glass walls and hitting us from every direction. Elias flinches with his enhanced hearing.

"Now that we got that settled, how much white do you all have in your closets?" Nix asks, to which everyone groans.

None.

White is a rare color down here for...*heavenly* reasons. And that's just what Raz wanted. To make it difficult.

Cain rubs his lips together in thought. "I may have a shirt or two...But definitely not enough for us all. Pants will be harder to find."

"I'll fucking go naked," Elias growls.

"Knowing Raz, he'll make you paint your body too," I respond and roll my eyes. All of us have our *things,* but Raz is just a pain in the ass.

"You're right," Nix adds. "I wouldn't put it past him."

Cain clears his throat. "I'll go. There's no need for us all to speak with him. It's better if Aria goes out as little as possible. She should stay here with protection." He's looking primarily at Elias and Dorian—which doesn't go unnoticed by me—but whatever. I don't want to stay behind anyway.

"I'm coming, too," I say. "Two sin demons is better than one. Especially when dealing with Raz's attitude."

"Make it three." Nix grins. "That is *if* you have enough white clothing for us."

Cain glances between us, seeming unsure about bringing me and Nix along, but he doesn't refuse it. Instead, he says, "I'll see what I can find."

CAIN

My younger brother's castle sits in the very middle of the Styxx river. He's made himself a little island there, the rapid water current just another way to deter visitors, on top of his ludicrous demands.

Unfortunately for him, I'm not afraid of wearing white. Nor am I afraid of getting a little wet.

As expected, it was hard to find pieces of appropriate clothing for us each to wear. I was lucky to have a white dress shirt and a pair of white shorts among all my darker colors. Don't ask me why I have them because I truly have no idea, but they're splattered with blood, which isn't uncommon for living down here. Hopefully the outfit meets my brother's approval, and the few red spots can be overlooked.

For Maverick, I was only able to find a nightgown, which is too short for him, and fits more like a woman's dress. While Nix is in a ruffled white blouse and a skirt—both things I'm sure were left from one of the many women I used to...court.

Even though Maverick has been scowling since we left my castle because of his new attire, Nix has been enjoying his a little too much, flashing Maverick his ass any chance he gets.

It seems the two have made somewhat of a friendship during my time away.

On the river's edge, Maverick side-eyes me. "We could fly across..." he suggests.

"That'll mean losing the only white clothing we have or stripping," I say. "And one of us will have to carry Nix."

"Swimming it is, then." He claps his hands together. "You can swim, right Nix?"

He waves a hand at him. "Of course I can."

"Then let's get this over with." Maverick is the first to dive in and paddle against the strong current toward Raz's castle. It's smaller than the others and made up of moss-covered stones he'd found at the bottom of the river. But like most things in this god-forsaken place, it's not what it seems.

Nix jumps into the murky water next and just manages to keep his head above the rapids. He's struggling, and ends up needing Maverick to haul him out on the other side.

It doesn't take me long to get across, but unlike the bodies of water on the living plane, the River Styxx's water feels more like slime across my skin. Thick. Sticky.

When I reach the island, I climb out, but the disgusting, mucus feeling remains on my skin.

"I'm going to need a shower after that," Maverick says, rubbing his arms.

We walk up to double doors.

"Remember," Nix starts, "everything you say needs to be made into a question."

I nod and use the giant metal door knocker to signal our presence.

It takes some time but, finally, the door cracks open. An old man dressed head to toe in white, with a frilled neck piece and exaggerated hips, stands on the other side.

"What do you want?" he asks. The clown-like getup means he has to be one of the unfortunates who have fallen prey to Raziel's stupid rules. He's been forced into servitude.

My mouth dries. Since I'll be the one carrying the conversations in hypophora, I'll have to think about my sentences carefully before I say them. "Is Raziel available?"

The man's hooded eyes dance over us, suddenly realizing who we are. He drops to a knee and his gray head bows.

"Can you tell my brother we'd like to speak with him? Now?"

When he stands again, he nods frantically. "Will I get him promptly?" Then, he turns and disappears, leaving the door open a fraction.

"This is stupid," Maverick grumbles, his voice low.

"It is, but it has to be done," I whisper back.

"Why is Raziel always such a pain in the ass—" The door opens wider, revealing our brother, looking as I remember him. Shorter in stature than me by a few inches, with gold curls, tan skin, and hazel eyes. There's no doubt women on Earth would fawn over him and his pretty-boy meets surfer looks. He's even wearing only a thin pair of white boxer shorts, as if he's been enjoying himself on a tropical island.

But we know better. The demon underneath is almost the opposite of his human form in every way. Slippery, scaly, and more like a man-eating monster than a person who enjoys the beach.

His unique powers can be quite handy, though. He can make any person fall asleep at the drop of a hat and then wiggle his way into their dreams. Even cause hallucinations if they're awake, making them see and believe whatever he wants with just a touch of his finger.

"What was that, Baby Brother?" Raz asks, glancing over our white outfits. "Was there a *question* you wanted to ask me?"

Maverick grinds his teeth. I can see the insults and curses he's trying to hold back, but he has to remember Raz likes playing these games. He wants to make you mess up; He wants there to be a reason to punish you.

I throw Maverick a glare. I am supposed to be the only one talking here. That was the plan.

Instead, Maverick says, "Yeah, why are you always such a dickhole?"

Raz laughs. "What could you possibly mean?"

"Maverick," I growl, "don't you think that's enough?"

He ignores me. "Making everyone talk as a question? What's up with that?"

"Ah…" A slow calculated smile lifts Raz's lips. "For the fun of it, Baby Brother. To see people like you suffer through it."

"Wait, was that a question?" Nix glances at me and Maverick.

"The rules don't apply to the one who made them, silly. Only to the players."

Maverick steps forward, ready to unleash verbal hell on him, but I whip out my arm to shut him up.

"We came here not to fight, did we not?" I ask and turn to Raz, who is watching me with one brow arched in interest. "And may we ask you a question?"

"Big brother Cain has come back home." He leans lazily against the doorframe and pretends to pick at his nails. "I almost didn't recognize you there. The living world really did make you weaker, didn't it?"

Anger begins to bubble up, but I suppress it, reminding myself not to fall for his traps. I keep my expression as smooth as possible.

"Let me guess…You're back to finish what you started? Or should I say, what you failed at the first time?"

"How can we have your help?" I asked through clenched teeth. "Don't you agree that it will take all of us—all sin demons—to defeat Lucifer?"

My tongue ties from reforming my statements into questions. What I really want to do is grab him by the shoulders, look him in the eyes, and tell him to put his damn ego aside for once. This is bigger than us. It's bigger than Hell. Grow the fuck up.

Raz seems unimpressed. He shakes his head, his curls dancing across his forehead. "You know, Lorcan warned me you may be stopping by. After you harassed Irno and stole the harp's pieces—"

"You mean the ones he stole from us first?" Maverick bites back.

But Raz waves that one away. "So, I had a feeling you'd be

knocking on my door, Cain, begging me to help you try and take Father's throne again."

Begging? Aggravation prickles up my neck. *I wouldn't go that far.*

His gaze flicks to Nix. "You're seriously going along with this?"

He opens his mouth to respond but closes it quickly to rethink his words. "Is-Isn't Father too unstable? Haven't you said that yourself before?"

Raz shrugs.

"Won't his antics end up killing us all?" Maverick asks next. "Including you and all of Hell?"

Raz peers up for a long moment, pretending to contemplate our words, but it's clear he's already made his decision long ago by his aloof attitude. "Well, I'm sorry to have wasted your time, Brothers, but I just can't join in your suicide mission this time."

Maverick is shaking with fury, his hands balled into tight fists. But I don't blame him. We'd have better luck reasoning with a corpse. At this point, if he goes to hit Raz, I may just let him.

"You know you're never going to get the throne...right?" Maverick adds on that last part to assure it still classifies as a question. "No matter what you and Lorcan have planned?"

Raz's gaze hardens on him, confirming Maverick's suspicions. If Lucifer takes us all out, he and Lorcan have plans to try and swoop in and share the crown. Only Lorcan, out of all of us, would *never* share power. He's the Demon of Envy, after all.

Either Raz is incredibly stupid or he's planned a double-cross of his own.

I shove all that nonsense aside. It's too easy to get caught up in the dirty politics and backstabbing of it all. It's just normal, everyday occurrences in Hell, and frankly, I don't have time for it anymore.

"Nice seeing you again, Cain. And may I say, you all look just show-stopping in your white outfits," Raz drawls as he pushes himself off the frame and starts to shut the door.

"You sonofa—" Maverick lunges, but Nix grabs him by the shoulder to pull him back.

Pausing with the door still open a crack, Raz grins wide. "Na-uh-uh, Mavie. Questions only."

"Yeah, well how about you suck my asshole, Raz? How's that? Question enough for ya?"

Raz slams the door shut, but his laughter booms from the other side.

Nix, Maverick, and I exchange concerned glances. There's no doubt we're all thinking the same thing.

Without Raziel and Lorcan's help, our chances of beating Lucifer are rapidly declining. We need all the sin demons to match his power, and without them...this plan very well could be a suicide mission.

But we do have one weapon now that we didn't have before. Aria.

She's the one who's keeping my hope alive. So, I won't give up just yet.

Fuck Lorcan and Raziel. There is still one more sin demon to recruit. Valdim. Gluttony. With his help, we'll be much better off.

I unleash my demon, my wings ripping through the fabric of my white collared shirt. Maverick follows suit next to me, grabbing Nix under the arms, and together we launch ourselves into the air.

After Cain, Maverick, and Nix came back from Raz's with the bad news, things aren't going in our favor. It's starting to remind me a bit too much of the first time we tried taking Lucifer out, and we definitely don't want a repeat of that failure. Especially since, this time, it'll most definitely end in death, not banishment.

Everything relies on the last sin demon of the seven. Valdim. Or Gluttony. So once they return and change clothes, we regroup to discuss what our plan is.

I, for one, am done fucking around and asking politely. Fuck the pleasantries and then getting the door slammed in our face. I say we start flexing our muscles more. It's the only way to get anything done down here.

Unfortunately, Cain doesn't agree with my methods, at least not yet. He wants to be civil with his brothers. For once.

I personally think it's to distance himself as far as possible from his father. That's my hunch anyway.

Before we can even make plans about how to handle Valdim, there's an ominous knock at Cain's castle door.

Every single one of us freezes in place.

Maverick glances at Nix from across the throne room. "Nix… Who else knows we're here?"

He shrugs. "I didn't tell anyone, if that's what you're assuming.

But you heard Raz. Hell's buzzing with rumors about you five. It was only a matter of time."

Aria's face pales. "You think it's Lucifer? He's found us?"

"This would be the first place he'd look," Nix replies, matter-of-factly.

"Shit, Nix." Maverick throws him a glare.

"What? It's true."

Cain holds up a finger to his lips to silence everyone, and the room grows still. Then, he whirls around and hurries down the hall into the foyer.

My ears prick up, listening for any sounds that could tip off an attack. Dorian and Maverick shift closer to Aria, too, waiting for my word. If things get nasty, they know to grab her and run.

But, to my surprise, I hear nothing but Cain's footsteps fading away, a rustle of paper, and then him returning. Stranger still, when he emerges from the darkness, he's holding an envelope in his hand. When he flips it over to the back, there's a purple wax seal that he pops open with a flick of his finger.

"You...got mail?" Aria asks in disbelief. "There are mailmen in Hell?"

"No mailmen," Cain begins, his eyes dancing over the script. His pinched frown has my chest tightening. "It's from Valdim."

"No fucking way." Maverick hurries over and snatches the letter from him to read for himself, and Cain doesn't protest. He reads it over too, and his face mimics Cain's. They both glance at Aria.

"What? What is it?" she asks, voice rising with fear.

"We've...been invited," Maverick starts hesitantly, "to a dinner party."

He's joking, right? He has to be joking.

"I don't understand. Is that bad?" Aria asks and glances around the room for some kind of comfort.

Cain answers, "He's asked for all of us by name. Including you, Aria."

"Me?" she chokes out.

"That means he knows we're all here in this castle. And that means Father knows," Nix says.

The seriousness of the situation slams into me and nausea roils in my gut. It won't be long before Lucifer comes busting through the door like he did in our home on Earth. This time, with his army of marble-made assholes. "We need to get out of here."

"I agree with dogboy." Nix points my way.

Anger mounting, I snarl at him and chomp my teeth. "I'll give you dogboy."

He ignores me and says, "We aren't safe here anymore."

"But where are we going to go?" Aria throws the question out that we're all thinking.

"We're going to Valdim's dinner party."

Everyone looks at Cain in disbelief.

"But, what if it's a trap?"

As always, his expression reads calm, but there's fire behind his eyes. "Then we kill Lucifer. It either happens now or it happens later. It won't change the outcome."

"But Cain—" Dorian tries to argue, but Cain cuts him off.

"If this isn't Lucifer, and Valdim is trying to reach out, then that means we have a better chance of him joining us. If it's a trap, we'll prepare for it." He glances at each of us. "Get dressed. We're leaving immediately."

That's it. That's Cain's final word on the subject.

He turns and walks out, disappearing down the hall again.

He's right, of course. If we take out Lucifer now or later, not much will change. Valdim's help is needed, but if this invitation is a trap, then we never had a chance for him to be on our side in the first place.

As I glance around the room, I take in the uneasy looks on everyone's faces. Especially Maverick's, who's still holding the invitation in his shaking hand.

I hope to hell what we're about to go to is only a dinner party. And that's one thing in my life I never thought I'd ever say.

MAVERICK

I feel like a jackass.

Here we all are, standing in front of Val's place, dressed to the nines, waiting for him to open the door like it's a family reunion or a holiday dinner.

Standing around, waiting, like a bunch of jerkoffs.

Does anyone else see how weird this is? Just me? And that's saying something, since I was just dressed in an old lady's night-gown when visiting Raz.

I sigh and peer down at my polished dress shoes. Why is it that I seem to feel like a fool a lot around these four? Now add Nix to the mix, and that's just a cherry on the vanilla frosted jackass-cake.

This is most definitely a trap. Has to be. With the way word travels in Hell, Lucifer has to know we're here and what we've been doing. He must know Valdim and Lorcan are the only ones we haven't visited yet, and by some simple process of elimination, he'll know exactly where to cut us off.

Although, if he really was the one to send the invite, why not just axe us off at Cain's place? Skip this embarrassing step? That was Cain's other argument when I tried to protest this plan on our way here, but still...Father does enjoy the game. And the torture.

So do I, but that's why I try to stay one step ahead of him. And my gut is saying T-R-A-P.

The door swings open wide, and who else is standing there but our brother, Gluttony himself, Valdim. Average height, slender build, with reddish hair and a wide smile that looks genuinely happy to see us. Which only makes me more suspicious. Val's always been on the more...extroverted side of us seven, along with Nix, but that doesn't mean I trust him any more than the others.

Somehow, Val manages to squeeze past the massive wall that is Elias and get right to Cain to wrap him in a hug, which Cain only awkwardly stands there for. Dorian edges a little closer, just in case he tries anything devious, but Val only steps back and looks Cain over from head to toe.

"You look good," he says and pats him affectionately on the arms. "Must be all that non-sulfuric air up there, hm?" His laughter booms, but no one returns it. We're all so tightly wound, waiting for the bang to come, but instead, Val's giving us friendly nods and hellos.

"You all got so dressed up!" He nods hello to me and Nix. "Brothers." Then, his eyes roam us all over and linger a little longer on Aria, for obvious reasons. She's absolutely stunning in a slinky black dress that's swooped at the neck and held up by thin straps. She didn't put on an ounce of makeup or do much of anything to her hair since we were in a hurry, but does she really have to? She's sexier than sin naturally.

And I should know. I'm a *sin* demon.

Val waves us all inside. "Come in, come in! We don't want the food getting cold."

I want to say I'm not sure how it could, seeing that Val's castle is built into the volcanic rock near the pits, a place where most of Hell's nastiest monsters thrive. So, of course, because of the steam geysers and pools of lava, it's hot as the dickens outside. And inside, it's like walking into an oven on broil.

I may have lived in Hell my entire life, but even demons have limits, and just stepping through Val's foyer has sweat dotting my forehead and upper lip. The air is so thick, it's hard to breathe, yet Val seems unbothered by the temperature.

"Excuse the ash," he goes on as he leads us through the open foyer and into a massive room with an actual wall of moving lava as the focal point. It falls like a waterfall from the ceiling, making it easy to miss the long table in the middle and the servants standing along the opposite wall, all waiting silently. "It's impossible to keep up with it all when living in more or less a volcano."

Aria leans closer to Elias and whispers, "Where's the food? I see eight places but no food?"

Elias glances at the people standing there silently. So, not servants, like I had thought. Souls waiting to be feasted on.

It must've registered with Aria too because she covers her mouth to quiet her gasp.

But something else strikes me—something else she'd said.

Eight place settings at the table...

I count them myself to find she's absolutely right. Eight. But why?

There's six of us, plus Valdim is seven. There's an extra.

Shit.

My heart falters.

Who else was invited to this dinner party?

A man strolls in at that second, wide at the shoulders with a bald head that's covered in demonic symbol tattoos.

Lorcan.

I knew it. This was a set up. Not with Lucifer, but still.

We all freeze in place. Elias's skin ripples as the power of the shift passes over him, ready to unleash his hellhound at the drop of a hat if necessary. Dorian's steps forward and bounces on his toes, itching for a fight. There's no doubt that if Cain said the word, he'd be on Lorcan faster than a blink.

My own demon surges to the forefront, wanting to tear into him for breaking into the mansion, stealing Azrael's relics, and making everyone believe it was me. Instead, I unsheathe my daggers and spin them in my hands.

Surprise flashes in Lorcan's gaze the moment he sees us all standing there, followed by blazing fury. His head whips toward Val. "What's the meaning of this? Why are they here?"

"Us?" I bark. "Why are *you* here?"

Lorcan glares at me. "I got a fucking invitation, asswipe."

Turning to Cain, I mumble angrily, "Give me one good reason why we aren't detaching his hard-boiled egg of a head from his shoulders right now?"

"Let's hear him out first," Cain replies calmly, and that only enrages me more.

"Hear him out? He. Stole. The. Relics. Or did we all forget? Because of him, you almost couldn't get down here again."

"Maverick..." Aria whispers in warning.

Am I the only one who wants revenge here? Lorcan almost fucked up everything for us. And he's right there. Why aren't we doing anything?

"Enough." Cain's voice is sharp and vibrates with power. He doesn't say much, but it's my cue to step back.

I don't want to listen to him; following orders has never really been my thing, but I've made my choice and pledged my loyalty, so I reluctantly put my daggers away.

Lorcan's head falls back and his laughter booms. "It's true? You've turned into one of Cain's lap dogs too, Mav? Nix?"

I clench my jaw as my rage continues to whip inside me like a violent storm.

"You have quite the circus there, Cain," Lorcan continues to hoot and howl like it's the funniest thing in the world. It only grates on my nerves. "A bunch of clowns."

Aria shouts over his obnoxious laughter. "And you keep sucking Lucifer's limp dick. Now *that's* hilarious, isn't it?"

Lorcan stops abruptly, his hateful gaze landing on Aria. His top lip curls over one of his fangs.

But she doesn't back down, only holds her head high and meets his glare head-on. Her ferocity and protectiveness make my heart pound harder. I love when she's fiery like this.

When Lorcan takes two threatening steps toward her, Valdim's hand shoots out to stop him from getting any closer.

"This isn't why I brought you all here," he says calmly and shoves Lorcan back.

"Yeah? Then why did you?" Dorian calls out.

Valdim's big smile is back, but this time there's a sinister twist to it. "Because, my incubus friend, I'm a glutton for many things. But being used as a pawn in someone else's game isn't one of them."

Lorcan rocks back on his heels, and even Elias and Dorian relax some.

"That's right. I knew you'd be visiting me soon regardless to try and sway me to your side for whatever nonsensical reason. But I decided to beat you to it."

"Nonsensical? This is life and death. The fate of the living and nonliving worlds," I protest. "This is the complete opposite of nonsensical."

Valdim only shakes his head. "I don't want any part in either of your plots to rule the underworld. I figured I'd cut out the middle-man, so to speak, and bring you all here to tell you directly."

"But he's working for Lucifer," Aria says, pointing to Lorcan. "And they're going to destroy everything—all of existence—if we don't do anything."

"That's where you're wrong, girl," Lorcan spits. "I only work for myself. Fuck Lucifer."

"Then why take the relics from us if you weren't doing his bidding?" I ask.

Instead of answering, Lorcan crosses his arms. Blatantly ignoring me.

What a massive prick.

"Come on, Lorcan. Fess up," Valdim says, but Lorcan only hisses at him, showing off his vampire-like fangs.

"What is this? A family therapy session?" I throw at Val. "And who the fuck do you think you are? You're just as fucked up as the rest of us."

Also ignoring me, Val turns to Lorcan again. "I'm asking you nicely, Brother. Explain your motives then, if you claim to not be under Father's thumb."

Still, Lorcan doesn't answer.

Val tsks and hold out his hand, palm up. "Alright then. We'll do this the hard way. *Dagger.*"

The prickle of magic caresses my hip, and when I glance down, I find my one sheath empty. There's a spark of light and, suddenly, it reappears in Valdim's waiting hand. He grips the handle and points the tip at Lorcan's neck.

Aria gasps, having never seen Val's power to summon things before, and I guess it could be seen as a nifty parlor trick to a stranger but, like most things, it comes with limitations. Still, it can be useful in a fight...or to tame an unruly brother, like now.

Lorcan sneers at him, craning his neck to keep away from the sharp blade. "Point that thing somewhere else," he warns.

Val responds by nicking his skin. Blood wells up from the small cut and drips down his neck.

Lorcan growls in defeat. "Without the relics, Cain couldn't come back. Without him, Raziel and I would take out Father and then take the throne."

Elias snorts a laugh. "You? You honestly thought you and Raz could kill your father? You're even dumber than you look."

"You underestimate me." He bares his gritted teeth. "You all do."

In one swift move, he throws up his arm, knocking my dagger out of Valdim's grip. It slides across the floor and I rush for it. But in a blur of speed, much faster than any creature alive or dead, Lorcan rushes me and slams all his weight into my chest. I fly backward and crash into the stone wall, so close to the waterfall of lava, that it singes my right arm and shoulder. I land on the ground in a heap, the pain making it hard to breathe.

I glance up to see the air shifting in a zigzag—another sign of Lorcan using his unique power of speed. He's so fast, it makes him hard to track, sometimes even seeming invisible to the naked eye. But there are things that give him away. A flash of darkness, a smear across the air...I've become accustomed to his tricks, and from the looks of it, he's heading straight for Cain.

"Cain! You!" I shout, the words raspy from my bruised ribs.

His demon snaps out of him and he leaps off the ground just before Lorcan's on him. He stumbles, tries to make a right turn, but gives away his location. Elias is there suddenly and manages to throw a punch in perfect timing and catches him right in the jaw. It sends him reeling back.

I hop to my feet, but since we weren't able to feed before our trip to Hell, my body's taking its sweet time to heal.

I may have lost one of my daggers, but I have another to spare. I rip it out of my belt, aim for Lorcan's bald-ass head—right between the eyes—and...

A resounding boom shakes the walls around us, and more ash rains down.

Everyone stops and looks around, confused.

Another earth-shaking boom. Lava spills over the table and red cracks line the floor at our feet.

"What's happening!" Aria asks and clutches Dorian's arm. "Earthquake?"

Hundreds of heavy, clunking footsteps come from outside the castle's doors, and dread seizes me. Not an earthquake. Much, much worse.

"Lucifer!" Val's panicked whisper confirms my fears. From his own horror, it's clear this wasn't on the itinerary for the dinner party. "And he's brought his guards! Hurry! You must leave!" He runs over to the lava and steps on a spot on the floor, triggering a secret escape route. The curtain of magma separates in the middle to reveal another doorway. "This way, Brothers!"

Lorcan and Nix rush for it just as we hear the crash of the castle's front doors being smashed through. Dorian shoves Aria forward, too, knowing that protecting her matters above everything else.

Lucifer's marble soldiers march into the room, weapons drawn.

With Elias transforming into a hellhound and Dorian freeing his own demon, they both dive into the fight without a second's hesitation. Chaos erupts as they clash, and Cain lands in the middle of it all, his massive wings taking out several of them at a time.

Spotting my missing dagger across the room, I sprint for it and snatch it off the ground just as a marble guard swings his broad sword down like a battle-ax. I leap out of the way, narrowly avoiding a wide gap in the floor that has more magma bubbling up and spilling over.

Shit! That was too fucking close.

The truth is, my daggers can't do much damage against an army of stone. The good news is, their heaviness and rigid stone bodies make them slow, so it's easy to I kick the sword right out of the mobile statue's hands.

Picking it up, I twist the handle in my hand.

Bulky, heavy, and clearly a weapon made for brute strength instead of skill.

Eh, it'll do.

With two hands, I swing it through the air and strike the guard right through the middle. When the metal hits the rock, the blow vibrates up my wounded arm, and I'm hit with another wave of pain.

The sword may have not sliced through the guard, but it causes it to teeter over and crash to the ground into a million tiny pieces. Only a small victory, since these bastards can't actually die; they can reform themselves like a giant evil jigsaw puzzle with some time.

I've got to move fast.

Sword in hand, I'm about to join the others in battle when a chilling thought comes to me.

Cain, Dorian, Elias...They're all there, locked in the fight with Father's soldiers. But where's Father?

Better yet...Where's Aria?

Terror ices me over.

I whirl around just in time to see Lucifer holding Aria captive in his arms on top of the dining table, her head flopped forward like she's unconscious. Or dead.

"No!" I bellow and run for them.

Lucifer smirks as his leather wings shoot out from his back and wrap around the two of them. Ditching the sword, I reach for my daggers, but I'm not fast enough.

They both pop out of existence right before my eyes.

Lucifer is in my face, his strong hand grasping my wrists, wrenching my arms over my head, and in seconds, cold shackles snap around them.

"Get off me," I yell, writhing against him.

His other hand grabs my jaw, stilling me, sharp nails digging into my skin.

He sneers, smoke wafting out from the corner of his mouth, and I'm on the verge of screaming because I've ended up as Satan's prisoner. This is what nightmares are made of...except he wants something from me, or I'd be dead already.

My back is plastered to the wall. Fear ripples over my skin as I stare into the eyes of this monster. I woke up in this dark room that smells of sulfur, with only the dim burning torches on the wall. Mud covers the floor, and it's stiflingly hot. I'm sweating profusely.

He's wearing a black suit with a matching dress shirt underneath, and as much as I hate him, the similarities between his face and Cain's are too close for my liking.

"All that hard work, sneaking into Hell behind my back, collecting your relics, and look where it got you," he snarls, his upper lip peeling over a perfect row of white teeth. And I can only guess they'd turn to fangs or something hideous if he wills it. His grip on my jaw tightens, and I wince on the inside, refusing to show him my fear. He's the kind of asshole who'd get off on it.

My teeth grind together, and I barely breathe through the bout of anger and dread consuming me.

"What? You're mad that you couldn't stop Cain from returning home?" I should shut my mouth, but my pulse is racing and I'm so furious, so scared, that my mouth does its own thing.

Fury dances across his face, darkness spreading over his eyes. I expect him to go full demon on me, but he doesn't. He just offers me a terrifying grin that curls on his thinning lips, which is a lot worse. He's holding back.

From the first time I met him, I knew Lucifer was unhinged.

He strokes his short beard, pulling back slightly. An air of regalness surrounds him, as it always has—the kind that belongs to an arrogant serial killer who thinks he's untouchable.

"Your words are empty," he barks. "And I will deal with my son soon enough, but that's not who I'm interested in right now." He reaches over and his nails scrape across to my collarbone, over to my shoulder, pushing the strap of my dress aside.

I swallow hard, trying really hard to not fall apart or cry. Within me, I sense Sayah stirring, sensing my dread. Hell has roused her since we arrived, making her more responsive. What I don't know is how she would stand up against someone like Lucifer...

Lunatics like Lucifer are full of ego and love to brag, and I am all for hearing his plans so I can help Cain overthrow him.

"We're going to play a game," he tells me, then fists my dress and rips it so hard, I lurch forward from the force. It tears down the front, and at the seams under my arms.

I gasp, earning me a deranged smile from him.

Shit, I really hate him. "Look, I get you're pissed at Cain, but your family squabble has nothing to do with me."

He just stands in front of me, not responding, and takes something out from his back pocket. It's a curved blade with a ring holder on one end, which he slides onto his middle finger. The flaming glint of the torches shine across the silvery blade.

Fear zips down my spine and I fight hard not to scream at the sight.

"This has nothing to do with Cain." He spits the words in my face like a venomous viper. "Everything I want is standing in front of me." He grazes the side of his weapon across the top of my breasts, then down between them.

I hold my breath. One wrong move and he'll cut me.

He pauses at my stomach, pressing the sharp tip against my flesh.

I tense, my heart hammering.

"It'd be easy to just gut you. Enjoyable too. Will that make your little shadow come out to play?"

It's a test.

This fucker wants Sayah.

I narrow my eyes at him, determined to give him nothing, and with that, I push down further on Sayah. She can't come out, not for this monster. I don't even want to know what he has planned for her...for me. But it can't be anything good.

"Go fuck yourself."

"I was hoping you'd say that," he says and slowly drags the blade across my stomach, slicing skin. Not deep, but it hurts like shit all the same.

The sting sharpens instantly, and I scream this time, my body convulsing.

"Now, that's the sound I like to hear." He lifts the blood-stained knife to my face, while my stomach is on fire, blood dripping onto my dress.

I jerk my head up, and the room seems to sway. "Y-you're a psychopath."

"Why, thank you." He huffs, pressing his knife to my cheek and slashes downward.

I hiss, clenching my teeth through the pain. "Your sons hate you. Each one of them fears you. There is no love."

He barks a laugh, while I tremble. Sayah's just below the surface, longing to escape, but I push her back. I can't let her. Not when I don't know what he has planned for her.

"Their fear is all I need," he snaps.

"Even if that means they see Cain as their true leader over you? That you destroy everything you touch?"

An ugly expression flares over his face, and he shows me the real beast with red eyes, protruding brow, fangs, and thick horns.

He's the creature of nightmares. Terror clings to my skin while blood drips down my jawline, my wounds scream with pain, but I hold Lucifer's stare. He's pissing me off.

"You'll get nothing from me."

"That makes this all the more fun. So, as I said before, let's play a game. It's simple. I will cut you, and when you want me to stop, release the shadow."

My body trembles on its own. "You're a fucking dumb piece of shit. Wasting your time with me." Distraction is worth a shot.

For a moment he pauses, churning over my words no doubt, but when the corners of his eyes wrinkle with his grin, I know he's beyond the point of insanity.

But if I show Sayah, then what? He'll kill me for her?

I keep thinking about how much easier she flows from me in Hell, how quickly she responds, and that somehow this place just resonates with her. Does that mean Lucifer will gain control over her easily?

If she really wanted to come out, she'd do it already, like she's done in the past.

She knows this bastard is dangerous to her and me.

Then he starts cutting—my arms, my chest, my stomach. The burning pain is like acid on my skin.

My cries fill my head, and I'm convulsing, teeth chattering. I don't stop even when he pauses. Fear crashes through me. I'm thrashing against the restraints on my arms.

Everything hurts so much, and I can't stop the tears drenching my cheeks.

But with all the dread, rage also surges forward, my thoughts filled with memories of Cain, Elias, Dorian, and even Maverick. How much they suffered, how we've bonded together, and it's worth all the agony in the world. I grew up with Murray, but there was no real love. Joseline was more a friend than a sister. My true family, my love, is with my demons. And for them, I will get through this. No matter what. I will survive.

I lift my head, blood dripping down nearly everywhere, and my stomach turns at the devil staring at me with such pleasure on his face.

"I have so much in store for you, Aria. So do keep resisting me. Your body will be marked with scars that will ensure you will never forget me...if I let you survive, that is. Though, I have been needing a new footstool."

"You don't scare me," I snap back, exhausted. I never want to become the girl who's too scared to fight back.

In a flash, the back of his hand flies to the side of my face. His knuckles crack hard, and my head is flung sideways, my world blurry. I cry from the throbbing ache zigzagging across my face and head.

He snatches my hair and yanks my head back up. "The tough ones are the most fun to break. Let's keep playing, shall we?" He releases me, and my head flops back down, my chin tucked into my chest.

I tense up, expecting more, but instead, the click-clack of heels hitting the stone floor catches my attention.

"What are you doing here?" Lucifer snarls.

"You think I'd miss this? No fucking way." Her voice has me instantly stiffening, and I raise my head, my gaze clashing with Serena's eyes.

What is she doing here?

She approaches us, flicking her blonde hair off her face. Her skin-tight, black bodysuit leaves nothing to the imagination. How is she not sweating up a storm in that?

I blink the blood and sweat out of my eyes as she pretends to show me pity.

"Oh, you're in a terrible state." She mocks.

I want to rake my nails down her face.

Lucifer raises his blade and I flinch against the wall behind me.

"You really are stupid," she drones on, while I'm shaking and bleeding.

"Just get out of my face," I hiss.

"I bet she doesn't even know how you found her." She chortles like a freaking hyena in Lucifer's direction, then glances at me. "It was me, in case you're too slow to work it out. When you hit me the ring cut me, and I smelled who you really were after that, human, along with it being Cain's ring. And I saw instantly that it was you... the bitch who took Elias from me. You were your own undoing."

I look at her, and one of my eyes is twitching, the eyelid not wanting to completely stay open. "What the fuck do you want? A pat on the back? And for your information, you destroyed your relationship by betraying him." I'm burning up on the inside over the fact that she ran straight to Lucifer.

I blink at her while grazing my thumb over Cain's ring. It felt amazing to smash my fist into her face, but knowing that was how Lucifer found me, I now regret it.

"Listen here, human filth. If you had half a brain, then you wouldn't be in this mess."

Lucifer cuts her a hard side glare, which she doesn't notice. She is so clueless, having no idea that Lucifer will betray her in an instant. But his look also tells me she has no clue why he really wants me...she thinks it's for her.

Ah, bless her black heart.

Serena laughs again and steps back, watching from the shadows.

I don't even have the energy to come back with a witty response. But when Lucifer presses the edge of his knife to my collarbone, the sharpness biting into skin, I start screaming. Darkness feathers around the edges of my eyes as he cuts me while he smiles.

Rather than fight it, I let myself fall.

<hr>

My EYES open and I groan with pain. Every inch of me aches, even my ears, which I don't understand.

I must have passed out, because Lucifer is no longer torturing me. Serena isn't around either. Thank fuck.

But when I glance down, I want to scream all over again. I am covered in blood and sweat, so are my clothes, with more blood dried across my skin. How long have I been out? Lucifer must have still cut me when I fell unconscious. Bastard.

My throat burns when I swallow. What I wouldn't give for a cold glass of water right now.

Or better yet, to get the hell out of here. I wrench my gaze across the room this time, just in case Lucifer or someone else remains in here watching me. I keep blinking to clear away the blur.

And now, instinct drives me. *Sayah*, I call to her in my mind. *Get me out of here. Please.*

Desperation is clinging to my thoughts because if Lucifer didn't get what he wanted, how long before he eradicates me?

She slips out of me like a rushing river, spreading out across the stone floor, then she rises before me like a storm, taking no particular form. She's fraying at the edges, and goosebumps cover my skin. It's not from fear, but from her surge of anger overwhelming me. She's furious that we allowed that prick to do this to me.

Escape. We need to get out before he gets us, I tell her. That's what matters now. Get back to my demons and pray to everything that they haven't been captured as well.

Sayah sweeps over the top of me. I crane my head up as she threads into the locks on my restraints.

In moments, the metal braces snap from my wrists. My arms fall by my sides and my legs wobble. They give out and I drop, my knees kissing the floor, my arms too numb to catch myself. I whine quietly from how much it hurts to move. How every cut stings like I'm on fire.

I raise bloody fingers in front of me, and anger billows to the surface. It bears down on me, almost crushing me from the inside.

Next thing I know, Sayah sweeps under my arms and around my middle. She lifts me up and off my feet. It feels like I'm on a rollercoaster. I have no control of my body when we move forward, which makes me queasy.

She opens the door and part of her slips into the dark hallway.

Everything swims around me, and I can't help but think I might pass out again.

Someone grunts up ahead, followed by something heavy hitting the floor. That doesn't sound good.

Sayah carries me around the corner seconds later, and that's when I spot three demonic, hairy goat-like creatures, complete with hooves, strewn on the floor. Their limbs are twisted, and blood pools around them. As Cain kept saying, no one really dies in Hell…well, except me. But these things will come back soon enough.

As if on cue and sensing my concern, Sayah rushes us forward.

We move fast now. I don't know where we are, but panic flares at the thought of being found.

Each time the wounds throb, I clench my teeth. My mind races with images of Lucifer in my face, how he was going to keep going until he killed me. My chest tightens again, and adrenaline thumps in my veins.

I never want to be alone with that maniac again.

And in that precise moment, an ear-piercing alarm goes off, blaring through the hallway, deafening me.

I flinch and look back, expecting guards, but there's only darkness. Shit!

"They know I'm gone," I mutter to Sayah. Desperation roars through me, and I'm wriggling to be free, to run faster, anything to escape.

My feet are skimming along the floor in the dark hallways, and I try my best to stand up on my own, but we never stop moving. Sayah takes the lead, but when we come to a dead-end, my stomach drops. My hands push against the wall, just in case there's a trap door...but nothing.

"Crap." My heart slams against the inside of my chest. I twist back around and, with Sayah still curled around my middle partially holding me up, we move again. We swing around another corner when thunderous footsteps sound straight ahead of us, shadows dancing at the end of the long hallway.

Sayah's hold around my middle constricts and she wrenches me backward into a dark passage.

Silence.

I don't dare take a breath while she spreads out in front of me like a shield, concealing me.

An army of soldiers storm past us—marble guards—and I feel the blood draining from my body remembering their attack from earlier and how I ended up being kidnapped in the first place.

Once they pass, we wait and I quietly try to catch my breath.

Then Sayah nudges me forward. I swing my attention to the left where the guards went...and we go right, hoping it'll lead us outside.

I stumble on my feet, holding onto the wall for balance. I'm walking faster now, almost running, when a flood of bright light comes from up ahead. Cautiously, I keep going and when we reach the turn, I peer around to find large double doors, sitting open, natural light spilling inside. Outside stands a large courtyard and more buildings nearby.

Nerves dance up my spine since I'll end up walking right into the open to be seen...but what other choices are there?

Sayah, still wrapped around my waist, tugs me in the opposite direction. I twist around to see her pulling open what appears to be a side door heading outside directly across from the courtyard.

You're amazing, Sayah. I frantically lunge after her just as the walls seem to tilt around me. I stumble and crash into one, then shake my head. I have no idea how much blood I've lost, but this is the worst place to pass out. I have to get my shit together.

I push my legs to move before they slip out from under me again. Time isn't on my side, but I can't stay here, so I step through the door with Sayah.

We find ourselves in a dingy passage encased by two granite stone buildings. Behind us is a dead-end, but up ahead a street runs adjacent to the building. I look back and quickly shut the door to not give away our position.

A way out. *Yes, please let it be the case.*

I've had so much bad luck that I'm desperate for something to go right.

I wobble awkwardly away from the door, my breath strangling my lungs with the burning hot air. My skin tingles, and a thrumming sensation fills my head. I feel Cain, Dorian, and Elias like they are just out of reach. Our connection flares awake now that I'm outside the building.

I'm drawn forward as though I'm magnetically pulled to them.

Our bond... It'll help me find them.

Sayah is stretching out ahead of me. But I don't need anyone spotting a huge shadow by my side and drawing unwanted attention. *Sayah, come back.*

She obediently complies.

At the end of the alley, I careen away, following the call to my men toward the left. I need to be as far from the prison or whatever the fuck this place is as possible.

But something dark suddenly falls over me.

Panicking, I raise my head just as I slam straight into a solid wall of muscle.

Panic flares over me, and I'm curling my hands, raising them, ready to defend myself.

But he snatches my wrists before I can even push away.

"Aria," he snarls with a deep husky voice I don't recognize and is already dragging me toward the street where a black car waits.

My heart lunges to the back of my throat so hard that I might pass out again.

NINETEEN

"Hush, I'm not here to hurt you. I'm helping," he says as he shoves me roughly into the back seat of a black car that looks like a hearse.

"Help how?" I hit the leather seat sideways just as the door slaps shut behind me.

What the fuck? I scramble back up and frantically pull at the door latch, but it doesn't budge.

Sayah's already edging out of me as the man wearing all black climbs into the driver's seat, and I hold her down so she's just brimming below the surface.

"I'm not going back to Lucifer," I yell.

He twists his head around to look at me with a downturned mouth. He's red all over, just like Lorcan's boyfriend. Thick, bushy eyebrows crown dark eyes, and he has a wide forehead, with thick stumps of sawed-off horns at his temples. His expression is one of permanent displeasure...or maybe he's constipated. Could be either one.

"Neither do I. But you want to see Cain again, right?" He eyes me in the rearview mirror and waits for me to respond. When I nod, he goes, "Then we need to go quickly before Lucifer comes after us."

My head spins, and he's already got the engine roaring. The car sounds more like a dragon than a motor.

One thing's for sure... I don't trust this guy.

"Let me the fuck out! How do you know who I am, or about Cain?"

"I'm a friend," he says quickly over his shoulder. "Cain came to my home and asked me to help find you. I drove past just as you rushed out of the building with your shadow. That's when I knew I'd found you."

The car is moving now. I'm huddled in the corner by the door, and panic curls in my gut. Sayah is begging to come out to hurt this demon. She doesn't trust him either. But, if I let her out, then what? I navigate through Hell in this car? I wouldn't be opposed to the idea, except with my luck I'd end up driving into a lava pit or something. Although, it wouldn't be much worse than the demon driving—he isn't even sticking to the road.

He swings abruptly between two houses, tearing up the ground, and we come out on a dirty path.

What the fuck?

I keep staring at this beefy, red man driving like a lunatic. He's taking turns fast and dodging fucking trees growing in the middle of the road so suddenly that I'm white-knuckling the door handle.

"You haven't answered my question," I snap. "Who are you? And don't bullshit me with your friend story." Not that Cain wouldn't have friends, but I doubt he'd trust someone he hadn't seen in years to track me down. "Why isn't Cain with you? For all I know, you're one of Lucifer's lackeys."

"Cain's searching for you, and we split up to cover more ground. Lucifer is a fucking bastard. He killed my wife, so I can promise you that I have nothing but loathing hatred for the demon." He growls as he turns left and takes us farther from the compound. "I tracked you down here because this is one of his homes where he takes pleasure in torturing anyone who crosses him."

"Well, sorry if I don't believe you. Let me out now!" I shout. "Or would you prefer to personally meet my shadow?"

I'm certain I hear him snarl under his breath, then the car comes to an abrupt stop. The motion throws me forward and I smack face-first into the back of the passenger seat.

I groan and push back. "Goddammit, warn a girl first." I rub my nose, worried it's bleeding again. Luckily it's not.

"You want to threaten me, then get out. Go!" He hits a button on the dashboard and my door swings open on its own. "Find your way back to Cain on your own. But keep in mind, Lucifer will be sending every guard he has to search for you. Then, if you manage to somehow outsmart him, the local demons will come after you. There are creatures roaming the streets, desperate for a feed." His eyes glint, and a forked tongue slips out from his mouth, licking his lips like the idea excites him.

Everyone here is so depraved.

I tremble and stare outside, the heat pouring over me like a furnace and burning my nostrils with each breath. There are no homes in this area, only block buildings with black charred trees everywhere. Roots have broken out of the ground and are growing wild. It reminds me of a post-apocalyptic movie.

The idea of going out there on foot alone makes me tense. I'd like nothing more than to prove this cocky demon wrong, but I have to admit that leaving the car now would easily be suicide.

When I don't move, he says, "My name is Bolgaun."

His dark gaze studies me, then settles on Cain's ring on my finger. It leaves me uneasy.

"Cain and I grew up together," he tells me. "I had a thing for getting in trouble back then, and he had helped me get out of a pretty long prison sentence, so, I owe him."

I square my shoulders, unsure if I should believe that. There's still one thing that bothers me. "Cain wouldn't tell you about my shadow."

The corner of his mouth curls upward, and I half expect him to change his story. Instead, he presses on, "He didn't have to. Lucifer put a target on your back. All hunters and assassins were called in and were told about a girl who could control a shadow. The reward was a massive number of souls."

My hopes of keeping low key are completely shattered. It shouldn't surprise me that Lucifer outed me once we escaped his clutches at The Ring. Though, dread fills me when I start to wonder if this red demon has any intention of being the hero for Lucifer.

"So, what are you going to do?" he asks, his eyes flicking to the open door.

I study the strong man, whose fingers are tapping his impatience on the steering wheel, and swallow hard. I understand his urgency to get moving, but that doesn't make it any easier to decide.

After running through all my options, I decide in the end that I am safer with him... At least I have Sayah if crap goes sideways.

"Let's go." I reach over to pull my door shut and notice half a dozen black creatures watching me from feet away. They're the size of German Shepherds, with six legs each and menacing fangs. I startle at the sight of them. When had they snuck up on us? And here I was with my door gaping open for the attack.

I grab the door and slam it shut, my heart in my throat.

Damn hell mutts. Damn demons. I hate everything in this place.

"I'm assuming Cain's castle is the best place to deliver you," he says, drawing my attention to him as we start moving again.

Bolgaun looks at me in the rearview mirror and waits for my confirmation. "I don't know where he is, but I can sense the direction, so keep driving and I'll tell you where to turn."

His gaze narrows. "Okay."

The pull in my body sweeps right. "Go right," I say.

Bolgaun abruptly swings in that direction, tearing down someone's fence as he zooms past their stone house and yard.

I jostle about in the backseat, madly searching for a seat belt, but find there are none in the car.

We're on a road again, and the sensation drawing me to my men seems settled in this direction.

"Keep going straight."

We fall silent as he drives like a maniac. I feel as though we're in a race car, and he's trying his best to hit everything he passes.

I settle in close to the door, my pulse still racing, and I stare outside as we pass through Hell. Part of me always imagined this world burning, with flames and terrifying monsters everywhere, but it looks nothing like that. Dried vegetation, stone structures, and dark mountains surround us. The sky is the only thing that looks like it's on fire, and they have paved roads and demons who live in homes. Like another city, just underground.

It's not what I'd expected at all.

I don't know how long we've been driving, but it feels like forever. But when we finally roll up to the magma pits and steaming geysers, I recognize the place right away. This is where Valdim lives, where we had come for dinner before Lucifer and his guards had attacked.

"This is it. Here." I sit upright, my gaze scouring the blackened grounds for any sign of my men.

Once we come to a complete stop, I push the car door open. The bond between me and my men pulls me to the mansion.

I turn to Bolgaun. "Thanks for the lift. I'll be sure to let Cain know of your help."

I exit the car and take quick steps to Valdim's front door on the volcano's side, but the bang of the car door sounds behind me. Looking back, I see Bolgaun coming in my direction, and I pause.

"What are you doing?"

"It'd be rude of me not to deliver you personally," he says with a nod. As he steps up beside me, I realize how tall he really is. He towers over me and is decorated with several sharp and deadly weapons.

"Maybe I should see if he's even here first, and I'll let him know." Despite all his help, there's just something about this demon that doesn't sit right with me. I can't quite put my finger on it, but even Sayah is uneasy.

He shrugs. "Did you forget I just saved your ass?"

I narrow my gaze at him. "Excuse me?"

Something flares behind his eyes, but the chance for him to respond is stolen when he glances at something over my shoulder. That's when I hear the creak of the front door.

"Aria!" Cain gasps.

I twist around, and I start to cry out his name, but Bolgaun grabs my arm, his grip squeezing hard. I struggle to break free and turn on him. "Let me go!"

"Bolgaun," Cain says, his voice as sharp as a blade.

It doesn't look like these two are friends at all.

I stomp my heel into his foot, which is just enough for his grip to loosen, and I wrench myself from his hold.

As I throw myself to Cain's side, his demon bursts forth— wings, dark veins beneath his skin, and black eyes appear all at once.

"Did he hurt you?" he growls as I stand pressed to his side.

I shake my head.

Bolgaun's upper lip peels back over fangs, and he puffs out his chest.

Cain pushes me to stand behind him, and then whirls on the demon. "What the fuck are you doing here?"

"He said he was your friend," I say.

"He's Lucifer's personal assassin," Dorian announces. He moves to stand alongside us, as do Elias, Maverick, Torryn, and Nix.

Assassin? My blood turns cold, and my stomach clenches painfully. His lies are so transparent now, and I kick myself for not noticing earlier.

But then, why save me at all? Why not take me back to Lucifer? It doesn't make sense.

A flash of something crosses Bolgaun's face... It almost looks like hesitation. Did he only expect to find Cain when we got back here and not his whole crew? Had his plan been to capture us both to become the big hero to his boss?

Bastard!

He sneers and starts to retreat.

"Six against one. Sounds like my kind of odds." Maverick cracks his neck and raises his fists, ready for a fight.

"I suggest you run home with your tail between your legs before you get yourself hurt," Dorian spits.

Turning to Dorian, Bolgaun's entire demeanor changes. His spine straightens and he fingers the handles of one of the knives on his belt. It's clear these two share some kind of history—real history. Not like the bullshit Bolgaun spewed before about him and Cain.

"Dorian," the assassin growls. "Still shining Cain's shoes, I see."

"And you're still wiping Lucifer's ass."

Maverick sucks in a sharp breath, loving the insult.

Bolgaun seems unimpressed. "You know, I wondered if I'd ever get the pleasure of seeing you again."

"Oh yeah?" Dorian scoffs. "You finally want some pointers on how to do your job properly?"

Oh, that's right. I'd almost forgotten Dorian had been an assassin too, once upon a time. His family was well known in Hell for it.

"Not exactly." He grins, and the sheer joy on his face has me hesitating. "I wanted to give you the news."

"News?" Dorian's brows pinch. "What news?"

His smile widens, consuming his entire face. "You know, after you were banished, Lucifer put a hit out...on your parents."

Oh shit...

Dorian's shaking now where he stands, the rage taking over.

"And I was the one to personally deliver them to him so they could be *eliminated.*"

Dorian roars and hurls himself at him. The two of them hit the ground near the enormous metal gates, coming together in a ferocious clash and rolling across the ground.

Without pause, Maverick and Elias leap into battle. Cain places his hand on my arm to keep me back, but I'm vibrating with anger myself.

The snarls and grunts of the fighting are deafening. Fists and blood flies. Metal flashes as Maverick and Bolgaun cross blades. Elias leaps out from behind and throws him across the ground. He rolls across the ash until he comes to a halt right before Cain's feet.

He doesn't move. Instead, he's slumped on his side and bleeding, his clothes torn and bloody. One of Maverick's blades sticks out of his back, too.

"Beg," Elias howls and stands over him. "And maybe Cain will show you mercy."

"Fuck that," Dorian says, chest heaving. "Did he and Lucifer show mercy to my parents?"

My hands clench, as I watch the agony flare across Dorian's face. I hear the grief in his words. Bolgaun deserves the worst kind of punishment.

"Fuck you." He spits blood at Cain's feet, and I glare at him. "Lucifer is the one true king."

In one swift motion, Dorian kicks the back of Bolgaun's head so hard, I hear the crack of bone breaking. "Shut the fuck up!"

The asshole drops to the ground, unconscious.

"He needs to die. We need the angel blade, now," Dorian demands. He's shaking violently and wearing a sheen of sweat over his face. Under the harsh, fiery sky of Hell, Dorian has gone pale, all the blood drained from his face. So lost, so angry, so heartbroken.

My heart clenches for him.

"My parents..." Dorian whispers, his gaze drifting up to the sky. Pain laces every word. "They're gone."

Unable to stand it anymore, I run to him. He takes me into his arms, and I hug him hard. He presses his face into my hair and inhales deep.

We stay like that for a while, saying nothing. No one dares break us up or disturb the moment.

After some more time passes, he pulls back and meets my gaze. "I'll be alright, gorgeous. But thank you."

I do my best to blink back any rising tears and step away from him.

Glancing at the fallen assassin still laying at our feet, Maverick snarls, "So, what are we planning on doing with him?"

Elias smirks. "I say we skin him. His red flesh would make an excellent welcome mat for me to wipe my muddy boots on."

Bolgaun surges up onto his feet like a missile, gripping a blade in his hand despite the one still in his back. He flies at me.

I freeze, my brain screaming at me to move but my body's locked in place. I'm paralyzed by my own fear.

As the blade arches down toward me, Sayah zips out of me lightning fast. Her black shadow gushes out, engulfing Bolgaun instantly.

One second, the blade is flying at my face, the next, a wall of darkness blots out the light.

Someone grabs me from behind, strong arms around my middle, and wrenches me away. I'm off my feet, Cain whipping me as far from the attack as possible.

But my gaze never leaves Sayah, who snaps around Bolgaun. The last thing I hear are his gurgled cries before she shrinks in on herself until she's a flat shadow on the ground.

Sayah breaks away and withdraws back into me.

My mouth falls open.

Bolgaun is gone. Where he'd been standing seconds earlier, now only two blades lay on the ground.

"Fuck," I gasp.

"She ate him!" Maverick blurts. "She fucking ate him!"

Death doesn't exist in Hell. Not without an angel blade. Healing is slow for those souls condemned here—it prolongs the suffering, since this is Hell, after all. But we all just witnessed Bolgaun die like the rest of the Nightwalkers and the hellhounds and imps. He was swallowed up by Sayah, gone into oblivion.

It was scary as shit when we were on Earth, but when the magnitude of what just happened hits, it's even more terrifying.

Aria's powers are stronger than we imagined. She can *kill* where no one else can. Not even Lucifer by his own hand, and that means she is more powerful than him.

We all stare at her in stunned disbelief, and my mind still whirls with everything that just happened. I can hardly keep up.

Somehow, my gorgeous girl escaped Lucifer by herself. We had even called in Torryn and Nix, and were about to fast-track our plans to storm Lucifer's castle, but she hadn't even needed us to save her. She and Sayah had gotten out of there on their own. Unfortunately, Bolgaun had tracked her down before any of us could find her, but his arrogance had been his undoing.

I'm glad he's dead. Red bastard didn't deserve such a quick death, but at least he's dead.

Bolgaun had always been in competition with me and my family, since we were in the same trade. He especially didn't like it when my father sliced off his horns during a fight and mounted them on top of our fireplace, like a trophy.

So, do I believe him when he said he had delivered my parents personally to Lucifer to be killed because of my allegiance to Cain? Yes. I do. The sick twisted smile he wore when he'd delivered the news said it all.

And why do I care if my family is gone? I'm asking myself that question over and over, but honestly, I don't have the answer to it. When I refused to carry out their wishes and become bounty hunters like them, they disowned me. They hadn't spoken to me in centuries for it, and I had vowed I hated them. I was just fine living my eternal damned life without them.

Yet, here I am, grief and fury lashing through my chest, knowing they're dead because of me.

When the silence and the weight of my parents' deaths are too much for me to stand anymore, I turn, pushing past Torryn, Elias, and Nix, and head back into Val's place.

"Dorian..." Elias calls out, but I don't hesitate. I need to be alone.

No one follows me as I walk further inside, stepping over the debris. There are fissures running across the floor, many oozing with lava. Blood splatters stain the walls and there are broken marble guards everywhere.

In the dining room, the curtain of magma is parted again, revealing the secret hallway beyond. As I step through, I'm instantly smacked in the face with a gush of hot air. The corridor swings around, and when I reach a descending staircase, the darkness creeps in. Slowly, I follow the steps into the underground. The temperature drops the deeper I go, cooling my sweat-slicked skin.

The moment I reach the bottom, the space opens up before me and the dark gives way to dozens of blinking lit candles. Besides the black molten rock wall, the place is equipped with several leather sofas, a stocked bar, pool table, and even a piano for entertainment. Underground bunker or demon bachelor pad? The place could pass for a little bit of both.

I stroll through the room and into one of two hallways that leads me to an unoccupied bedroom.

Running a hand through my hair, I slump on the edge of the king-sized bed. Bolgaun's words run rampant in my mind. The enjoyment in his voice destroyed me. My arms tremble and I lean forward, elbows pressed into my thighs, my head in my hands.

It's been so long since I had anything to do with my parents, and yet the news is like someone had wrenched open the old wounds...pain that I'd worked on forgetting.

They rejected my decision to not join their bounty hunter business. They disowned me as a result. It was bullshit and I hated them for a long time. I still do...so the conflict warring inside me only confuses me more.

Fuck!

I don't know how long I sit there, but the lights switch off. Only the glow from the main room glints in the doorway.

When the soft tap of footsteps approaches, I don't look up.

"Are you sleeping?" Aria whispers.

"No." I frown, even if she can't see it, and push myself up.

"You sound croaky like you *were* sleeping," she teases, with that sing-song voice of hers. I can't help but grin.

Instead of replying, I tap the bed and motion for her to come on over.

She strolls through the dark and flops down beside me before taking my hand in hers. The silence stretches between us. Her hair is wet and slicked back, like she's just taken a shower. She's wearing a loose black tee that looks too big for her, and it hangs off one shoulder where her cuts have been bandaged. The one on her cheek is red and slightly puffy.

"I'm fucking furious at myself for not getting to you before Lucifer hurt you." I tense, hating how fucked up things have become.

"I survived," she answers, putting on a brave smile, which I adore. "Besides, there was nothing you could do. We are on his turf."

My heart constricts and I move to embrace her, taking her into my arms.

The quiet between us is a mix of understanding and thoughtfulness, coupled with the kind of tenderness I've become accustomed to from Aria.

She cares for all of us, ready to fight to keep us protected, as much as we look out for her. Her passion radiates from every word and action she takes. And there is no doubt in the way I feel about her.

"Do you...want to talk about it? About what Bolgaun said?" she asks cautiously.

"I'm not sure I can even make sense of it myself."

A flicker of a smile crosses her lips. "Maybe I can help?"

I let out a long sigh. "I'm pissed. Livid. I want revenge. But I'm also confused. Hopelessly confused. I shouldn't give a shit that my parents were killed. They booted me out when I needed them the most. But their death fucking stings, especially since they died because of me."

"It's not your fault."

Looking down at our intertwined fingers, I swallow hard. "Lucifer killed them to get revenge against me. He punished me for going to Earth with Cain."

"Lucifer's a sick bastard. That's not on you."

"Yes, it is." My tone is harsher than I intended, but I push to my feet and walk across the room. My skin crawls with my guilt, and I fucking hate it. Pacing in front of the bed, I try to calm myself down.

Rubbing my pounding temples, I say it again, only softer, "It is..."

Aria's on her feet and touching my arm. "I hated my parents for a long time, thinking they left me. That I wasn't good enough." She dips her head to try and capture my gaze again. "But it doesn't change who I am or what I choose to do with my future."

Her words spin in my mind... I know she's right, but the ache drowning me isn't letting go. Perhaps I just need time to let it all sink in, to accept their fate.

I draw her into my arms, and she wraps me in her embrace. With her tucked against my chest, I kiss the top of her head. Our pasts are just as broken, which makes her so much more special in my eyes.

For many years, I had assumed that the most I needed out of a partner was sex, and to feed my arousal. After all, my parents showed me that love was a useless emotion. I thought I had it all worked out, except I'd been wrong.

What I have with Aria is the true definition of heaven, which is so ironic I could laugh.

"We can't control what other people do, as much as we may want to," she goes on gently. "We can only control what *we* do. How we live our lives."

I arch a brow at her, impressed.

"Everything you're feeling is real and valid. It's like when Murray died. I didn't want to care, but I did... I still do." Her voice cracks. "I can't help it."

I give her a small smile, and she presses up against me, lifting herself up on her tippy toes. Her breasts are crushed between us, and they are all I can focus on at first. Until she fists my shirt and pulls me down to her lips. Our mouths clash, and she kisses me like someone who knows what they want...and what she wants is me.

There's never any doubt in my mind what I want, too. Not when it comes to my gorgeous girl. Arousal awakens within me, flaring and burning through me.

I adore the way she licks my lips. My cock twitches, wanting her.

I grab her by the back of the neck, holding her closer, and kiss her like I mean it, my other hand following a trail to her breast.

She moans against my mouth, and I love the sounds she makes. But when she winces, I pause and break our kiss.

"Did I hurt you?"

"No. I'm just a bit worse for wear after Lucifer's torture session."

"Come sit down," I say. "I'm being fucking selfish and should be waiting on you hand and foot."

She giggles. "I'll hold you to that once we get out of here. But who said we can't just have a bit of fun now?"

I reach over and push a loose strand of hair back off her face. "You are a temptress."

She laughs, then flashes me a smile that has me caving in.

"I want you naked," I say, reaching for her shirt, my mouth on the curve of her neck.

"How about you go first," she moans as I lick all the way up to her earlobe.

She shudders against me, and I make quick work of stripping her from the tee and leggings.

In moments, she stands naked in front of me and she's the

most beautiful thing I've ever seen. Even with bandages across her stomach and over the top of those sexy tits, she still destroys me.

"I promise to be gentle."

"Please don't," she answers quickly, batting her eyes at me while pulling savagely at my shirt.

I drag her to me and kiss her, taking her tongue into my mouth while I rip my clothes off. She tugs at the button and zipper on my pants, and I shuffle out of them, along with my boots.

It's a frantic rush, both of us breathing like we've just finished racing a marathon. "Tell me to stop if I hurt you."

"I'll tell you when you're not hurting me," she teases, then kisses me hungrily. She's beautiful, and everywhere her hands touch, she leaves a streak of fire on my body.

My hands are on her breasts, squeezing them while my thumbs roll over her stiff nipples. Then we're kissing again and I walk her to the wall, our bodies plastered together. She shudders against me like she's been waiting for this, craving it.

My fingers trace the sides of her body and they glide over her ass, then I scoop my girl off her feet. Immediately, her legs curl around me. She's moaning, her nails digging into my shoulders, our kiss all consuming. Her body, her kiss, and her taste are all intoxicating, and I can feel my soul drawn to her. I'd give her my life if she asked for it.

Her gaze fixes on me as I shift and my cock presses to her entrance. She draws in a sharp breath, her body quivering. We kiss and I push all the way into her in a swift motion. Her moans drive me crazy.

"I want every inch of you," I growl against her mouth. "I will never get enough."

I drive into her. There's pure euphoria over her face, and I feel the heat and wetness over my cock. My world is floating and nothing else matters but us two.

"I love you, Dorian, so much," she breathes the words that wrap around my heart. Words I've wanted to hear for too long.

Pausing, I press my brow to hers, both of us drawing in air rapidly. Our chests are pumping, and her sweet pussy is squeezing down on my cock.

"Oh, Aria. I've loved you for a long time. This is everything I've wanted."

She grins at me. "I love hearing you saying it."

I pull and push back into her, coaxing her moans out. "I love the way you grin, I love the way you smell when you're turned on, I love fucking you. I love that you fight back, that your passion for those close to you is vicious, and most of all, I love that you love me."

"Dorian," she whispers. "You're going to make me cry."

She holds the sides of my face and gives me the kind of kiss that makes me lose myself completely. Even when the world falls apart around us, all I think about is her.

Possessiveness rising through me, I carry her over to the bed and lay her down. Covering her body with my own, I ask her, "Do you want more?" My hand is already moving down between our bodies.

"Please," she begs, those sweet lips and voice ruin me.

I draw out of her and exhale, the tingle at the base of my groin growing. When she raises her head up to take a look, she notices that both my cocks are now alert and so ready.

"Two," I say. "In one hole." I wink at her and rub my finger over her spread pussy. She's drenched already.

"Don't just talk about it," she says, then spreads her legs wider, lifting her gorgeous ass. With my cocks stacked on top of each other, it's easier to grab them together, then push against her opening.

She's gasping for air but doesn't flinch. Fuck me, it's a tight squeeze...but I work my way in slowly, gradually widening her.

Her cries are escalating, her chest heaving for breath. I look down, absolutely loving the way her pussy is swallowing both my cocks at once. How she greedily sucks on them, seeming to pull me in.

I push all the way in, and her eyes are glazed over. She pinches her nipples. "Fuck. I'm going to come so quickly."

A thrill rushes down my back.

"You're mine, gorgeous. All mine." I rock my hips back and forth into her, hard and fast, giving her everything she desires. My power cascades over us, heightening the pleasure even more as our bodies rock back and forth.

Her moans escalate while I'm pounding into her.

I growl, my balls tightening, and it's a losing battle. The sensation of her tight pussy is destroying me.

The horny little sounds she makes make me harder and the buildup comes fast.

She suddenly screams, her whole body shuddering. Her pussy clamps down and constricts my cocks. And that sets me off.

I snarl, buried deep inside her, spilling my seed. We're both sweating and gasping for air.

Losing track of how long we float on ecstasy, I finally look down at Aria. She's breathing heavily and staring at me with a delicious grin.

"Damn, this whole time we could have been having sex with both your cocks inside me? Why have you been holding out on me?"

I laugh and draw out of her. "Let me clean you up." I head out, crossing the hallway, and grab a towel from the bathroom. On the way I notice the bright light of the main room where I see the back of Elias, and there are others with him. Waiting for us, no doubt.

Back in the bedroom, Aria is spread and divine. I wipe the mess from her sweet pussy and her thighs, then toss the towel aside. Taking her hands into mine, I draw her to her feet.

"Thank you," she says. "It was everything I needed."

"I wish I could drag you into my arms and have you fall asleep there, but I think the others are waiting for us now."

"I know." She hugs me tight and I embrace her, kissing the top of her brow. "My stomach is so antsy. Is this how it feels before big battles?"

"They say being nervous before a fight gives you an advantage."

"Fuck, I hope so," she answers and breaks away from my arms. There's a bittersweet sensation rolling over me. After such a perfect moment, the last thing I want is to dive into battle.

The hum of voices dances in from the main room of the bunker.

We quickly get dressed and step out of the bedroom. She takes the lead and I'm close on her heels, heading through the dimly lit hallway, soon emerging in the main room of the bunker.

Six sets of eyes are on us instantly... And with the wicked grins on the faces of Val, Nix, and Torryn, I'm going to say they've all been privy to all the sounds from the bedroom.

Aria moves to the bar without a care in the world, pouring herself water from a pitcher.

"So, what's the plan?" I ask, wanting their attention on me, not on her.

"Well, we're ready to head out," Cain answers in a clipped tone.

"Good thing you two were so quick," Maverick pipes in. "I'd be happy to give you some pointers on how to make it last longer in the bedroom. I'm pretty sure I counted less than three minutes."

Nix and Torryn burst out laughing.

"Fuck off," I grind out.

Elias is howling in laughter, while Cain strolls over to Aria by the bar.

"Are we leaving or what?" I declare. "Let's take this show on the road."

Everyone moves toward the stairs. When I realize Val took a detour to the bar to mix himself a drink, I pause.

"Calming last minute nerves?" I ask him, confused.

Val shrugs. "I'm sitting this out, taking neutral ground."

I bristle. *Neutral* ground? Is there even such a thing in Hell? "I knew you were a lot of things, Val, but I never took you as a coward."

Gaze lowering to his drink, he shrugs nonchalantly, which only irks me more.

I'm about to curse him off, but Cain appears on the steps ahead of me and gestures for me to follow him upstairs. With one last glare Val's way, we head out of Val's home, another sin demon down.

TWENTY-ONE

This is it. This is what I've—*we've*—been waiting for. Everything's come down to this.

Today, my father will fall.

We stand in front of Lucifer's castle gates. As Hell's biggest and center feature, it looms over his mighty kingdom with high peaks and stone walls. Black smoke billows from the underground crematorium, where Father likes to set fire to his victims that can never die. It's running double-time today, the pungent scent of burning flesh and singed hair poisoning the air.

The last time I was here, things went to shit fast. I was sure I'd let everyone down for convincing them to be a part of my plans to overtake my father and then failing. I blamed myself for decades for getting Elias and Dorian banished and stuck with me on the living plane.

And here we are again.

But I've grown a lot since then. I've learned that I didn't need Hell or my father's stupid crown to be someone. Elias, Dorian, and I—we built ourselves up from nothing. We made an empire from the ashes and became kings among the living. And because of Aria, I discovered what love is, how powerful and consuming it can be, and those are things I'd never thought possible for a demon.

I'm not the same sin demon I was when I left here.

I'm stronger. Wiser. Better all around.

I look to my left. There's Aria, dressed for the fight in ripped jeans and a tank top, a sword in her hand. I wish I didn't have to include her in the upcoming danger, but she's proven time and time again that she can hold her own in a fight. And with Sayah, I know she's protected.

Beside her is Dorian, my oldest friend. Like the rest of us, his demon is out and his gaze is locked ahead of us. Determination crinkles his brow, and the tattooed runes on his chest glow bright as his power heightens.

On my right, there's Elias as his hellhound—a massive black beast with lips curled over fangs and hackles up. My brother, Maverick, spins his daggers expertly in his hands on the other side of him. He glances over at me and gives me a stiff nod. He knows what lies ahead, and this time he's not going to run. He's going to fight at my side.

I turn to see the others who've chosen to join us. In his demon form, Torryn is an impressive sight. He's a ten-foot monster—part man, part bull, with long horns, a stretched snout, and hooved feet. Behind him are his legion of minions. Like with Lucifer and his marble soldiers, Torryn can call on and command hundreds of damned souls and make himself an army. It's one of the unique sin demon gifts he was given and, most importantly, it allows our numbers to rival Father's.

Even though Nix's power to shapeshift is more on the defensive side, he's still one hell of a fighter. Maverick even convinced him to use one of the weapons in his collection. He picked a battle axe.

Of course, I wish my other brothers were here. Lorcan, Raziel, and Valdim. I wish they had seen that we all have a place in this battle, but I know now that their loyalties lie only with themselves.

And when this is over and we win, they're going to have to beg for mercy.

Everyone is waiting for my word. They're looking to me for guidance, and it's time for me to be the leader they need me to be.

It's time to give Lucifer hell.

My wings whip out, spreading wide, and the darkness inside me roars to life. Hellfire blazes in my fists. *"Donec ipsum finem!"*

Until the very end.

And with that, we charge.

Torryn's thunderous bellow shakes the ground. Maverick and I take to the sky, while everyone on the ground rushes toward the castle. With one swing of his arm, Torryn breaks the magical and non-magical locks holding the gate closed and his legion of tortured souls spill into the overgrown courtyard.

Lucifer's castle is surrounded by vine-like thorn bushes, with points as sharp as a surgical scalpel, and they crawl all over the ground, walkway, and up the sides of the monstrous building. Hovering above, I spot Aria struggling to avoid the branches. A thorn catches her and slices across her arm. She gasps, leaping back, and is about to stumble into another patch when Elias appears and, mid-stride, throws her onto his back. As they head toward the front door, she grips onto his fur and ducks her head down low.

"Cain!" Maverick shouts, and when I look his way, I see he's pointing at the stones on Lucifer's castle. And they're shaking, quivering before our eyes.

What the fu—

Suddenly, the stone-men pop out of the walls—dozens of them—and leap onto the ground below.

"Watch out!" Maverick shouts.

The stone soldiers swing their weapons, taking out many of Torryn's men at one time.

Shit.

Maverick flies at the wall, knives slicing the air, and when I realize another wave of stone guards are about to come to life, I throw a blast of hellfire their way. But it only sends them back instead of stopping them. The second my fire extinguishes, they push themselves off the wall and leap into the battle, now glowing orange-red and blazing hot.

Well, that's not going to work. I've only made them more dangerous.

When the next group of guards start to wiggle their way out of stone, I throw my body into one, smashing it to rubble.

"Ah, brute force. Sometimes that's the best way," Maverick says, sheathing his daggers, which hadn't been making much progress against solid rock, and follows my method. We slam ourselves into the wall over and over, and it isn't long before numbing pain shoots up and down my arm.

As if we're on the same mental wavelength, Maverick yells, "We can't keep this up forever. They won't stop coming."

He's right, and I know it. We're just wasting time.

Flying backward, I glance at the castle turret. There's a window at the very top. We can use it to get in and weed Lucifer out from the inside, while Torryn and Nix try to get through those doors. We'll surround him.

"Dorian! Elias!" I shout. Both their heads perk up to find me hovering above them. I point to the window to leave our new plan unspoken but clear. It doesn't need to be said; we've fought alongside each other enough to know how we each fight.

With Aria still on Elias's back, the three of them round the castle and do all they can to get past the soldiers and the prickly vines.

I turn to Maverick. "We need to help them get up here."

He nods, understanding, and we swoop lower.

Elias shifts rapidly, and Aria drops to her feet. Without much effort, I scoop her into my arms and beat my wings against the air to gain altitude again, while Maverick tries the same for Elias. His takeoff's a bit more wobbly because of Elias's size, and he curses as he struggles to get them higher in the air.

"Shit, man. You need to go on a diet or something," he grumbles. "You're too fucking heavy."

"Shut the fuck up," he growls back. "It's 'cause I eat baby demons like you for breakfast."

Dorian chuckles as he scales the side of the castle like an overgrown primate with the grace and pose of a feline. Holding Aria tight, we swing toward the window. Dorian beats us there and punches through the glass, swiping away the rest of it so that I can help Aria inside without injury. Once she's in, I climb in next only to hear a loud thud and Elias cursing wildly. A second later, Elias is thrown through the window and tumbles across the dusty floor. He lands with his naked ass in the air.

Maverick slides in next, his wings folding into his back. "Next time, you get the gorilla and I get the girl."

"You little shit." Elias stands and goes toward Maverick, but Dorian presses a hand to his chest.

"Focus, King Kong. Focus," he teases.

My gaze roams the room. It looks like we've ended up in some forgotten attic space. There are abandoned furniture pieces covered in white cloth, a broken chandelier, and a grand piano from what I can see. When I find Aria, she already has her hand out, the ominous orangey-yellow light sparkling around it. At her feet, Sayah's dark tentacle wiggles across the floor and down the spiral staircase.

How very clever of her. Having Sayah check for danger is the safest way to go on from here.

Outside, the sound of fighting intensifies, and the walls around us quake as more of Lucifer's stone soldiers manifest and join the battle.

The only way to get them to stop is by defeating Lucifer—whatever that entails. Killing him or capturing him and having him renounce his hold on Hell. We are hoping for the later, but knowing the devil, we're expecting the former.

When Sayah zips back into the room and back into Aria, her power's light dims. She glances at all of us. "She says it's safer for us to go down the west wing. And Lucifer is in the throne room."

"Of course, he is," Maverick says with a dramatic roll of his eyes. "He's waiting for us there. Probably has traps set up for us."

"Probably. But what other choice do we have?" Dorian asks.

"Actually..." Maverick starts, an idea forming, "the element of surprise may still be on our side." He makes a beeline for the broken window and unfurls his wings again.

"Where the heck are you going?" Elias barks angrily.

Hopping on the ledge, Maverick looks back at us. "Trust me on this, okay?"

Elias growls, "Trust you? What the fuck is that supposed to—hey!" But Maverick jumps out, cutting him off mid-sentence. His gaze whips to me. "What the fuck? He just bailed on us."

"He did say he has a plan," Aria chimes in.

"It would've been nice for him to let us in on it, don't you think? Our asses are on the line here."

I don't know what my brother's intentions are, but fleeing or not, I agree with Elias. He should've told us of his plans.

I guess Maverick still has some work to do when it comes to being on a team. But I can't worry about him now. I can only hope that whatever he's doing, it doesn't get him or any of us killed.

"We go on without him," I tell everyone else. "Our objective hasn't changed."

Dorian nods. "Take out Lucifer. Don't get killed. Got it."

I turn to Aria. "Can Sayah lead the way?"

As if hearing me, her shadow elongates and spreads across the stairwell.

"I'll take that as a yes, then," I say, and together we follow Sayah's shifting form to the lower levels.

Besides the commotion raging outside, every floor we pass is deadly silent. No marble guards, no screams of torture or of ecstasy...all the familiar things I have come to expect when visiting his home. This time, there's no movement, no sounds, nothing.

It's looking more and more like Maverick's mention of a trap awaiting us is right.

Sayah stops suddenly at the very bottom of the steps, making us all halt. We wait for Aria to translate the Leviathan's thoughts to us.

"Lucifer's through there, across the foyer, in the throne room," she whispers so low she barely makes any sound at all. "He's alone."

"Bullshit," Elias replies, only to be shushed by Dorian.

Aria shrugs. "That's what she says."

My first thought is that it's impossible—his guards must be waiting in the walls for his command—but then I realize this must be a test of some kind. A power play to show us that he isn't afraid and that he can squash our coup for a second time without much effort at all.

It's something I would do if I was in his shoes, and what does that say? It's his pride getting in the way of logic.

I should know. I'm made from that part of him.

But unlike him, I've evolved past that baser part of myself. We can use his ego against him.

"I'm going alone," I say, and pull back my shoulders.

"What?" the three of them snap in unison.

I lower my voice even more. "Listen to me. I know Father. His inflated ego is refusing to let him show weakness, so he's pretending that this—all of this—doesn't matter to him. It's nothing but a mere nuisance. A pestering fly he intends to catch and squish."

"Wrap it up Shakespeare," Dorian says and whirls his finger in a winding motion.

"He's playing a game. Don't you see it? One he thinks only he can win. And we need to use it against him."

"I still don't understand why that means you have to sacrifice yourself," Aria answers in a panicked rush.

"I'm just going to talk to him. Distract him. He knows we're coming, but if I can keep him busy long enough, maybe you three can get the angel blade. With it, we'll have the power we need to kill on this plane."

"And what about Sayah?" Dorian asks. "Can't she just... swallow him up too?"

"I don't know." And it's the truth. I don't know the extent of Sayah's powers and what will and will not work against the king of the underworld. "Lucifer's an entirely different animal than Bolgaun. We don't know what will happen if Sayah faces him. Or what it'll do to Aria."

That is my main concern, of course. Will consuming the most evil being in all of existence affect my beloved in a negative way? I don't want to find out if we don't have to.

"We try to dethrone him without Sayah at first, just in case using her hurts Aria. But if it comes to it, then we let her do what she must."

Everyone nods in agreement.

"I am trusting Sayah to keep Aria safe from any harm," I say carefully, knowing the creature in her is listening, too. "Am I right?"

Aria sighs. "She's got the message."

"Good." My gaze passes over all of them one last time, and my chest clenches with fear. They mean so much to me. I love them each in their own way, which is something I once thought I could never feel for another being, let alone three. We've been through a great deal together, and I hope that by the end of the night, I don't have to mourn the loss of any of them.

Then, retracting my demon and trying to rebutton what's left of my shirt, I leave Elias, Dorian, and Aria behind and walk into the throne room alone.

I find him sitting on his high-backed throne, twirling his unholy crown of bones and gems around his two fingers. As suspected, he's not surprised to see me. His dark eyes find me and a tight-lipped smile curls on his face.

"My first born," he purrs. "How nice of you to give your old father a visit while in the neighborhood."

"You know why I'm here," I say, not wanting to play into his games.

"I do." He jumps to his feet. He tosses the crown onto the chair and hops down the steps. "And I have to say, I'm a bit disappointed. Not surprised, just disappointed."

I watch as he walks around the room, circling me like a predator. His eyes flash red, the evil creature within him wanting to come out to play.

"So, what now, Son? You try and kill me again? Take my throne? Hell? Become king?"

"I don't want the throne for myself," I reply. "I just want you off it, so either you come with me willingly, renounce your claim to Hell, and live out the rest of eternity in a cell somewhere, or I will remove you forcefully."

His head snaps back and his laughter booms like a gunshot. "And you honestly think you can do that? You?" He glances around the room. "Where are your little friends? The girl? Aria."

Hearing him just say her name has my temper flaring. And he sees it. He knows how I feel about her, and it only makes him smile wider.

"I expected something like this from your brothers. This weakness. Letting your dick guide you into disaster. It'll be your undoing."

"You know nothing about me."

He stops and rocks back on his heels, looking down at me. "You're right. When I ripped you from my own flesh and bone, I expected you to be just like me. Strong. Powerful. Ruthless. You've done nothing but prove me wrong. You're pathetic."

I clench my jaw and tell myself he's trying to get a rise out of me. That's all.

Unsatisfied with my lack of response, he continues to circle me, his hands clasped behind his back. "Apparently banishing you the last time you tried to dethrone me wasn't enough. You learned nothing."

At the corner of my eye, I see movement in the shadows of a doorway. Aria, Elias, and Dorian? Or more of Lucifer's guards?

My heart beats a little faster.

"I'm going to have to go a little darker with my punishment." He taps his chin in fake thought. "Something involving the girl, perhaps?"

My thoughts jump to the worst possible scenarios, and my stomach lurches in fear. How could they not? I know Lucifer and the way his deranged brain works. He'll torture me by torturing her. Raping her. Making her suffer while I watch.

My demon shoves forward without my say-so, my hellfire surging to my hands and my wings snapping out from my spine. Whatever was left of my shirt falls to the ground, and my vision sharpens as my eyes go black.

But Lucifer only grins, pleased. "Ah, there you are. Now this fight will be more fun."

Closing his eyes, he rolls his shoulder back and tilts his neck side to side. The muscles underneath his skin shift and move. His body stretches upward, gaining height until he's towering over me. Skin graying, his clothes rip at the seams as every inch of him expands and two horns push from his forehead.

Then, when his eyes snap open again, they're a hellish, fiery red.

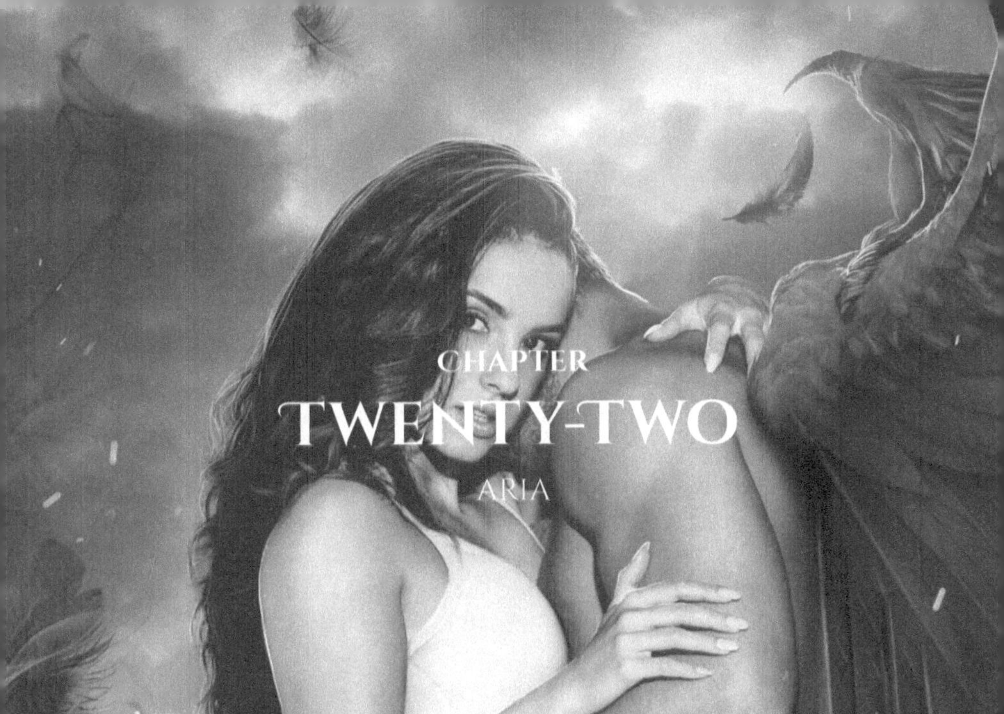

Lucifer's real demon form is terrifying. He's a monster with thick gray skin with black veins lining every inch of it, like Cain's. He's grown two feet taller, and with his clothes in shreds on the floor, it's clear his body is rippling with solid muscle.

The true King of Hell.

A shudder runs through me, and any confidence I had of us winning this dwindles. We're watching from the shadows of a doorway, waiting for our time to spring into action. It'd be nice to have Torryn, Nix, and the undead army to help right now, but they're still fighting the stone soldiers outside.

Lucifer grins eerily at Cain, showing off a mouthful of fangs. Then he holds out his hands as if introducing himself for the first time.

"Let's get this over with," he says, the beast's voice much deeper than his other form. Then he rushes Cain, and they crash into each other in a blur of punching fists, slashing claws, and whipping wings. Snarls erupt, blood splatters, and it's not long before I turn to Elias and Dorian, unable to watch the fight anymore.

"We need to help," I say. "We can't let Cain do it all alone."

Elias's heavy hand comes down onto my shoulder. "We will.

We need to figure out the best time. When Lucifer is distracted enough, and we can do the most damage."

"Does anyone see the angel blade?" I ask, scanning the room.

Dorian peers around the corner more and curses. "There. On the throne. Under the crown."

It's in the middle of the room, up on the dais, in plain view.

So much for sneaking our way to it.

"How are we handling this?" Elias asks Dorian in a rushed whisper. "Cain won't be able to fight him off for too long alone. Not when he's in this form."

"I'm thinking. I'm thinking!" He hits himself in the forehead. "Cain's usually the one that makes the plans."

"Well, considering he's getting sucker punched in the stomach right now by a red-eyed, two-horned monster, I'd say he's a little busy."

"Can you two stop?" I snap at them. This bickering definitely isn't what we need right now.

I rub my lips together and try to think of what we can do without getting ourselves or Cain killed.

Sayah wiggles inside me, giving me my answer.

Shit, why hadn't I thought of her before?

"Sayah," I call to her, and she pulls out of me instantly. "Can you grab that blade for us?"

Her ghostly forms spreads across the floor, giving me my answer.

"Quick. Try not to be seen."

She zooms outward toward the throne. As she lifts off the ground, her form begins to solidify, and I can feel the familiar tug of her using my energy to become real. Now that I can control her, it's not as draining as it used to be, but tiredness does seep into my bones. Especially when the orange sparks dance along our tether as more power transfers from me to her.

Elias grips my arm to help keep me upright, which I am thankful for. But the moment Sayah pulls out the dagger, Lucifer spins around, finding her there.

I gasp. *Shit!*

His eyes widen at the sight of Sayah, a life-sized shadow with a shifting form holding the angel blade.

"What the—" He follows the dark string linking us, and when

his gaze lands on me, Dorian, and Elias hiding in the wings, his nostrils flare.

Double shit!

Cain tries to use the distraction to his advantage and punches Lucifer hard in the face and follows with a roundhouse kick to the ribs. Lucifer stumbles back a few steps and blood leaks from his mouth, but it doesn't do much damage and the next time Cain comes at him, he grabs his fist mid-swing, wrenches it back until bones snap. He then uppercuts him so hard, Cain flies backward, skidding across the smooth marble floor.

"No!" I shout automatically. My panic causes Sayah to drop the blade and yo-yo back into me so fast, I jerk back into Elias's chest.

Lucifer's eyes are still pinned on us, disbelief and excitement flashes in them. "No way. A Leviathan? She's a Leviathan?" He laughs, the terrifying sound grating against my eardrums. "Things are getting interesting now!"

When he trudges our way, Dorian grabs me and pushes me back. "Well, looks like hide and go seek's over. Let's go, Elias!" He and Elias run out and tackle Lucifer at the same time. Cain stands again, shaking off his healing wounds, and joins the tussle. But despite all three of them taking on Lucifer, he's still able to fight them off easily.

Without the angel blade, there's no way to really hurt him.

I withdraw my sword, wondering if I should just burst out of here and make a run for it. Or should I risk Sayah again?

Fuck. Fuck. Fuck.

I can't just stand here and watch the demons fight for their lives.

Boom.

The ground shakes under our feet and the thunder of footsteps pour into the foyer. Seconds later, Torryn's bull-like demon shoves his way into the throne room, taking most of the doorway with him. His zombie soul minions spill in from behind him, followed by Nix.

Lucifer roars and somehow manages to throw Cain, Dorian, and Elias off him.

"Spoiled, ungrateful children!" He stomps his foot, and the marble splinters and cracks in every direction under him. The ground shakes again, and the tingle of dark magic caresses my skin.

Suddenly, spots in the walls around us move. Pieces chip away and crack off, forming more of those terrifying marble guards we've fought before.

"Teach my sons a lesson," Lucifer barks, and the guards surge for the demons. They clash, and fighting erupts once again.

Where the fuck is Maverick through all this? I really hope Elias isn't right and he abandoned us. But I can't really focus on that right now. I need to get that blade.

"Alright, Sayah." She slides from me again, taking over my real shadow. "Are you ready for this?"

Her head nods.

"Okay, let's do this." Gripping my sword tighter, I dart out into the chaos.

A marble man's spear swings at me, and I spin, narrowly avoiding it. With a mighty howl, Torryn stampedes across the room, crushing many of them and almost me too. I leap out of the way just in time.

I feel Sayah's warning zip up our connection, and I turn to see two more guards charging at us. Sayah lifts off the ground and overtakes them before their weapons can reach us, swallowing them whole until nothing's left.

"Thanks," I pant. Another guard appears to my right, and I swing my sword. It hits its shoulder, but the strike does nothing but reverberate up my arm.

Man, these things are hard to break.

I swing again, crossing my sword with its spear, but it over-powers me easily and shoves me back. Falling on my ass, my sword skitters out of my hand and across the floor.

I curse as pain skirts up my back from the hard landing. I don't even have time to see where my weapon went because the spear's tip is pointed at my throat.

I freeze.

Lightning fast, Sayah flies around me and wraps the guard in her darkness, engulfing it, too. It's there one second, and the next it's not.

As she stands in front of me, waiting for me to get up, I hold up my hand. "Let's call our friends and reduce some of Lucifer's numbers, don't you think?"

I can feel her giddiness through our link, and I waste no time reaching down into myself and awakening our power. Light flares in my palms, the magic tickling me, and soon, the shadows around the room begin to shift and come to life.

Closing my fists, I give them all the silent command to feed. Consume. Destroy.

Like Sayah, they attach themselves to me, using me as their power source, and then dart around the room like mini phantoms. One by one, they pick off the marble guards, moving so fast, they appear as nothing more than a blur.

Perfect. This'll give us a better chance.

A cold hand grabs my arm then and tugs me closer to the wall. It severs my links to the shadows, and, disjointed, they're forced to zap back into their normal places, losing their sentience completely.

Dread seizing me, I'm about to lash out with a fist when I see it isn't another guard holding me. It's Valdim, Cain's brother.

But what is he doing here?

"I apologize for startling you, but there is only way to end this, and it is with the angel blade," he murmurs.

I nod. *Tell me something I don't know.*

"I thought you wanted to stay out of this fight. Stay neutral," I whisper in a rush.

"Can't a demon change his mind?" He opens his palm. "*Angel blade.*"

There's the familiar tickle as magic washes over me and there's a flash of light. When it diminishes, the angel blade is in Valdim's open hand.

Wow, I almost forgot he could do that. Talk about a handy power.

He grips the handle. "Transporting something powerful like this, my gift will need to recharge, so we have to—"

From the corner of my eye, there's a flash of silver and he pushes me out of the weapon's path at the last second. I roll roughly across the floor, and when I come up, I see Valdim fighting off a marble guard, the blade no longer in his hand.

Fuck! Where did it go?

I spin and collide with something solid. Peering up, I lock eyes with Lucifer himself, and my breath locks in my chest.

"Hello again, Aria," he says with a fangy smile.

I feel Sayah rushing to leave me again, to protect me, but then there's only pain. It's so sharp and sudden, I don't even register what's happened right away until I glance down and see Lucifer holding the heavenly dagger's handle, its blade embedded in my stomach.

When he yanks it out, I shift backward, clutching my middle and instantly feeling warm blood covering my hands.

The pain is all I can think about. It's fiery, burning, searing, and it steals everything from me. My knees give out, and I fall at Lucifer's feet.

"Such a pity," he says smugly. "I had big plans for us, Aria. Big plans."

Sayah... I call to her internally, but I can't feel her essence within me anywhere. Panic seeps in. *Sayah! Where are you?*

Still, she doesn't respond.

Besides the pain, all I feel is emptiness. Even when she was hiding from me, I knew she was still there, but now, I can't feel her at all.

It's like...she's gone.

Exhaustion weighs heavy on me, and I know I'm losing too much blood. Unable to move, all I can do is glare up at Lucifer, hatred burning in my gaze.

"What-What did you do?" I shout at him. Saying anything is a huge effort, and my head whirls.

"Simple. I rid you of your demon," he says. "And soon, you'll be rid of your life too."

My body begins to shake without my doing, and I know it's from the blood loss and pain. I fight to keep my eyes open. Even when Lucifer raises the angel blade again, like he's about to use it to chop off my head.

Sayah... I search for her again but find nothing. Not a damn thing.

Roaring, Lucifer's arm swings down, and suddenly Cain's there and rams into him with all his strength. The blade clatters to the floor somewhere out of sight as the two wrestle on the floor, tearing into each other and spilling more of the other's blood.

There's a blast of heat to my left and when I look, black flames erupt from the massive fireplace. I keep myself blinking through the pain, knowing that if I let my eyes close for even a second, they will never open again.

Through my blurry vision, I see the outline of a man in the middle of the flames. With so much carnage and chaos happening all around me, no one sees the stranger emerging from the hearth, but when I spot the silvery white hair and boyishly handsome face of Maverick, my heart skips with relief.

So, this had been his plan all along... Use the magical passage he and Lucifer shared.

With daggers in both hands, he bursts from the fireplace, feathered wings out, and sails high above the action. Then he dives straight for Lucifer and Cain who are locked in a fierce battle of their own.

Before Lucifer can turn around, Maverick plunges his knives into his shoulders, sending him reeling back and roaring like the monstrous beast he is. Unable to hold on, he's bucked off and lands hard on the marble floor.

Cain uses his chance to spear Lucifer through the chest with his wing's talons, and as he pushes them in deep, Lucifer's eyes widen in shock and pain. Black blood from his own internal wounds stains his teeth and drips down his chin as he screams with all the hatred and rage burning inside him.

For a second, it looks like Lucifer is too weak to stay standing. He sways on his feet and his eyelids droop. But suddenly, he grits his teeth, clutches Cain's wings, and yanks the sharp talons out of him with an annoyed grunt.

The look of terror on Cain's face ices me to the core. A normal man wouldn't have that strength, especially with his injuries. Hell, a normal demon wouldn't either. But Lucifer isn't either of those, is he?

No. He's evil incarnate.

With flaming red eyes, his hand clamps down on his arm and the other grips his wing. Then, while looking him dead in the eye, he twists the leathery appendage hard and tears it right off Cain's back.

My stomach roils as vomit threatens to come up. The sound... The disgusting, fleshy and wretched sound. I'll never forget it.

Then comes Cain's screams of agony, of absolute horror as Lucifer carelessly tosses the wing away like it's nothing but an oversized piece of trash.

Unable to bear it, Cain collapses onto his knees, his demon forced to return and his blood turning crimson as it continues to spill from his wounds.

Lucifer reaches up and pulls out Maverick's daggers from his shoulders without so much as a wince. Chucking them to the side, he whirls on his youngest son next, his gaze shining with vengeance.

"You're fools. All of you!" he spits, stepping closer to Maverick. He scrambles to get away, crawling backward across the floor, but Lucifer keeps coming.

"I brought you into this hellish world, and I can take you out of it just as fast."

Sayah, I plead with her again in desperation. *Sayah, please. Our demons are in danger. They need our help. Please!*

But I can't feel her at all anymore. There's not even a flicker of her dark presence inside me.

Sayah!

Tears spring to my eyes as the realization finally sinks in.

She's gone. I've lost her. And now I am going to lose my demons too.

Maverick's pain-filled cry has me panicking. Lucifer has stomped on his leg, crushing the bones in his knee. But still determined to get away from his father's wrath, he hauls himself up the steps of the dais.

A tingle of familiarity wiggles through me at the scene.

I can't think too long about it because there's a flash of dark fur and Elias's massive hellhound leaps onto Lucifer's back, clamping his jaws into his neck. Cursing, Lucifer spins, grabs Elias by the scruff, and wrenches him off. Elias's jaws take away a large chunk of his neck, but it doesn't seem to matter. Despite the blood gushing down his back, Lucifer's still able to hurl Elias into a column so hard, it crumbles all around him. As does a part of the ceiling, which rains down chunks of marble.

Dust erupts, cloaking the room in a dense cloud.

"Damn mutts," Lucifer growls.

A scream tears from my throat. I can't see Elias, but I can hear his hound's soft whines from under all the rubble.

For what feels like the millionth time, I try to push myself up, but my body feels too heavy and I am too weak. It was ungodly painful when Lucifer stabbed me through the stomach with the angel blade, but its magic is relentless. Blazing like fire, like it's burning me from the inside out.

Blue light cuts through the dust cloud, and when I see the ghostly glow of Dorian's rune tattoos, I hold my breath. He rushes at Lucifer at full speed, claw-like fingernails aimed for his face, but Lucifer somehow snatches him by the neck.

He lifts him off the ground with one meaty hand, and even though Dorian slashes at his arms desperately, he doesn't let go. Instead, he squeezes his throat hard.

Dorian gasps for air, his eyes bulging from their sockets, and all I can do is scream and cry. Helpless. Completely helpless.

It takes only seconds, but Dorian's body goes limp and Lucifer drops him. He lands in a heap, unmoving. Lifeless.

"No!" The pain in my chest is paralyzing. My world comes crumbling down all around me. Cain, Dorian, Elias, Maverick... And Sayah. I'm going to lose them all.

As if remembering me, Lucifer's head whips my way. His red eyes brighten, and a malicious smile twists his mouth. My heart drops.

He stomps towards me.

Frantically, I search around for a weapon—something to help protect me from this raging monster coming right at me—but find nothing other than some pieces of broken rock from his fallen marble guards.

To my surprise, Lucifer stops mid-step, nostrils flaring, his face pinching in anger. He spins on his heel.

"No!" he bellows.

That's when I see what he's staring at. Cain's there on the dais, blood painting every inch of him. His one wing is out, the missing one nothing but a gaping hole in his back. Maverick's near the throne, laying on his back, and looking up at his brother, eyes wide in terror.

Oh my god... Recognition slams into me, making my head whirl. I've seen this scene play out before. Not exactly like this but close enough. When we were on top of mount Kirkjufell and we had touched the foot relic of Azrael's harp.

Acid burns its way up my throat as I remember how that ended. With Cain and Maverick dead.

As a last-ditch effort to win this war, Cain's going to kill himself and his brother to weaken Lucifer.

But he can't... He can't!

"No! Cain!" I yell as panic surges forward. "No!"

Cain lifts his hand and something metal glints in his hand.

A dagger. The angel blade.

"I'm sorry, Brother..." he whispers, pain lacing his voice.

Knowing what's coming next, I rip my gaze away. I hear the blade cutting through the air, and then the final thud, my heart seizing. I choke, more screams trapped in my throat, and when I glance up, Cain is wrenching the dagger out of Maverick's chest.

Oh my god...

Lucifer stumbles, as if struck by an invisible sledgehammer. "You fool! You'll kill us all!" he shouts, furious.

We were right. He's getting weaker.

"I plan on it." With hands covered in blood, Cain turns the blade on himself. Lucifer snarls and charges him.

My heart twists. Time seems to slow in that moment, and Cain's black eyes flash my way and automatically change to their beautiful crystal blues. I expect the same sadness I saw in the vision, but to my surprise, I see nothing but fierce determination.

Those eyes flick right, then back at me, and that's when I realize he's trying to tell me something.

I follow his gaze and see the hint of something silver under the fallen rubble.

What the...

Is that...?

But if that's the angel blade, then what is Cain about to stab himself with?

My brain scrambles to catch up with everything, but I don't have time to sort it all out now. Cain thrusts the dagger into his chest and I'm up and crawling madly across the floor. Clutching my stomach, the pain is unimaginable; every part of me screams to stop, but I can't. Too much depends on this.

Lucifer wobbles on his two feet, and his monster starts to

recede. His horns retract and his massive form shrinks right before my eyes.

As I reach the spot, I grit my teeth against the pain and force myself to shift through the rocks. Underneath the mess is the modestly engraved handle and curved blade of Heaven's *real* weapon.

Cain faked him out. If he hadn't used the angel blade to stab him and Maverick, they would heal. And that means Lucifer's weakness is temporary. I'll have to be quick.

"Aria..." The deranged sing-song way Lucifer says my name makes me wince. Breathing frantically, I glance over my shoulder to see him still stuck in mid-transformation, his skin gray and scaly, his brow protruding and twisted horns shrinking further into his head, his body the size and shape of a normal man. He rolls his neck and bones crack. "Finally. You're mine now."

Then, he comes for me with arms outstretched.

I wrap my hand around the angel blade's hilt and wait, licking my lips. He's tried to take everything from me. Made my life and my demons' lives a living hell for far too long.

Not anymore.

No more running.

This is it. With no help from the demons or Sayah, it's only me.

And I'm going to kill the devil.

"Come and get me," I growl at him, my anger giving me the courage and strength I need.

Right then, Lucifer lunges for me, and I yank the angel blade from its hiding place and thrust it upward, right into the evil bastard's blackened heart.

His eyes widen in shock and confusion, and I drink it in. All of it.

"No..." he croaks, his face paling. "How did you... The Leviathan..."

"No Leviathan here. Just little ol' me. An Ordinary." I push the blade deeper, loving the way he grunts as pain consumes his expression.

The brightness to his red eyes dims as it scans my face in disbelief.

"Bitch..." he whispers on his last breath.

I pull out the angel blade as his body slumps and crumples to the ground.

Dead.

Around me, the marble guards crumble and disintegrate to dust. Torryn, Nix, Val, and the others stop fighting and all look at me kneeling over Lucifer's unmoving body.

Torryn's back in his human form and staring at me with wide eyes. "You... You killed him."

I stand there for a while, my heart thundering in my chest, letting the victory sink in. Then, I lift the angel blade to see Lucifer's and my blood coating it.

"She did!" Nix shouts and runs over to me. He grabs me by the shoulders and kisses both of my cheeks. "She did!"

"Well done, girl," Val says with a smile.

I want to smile back—it tickles across my lips—but remembering Cain, Maverick, Dorian, and Elias, I whip around instead and limp for the dais.

As I collapse beside Cain, he and Maverick begin to squirm. Their eyes flutter open, both finding me at the same time.

"Ar-Aria..." Cain groans with a smile. "You did it."

Relief washes over me, and now the smile comes naturally. For a moment, I'd thought I'd lost them all, but especially him and Maverick.

"That was a pretty clever thing you did," I whisper, stroking his blood-matted hair away from his face. He presses into my touch.

"Clever and extremely painful," Maverick grumbles and rubs his chest where the wound has already knitted together. "Would've been nice if you told me what your plans were before this."

"It wouldn't have been believable if I had," Cain explains.

I chuckle and watch his skin knit back together before my eyes until only smooth skin and muscle remains.

"I don't know. I think you may have enjoyed killing me a little too much." Maverick sits up and winces, obviously still in pain.

"Maybe."

The sound of rocks shifting has me looking across the room. Elias climbs his way out of the rubble, dust covering him from head to toe. He shakes his head like a dog, long hair whipping across his face. "Where's Dorian?"

"Here." Dorian rolls onto his back and folds his hands over his chest, mimicking being dead. "But I'm going to need a kiss from a princess to wake me up."

He puckers his lips, and I laugh.

I'm about to walk over to him when the pain in my stomach spikes again and sends me onto my knees. The angel blade clatters to the floor next to me.

Cain and Maverick are next to me in the next second, Elias and Dorian striding across the room to us.

"She was stabbed with the angel blade," Cain reminds everyone. "She won't heal here."

"Sorry..." I breathe and pull away my hand to show them that it's covered in blood. "Rain check?"

Dorian frowns. "You bet, gorgeous... Let's get you fixed up first."

Gingerly, Cain scoops me up and cradles me against his chest. "Cain..." I whisper, my voice as weak as I feel.

"Yes, my love." He begins to walk me out of the throne room, all the other demons following behind us.

"Sayah... I think she's gone." Tears sting my eyes, and I'm not even sure why. The moment Lucifer stabbed me, it felt like I'd lost a part of me. Like I wasn't myself anymore.

His tone is gentle, his gaze full of worry as he searches my face. "Why do you say that?"

"I can't feel her anymore. I think the blade..."

He hushes me softly. "Let's get you feeling better first, and we'll figure out Sayah after. Okay?"

I dip my chin in a nod. Being this close to him, I can see the real damage to his severed wing, and I wonder if something like that will grow back. It's a missing limb, nothing like a stab wound. I'll have to remember to ask him about it later.

For now, I lose myself in the warmth of his skin, the rhythmic sound of his heartbeat against my ear, and let my eyes drift closed. Despite everything we've been through, the pain, and all the unknowns still to come, we are finally rid of Lucifer. Hell is free and so are we.

We won.

TWENTY-THREE

"Fuck yeah, Lucifer is dead!" Torryn roars, breaking into hysterical laughter.

His brothers cheer. Under any other circumstance, it'd be strange to see siblings celebrating the death of their father. But Lucifer deserves everything he got.

The leather chair I sit on groans like no one has sat in it for centuries. Which might very well be the case, considering we're back in Cain's castle. We've come together in the throne room, where I lounge listening to the five sin demon brothers, Elias, and Dorian discuss who will be the new leader of Hell.

I'm just happy to be able to sit down after laying in a bed for a week straight.

Despite being patched up and magically worked on by any spellcasting soul the demons could get ahold of down here, every inch of me still aches. The magic in the angel blade is resistant to other magic apparently, and although we were able to stop the bleeding and sew me up, healing properly will take a while. I'm just lucky Lucifer hadn't hit any major organs when he'd run me through. Otherwise, I'd be dead.

Cain appears at my side, his face a permanent image of concern. Even though all his injuries are healed, there is one thing he'll never be able to get back. His wing.

Being Cain, he tries not to make a big deal of it, but I know better. To no longer be able to fly? That's soul crushing. He must feel like he's lost a major part of himself.

It would to me.

Like me...with losing Sayah.

Still, he's been doing all he can to focus on me and my recovery and not himself. And every time I try to bring up the subject, he changes it. So, I figure I'll let him talk about it when he's ready. That's all I can do for now.

"How are you feeling?" he asks.

"You just asked me that five minutes ago," I tease him.

"I know. But I want to make sure things haven't changed."

"I'm fine," I assure him for the millionth time. "Sore. Achy. But I'm alive so I'm *fine.*"

He still doesn't seem completely satisfied with that answer, and I offer him a small smile to really sell it.

"Come on," I say. "This is a big day for you. You should be happy."

His brows pinch. "Big day? What do you mean?"

I lower my voice and glance around the room to see everyone else tied up in their own conversations. "You know...coronation day. You're the oldest sin demon. You lead us all. Because of you, Hell is free. There's no doubt they'll pick you to wear the crown."

Standing a little straighter, his expression smooths over. Not exactly the reaction I expected from him, but it's clear something is bothering him. Something he's not ready to talk about yet.

He walks to the front of the room, in front of his own throne where Lucifer's crown sits, and clears his throat. Everyone quiets down and they all turn their attention to him.

He clears his throat and speaks loudly, demanding everyone's attention with just his voice, like a true king would. "I know we've all already agreed that Raziel and Lorcan will be apprehended and punished for treason, but we still need to discuss who will rule in Lucifer's place now that he's gone."

"It should be Cain," Dorian shouts. "He's the one who first had the guts to stand up to his father and gather us all."

Cheers erupt from the rest of the brothers agreeing, and I clap from my seat.

But Cain holds up a hand to stop them. Then he turns, picks up the crown of bones, and holds it up for everyone to see.

"Come on, Brother! Put it on!" Torryn shouts and raises his fist in triumph.

I can't help myself. I'm smiling from ear to ear. I'm so proud of Cain. He deserves this—all of it. Hell, the throne, the power... He's sacrificed so much for this. Plus, he's a real leader, one who will care for his people instead of ruling by ruthlessness and fear.

Nix joins in. "Put it on! Put it on!" he chants, and soon, Val's wrapping his arm around him and adding his voice to the chorus too.

Despite their praise and encouragement, Cain's eyes fall onto me. He closes the distance between us, and the room falls silent again.

Then he does the unthinkable and places the crown on my head.

When he steps back, a smile lifts his lips. "I cannot accept the crown because it does not truly belong to me," he says. "Aria killed the devil when none of us could. And she did it without magic or special powers of any kind. She is stronger and braver than any of us, and she is the ruler Hell deserves."

"Wha-What?" I can't believe what he's saying. Me? Queen of Hell? "No. No way."

Murmurs come from the other brothers, and uneasiness stirs inside me. I can't be queen. I'm not even a demon. It doesn't seem right.

"I don't even have Sayah anymore," I go on, and reach to take off the crown. "The Leviathan's gone. I'm human now. An Ordinary."

"And that's all the more reason you should lead us," Cain says. "You have the compassion and the insight demons lack. For so long, I thought I was only capable of destruction. You changed me for the better."

"And me," Dorian chimes in and steps forward.

Elias follows suit. "Me too, little rabbit."

"And me," Maverick says from the corner of the room, where he's leaning against a pillar, observing all this from afar. "Which is quite a feat in itself, I'd say."

"And if we want things to change here, too, then it's time we start thinking differently." Cain stops me from taking off the crown and instead adjusts it on my head. Then he holds out a hand to help me up. Elias and Dorian come over, and all together, they help me walk up to the throne.

I still can't believe this is happening. I want to reject it, to argue that Cain is a much better fit for this role than me, but with the three of them beaming at me with such pride and devotion, it's hard to deny them.

When I sit on the large throne and look out at Torryn, Nix, and Val, I see them smiling up at me with the same certain looks on their faces.

Maybe I *can* do this. They all seem to think so. And, if they believe in me, then goddammit, I should too.

Sayah would think so, too, if she were here.

My stomach twists, her absence a heaviness I've been carrying with me since the battle. She hasn't come back; I still can't feel her, and that's only confirmed my fears that the angel blade stole her from me.

After having her with me for so long, it's weird not to anymore. The only way I can describe it is as if my best friend died. But, she took part of me with her. I don't know if I'll ever feel whole again without her, but after everything, I am thankful she did choose me to attach to.

"I think this calls for a celebration! A feast!" Valdim shouts, which snaps me from my grief-ridden thoughts. All the other brothers groan.

"You and your parties," Torryn chuckles and slaps his brother playfully on the back.

"It is sort of my thing," he replies.

With everyone's merriment, I remind myself that I'm not alone in this...even without Sayah. I have my four lovers, my demons, my soulmates. And that's all I really need.

The day goes on and Val gets his party. There's food and music and laughter. Everyone reminisces about the fight or about past memories, and I marvel at how these men went from fighting each other to being thicker than thieves in no time.

Dorian and Elias are chatting loudly. Cain's chatting with Torryn, and from the looks of their hand gestures, it's about fighting techniques. Go figure.

My gaze swings around the room again, and this time, I catch

Maverick's eye. He's leaning against the same pillar as before, staring at me with a wicked smirk.

Since moving is still difficult for me, Maverick walks over and hops onto the throne's armrest.

Stretching his legs out, he points to my crown and says, "I like it. It suits you."

My face heats up, and I'm not really sure why. "Thanks."

He's definitely managed to crawl into my heart. I just can't believe how quickly it happened.

"It's still a bit surreal," I confess.

"What is?"

"You know. Being queen and all."

He waves a hand at that. "Nah, you were made for this."

I snort a laugh. "This is *me* we're talking about here. *Me.*"

"Yeah, I know. And I still won't change my answer." His hand is in mine suddenly, and he squeezes it lightly. This gorgeous man with golden flecks in his deep, chocolate eyes studies me. We'd been through so much, discovered each other's darkness, and despite being enemies at first, I have found four men who adore me unconditionally. That is the true gift I gained.

He begins, "I would never have guessed things would turn out the way they have." He raises the back of my hand to his mouth and kisses it, before leaning in closer. "And I should have told you this earlier, Aria, before things got...crazy, but I'm going to say it now before I lose my nerve."

"Yeah, what's that?"

"I'm falling in love with you."

My breath catches in my throat.

He really said that? Really?

"This is new for me," he explains and rubs the back of his neck shyly. "All of it... Feeling this way. But Cain's right. We are capable of being more than our sin, more than what our father created us for. It just took me a bit longer to see it."

My chest warms, and I don't know what else to say besides the obvious. "I love you so much," I whisper back, and my eyes are close to tearing up.

"All the fear and death is over now," he says. "It's just about the future. About all of us."

Tilting my head up, he closes the distance for a kiss. I love his words and the inclusion of my other men, too. And, for the first time, I think this can actually work, with all of us being happy together.

Someone clears their throat, and we break apart. Everyone is staring at us now.

"Uh..." Who knows how long they were watching.

"So, what is the plan now?" Maverick asks quickly to save us from the awkwardness settling in. "Are we all moving into Cain's castle to rule Hell?"

Oh shit. I hadn't even thought about that. That's going to be a pretty big problem.

I straighten in the chair, facing Cain. "I don't think I can leave Earth behind for good. What about Cassiel? I can't leave him. And Charlotte? What about your clubs? And rebuilding Purgatory?" It's all rushing out of my mouth now. Word vomit. "I am still human after all, and without this ring..." I show his crimson ring, still on my finger, "I wouldn't even be able to be here. How is any of this going to work?"

He answers by pulling out something from his pants pocket. When he unfurls his fingers, another ring is sitting in his palm, not too different from his. The band is made of crisscrossing tiny bones, and it's crowned with an onyx gem.

I've seen it before...

"Is...is that Lucifer's?" I ask.

He nods. "And now, it belongs to you. It will keep you protected in Hell, body and soul."

I blink at the ring, unsure if I should take it.

Taking my hand in his, he pushes the ring onto my middle finger. The bones shrink to match my size, cradling around my skin with a perfect fit.

He then removes the one that belongs to him and slips it back onto his finger.

As I continue to study Lucifer's old ring, I shift my hand side to side, and find that when I do that and the dark stone catches the light, a hue of different colors shine back at me. Like a rainbow has been trapped inside.

"You have been given a great responsibility," Cain adds, looking at me.

"I understand."

"Which means you cannot dismiss your role," Torryn says. "Everyone will expect you to stay here."

"They will," Nix agrees with a firm dip of his head. "Without a ruler, Hell will erupt into utter chaos."

More than it naturally is? I couldn't even wrap my head around what that would look like.

Swallowing hard, I glance over to Cain again. He's staring at me intently, thinking. Then my gaze sweeps over my other men.

I shouldn't be surprised. Of course, I'd have to stay here in Hell to be queen.

But to leave the living world... My friends? Work? The life we'd built in Glenside?

My stomach knots just thinking about it.

I remind myself that this is what my demons wanted. Ever since I met them, their goal was to return home. To Hell. I can't take that from them, either, and I certainly can't live without them.

Cain must see me struggling because he whispers sympathetically, "It's whatever you decide. We support your decision either way. "

"I've grown rather fond of living on Earth," Elias mentions, which surprises me. "Don't even mind the cold of Vermont anymore. And our house is in the middle of a wild animal's paradise. The woods, the lake..."

"I agree with you there, except Nix is right. Shit will go sideways here, and fast, if we leave," Dorian pipes in.

"Someone else will jump at the chance to steal the throne," Nix replies. "War will break out, a division among all the ranks."

Cain's silent, lost in his head, but his frown deepens. He wants to make me happy, but Hell is just as much his home as Earth is mine. And leaving Hell without a ruler could cause another tyrant to rise in Lucifer's place. I can see the two sides of his thoughts warring with each other through his expression.

My own anxiety climbs. What can I do to give everyone what they want and need?

Then an idea strikes. A crazy one, but it's the only thing I can see that might work.

"I have an idea," I suggest, raising my voice over the growing noise in the room. "What if we stayed six months in Hell, and six months on Earth? We have two homes, and get to enjoy the best of both worlds?"

I don't know how much the word *enjoy* applies to Hell, but with me in charge, I intend to bring about some changes. Maybe a café built in town, or a library. And there's no way I'm staying in Lucifer's castle. That's coming down.

Oh, and air conditioning.

Yeah, I'm definitely installing central air wherever we live.

"And what about the six months you're not in Hell?" Torryn presses, distracting me from my thoughts. "That doesn't solve you being absent for a significant amount of time. What stops total anarchy from reigning?"

Fuck, true.

"Well then…" I pause for a moment, racking my brain for a solution. Then I glance from one man to another. From Torryn, to Nix, then Val. They'd done so much to help us, had bravely fought by our sides despite the risks… They deserved something, too. "Then, during the six months we are on Earth, Torryn, Val, and Nix will keep things in check. We'll make this more like a democracy than a monarchy. You three will help while I'm away, but keep me in the loop of everything, of course." I look over to Cain. "How does that sound?"

At first, no one responds, and in their silence, my worry peaks.

But then Cain lifts his chin and a slow smile spreads his lips. "A shared responsibility. We keep us all accountable."

I can't help myself. There's just something about when the sin demon smiles… It makes my heart flutter. "Yes. Exactly. I was thinking since we work so well when we cooperate. As a team, maybe we can extend that into Hell and prevent another dictator."

"Spoken like a true leader." Cain's eyes spark with pride, and my chest warms. Looking over at his brothers, he nods once. "Would you three be willing?"

"Work with these two idiots?" Nix grumbles and tosses his long hair over his shoulder. That wins him a slap in the back of the head from Torryn.

"We can do it, of course," he says. "Especially since we cut off the dead weight."

He means Raziel and Lorcan.

"There will be a trial period," Cain goes on, "to work out any issues and to make sure the people of Hell are respecting the changes."

The three brothers nod in unison.

Cain's eyes narrow in warning. "And if any of you disobey or try to take too much power..."

"Don't worry about that, Brother. We love Hell and its people. And we don't want another Lucifer," Val says.

"Not to mention we all saw what Aria can do with the angel blade," Nix chuckles. "I like my eternal life, thank you very much."

Laughter bubbles up inside me, too. And it's not long before Elias and Dorian join in.

"Good then, so we have a plan." Maverick dusts his hands like all's well and done. He, Elias, and Dorian walk over to the others and begin to talk about new living arrangements, but when I try to listen in, Cain draws my hand to his chest, capturing my attention fully.

"Thank you," he says, the softness in his gaze making me melt. "I know this isn't truly your home, so thank you for the compromise."

"It's not my home *yet*," I say and smirk. "Maybe with a few little changes here and there."

He raises an eyebrow. "I want to hear all about it."

Cain laughs, and I don't think I will ever grow tired of hearing that sexy sound.

WE DECIDE that before we take over the reign of Hell officially, we have to return to Earth to pack a few things, work out what we are bringing with us, and tie up some loose ends, like Cain's club.

We are barely in the foyer of our home when power dances up my arms, the kind we all recognize at once.

Elias growls just as the air in the room vibrates, and with a snap of energy that cracks at the back of my nape, archangel Gabriel materializes in the middle of the room. He's wearing a white tunic that falls to his knees, a golden rope tied loosely around his waist, and his wings are tucked into his sides. Unlike his previous visits, there is a sense of relief on his face.

"I guess you've heard the good news," Cain announces, squaring his shoulders.

"Everyone in Heaven felt Lucifer's death the moment it happened," he says with a grin that makes him look creepier than normal.

"I'm picturing all the angels up there, dancing merrily," Maverick says, his eyebrows raised.

Gabriel gives him a deadpan look, and I might have laughed if I wasn't frozen on my feet, knowing exactly why he's paid us a visit.

Dorian adds, "Hey now, let Gabe have his little merriment. This may be the only time he finally gets to jerk off in peace." He stares at Gabriel, grinning. "If angels do enjoy the pleasure of the flesh, that is."

"Filthy Hell-vermin. You dare talk to me in such an irreverent manner," Gabriel roars. "I could rip your soul out for such impious words and smite you where you stand."

"I take that as a no," Elias mumbles under his breath. Maverick sniggers.

With a sneer, Gabriel turns his attention to Cain and me. "My time is being wasted. I must deal with the Leviathan."

I loathe the way he refers to me by that name... Sure that might be what Sayah was, but it's not me or my choice that I ended up cursed.

"You're too late," Maverick interrupts.

"What does the demon refer to?" Gabriel asks, not even bothering to look Maverick's way.

"She's gone," I reiterate. "During the battle with Lucifer, I was stabbed with an angel blade and it must have been vanquished because she's no longer inside me. I don't feel her."

Frowning, I reach into myself just to confirm she's really gone for the millionth time.

Gabriel's face twists into a scowl. "Her? Next you'll tell me you named it. Such a weak human trait."

"Hey," I say, louder than I intended, but I'm tired of his arrogance. "Just remember, I didn't create her, but was cursed, and I learned to make peace with her. Maybe you should show respect that I, a mere mortal, survived with a beast created by God living inside me."

His lips thin and eyes narrow, showing no sign of remorse. "I will lay my hand on you to check for myself that what you say is true."

I flinch back, and Cain steps in front of me. "Her word is enough," he growls, a direct threat against an archangel. "We defeated Lucifer, and did your work for you in protecting Heaven. That is proof enough."

"I don't trust your kind. And don't ever challenge me, sin demon," Gabriel bellows, his wings snapping out so wide, the tips touch the walls on either side of us.

I don't know who would win, but I don't want to find out after what we've just been through. I step around Cain.

"We have nothing to hide, so I give you permission," I state, lifting my chin, even if I am slightly trembling.

I sense my men all watching me, Cain shifting closer to me, and I know they don't agree. "Gabriel is not our enemy," I say. "He helped us protect our home from Lucifer's attack."

Besides, we just got Lucifer off our tails, and I don't want to worry that a gang of angels will be lingering around.

Gabriel steps toward me, towering over me like a mountain.

Without warning, he places his large hand on the top of my head.

Instantly, a zap of energy snaps through me, where my whole body feels like jelly, and my mind flashes with images as if on fast forward. They speed past my mind's eye, but I see them regardless, running through every memory in my mind, everything I've experienced. From being left at the hospital as a baby, to the foster home with Murray taking me in and promising to keep me fed and warm, to meeting Joseline and how quickly we clicked, to learning to steal to survive.

Even stealing Sir Surchion's orb—little did I know that night would set in motion so many events.

Days and months zip by so fast, and seeing them again rattles me. My heart pounds in my chest, tears pooling in my eyes at seeing my life flash before me. Murray sold me to the demons, all the fear, excitement, and adventures we underwent, down to how I fell in love with each of my four men. It all rushes through my thoughts all the way to the final battle with Lucifer.

Then, in a crack of power that prickles over my skin, Gabriel releases me.

My knees give way under me, and I drop to the floor, tears flooding my cheeks, my chest close to breaking from seeing everyone in my life. All the emotions, the heartache, the grief. I was rejected by my family and, despite all that, I found love as though someone always looked out for me.

Unbelievable warmth spreads through my body, flooding me with the kind of intense sensation that promises me, wholeheartedly, passion and love.

I cry into my hands, unable to remember the last time I cried from sheer happiness.

Cain's at my side, crouching low, wrapping his arms around me. "Are you okay?" I sink against him, letting him hold me, and despite my tears, I'm smiling.

"What did you do to her?" Dorian barks.

"Four against one archangel sounds like good odds to me," Maverick snarls.

"What I said I'd do," Gabriel says calmly. "She speaks the truth and is clean. With Lucifer gone, our business here is done."

"Then leave," Elias warns.

"Aria," Gabriel states, and I lift my head in response, tears streaming down my face. "What is meant to be, will always find a way to happen. Even love with the unloved. Even taming the most dangerous creature God created. Everything happens for a reason. Remember that."

Then, in a flash, the air sparks from his energy, and Gabriel pops out of the room.

Goosebumps race down my arms, and I wipe my eyes. My four men are kneeling in front of me in a semicircle, each of them reaching out and touching me.

"What did he do to you?" Cain asks.

I sniffle and lift my gaze to each of my men, drowning in the devotion in their eyes. How did I get so lucky to find them? And, with that thought, Gabriel's words swirl in my mind.

Everything happens for a reason.

What if a great power had a hand in my fate?

"Gabriel's touch showed me my whole life in a flash. It was incredible and heartbreaking." My breath hitches, and Dorian wipes the loose tear running down my cheek. "It made me realize that despite my family giving me up, I deserve love too." I half laugh. "These damn tears won't stop. I think Gabriel did something to make me cry."

"Right, I'm ready to take down that jerk." Maverick rolls up his sleeves, and it only makes me laugh louder.

"I loved you from the first time I laid eyes on you," Cain confesses. "I just didn't realize it at the time. Of course, you deserve all our love."

"You will always have us," Dorian says.

"We are fated mates, after all." Elias squeezes my hand.

"And I may be late to the party, but I never thought I'd find love. Not until you came into my life." Maverick gives me one of his gorgeously wicked grins.

"That's why I'm the luckiest girl in the world, because I love each one of you. And, after everything we've been through, how about we draw a line in the sand and start our lives properly from here? No more end-of-the-world adventures?"

Elias howls with laughter. "I'm down for this."

The other three agree, and I lean forward to hug them all. I take a deep breath and smile easily, knowing that, for once, my life might just be normal. Well, as normal as ruling the realm of Hell will permit. But it doesn't scare me. Not when I know I'll never be alone again.

The click of nails scraping the wooden floorboards draws our attention over to the doorway.

Cassiel charges in just then and leaps at us, tongue out, and I swear he's smiling. When he crashes into Elias first and knocks him over, I burst out laughing.

This...this is exactly what life should be. Laughing, chasing a lynx cat through the house for hugs, and wondering if there is a bathtub big enough for five people I can order online.

Grab Your Copy of Sin Demons Book 7 Today

EPILOGUE

ARIA

"Aria, hurry up, we're going to be late," Dorian calls from downstairs. "We're all waiting on you."

I roll my eyes before yelling back, "Give me a sec."

Exhaling loudly, I glance back at myself in the mirror, and apply the scarlet red lipstick, trying not to smudge it. I don't normally wear a lot of make-up, so I'm a lot slower at getting ready. Give me a demon to fight any day over keeping a steady hand while using an eyeliner pen.

Making kissy lips, I pull back and look at myself. It's hard to believe I look so hot in all honesty. I still recall the red dress Cain gifted me to wear to Purgatory when I first arrived at the mansion. I looked stunning but completely virgin in it. And when it came to the heels, I'd been a complete klutz.

The dress I wear now is black and flecked with tiny Swarovski diamonds. It hugs every curve of my body, from my bust to my hips, and gives me a true hourglass figure. My hair is pulled up and off my face with only a few loose strands hanging down, making the whole ensemble more dramatic.

It isn't everyday you are invited to a friend's wedding. So, only the best would do.

Besides, I am the Queen of Hell now, aren't I? I need to look the part.

I smile and spritz myself with perfume, then hurry to the men before they holler after me again.

With all the fabric sashaying around my legs, I take my time coming down the steps. When I glance up, I meet the eyes of my four men, each of them visually devouring me.

My demons are all dressed in fitted suits, each with different colored shirts. My heartbeat speeds up automatically at the captivating sight of them all. I've always thought they resembled gods, but dressed up, it's like they're gods who've just stepped off the catwalk.

"Absolutely stunning," Cain mutters, his crystal blue eyes glinting as they roam over my body. "We may need to go out more often just to see you dressed up like this."

"If you keep buying me dresses like this, you have a deal," I reply, feeling incredibly beautiful.

Once I reach his side, all four of them surround me like predators and study every inch of me.

"I-I thought we were in a hurry," I stammer, the heat from their closeness making my pulse thunder.

"I'm suddenly thinking it can wait," Dorian says, his hand sliding to my ass. He whistles approvingly. "Wait, gorgeous, are you not wearing underwear?"

"Fuck me, Aria." Elias sweeps his hands on my waist, pressing the bulge in his pants against my side.

My head whirls at how amazing he feels, and I'm starting to wonder if there's any way we really can show up late to the wedding. Just a little.

No, stay focused.

"How can you be so cruel?" Maverick leans in, his warm breath feathering across my neck and making me woozy with desire. When I see him grabbing himself through his trousers, I have a hard time swallowing. My throat's suddenly too tight.

"Or," Elias chimes in, "we can bend you over now and get this out of our systems before you give us all blue balls."

I laugh, though I'm well aware he's being completely serious.

Cain's watching me with an arched eyebrow, while that primal hunger I know all too well flares in his gaze. Is he actually considering Elias's proposal?

"You too?" I ask him.

His lips quirk up at the corner. "You have no idea how fucking delicious you look and smell."

As tempting as this sounds, Charlotte would *kill* me if I missed the wedding.

I push past all of them and head to the front closet.

What am I looking for? My thoughts are a jumbled, sex-crazed mess.

Oh yeah, my coat. That's right. Coat.

"Maybe after the party," I say, trying to hide the trembling in my voice. "But first—"

"Oh, in one of the new VIP rooms?" There's a mischievous smirk on Dorian's face when he glances at Cain.

"There's an idea," he replies, and a growl of approval rumbles in his chest. "I did want to try out those new beds we just had customized and installed. With the racks and ties."

Oh boy. I'm in trouble.

The ravenous desires on all their faces has me struggling to not give in to the pleasures they promise. Arousal is already thumping in my veins. It's hard to ignore.

An abrupt knocking at the front door douses me with imaginative cold water and shakes me from my dark thoughts.

Is that Ramos? How late are we?

Cain marches past us and opens the door.

To our complete surprise, the Seer, Miranda, stands on the front steps, wearing that lecherous grin. She's dressed in a black coat with faux fur around the collar, and her hair is tucked in a matching hat, like she's just flown in on Krampus' sleigh. The cold instantly rushes inside, chilling me to the bone.

"What are you doing here?" Cain growls.

She slinks into our home without an invitation, looking too comfortable for my liking, and dusts off the snow clinging to her shoulders. "We had a deal, remember?"

Anger instantly stirs in me. That *deal* she's talking about involves being Cain's bride after he dethroned his father and took over Hell. Against all our pleas, Cain had agreed to it, and now Miranda is hoping to collect on her prize.

There's no way in Hell I'm going to let that happen.

I step forward, but Elias's big hands are on my shoulders,

pulling me back against his chest. He's radiating heat, but I'm already burning up with fury, and sweat slicks down my back.

When her gaze sweeps over us, she sneers. "Got a big night out planned?"

Bitch.

Elias holds me tighter.

When she turns back to Cain, she fakes a smile. "It's a shame you're going to have to miss it," she says.

Jealousy flares in my chest, and I shrug Elias's grip off me. As I step up to Cain's side, his hand slides across my back.

"I suggest you leave," he tells her firmly, chin lifted high.

"I've come to secure my contract."

"You heard him. Leave," I push through a stiff jaw.

Anger flashes in her gaze.

"My business is not with you," she snaps at me, then reaches toward Cain's chest. But he blocks her by pushing her hand away.

"We had a deal. Signed in blood," she snaps. "Or did you forget?"

I go over what I know of the deal again in my head. She was to rule Hell beside Cain when he got the crown. But he didn't get the crown, did he?

I did.

So, that would mean the contract holds no power anymore. It's null and void.

It's the loophole we've been hoping for.

Grinning, I link Cain and my hands together, trying hard to make a show of it. I want her to see the onyx Hell ring on my finger and know that Cain's chosen me as his eternal bride.

Once her gaze focuses on it, her eyes widen in shock. "Wait... is that Lucifer's ring?"

"That's right, baby doll," I reply with fake sweetness. "I killed the King of Hell. Me."

Her mouth tugs down into a tight frown. "That's-That's impossible. That would mean..."

"She's queen," Cain finishes for her. Lifting our joined hands, he places a kiss on the back of mine. "My queen and Hell's."

An excited shiver runs down my back. I do like the way he says that.

"Impossible." She shakes her head. "I translated Lucifer's diary. I did my part, now you need to hold up your end."

"It's over, Miranda." Cain is as calm as ever, and it only seems to annoy Miranda even more. "Your terms were to be held on the condition of me being king. Which I am not. Therefore, the contract holds no power."

Elias wastes no time in moving toward the doorway, as does Maverick and Dorian, flanking Miranda.

She notices but doesn't retreat.

"In layman's terms that means you can fuck off," Maverick says.

"You heard him," Elias snarls and shows fangs. "Out."

Her face blanches, and dread slides over her expression.

Just then, Holmes pulls up in the limousine. When Ramos steps out of the passenger seat wearing a tuxedo, I can't help but think that the albino dhampir cleans up pretty well, too.

Cain instantly waves for Ramos to come over. "Help the Seer off our property, will you? I think she's a little lost."

Ramos moves fast and grabs Miranda by the arm, wrenching her back into the freezing night. She struggles against him at first, spitting curses at me, but once she's out of sight, her shouts silence abruptly.

Good riddance.

"Well, that was a bit of fun," Maverick says and readjusts his suit jacket. "I can't wait to see what a vampire wedding brings."

"Hopefully a happily *forever* after," I reply.

He chuckles, and with that, Cain, Maverick, Elias, Dorian and I head for the limo.

"I'VE NEVER BEEN to a wedding before," I whisper quietly to Cain as we enter the newly built club. Seven is the name Cain settled on, to honor his brothers.

It was better than Dorian's suggestion, which was unapologetically, "Lucifer's Limp Dick." That one got Elias's approval... but no one else's. For obvious reasons.

Seven is much bigger and badder than Purgatory was with a more modern, sleek, and sexier feel. It's two stories—well, technically three—with all the offices in the basement, the club and bar on the main floor, and the new VIP rooms upstairs. Antonio and Sting have full range of the bar, which stretches across the entire back wall and also doubles as a second stage for dancers. The dance floor is massive and has smoke effects and underlighting to really enhance the experience.

For today, the club's gotten even more of an overhaul with the dancefloor being transformed into a wedding ceremony space. With the lights dimmed, hundreds of flickering candles add to the romantic ambience, and a carpet of rose petals line the aisle between the rows of chairs for guests.

My demons and I have picked spots by the front, and excitement makes my knees bounce.

"This will be my first human wedding too," Cain answers.

"It was really nice of you to let them use the club."

"Charlotte and Viktor are good friends. It's an honor, really."

Antonio and Sting sit in the row right behind us, sporting matching white suits and bowties. Antonio already has misty eyes, but he's trying his best to pretend like he's tired by yawning and being dramatic about it. Sting only pats his arm affectionately.

My cheeks hurt, and I realize it's because I haven't stopped smiling since we got here. Cain was able to hire all the old workers from Purgatory and I see so many familiar faces... it truly feels like I have a family here.

It makes me think of Joseline, and how much I miss her. Without Maverick's soul contract anymore, I wonder how she's doing and how her life in a new city has been treating her. I promise myself I'll send another messenger bird tomorrow and see if we can meet up.

Elias reaches over and places a warm hand on my bouncing leg. It stops instantly, and when I peer up at him, he gives me a warm smile.

More guests pour into the club, making it a full house.

As music begins to waft from the speakers, Dorian leans forward in his seat behind us, next to Maverick. "Time to start the show," he says.

On cue, Viktor emerges from a hallway, and everyone falls silent. His smile has me grinning, and just seeing how elated he is has my own eyes prickling with tears. In true Viktor fashion, he wears a traditional Dracula ensemble, with black tails, ruffled shirt, cape, and all.

I mean, the man knows what he likes. And not to mention, he can rock a cape pretty damn well. Not many people can say that.

After making his way up the aisle, he turns to the crowd and says in a strong voice, "Thank you my friends and family for attending. Today is a dream come true for me, and it means everything to Charlotte and I that you could join us." Despite his confident words, he's fiddling with his hands and glancing around.

He's nervous. How adorable.

I clap, as do a few others, and he takes his place beneath an arch made of vines and red roses. Behind him stands Ramos, who was given the task of marrying them.

I know Cain, Elias, Dorian, and I performed the binding ritual, or Hell's equivalent to marriage, but all this love and ceremony has me wondering if I will ever be walking down the aisle too. I've already met the men of my dreams. If they asked, I wouldn't hesitate to say yes, but demons have different ideas about marriage. Cain and I may have talked briefly about it before, but who knows if something like this is even on the table for me.

As if sensing my thoughts, Cain runs his hand over mine and begins to twist the Hell ring on my finger. He's watching me intently, and behind his gaze, I can see the same questions hovering there.

He offers me a warm smile, and butterflies dance in my stomach. Forever is a long time, but there's no one else I'd rather spend it with than the four of them.

Just then, the lights dim and the music changes to a soft piano tune. I twist in my seat, anticipation skittering through me to finally see the bride.

A spotlight flashes at the back of the room and Charlotte steps out of the dark, making her appearance.

My mouth falls open.

Blonde curls cascade over her shoulders, framing the most beautiful face. Her lips are painted red and match her form-fitting and nearly sheer bridal gown. With all the crystals on the bodice and long train, her dress glints like stars in the sky.

She is spectacular.

She glides past us to her lover, unable to look anywhere else but his face, and my chest tightens with happiness. As Charlotte and Viktor hold each other's hands, their faces are aglow with joy and love.

Cain's hand squeezes mine, and I realize that I'm captivated by the love in their eyes because I feel it too, times four. I went from having no one to love me to have four of the most incredible demons in my life.

Who would've thought I'd find my heaven in the darkest pits of Hell?

Despite all the shit we've been through, things really have turned out perfect.

Well, besides losing Sayah. If I had the power to change anything, it would be getting her back. Her absence is like a hole in my heart.

I exhale deeply, my body relaxing into the seat as I watch the ceremony go on.

"I wish you could see this, Sayah. I wish you could share in this happiness, too." I shake my head, realizing I'm talking to someone who's no longer there. But she was with me for so long, it's been a harder habit to break than I thought it would be.

Leviathan or not, she was my best friend.

A strange sensation wriggles up my spine. A familiar one and I stiffen.

No... it can't be. It can't.

Impossible.

It happens again, this time stronger. A swirling of ancient magic deep, deep inside me.

Unable to believe it, I gasp under my breath.

Leaning in close to not interrupt the vow exchange happening up front, Cain whispers, "Everything okay?"

I nod, unable to make what I'm feeling into words.

No way.

No. Way.

But, when I reach into myself again, I find the same pulse of living darkness, the one I'd lived with my entire life.

It's her. My shadow...

She's back.

"Sayah?"

HELL OF A GOOD TIME

SIN DEMONS

BONUS SCENE

A deliciously captivating reverse point of view scene of Aria and Cain from book 6, Hell on Earth.

HELL OF A GOOD TIME

ARIA

"Consummation."

Something about the way Cain said the word has goosebumps flaring over my skin. A simple word, yet it awakens desire in me so powerful, I'm practically trembling on the spot. He has that effect on me. Always has. The only difference is that now, I'm not afraid of it.

I'm full of anticipation.

After taking his cellphone out of his pocket, he types out a text to someone with expert and speedy fingers before pushing it back into his jacket. Then, he wraps his arm around my waist, tugs me in close, and crushes his mouth against mine.

My head fogs, all other thoughts evaporating into thin air. When his tongue slides between my lips and tangles with mine, a whimper escapes without my permission. Even through his layers of clothing and mine, he's burning up, the hellfire in his veins making me sweat. As he kisses me, I can feel his hard cock pressing against my stomach, promising sex that's dominating and merciless, like everything else about him.

When he finally pulls away, we're both panting and shaking with need.

"You're mine, Aria," he says, the rising demon within him making his voice deeper. "You know that, right?"

"I think Dorian and Elias might have something to say about that," I reply.

A smirk curls the corner of his mouth, and for a split second, I'm reminded of his younger brother, Maverick. My heart starts pounding even harder.

"You're mine. Heart, body, and soul," he says.

He's not wrong there.

I push up onto my toes, about to capture those devilish lips again for a fiery kiss, but the sound of a throat clearing snaps both our attention to the glass doors.

Dorian stands there, arms crossed, and leaning against the doorframe in a casual way. But there's mischief in his eyes.

"You starting the party early?" he asks.

I glance at Cain. "Party?"

Was Dorian the one he'd texted?

Better yet, will he be...*joining* us?

Cain doesn't answer me, only seizes me by the hand and tugs me past Dorian, through the hallway, and up the stairs. Dorian follows on our heels, throwing me a wink whenever I glance at him over my shoulder.

My stomach flutters with nerves.

Not saying a word, Cain guides me toward Elias's bedroom. A quick knock and it opens, revealing the massive hellhound of a man. As if he's just come in from a run through the woods, his hair a mess and his t-shirt and sweats torn are covered in mud.

Cain mutters quick words to him in a tone too low for me to hear, and nodding, he joins us in the hall a second later. His amber eyes land on me, and a predatory grin appears.

Uh oh... What are these demons up to?

"Are you ready, little rabbit?" Elias asks.

"Ready for what?"

"You'll see," he says.

With my hand still in Cain's, Elias and Dorian take their places on my other side and behind me as we stroll further down the corridor to Dorian's bedroom this time. When Cain opens the door and we all file in, my gaze lands on another person—another *demon*—in the middle of the room.

Maverick.

He's sitting on the leather couch, smirking like he always does, and I quickly glance at Cain for answers. I want to know what he's doing here, what we're doing here, but Cain only pulls me toward Dorian's bed.

"So?" Maverick starts, sounding annoyed. "What's this all about?"

Standing at the opposite side of the bed as Elias, Dorian smiles wickedly, like he's full of secrets, and when he and Elias begin taking off their clothes, the temperature in the room jumps up a few more degrees.

Uh, Cain," I ask him. "What's going on?"

"Do you remember us talking about humans and their wedding rituals?" he explains.

Of course I do. I haven't stopped thinking about it since he brought it up. "The wedding night."

"Consummation," he clarifies. "Yes."

I glance at the bed, at Dorian and Elias, who are both now naked, and then Maverick. My pulse picks up pace. Are all three of the demons planning on having sex with me at the same time, like during the ritual? Here? But then, why is his brother here?

"Wait, now?" My voice rises with my nerves. "But Maverick—"

Before I can finish my question, Cain yanks me into his embrace and our mouths clash in a possessive kiss. I can't help it; I melt against him, instantly lost in his hunger, his desire again.

He breaks away for only a second and whispers against my lips, "If my brother wants to be a part of this cause, then he is going to have to know his place."

A shiver races down my spine at the possessiveness in his tone. Whatever he, Dorian, and Elias are planning here, it's meant to be more than just sex. It's a power move. And I should be appalled they're using me as a pawn in it, but the need my body has for these three demons wins out every time.

I can't say no.

Fuming, Maverick pushes to my feet. "This is fucking stupid," he bites out. "There's no way I'm sitting here while you...while you..."

"Ah, but you don't have a choice," Dorian interrupts him.

"You leave, you're deemed the enemy," Elias adds with murder in his hard gaze. "Which means, all bets are off."

There's no doubt in my mind Elias will kill him. Without even blinking an eye.

Glancing over at Maverick again, uneasiness clenches my chest. Sure, the demons have brought out more confidence out of me than I ever thought possible but voyeurism? I'm not sure...

Maverick wants no part of this either—I can see it on his face—but even knowing Cain's reasons and what's about to happen, he drops back onto the couch and crosses his arms, forcing boredom into his expression.

"Let's make this quick, then," he says. "We got shit to do."

Cain touches my chin, turning my head so that he can start kissing me again. His tongue sweeps into my mouth, and when his hands start to peel away my clothes, I forget all about our audience.

It's like he's hypnotized to me. Everything about it calls to me, and I'm his for the taking. Completely lost. And it isn't long before he's stripped me down to nothing but my lace panties.

His fingers tangle in my hair and wrench my head back. Pain shoots over my skull, adding fuel to my desires, and a groan escapes.

Damn, I love it when he's rough like this. Dominating. Taking what he wants without remorse or hesitation. It drives me wild.

Wanting more of him, I slowly lower to my knees. Cain's fingers stay locked in my hair, holding me in place as I face huge the bulge in his pants.

Fuck, I want to taste his salty sweetness. I want him to lose himself in the way only I know how to do for him. Peering up at him through my lashes, I lick my lips, and when I hear his sharp intake of breath, I smirk.

That's it, Cain. Give me that cock. All of it. You know I can take it.

I undo his belt and tug his pants down. When his dick springs free, I grab it and lower my lips to its hardened tip. The entire time, I watch him—watch his icy blue eyes darken two shades as my tongue swirls around the head and along the base. Then, using his hold in my hair, he guides his cock and my mouth to the right spot and pushes me down so that I can take the entire length of him.

Cain's not small by any means, and when he hits the curve of my throat, it takes full concentration from me not to gag. He pushes himself even deeper, testing my limits, and when he finally yanks me off, salvia drips from my mouth.

I feel so dirty, so naughty, but I don't want to stop. I need more.

As if hearing my silent plea, he does it again, pushing my mouth down, all the way to the base. Eyes tearing, my nails bit into his hips, urging him on, and he tilts his hips, somehow fitting more of his cock inside me. I can't help it. I gag, and Cain jerks me off him from his fistful of my hair just as rough and fast as before.

I moan.

He doesn't need to stop for me. I'm enjoying this dance between pleasure and pain. I never thought giving a man a bj could arouse me so much, but this one is. My panties are soaked, and I'm squeezing my thighs together to try and sedate the building ache there.

Without permission, I lean forward and take Cain's cock back into my mouth, this time devouring him. I suck hard, my head bobbing, while my tongue laps at his underside. The sounds of my slurping and sucking fill the room, and Cain's head rolls back in ecstasy.

I'm itching to touch myself, my fingers trailing over my breasts to my hardened nipples. I pinch them, another moan rising within me.

Again, Cain yanks me off him, but then he forces my head in Maverick's direction. He's sitting there, fists clenched on his thighs, and his obvious erection straining against his pants. Our eyes lock.

"How do I taste, my love?" Cain asks in a husky tone.

My heart hammers, but my gaze is still glued to Maverick's. His lips part, and his hunger shines in his eyes. He's liking this. More than he wants to show, and just knowing that coaxes a whimper out of me.

"Tell my brother how much you love it when I fuck your throat, Aria," Cain says, leaning closer to my ear. His breath fans across my cheek.

It's like I'm drunk on lust, and I'm panting. "I do. I love it."

"Do you want more?" he presses.

Oh yes.

I nod.

"Beg for it," he commands.

Unable to look anywhere else but at Maverick because of Cain's grip, I say, "Please... Cain." I swallow roughly in anticipation. "Fuck my throat."

He grabs me from under my arms, lifting me off me feet, and throwing me onto the bed. Elias and Dorian descend upon me in an instant. Dorian flops onto his back, upside down, and pulls my body over his.

My panties are torn off in a flash, my pussy hovers right over his face. Like a starving beast, he starts to devour me. I cry out, my legs quivering.

Elias moves closer behind me, to my rear. I can hear him spitting on his hand, and when he presses his two wet fingers into my ass, I gasp.

Undoing his jacket, Cain undoes his shirt's buttons and he tugs it off. He takes his place in front of me again, and his stiff cock bounces in front of my face.

His finger runs up my throat to my chin, and a smirk lifts his lips. "My sweet, sweet Aria," he whispers. "I don't think he heard you. Say it again. Louder."

My back arches as Dorian grips my legs and sucks on my clit. Colors dance before my eyes as the delicious pressure of an orgasm builds. At the same time, Elias continues to finger-fuck my ass while stroking himself, and with so many amazing sensations warring through me, I'm not sure how much longer I can keep myself upright.

"I... I..." I'm trembling. I can barely get the words out. When Elias removes his fingers and rubs the tip of his length along my crack instead, I gasp, "Oh fuck."

"Come on, Aria," Cain urges me. "Say it. Look at Maverick and say it."

Doing as I'm told, my heavy gaze swings his way again. Sweat beads on his brow, and it looks like it's taking all his control not to join the four of us at this moment.

I wish he did.

As Dorian's tongue flicks over my clit expertly and Elias presses his massive dick deeper into my asshole, I rasp, "Fuck me... Fuck me, please."

Giving in to my pleas, Cain, Dorian, and Elias readjust themselves and do exactly what I've ask for. Elias sinks himself inside me, groaning, while Dorian continues to lap at my sex until I'm coming undone. Screaming.

Every time Elias rams into me from behind, my head spins. I'm thrown forward with each thrust, and Cain takes the opportunity to grab my head with two hands and thrust his cock into my mouth.

Holy shit.

Yes!

They're all fucking me at once, and honestly, what more can a girl ask for? They're merciless, pounding, licking, thrusting, and I take it all, moaning loudly.

When Cain pulls away from me, I switch my attention to Dorian's erection, taking him into my mouth instead and tasting him from base to tip.

"Ssssshit," he hisses in surprise.

Cain steps away, and for a moment, it's all about Dorian and Elias. And they worship me—Elias speeding up so that my ass slaps against him with every thrust and Dorian dipping two fingers into my pussy.

Wanting to return the favor, I use both my hands and my mouth on Dorian. Quickening up my pace, I massage him, up and down, and swirl my tongue around the tip.

Suddenly, my orgasm slams into me, causing me to cry out and my vision whites out. My elbows give out, but Dorian hands are on the back of my head, keeping me still as he continues to thrust his hips up to fuck my mouth through it. His cock mutes the rest of my screams.

He thrust once more, and with a grunt, his hot seed fills my mouth and shoots down my throat. I swallow all of it down. Simultaneously, Elias pounds into me two more times before he pulses inside me too, reaching his end.

We all sag into the mattress, leaning on each other for support, but when Cain steps forward, his demon fully out, I know my part in this sexcapade isn't over yet.

His leathery wings are tucked into his back, and his marble-like skin is lined with dark veins. He looks me over with inky black eyes as he steps closer to the bed, and I shiver all over. He's a figure of absolute power. Of darkness. And he's all mine.

Dorian and Elias move away to give him space. He grabs me by the ankles, and rolls me onto her back at the center of the bed. Then he crawls over, his wings and my legs spreading open wide.

I can hardly breathe.

Without warning, he thrusts into me. Hard. I scream as the entire bed shakes underneath us. The headboard bangs against the wall, sending a loud boom throughout the room.

As he rams into me again, pleasure bursts through me. I'm still weak from the explosive orgasm by Dorian and Elias, but I grip his shoulders, holding on for dear life.

His thrusts gain speed, and his cock hits deep, *deep* inside me every time, making pain heighten the bliss.

Faster. Faster.

Harder. *Harder.*

Plaster falls from the damaged wall above us.

I'm going to come again. I can't help it. The orgasm is coming too fast.

"Fuck, Cain! Fuck!" I yell.

The sound of the bedroom door shutting steals my attention for a millisecond, telling me Maverick has left.

But Cain quickly barks above me, "Look at me, Aria."

I do and watch as the darkness recedes from his eyes, giving way to the blue again.

"You're mine," he growls.

His words open the floodgates, and I swear my heart stops as my orgasm seizes me. Cain's wings stretch as wide as they can, blocking out all the light and filling most of the room, and his body tenses as he finishes too.

We're gasping for breath, and with his hands on either side of my head, we stare at each other, the magic of the moment washing over us.

"You're mine," he repeats, his voice breathy, and his gaze softer. He dips his head to capture my lips for a passionate kiss, and our tongues tangle.

Fuck, I love this demon—love all three of my demons. More than I ever thought possible. Cain, Dorian, Elias... I can't imagine my life without them. They're a part of me now.

As Cain pulls back, I cup the side of his face, stare deeply into his eyes, and whisper, "Heart, body, and soul..."

SNOWBALL'S CHANCE IN HELL

SIN DEMONS #7

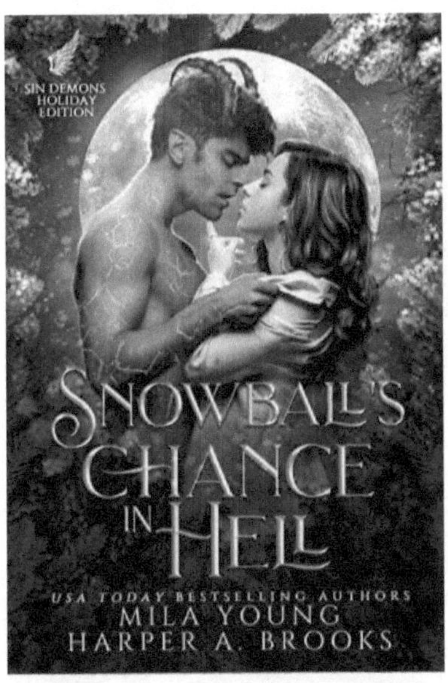

Four demons for Christmas? It pays to be naughty.

Being the Queen of Hell has its perks... Like having four sexy demon lovers at your beck and call, and the power of the underworld at your fingertips.

It has its downsides too, like everyone trying to kill you for your throne. And that includes Krampus.

But when the winter demon steals someone close to me, my family and Christmas are thrown into the fire.

Looks like it's time to rain Hell on this Hallmark holiday.

There's a snowball's chance in Hell I'll let anyone take what's mine.

A holiday epilogue novella with a little bit of sugar, spice, and A LOT of sin. Don't wait for Santa. Grab your copy now!

Snowball's Chance in Hell is a book Holiday Special Edition of the Sin Demons Series.

Hell or Highwater

Sin Demons #8

HELL OR HIGHWATER is Coming Soon!!

There's a baby on the way for Aria and her four demon lovers...so how about a tropical getaway before all hell breaks loose? What could go wrong?

SIN DEMONS SERIES

Playing With Hellfire

Hell In A Handbasket

All Shot To Hell

To Hell And Back

When Hell Freezes Over

Hell On Earth

Snowballs Chance in Hell

About Mila Young

Best-selling author, Mila Young tackles everything with the zeal and bravado of the fairytale heroes she grew up reading about. She slays monsters, real and imaginary, like there's no tomorrow. By day she rocks a keyboard as a marketing extraordinaire. At night she battles with her mighty pen-sword, creating fairytale retellings, and sexy ever after tales. In her spare time, she loves pretending she's a mighty warrior, walks on the beach and cuddling up with her cats.

Ready to read more and more from Mila Young?www. subscribepage.com/milayoung

www.milayoungbooks.com

For more information...
milayoungauthor@gmail.com

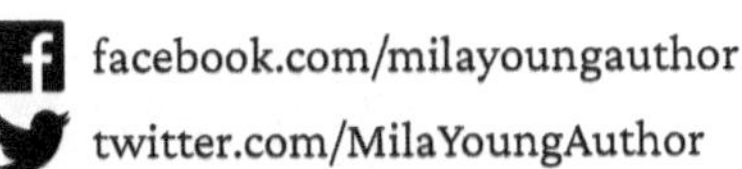

facebook.com/milayoungauthor

twitter.com/MilaYoungAuthor

instagram.com/mila_young_wicked

About Harper A. Brooks

Harper A. Brooks lives in a small town on the New Jersey shore. Even though classic authors have always filled her bookshelves, she finds her writing muse drawn to the dark, magical, and romantic. But when she isn't creating entire worlds with sexy shifters or legendary love stories, you can find her either with a good cup of coffee in hand or at home snuggling with her furry, four-legged son, Sammy.

She writes urban fantasy and paranormal romance.

RONE AWARD WINNER
USA TODAY BESTSELLING AUTHOR
INTERNATIONAL BESTSELLING AUTHOR

Want to read more from Harper A. Brooks?
Subscribe to Harper's newsletter and get *Halfling for Hire* for free!
http://BookHip.com/MCBDCN

Join Harper's reader group for exclusive content, sneak-peeks, giveaways, and more! www.facebook.com/groups/harpershalflings

www.ingramcontent.com/pod-product-compliance
Lightning Source LLC
Chambersburg PA
CBHW030833190726
48285CB00004B/1207